LEGENDS OF THE SHADOW WORLD

Chapter illustrations
by Adam Stower

THE SECRET COUNTRY
THE SHADOW WORLD
DRAGON'S FIRE

Jane Johnson

Simon & Schuster Books for Young Readers
New York   London   Toronto   Sydney

For William

SIMON & SCHUSTER BOOKS FOR YOUNG READERS

An imprint of Simon & Schuster Children's Publishing Division

1230 Avenue of the Americas, New York, New York 10020

This book is a work of fiction. Any references to historical events, real people, or real locales are used fictitiously. Other names, characters, places, and incidents are products of the author's imagination, and any resemblance to actual events or locales or persons, living or dead, is entirely coincidental.

First Simon & Schuster Books for Young Readers paperback edition February 2010

The Secret Country text copyright © 2005 by Jane Johnson

The Secret Country illustrations copyright © 2005 by Adam Stower

The Shadow World text copyright © 2006 by Jane Johnson

The Shadow World illustrations copyright © 2006 by Simon & Schuster UK Ltd.

Dragon's Fire text copyright © 2007 by Jane Johnson

Dragon's Fire illustrations copyright © 2007 by Adam Stower

These titles were originally published individually in Great Britain by Simon & Schuster UK Ltd.

All rights reserved, including the right of reproduction in whole or in part in any form.

SIMON & SCHUSTER BOOKS FOR YOUNG READERS is a trademark of Simon & Schuster, Inc.

For information about special discounts for bulk purchases, please contact Simon & Schuster Special Sales at 1-866-506-1949 or business@simonandschuster.com.

The Simon & Schuster Speakers Bureau can bring authors to your live event. For more information or to book an event, contact the Simon & Schuster Speakers Bureau at 1-866-248-3049 or visit our website at www.simonspeakers.com.

Book design by Tom Daly

The text for this book is set in Garamond.

Manufactured in the United States of America

1209 OFF

2 4 6 8 10 9 7 5 3 1

Library of Congress Cataloging-in-Publication Data

Johnson, Jane, 1960–

Legends of the Shadow World / Jane Johnson.

v. cm.

Previously published as three separate works.

Contents: The secret country — The shadow world — Dragon's fire.

ISBN 978-1-4169-9082-6 (pbk. : alk. paper)

1. Children's stories, American. [1. Magic—Fiction. 2. Cats—Fiction. 3. Space and time—Fiction. 4. Fantasy.] I. Title.

PZ7.J632162Ei 2010

[Fic]—dc22

2008055390

THE SECRET COUNTRY

Contents

Part One

Here

Chapter One

Mr. Dodds's Pet Emporium

Ben Arnold was not a remarkable-looking boy. Not unless you looked closely. He had unruly straw-blond hair, thin legs, and quite large feet. But his eyes had a faraway expression; and when you got close enough to notice, you could see that while the left one was a sensible hazel brown, the right shone a wild and vivid green. Ben believed this oddness to be the result of a childhood accident. One day, his mother had told him, while being pushed up the High Street in his stroller he had stuck his head out unexpectedly and banged it hard on a lamppost. He had been rushed to the hospital and when he came out one brown eye had gone green. It was as simple as that. Ben couldn't actually remember the accident, but he had long since stopped wondering about it. He had other things on his mind, after all.

Which was why, this Saturday morning, he found himself walking briskly along Quinx Lane, his heart thumping with excitement. It had taken him weeks to save up for this. One day on his way home from school, when pressing his nose up against the glass of Mr. Dodds's Pet Emporium, he had seen something so special he had been obsessed ever since. Amongst all the colorful paraphernalia of the Pet Emporium, looking as wicked and shiny as jewels, switching back and forth in their brightly lit tank, their fins fluttering like the pennants on a medieval knight's lance, were two Rare Mongolian Fighting Fish, as a neon-orange cardboard sign announced. Did they live up to their name? he wondered; and if so, how did fish fight? He had taken a deep breath and gone into the shop there and then to ask how much they cost. He had nearly fainted on the spot when Mr. Dodds told him, and so had headed home, grim and silent with determination, moneymaking schemes careering round his head.

Every day since, he had checked to make sure the fish were still there. He wanted to own them more than he had wanted anything in his life.

Mongolian Fighting Fish!

He desired them. He coveted them, a word for which he had had till then only the vaguest of Biblical associations. Before he went to sleep each night, he pictured them swimming around in a tank mysterious with soft light and fronds of weed. When he slept, they swam through his dreams.

He'd saved his birthday money (twelve at last!), his pocket money, and whatever he could make from extra errands and odd jobs. He'd cleaned his father's car (three times, though it was an ancient Morris, and polishing it just seemed to expose the rust patches); he'd mowed next door's lawn (and a flowerbed, when the mower got out of control, but luckily they hadn't seemed to notice); he'd peeled potatoes and washed windows; he'd vacuumed and dusted and ironed, and even (and this had been *really* horrible) changed his youngest sister's diaper, which made his mother very happy indeed.

Before long, he'd gathered quite a tidy sum, which he carried around with him, to keep his elder sister off it.

"I can tell it's burning a hole in your pocket!" his mother had teased him gently.

What would happen, he wondered, if it *did* burn a hole in his pocket? Once it had done that, would it stop at his leg? Or would it keep on burning, right through his leg, into the road, down through the sewers and into the core of the Earth? Goodness knows what might happen if he didn't buy his fish: Failure to do so might bring about the end of the world!

He turned off the High Street and into Quinx Lane; and there it was, squeezed between Waitrose and Boots the Chemist. The great ornate gold letters above the shopfront announced it grandly: Mr. Dodds's Pet Emporium. A throwback from a bygone age, his father called it, and Ben sort of knew what he meant without being able to put it into words. It was a shop full of clutter and oddities. It was a shop full of wonders and weirdness. You never knew what you might step on next: in amongst the shiny silver cages, the collars and

leashes and squeaky toys, the dog baskets and cat ham-
mocks, the sawdust and sunflower seeds, the hamsters
and talking birds, the lizards and Labrador puppies,
you had a vague feeling you might just stumble upon
a tangle of tarantulas, a nest of scorpions, a sleeping
gryphon, or a giant sloth. (He'd never yet done so, but
he lived in hope.)

Holding his breath, Ben gazed in through the
murky window. They were still there, at the back of the
shop: his Mongolian Fighting Fish—swimming
around without a care in the world, little realizing that
today their lives would change forever. For today they
would be leaving Mr. Dodds's Pet Emporium and
traveling—in the finest plastic bag money could buy—
all the way to Ben's bedroom, First Door on the Right
on the Upstairs Landing, Gray Havens, 27 Underhill
Road, just past the Number 17 bus stop. And that
afternoon Awful Uncle Aleister was coming over to
drop off an old fish tank for which they no longer had
a use. ("Awful" had become an automatic part of his
name as far as Ben was concerned, for very many reasons not unrelated to his braying laugh, loud voice,
and complete insensitivity; and the fact that he and
Aunt Sybil had spawned his loathed cousin, Cynthia.)

Feeling the weight of destiny in his hands, Ben pushed open the heavy brassbound door. At once he was assailed by noise: cheeps and squawks and scratchings; rustlings and snores and barks. It was really quite alarming. Thank goodness, he thought suddenly, that fish were quiet. Surely even Mongolian Fighting Fish couldn't make much noise? A badly behaved pet would be a terrible trial to his poor mother, as Aunt Sybil had reminded him. Frequently. And she did have a point; for Cynthia's piranhas had not been the best behaved of creature companions. But that was another story.

Ben's mother had not been well for some time now. She had complained of tiredness and headaches, and the skin below her eyes was always thin and dark. No one knew what was the matter with her, and she just seemed to get worse and worse. She had, as Ben's father said, always been "delicate"; but in the last few weeks she had declined suddenly, and now she found it easier to use a wheelchair than to walk. It made Ben very sad to see how tenderly his father picked her up at night to carry her to their room.

Sometimes Ben would find his father sitting quietly at the kitchen table with his head in his hands.

"It's as if she's allergic to the whole world," he had once said helplessly.

But she wasn't allergic to animals. Ben's mother loved animals. She had, as people say, a way with them. Stray cats came to her as if from nowhere. Dogs walked up to her in the street and laid their heads in her hands. Birds would settle on the ground in front of her. Ben had even seen a pigeon land upon her shoulder, as if it had something to tell her. She had encouraged him to save for the fish. "Looking after other creatures teaches us responsibility," she had said. "It's good to care about someone other than yourself."

A man pushed in front of Ben, and for a moment he was terribly afraid that he would stride up to the counter and demand that Mr. Dodds's assistant pack up Ben's fish; but instead he grabbed a sack of dried dog food, slapped a ten-pound note on the counter, and left without even waiting for his change. Outside the shop, its thick leash tied very thoroughly to the brass rail, a huge black dog glared at the man, its red jaws dripping saliva onto the pavement. Anxiously, Ben stepped over a heap of spilled straw, avoided a collection of oddly shaped and buckled tartan coats, threaded his way between a narrow row of cages, one of which contained a noisy black bird with orange eyes, and—

Stopped.

He tried to step forward a pace, but something—someone?—was holding him back. He stared around, but there was no sign of anyone behind him. Shaking his head, he started off again. But again he was pulled back. He must have snagged his jacket on one of the cages.

He turned around carefully so as not to make the snag any worse. It would not do to return home with a pair of Mongolian Fighting Fish and a ripped coat. He fiddled with the area that seemed to be caught, and found, not a spike of wire or a sharp catch, but something warm and furry and yet hard as iron. Skewing his head around until his neck hurt, he stared down. It was a cat. A small black and brown cat with shiny gold eyes and a remarkably determined arm. It appeared to have reached out of its cage and snagged its sharp little claws in his jacket. He smiled. How sweet! He made an attempt to pry it loose, but the cat clamped its fist together even harder. The fabric of Ben's jacket became rucked and furrowed. Ben's smile became a frown.

"Let go!" he said under his breath, picking at its powerful claws.

The cat looked at him, unblinking. Then it said very distinctly, in a voice as harsh and gravelly as that of any private investigator with a bad smoking habit, "There's no way you're leaving this shop without me, sonny."

Ben was shocked. He stared at the cat. Then he stared around the shop. Had anyone else heard this exchange, or was he daydreaming? But the other customers all appeared to be getting on with their business—inspecting piles of hamsters sleeping thoughtlessly on each other's heads; poking sticks at the parrot to try to make it say something outrageous; buying a dozen live mice to feed to their python . . .

He turned back to the cat. It was still watching him in its disconcerting way. He began to wonder whether it actually had eyelids or was just saving energy. Perhaps he was going mad. To test the theory he said, "My name is Ben, not Sonny."

"I know," said the cat.

Chapter Two

A Sudden Change of Heart

"I came here to buy some fish," Ben said firmly. "Mongolian Fighting Fish." The cat still hadn't blinked. "Over there, see."

The cat's eyes flicked boredly across the bank of glass tanks on the far wall of the shop. It still held on to his jacket tightly. "Oh, fish," it said. "You don't want fish. Who wants wet pets?"

"I do," Ben protested hotly. "I've been saving up for them for weeks."

"But what can fish *do*?" said the cat in a tone of ultimate reason. "They just swim up and down all day." It thought for a moment. "And sometimes they die and float to the surface. It's not a lot to boast about. It isn't as if they have much effect upon the world."

"These," said Ben proudly, as if he owned them already, "are Mongolian Fighting Fish. They . . . fight."

The cat regarded him askance. He could have sworn it raised an eyebrow, but because cats' faces have fur all over and not just as eyebrows, it was hard to tell.

"Obviously," the beast said, this time with a clear edge of contempt, "you know very little about fish. Mongolian Fighting Fish indeed. There's no such thing. It's just a marketing strategy. So many pretty fish to choose from: How do you persuade a boy to part with his hard-earned cash? You give your fish an exciting name and let your customer's imagination run away with itself."

At last it blinked.

Ben was furious. "That's not true! I saw a picture of them in *Fish: The Ultimate Encyclopedia*—"

"And who was the author of that esteemed tome?"

Ben concentrated hard. He pictured the cover of the book, with its gorgeous angelfish and archerfish, its dogfish and catfish and rabbitfish, thornbacks and triggerfish, its groupers and gobies and grunions. And in the middle of them all, swimming in a sea of fins and scales in long black letters as sleek as any shark, the name A. E. Dodds . . .

His face fell.

"You mean, it's a trick?"

The little cat nodded. "Worst sort of untruth." It eyed him solemnly. "Mongolia's landlocked and mainly desert, anyway. Nowhere for a fish to live."

"Next you'll be telling me they don't fight, either."

The cat shrugged. "They might argue a bit, I suppose."

A shadow fell across him.

"I beg your pardon, laddie," the shadow said. "What don't fight?"

Ben looked up. Mr. Dodds was standing in front of him. Or possibly, since he was a very tall man, looming over him. He didn't look as you might expect the owner of a pet emporium to look. He wasn't old and benign-looking, and he didn't wear overalls covered with dog hair. He didn't have little half-moon spectacles, or smell of rabbit food. No, Mr. Dodds wore a sharply cut Italian suit with narrow lapels and very shiny buttons. He had a bowtie made from some sort of weirdly patterned fur, like luminous leopard-skin, and his smile was as white as a television adver-tisement for toothpaste.

Ben quailed slightly. Mr. Dodds had that sort of effect on you.

"Er, the Mongolian Fighting Fish?"

"Nonsense, laddie! They fight like demons. Not in here, of course—too many distractions; but get them home to a nice quiet room and they'll be at each other's throat in no time. Lovely family pets."

Ben was beginning to have serious doubts about his dreams of the last several weeks. Even if Mr. Dodds was truthful, the idea of owning a pair of fish that actually wanted to hurt one another was becom-ing less attractive by the minute. Bravely, he looked the pet shop owner in the eye. Mr. Dodds had large eyes, eyes so dark they seemed to be all pupil and no iris, as if all available light were being sucked into them with not even the slightest hint of a reflection.

"I had heard," Ben started nervously, "that some creatures don't always live up to their names. And also," he went on quickly, "that Mongolia has no ocean, and therefore no . . . fish. . . ."

Mr. Dodds' eyes widened slightly. A second later and his smile followed suit, but the expression that had crept onto his face was not amused.

"And who might have given you this remarkable information, laddie?" he inquired gently.

Ben looked down.

"Well, go on then, Ben," came the gravelly voice of the cat, "tell him who told you." It grinned at him unhelpfully.

Ben looked up and found Mr. Dodds fixing the cat with a gimlet glare, a glare that suggested he would like to strangle it, or maybe just swallow it down, fur and all, in a single mouthful. Even so, it was hard to tell whether he had been a party to their conversation, or just wasn't very fond of this particular item of stock.

"Er," floundered Ben, "I can't remember. Maybe I read it in a book."

"Oh, yes," said the cat sarcastically. "That would be Mr. Dodds's *Great Big Book of Lies*, then, would it?"

The pet shop owner reached out with sudden shocking speed and did something that made the cat wail. Ben whirled round in horror, only to find

Mr. Dodds extricating the creature's claws, with seeming care, from the back of Ben's jacket.

"Whoopsadaisy," Mr. Dodds said lightly. "This little fellow seems to have got himself caught up with you."

So saying, he gave the final claw a spiteful twist and pushed the cat away with an uncompromising finger. It hissed at him, ears laid flat against its skull, and retreated into the cage.

Mr. Dodds straightened up. He seemed taller than ever.

"You've got to go with your heart, laddie, follow your heart's desire. It does no good to hanker after a dream and not pursue it to the ends of the earth." He leered at Ben, gave him an encouraging wink. "Do the right thing, son: Spend the money you've saved all these weeks. Can't have it burning a hole in your pocket, can we?" He moved toward the fish tanks, reached up to collect the little plastic scoop to remove the Mongolian Fighting Fish, and regarded Ben expectantly.

Ben looked at the black and brown cat. It was crouched at the back of the cage with its paw cradled to its chest. When it looked back at him, its eyes were hot with misery, and at the same time a barely suppressed fury. He sensed a challenge, an invitation. He looked at the fish. They circled sweetly through the miniature bridge with which someone had decorated their tank, entirely unconcerned by the world and its ways. One of them swam up to the surface, the artificial lighting making its scales glow like rubies and sapphires, and banged its head on the air pipe. They were, he decided, very pretty, but possibly not very bright. He looked back at Mr. Dodds—who was standing there like a waiter in a posh restaurant, fish tank lid in one hand, scoop in the other, ready to dish out his order—and made a momentous decision.

"How much for the cat?" he asked.

Mr. Dodds was not to be deterred. "That little beast's not a suitable pet for a nice boy like you, laddie. Vile temper it's got."

From the cage behind him came a hiss.

"Don't believe a word he says." The cat was sitting at the front of the cage, grasping the bars with its paws. "I've never bitten anyone." It paused, then growled, "Well, no one that didn't deserve to be bitten." It gave Mr. Dodds a hard look, then turned imploring eyes to Ben. "You have to get me out of here—"

A heavy hand fell on Ben's shoulder. He looked up to find the pet shop owner beaming at him benevolently. It was an unsettling sight. "Tell you what, laddie," said Mr. Dodds, drawing Ben away from the cat's cage. "I'll do you a special deal on the fish: two for the price of one—how's that? Can't say fairer, can I? Mind you, I'll go out of business if I keep letting my better nature get in the way!" The beam became a full, open grin. Mr. Dodds's teeth were remarkably sharp, Ben noticed: more like a dog's teeth than a human's. Or even a shark's . . .

"No, sir, Mr. Dodds, I've changed my mind. I don't want the fish anymore, I want the cat. It's"—he searched for a persuasive description—"really pretty."

"*Pretty*?" The cat fairly squawked with indignation. "You might leave a chap a bit of dignity! Pretty, indeed. Bast's teeth! How'd you like it if I called you pretty, eh?"

Mr. Dodds was frowning now, and his polite smile looked less than sincere. "Sorry, laddie, but you can't have the cat," he said through gritted teeth. "I've promised it elsewhere, and that's that."

"It hasn't got a sold sign on it," Ben pointed out reasonably.

26

The pet shop owner leaned toward him, his face dark with blood. "Now look here, laddie: This is my shop and I shall sell my stock to whomsoever I please. And I do not please to sell you this cat. All right?"

A terrible wail came from behind them. Everyone in the shop stopped what they were doing and stared. The cat was writhing around the cage, clutching its stomach and howling bloody murder. Ben ran to the side of the cage.

"What's wrong?"

The little cat winked at him. "Don't worry, I've a few tricks of my own up my fur. . . ." Its voice rose in an earsplitting shriek.

Mr. Dodds glowered down at it. Then he bent down till his face was on a level with the cat's and said quietly to it, "Don't think this will save you. I know your game."

A young woman carrying a baby in the crook of her arm looked very shocked at this hard-heartedness. She whispered something to her husband, who tapped Mr. Dodds on the shoulder.

"Excuse me," said the man, "the kitten doesn't look very well. Shouldn't you be doing something for it?"

Mr. Dodds gave the man an oily, but forbidding, smile. "Terrible little playactor, this cat," he said. "It'd do anything for a bit of attention."

A big, elderly lady with colored spectacles bustled up and joined in. "Nonsense!" she cried. "Poor little thing. Animals always know when there's something wrong with them." She stuck a pudgy finger through the bars. The cat rolled weakly onto its side and nudged its head against her hand. "Aaaah," she said. "They always know when a human is their best chance of survival too."

Ben saw his chance. "I want to buy it and take it to the vet's," he said loudly. "But he won't let me— keeps trying to sell me some expensive fish instead."

Quite a crowd had gathered around them now and there was a lot of muttering and shaking of heads. Mr. Dodds looked angry and beset. The cat flashed Ben a knowing look.

"Oh, all right then," Mr. Dodds said at last, gritting those terrible teeth. He smiled around at the crowd, then dropped an avuncular hand back onto Ben's shoulder. Ben could feel the man's fingernails biting into the skin beneath his jacket. They felt as hard and horny as claws. "Have the creature, then."

When the other customers had drifted out of earshot, Mr. Dodds named his price. Not only did it include all the money Ben had saved for the Mongolian Fighting Fish, it also meant handing over his bus fare. Mr. Dodds took it of him with very bad grace and stomped off into the back of the shop to fetch a cardboard carrier. Ben leaned down to the cat. "I've no idea what's going on here," he said as sternly as he could manage. "So as soon as we're out of here you've got some explaining to do. It's taken me weeks to save that cash, and I don't know what my parents will say when I come back with a talking cat and no fish."

The cat rolled its eyes. "Just regard it as the first step to saving the world, okay? If it makes you feel any better. Now here he comes, so shut up and behave like a grateful customer."

Ben did as he was told so well that in the end Mr. Dodds felt obliged to give him two free cans of cat food—"as a goodwill gesture"—and two minutes later Ben was out in the street with a cardboard box in his arms and the two cans balancing precariously on the top. As he walked slowly down Quinx Lane, Ben could feel Mr. Dodds's eyes boring into his back until he turned the corner onto the High Street, where the bustle of traffic and shoppers made the last half hour feel even more bizarre. Ben was beginning to think he had experienced some sort of fit or waking dream when the box spoke to him.

"Thank you, Ben," it said, and the unmistakable, gravelly voice was solemn. "You have, literally, saved my life."

Ben held the box away from him so that he could peer in through the airholes. As if in response, a small pink muzzle emerged, sniffed once or twice, and withdrew again.

"You *can* talk, then," Ben breathed. "I thought I might have been imagining it."

"Everything talks, Ben," the cat said enigmatically, "but it's not everyone who can hear."

Chapter Three

Cynthia's Piranhas

Gray Havens, 27 Underhill Road, was an unremarkable semi-detached house in a long row of other unremarkable semi-detached houses on the outskirts of town, but Ben loved it. Always warm in the winter and cool in the summer, it was filled with comfortable furniture and secret, dusty nooks and crannies; and out in the back garden there grew the largest apple tree he had ever seen, a tree that produced hundreds of delicious green-and-red apples every summer and still had the generosity to let him climb into its branches and build a tree house. He had lived at Gray Havens all his life, and it usually made his heart lift when he rounded the corner by the soccer pitch and caught sight of his home. Today, though, as he plodded up Parsonage Road and turned into Underhill Road, his heart sank; for there, in front of his own house, and blocking the driveway to Number 28, was Uncle Aleister's gleaming black Jaguar car.

"Oh, no," breathed Ben unhappily.

Ben was not fond of his mother's awful brother, or Uncle Aleister's wife, Sybil. And he was especially not fond of their daughter, the awful Cynthia. They lived on the other side of town, past Aldstane Park, on one of the new "executive" estates: huge houses masquerading as genuine Tudor mansions, with lawns like smooth green carpets and flowers that grew exactly when and where they were supposed to. There was never a weed to be seen at Awful Uncle Aleister's: No weed would dare to spoil that perfect symmetry. Everything in the house looked brand-new—bright white carpets and pale pink leather sofas and armchairs—as if the plastic wrappings had just been whisked off as you rang the bell (which played a fetching version of "Greensleeves"). Ben's mum often muttered darkly that she thought that was exactly what Aunt Sybil did, for she couldn't for the life of her understand how anyone could keep such a color scheme so immaculate and still live there like a proper family. There was none of the comfortable clutter you would find at their house—newspapers and books, packets of cookies, half-finished drawings, games and postcards, and bits of wood or pebbles they had collected on their walks. No, at Uncle Aleister's house you sat awkwardly on the edge of the sofa (unless it was a particularly hot day and Aunt Sybil suggested she put a cloth down first, in case you sweated into the leather) and clutched your glass of bitter grapefruit juice and stayed silent while the adults made polite small talk, which mainly consisted of Uncle Aleister puffing on a fat cigar and boasting about how he'd made yet another fabulous sum of money on one of his deals. ("That sort of money," Ben's father would say, once they were back in their car, "could only possibly come from someone else's misery." And though Ben had no idea what sort of job his uncle had, he would nod his head sagely.)

The other torment of visiting their relatives was being made to accompany Cousin Cynthia upstairs to see her latest acquisition.

The last time it had been piranhas.

Cynthia never seemed to have normal pets. Or rather, if she did, they never seemed to last long. She had once had a very playful collie puppy, but it had mysteriously disappeared the day after it bit her. Her rabbit had made a successful bid for freedom by tunneling out of its run in the backyard; her tarantula appeared to have committed suicide by hurling itself in front of Uncle Aleister's Jaguar; and the boa constrictor she had had the previous year was last seen disappearing down the toilet. The piranhas, though, were something else.

There had been eight of them to begin with: ugly little brutes with bad overbites and overlapping teeth. Cousin Cynthia—a painfully thin girl with green eyes and mean elbows—had invited Ben and his sister Ellie round for tea to show them off. "Look!" she had cried, gleefully dangling a goldfish over the tank. (The goldfish was the last remaining one of six she had "won" from a local fair.) The goldfish had rolled its eyes and struggled: It knew what was coming next. Ben was appalled. He stared at Cynthia, his mouth open in protest, but before he could stop her, she had smiled and dropped the goldfish, and when he looked down, the water in the tank was murky and churned.

When at last the water cleared, there was no sign of the goldfish; but oddly enough, there seemed to be fewer piranhas, too.

Ben counted them. It was difficult, since they kept trying to confuse him by swimming around, but he stuck at it. One, two, three, four, five, six . . . seven . . . He counted them again. Still seven. Definitely only seven. The eighth had vanished along with the gold-fish. The remaining piranhas stared back at him blankly as if to say, "Well, what did you expect? We're piranhas, after all." After this, he'd quite gone off the idea of fish-and-chips for tea and had mumbled his excuses and gone home. By the weekend there had been only one piranha left, as Cynthia cheerfully con-fided to him at school. One great big, very satisfied-looking piranha.

And then, she told him, it got so hungry that it ate itself.

Ben could never quite work that one out; but since it was the tank it had occupied that Uncle Aleister was going to be installing in Ben's bedroom as a home for his new Mongolian Fighting Fish, it was clear that Cousin Cynthia's last piranha no longer had a use for it.

He walked down the road slowly, not looking forward to explaining that he no longer needed the tank. When he arrived home, he put the box down carefully outside the front door. "I won't be long," he said softly. "Just stay here and don't make any noise."

He could smell Awful Uncle Aleister's cigar smoke even before he opened the door; and as soon as he did, an awful laugh rang out. For one wonderful moment Ben thought that maybe he'd come around to say Ben couldn't have the fish tank after all. But no: He opened the door, only to hear his uncle exclaiming, "Marvelous tank that, Clive." (This being Ben's father.) "Top of the range. If it could hold all those piranhas, I'm sure it can manage two tiny little Siamese Dancing Fish."

"Mongolian Fighting Fish," Ben amended automatically.

Uncle Aleister turned around and glowered at him through a cloud of smoke, but since Uncle Aleister had huge black eyebrows that almost joined in the middle to make one great furry caterpillar of an eyebrow, it could be quite hard to tell when he wasn't glowering. "Don't you know it's not polite to contradict your elders and betters, Benny?"

"But . . . ," Ben started, only to go quiet when his father shook his head at him. "Yes, sir."

"Come along then, Benny," Awful Uncle Aleister said benevolently, taking him firmly by the shoulder and leading him back out into the hall. "Let me show you the beautiful tank your father and I have just spent two happy hours installing for you, a tank in which your fish can dance their little hearts out."

Ben stared helplessly back over his shoulder at his father, who, shielded by Uncle Aleister's back, was rolling his eyes heavenward. "Up you go, son," he said. "We've done a lovely job."

They had. The tank was exactly where Ben had imagined it, on top of the chest of drawers and in front of the window, so that the afternoon light played through the emerald green weed and lit each air bubble that issued from the complex filtration unit to a perfect silvery sphere.

"That's, ah, amazing," he said at last.

Uncle Aleister beamed. "Isn't it just? And a proper

bargain for you, Benny, since it cost the best part of three hundred pounds only last Christmas. Your father's kindly agreed to come and trim our hedges in exchange. Marvelous with his hands, your father.' He ruffled Ben's hair, a gesture Ben particularly hated, but not as much as he hated being called Benny. "So talented. I always say to him if working with your hands was as highly valued as running a successful import business, then it'd be him who was a millionaire living in King Henry Close, and me who'd be living here in this dreadful hovel. Ha-ha!" His uncle's awful laugh rolled out round the room and Ben's father, appearing suddenly at the door, smiled weakly.

"Well, where are your fish, then, son?" he asked, to get Aleister off his favorite topic of conversation. "Let's see how they like their new home, shall we?"

Ben was stumped. He couldn't think of a word to say or a thing to do. Instead he mumbled something inaudible and fled downstairs in panic. Not only would Uncle Aleister kill him for causing him so much needless bother, but his poor father would have to spend hours working in the garden at King Henry Close, with Awful Auntie Sybil flapping around him and asking, "Please, Clive, not to trample the grass . . ."

At the foot of the stairs Ben's mother appeared, silently, as if by magic. Her new wheelchair was remarkably free of squeaks and squeals. She was a small, tired-looking woman, with pale gold hair and lively eyes, and in her arms she carried Ben's tiny little sister, Alice. By now Ben had just started working on his best excuses for arriving home without the fish: Someone had stolen them right out of his hands outside the pet shop? The fish had somehow contracted a rare disease and weren't well enough to travel? The pet shop had sold out of Mongolian Fighting Fish and were going to have to send to Mongolia to get some more, which could take at least six months? . . . He was concentrating so hard he almost tripped over the wheelchair.

"Oops, sorry, Mum!"

In reply, his mother dropped him a long, slow wink. She did this sort of thing from time to time, and Ben wasn't entirely sure what she meant by it, though it always made him feel as if she could see right through him, into the very depths of his soul. It was useless trying to lie to her.

Even so, he couldn't imagine she'd welcome the addition of a cat to the household. Still racking his brains, he opened the front door.

The cardboard box was exactly where he had left it, but someone had artfully placed a transparent plastic bag in the middle of the doorstep. The bag was ripped and water was puddling around it and dripping off the step, where it ran in a long thin runnel down the garden path. At the end of the path, a big ginger tomcat sat licking its paws thoughtfully. Ben wrinkled his forehead. What on earth was going on?

"Don't say a word." The voice came from very close to the ground. "Just look upset. Everything will be fine."

Ben knelt down to interrogate the box further, but at that moment there was the sound of running feet, and his sister Ellie and Cousin Cynthia appeared, wearing a strange assortment of gaudy fake furs (which clashed horribly with Cynthia's bright orange hair and green eyes) and scarves and ridiculously high-heeled shoes. Cynthia took one look at Ben's shocked face, then at the ripped bag, and finally at the cat licking its paws. And then she started to laugh. It was the sort of laugh that brought to Ben's mind the image of someone poking a piglet with a broomstick. It was a laugh that brought Ben's mother to the door. She surveyed the scene with a single raised eyebrow.

"It sounds as if someone's having fun!"

Cynthia was laughing so hard that she fell off her shoes. Even that didn't shut her up. Tears of mirth were rolling down her cheeks, but Ben was still mystified. "Oh, cats!" squealed Cynthia. "They're so . . . cruel!"

Mrs. Arnold cast a contemptuous gaze at her niece, now sprawling on the lawn, clutching her sides. Finally her gaze came to rest on the step. "Well, well," she said. "It looks as if someone's dropped something there."

Cynthia giggled harder. "That cat . . . ," she indicated the big ginger tom, now threading its way sinuously between the palings of the gate, its tail curled over like a great big question mark. "He"—she snorted with laughter—"he's eaten Ben's new fish!"

Ben started to say something, then stopped. He stared at the wet doorstep; then at the retreating tomcat; then at the cardboard box, which offered no help at all, other than a few white whiskers that poked briefly through one of the airholes then quickly withdrew from sight.

"Oh, Ben . . . ," said Ellie, for once at a loss for words.

"All that time," said his mother. "All that effort . . ."

But Ben's head was bent, which was just as well, since a wide, secret smile had started to spread itself across his face.

His relief was not to last for long.

"And look!" cried Cousin Cynthia, picking herself up with alacrity and swooping upon the cardboard box. "What's this?"

Ben's heart fell like a stone to the bottom of his sneakers.

"Ben's bought me some food for my new pet!"

A short while later Cynthia and her father left, Uncle Aleister huffily reinserting the piranhas' tank and filtration unit into the trunk of the car, Cynthia grasping her two ill-gotten cans of Kit-e-Kat to her meager chest. There seemed to be something wrong with her face, but Ben couldn't quite work out what it was. With a loud honk and a squeal of brakes, the Jag sped off down the road in the direction of town. Ellie, Ben, and their parents watched it go in silence. Then Mr. Arnold shook his head. "I know he's your brother, Izzie, love," he said to Mrs. Arnold, "but I just can't stand the man. All he talks about is money."

"Ah, but Clive," Mrs. Arnold said, patting his arm, "I'm sure he's none the happier for it."

"Not with a daughter like Cynthia," Ben said, very quietly.

Ellie stifled a giggle.

For a moment neither of their parents said anything. Then his father laughed. "No wonder the piranhas ate each other," he said. He kissed the top of his wife's head. "I'll make us a cup of tea."

"What about you, Ben?" his mother asked gently. Her eyebrow rose again into what Mr. Arnold called her "quizzical" expression.

"I'm all right," Ben replied. "I'm just going to walk around the yard for a bit."

As his father pushed the wheelchair down the hall toward the kitchen, Ben, still puzzling over the mystery of the disappearance of the phantom fish, thought he heard his father say something about Cynthia and a cat, but he couldn't quite make it out.

Chapter Four

The Secret Country

As soon as they had all disappeared into the kitchen, Ben picked up the cardboard box. It came up into his hands so easily that he almost overbalanced. Something was wrong, his head told him. It was too light. . . .

It was empty.

Ben stood up and stared wildly around, but he could see neither hide nor hair of the cat. He wondered whether Cynthia had stolen it, or if it had somehow escaped from the box and wandered off. He thought about calling out for it, but then realized that he had no idea of its name. Instead, he walked around the front yard, calling "Kitty, Kitty!" but this sounded plain ridiculous; besides, within a few minutes it seemed that several other cats answered to that name, since they kept appearing stealthily: on the front wall, beside the gate, on the fence, poking their heads through the hedge. Ben looked at them crossly.

"Go away!" he said fiercely. "You're not my kitten."

A thin white cat with a sharply angled head and pale eyes slid through the gate.

"You're a very rude boy," she said, quite distinctly.

Ben stared at her. After a moment he pulled himself together and said, "So you can talk too."

The white cat laughed. So did all the others. A fat brown cat with a patch of gold over one eye waddled across the lawn and wheezed up at him, "Of course we can talk. How'd you like it if we treated you like a complete idiot? Show some respect."

Ben frowned. "Eh?"

"Hay is for horses," said the white cat primly. "Didn't your mother teach you manners? You should beg his pardon."

"Sorry," said Ben automatically. He ran a hand across his forehead, and it came away beaded with sweat. Whatever was he doing, apologizing to a group of cats? He stared around in case his father came out and saw him. (His mother would think nothing of it: She talked to things all the time, animate or inanimate—she talked to flies and spiders and plants; she talked to the car, to the vacuum, to the washing machine; once he'd even caught her lecturing a fork.) "I must be going mad," he said to himself. "Completely and utterly bats. It's probably genetic."

"In my opinion, all humans are mad." This came from the big ginger cat he had seen earlier. It was standing at full stretch up against the garden gate with its elbows on the top, a most bizarrely humanlike posture. As if to allay suspicions, it dropped at once to all fours.

"What do you mean?" Ben wondered, feeling obscurely insulted.

All the cats laughed like a pack of hyenas, as if they'd all been waiting for this.

"Humans!" proclaimed the big ginger tom. "Humans are big and slow and completely devoid of magic."

Ben decided to change the subject. "I'm looking for my kitten," he said. "It was in that box over by the door just a minute ago. Have you seen it anywhere?"

The white cat tutted. "It," she said. "It, indeed. You wouldn't think us very polite if we called you 'it,' would you?" Then she winked at him. Or perhaps she just had something in her eye. "Besides," she added, "I don't think he'd thank you for calling him a kitten!"

"I'm sorry," said Ben. "I don't know anything about him. I just bought him from Mr. Dodds's pet shop. He is a bit scrawny, though, for a grown-up cat. . . ."

A hush fell over the group. Four or five of them went into a secretive huddle and began whispering urgently. At last the group broke apart. The fat brown cat appeared to have been elected the cats' speaker, for he bushed out his tail in a rather self-important fashion, cleared his throat, and said, "No one can ever own a cat, young man, so we regret we cannot aid you in your search. It would be a grave disservice to catkind for another of our number to fall under human oppression. Too many cats have been bought and sold against their will, only to be labeled and collared in a most demeaning fashion." He indicated his own collar—a handsome affair of red velvet, complete with a silver bell and a plastic name tag.

The ginger tom leaped gracefully over the front gate and landed at Ben's feet. He stared insolently at the fat brown cat and said in a dismissive tone, "There's no need for any of this nonsense. I know exactly where the Wanderer is. Follow me."

So saying, he trotted quickly through the front garden, past the Morris and the bins, one of which was lying on its side with its contents strewn around on the paving stones, and through the alleyway into the backyard. He went unerringly across the lawn until he stood at the base of the apple tree. "He's up there," he said, indicating the tree house.

The little cat was waiting for him. He had made himself comfortable on an old blanket and was grooming nonchalantly. Ben hauled himself up through the hole in the tree house floor and regarded him wearily.

"Right, then," he said. "Tell me exactly what's going on—why did you stop me buying my fish? What does the world need saving from? And what was all that with the burst bag on the doorstep?" He stopped to draw breath. The Wanderer just smiled.

"And how come I'm suddenly plagued by talking cats? And who are you, anyway?"

"Now calm down, Ben," the cat said in a cowboy drawl. "Let's take this one step at a time, shall we? In the first place, I didn't make you do anything; you chose to rescue me—even if it was in response to my heartfelt plea—and it was extremely kind of you to give up all your savings in order to do so.

"We'll come to saving the world later, shall we? And as for the fish—well . . ." He grimaced. "They weren't exactly as advertised, as is so often the case in life, and especially in Mr. Dodds's Pet Emporium."

The Wanderer stretched out a leg and started to groom in a finicky fashion between his spread toes.

"Keep going," said Ben fiercely.

"Just being polite," said the cat. "I mean, if we're going to do proper introductions, you don't want to shake hands while I've still got the stench of that pet shop on me, do you?" He sniffed his foreleg again, gave it a final lick. "That's better. Just smells of cat spit now." Grinning evilly, he extended a paw, but Ben was not the sort of boy to be put off by a bit of saliva. Grasping the cat by the paw, he gave it a firm shake, just as his father had taught him.

The cat winced. "Ow, no need to try and break my leg."

"Sorry," said Ben. "Look, this paw-shaking is all very well, but you know my name and all I know about you is that the ginger cat called you 'the Wanderer.'"

The cat smiled proudly. "Yes, indeed. I was born into a family of great explorers. My father was Polo Horatio Coromandel, and my mother the famous Finna Sorvo Farwalker. We are well known for our expeditioning. My father climbed Cloudbeard, the highest mountain in Eidolon, the year before I was born; and my mother, well, she founded a colony in the New West before sailing on to discover the Unipeds of Whiteland. She was the one who discovered the highway that leads into your Valley of the Kings."

"Sailed?"

"With her great friend Letitia, the giant otter."

This all sounded very impressive and entirely fictional. "And what have you done to earn *your* title?" Ben asked.

The cat looked uncomfortable. "Ah, well, you know, wandered about a bit. Made some long journeys. Came here . . ."

"Obviously."

The little cat cleared his throat and changed the subject quickly. "I am going to give you a gift, because of who you are. I would not entrust my name to just anyone, for the gift of a true name carries with it a responsibility as well as power over the giver."

Ben was rather lost by this, so he said nothing.

The cat looked him steadily in the eye. "Our fortunes are bound up together," he said. "I can feel it in my marrow. Can I trust you, Ben Arnold?" He reached out and placed a paw on Ben's arm. Ben could feel the points of the claws cool and sharp against his skin. He nodded dumbly. Then something struck him. "I didn't tell you my name, so how do you know it?"

In response, the little cat tapped the side of his nose. "That's for me to know and you to find out," he said irritatingly. Then he tightened his grip on Ben's arm, the claws digging in like needles.

"Ow!"

"Now give me your full name."

Ben hesitated. If names really did give someone power over you, could he trust this strange little cat, who had already played a number of tricks on him?

He regarded the creature solemnly. The cat stared back, unblinking.

Ben made his decision.

"Benjamin Christopher Arnold."

"Benjamin Christopher Arnold, I thank you for your gift, and hereby entrust to you in exchange my own full and secret title and the power it has over me." He took a deep breath. "My name is Ignatius Sorvo Coromandel, also known as the Wanderer. But you can call me Iggy."

"Iggy?"

The little cat shrugged. "You have to admit the other's a bit of a mouthful. All cats have a short name they give freely to others. You may know a couple of the local cats as Spot and Ali. But their true names begin respectively as Spotoman and Aloysius."

Ben nodded consideringly. "Okay—Iggy," he said. "That's all very well, but you've still got a lot of explaining to do."

Iggy grinned. "Let's deal with the doorstep trick first, shall we? Then we can get on to saving the world." He tucked his cleaned toes back under his belly. "It was clear that you were about to get yourself in a right old pickle coming home without your famous Mongolian Fighting Fish, what with your loud uncle booming away about the expensive tank he'd brought for you, and all. So a swift plan was hatched."

The Wanderer's topaz eyes glinted mischievously.

"I couldn't get out of the box without making a terrible racket, since some idiot had left some heavy cans on top of it, so Aby—that big orange tomcat—went off and raided your trash cans; came back with a plastic bag, just like the ones Dodds puts his fish in. I suggested he fill it with water from the birdbath, drag it back across the grass, and give it a good going-over with his claws on the doorstep. Brilliant, eh? Certainly fooled those scary girls."

"Well, yes, you fooled us all." And then Ben's heart lifted. Not only did he not have to worry about the fish or the tank, but it also meant that his father wouldn't have to go around to King Henry Close to cut Awful Uncle Aleister's hedges!

The cat watched him closely. "Now, Ben, what I am going to tell you is very dangerous information. There are only a handful of people in this world who know; and of those, most are enemies. The very fact that you can hear me singles you out, for only those with a touch of magic in them can hear what cats say. For that reason alone, I have decided to place my trust in you. That, and the goodness of your heart. I do believe, Ben, that you have a good heart."

Ben felt himself blushing.

"Listen carefully to what I tell you, for it is a remarkable story."

Iggy shuffled around on the blanket until he had made himself fully comfortable, then he began: "There is a Secret Country, which no true human being has ever seen. It lies between here and there; between yesterday, today, and tomorrow; between the light and the dark; it lies tangled between the deepest roots of ancient trees, and yet it also soars among the stars; it is everywhere and nowhere. Its name is Eidolon, and it is my home."

This all sounded rather peculiar, and to be honest, Ben thought, a trifle excessive. But Eye-do-lon. It had a certain resonance. . . .

"It is a land of magic. . . ."

Now Ben looked disbelieving.

"Long ago," continued the Wanderer, "there was only one world. It was a wonderful place, full of extraordinary beings. Every creature you could ever

imagine lived there: dogs and rabbits, cats and elephants, horses and frogs, fish and birds and insects.
But there were also those that you humans think of as
mythical—like the dragon and the unicorn, the
gryphon and the satyr, the centaur and the banshee
and the minotaur. And those you regard as 'extinct'—
dinosaurs and dodos, mammoths and saber-toothed
tigers and giant sloths. People lived there too, but in
many different forms: giants and goblins, fairies and
elves, trolls and mermaids and witches and dryads and
nymphs. Then a great comet came flying through
space and hit it so hard that it flew apart. And when
it came back together, it was as two worlds. All the
magic that had ever existed fell away into the Shadow
World, the place we know as Eidolon, or the Secret
Country. The world in which you live is what was left
when all the magic was gone from it."

Ben laughed. "I don't believe in magic. Tricks, yes,
but not real magic. I've seen those TV programs where
they show you how magicians fake their illusions—all
those mirrors and false floors and invisible string and
stuff."

"Mummery and legerdemain have always existed,"
Iggy said mildly. "But that's not what I mean. You

would need to come to Eidolon to see real magic at work. Here it fades to nothing more than shimmer and shine. Oh, and the ability to speak with beasts." He regarded Ben quizzically.

"What are you saying? That because I can speak to you and hear you talking to me I must have magic in me that comes from this other place?"

"From the Secret Country, Ben; yes. As I told you, it is my home. But in some part, it is also yours. I knew it as soon as you walked into the shop. You smell of Eidolon."

How rude! Ben stared at him.

"I do not. I wash every day. Well, almost."

The cat grinned at him. "I have a remarkably good nose."

Chapter Five

Instances of Magic

"Who are you talking to?"

Ben stuck his head down through the hole in the floor of the tree house. His sister Ellie was standing at the bottom of the apple tree, staring up at him.

At the sound of her voice, Iggy began to burrow frantically under the old blanket until he eventually disappeared from view, apart from the very tip of his tail.

Ellie started to climb the peg-ladder that led up the tree.

Ben flicked the blanket over the twitching tail and then flung himself down next to it, carefully masking the bulge of the Wanderer with an opened comic.

"Er, no one."

"Talking to yourself is considered mad in most civilized circles, you know."

Ellie's head appeared, truncated at the neck by the tree house's decking. She was four years older than her brother, and those years made a world of difference. All she was interested in, it seemed to Ben, was fashion. Her room was scattered with magazines and scraps of fabric, the walls invisible beneath a papering of sullen models in bizarre garments, and about a million mirrors, in which she checked her face and hair every three seconds. (In contrast, Ben's room contained piles of books and comics and a jumble of objects: a piece of flint that looked just like a dragon's claw, fossils and star charts, unusually shaped bits of wood. There was a mirror in there somewhere, but Ben never used it.) Ellie's room smelled of perfumes and powders, lotions and nail polish. Today, it seemed, Ellie and

Cynthia had been experimenting with makeup, for his sister's eyes had acquired a startling and unsettling definition. (Which would explain why Awful Cousin Cynthia had looked even more awful than usual.) Unfortunately, whatever effect Ellie had been trying to achieve was rather spoiled by a long smear of mascara beneath one lower lid, which had given her a slightly lopsided look, as if her face wasn't entirely in control of itself, and by the hideous shade of purple glitter-shadow she had applied to the upper lids.

"Gross!" said Ben. "You look as if someone's smacked you in both eyes!"

Ellie curled her lip at him. It was smudged a livid and slippery pink. So were her teeth. "It's Dior," she snarled, as if this explained everything. "You wouldn't understand."

"Anyway," said Ben, "what do you want?"

"It's time for tea. Mum and Dad have been calling you for ages."

"I'm not hungry."

"No?" Ellie raised a badly penciled eyebrow. "It's shepherd's pie. And Mum's melted cheese on top."

"I'll be down in a minute, okay?"

61

"Why, what are you trying to hide from me?"

With an arm swifter than a striking snake, she snatched the comic out of his hands.

"It's a graphic novel," Ben said. He maneuvered himself squarely between her and the lump now revealed in the blanket. "*The Sandman*. It's about Morpheus, the Lord of Dreams, who rules over the world we enter when we sleep. It's famous. It's won awards."

"Another world? Really?" Ellie riffled through it. She stopped at one page, turned it sideways, and scrutinized the illustration. For a moment, curiosity softened the mask of superiority she usually adopted. Then she tucked it under her arm. "Right, I'm confiscating this!"

And before he could say anything, she swung herself back down the peg-ladder and ran toward the house. Ben watched her go and felt no irritation, no anger; nothing but relief. He lifted a corner of the blanket.

The cat's nose quested out and sniffed the air once, twice, three times. Then his head emerged.

"It's all right, Iggy, she's gone."

"So that's your sister, is it, Ben?"

Ben nodded. "Ellie, yes. Eleanor."

"Eleanor Arnold."

"Eleanor Katherine Arnold," Ben said suddenly, then clapped his hands over his mouth. What had he given away?

"Eleanor Katherine Arnold," the Wanderer said softly, as if committing this to memory. "Ah, yes."

"I have to go now," said Ben. He reached out to the little cat but Iggy flinched away.

"You should never touch a cat—or indeed any creature—unless invited," Iggy said sternly. "Humans can be so ill-mannered."

"I'm sorry," said Ben. He seemed to be spending his whole day apologizing to cats. "Can we talk about saving the world later?"

"You'll have to bring me something to eat," Iggy said pragmatically. "Otherwise I'll have to raid a trash can or two. It can make a bit of a mess, and I wouldn't want you to get into any more trouble."

"That's blackmail!" Ben thought regretfully of the two tins of catfood Cousin Cynthia had swiped. Heaven knew what else he could find.

Ignatius Sorvo Coromandel shrugged. "That's life." His eyes glowed enigmatically.

• • •

By the time he got inside, though, Ben could hardly eat, he was so excited by the day's strange events. Luckily, no one was paying much attention to him, since Ellie was getting lectured on the overuse of cosmetics. "It's just not attractive, darling, plastering yourself like that," his mother was saying. "Besides, I thought the natural look was in."

"This *is* the natural look," Ellie said sulkily. "I could have put loads more on if I'd wanted to. Cynthia did."

"Natural, if you want that 'I've-just-gone-ten-rounds-with-Mike-Tyson' sort of look, I suppose," Mr. Arnold muttered.

Ellie flung down her cutlery. "Honestly, it's like living in the Middle Ages round here—you have no idea!" Sighing theatrically, she flounced off to the sofa and switched on the television.

The six o'clock news had just started. A woman in a buttoned-up blouse and a sensible jacket was looking seriously out of the set and explaining to viewers that main street shops were reporting a slight rise in their earnings this month.

"That'll be a result of all the money Eleanor's spending on eyeshadow," Mr. Arnold said very softly to Ben, making sure that Ellie didn't hear. Ben smiled. Since the doorstep incident, his parents were being extra kind to him, he noticed: His father had given him the largest helping of shepherd's pie, with the crispiest cheese, and his mother had yet to suggest he tidy his room, his usual Saturday chore. And no one had mentioned the Mongolian Fighting Fish at all.

"And finally," came the voice on the television, "the Test Match at Lords was interrupted this after-noon by a rather unusual pitch invasion."

Ben craned his neck. The screen showed a wide expanse of brilliant green field, dotted with white-clad cricketers. Instead of concentrating on the play, they were all staring at the far end of the ground, where there was a bit of a commotion. A lot of people were running around with their arms outstretched, as if try-ing to catch something. The camera zoomed in for a close-up. It appeared that a small white horse had somehow gotten on to the pitch and was now in a panic because of all the attention it was receiving. It reared up, and for a moment Ben could have sworn that it had a tall, spiraling horn attached to its fore-head; then it bucked and darted for the edge of the field and disappeared into the crowd. Spectators scrambled out of its way, and a few seconds later it was gone.

Mrs. Arnold watched it, her green eyes wide with what might have been amazement, or shock. "Oh," she said, her hands pressed against cheeks that had gone ivory white. "Oh, no . . ."

"Typical," said Mr. Arnold. "It's the only way England can get a draw. Unicorn stops play. Whatever next?"

"It *was* a unicorn, wasn't it, Dad?" Ben asked earnestly.

Mr. Arnold grinned. "Of course it was, son."

From the sofa came a great howl of derision from his sister. "Don't be stupid! Of course it wasn't a unicorn—they don't exist. It was just some poor sad little pony someone had tied a whopping great horn on for a joke."

"They do exist!" Ben said crossly. "In . . ."—he hesitated—"another world."

Mrs. Arnold stared at her son, her eyes sparking green fire. She opened her mouth as if to say something, then closed it again.

Ellie laughed. She held up the graphic novel she'd taken from him and waved it around. "You'd better tell him to stop filling his head with this garbage. He'll rot his brain."

Ben charged from his chair and hurled himself over the sofa on top of his sister. After a lot of scuffling and hair-pulling, he emerged triumphantly with *The Sandman*, now rather bent and battered, tucked under his arm. From the other side of the room, a terrible high-pitched wail broke out.

"Now you've woken Alice!" his mother cried. She looked pale and drawn, as if she might faint at any moment. Tears sparkled in her eyes and at once Ben felt terribly guilty.

"Sorry, Mum," he gulped, hanging his head. When he looked up again, hoping she would give him her usual smile, he found she wasn't looking at him but was staring at the television as if it had in some way betrayed her.

Mr. Arnold intervened. "I won't have you two fighting like cat and dog! See how you've upset your mother. You can both take the rest of your dinner and go up to your rooms. I don't want to see you down here again before breakfast."

Even though he wasn't feeling hungry any longer, Ben grabbed his plate and a fork from the table and went slowly up the stairs. When he reached the landing, he gazed out of the tall, arched window that overlooked the backyard. The tree house showed no sign of its new occupant. Nothing stirred, except for a big blue dragonfly lazily quartering the air above the lawn, hunting down unwary insects. Ben watched it for a while, entranced by its graceful aerobatics and by the way the rays of the setting sun made its body shimmer and shine; then he opened the door to his room and shut it carefully behind him.

The window in Ben's room opened on to the alley at the side of the house. It was also conveniently close to the large black drainpipe that ran from the bathroom down the brick wall to the ground. Ben gave the drainpipe a good, hard stare. A few minutes later he heard Ellie's door slam shut and the latest Blue Flamingos album come on. Alice had stopped crying, and the only noise coming from downstairs now was a comfortable hum of conversation and canned laughter from some television sitcom.

For the next hour Ben forced himself to concentrate on his math homework.

The sun went down and the moon rose to take its place amongst the clouds. A dog howled and a car pulled out of a driveway farther down the street. Inside the house all was quiet.

Ben slid the remains of the shepherd's pie into the only container he could find in his room—a baseball cap advertising the local newspaper for which his father worked (*The Bixbury Gazette*)—and lowered it out of the window on a length of string. Then he swung his legs out over the sill and transferred his weight gingerly onto the drainpipe, gripping the slick plastic tube tight between his knees. His heart hammered with the anticipation of an adventure about to begin. The drainpipe creaked and the metal brackets holding it to the brickwork rattled, but it seemed secure.

Ben hated games at school. He was hopeless at rugby (all those people kicking you), didn't like swimming (cold, wet, and no matter what he did, he always sank to the bottom like a stone), and as for gym, how tedious was it to go up rope after rope, or jump endlessly over tattered leather "horses"? But curiously enough, all those hours of rope-climbing seemed to have paid off. He jammed his sneakers into the space between the drainpipe and the wall and, shifting his balance carefully, worked his way down hand over hand, in excellent style.

At the bottom, he retrieved the baseball cap and its

gooey contents and ran silently down the passage. The poor cat must be starving by now. Did cats eat shepherd's pie, he wondered, and if so, would they eat a congealed one with cheese on top? Had Ignatius been a dog, he would have had no qualms at all, for dogs seemed to eat anything, including things no right-minded creature would touch, but he wasn't too sure about cats.

At the end of the alley, he came out into the backyard. Pale moonlight silvered the grass and filtered through the apple tree to send shadows stretching toward him like long, spiky fingers.

Even in the wan light, he could see there was something lying in the middle of the lawn. From where he stood, it looked shiny and metallic, a bit like a crumpled chip packet. He glanced back at the house to make sure no one was watching him, then crept quietly across the grass. When he reached the middle of the lawn, he looked down. Whatever it was, it was certainly not a chip packet, that much was clear. He knelt to examine it closer. Four great glistening wings were curled over a long, still, iridescent body. He felt a moment of pure sadness when he remembered how magnificently the dragonfly had swooped and cruised around the garden. Clearly it would never fly again. He touched it with a finger. Perhaps it was asleep. Did dragonflies sleep? The middle of someone's lawn was probably not the best spot to choose, he thought, especially with a hungry cat only a few yards away up a tree.

As if in response to the gentle pressure of his finger, the dragonfly stirred briefly. One of the gauzy wings fell a little to one side, and suddenly Ben found himself staring down at the most extraordinary thing he had ever seen.

It was not a dragonfly at all.

It was a fairy.

Chapter Six

Twig

Ben could hardly believe his eyes. Whatever was happening in the world? Or should he say, *this* world? A unicorn on the television news, a talking cat up in the tree house, and now a fairy on his very own lawn . . .

He picked it up gently. It was lighter than he expected, and dry-feeling, like a dead leaf. He hardly dared close his hand on it; it seemed so fragile, for all its size. Already the iridescence on its body and wings was fading, just as the scales of a freshly caught fish quickly lose that glossy sheen that made you want to catch it in the first place. Cradling the fairy in one arm, he approached the tree house. He put the baseball cap on the ground at the foot of the apple tree, wrapped the string attached to it around his hand, and climbed up the peg-ladder, being careful not to bump the fairy on the way.

It was very dark inside the tree house; so dark, in fact, that he did not see Ignatius Sorvo Coromandel until he trod on his tail. The dozing cat yowled so loudly that Ben, in fright, almost dropped the fairy. He juggled it desperately, caught it by a wing, and scooped it back into his arms. Iggy, disoriented and furious, his hackles sticking out like the ruff of a frilled lizard, was dancing high on his toes, tail bushed out to the size of a feather duster. Moonlight reflected from eyes that looked mad for battle. At that moment he did not much resemble Ben's fond ideas of what a fluffy pet cat should be.

"I'm really sorry," said Ben. "I didn't see you."

"Again the boy apologizes," Iggy sighed. "Humans," he muttered darkly. "They're all the same. Completely useless."

"I'm not useless," Ben said huffily. "I've brought you two things you'll be very interested in."

The cat's eyes gleamed.

"Food?" he asked hopefully.

"That might be one of them," Ben conceded. "But first, look at this. I found it on the lawn."

He knelt and laid the fairy carefully at Iggy's feet. The cat took a swift step backward. "By the Lady! A wood-sprite. Where did you say you found it?"

Ben pointed down through the hole. "Over there. I saw it flying around earlier on, but I thought it was a dragonfly."

Iggy sniffed at the wood-sprite. "Still alive, though barely." He opened his jaws wide and shoveled at the creature's body. After angling his head awkwardly several times, he said, "He's quite big, isn't he? For a wood-sprite."

In the darkness, Ben grimaced. "I don't know. How big do they get?"

The little cat sat back on his haunches. "Oh, some are so long. . . ." He stretched his front paws out wide. "But most are about this size. . . ." He brought them closer together. "But you should see some of the goblins in Darkmere Forest. . . ." He whistled through his

75

teeth. "You don't want to meet one of those on a dark night."

His stomach rumbled so loudly that it reverberated off the walls of the tree house. "Whoops, sorry. Better attend to this little fellow, then you can show me what else you've brought for me. I'm so hungry, I could eat my own tail."

Ben picked the wood-sprite up and carried it across to the blanket, where Ignatius crouched over it, his back to the boy. In the gloom, Ben could not quite see what the cat was doing; but after a while he heard the wet, clicking sound of a mouth hard at work, and for a terrible moment he thought Iggy's hunger had got the better of him and that he was eating the fairy. He must have made a noise, for Iggy's head came up sharply. The cat licked his lips. "Cat-spit mends all," he said. "According to my mother . . ."

Ben eyed the cat skeptically. "You can't just lick someone back to life."

But against all the odds, the wood-sprite was stirring. Dopily, it raised itself onto one thin elbow. It rubbed its face with a spidery hand and its eyes came open. Even in the dark, Ben could see that its eyes were remarkable: prismatic, many-colored, as round as Christmas baubles. It said something in a tinny, scratchy voice, then sank down again, exhausted.

"His name is . . ." Iggy made a sound rather like the creaking of a branch. "You'd better call him Twig. He says he is dying."

"What's the matter with him?"

"He's dying of being here."

"Why?"

"There isn't enough magic here to sustain him. A wood-sprite is a creature that can live only in the element for which it is adapted, and that's the woodland of the Secret Country."

"But how did he get here?"

"I wish I knew. The only way in and out of Eidolon is by way of the wild roads—"

"What?"

Iggy sighed. "Questions, all the time, questions." He rubbed his face wearily. "I will tell you what—feed me and then I'll try to explain. You probably won't understand it all, but that's because you're largely human—"

Ben started to complain, but Ignatius held up a peremptory paw, then pointed to his open mouth. "Food first, sonny."

Gritting his teeth, Ben hauled up the baseball cap. It seemed heavier than before, and when he got it over the lip of the entrance, he understood why. It was full of slugs. "Ugh!"

"Well," said Ignatius reasonably, "whatever do you expect, leaving such a feast lying around unattended like that?" He bent his head to the cap and sniffed. "Smells good. No, I take that back: It smells wonderful!"

Ben wrinkled his nose in disgust. He'd always thought cats were such fastidious animals, the way they groomed and fussed over themselves. Now he was beginning to have his doubts.

Ignatius was whispering to the cap. After a few moments, the slugs started to wave their antennae at one another as if in debate, then one by one they slithered up out of the baseball cap and trundled off down the tree. The paths they had made to the exit glittered, all silver slime in the moonlight.

"What did you say to them?"

"I told them you'd eat them if they stayed."

Ben looked appalled. "Me? Eat a slug?"

"I'd heard that humans ate all manner of peculiar things," Iggy said indistinctly, through a mouthful of cold shepherd's pie. "I'm sure I heard somewhere of people eating slugs."

"That's snails, and I'm not French," Ben said shortly.

"Ah, well," said Iggy, sounding a lot more cheerful, "did the trick, though, didn't it? Not very bright, slugs, get a bit confused sometimes. They rather aspire to being snails, having their own houses, and all." He ate in relative silence for a while, his head disappearing farther and farther into the baseball cap. Surely he wasn't going to eat the lot? But then there came the clear sound of the rasp of tongue against fabric, and Ignatius Sorvo Coromandel emerged with a deeply satisfied expression on his face. His belly bulged as if he had swallowed a rubber ball whole.

"Now then, where were we?"

"Wild roads," Ben reminded him.

"Ah, yes. The magic highways. Cats are by nature curious creatures, and also great explorers; so when the worlds separated, it was cats who nosed around and found that there were places where the worlds touched, and that if you had a good enough nose, you could find a way through from one to the other, and even back again. If enough cats followed the same path, back and forth, a wild road was made. We cats like to have the best of both worlds, you know." He grinned at his feeble joke. When he realized Ben wasn't smiling, he went on with a more authoritative tone, "The trouble is, there are others who can use the wild roads, others who can exist in both worlds. But they must own a dual nature, for if they do not, they sicken and die."

"What do you mean?" asked Ben, frowning, "by a dual nature?"

Iggy regarded him with his head on one side. He looked from Ben's green eye to his brown eye and back again and became thoughtful. After a moment he said, "Some creatures, like cats, are both wild *and* tame, both magical and mortal, though a pet cat may seem more tame than wild to you as it cries for its tinned food and rolls on its back in play. But don't be deceived: In even the soppiest of pets lies the wildest of hunters and explorers. We live by day and by night; we can see by sun or by starlight; we can be visible to the human eye one moment, the next we're . . ."

The word "gone" hung for a moment in the night air, then there was a sudden scuffle of movement that had Ben spinning around for the source of the noise.

When he turned back, Iggy had vanished. Just like that. And here he was, all on his own with a dying fairy. Typical.

"Where are you?" he called crossly.

There was no reply. Ben's eyes strained against the thick darkness, but it was impossible to see anything. To make sure he did not accidentally tread on Twig as he had on the cat's tail, he picked him up, cupping him gently in both hands. The wood-sprite's eyes flickered at Ben's touch, and then, as if by magic, an eerie blue-green light pulsed out of his body. It illuminated every nook and cranny of the tree house, but there was no sign of Ignatius at all.

"All right, Iggy, very clever. Now come back!"

Silence.

Then: "Cat . . . up . . . there . . ." The words were quite unmistakable. Ben stared at the wood-sprite in amazement.

"What did you say?"

Twig sighed, a small sound like a breeze through leaves. Feebly he pointed above Ben's head, but before Ben could say anything, a bizarre croaking sound split the night. Ben stared up, and Ignatius Sorvo Coromandel was revealed, bathed in Twig's uncanny light, hanging by his claws from the ceiling. He dropped neatly to Ben's feet and burped.

"Oops, sorry! Still, better out than in."

"That was just a trick, and not a very good one. I can't see what it's got to do with wild roads at all."

Iggy shook his head. "I knew you wouldn't understand," he said. A hiccup escaped him, racking his whole body. Then another, and another. Ben stood there with the wood-sprite in his hands, regarding the cat unsympathetically.

Twig's eyes flickered, and the green light began to fade. Ben lifted him up and blew warm air onto his face, but the little creature only stirred weakly, twisting away from him, then lay still once more. "Iggy, he's dying again!" he cried in panic. He laid the wood-sprite down on the floor in front of the cat, who scrutinized him closely.

"It's better that you don't touch him too often," the cat said gently. His hiccups appeared to have subsided. "You probably squeezed him a bit hard when you picked him up. Wood-sprites tend to shine like that when they feel under threat, but it uses up their strength."

"But I wouldn't hurt him for the world—," Ben started miserably.

"This world—and everything in it—is a threat to him, as it is to all the creatures of the Secret Country. And that's the problem we have to fix."

Another scratchy sound. "Tell boy didn't hurt . . . dozing . . . pick me up . . . panic."

Ben was silent for a moment. Then he knelt beside the sprite. "I'm really sorry, Twig," he said.

Twig made a grimace that might have been a smile, showing two long rows of tiny teeth that shone as sharp as needles and looked as if they could give you a nasty nip. Then he closed his eyes. "Sleep . . . now," he said indistinctly.

Ben turned to the cat. "Is that true of unicorns?"

"Eh?"

"Hay is for horses," Ben corrected sternly, remembering the little white cat. "Though I suppose unicorns might eat hay too."

Iggy frowned. "Unicorns?"

That got him, Ben thought, with grim satisfaction. "If this world is a threat to all the creatures of the Secret Country, then how come the unicorn I saw on TV this afternoon looked just fine?" he asked. "There it was, kicking up its heels, interrupting the cricket."

"Cricket?"

"It's a game with two teams of eleven players, though they're not all on the pitch at the same time . . . in fact, there are only ever thirteen players on at once—unless one of the batsmen's using a runner; though I suppose technically both of them might be, which would make fifteen; oh, and the umpire, of course. He's the one covered in sweaters. And they use bats to hit a ball around a big field."

Iggy looked horrified. In his confusion he saw a crowd of crickets and grasshoppers cornering a victim, the so-called umpire, and leaping up and down on its body. And those poor bats . . . What a terrible place this world was. He shivered. "I hesitate to ask, but how does the unicorn come into this?"

Ben explained what he'd seen.

"A unicorn, here . . ." A fearful light shone in the little cat's eyes. "Someone is up to no good; and I know who!" He clutched Ben by the arm. "We must leave at once."

Ben drew back. "We?"

"Someone must carry the wood-sprite."

"And go where?"

"Why, to Eidolon, of course."

"To the Secret Country?"

"At once."

"For how long?"

Iggy shrugged. "A few days? A week? A month?"

"But I've got school on Monday!"

Iggy's claws tightened on his arm. "The natural balance of two worlds is under threat, Ben, and you worry about school?"

An unreadable expression crossed Ben's face. Then he grinned.

"Great!" he said. "I'll miss swimming!"

Chapter Seven

Something Fishy

If he was going to the Secret Country, Ben thought, he'd better leave a note, or his parents would go postal.

He rummaged around in his treasure chest (an old wooden box he used as a seat) and emerged eventually (after casting aside a one-armed Gollum, a Dalek with no antenna, and a headless Incredible Hulk; a dozen tattered comics; a much-thumbed copy of *The*

Hobbit, a half-eaten Mars bar, and some poster paints) with a spiralbound notebook, a chewed pen, and (triumphantly) a pound coin. First of all he wrote:

> Dear Mum and Dad,
>   Ellie is in league with Cousin Cynthia. If I stay she will sell me to her as pet food for whatever monster she owns now, so I have run away to sea.
>   Love,
>   Ben

He crossed it out; knowing his mother, she'd think it was true.

He started again.

> Dear Mum and Dad,
>   I met a talking cat and a dying fairy who come from another world called the Secret Country. I have to help them find their way back, or Twig will die.
>   Remember that unicorn? It was real! See you soon.
>   Lots of love,
>   Ben

Then he tore that up too—you never knew who might find it, and it was giving away a lot of important information.

After several more attempts (it was hard to write when you couldn't see what you were doing and the cat would not allow you to use the wood-sprite even for a moment's illumination) Ben wrote:

> Dear Mum and Dad,
>   Please don't worry about me. I'll be
> back soon. It's a matter of life and death!
> (Not mine, I hope.)
>   Lots of love,
>   Ben

He left the note on the front doorstep with a stone on top to prevent it from blowing away. Carrying Twig in the roughly cleaned baseball cap, and with his notebook and pen in his pocket, he followed Ignatius Sorvo Coromandel out of the garden, tiptoed up the path, opened the creaky gate, and closed it behind him as quietly as he could. Out on Underhill Road the streetlamps bathed everything in an eerie orange glow, so that the whitewashed houses looked as if they'd been drenched in stale Tang.

"Right, then." He looked at Iggy expectantly. "Where's this wild road?"

The cat shrugged. "I don't know."

"You don't know?"

"It's not that simple. They're a bit of a maze. You have to get the right one to start off with, or you could end up anywhere. You could get well and truly lost—find yourself in Outer Mongolia in 1207." He shuddered.

Ben thought hard for a moment. "Genghis Khan—brilliant!" His eyes gleamed. "The Golden Horde, sweeping down through the Asian steppes, killing everyone in their path. Wow! I'd love to see that."

Iggy regarded him dubiously. "You're a very bloodthirsty young man. That's why you fell for the so-called Mongolian Fighting Fish, is it? Reminded you of all those blood-and-guts tales of the Great Khan, did they?"

Ben's face fell. "Sort of."

"Well, I can tell you, sonny, that he was not a very nice man. He smelled like a yak and"—he leaned toward Ben, grinning like a demon—"he turned out to be terrified of cats!"

"I don't believe you," Ben said stiffly. "You're making this up."

"Believe what you like," Iggy said crossly. "I was there and I saw him climb up his tentpole. Now then," he said briskly. "My best suggestion is that we start with Mr. Dodds's Pet Emporium, since that's the first place I remember when I woke up in this terrible place."

It was exciting to be out on the deserted streets of Bixbury, which seemed at this still hour rather like a secret country itself. Exciting too, though he tried not to show it, to be caught up in Ignatius Sorvo Coromandel's adventure. Iggy explained as they went what had happened to him. While exploring on the edges of Eidolon's northern continent, searching, he explained, for the legendary three-tailed mouse (which no one had seen for a while) he had stumbled upon an unusual wild road. He knew as soon as he stuck his head in that it was unusual: The winds inside it all blew in the wrong direction, carrying with them bizarre aromas, aromas not familiar to an inhabitant of the Secret Country. And so he had followed his nose, driven by the curiosity of his species, and had eventually emerged here in Bixbury, of all places. But no sooner had he arrived in this world than someone had clubbed him over the head. When he woke up, he found himself in a cage, and shortly after that, Mr. Dodds had put him on sale. He showed Ben the lump on his head, just below his left ear.

"I didn't see who did it, but if I smell them again they'll be sorry." He flexed his claws. "I gave Mr. Dodds a nasty bite anyway, just to be on the safe side," he added cheerfully. He thought about that for a moment, his face suddenly queasy. "Though I wish I hadn't. He tasted simply awful."

On Quinx Lane, the Pet Emporium was dark and silent, as if everything in it—the birds and hamsters, fish and gerbils—had all been turned off along with the lights. Ben pressed his nose to the window and watched his breath flower and fade on the cold glass.

"What now?" he asked.

"We go in."

"But the door's locked," Ben said, giving it a push.

Iggy showed his teeth in what might have been a grin. "Cats can get in anywhere." So saying, he bunched his legs beneath him and leaped fluidly up onto the canopy above the shop's signboard. Another jump took him onto the upstairs window ledge, and from there he disappeared through an open fanlight. Ben had to admit he was impressed.

A minute or so later there came a rattling sound from overhead, and one of the windows came open. Ben stepped smartly into the shadows in case it was an annoyed tenant who'd had their sleep disturbed.

"Pssst! Ben!"

It was Iggy. He had no idea cats could be so dexterous.

"Come on," the Wanderer said.

"What, me, climb up there?"

The cat nodded vigorously. "Quickly now, before anyone sees you."

Ben gulped. "What about Twig?"

"Put him down whatever you call that thing you're wearing."

"My sweater?"

"Yes, yes. Now get on with it."

"But I might fall and squash him."

"We'll just have to take that chance, sonny."

"The name's Ben," Ben said crossly.

He wrapped the baseball cap closely around Twig

and slipped him down inside his sweater, which he tucked securely into his jeans. Then he examined the exterior of the pet shop. There was, of course, a drainpipe running down one side of the building. Looking up and down the street to make sure there were no witnesses to this blatant example of breaking and entering, Ben took a firm hold on the drainpipe and, wedging his feet solidly on either side, went up hand over hand till he reached the window ledge. He made the tricky transition from the pipe to the sill with his heart in his throat, and stepped cautiously through the open window.

Inside, there were a load of boxes stacked one on top of the other. Most were of the cardboard variety and had brand names of pet food stamped upon them: ToothyDog Chews; Gourmet Fishlips, Eyelids, and Earholes; Tweetiepie's Cuttlefish Heads; Stegosaur Steaks; but some were more substantial and, even to Ben's nose, smelled strange. Ignatius was poking around at the back of the room, only the tip of his twitching tail visible between the boxes.

"What are you doing?" Ben whispered. He wanted to get out of there before someone caught them.

Iggy's eyes were brilliant in the moonlight. "Look!"

Ben clambered over obstacle after obstacle to reach him.

"This is the cage they put me in. . . ." He indicated a small metal container with a hinged, slatted door. A tuft of tortoiseshell fur was still trapped in the hinge. He sniffed sadly about the cage. "I can smell the Secret Country on it," he said. "I can smell my home."

For a moment he looked so forlorn that Ben actually wanted to hug him, but Iggy came over brisk and purposeful.

"Come on," he said. "Let's see what we can find downstairs."

Ben followed him to the door and was about to open it when he trod on something hard and flat. He bent to pick it up, and his fingers had just closed on it when he heard a noise downstairs. At once Iggy became as still as only a terrified cat can be. The noise grew louder, then resolved itself into the creak of a door opening and the sound of voices. Ben shuddered.

It was Mr. Dodds.

"Hide," Iggy hissed urgently.

"Where?" Ben stared desperately about the stockroom. The boxes were too small for him to crawl into, but in the farthest corner they had been stacked up to make two tottering piles that he might just crouch behind. . . .

Footsteps on the stairs.

Iggy leaped into the cage in which he had been captured and huddled up into a ball, his eyes gleaming balefully. Ben tiptoed toward the corner, wincing at every creak and scuff his feet made on the dusty boards. The voices got closer. There was a lot of huffing and puffing, as if whoever was coming up was carrying something particularly heavy and cumbersome. Someone said, "No, you go backward," which was followed by stumbling feet, and then the door handle began to turn. . . .

Ben ran for the cover of the boxes, heart beating like a bird trapped behind his ribs. Silently, he cursed Iggy for getting him into this situation; then, rather more fairly, cursed himself for being so stupid as to follow a cat. At that moment Twig started to wriggle under his sweater. *Poor thing*, Ben thought. *He probably can't breathe down there.* He eased the sprite toward the V-neck so that it could get some air, but as soon as he did so, Twig started to glow—an eerie green that sparked like a warning beacon. It illuminated Ben's face and the expression of pure panic upon it. "No, Twig, no!" he whispered, pushing the wood-sprite back down into the depths of the sweater. "Not here!"

He stared at the two figures making their way awkwardly through the opened door. The one facing him was Mr. Dodds, no longer in his Italian suit; but he couldn't quite make out who the other man was, since he had his back to him. Luckily they were both too preoccupied with whatever they were carrying to have noticed the wood-sprite's glow. He looked down. Twig was still giving off a faint radiance, a pale green light that pulsed between the fibers of his sweater. Frantically, Ben undid some buttons on his shirt and shoved the poor wood-sprite under that as well. Twig's glow was now so feeble as to be invisible.

"Put it down there," said Mr. Dodds. "I'll ship it out in the morning."

There was more shuffling of feet as the two figures maneuvered.

"Do you think we should give it more water?" It was the other figure who spoke, but its voice sounded muffled.

"I'm exhausted. It'll survive till morning," Mr. Dodds said callously.

There was a thump as the crate they had been carrying hit the floor, then Twig sneezed.

"What was that?"

Ben held his breath. He clutched at the wood-sprite in case it sneezed again. Pale green light oozed past his fingers.

Mr. Dodds strode to the light switch and flicked it on. Nothing happened.

"Darn bulb's gone!" He reached into a pocket of his overalls, took out a flashlight, and shone it negligently around the room. Ben thought his lungs might explode. His blood thundered in his head. Surely they could hear him? But Mr. Dodds tutted, clicked the flashlight off, and stuffed it back in his pocket. "You're getting paranoid. Time to go." He gave the box a kick. "We'll be back for you tomorrow," he promised.

Out they went then onto the landing. The door closed, and the sounds of footsteps and voices receded. Ben began to breathe again. He reached under his clothing and brought the wood-sprite out. It lay in his hand, its chest shuddering feebly up and down, its eyes squeezed shut as if in pain.

"Oh, Twig, I'm sorry. . . ."

At this, the sprite's eyes came open. All the color

had gone out of them in fear. It stared about blearily, then focused on Ben. "Gone?" it asked.

Ben nodded. The wood-sprite struggled to sit up. It blinked, and the last of the green light went out of it. "Know . . . them," it said. "Hurt . . . me." Then it lay back down with its arms wrapped around itself.

"Help!"

Ben jumped, startled. The noise came again, louder this time.

"HELP MEEEE-OWWWW!"

It was Iggy. Ben put Twig back inside his sweater and crossed the stockroom. He stared down at the cage. "What's the matter?"

Ignatius Sorvo Coromandel stared up at him sheepishly through the slatted metal. "I'm, er, stuck."

"How can you be stuck? You put yourself in there."

"How would I know the door had a spring on it?"

Ben shook his head. If this was the level of expertise possessed by their expedition leader, they were in a lot of trouble. He knelt down and fiddled with the catch on the cage door. It wouldn't budge.

"Oh, Iggy . . ."

"What is it?" The cat's voice held a rising note of panic.

"It, well, it seems to be locked."

"Locked?" A shriek this time. "How can it be locked? Do you think I reached out through the door and locked myself in with some invisible key? Do you think I like being in a cage? Do you think I've got some sort of imprisonment fetish?"

Ben rattled the door again, but there was no question about it: The cage was locked, and Iggy was trapped inside it. "Look," he started in the most reasonable tone he could muster, "there must be a key somewhere. I'll go downstairs and see if I can find it—"

"Don't leave me here!"

Ben wiped a hand across his forehead. Then he tried to pick up the cage, managed to move it a few inches, but the effort was too much and he dropped it rather less gently than he'd meant to.

A howl of protest came from the trapped cat.

"I'm sorry, I'm sorry. It's just really, really heavy."

"And you think that's *my* fault, do you?"

Ben didn't, but he said, "Well, you did eat all that shepherd's pie. . . ."

Iggy began to wail.

"Sssh. Please. Just for a minute or two. I'll leave you Twig for company." He laid the wood-sprite in his baseball cap on top of the cage and went swiftly out of the door before Iggy could say another word.

The pet shop was dark, but Ben didn't dare try any of the lights. He felt his way around the hall downstairs until he came to what seemed to be the office. Inside, a wash of moonlight illuminated a desk piled with paper, two wooden chairs, and a couple of old metal filing cabinets. Ben went to the desk, thinking that Mr. Dodds might keep keys in one of the drawers.

He was just about to open one when his eye was drawn by a letter lying on the desk. It had a very smart letterhead with a sort of a crest in dark ink running along the top of it.

Dear Mr. Dodds, he read.

Many thanks for delivering the merchandise as requested. However, I have to say that it is not in the sort of condition I would expect, given the large sum of money I have paid you for it. Indeed, a number of its scales have already fallen off and the rest are looking decidedly unhealthy. In addition, it mopes about all day and doesn't appear to have the strength even to burn newspaper. Quite what use it is going to be as (and I quote your recent advertisement in More Money Than Sense *magazine) "a superbly ecological garden incinerator" I can't imagine.*

I would be grateful if you would remove the item and refund my £1,500 at once. Otherwise I may be forced to call in the Trades Descriptions people.

I shall look forward to hearing from you by return post.

Yours,

Lady Hawley-Fawley of Crawley

Ben stared at the letter. One thousand five hundred pounds? What on earth could possibly cost one thousand five hundred pounds? Maybe an elephant, he reflected. But elephants didn't have scales. Or did they? And how could any animal possibly be a "garden incinerator"? Who would want to burn their garden, anyway? He couldn't imagine what it all meant. He was now beginning to feel so tired and confused by events that he couldn't think straight.

There were a lot of keys in the desk drawer. Just to make sure, Ben took them all. The fifth one he tried opened the cage, and the little cat flew out, fur bristling. Ben stroked him until he calmed down enough to start purring.

"I've been thinking," said Iggy at last. "Twig might be able to help us. Wood-sprites have an amazing sense of smell, and if they smell something they love, they glow pink all over. So when we find a wild road, we can make sure it's the right one with Twig! If you were to hold him out in front of you, he'll start to glow if we've found the one that leads to his home. At least then we'll be back in the right time zone."

"What, like divining for water?" Ben remembered seeing some people on TV once holding hazel twigs in their hands, twigs that jumped and twitched when they passed over water. Perhaps it was something twigs did.

Iggy looked at him as if he was mad. "I haven't the faintest idea what you're talking about," he said.

"Water . . ."

It was a faint voice, high and thready. Ben turned around and stared into the gloom.

"Water . . . ," the voice came again. Ben could have sworn it came from the container Mr. Dodds and his accomplice had brought up to the stockroom. He and Iggy went over to it. It was a big box, about five feet long and almost two high. Rather like a small coffin. Ben tapped on it.

"Hello?" he called. "Is there someone in there?"

In response, the box began to rock and creak. Ben and Iggy leaped backward. The cat's nose started to twitch frantically. "Whoever it is comes from Eidolon," he said.

"I need water!"

Whatever it was, it sounded very demanding. "If we let you out," Ben said carefully, "will you promise not to hurt us?"

"Did you put me in here?"

"No."

"Then I won't hurt you."

Which seemed fair enough. Ben took a close look at the lock, then sorted through the pile of keys. This time, the second one he chose worked. He was getting good at this. As soon as the lock clicked, the lid of the box sprang open.

Inside was something large and mottled and sleek. It had huge, wet, dark eyes and flippers. It was a seal. In a sea green dress.

At the sight of Ben and Ignatius, its eyes rolled and it began to quiver all over. What happened next might have been a trick of the moonlight, or what happens when you should have been in bed asleep for hours, but when Ben looked at the seal again, it appeared to have turned into a girl.

Chapter Eight

Wild Roads

Ben blinked rapidly, in case it was a problem with his sight. But when he focused again, it was still a girl, even if it still had flippers and a rather whiskery face.

"What is it?" he said, in his alarm forgetting his manners entirely.

Iggy smirked. "The creatures of this world are so dull in comparison with those of Eidolon. This young lady is what is known in the legends of your Scottish Isles as a selkie."

Ben stared at him. "A what?"

"Must you talk about me as if I wasn't here?" the girl/seal asked suddenly. "Help me out of this box." Her voice was as musical as the sea on a calm day, and her eyes were as shiny and bright as wet beach pebbles.

Ben did as he was told and found himself clutching what appeared to be a large piece of flexible, damp black rubber. "My name"—the selkie said, coughing delicately into her other flipper—"is She Who Swims the Silver Path of the Moon, daughter of He Who Hangs Around on the Great South Rock to Attract Females; but you can call me Silver."

After a pause while he took this in, Ben replied, "I'm Ben Arnold. But my father is just called Mr. Arnold. I'm a human boy. Although Iggy here says I'm also from Eidolon, which I don't understand. What sort of creature is a selkie?"

She laughed, and her laughter was the sound of tiny waves trickling over shingle. Ben was beginning to get a bit fed up with all this sea imagery.

"I am, as this beast just explained, a child both of the water and of the air. . . ."

Out of the corner of his eye, Ben could tell that Ignatius was bridling at being called a beast. It served him right. Ben began to like the selkie better.

"I am mostly a seal who swims and plays in the briny deep, but when removed from my natural element for too long, I take on the form you see before you." She began to cough again, and now it was a terrible racking, hacking sound that made her whole body shake. "I believe," she said at last when the fit subsided, "your legends tell of magical cloaks of sealskin which, if removed, deprive the wearer of being able to change back into a sea creature." She laughed, and flung her arms wide. "Nothing so dull, as you see. Wet: a seal; dry: a girl. Well, almost. I can't seem to get my flippers to change." She clutched them to her thin chest and stared around, wide-eyed with fear. "What is this awful place? It smells of death and despair, and no magic at all. If I stay here I'll get stuck in the form of a girl, and that would be terrible. I need water to be a seal again, but if the water here is as bad as the air, it won't do me much good."

"Just like Twig," Ben said softly.

"Twig?"

Ben indicated the wood-sprite on top of the cage Iggy had been trapped in. "I found him on my lawn."

Silver gazed at Twig sorrowfully. "He certainly doesn't look well. Perhaps we are both ailing for the same reason."

Ben grimaced. "My world is bad for you?"

She shuddered. "There is no magic here," she said. "Everything feels flat and dull and lifeless. And without magic, we cannot survive."

"We'll have to find our way back into the Secret Country," Iggy added, "as soon as possible. The trouble is," he confided, "I don't know where the entrance to the correct wild road may be; and you know what they're like: We could end up anywhere if we get the wrong one."

The selkie looked at him pityingly. "Can't you cats navigate?"

"They call him the Wanderer," Ben piped up helpfully. "Because he's a great explorer."

Iggy looked embarrassed. "Well, yes. But"—he searched quickly for a face-saver—"the men who caught me knocked me over the head before I had a chance to get my bearings."

Silver looked terrified. "Then we'll die!" She

grabbed Ben by the arm with one strong flipper. Even through the sleeve of his jumper, Ben could feel the cold of another world's sea. "You must help us!"

"Whatever I can do, I will," he said simply.

"You will be my hero." The selkie closed her eyes. A vertical line appeared on her forehead, as if she was thinking very hard. "When they carried me through the way-between-worlds, the smell changed and I knew I was no longer in Eidolon. When I opened my eyes all I could see was a lot of dark bushes, a large pool of water with little colored wooden things on it, a tall rock, a winding pathway . . ."

Now it was Ben's turn to frown. Dark bushes. A large pool of water . . . a big rock . . .

The standing stone! "Aldstane Park!" he blurted out triumphantly. "The big rock—Aldstane is Old English for the Old Stone! And there's a boating lake there, and lots of trees and bushes!"

Aldstane Park lay behind King Henry Close and was the scene of many a family picnic presided over by Awful Aunt Sybil. Ben hated these outings with a passion, but he remembered one particular picnic all too well. Cousin Cynthia and his sister Ellie had made a secret camp and disappeared into the middle of the forest of rhododendrons, hollies, and hawthorns in the park, leaving Ben behind. At seven, Ben had found this both hurtful and annoying. With grim determination, he had searched for them, creeping around the bushes, tripping over roots, being startled by stray dogs. And when he at last tracked the hideaway down, the girls had ambushed him and left him tied to a tree till the moon came up and he was found by the park-keeper, who thought it all a great joke. Even now, the memory made him blush with shame.

As a hero, he had a lot of ground to make up.

Suddenly the selkie slumped to the floor, her breath sounding ragged. Iggy began to lick her face, but she pushed him feebly away. "Water . . . ," she moaned.

After a moment's thought, Ben ran downstairs. In the pet shop, the fish tanks were eerie with neon light. "Sorry," he apologized to the Mongolian Fighting Fish. He pulled off their lid, scooped the two bemused fish up in the net that hung beside the tank, and deposited them in a huge tank full of goldfish. Instead of setting about conquering this new territory with the fervor you would expect of creatures from the land of the Great Khan, they immediately swam to the bottom of the

112

tank and cowered, quivering with terror, beneath a decorative arch, while the goldfish swam round and round, staring at them, their mouths opening and closing with curiosity. Ben unplugged the empty tank and lurched upstairs with it, water sloshing all over his sweater. He staggered through the stockroom door and with superhuman effort upended the contents of the tank all over the selkie. Water went everywhere—over the floorboards, his feet, the boxes, and the cages. Unfortunately, quite a lot of it also went over Ignatius Sorvo Coromandel, who yowled in outrage and leaped for safety. From the top of a teetering stack of boxes, he bubbled and hissed like a kettle on a stove, his fur sleeked to his skin, not looking much like one of the greatest feline explorers in two worlds.

At the touch of the water, Silver's skin began to mottle and shine. She sighed and rolled, and her movements became ever more sinuous and seal-like. At last, rubbing her face with her flippers, she sat up. Bristles had sprouted all round her mouth: her eyes were round and dark.

"Thank you," was what Ben heard in his head, though what he heard in his ears was more like a sharp barking noise. He stared at the selkie—now definitely more seal than girl—and wondered how on earth he was supposed to get a seal, a cat, and a wood-sprite to a park over three miles away. But even as he wondered this, the selkie was changing again: The whiskers started to recede, her head began to change shape, mottled hide gave way to skin and a thin, green cotton shift. But the flippers remained, a defiant and rubbery black.

"We'd better leave now," Ben said. "Quickly. Can you walk?"

She could, after a fashion. Ben gave the shivering Iggy a quick rubdown with his sleeve; slipped Twig, complete with baseball cap, back inside his damp sweater; grabbed up a dustsheet draped over some crates and wrapped it around Silver's head and shoulders. She looked pretty odd in it—like a rather cumbersome ghost—but, thought Ben, anything was better than being seen marching a seal around Bixbury in the middle of the night. Questions would be hard to answer.

They slipped out through the shop, leaving a frenzy of twitching noses and blinking eyes behind them. Out on the street all was silent, and even though it was the beginning of summer, there was a distinct chill in the air.

The selkie stared skyward. She smiled.

"Look!" She pointed to where a constellation rather like a saucepan with four legs and an extended handle rode the starry sky. "The Great Yeti!"

Ben followed the line of her finger and frowned. "Um, don't you mean the Great Bear?"

Silver laughed. "Not where I come from. And above it is the Pole Star."

"We call it that too!" cried Ben excitedly.

"By some strange miracle, your night sky is the same as ours," said the selkie.

They crossed the High Street and the old market square, where the moonlight fell over the war memorial. There was not another soul to be seen. The town appeared to have been abandoned, as if everyone had left suddenly to go somewhere else, been beamed up by aliens, or devoured by giant plants. Ben was visited by the unwelcome realization that Bixbury's current state somewhat echoed the growing emptiness he felt inside. Perhaps it wasn't even his true home. Perhaps he didn't belong anywhere.

He was just thinking this when there was a distant rumble. Ben stared up the road. "It's the night bus!" He ran up the street a little way and stuck his arm out.

Silver and Iggy followed uncertainly. The bus slowed and came to a halt with a screech of brakes. The automatic door opened with a sigh, and the driver stared at the motley crew at the bus stop.

"Do you go anywhere near Aldstane Park?" Ben asked.

The driver tried to peer around him at his companions.

Ben dodged sideways.

"Would King Henry Close do you?"

Ben nodded vigorously.

"Fancy-dress party, was it?" the driver asked suspiciously, still trying to get a good look at Silver and Iggy.

"Er, sort of. Two halves, please, and a cat." Ben fumbled in his pocket for the pound coin.

The driver drew himself up. "I'm afraid I don't take animals on my bus unless they're properly restrained by a leash or carried in a suitable container."

Ben stared around in anguish, but curiously there was no sign of the cat at all. Silver had edged forward and seemed to be having problems with the steps. On the pretext of helping her up, Ben leaned over and hissed, "Where's Iggy?" In response, Silver lifted

a finger to her lips. Then she twitched back the volu-
minous sheet. Iggy was clinging to the inside of it for
dear life.

Ben turned back to the driver. "Just the two halves
then, please."

Silver hauled herself up the steps, waddled past
Ben, and found herself a seat out of the driver's view.
Apart from a young couple entwined around one
another at the back, the bus was empty. When Ben
came and sat down beside the selkie, Iggy peered out
from the cloak and purred at him. Silver tucked her
flippers out of sight and gave a little smile.

Ten minutes later, the bus dropped them off on the
corner of King Henry Close. But when they reached
Aldstane Park, the gates were locked. Ben rattled them
uselessly. He tried to shimmy up the tall railings on
either side, but each time slipped back down, burning
his palms. "What shall we do?" Silver wailed. Her
voice tailed off into a haunting, dolphinlike cry. She
slumped to the pavement, coughing.

Iggy wove around her in disconsolate figures-of-
eight, mewing, "Now, now, She Who Swims the Silver
Path of the Moon, don't worry, Ben will think of
something."

At this, Twig began to stir too. Ben took him out of his sweater and laid him on the ground between them. The wood-sprite seemed listless. He kept twisting around in the baseball cap as if he couldn't find a comfortable position.

Ben sat down with his chin on his knees, feeling responsibility pressing down upon him. He remembered what his mother had said, that looking after other creatures taught you responsibility—which was all very well; but what it didn't teach you was what to do at times like this. He was out of his depth here. He looked up, about to admit defeat. In the moonlight, Silver's skin and hair appeared colorless. Now she really looked like a ghost. For a moment Ben found himself wondering if he were dreaming all this; then she put a flipper on his shoulder, and again he felt the strange coolness, as if someone had draped seaweed upon him. "You will think of something," she said between coughs. "I know it, Ben Arnold."

It was as if the saying of his name gave Ben the power he needed to solve the problem.

"Can you climb?" he asked the selkie.

Silver smiled. "I will follow you anywhere."

Ben jumped up and pulled her to her feet. "Come on," he said. "I have an idea!"

At the western wall of the park stood a great ash tree, with branches that swept low on either side of the fence. The ash lay silhouetted against the sky like Yggdrasil the World Tree from Ben's favorite book of Norse legends, the tree whose roots lay in the underworld and whose branches swept the heavens. *Had the ancient peoples somehow known there was another world, a secret country, touching our own?* Ben wondered.

He stowed the sprite in his sweater again, grabbed hold of one of the low-slung branches, and swung himself up. It was surprising to see that all that gymwork was really beginning to pay off. Perhaps there were other aspects of school that might yet come in handy, though it seemed unlikely.

Iggy leaped past him, ran lightly to the junction with the trunk, and sat there, smiling smugly. It was a bit of a struggle (he had no idea that a selkie could be so heavy), but Ben managed to haul Silver up beside him. They edged along the branch and stared down the other side of the fence. The selkie cried out in sudden delight. Stretching away from them in the moonlight was the boating lake, shining like a mirror in the center of the park. Ben helped Silver to clamber along the branches, and when they reached a great down-swooping branch on the park side of the ash, Iggy and Ben jumped to the ground.

Silver lay on her stomach across the branch and looked down. "I'm not sure I can jump so far."

Ben grimaced. He placed Twig carefully between the roots of the ash tree and went to stand beneath Silver, arms outstretched.

The selkie wriggled awkwardly into a sitting position and swung her hind flippers over the side of the branch. A bout of coughing made her double up in pain. When she opened her eyes again, they were watery with what might have been tears.

"Just let go and I'll catch you," Ben said with a confidence he didn't feel.

Silver shut her eyes and pushed herself away from the branch. As if in sympathy, Ben found his own eyes shutting. He waited for the impact, but none came. Instead there was a rush of movement, followed by the sound of tearing fabric, and then a soft thump. He opened his eyes to find the torn sheet hanging from a snag on the branch, and Silver, her fall broken by the ripping cotton, safe and sound beside him.

"Luck is clearly running with us," Iggy breathed.

Silver took one look at the boating lake and started to lumber toward the shining water. Her flippers slapped against the grass. At the edge of the lake, she slipped out of her sea green shift and a moment later there was a splash. The water closed seamlessly over the selkie's head. The moon shone down on the dark surface and traced in silver the progress of the concentric ripples spreading away to the shore. Ben held his breath. At last there was a disturbance beneath the surface and something reappeared. It was not the head of the girl who had gone in, but of a seal, slippery and whiskery and liquid-eyed. The seal dived and resurfaced, dived and resurfaced. It swam with a sinuous, lithe grace that filled Ben with envy.

Iggy, however, watched the display with a look of disgust. "Ugh, water," he said, and turned away, shuddering.

At last the seal swept across the lake, flopped inelegantly out onto the shore, and blinked its large, wet, round eyes at them.

Even in the cool of the night, the water began to evaporate at once. Ben watched in amazement as the water dried; for where there had been sleek, mottled sealskin, areas of pale pink were beginning to show through. The seal reached a flipper to the scrap of sea green fabric on the ground, and as she did so the flipper began to lengthen and refine its shape and eventually become an arm, albeit with a rather blurred, dark mass on the end that was neither quite flipper nor hand. Ben was so mesmerized by this transformation that he missed the exact moment when seal became girl. When he looked up again, Silver was fully clothed and gazing at him with a delighted smile. She was, he realized suddenly, quite beautiful, with her pale hair and her huge eyes restored to some vestige of health.

"Thank you," she said.

"It was nothing. It's not much of a lake," Ben replied.

"Not for that, though I am grateful indeed. No, I thank you for your chivalry."

"My what?"

"For not staring at me unclothed."

"Oh, that." He hadn't even thought to do so. "No problem."

"You are a true friend, Ben Arnold."

Ben felt himself go pink with pleasure.

Feeling rather left out in this exchange, Iggy cleared his throat. "And what about this wild road?" he said.

The selkie smiled at Ben and he felt as if his heart had grown to twice its normal size. She stared up into the night sky, then turned around. "Over there, among those bushes."

Ben followed the line of her arm to a great forest of irregular black shapes. He shivered. He remembered those bushes well. "Are you sure?"

The selkie nodded.

Ignatius Sorvo Coromandel interposed himself between them. "Better let me go first. The eyes, you know." And indeed his eyes were glowing like headlights in the moonlight.

They followed him into the midst of the rhododendrons. Beneath the canopy of leaves it was very dark, and cooler than it was in the open. Ben held Iggy's tail with one hand; Twig twisted and turned on the baseball cap in his other hand; and Silver brought up the rear, holding on to Ben's jumper and shuffling noisily along amongst the dry leaves; and in this strange configuration they wove between the shrubs and bushes for several minutes.

At last Iggy stopped.

"What?" said Ben.

"Er, nothing," Iggy said, rather uncertainly, and led off again.

Some minutes later they found themselves back in the same place.

"We've been here before," said Silver.

"I thought they called you the Wanderer because you were a great navigator," Ben exclaimed, rather crossly.

"Hmmm. Yes," said Iggy, and did not elaborate.

He sniffed the ground with an air of scientific precision, then led them off in a different direction. They ducked under branches and suddenly found themselves in a small circular clearing.

As they did so, a weird red illumination sprang up around them, painting their faces and the undersides of the trees with a wash of scarlet. Iggy's eyes flared like a demon's. Silver gave out a tiny shriek of alarm, and Ben gazed wildly around, trying to determine the source of the phenomenon. The light was suddenly accompanied by a scratchy, high-pitched humming, rather like the whine of a giant mosquito. Ben stared at his hand. It was Twig. The little wood-sprite was sitting bolt upright, his whole body vibrating like a tuning fork. He was singing. The strange red light shone out from every pore of his body. It fled away from the wood-sprite, out along the dusty ground like a running fuse, sparking off roots and dead leaves, until at last it lit up against a great slab of rock partially hidden among a grove of hawthorns.

Ignatius Sorvo Coromandel grinned, and his teeth flashed as red as blood. "You see? I've found the entrance to the wild road." He bent his head and began to sniff energetically along the path of the light. When he reached the rock, he came to a halt. He walked three times around it, stepping carefully in and out of the thorny bushes, then stopped and walked back the other way. "It's the one," he declared. "No doubt about it."

Silver shuffled forward. "Let me see." She dropped to all fours, then gave a whoop of delight, which was followed by another coughing fit.

"What is it?" Ben was at her side at once.

Iggy craned his neck, ever curious.

The selkie was fiddling with a branch of hawthorn. Caught on the thorns was a scrap of red fabric. "Help me," she said breathlessly.

Ben folded the wood-sprite back into the baseball cap and slipped him down inside his sweater. The red light subsided to a gentle glow, and the strip of cloth changed color to a pale pinky-green. Ben disentangled it from the hawthorn and held it out to Silver.

"It's from my dress!"

She twirled around to show Ben and Iggy the back of the flimsy sea green tunic. Near the hem there was a small zigzag of fabric missing, as if torn violently away. The scrap she held fitted the hole perfectly.

"Wow," said Ben, overwhelmed.

"This is where they carried me through to your world," she said. "This is where I was imprisoned in the box."

"It's where I came in too," said the cat. He gave a low growl. "There are human footmarks here, and I remember the smell of the stone."

Ben ran his hands over the rock. It was pitted with age and patched with lichen and was sunk deep in the earth, deep in the leaf mold. It seemed that, like an iceberg, there was more of it below the ground than appeared above. Ben's fingers traveled across it as if remembering something. He stopped, then took Twig out of his sweater. Holding the wood-sprite close to the rock like a torch, he examined the surface closely.

Obscured by lichen and the corrosion of rain, a pattern was still visible. Someone had carved a word into the stone. It consisted of a lot of straight lines and angles, and for a while Ben could not quite make it out. Then . . . "Look!"

They crowded around.

"It's the Old Stone!" Ben exclaimed. "It's a sort of way-marker. . . ." His fingers traced the marks as he spelled them out: "E-I-D-O-L-O-N." And someone had rather more recently chalked an arrow on the Aldstane, pointing down into the ground.

Ignatius Sorvo Coromandel stepped around to the back of the stone, where the hawthorns made a dark hollow. There he did something with a front foot. It disappeared. Ben stared. Iggy pressed his face close to the ground where his foot had gone. A second later, his head had disappeared as well.

Ben's breath hissed out in alarm.

A few seconds later, the cat reemerged intact. "I can smell it!" he cried. "I can smell our home!"

The wood-sprite was sitting up now, his huge prismatic eyes gleaming red, like raspberries lit from within. All his deathlike lethargy had dispersed with the possibility of returning to the Secret Country. He looked . . . well—*spritely*, Ben thought. Then he thought, How did people know what spritely meant, when there were no sprites in this world?

This pondering was interrupted by Silver tapping him on the shoulder. "Come with us, Ben Arnold," she said.

The cat stood poised on the edge of the wild road.

"Come with us to Eidolon, Ben," Iggy exhorted. "Come and learn your destiny."

The Secret Country: a place filled with magic and wonders; a world that was in some way also his own; a world that bordered his like a shadow. A world that could be entered only by a wild road. Ben shivered. Did he really want to go to such a place? What if he couldn't get back again? Would he start to ail as Twig and Silver were ailing in his world?

Iggy started to shuffle impatiently.

Ben thought of his family. He thought of his sisters: Ellie, so sarcastic and touchy, who had, for all her faults, saved up and bought him the perfect gift— *Fish: The Ultimate Encyclopedia*—for Christmas last year; baby Alice, who would clutch his finger in her tiny hand as if her powerful grasp was the only way she could communicate her love. He thought of his father: so busy with his job on the paper, cracking jokes as he did the dishes; his father, who had volunteered to cut all of Awful Uncle Aleister's hedges in exchange for a fish tank to make Ben happy. And then he thought of his mother. He did not think of her exhausted and wheelchair-bound, but of the brightness of her green eyes, the quirk of that single raised eyebrow before she dropped him one of her slow, conspiratorial winks.

"I can't leave them," he thought. "I just can't."

Then he realized he had spoken these words out loud, for Silver had burst into tears. She came to him and hugged him. He felt her strange coldness around him, and it was like being at sea.

"I know that I will see you again, Ben Arnold."

Ben nodded mutely. He couldn't speak, since a huge lump had risen in his throat.

Twig, his red light at last extinguished, flew up in front of Ben's face, dragging the baseball cap. It was clearly a great effort, but the wood-sprite was smiling, showing two rows of glittering, sharp teeth. He deposited the cap (slug slime and shepherd's pie remnants and all) on Ben's head. "Thank you, Ben . . .

saved me . . . never forget . . ." Then he fell to the ground with a thump, exhausted.

The selkie bent and picked Twig up gently in her great dark flippers and cradled him against her chest.

Ignatius Sorvo Coromandel dragged himself away from the entrance to the wild road. "Are you quite sure that you will not come with us, Ben?"

Ben nodded, and a single tear squeezed itself out of one eye. He rubbed it away angrily. "I'm sorry, Iggy. I can't. My mother's ill. I can't leave her."

The little cat looked sad. "Eidolon is your destiny, Ben, and I would like to show you your other home."

Ben smiled, a little lopsidedly. "Even so."

Iggy rubbed his head against Ben's leg and a huge purr rumbled through the grove. Ben dropped to one knee and held the cat against him so hard, he could feel its heart beating against his hands. "I will miss you, Iggy."

In the darkness, the little cat grinned. "I own your true name, Benjamin Christopher Arnold," he said in his gravelly cowboy voice. "I can call you anytime." Then Iggy disengaged himself and stood before the entrance to the wild road. He looked back over his shoulder at Ben and reminded him, "And you have my true name and can do the same. Though you can do it only three times, so don't waste it!" Then, like the Cheshire Cat, he disappeared gradually from sight, until not even a grin was left behind.

Silver leaned forward suddenly and kissed Ben's cheek.

Then she stepped behind the Aldstane and vanished.

Ben stood there alone in the dark for a long time, rubbing the cool trace of the selkie's lips against his cheek. Then he turned, parted the bushes, and came out once more into the park. The moonlight showed the pattern of their path across the dewy grass as a snaking, dark trail. He followed it to the oak tree, climbed back to the road, and began the long walk home.

The London Daily Tribune

UFO seen over Parliament

Late-night pedestrians crossing Westminster Bridge reported sightings of an unidentified object flying across the face of Big Ben.

"It was much larger than any normal bird," said Paula Smith (34), a practicing herbalist. "I've never seen anything like it."

A group of Japanese tourists took several

photographs of the object. It is somewhat indistinct, caught between the illuminated face of the clock tower and the light of the full moon, but it is the opinion of this newspaper that the object is probably either a heron or the result of a hoax.

Professor Arthur James Dyer from London University's Department of Extinct Animals disagrees.

"It's certainly a great deal bigger than a heron, and the set of the wings is not obviously avian. As far as I'm concerned, there's no doubt about it: it's the first clear sighting of a live pterodactyl."

This is not an isolated incident. There have been several instances in recent weeks of witnesses purporting to have seen unusual creatures in the vicinity of our capital city.

Last Tuesday, revelers on Hampstead Heath saw what they described as a large, dark, hairy animal running into the undergrowth on the eastern edge of the heath. One of the witnesses stated that he had had a very clear view and that the creature had "the head and torso of a horned man" and the "legs and nether regions of a goat." It was, he claimed, "quite clearly a satyr."

This sighting has generally been dismissed as the work of a fancy-dress trickster.

The Kernow Herald

LOCAL MAN IN HOSPITAL

The Beast of Bodmin:
Fact or Fiction?

Ramblers returning from a walk around the Sibleyback Reservoir on Bodmin Moor on Sunday morning scattered and ran for their cars when surprised by a loud roaring noise from behind a drystone wall.

Mr. B. Wise of Daglands Road, Fowey, did not live up to his name by staying in his vehicle. His wife, Barbara, blond, 43, recounted for us her version of events:

"There was this terrible roaring, and Bernard said to me, 'That's the Beast, that is. I'm going to get some piccies for the newspapers and make my fortune.' The next thing I know, he's grabbed his camcorder and slipped out of the car. Then he started climbing the wall. My Bernard's never been that fit, but he got nearly to the top and—well, what happened next was a bit of a blur. I saw a large black shape rearing up, and then a chunk of the wall came off in Bernard's hand and he fell over backward and hit his head. I got him to Emergency at Callington Hospital, but he's been out cold ever since."

A hospital spokesperson told us that Mr. Wise is now out of Intensive Care and is "as well as can be expected." Nurse Samantha Ramsay added, off the record, that he was probably lucky that the wall had got him rather than what was behind it.

There have been stories about a "Beast on the Moors" for decades now, but in the last month rumors have spread like wildfire. There have been over twenty reported sightings of what is believed to be a very big cat, and local farmers have lost a number of sheep. Experts called in from London Zoo's Conservation of Dangerous Animals Department examined the remains of some of the victims and were surprised by what they found.

"We thought it might be an escaped puma or leopard," said Dr. Ivor Jones. "But really, the width of jaw indicated by the bite marks suggests a very much larger animal, probably with enormous canine teeth, possibly even as large as those of a smilodon."

Since smilodons (saber-toothed tigers) became extinct during the Tertiary period, and there is no living cat with a similar bite pattern, Dr. Jones's opinions have provoked considerable controversy.

Part Two

There

Chapter Nine

At Awful Uncle Aleister's

In the days that followed, Ben regretted his decision not to follow his companions to the Secret Country. He thought about it when he was awake, his mind wandered in class, and at night he saw Iggy and Twig and Silver in his dreams: a small black and brown cat with shiny golden eyes staring out across an unfamiliar landscape from the top of a stone tower; a woodsprite, grinning from ear to ear, chasing dozy moths in and out of the branches in a dark forest. Most of all he dreamed of She Who Swims the Silver Path of the Moon, swimming with a lazy flick of her tail from the murky ocean depths to the surface of a shining sea.

But some nights his dreams were less serene. Once he dreamed of a terrible tall figure stalking across the land, its huge dog-head silhouetted against the moon, its sharp white teeth glinting in the pale light; and he heard the cries of terrified creatures dwindling to moans as if they were being dragged down some great, long tunnel.

Sometimes when he woke from these nightmares, it was to the sound of his baby sister wailing in the dark, and a vague sense that he was guilty of something, as if there was some important task he had left undone.

At school he tried to put such thoughts behind him, but in every class something would crop up to remind him of the Secret Country: In English they were given an essay entitled "Imagine your pet was suddenly given the power of speech"; in technical drawing they drew bisecting circles that made Ben think of the moment Iggy had described of Eidolon being jolted away from Earth; and in biology when Mr. Soames told them about the dinosaurs being dead, Ben, unthinking, piped up with, "No they're not, sir: they live in . . ."

Luckily his mate Adam saved him from further embarrassment by adding ". . . Transylvania!" which made the rest of the class laugh and jeer.

Ben was desperate to tell someone about his adventures. The pressure of his secrets was building up inside him until he thought he would burst. He'd thought of saying something to Ellie, but he knew she'd shriek with laughter, tell all her snotty friends (particularly Cousin Cynthia, with whom she was thick as thieves), and tease him mercilessly about it. His father was more preoccupied than usual. Mr. Arnold told Ben he was "onto something that could turn out to be a big story" and spent a lot of time out of the house doing "research." Several times he came close to telling his mother; but she seemed so tired and ill that although she was the most likely member of the family to believe him, he felt sure it would just make her worry about him, and that would make her even more tired. So he'd gone out one morning, looked around to make sure no one could hear him, and approached the thin white cat with the slanting eyes.

"Look," he'd said in as reasonable a fashion as he

could manage, "I've got to talk to someone about this or I'll go mad. You're a cat; you're supposed to know about Eidolon and the Wanderer and wild roads and stuff. Is it true, or did I dream it all?"

The cat gave him a sharp, rebuking look, then arched her back and stalked away.

Well, thought Ben. *How rude.* Then he thought, *Perhaps she's a bit deaf.* He shouted after her, but she slunk under the fence and disappeared. So either his ability to converse with animals had evaporated along with Ignatius Sorvo Coromandel, or he'd imagined the whole episode.

But who would make up a name like that? Who in their right mind would concoct such an unlikely tale?

When he went back into the house, his mother called his name. She was in the kitchen, slumped in her wheelchair. The clothes she had been trying to load into the washing machine lay strewn across the floor.

"Oh, Ben," she said when she saw him, and her voice had a defeated air.

The jeans he had worn on the night he had taken Iggy and Twig and Silver to Aldstane Park lay across her knees, and she was holding something small and dark in her hand. Her face looked pale and drawn and her eyes had a faraway look, but her voice was fraught with anger.

"Where did you get this?"

She opened her hand. The object she held was brown and almost oval in shape, and one end was sharper than the other. There were small wrinkles and striations on one side, while the underside appeared smooth. It looked like a piece of fir cone, but whatever it was made of wasn't wood. It took some moments before he could remember where he'd found it.

"Well? I'm waiting for an answer, Ben."

How could he tell his mother that he'd broken into Mr. Dodds's Pet Emporium and found this strange thing on the stockroom floor? He knew that although his mother hated cruelty to any creature and would be horrified to hear about Mr. Dodds's terrible trade, she would be very angry with him.

"I . . . I don't know what it is," he said, hoping to deflect her.

"Ah, but I do, and it shouldn't be in this world at all." She closed her eyes as if overcome with exhaustion. "Too late," she whispered. "I should have gone back, but I left it too late. . . ."

Ben felt his heart contract. "What is it, Mum? Are you okay?"

Mrs. Arnold gave her son an anguished look, tried to wheel herself toward the back door, and collapsed.

Ben dropped to his knees beside his mother. "Mum, what's the matter?"

Her eyes flickered over him, but she didn't seem to see him. Her mouth moved as if she was saying something, but no sound came out.

Ben felt helpless. He caught up his mother's wrist, and the object fell from her hand. He stuffed it back in his pocket, then found her pulse and counted, just like they had taught him to do in the first aid course at school.

One hundred and fifty. That couldn't be right.

The next time he tried it was two hundred. Ben rushed out into the hall. Should he call an ambulance, or his father? In the end he did both.

No one knew what was wrong with her. At the hospital they kept her in isolation and hooked her up to all sorts of tubes, but she got no better. A friend of hers came and took baby Alice away. Awful Uncle Aleister and Aunt Sybil offered to look after Ben and Ellie so that Mr. Arnold could spend time at his wife's bedside.

"Dad . . . ," Ben began pleadingly, but his father turned a face full of misery to him, and after that he couldn't refuse.

"It'll only be for a week or so, till she's over the worst of it," Mr. Arnold said, as if he believed it.

It was awful at Awful Uncle Aleister's. Ben had known it would be, with a sort of vague dread that failed to focus on specific details. Imagination had never been his strong point, and so he was very unprepared for what was to come. First of all, Aunt Sybil took his shoes away from him at the door before letting him inside ("mustn't spoil the carpets"); then she made him have a bath and wash his hair with some vile-smelling concoction that would, she promised with a nervous laugh, "get rid of any nasty little unwelcome visitors."

Ben had no idea what she meant by this, though the idea of visitors in his hair, partying away, having a good time, invisible to the rest of the world, was rather appealing. Even so, he did what he was told, though the shampoo made his eyes water and his scalp sting. It was only when Cynthia sneered at him and said something about lice that he realized what Aunt Sybil had meant, and after that his head itched all night.

He had been given a supper of kidneys and boiled potatoes and stewed cabbage that had tasted so awful he couldn't eat it, despite being ravenous, and as a result he had been sent to bed early with his plate of horrid food, to what Aunt Sybil called "the box room." He supposed that was because there were a lot of boxes in it. So many boxes, in fact, that there was hardly room for a bed. They were brown cardboard boxes, and they were piled high in a higgledy-piggledy sort of way. None of them were labeled, and all were bound with brown packing tape. The first one he tried to lift was so heavy he couldn't move it; but the next was oddly light, as if someone had taped up a boxful of air. When he shook it, he could hear nothing inside.

He sat on the edge of the rickety camp bed and stared at the plate. Then, slowly, he ate all the potatoes. But the cabbage was gray and slippery and smelled like old pondwater; and as for the kidneys . . . Defeated, he found a plastic bag and shoveled the rest of the food into it, then stowed the bag in his rucksack.

Tomorrow he would smuggle it out to the bins before Aunt Sybil found out. Then he thought about sawing open one of the boxes with the penknife Aunt Sybil and Uncle Aleister had failed to confiscate from him, but decided they might keep feeding him kidneys and cabbage if they found out. Or worse. Then, for a long while, he thought about his mother. Tears threatened. To distract himself, he took the odd object he had picked up at the pet shop out of the pocket of his jeans and turned it over and over in his fingers, feeling its strange serrations and the smooth curve of its inside face. He was holding it at arm's length and wondering just why his mother had been so affected by it when the door came slightly ajar and a creature appeared at the foot of it. It was a small and hairless creature with a pointy face and large ears and uptilted eyes of amber yellow. Wrinkles of skin pooled around its feet and bagged at its joints. Nudging the door harder with its head, it came into the room and stood there, staring at him. Ben was so surprised by the sight of it that he dropped the thing he had been holding. It skittered across the uncarpeted floor and came to rest in front of the hairless creature, which stepped

145

back nervously. Then it took a step closer and sniffed it. Its head shot up in alarm. At last it bashed the object with its paw and hissed so that its face became one big wrinkle.

It was then that Ben realized this strange creature must be a cat: to be precise, Cynthia's new cat. But cats were supposed to have silky coats from head to toe. What new atrocity had Cynthia subjected the poor beast to?

He put out his hand. "Here, Kitty, Kitty," he said softly.

The cat—or whatever it was—gave him an evil look.

"Don't 'Kitty' me," it said, its voice high and scratchy.

Ben grinned. "You can talk! I was beginning to think I'd imagined all that. What's your name?"

The cat smiled. "You won't catch me like that." It stalked across the room, squinted up at him, then leaped up onto the windowsill behind him. Ben could feel its eyes on him like a cold shadow on the back of his neck. He shivered and turned around.

"Are you a cat? What happened to your fur?"

"So many questions."

"Did Cynthia do something to you? She doesn't always look after her pets—"

The cat hissed at him. "Petssss? I am no pet. I am a Sphynx."

Ben raised his eyebrows. It sounded pretty impressive, but the only sphinxes he knew were the ones that guarded the Great Pyramid of Cheops, and this wizened, wrinkly little beast looked more like Yoda than a grand Egyptian carving.

As if it could read his mind, the cat rolled its eyes. "We Sphynxes are hairlesss, not covered in smelly fur like common catsss." It looked sly. "Unlike the Wanderer."

"You know the Wanderer?"

The Sphynx began to groom a paw in a peculiarly catlike fashion. "Oh, yesss, I know the Wanderer." It examined its spread toes, then lifted innocent eyes to Ben. "You don't happen to know where he isss, do you?"

"No. The last time I saw him—" Ben stopped. "Why do you want to know?"

"He'sss a . . . friend."

Something about the way the Sphynx said this made Ben doubt the truth of this statement. "Er, he went wandering," he finished lamely.

The cat regarded him suspiciously.

"In Eidolon," Ben added, to test the creature's reaction.

The Sphynx's ears went flat to its skull. "Sssssssssss! What do you know about the Shadow World?"

"Oh, this and that," Ben said airily. "How to get there—that sort of thing."

Now the cat looked fearful. It jumped down from the windowsill and slunk around the edge of the room as if keeping as much distance as possible between itself and Ben. "She'sss sent you as her ssssspy," it muttered. "I should have known." It narrowed its eyes at him. "You should not involve yoursssself in thingsss that do not concern you, Ben Arnold. It could be very dangerousss."

And with that, it disappeared.

Ben sat on the bed for a while, feeling distinctly uncomfortable. He wished Iggy were there to talk to. Then he got up, crept over to the door, and peered around it down the corridor. There was no sign of the Sphynx, nor of anyone else. Closing the door quietly, he picked up the thing he had taken from Mr. Dodds's stockroom and stared at it again.

It looked so ordinary, but the cat had seemed frightened by it.

And he remembered how his mother had reacted when she had found it in his jeans pocket.

What on earth could it be?

He turned it over and examined the underside, but got no more clues from that. He rubbed it between his fingers and found it rough on one side and smooth on the other. Under closer scrutiny it looked as if it might once have been a reddish color, but it had somehow faded to this rather uninteresting brown. He sniffed at it, and it smelled slightly musty, like something that had once been alive.

Frowning, he climbed into bed and tried to get comfortable. His thoughts circled around his mind like bats in a cave.

Ben slept badly that night. It might have been because the camp bed's mattress was so lumpy. It might have been because he was in Awful Uncle Aleister's house. It might have been because he was hungry, or because Cynthia and Ellie were giggling away in the room next door. Or it might have been because of what the Sphinx had said.

At any rate, he found himself suddenly wide awake in the dead hours of the morning. Outside, an engine was running, low and rumbly. He got up and peered through the window. A truck had backed up into the driveway. Its tailgate was open, as if someone were loading or unloading from it. Ben squinted into the darkness. For a long time he could see nothing at all, for there was no moon; but he had the sense of there being a lot of activity, for he could hear the scuffle of footsteps on the gravel and even a murmur of voices. A few minutes later his patience was rewarded when something moved close to the house and the security light came on. Two figures with hooked noses, hunched bodies, and clawed fingers . . .

The security light went off.

Ben sucked in his breath, blinked, blinked again. He rubbed his eyes. Surely he hadn't seen what he thought he'd seen? But the light did not come on again, and a little while later he heard the trunk being banged shut, then someone climbed into the cab and drove the truck out into the road. He watched as its red brake lights dwindled into the distance.

Perhaps he was still dreaming. That would explain everything.

But as he moved away from the window he stubbed his toe on the bed leg, which made him painfully aware that he wasn't dreaming at all.

And that the figures he had seen loading boxes into the back of the truck really had been a pair of goblins.

Chapter Ten

A Remarkable Discovery

At breakfast the next morning Ben found that Cynthia was watching him warily, which was unusual, since she rarely looked at him at all except to glare. Even Ellie seemed subdued. This meant that the conversation was left to Awful Uncle Aleister and Aunt Sybil, who were planning some sort of outing. Ben wasn't paying much attention—partly because the subject sounded really very dull (a customer had been complaining about some faulty goods the company had supplied) and partly because Cynthia's cat, the unnamed Sphynx, was sitting right on top of the bookcase like a particularly unpleasant bookend, staring at him with its unblinking yellow eyes.

"Well, what do you think?" Aunt Sybil asked brightly. "Shall we all make a day of it?"

Uncle Aleister did not seem too happy at the idea of the entire family accompanying him on his errand. "You'd be very bored," he kept saying.

"But," said Aunt Sybil forcefully, "I believe the house is one of the finest examples of Tudor architecture in the country. It would do the children good to acquire a bit of culture."

Her husband rolled his eyes. He knew when he was beaten.

"Is there a shop?" The girls wondered. It was all Ellie and Cynthia were interested in.

Aunt Sybil smiled and avoided the question. "It has lovely grounds. And a knot garden."

Cynthia curled her lip. "Do I look like someone who cares about knots?" she snarled.

"And some very famous Whistlers."

Now even Ellie was rude enough to snort with

laughter. "Who wants to listen to some idiots whistling?"

Aunt Sybil became flustered. "No, no, dear— they're paintings. . . ."

Of course that didn't do the trick either.

Ben, who had for a moment been quite curious about a team of whistlers, found his attention straying back to the goblins he had seen last night. What had they been doing here, at Uncle Aleister's? It was all very odd. Rather than go to some crumbling country house full of musty furniture and old paintings, he thought he'd rather stay behind and search for clues. And he wanted another chance to talk to the Sphynx.

"Right then, no more arguments from you lot!" Uncle Aleister announced. "We're all going and that's an end to it. Chop, chop! We can't keep Lady Hawley-Fawley waiting."

Ben's ears pricked up. "Would that be Lady Hawley-Fawley of Crawley?" he ventured.

Awful Uncle Aleister regarded him disdainfully. "What on earth would a boy like you know about the aristocracy?"

Ben floundered. "Er . . . I . . ." He thought desperately, then said the first thing that came into his head. "I hear she has a world-famous collection of shoes."

Why on earth had he said *that*?

"Shoes?" Ellie's face lit up.

"Fantastic," said Cynthia.

And that was that. Half an hour later they all piled into Aunt Sybil's Range Rover and drove to Crawley.

All the way there, Ben tried to remember exactly how he knew Lady Hawley-Fawley's name. It wasn't as if he'd ever met any lords or ladies. Perhaps his father had mentioned her when working on one of his stories for the newspaper. But that didn't sound right either. It was only when Uncle Aleister said something to his wife about the faulty item being a garden incinerator that something clicked into place.

He remembered a letter with an embossed crest lying on the desk in the Pet Emporium's office. But that letter had been addressed to Mr. Dodds.

So if that was the case . . .

He stared very hard at the back of Awful Uncle Aleister's head and thought about the implications.

• • •

Rather than follow the rest of them into the grand mansion, Ben made an excuse of wanting to explore the gardens instead. To his surprise, no one argued with him. Uncle Aleister had his appointment, and Aunt Sybil, Cousin Cynthia, and Ellie were far too excited about the famous shoe collection to mind that he was going off on his own. Which was another good reason to disappear for a while.

First of all, he saw a sign for the knot garden and went to have a look, but it was a rather disappointing affair made up of low green hedges and colored gravel, and there was no sign of any knots at all. The fountains were turned off and some fat pigeons were sitting around the edges, looking bored. He followed the path past the ornamental ponds where fat orange goldfish meandered lazily through the weed like miniature submarines, and found himself at last in an orchard. Last year's leaves were strewn on the grass between the fruit trees, making the area untidier than the rest of the grounds, but Ben preferred the wildness here. He kicked some leaves around and watched the way they spiraled in the breeze. He picked up a fallen apple and, after giving it a cursory polish on his jeans, bit into it; but the fruit was tart and unripe, and when he looked into the bite mark he'd made, he spied something white and wriggly near the core. "Ugh! Maggots!" He threw the apple away from him as hard as he could and walked on.

Beyond the orchard was an area of trampled grass and scattered brown objects that crunched underfoot like the dried husks of beechnuts. Within feet, the trampled grass gave on to an even scruffier area where rusting machinery, bales of hay, rolls of wire netting, and tree-stakes lay tumbled between weathered sheds and lichen-streaked outhouses. There were broken plant pots, bags of rotting compost, and garden implements. Old crates, a bicycle missing its front wheel; and a dragon.

Ben came to a halt, his eyes bulging.

He had never seen a dragon before, except in books. There, they were sheathed in glorious color, breathing sheets of fire that turned maidens to Kentucky Fried Chicken in seconds flat. Or fighting bold knights who had come to slay them. Or curled around hoards of gold in mountain caves, guarding their treasure from thieves. They were creatures from the world of legend, powerful, cruel, and magnificent, soaring and swooping in the twilight skies of mythology.

This dragon did not look as if it had ever soared, or fought a knight, or even cooked a maiden. It was small (for a dragon), and it had a heavy collar around its neck, which someone had tied to a fence post with a length of frayed rope. It sat hunched up with its scaly tail and a pair of thin, leathery wings curled around its feet like a domestic cat. Its hide was patched and mottled. Its head hung down dejectedly. It did not even look up as he approached.

"Hello," said Ben.

The dragon lifted its head very slowly, as if the weight of it was more than it could manage.

Its eyes were purple and seemed to have several rings of iris rather than the usual one. Ben felt that if he were to stare into them for any length of time he would become very confused indeed.

When it saw that its visitor was a mere boy, the dragon hung its head again and sat there contemplating its long, scaly toes.

Ben walked up to it cautiously. He knew he should feel afraid, since the dragons in the books he had read had been terrifying monsters, but all he felt for this one was curiosity and a sort of pity. The dragon looked not only unthreatening, but defeated, and rather sad. He wanted to hug it. He wanted to untie it from its post and set it free.

His fingers closed around the thing in his pocket, and suddenly he knew exactly what it was.

"Excuse me," he started again, it seeming a good idea to be as polite as possible. "Is this yours by any chance?"

He took the scale out of his pocket, held his hand under the creature's nose, and watched as its nostrils flared. Then two little protuberances on top of its head, which he imagined might be ears, started to twitch. He took a step back, just in case it was preparing to barbecue him.

"Another one," the dragon said gloomily.

"I beg your pardon?"

"You found another one, then," the dragon repeated.

It nodded its head around in a vague sort of way, and Ben knew he'd been right. The things that looked like husks of dried nuts were scales that had fallen off into the trodden grass and dust, and the mottled effect of the dragon's coat was because many of the scales had peeled away in patches, exposing areas of gray-brown hide. Even those that remained were dull and dead-looking.

"Are you ill?" he asked suddenly. "You don't look very well."

"I'm very tired," the dragon said slowly. It fixed Ben with its strange eyes. "And I'm very hungry."

Ben laughed nervously. "Don't they feed you, then?"

The dragon wearily lifted a front foot and indicated a pile of cabbage leaves and potato peelings rotting away by one of the sheds. "If you can call that food."

"What would you prefer? Perhaps I can get it for you."

The eyes flashed for a second. "I was always rather partial to the odd warm-blooded mammal," the dragon said. It assessed him slowly. Then it gave him a crocodile smile. "Lucky for you I don't have the strength to roast a rabbit at the moment. Or even a dingbat."

"A what?"

But the dragon was staring off into the distance, looking wistful.

Ben had an idea. He took off his rucksack. Inside was the plastic bag containing last night's congealed supper. He had meant to put it in a bin, but now he upended it in front of the dragon. "You

161

might like some of this," he suggested, though it was hard to imagine that anyone would, even a starving creature from another world.

The dragon sniffed at the gooey pile. It nosed about in it for a bit, separating the cabbage from the meat. Then a long gray tongue—just like a snake's, but much, much bigger—shot out, and two seconds later all the kidneys were gone.

The dragon regarded him hopefully. "Mmmm," it said. "That was delicious. Is there any more?"

Food in the Secret Country was obviously a lot less appetizing than food in this world, Ben decided, remembering how ravenously Iggy had scoffed the shepherd's pie.

"No," he said. "Sorry. That's all there is."

He was just thinking about how excellent it would be to hide the dragon in Awful Uncle Aleister's garden to dispose of his unwanted dinners, when he heard voices. Two people were coming through the orchard, and by the sound of his booming voice, one of them was Uncle Aleister.

Ben grimaced. Then he grabbed up his rucksack and the plastic bag and fled around the back of the nearest shed. Behind him, he heard the dragon mutter,

"Very rude. Really, how very rude. Not even a good-bye. Or, in fact, an introduction . . ."

"It's completely useless, I tell you," came the voice that was not Uncle Aleister's. "It's not worked properly since Day One. All it does is sit there and look miserable—as you can see it's not burned a single leaf in all the time I've had it. The orchard's a disgrace! I can't even show the thing orf to my guests, it's so ugly; and I'm quaite sure it's sick, for as you'll perceive, all its scales are falling orf."

The speaker was a tall, thin woman wearing a brightly colored headscarf. She had a long narrow nose, long narrow arms, and a long narrow skirt that almost touched the ground. Walking beside her was Awful Uncle Aleister. He looked, Ben thought, peering through the baler twine and rolls of netting, rather red in the face, as if he wanted to say a lot more in response to the woman than good customer relations would allow.

"Let me take a look at the beast, Lady Hawley-Fawley," he said at last, tapping some ash off the end of his cigar. "I'm sure it's just off its food. These exotic creatures do take a little while to settle in to their new surroundings, you know." He stood there for a moment looking at the dragon apprehensively. Then he put a hand out to it.

The dragon regarded him with considerably more interest than it had previously shown, then bared its teeth—all its teeth, of which there were a lot—and gave a low growl. Uncle Aleister took a swift step away again.

"I want my money back!" the woman demanded crossly. "All fifteen hundred pounds of it, and no argument, my good man."

"If you'd read the small print carefully—" Uncle Aleister started.

"Don't you 'small print' me," said Lady Hawley-Fawley. "I know my rights. Money back, or a brand-new replacement—at once!"

"We . . . er . . . haven't any more in stock at the moment."

Lady Hawley-Fawley put her hands on her hips. "If that's your attitude, then I shall be calling the city council. And the Trades Descriptions people. And the ombudsman. And my lawyer."

And when Uncle Aleister still had nothing to say for himself, she added, fixing him with an uncompromising glare, "And the police!"

"All right, all right. I'll get you a new one."

"And dispose of this one—I don't want it cluttering up my garden anymore, and I certainly don't want the damned thing dropping dead. I can't imagine what the SPCA would have to say about that."

Uncle Aleister nodded tiredly.

"And you can remove yourself and your mad family, too. Famous shoe collection, indeed—whatever do you take me for!"

Then off she flounced, if it was possible to flounce in a long narrow skirt and a pair of large green galoshes, leaving Awful Uncle Aleister (apparently) alone with the dragon.

"Now, then," he said, wiping a trickle of sweat off his forehead. "Just come with me, there's a good dragon."

The dragon didn't even look at him. Instead it nosed at the ground where Ben's dinner had been in a questing sort of way. It licked at a bit of grass. Uncle Aleister took a step closer, then another, and another. He put his hand on the beast's neck. A tiny puff of smoke emerged from one of its nostrils.

Looking alarmed, Uncle Aleister dropped his cigar. "Now, now, no need for that," he said hastily. "Just stay here, there's a good fellow, while I fetch the car." And dashed off through the orchard.

Ben waited until he had gone, then emerged from his hiding place. "You're coming home with us," he said gleefully.

"Home?" said the dragon. "There is no home for me in this world." It looked at Ben. "I miss my home. And I fear I shall never see it again. They will take me to some other terrible place and either they will kill me because they cannot profit from me, or I shall die from lack of care. Or from the sorrow of never seeing my wife and kits again."

A single fat tear gathered at the corner of one of its purple eyes and spilled out onto its cheek. Ben had had no idea a dragon could cry. He had heard about crocodile tears, which he knew were tears cried for effect rather than genuine feeling, to trick the unwary into trust so that they could be snapped up by those long jaws. The dragon did look more like a crocodile than any other creature he could think of, but it seemed so sincere and so mournful that he felt his own eyes well up.

Quickly he made a decision. "Right, then. We must get you back to your home. We must get you back to Eidolon."

The dragon blinked. "You know my home?"

"I've never been there," Ben admitted. "But I do know a way in." For now he had a plan. And the real beauty of it was that Awful Uncle Aleister would help with it without even realizing he was doing so.

It took twenty long minutes for Uncle Aleister to maneuver the dragon through the back doors of the Range Rover, for the smell of the exhaust, the oil, and the fuel made the poor beast faint with terror. He undid the rope from the post and hauled on its collar. That didn't work. He put his shoulder against its haunch and shoved, and that didn't work either. Eventually, more to get rid of its tormentor than for any other reason, the dragon bolted into the back of the vehicle and crouched there, its sides heaving, its purple eyes watching balefully as Uncle Aleister picked himself up out of the dust, swearing at the state of his suit. But at last it lay down and allowed the man to cover it with a plaid blanket, so that it looked as innocuous as a pile of rubbish.

Ben watched the vehicle meander off along the path, its back end weighted down in a rather alarming fashion, and then took to his heels. He ran through the orchard, past the ornamental fishponds, through the knot garden, and arrived in front of the house just in time to see the Range Rover appear from the road that curled around the back of Lady Hawley-Fawley's estate. Aunt Sybil, Cousin Cynthia, and Ellie were already waiting there. They did not look very happy.

"What an embarrassment!" Aunt Sybil scolded as soon as she set eyes on Ben. "I have never been so mortified in all my life."

"There wasn't any shoe collection, Benny-Boy," Cynthia jeered, digging her fingers painfully into his arm.

"Ow," said Ben.

"Leave him alone," said Ellie. "He's *my* brother, not yours. Only I'm allowed to claw him." Secretly, she had quite enjoyed the scene between Lady Hawley-Fawley and their awful aunt.

Cousin Cynthia was so surprised that she got into the back of the Range Rover without another word.

It was odd being in league with Uncle Aleister, even if his uncle did not know they shared a secret. When the dragon shifted suddenly as they rounded a sharp bend, the Range Rover veered and Aunt Sybil berated her husband for his poor driving, which caused a row and made Ben smile to himself. When the dragon let out a great huff of a sigh, Ben pretended it had been him, so that everyone gave him odd looks, even Uncle Aleister in the rearview mirror. On the motorway, they hugged the inside lane and even the slowest and most battered old jalopies overtook them. At last, when they were overtaken by an ancient three-wheeler, Aunt Sybil could stand it no longer.

"I don't know what on earth's the matter with you!" she cried. "You're driving like an old woman. Pull over and let me drive at once."

There was no point in arguing with Aunt Sybil when she got the bit between her teeth. At the next service station, they switched over and she drove them back onto the motorway.

Soon she had her foot flat to the floor, but still the Range Rover labored under the unaccustomed weight. "Well!" Aunt Sybil burst out at last. "There's obviously something wrong with this vehicle. I think it must have blown its turbo. It's so *sluggish*!"

Ben had little idea of what she meant by "blowing its turbo," but he loved the description of the car being sluggish. He was tempted to look out of the back window to see if they were leaving a glistening silver trail behind them, a trail that marked his progress into a world of magic.

Chapter Eleven

Xarkanadûshak

Ellie, Cynthia, and Aunt Sybil were arguing about the relative merits of Versace, Oscar de la Renta, and Christian Lacroix in the kitchen. To Ben, who had no idea what they were talking about, the names sounded like those of foreign soccer players; but knowing Ellie's absolute scorn for all sport, he realized that was unlikely. When the discussion got heated, Ben slipped out of the back door and into the rhododendrons so that he could spy on what Uncle Aleister was doing with the dragon. He didn't have to wait long before his uncle came out to the garage, unlocked the back door of the Range Rover, and unceremoniously dragged the dragon down the path to what Aunt Sybil referred to as her "gazebo," but that looked to Ben distinctly like a very ordinary garden shed.

"And don't even think of trying to burn it down!" Uncle Aleister warned the dragon menacingly as soon as he'd got it in there. "If you so much as scorch this place, you'll be dogmeat, I promise you."

He stepped smartly out of the shed and banged the door shut. "In fact," he added, through the slats, "that's probably the best plan. I bet Dodds can get a pretty penny out of some of those Doberman owners for a nice dragon steak or two."

"Dobermans," came the dragon's voice. "I used to eat them for breakfast."

Uncle Aleister laughed cruelly. "I doubt you could manage a Chihuahua in your current state." Then, still laughing to himself, he stumbled back up the dark path to the house.

Ben watched him disappear. Then he tiptoed to the shed, unlatched the door, and peered in. The dragon was curled up on the floor with its head on its front paws. It was shivering.

"Are you cold?" Ben asked softly, creeping inside.

The dragon lifted its head. In the darkness, its eyes glittered like jewels. "Dogmeat," it snuffled. "He wants to feed me to dogs."

"I'm sure he didn't mean it," was Ben's automatic response. Except that knowing Awful Uncle Aleister, he probably did, especially if there was any money to be made out of it. Then he suddenly realized the significance of what he had just witnessed.

"He could hear what you said—you talked to each other!"

"Oh, yes," said the dragon sarcastically. "We're close friends, despite all appearances to the contrary."

"No, I mean I thought it was only me."

"Oh, he can hear you, too, can he?" said the dragon. "Wonderful. Good for you."

"No, no," Ben whispered. "I mean, I thought it was *only* me who could hear the creatures of Eidolon talking. But if Uncle Aleister can hear you as well . . ."

"They're all in on it, all those traitors," the dragon said heavily. "Him, the Dodman, and their allies. They always wanted the power your world offered. We should have stopped them while we had the chance, but we never realized how ambitious they were."

Ben frowned. "Who's the Dodman?"

The dragon gave him a hard stare. Even in the night shadows of the shed, Ben could feel its gaze upon him. "Are you deliberately trying to aggravate me?"

Ben felt himself blush. He was glad it was dark. "Mr. Dodds?" he hazarded.

"Oh, that's what you call him here, is it?"

"Why do you call him the Dodman?"

The dragon closed its eyes. "Just pray you never find that out. Now you'd better leave me alone. If they find you talking to me, they'll turn *you* into dogmeat too."

Ben shuddered. "I'm not going to let them do that," he said firmly. "To either of us." He got up and moved to the door. "I'll be back later," he promised. "To help you get home."

The dragon opened one eye and looked at Ben disbelievingly. "What chance does a boy like you stand against them? It's too big for you, all this. You'd best save yourself and forget about me."

"My name's Ben," said Ben, taking a deep breath. "Benjamin Christopher Arnold. And I mean what I say."

The dragon opened its other eye.

"Well, that was brave of you, giving your true name to a dragon," it said after a while. "Thank you. It's a comfort to me to have found one friend in this terrible place, Ben. Even if you're the last friend I ever make." It laid its head down on its claws again in a defeated manner and closed its eyes.

"So that's it, then, is it?" Ben said, feeling sudden anger. "You're just going to give up, are you? Without even bothering to tell me your name?"

The dragon sighed. "What's the point? You wouldn't be able to pronounce it anyway."

"Try me," Ben said defiantly.

"Can I trust you?" The dragon fixed him with its extraordinary eyes, which seemed to spin and spark until Ben felt as if he might faint. Then the dragon sighed. "It seems I must, for you are one of her own. But so young . . . All right then, my name is Xarkanadûshak."

"Oh."

In the darkness of the shed, a long row of white teeth glittered briefly. After a moment of suppressed panic Ben realized the dragon was smiling.

"If you must, you can call me Zark."

"Zark," Ben echoed. He reached out and touched the dragon's head, very slowly. The scales there felt dry and cool under his palm; like snakeskin, but harder. Not knowing what to do then, he gave the dragon a gentle pat, as he might a dog. "I must go now before they miss me, but I'll bring you some food later."

"No cabbage," said Zark.

"No cabbage," Ben promised.

Dinner that night was a salad. Ben picked disconsolately through all the greenery, trying to find something he recognized as food. Both Ellie and Cynthia had declared themselves to be on diets, though both were skinny as rakes, and Aunt Sybil had joined them, since Awful Uncle Aleister had gone out to see a business colleague. Ben suspected it was probably Mr. Dodds—the Dodman.

He went to bed starving. No wonder, he thought as he lay there feeling his stomach complaining, the dragon was so tired and bad-tempered. It had spent several weeks on the Hawley-Fawley Diet: potato peelings and cabbage. He wondered if he might suggest it to Cousin Cynthia.

At last the house fell silent and dark. Uncle

Aleister's Jaguar was still missing from the driveway, but Ben decided he could wait no longer. He crept along the landing, taking care not to tread on the loose floorboard, and slid down the banister rather than using the creaky stairs. Dressed for stealth in a pair of black jeans, a black sweater, and his black fleece, he felt like James Bond.

His first raid was on the fridge. It was a vast silver appliance with double doors, like a wardrobe for food. For a family on a diet, it contained a ludicrous amount of stuff. Ben grabbed a backpack and filled it with a whole roast chicken, two fillet steaks, a slab of boiled ham, some smoked salmon, a big hunk of cheddar cheese, two packs of bacon, a large sloppy bag containing what he suspected to be more kidneys, and a shoulder of lamb. That should do the trick. Then, for good measure, he added a large tub of ice cream and a spoon.

Down the garden path he crept. When he got inside the shed, he found the dragon on its feet, waiting expectantly. It had its head in the backpack before he had even closed the door behind him. Soon the entire contents of the bag were strewn around the shed.

"Mmm," said the dragon appreciatively. "Cow. Pig. Sheep. Fish. Fowl. Excellent: all the major food groups." It nosed at the ice cream carton. "But what's this?"

"Ben and Jerry's Chunky Monkey," Ben said, grabbing the spoon.

The dragon gave him an odd look. "Funny," it said. "It doesn't smell much like monkey to me."

While Zark ate the roast chicken, the steaks, and the joint of lamb, Ben swiftly made his way through the tub of ice cream. Then he helped the dragon open up the packs of bacon, salmon, and kidneys, and watched in awe as it gobbled up the lot.

Ben thought about eating the cheese, then realized that the very idea of eating anything else after all that ice cream made him feel quite ill. He stashed it in his pocket for later. It could be a long night.

At last, Xarkanadûshak had eaten everything other than the backpack. He gave a contented belch and settled down on the floor of the shed with his claws folded over his belly.

"Hey!" said Ben. "You can't go to sleep now."

"Just a little nap," said the dragon, yawning.

"We haven't got time. Uncle Aleister could be back

at any moment. Do you *want* to be turned into dog food?"

All he got in response to this was a snore, followed by another, and another. The whole of the gazebo reverberated with them, as if someone had started up a lawn mower.

Ben grabbed up a garden rake and poked the dragon hard with it. "Wake up!"

Zark growled. Little flames escaped between his teeth, illuminating the inside of the shed.

Ben gasped.

"What?" said the dragon crossly. "What is it now?"

"Your scales. They're . . . glowing."

"That's what they do. When I'm getting ready to roast someone."

Ben backed away. "Well, roast Uncle Aleister, then," he suggested. "Or Mr. Dodds, not me. And if you don't want to go home to Eidolon, then I'm going back to bed."

At the mention of the Secret Country, the dragon's eyes went quite misty. Slowly, he lumbered to his feet. "Come along, then," he said.

Now that the dragon was refueled, making their way the short distance from King Henry Close to

Aldstane Park looked as if it should be less difficult than Ben had envisaged; but he was wrong. First of all, Zark demolished the back gate, because now that he was full of food he was simply too large to fit through it. Then he stopped at the garage and sniffed at the door. "The monster's in there, isn't it?" he asked.

"Monster?"

"The beast they brought me here in."

"Oh, you mean Aunt Sybil's Range Rover?"

The dragon regarded him suspiciously. "That monster, yes. I have a score to settle there."

And before Ben could say anything to stop him, Xarkanadûshak had shoved his head through the garage door and melted all the vehicle's tires. The smell and the smoke were terrible.

"When all's said and done," the dragon said with satisfaction, "they're nothing but cowards, these creatures. Hardly put up any sort of fight at all."

The skin on the back of Ben's neck prickled as if they were being watched, but when he turned around, there was no sign of anyone. "We'd better run," he said nervously, watching the column of black smoke spiraling up into the night sky.

"Run? Dragons don't run, boy; chickens run. Dragons *fly!*"

"That's all very well, but I can't."

"Of course you can," Zark said kindly. "Get aboard." It lowered a glowing red wing to him.

"Really?"

"Really."

Ben climbed onto Xarkanadûshak's back, with the niggling sense that there was something he hadn't thought through. But before he could think what it was, the dragon gathered its powerful rear haunches beneath it and leaped upward with a great whoosh. Ben nearly fell off. He grabbed hold with everything he had—his hands, his knees, his feet. Then he realized what it was he had failed to think about: (a) dragons don't have much for a boy to hold on to, and (b) flying meant being high up in the air.

Ben made the mistake of looking down.

Below—a long way below—he could see King Henry Close receding till each of the huge executive houses looked no bigger than a matchbox. Even so, his eyes were sharp enough to spot Uncle Aleister's Jaguar pulling into the driveway. Their escape had been very narrow indeed. Now the dragon wheeled and soared and the cold wind whistled past Ben's ears. His fleece filled with air and flapped alarmingly. A moment later the cheese worked its way out of his pocket and plummeted to the ground. Ben had the nasty feeling he might follow, if he couldn't get Zark to land soon. He didn't feel much like James Bond now.

"Down!" he yelled to the dragon. "Go down!"

But Xarkanadûshak was in ecstasy. He hummed to himself as he flew, and as he hummed his scales changed color. In the moonlight, Ben could see them go from red to purple to blue to green, from green to yellow to gold and orange, and back to red again. It was an impressive display; even in his state of rigid fear, Ben recognized that. But it also made them rather visible to anyone who chanced to look skyward at that late hour.

"Zarka . . . Zarkan . . ."

He couldn't remember the dragon's true name.

"Zarnaka . . . Zarkush . . ."

The dragon rolled sideways with a gleeful roar and the air whisked Ben's voice away. Briefly, he saw the tops of trees skimming past and then a surprised-looking owl banking suddenly away from them.

Panic dislodged the word at last.

"Xarkanadûshak!" Ben cried desperately. "We must land in the park. Now!"

At last he had the dragon's attention. It growled, and a little red fire escaped its jaws and expired in the darkness. Then, as if defeated by the use of his name, Zark extended his wings and circled Bixbury like a seagull planing on a current of sunny air. Ben edged a little way up Zark's neck and shouted into the prominence on his head he thought might be an ear, "See that lake there, to the left? Land near there."

Folding his wings like a hawk stooping to its prey, Zark headed downward and the ground hurtled toward them at an alarming speed. There were boys who would be shrieking with excitement at such a ride, but Ben was not one of them. He squeezed his eyes tightly shut and held on for dear life. Luckily, dear life stayed with them that night. There came a moment when he felt the dragon pull up swiftly, then a lurch and a thud; and when he opened his eyes, they were on the ground, in Aldstane Park.

"Not a bad landing, considering," Zark mused. "Rather an awkward yaw to the right as we came in on the final approach. Losing all those scales has rather spoiled my aerodynamics; but it was pretty decent all the same, given that I haven't had much practice lately."

Ben slid from the dragon's back, feeling rather weak at the knees. It felt as if the ground were still swaying and swooping beneath his feet.

"I feel like a new dragon," Zark boasted. "The great Xarkanadûshak is alive and well!" He inhaled a huge breath so that his chest swelled out like a sail full of wind. Then he let it all out in a whoosh. Unfortunately, a great sheet of flame came out along with the air; and all of a sudden where there had been a park bench there was nothing but a smoking iron frame and a pile of black ashes.

"Oh, Zark—"

Ben was about to lecture the dragon on the irresponsibility of setting fire to other people's property when he heard a shout. Drawn by the sudden gout of flame in the black of the night, several figures were scaling the park gates.

It was Awful Uncle Aleister, Mr. Dodds, and the goblins.

Chapter Twelve

Eidolon

"Zark! Hurry!"

The dragon's head swiveled to regard him. "What is it now?" he demanded in an annoyed fashion.

Ben pointed toward the gates.

"Ha! The Great Xarkanadûshak will roast them all."

"I don't think that's a very good idea," Ben began. Even though he detested Uncle Aleister, when all was said and done he was still his mother's brother.

Zark took a deep breath as if stoking his fire. Then the moon emerged from behind a cloud, illuminating the figures at the gate, and his expression changed from proud bravado to terror.

"The Dodman," he breathed, and all that issued from his mouth this time was the tiniest wisp of smoke.

Ben's heart clenched. "Like it or not, now you must run! Come on, follow me!"

Across the park they fled, boy and dragon, toward the dark bank of bushes, toward the Aldstane. But this time there was no wood-sprite to light the way. Once inside the rhododendrons, Ben was lost. He had a vague memory of where the stone lay, but in the darkness and the confusion he could not immediately find it. Zark blundered behind him, crushing bushes, breaking branches, leaving a swath of devastation in his wake. Looking over his shoulder, Ben could see Mr. Dodds's minions gaining on them, and with an easy path to follow.

The dragon turned too. "Vile goblins!" he roared. "I shall burn them!"

"No!" Ben grabbed his wing, tugging it frantically. "You'll set the whole park alight!"

On they ran, Ben staring to left and right for the little clearing in which the Aldstane stood. He could picture it as clear as day in his mind, but it was, unfortunately, not as clear as day.

The next time he chanced a look over his shoulder, he could make out Awful Uncle Aleister and Mr. Dodds, too, just behind the two goblins, which must surely have been the creatures he saw loading the truck in the driveway.

He picked up a broken pine branch from the ground.

"Zark!" he cried urgently. "Can you be very, very careful and light this, and only this?"

The dragon gave him a hurt look, then breathed very gently on the stick. A moment later, a flower of fire blossomed at its tip. On Ben ran with his torch held high like an Olympic flame-carrier.

Now he had his bearings.

"This way!" he yelled, charging through a particularly dense stand of bushes. Hawthorn brambles snagged his fleece and dragged at the fabric of his jeans. He could hear the dragon behind him, breathing hard. He hoped it wasn't burning its way through.

And then, suddenly, there it was: the Old Stone, the way-marker to Eidolon.

Now that he saw it, the old qualms returned. Did he dare enter the wild road to the Shadow World, from which he might never return, or should he push the dragon through and take his chances in this one? But he did not think he could outrun the goblins, even if he could evade the men; and he dreaded to think what might happen if they caught him. Swallowing his fear, he ran to the back of the stone, to where Ignatius Sorvo Coromandel and his friends had disappeared.

The dragon cannoned into him, almost knocking him down.

"Why have you stopped?" Zark demanded. "They're gaining on us."

"Look." Ben held the burning branch up to the surface of the stone so that the leaping light illuminated the carved letters.

The dragon stared at the stone, then at Ben. "What?"

Ben ran his fingers over the word. "Can't you see? It spells Eidolon."

Xarkanadûshak gave him a withering look. "Do you honestly think dragons can be bothered with such things as reading?"

There were a lot of answers Ben could have

thought of to that, for he loved books and stories, but now was not the time.

"You, boy, stop!"

Ben's head shot up.

It was Mr. Dodds; somehow he had outstripped even the goblins. He stood now at the edge of the clearing, and his face was contorted with fury.

"Where do you think you are going with that dragon?"

Ben felt his heart thumping, but he grasped his courage. "I'm taking him back to Eidolon!" he said defiantly. "Where he belongs."

"He belongs to me," said Mr. Dodds. "And I have all the paperwork to prove it!" He flourished a bundle of documents.

Xarkanadûshak raised his head and roared. A line of red flame lasered the night, and a moment later the papers were fluttering away as tiny black ashes on the breeze, and Mr. Dodds was swearing and holding his injured hand to his chest.

"You'll regret that!" he promised, and it seemed to Ben as if his teeth had grown longer and sharper. "Both of you."

"Quickly, Zark, into the wild road!" Ben urged.

He thrust out his hand and they both watched as it disappeared from view.

The dragon blinked. Then he took a step backward.

"But I don't want to disappear," he said uncertainly.

"It's the only way back to your home!" Ben cried desperately. "It's the only way I know into Eidolon."

By now, Awful Uncle Aleister and the goblins had joined Mr. Dodds. Uncle Aleister was red in the face and puffing like a sick dog. There was a bruise on his head, and several crumbs of what looked suspiciously like cheddar cheese on his jacket.

He stared when he saw Ben, and for a moment he looked afraid. Then he puffed himself up and bellowed, "Benjamin Arnold, go home and go to bed at once! You've no business gallivanting around a park in the middle of the night!"

Mr. Dodds turned to him. "Benjamin Arnold? Your nephew?" He looked from Uncle Aleister to Ben and back again. "*Her* son?"

"Izzy's boy, yes."

Mr. Dodds grimaced so that his teeth shone in the darkness. "I might have known," he hissed. "And indeed, Aleister, you might have told me." He paused. "It is so much easier to have enemies than allies; at least you always know exactly where you stand with them." He fixed his gaze on Ben once more. "You do have a look of her," he said grimly. His eyes narrowed. "But aren't you the boy who bought that blasted cat from me?" he asked suddenly.

Ben nodded uncertainly.

"Damn the meddler!" Dodds howled. "What a mess. We'd better sort this out, Benjamin Arnold, once and for all. Before it gets out of hand." He took a step forward.

Ben pushed the dragon. "Go!" he said urgently. "Go on . . ."

One of the goblins giggled, showing a lot of black teeth, which complemented its long black claws perfectly.

"Let us eat him," the goblins begged Mr. Dodds. "Lovely fresh boy."

"Oh, no," said Mr. Dodds. "I have other plans for him. You will capture him but draw no blood. I know what you are like when you draw blood." He pushed back his suit sleeves and extended hands like claws.

Ben blinked. They *were* claws.

"Get in the wild road, Xarkanadûshak!" he yelled.

Compelled by the use of its true name, the dragon gave Ben an accusatory look, then took a tentative step into the wild road. One foreleg shimmered and disappeared, followed by part of his head. Then, with a bound, the dragon gathered his haunches and sprang, and just like that he was gone.

At the moment when the tip of Zark's scaly tail vanished behind the Aldstane, someone grabbed Ben's arm.

It was one of the goblins, its wicked little teeth bared in a vicious grin. "Got you!"

In a gesture born more of panic than intent, Ben thrust the flaming pine branch into its face. With a shriek, the goblin released its grip, and in that second, Ben threw the torch at the other goblin and dived into the wild road.

All at once he felt as though he had been caught up by a whirlwind and hurled over and over, a tiny speck of life in the grip of something scary and elemental. The world flashed past in a rush of color, a blur of shapes, a flicker of light and shade. The question was: which world?

Perhaps, thought Ben, suddenly afraid, only those who fully belonged to the Secret Country could survive the transition. He would perish, and no one would know. He thought of his mother lying in her hospital bed, hooked up to tubes and monitors, her paper-thin eyelids closed, and bitterly regretted his decision. But even as he pictured her thus, her eyes opened wide. "Oh, Ben," she whispered. "Be brave, be careful. Take heart. . . ."

It was only a dream, a wish; but even so, it made all the difference. Ben gritted his teeth and took heart.

The world stopped spinning.

He took a deep breath and looked around. It was night here and he was in a forest, next to a standing stone that looked very much like the one he had just stepped into. But everything *felt* different. He could not define it, but it was as if he felt more alive, all over. His skin tingled as if an electric current had been passed through him. Was this what magic felt like? Or was he just scared? He turned around and stared into the darkness. Where was the dragon? There was no sign of it at all. He found that even though there was not much moonlight, he could see remarkably well. But only out of one eye. If he closed his green right eye, he found, the world became dim and obscure; but if he closed his brown left eye and looked with his right it came into sharp focus.

How curious.

But Ben did not have time to ponder this oddity, for there came a great din through the air and then he heard the voice of Mr. Dodds, strangely amplified so that it boomed like a bloodhound's baying: "Benjamin Arnold, come to me!"

First Ben thought, *He must be joking!* Then he thought, *He's trying to make me do what he wants by using my true name.* And finally he thought, *Thank goodness he doesn't know it.*

But Mr. Dodds was with his uncle. An icy hand of fear gripped Ben's heart. Did Awful Uncle Aleister know his full name? Given that his uncle tended to address him as Benny, and never Ben or even Benjamin, he rather thought he might not. But he could not simply trust to luck. Head down, using the good eye to spy his way between the tangle of trees and brambles, Ben ran.

He stared uncertainly up into the mysterious darkness, scrutinizing the black, abstract patterns for the sign of any predator, ready to run for his life. His skin prickled. He could *feel* something watching him, as if the magic in this place made him unnaturally alert. Branches, leaves, sky, moon, branches . . . And a pair of eyes!

Ben felt his heart stop, then jump into rapid rhythm. Eyes were watching him: a pair of wide, amber eyes that belonged to something other than an owl.

Terrified, he chanced a glimpse back over his shoulder: Perhaps a safer route through this strange and frightening place lay on the other side of the thicket. But then a shattered rainbow of light bounced off the trees behind him, and for a second, very clearly outlined by that unearthly glow, he saw four figures. The first two were the goblins; the third he could hardly make out at all; but the fourth was so terrifying that he forgot to turn back to see where he was going and tripped and fell headlong, hitting the ground so hard he could not help but cry out.

The next thing he knew, one of the trees had grabbed him.

Chapter Thirteen

Captive

Ben struggled, but the tree just held him tighter. *Oh, no,* he thought in despair, *if even the trees are in league with Mr. Dodds, what chance do I have?*

As if in response to Ben's growing panic, one of the tree's branches wrapped itself around his neck, its twigs like fingers holding his mouth closed, while others twined around his ankles and knees until he could not move an inch.

All he could do was stare, wide-eyed, as his pursuers came through the forest in search of him. The goblins ran ahead, their eyes glinting in the gloom. They looked exactly the same as they had before, but the two figures behind them hardly resembled Awful Uncle Aleister or Mr. Dodds at all. The smaller of the two was hunched and bald, his face wizened, his teeth and nails horribly overgrown. He looked, Ben thought, like his uncle might look if he were about three hundred years old, except that he moved with an unsettling vigor. But he had a bruise in exactly the same place as his uncle's, and Ben thought that if he squinted he could see crumbs of cheddar on the shoulder of the robe he wore. Behind him was the figure that had so transfixed Ben: no longer Mr. Dodds in this world, but surely the Dodman himself.

Looming eight feet tall and more, he strode through the undergrowth, looking to left and right. To the shoulder he was a man; but from the neck up he had the head of a great black dog, like an Egyptian god Ben had once seen in a book. Like the figure he had seen in his nightmare.

Ben started to tremble at the sight of his uncle and Mr. Dodds in their shocking new Eidolon forms, which seemed to reflect their inner natures in a most disturbing way. The tree squeezed his ribs so that he could hardly breathe.

As the dog-headed figure walked, he sniffed; with his nose, his mouth open as if he were tasting the air. Moonlight gleamed on twin rows of razor-sharp teeth.

Leaves curled themselves around Ben's face and he felt his legs being encased in bark. It was hard to know which was worse: to be eaten alive by a tree, or to be found by the thing that the dragon had called the Dodman, and the horrible old man who had once been his uncle. Ben closed his eyes.

"I can smell you, Benjamin Arnold!"

And now the Dodman looked in his direction and smiled.

"Nothing can save you, Ben, not in my world."

He stared around, his great, black, doglike eyes silvered by moonlight so that it seemed that they had been replaced by a pair of shiny steel ball bearings. His gaze fixed itself on a point to Ben's right and his ears flicked—once, twice—as if he were listening to something beyond the range of ordinary hearing. Then he walked right up to the tree in which Ben was imprisoned. Ben could feel his hot breath even through the veil of leaves.

"Release him!" he ordered the tree.

Ben felt the tree quiver, as if a great wind had caught it and shaken it to the core; but still it did not let him go. And now that he saw the Dodman up close, towering over him, Ben decided he would rather be absorbed into the tree than taken by such a monster.

Now the Dodman lashed out at the tree with a booted foot and Ben heard it moan, as anyone might who'd been kicked by a bully.

"Let him go!"

"I shan't!"

Ben tensed. The voice—which was light and gentle, and female, and very determined—seemed to have come from above him, and yet all around him, as if the tree itself had spoken. Which was impossible, wasn't it?

"If you do not, it will be the worse for you, Dryad."

Dryad? Ben puzzled over this. It was a word he half remembered from his books of mythology.

"Leave him be," said the voice of the tree. "I have offered him the protection of these woods, and if you do not go, it will be the worse for *you!*"

"You do not know this boy, or what he has done, so why would you risk your welfare for him? He is a thief and a renegade," the Dodman growled, "and *you* will give him up to me."

"Elves and wood nymphs have a kinship; and if this young elf is being chased by one such as you, then I know who is more likely to be in the right," the dryad retorted defiantly.

Now things were taking a very odd turn indeed. Talking trees were one thing, but wood nymphs and elves? What was she talking about?

"The boy is only half elven, which lessens your ties commensurately," the Dodman said smoothly. "And he has meddled in things that are not his business. Now, if you will not give him up to me willingly, perhaps a show of force is required." He turned to the old man. "Aleister, I believe a little fire is called for: you have some matches?"

And now Ben felt the tree shiver in a kind of dread.

Clutching what appeared to be an ordinary matchbox in his gnarled hand, the awful old man stepped to the foot of the tree and tried to strike a match. In his own world, Uncle Aleister could light a cigar even in a high wind; but in the Shadow World his horrible long nails got in the way—he fumbled the first match, dropped it on the ground. He managed to strike the second, but almost set fire to his robe. The Dodman looked on, unimpressed. "Give the matches to the goblins!" he hissed, but they shook their heads and backed away.

The Dodman snatched the box from Awful Uncle Aleister's ancient hands. But his fingers were claws, with hard black nails just like a dog's, and they were not made for the delicate task of striking a match.

The Dodman's eyes flashed in frustration; and for a moment Ben thought that, having lost face so, he might just give up and go away. It was a foolish hope. A moment later, the dog-headed man threw back his snout and roared up into the sky, "Xarkanadûshak!"

Ben's heart missed a beat, then fell like a cold stone into his stomach.

On the other side of the clearing, a black shape rose in the sky and beat its wings slowly as if making up its mind whether or not to heed the call, then it wheeled and dived into the dark canopy of the forest. Moments later there came a great snuffling and rustle of undergrowth, and the dragon emerged between the trees. It looked puzzled and ashamed, and when the Dodman turned to it, it shuddered.

"You summoned me," Zark said dully.

"Ah, yes." The Dodman's great black muzzle wrinkled with distaste, and perhaps a little mirth. "I have a job for you. I want you to burn down this tree."

Zark raised his head reluctantly and regarded the ash tree. His eyes narrowed, then gleamed. "I cannot burn a dryad," he said. "She is a sacred creature."

"If you do not, I will bind you to me as my slave for the rest of your days. And I hear dragons' lives are long. . . ."

Xarkanadûshak hung his head.

The tree's hold on Ben slackened minutely as the dryad realized the implications of the Dodman's threat. Taking this chance, Ben thrust his chin free from her branches and shouted, "No!"

Everyone stared at him.

For a moment, Ben felt as if he were two people in one skin: one, a frightened boy lost in a world he did not understand, menaced by creatures beyond imagination; the other, a proud and angry denizen of Eidolon, whose birthright it was to walk the Shadow World freely and without fear.

"Release me, Dryad," he said at last. "I can't allow them to hurt you just to save my own skin; and I can't let my friend Zark, whose true name I so stupidly allowed the Dodman to hear, to be used in such a way."

"But he will hurt you," she said softly, so softly it was like the sound of leaves rustling in a breeze. "He is the Dodman and his companion is Old Creepie. They hate all magical things and are doing everything they can to bring the world to ruin."

"Even so," said Ben, trying to sound brave even though his knees were trembling. "Two wrongs don't make a right." It was another of his mother's sayings. "Thank you, Dryad, for trying to save me, but I don't want to put anyone else in danger. Please let me go."

"Ahhhh . . ." The dryad sighed.

Then, very slowly, the tree released its grip upon him. Vines and bark unfurled from his legs; branches unpeeled themselves from his arms and chest. At last he stood on his own two feet on the forest floor. But even though Ben felt the Dodman's compelling gaze upon him, he could not resist turning to see what a dryad might look like.

At first, all he could see was an ash tree; a tree that looked very similar to the ash that stood on the border of Aldstane Park. Then he closed his left eye and focused with his right, and at once he could discern a shadowy form within the gnarled bark of the tree. As if in response to his interest, the dryad moved, and Ben saw the shape of a lithe, brown-skinned woman within the tree. Her eyes were the bright green of new buds. Tears stood in them like dew. She sighed.

"At first I thought you one of my elves; but even as I held you, I knew you were more. When the Dodman called you half elven, I realized my error," she said. "And now I have let you fall into the hands of our enemy. Your mother will never forgive me."

Ben frowned. "My mother?"

From behind him came a caterwaul of laughter.

"It seemsss the boy knowssss nothing after all! How amusssing!"

Ben whirled around. It was the Sphynx, as he had known it would be, wreathing its skinny body in and out of the Dodman's legs. He had sensed something watching them as he and Zark had escaped from Awful Uncle Aleister's; had sensed eyes on him from up in the trees of the Shadow World as he ran through the forest. The little spy . . .

The Sphynx's eyes shone with amusement.

"You sssee?" The hairless cat said to its master. "He

isss just a ssstupid boy, despite the eyesss and all the trouble he has given usss."

The Dodman grimaced. "I thought you said he knew all about the Shadow World. That he had been talking with that infernal cat."

"The Wanderer? The Wanderer isss an idiot. He did not even recognise hisss own Queen, not even when he wasss in the boy's houssse!"

"But . . . the Wanderer never came into my house," Ben said slowly, trying to piece all this strangeness together. He turned to the dryad again. "Who is my mother?" he asked, his heart pounding. *And who am I?* he wondered.

"Your mother is Queen Isadora," said the dryad. "Long ago, when she was barely more than a girl, she was dancing in these woods—they were different then, you understand, with sunlit glades and ponds full of nymphs, not gloomy and grim as they are now—and she danced a wild road into existence, a way between worlds. The next thing she knew, she was in a different sort of wood entirely, a place where it seemed no magic existed at all. But by some strange chance or fate, a new kind of magic overtook her, for there she met an inhabitant of this other world, and they fell in love. . . ."

"Ah, such a sweet tale." It was the old man who spoke, but his face was at odds with his words, for it was twisted into a grimace. "My stupid sister, falling for that good-for-nothing human lump, Clive Arnold!"

Ben's mouth fell open. Clive Arnold, his father? Now he was very confused. His mother was a queen? He was an elf—or, actually, half elf? And as for dancing wild roads into existence . . . Part of him felt adrift and bemused; but another part of him accepted these strange offerings as facts, facts that began to bring the two parts of himself into clearer focus.

"She should have been mine!" Now it was the Dodman who spoke so bitterly, and a red light flickered in his eyes like little fires. "She is wasting in the Other World now; but she shall be mine, when she is too weak to resist me any longer!"

The dryad regarded the dog-headed man in disgust. "You may steal the magic out of Eidolon; you may disperse it through the wild roads and destroy the delicate balance between the worlds; you may bring Isadora to the brink of death by your cruel trade; but she will never love you!"

The Dodman narrowed his eyes at her. "Love?

Who speaks of love? Love is for weaklings and fools. I shall take her without love, and make her magic mine; and then I will be the Lord of Eidolon."

The dryad laughed, but there was no humor in the sound. "She is stronger than you think, Dodman. Love and its consequences will defeat you in the end. For when Isadora left our world and fell in love with the human man Clive Arnold, she stayed to have his children and thus began to fulfill the ancient prophecy." She turned her luminous green gaze upon Ben. "Ben Arnold, Prince of Eidolon, I am sorry I have failed to save you. Perhaps your mother could forgive me, but I do not think I can forgive myself."

And she buried her face in her hands and wept.

Chapter Fourteen

The Castle of the
Gabriel Hounds

Then the goblins came cackling toward him carrying
two lengths of flexible vine.

"Bind his hands!"

"And his foots!"

"Feet!"

"Foots!"

"Fools!" cried the Dodman. "If you bind his feet, how will he walk?"

The goblins looked at one another.

"Idiot!"

"Numskull!"

"Featherhead!"

"Toad-brain!"

Ben regarded them with his jaw clenched. They had sharp noses and cruel little red eyes that sparkled in the gloom. Was this Darkmere Forest, and were these the goblins Iggy had warned him about, the ones you wouldn't want to meet on a dark night? It *was* dark in the forest, and he fervently wished he had not met them. He wondered how far and how fast he could run if they tried to grab him. At school he had always come second to his friend Adam when they ran the hundred meters, but he could beat Adam if the race was over two hundred meters. Of course, that was on the flat, in the daylight. And in another world.

"Don't even think about trying to get away, Ben Arnold," snarled the creature who had once been his Uncle Aleister, but whom the dryad had called Old Creepie. Old Creepie suited him well, Ben thought, with his sallow skin and his bent back, his big bald head and those horrid long nails and teeth. "Goblins can run much quicker than human boys and as fast as an elf; and since you are only half of one and half of the other, I would not think you have much chance against them."

"Besides," said the Dodman, offering Ben a ghastly grin, "if you try to escape, I will make sure your friend here suffers." And he gave the dragon a look of such malice that Zark began to shake with fear.

Slowly, Ben offered his hands up to the goblins. There was nothing else he could do. The goblins tied the vines with swift expertise, as if they had had a good deal of practice at subduing captives.

It seemed that being an elf, or even a prince, in the Shadow World didn't give him much in the way of special powers or privileges—if any of it was true, and not just a fairy story. Ben shuffled along behind the Dodman and poor Zark, aware of his transformed uncle and the pair of goblins at his heels.

He wanted to talk to the dragon, to ask him questions about this Secret Country; but when he softly called Zark's name, the dog-headed man turned around and glared, and the dragon looked imploringly at Ben and gave him the tiniest shake of the head. It seemed that the Dodman had broken his spirit.

Ben felt very alone. He was anxious, too—anxious about being a captive in the hands of the frightening Dodman, and anxious about being in a world he didn't understand. *Maybe*, he thought to himself, *if I can think about my circumstances as more of an adventure than a trial, I might cope with them better*. And so, determined not to feel too sorry for himself, he started to take in his surroundings, trying to see if he could make that strange shift with his eyes happen again.

It worked.

He found that if he stared at the Shadow World with his left eye it looked slightly out of focus, as if he needed glasses. He saw things in terms of the world he thought of as home: trees and birds and flowers and shifting patterns of light and shade as the sun slipped over the hills and moved higher in the sky.

But when he looked at the same scene with his right eye, he nearly cried out! For now the view took on a far more distinctive and unsettling character. First, the things he had thought were buzzards planing high up among the wispy clouds now looked suspiciously like pterodactyls, dinosaur-birds that had

been thought to be extinct in his own world for millions of years. The trees had faces, and one of them
winked at him as he passed, while another waved
twiggy hands at him and made a silent roar. Some of
the flowers *were* flowers, though of strange shapes and
colors; but others cast out what looked like tongues
and tentacles, as if searching for something tasty to
eat. And in the shifting patterns of shadow beneath
the trees were other sorts of creatures entirely.

He saw a group of gnomes gathered in the midst
of tall, spotted toadstools; but they did not look much
like the benevolent plaster gnomes that some people
kept in their gardens back home in Bixbury, with their
merry belled caps and bright trousers and fishing rods.
No, these wore no clothing but long shirts of woven
grass, and had eyes as black and glittery as anthracite
as they watched him pass.

Indeed, many eyes watched the strange procession—from up in the branches, from stands of giant
fern, from burrows in the ground: an elf-boy pulled
along by two Darkmere goblins, followed by the
Dodman, a dragon, and Old Creepie. At the sight of
the dog-headed man, many of those onlookers bolted
for safety and watched from a distance, or took wing

if they could. They had over the past months become used to seeing creatures leaving the Shadow World, not being brought into it. Only one, a tall figure wearing the antlers of a great stag, watched boldly and did not hide his face.

Ben stared at him, and a little shiver ran down his spine—as if a memory had stirred, somewhere so deep inside him that he could not quite catch hold of it. Surely he had seen him somewhere before? He was about to ask Zark who the antlered man might be when the figure stepped out from the deep cover of the trees and dappled sunlight fell upon him. He wore nothing but oak leaves, Ben saw, and his skin had a greenish cast to it.

"This is my woodland!" he cried, addressing the dog-headed man boldly. "You have not asked my permission to traverse it, Dodman. And you of all folk know that you are not welcome in my domain, alone or in company. I have heard tell that you have been stealing away the creatures of Eidolon and removing them from our world. Is this true?"

He paused as if waiting for a response to this accusation; but the dog-headed man looked away.

"I know that it must be," the antlered one continued,

"for I have sensed the balance of nature changing. And I have seen the effects of this theft." He cast his arms wide. "My woods are not as beautiful as once they were and my creatures are afraid. They cower from strangers where once they walked freely and without fear, as is the right of all the folk of Eidolon. I tend my own as well as I am able, but two of my unicorns and a number of my sprites are missing. The goblins have always been a law unto themselves, but it pains me to see a pair of them in your thrall. I hear that in the wider world things are far worse, and yet the Lady has not returned to halt the damage. What have you done with her, Dodman?"

The dog-headed man smiled now, and his teeth glittered in the sunlight. "I? I do not have her," he said, as if in indignation. "Do not blame me for her absence, Horned Man."

The Horned Man stared hard at the Dodman until he looked aside. Ben could feel his captor's anger boiling like the heat from a radiator. And something else, too. Was it a kind of fear?

Now the Horned Man turned his attention to the creature who was, in another world, Ben's uncle. "And you, Old Creepie!" he challenged. "You are her brother. You must know where our Queen is, and why she has not come back to us?"

But the dreadful old man merely showed his horrible slimy teeth and laughed. "Isadora chose to go away. And she's never coming back!" he cried triumphantly.

"No!"

Ben surprised himself by his outburst. Everyone stared at him. He started to say something else, to tell the Horned Man where his mother was, when the Dodman took a step toward him and pulled him into a hot, foul-smelling embrace, stifling Ben's words. "Ha! Ignore the lad," he said fiercely. "He's a simple-minded creature and entirely dim-witted: The nonsense he spouts, you never know what he's going to come out with next!"

"Where is it you are taking the boy, and why have you bound him?" the antlered man demanded.

Now the Dodman lost his temper. He gave a low growl. "Go back to your folk, and do not seek to challenge me. The boy is a thief and must be punished. He has nothing to do with you."

The Horned Man narrowed his eyes. "I'd say he has a look of the Lady about him."

But the Dodman would say no more and, wrestling Ben ahead of him, hurried them past.

Ben could feel the eyes of the Horned Man on the back of his head as they moved away from him. For a brief moment he thought about breaking from the dog-headed man's grasp and fleeing to the antlered man's side; then he remembered that the Dodman held Zark captive, and would probably burn the whole forest to take him back. And so, with all sorts of confusing thoughts charging around his head, he stumbled on, away from the only allies he seemed to have in this world.

They walked through forest for what seemed like hours. When they finally emerged into open land-scape, Ben gasped.

Woodland gave way to rolling green hills, which in turn became a hazy purple moorland. In the far distance a line of majestic mountains rose into the clouds. It was the most beautiful place Ben had ever seen. The colors were brighter than they were in his own world, and the birdsong was louder.

He watched a pair of larks high up in the blue air, dancing and diving, their trilling calls a beautiful, sharp song. But when he closed his left eye to focus on them better, he realized they were not larks at all but some sort of sprite or fairy. He grinned as they chased one another, zigzagging like swifts. It was nice to see that someone in Eidolon was having a good time.

He smiled and chanced a look at Zark, but the dragon had his head down in undisguised gloom.

The sprites darted closer—too close. With a sudden leap and a twist that carried him ten feet or more into the air, the dog-headed man caught one of them and held it, squirming, its legs kicking, its wings flapping uselessly, in his clawed hand. For a moment the Dodman stared at the tiny creature dispassionately; then he looked up and sneered and, never taking his eyes from Ben's face, crushed it in his fist and let it fall to the ground. It lay there motionless, its lovely wings all mashed and broken.

Ben was aghast. He dropped to his knees beside the fairy and scooped it up in his bound hands. But its eyes were closed and its chest unmoving. He stared at the dog-headed man with tears in his eyes. "You killed it!" he cried.

But the Dodman's smile merely widened. "It was no

great loss," he said. "They fetch so little in your world, and die so quickly."

Ben gazed at the dead creature, remembering how he had once held Twig. Above him, the second sprite flew as close as it dared, its movements jerky with shock and distress. At last it gathered its courage and darted swiftly to take hold of its dead companion. Flapping its wings with immense effort, it managed to drag the body of the dead sprite out of Ben's hands and up into the air. Ben watched the tiny figures diminish into the blue, blue sky, then pushed himself to his feet, brushing away on his wrist the tears he would not let the Dodman see. As they walked on, he watched the dog-headed man's wide black back with loathing.

"And so another of the Secret Country's folk has passed from the world and the sum total of magic is diminished," Zark said softly. "This is how the world will fail, Ben—with just such careless cruelty. And if a prince and a dragon dare not prevent the killing of one small fairy, what chance is there for Eidolon?"

He was about to say more, but the Dodman kicked him hard on the leg. "Stop moaning, dragon," he growled. "Your precious home can withstand a little more damage yet."

On they went, and with each step Ben's heart sank further; for although the scenery of the Secret Country continued to amaze him with its beauty, he found that all looked well only when he gazed around with both eyes open; when he used only his right eye it seemed that wherever he looked, something was subtly wrong. The grass they walked on was withered, its tips brown and dry. Mildew had coated the leaves of some of the bushes; briar roses in a hedge bore blooms that were rotting on their stems. Insects buzzed indolently; pungent steam rose from brackish water, and fungus grew in the shade—not the handsome stands of boletus his mother had shown him in the woods at home, nor the fresh white horse-mushrooms they had picked in a field, but spindly, slime-capped toadstools and lurid bracket-fungi, things with waving spores and poisonous-looking spots.

They walked for a while beside a stream in which the water was so clear Ben could see every stone and pebble in its bed. But he also saw the dead fish that swept past in the current, white bellies turned up to the sun. On an outcrop beside a rock pool there sat the hunched shape of a girl, combing the tangles out of her hair with long white fingers.

She turned her head toward them as they passed, and Ben saw that she was not a girl at all, but a crone, and that her eyes were glazed white, just the way a trout's eyes turn when it is cooked. As they approached, she slithered off the rock and into the pool, and Ben thought for a moment that she had a fish's tail instead of legs; but before he could look more closely, she had vanished from sight amongst the rushes and weed.

At last they came to the edge of a great lake. By now, the clouds had drawn across the sky like curtains, shutting out the light. The surface of the water looked dull and smooth and somehow tarnished, like an old pewter tray in the kitchen at home that had belonged to Mr. Arnold's mother.

On the other side of the lake stood what appeared to be a castle of tall white stone, with brave pennants fluttering at its four towers. Ben liked castles; he had lots of books about them, and had visited some with his father: Warwick Castle and Carew Castle, the White Tower of London, the ruins of Restormel in

221

Cornwall, Carnarvon and Harlech and Stirling. This looked like none of the castles he had seen, yet somehow it looked like all of them at once. It was sort of blurry, as if it were shifting in and out of two worlds at the same time.

He closed his left eye and stopped in his tracks.

With his right eye—the eye he had come to think of as his Eidolon eye—the castle did not look like a pretty place at all. It was solid and grim, black with lichen and stains; and the pennants that he dreamed he had seen at its towers were nothing more than ragged clouds. He shivered. It looked a dark and forbidding place.

As they reached the shore, the Dodman lifted his head and howled, a mournful sound that swept across the lake like the call of a wolf pack. Seconds later the cry was taken up from beyond the walls of the castle and then the sky above the castle began to ripple.

Zark stopped in his tracks, and his haunches quivered with fear.

"What is it?" Ben whispered, but the dragon would not say a word.

Ben looked carefully with his Eidolon eye. There, in the air above the castle walls, something was materializing. He squinted and tried to make it out, but the image was so bizarre it made no sense to him. For a moment it looked as if a team of spectral dogs had leaped over the battlements, drawing with them what appeared to be a sort of cart, and were streaming across the sky between the castle and the shore in a burst of light.

As the apparition came closer, Ben realized that this was exactly what he was seeing. He watched them draw near with a fearful fascination.

"Ghost-dogs," he breathed.

The Dodman laughed. "Ignorant boy. They are the Gabriel Hounds, the curs of the wild hunt, and they answer only to me. I have harnessed them for the first time in history. I am their master."

But it did not seem to Ben as if the ghostly dogs much liked their master, for they arrived snarling and wild-eyed, and when the Dodman stepped into the chariot, their hackles rose and their tails curled down between their shaggy legs.

When it came to Zark's turn to get aboard, he drew back, his nostrils flaring unhappily. "Will you not release me now?" he asked miserably.

"Ah, no," said the dog-headed man. "You know

too much. I think you must come with us."

"If I must come with you, let me fly," the dragon implored.

The Dodman regarded him steadily. "Try to escape and you will regret it—I can force you to my will, as well you know. Land in the courtyard and await us there." He waited until the dragon had soared into the air before adding softly, with his ghastly grin, "And then, my faithful hounds, I shall reward you with some fine dragonmeat!"

"You can't!" Ben was horrified.

"But the dogs must eat, laddie." The Dodman showed Ben his unpleasant teeth. "We all must eat."

Ben watched the distant shape of the dragon circling the castle and descending in a flurry of wingbeats. There must be something he could do to save Zark. As the Gabriel Hounds drew the chariot through the chilly air above the lake, all Ben could think about was his friend, who had been so ill-treated in two worlds. The injustice of it made his eyes sting with tears, and he blinked them away angrily. He would not let these terrible creatures see him cry.

So as soon as the hounds began their descent into the castle's courtyard and he was within earshot of the dragon, he stood up in the chariot and yelled with all his strength, "Xarkanadûshak! Save yourself: Fly away home!"

The dragon regarded him wonderingly with his swirling purple eyes, and for a moment Ben thought the use of Zark's true name was no longer having any effect. Then, just evading the snapping jaws of the Gabriel Hounds, Zark bunched his haunches and leaped skyward, beating his wings with all the power he could muster.

The Dodman watched the dragon go with narrow eyes. "Since I may command the beast only thrice, I shall let him go for now," he said. "It is not a gift to be wasted."

With a painful stab of regret, Ben realized he had used up all his chances to invoke the dragon's true name: first, to make Zark land in Aldstane Park; second, to compel him to enter the wild road; and last, to set him free. Now he was all alone in this terrible place. Literally, it seemed, without a friend in the world.

Chapter Fifteen

The Rose Room

As he was marched through the castle by the goblins, Ben looked at his surroundings first with one eye closed, then the other. The goblins' spiky little claws dug into his arms every time he paused to peer through an open door, but he still managed to glimpse the faded grandeur of a bygone age as they passed. Beautiful brocades, splendid carpets, and fabulous tapestries caught his attention, but with his

Eidolon eye he could see that now they were hung with cobwebs, smelled of mildew, and were covered in dust. Many rooms were dark, the shutters closed against the day. Still others were locked shut. Everywhere was deathly silent.

"Where shall we put him?" the Dodman asked the hunched old man who had once been Awful Uncle Aleister.

Old Creepie giggled. "Why not the Rose Room?" he suggested. "It used to be his mother's."

"Perfect." The dog-headed man grinned.

They climbed another flight of stone stairs and the old man produced—out of nowhere, it seemed—a set of rusty keys and opened a door at the top. The goblins pushed Ben inside.

The Dodman's eyes glinted. "Badness knows what we shall feed you on, boy. But I dare say we can find you some giant cockroaches or a basilisk or two." And he slammed the door so hard that its hinges creaked in protest.

Ben heard the key turn in the lock and the footsteps of his captors echoing away down the corridor. Then he set about exploring his prison.

As prisons went, it seemed rather nice. There was

a huge four-poster bed covered with a heavy canopy. There were bookshelves crammed with books. The cupboards were full not just of old clothes but of odd and rather interesting items—feathers and stones and pieces of driftwood—all the things his mother loved to collect in his own world. And the narrow stone windows looked out over the lake.

But it seemed a sad place, emptier than an empty room should be, as if it were in mourning for its previous occupant. What it felt like, Ben decided, was lonely. And no wonder, for it was as if no one in the world came to the castle; no one but the Dodman and his helpers.

What a waste, Ben thought, staring out of the window. If he closed both eyes, he could imagine the castle in better days, when his mother had lived here; when it must have been teeming with life. Laughter would have echoed down its hallways, the Princess Isadora and her friends would have played on the stairs, and people—and all manner of wonderful creatures—would have swum in the lake. In the courtyard, which now appeared to be the province of the Gabriel Hounds, since it was scattered with bones, there must have been fruit trees to steal apples and pears from, fountains to splash in, and lots of fishponds—filled with anything but Mongolian Fighting Fish.

Somehow the castle had been reduced to a ghost of itself.

When Iggy had described the Secret Country, Ben had imagined it to be a land stuffed full of wonders, rather as he had once believed the Pet Emporium to be. But now he realized he had been naive. Just as on closer inspection the pet shop had turned out to be a shoddy front for Mr. Dodds's wicked trade in creatures he had no business transporting between worlds, so Eidolon was no longer the glorious haven of magic Ben had expected.

Neglect and greed had diminished it.

Ben thought about the creatures he had encountered from the Shadow World: the Wanderer, the wood-sprite, the selkie, the dragon. Other than Iggy, who seemed able to adapt himself to whichever world he walked in, the others had fallen sick when they left Eidolon and became sicker the longer they were away.

And at the same time the Secret Country itself was suffering. He thought about the mildew and the fungus, the brittle grass, the dingy forest. He thought about the fish floating belly-up in the stream, and about the ancient mermaid with the blank white eyes; about the creatures that had run away and hidden at their approach; about the dryad's tears, and what she had said.

Perhaps if Eidolon had once had a queen and she had gone away, this was what happened, he thought. Her absence enabled the Dodman to do what he liked, for there seemed to be no one to stop him—not even the Horned Man, through whose woodland realm they had passed, who had seemed so regal and imposing. It allowed Awful Uncle Aleister to sell poor Zark as a garden incinerator and to make tons of money from the sale of the Shadow World's creatures, and thus drain the magic out of Eidolon.

He remembered what Zark had said about the death of the fairy: *"And so another of the Secret Country's folk has passed from the world and the sum total of magic is diminished. This is how the world will fail, Ben—with just such careless cruelty. And if a prince and a dragon dare not prevent the killing of one small fairy, what chance is there for Eidolon?"*

Ben knew it was true.

He turned away from the window and sat down

on the bed. His mother's bed. At once a great cloud of dust rose up around him, making him cough. When the dust cleared he thought he could smell her scent, faintly, in the air of the room: a delicate scent, just like rose petals. The loss of her and of his family and his world seemed overwhelming.

Take heart, Ben.

The sense of the girl his mother had once been, here, in this room—the shape of her absence—made something fall into place in his mind, like the last piece in a jigsaw puzzle. He realized, suddenly, that everything the dryad had said must be true. His mother *was* the Queen of the Secret Country: and that was why in the other world she had been getting sicker and sicker. The longer she was away from her world and the magic that sustained it, the worse she got. And the worse Eidolon and its creatures fared, too.

But if that was the case, then he was to blame. He and Ellie and Alice. And his father. If it hadn't been for them, she would be in Eidolon, and all would be well.

Ben curled up on the musty old bed and hugged himself miserably. He was the only one who knew the truth and could pass between worlds, other than Mr. Dodds and Awful Uncle Aleister and the goblins; and he was here, locked in a castle in the middle of a lake, and there was nothing he could do to save his mother, or Eidolon, or its creatures.

Self-pity enveloped him; and darkness began to draw down.

Nothing to be done . . . No one else who could pass between worlds . . .

Ben sat bolt upright. "Idiot!" he cried. He laughed. He leaped up from the bed. He danced around the room. He turned a cartwheel and grinned and grinned.

There *was* something he could do. There *was* someone who could make the journey.

Then he sobered. It would be dangerous.

But there was no choice, and so he crossed to the window, leaned out of it, and shouted out into the night: "Ignatius Sorvo Coromandel! Wherever you are, come to me now!"

Chapter Sixteen

Ignatius Sorvo Coromandel

Ben waited. He stared out of the window at the darkening lake and waited. He sat on the bed and dangled his feet and waited. He paced around the room, listlessly opening and shutting cupboard doors, and waited.

There was no sign of Iggy at all.

Then he cursed himself for his stupidity. Even if Ignatius Sorvo Coromandel had heard his call, how would he find him? And even if he did find him, how would he cross a lake? It would be nearly impossible, especially for a cat like the Wanderer, whom Ben knew in his heart to be a rather inept sort of explorer. By now Iggy could be anywhere: He could have taken the wrong wild road and ended up in ancient China; he could be scaring the wits out of the Emperor Napoleon on the eve of Waterloo; he could be stuck on top of Ayres Rock in the middle of the Australian Outback.

Or he could have been dragged here unwillingly and set upon by the Gabriel Hounds.

Ben put his head in his hands.

Footsteps sounded on the stairs.

Ben stared at the door as if by sheer force of will he could employ X-ray vision and see exactly who was out there. The next thing he knew, someone was fitting a key into the lock and the door was creaking open.

It was Old Creepie and the goblins. One of the goblins carried in a plate, the other a mug and a lit candle. Ben's stomach rumbled; but when he scanned the contents of the plate, he realized the Dodman had not been joking.

"Eat up, Benny-boy! Very nutritious, these giant Malaccan cockroaches. Bit crunchy, but I'm sure you'll get used to them," Old Creepie chortled. "You'll have to: It's all there is in this dump. I'll be off home later for a nice steak and chips; but don't worry, Boggart and Bogie will take care of you—make sure you don't try to escape or anything silly like that."

Ben stared at the wizened old man, who in another world was his awful uncle; at his unblinking black eyes and his overgrown teeth, his whiskery chin and sharp beak of a nose. It was hard to see the family resemblance, but even so, he couldn't help saying, "But if you're her brother, how can you bear to let her die?"

Old Creepie wheezed with laughter. "Haven't you worked it out yet, Benny-boy?" He looked over his shoulder in case anyone was listening, then leaned in toward Ben and lowered his voice. "When Isadora is dead, I will bring my Cynthia here to take her rightful place as the Queen of Eidolon."

Awful Cousin Cynthia, Queen of Eidolon? There would be no hope for this world if that ever happened.

At the sight of Ben's horrified face, the old man

rubbed his hands together in glee and gave the horrible, braying laugh Ben hated so much.

Now the old man was addressing his henchmen. "I want you downstairs in two shakes of a salamander's tail," he said, employing exactly the same officious tone he used with Ben and Ellie when telling them to do some unpleasant chore around the house. "We have to go and trap a replacement for Lady Hawley-Fawley's garden incinerator. Just give the boy his meal and make sure he eats it, then join me in the courtyard."

Then he turned on his heel and left the room, banging the door behind him.

The goblins leered at Ben with their little shiny eyes. They put the plate and mug down on the chest at the foot of the bed and stood there looking down at them rather enviously.

"What's in there?" Ben asked, pointing at the mug.

The goblins looked at each other.

"You tell him, Bogie," said the one on the right.

"No, you tell him."

"You!"

"No, you!"

"Rats' blood," said Boggart at last. "Lovely rats' blood."

Ben felt his stomach heave. "You can have it if you like," he said, more kindly than he felt.

The goblins licked their lips with slithery black tongues.

"We couldn't!"

"You could."

"No, we couldn't. The Dodman would skin us."

"I won't tell him," said Ben.

"You will."

"I won't."

This was all becoming tedious; Ben felt as if he had somehow landed onstage in a rather bad pantomime. All it needed now was for someone to yell, "He's behind you!" and the scene would be complete.

As Boggart reached for the mug, Bogie's eyes went wide and round.

"He's behind you!" he hissed.

Boggart snatched his hand away as if burned.

The Dodman was in the doorway.

"Tell me what?"

"Nothing," said Boggart.

"Nothing," said Bogie.

They watched Ben warily.

"Tell you that my mother will punish you for

what you have done to her creatures," Ben said.

The goblins exchanged terrified glances and ran away before the dog-headed man could lose his temper.

The Dodman shrugged. "Soon, she will not be strong enough to punish me for anything," he said cruelly. Then he smiled. "I brought a companion for you," he said.

He reached beneath his long black coat and brought out a dripping, struggling shape. For a moment Ben was not sure what he was looking at; then he realized it was a cat.

"Oh, Iggy," he said miserably.

The cat wrenched itself from the Dodman's grasp and fled, sleek as a rat, under the bed and sat there shivering, a pair of eyes in the dark.

The Dodman laughed. "The Wanderer and the Prince of Eidolon. What a heroic picture you make. If this is the sum of the resistance that stands against me, I have little to fear. Another consignment of Isadora's creatures shipped into the Other World should break her forever. Then I shall take the throne!"

Ben thought fast. He remembered what Old Creepie had said about his awful cousin. Perhaps it was time to sow some discord between the Dodman and his henchman. "But Uncle Aleister said that Cynthia would be the Queen," he said, and watched in satisfaction as the Dodman's head swung around dangerously, his eyes glittering in the candlelight.

"Did he now? Did he indeed? How very . . . interesting."

Without another word, he turned and left. Ben heard the key grate in the lock; then there was silence.

Ignatius Sorvo Coromandel emerged from his shelter looking like a waterlogged squirrel. Draggles of water followed him, puddling on the floor. Iggy set to licking himself dry with surprising energy.

"I'm sorry I brought you here, Iggy."

"I should hope you are. I was having a thoroughly pleasant time watching the sun set on the Western Sea with a very pretty six-toed Jamaican cat it had taken me three days' solid work to get close to, when your summons came through loud and clear and I was off and running for the nearest wild road and no time even to say good-bye." He gave Ben a dark look. "If she won't speak to me when I get back, it'll be all your fault. And if that wasn't bad enough, then I had to swim a lake and deal with a pack of sky-yelpers. For ghost-dogs, they have remarkably sharp teeth." He turned so that Ben could see his tail, the end of which looked bent out of shape. "If it hadn't been for that last one, I'd have been free and clear; but their noise alerted the Dodman. . . ."

"I didn't know cats could swim."

Iggy gave him a narrow-eyed look. "Only Turkish Van cats and tigers do so by *choice*," he said. "Water is cold and wet and it ruins your fur. But I should imagine I'm still a better swimmer than you are, Ben Arnold."

Ben grinned. "That wouldn't be difficult: I swim like a brick!"

Iggy shook himself with sudden vigor. "Right, then," he said. "Better make it all worthwhile and start saving the world, hadn't we?" He regarded the dinner the goblins had brought with an acquisitive eye. "Do those belong to you?" he asked as nonchalantly as he could manage.

Ben looked from Iggy to the plate of cockroaches and back to the cat again. The expression on his face spoke volumes.

"They're all yours," Ben said, and had to look away as Iggy dispatched them swiftly, crunching cheerfully through the lot.

• • •

"Have you got it now? You know what to say?"

"Who's going to listen to a talking cat?"

"I did."

Ignatius Sorvo Coromandel winked. "True."

"You're the only chance we have of saving Eidolon and my mother. Just make sure that Awful Uncle Aleister, and Aunt Sybil, and Awful Cousin Cynthia and her awful hairless cat are out of earshot."

"A hairless cat, you say?"

Now Ben remembered something. "He said he was a Sphynx, and I think he's the Dodman's spy. He did seem to know you. . . ."

"Indeed." Iggy's eyes sparked topaz fire. "I have a score to settle there."

But if Ben was hoping for a story, the cat was disinclined to indulge him.

"Best be off, then," Ignatius Sorvo Coromandel said, giving himself a final shake; though why he should bother when he was going to have to get so wet again, Ben could not understand.

"Be careful, won't you, Iggy? Don't drown or . . . anything."

The little cat showed his teeth. "It really wasn't what I had in mind."

Ben looked around the room: at the locked door, at the leaping shadows made by the candle, at the night beyond the windows. "But how are you going to get out?"

By way of response, Iggy leaped elegantly onto the nearest sill and meowed something scratchy and strange into the darkness.

For a time there was no sound at all. Ben found that he was holding his breath, and the cat sat on the sill staring out into the night as if he were a stone carving.

Then a faint orange glow showed in the air and reflected in the still waters of the lake below it. Ben ran to the window and stared out, nearly knocking Iggy off his perch in his excitement.

What looked like a cloud of fireflies was making its way across the lake. Moonlight shimmered off a storm of diaphanous wings, silvered heads, and antennae.

At last one of the creatures broke from the pack and came flitting into the room, where the candlelight made a golden haze of its busy wings.

"Hello, Ben . . . hello, Iggy!" came a familiar,

scratchy voice. The tiny face was split by an enormous, sharp-toothed grin.

"Twig!" Ben cried in delight.

"And, see: He has brought his entire family," Iggy said proudly. He looked down at his portly stomach, now full of chewed Malaccan cockroach, then back at the approaching wood-sprites. "I hope there are enough of them," he added nervously.

The wood-sprites darted through the window one by one until the whole of the Rose Room was aglow with them. Between them, they carried a tangle of vines.

"We thought you might make a basket," Twig said hopefully. "To put the Wanderer in . . . so we share his weight." He looked at the cat dubiously. "Though he seems . . . larger than I remember." He shook his head sadly. "I was not well then."

Ben stared at the vines. Basket-weaving had never been at the top of his list of accomplishments. Or even close to the top. In fact, if forced to admit to it, he had not the faintest idea how to set about such a task. And yet the Wanderer's fate depended on this. He took the vines from the sprites and sat down on the bed with them.

Half an hour came and went, and all Ben had to show for his efforts was a lot of broken bits of leaf and vine and a worse tangle than there had been before. He grimaced. "Er, this isn't going well, Iggy."

The cat gave him a hard, flat-lidded look. "I realized that a long time ago." He wandered off across the room, dug a claw into the first wardrobe he came to, and casually flicked it open.

Inside was a jumble of dresses and shawls, capes and hats. Ben leaped to his feet, scattering vine everywhere, and ran over to root through it all. At last he emerged triumphant with a frilly, wide-brimmed, lace-trimmed bonnet. "There you go!" he declared. "Perfect!"

Iggy eyed the bonnet with distaste. "I wouldn't be seen dead in it."

"You're not going to wear it, stupid," Ben said impolitely. "You're going to sit in it, and Twig and his family will carry you."

"I'll look ridiculous."

Ben put his hands on his hips—a gesture of his father's when he was mildly annoyed about something, a gesture he had not even known he had inherited. "Does that really matter?"

The cat took one more look at the lacy mon-strosity, then shrugged. "I suppose not." He paused. "But you'd better not tell a soul." He thought about this for a moment. "If those Gabriel Hounds see me, I'll never live it down. The Wanderer in a bonnet. I ask you . . ."

It made a very odd sight, Ignatius Sorvo Coromandel carried across the surface of the black lake in a white lace bonnet, by a dozen (rather strug-gling) wood-sprites. For a moment, Ben wanted to laugh. Then he found that he felt more like crying and had to bite his lip. For his part, Iggy stared straight ahead, like an admiral at the bow of his ship, and tried to look as dignified as he could. Ben watched the strange progress until it disappeared from sight on what appeared to be the other side of the water.

Then he went and lay down on his mother's bed and hoped with all his might that the Wanderer's mission would succeed.

Chapter Seventeen

The Messenger

Aldstane Park was as silent as the grave as one small black and brown cat with shiny gold eyes emerged from the rhododendrons into the dew-beaded grass of a very early morning. In this world, the sun was not quite up and the dawn chorus was just beginning to stir.

Ignatius Sorvo Coromandel regarded with passing interest a sleepy blackbird on a low branch of the great ash tree, then forced his mind back to the job at hand. (Or paw.)

Ben had done his best to explain where King Henry Close was, but Iggy found that his mind tended to go all vague and hazy when anyone tried to give him instructions: he preferred to trust his instincts. And his luck.

So he trotted smartly along the road, looking to left and right, and tried to remember what Ben had told him about Uncle Aleister's house. Something about a shiny, big, black Jaguar that sat outside on the driveway . . .

After quartering the residential streets of Bixbury for the best part of two hours Ignatius Sorvo Coromandel had very little to show for his efforts, other than four very sore feet. Nowhere had he spied a Jaguar; or any kind of great cat at all. There had not even been a whiff of one. And he was well and truly lost.

He jumped up onto a brick wall and licked his paws sadly. So much for being the son of Eidolon's two greatest explorers. So much for being the famous Wanderer. He would fail Ben; he would fail Queen Isadora; and he would fail Eidolon—all because he could not find the right house. He hung his head.

"Get off my wall!"

His head jolted up. On the lawn below him, a large marmalade cat was watching him with furious yellow eyes and much of its fur sticking out in spikes.

"Off, I said. Now!"

Iggy stared at the other cat. "You might say please," he started, in a rather aggrieved fashion.

It was not a good idea. Before he knew it, the marmalade cat had leaped up onto the wall and had most of Iggy's head in its very large mouth. He felt its teeth digging into the top of his scalp.

"Ow! Let go!"

The orange cat said something indistinguishable (mainly because its mouth was full) and then batted him with one of its paws. They fell squalling onto the lawn, where Iggy managed to extricate himself for long enough to say, "My name is the Wanderer, and I need your help!"

His aggressor removed his teeth slowly, as if he could do so one by one, from Iggy's skull. Then he backed away and stared at the small black and brown cat in an unfriendly fashion, with his ears flat and his nose wrinkled.

"I've heard of you," he said. "How do I know you are who you say you are?"

"Would one cat lie to another?" Iggy questioned poignantly.

Then he said, "I'm looking for a girl called Ellie. She is staying in a house where a big black Jaguar lives outside. But I have searched everywhere and haven't even sniffed one. Nor even a lion or a tiger or a lynx . . ."

The marmalade cat howled with laughter. He regarded the Wanderer with derision. "What great cat worthy of the name would sit quietly outside a human's house? It's a car, you idiot—a Jaguar, a sort of car! You must come from another world if you don't know *that*!"

Iggy shifted uncomfortably. His insult was dead-on, but no cat likes to seem a fool. "Well, then," he said crossly. "Where do I find this car?"

His antagonist got up off the grass and dusted itself off. "I don't know."

"You don't *know*?" Iggy was enraged. After making himself the butt of the marmalade cat's humor, this was just too much.

"Look around." The other cat gestured to the

roads beyond the garden. "There are cars everywhere. That's the trouble with cars: They move around."

It was true: There were cars everywhere, moving around, and a lot of them were black. By now the streets were busy with them as people made their way to work, entirely oblivious to the fact that two worlds were in jeopardy. Iggy sighed, defeated.

"Don't you have any other information that might help?" the marmalade cat asked more kindly.

Ignatius Sorvo Coromandel racked his small brain. "Well," he said. "The person I'm looking for is living with someone called Awful Uncle Aleister, a girl called Cynthia, and a hairless cat. . . ."

The orange cat looked startled. "A hairless cat?"

"You know it?"

"I do." The marmalade cat was suddenly grim-faced. "If anything is evil in this world, or in yours, it is that Sphynx. If the person you are looking for is anywhere near that creature, you may as well give up now."

"I can't do that."

"I will take you to the end of that road," the orange cat said. "But I will go no closer. Beware the Sphynx, and the people in its house; their cruelty is well known." He dropped his voice and looked over his shoulder as if afraid of being overheard. "They keep animals in boxes and send them off to goodness knows where in trucks. A lot of them simply die in transit. It's said that they sell the bodies for pet food. Food that makes you ill. I won't eat anything that's not out of a can, now." He thought about this for a moment. "Apart from the odd mouse, you know." He shrugged helplessly, gave Iggy a lopsided grin. "Cats will be cats."

The two of them trotted along together in silence for what seemed to Iggy, with his sore feet and impatient nature, a very long time, back the way he'd already traveled that day. Soon the trees of Aldstane Park were visible above the rooftops. He felt even more of a fool than he had before.

At last the marmalade cat stopped beside a tall red object on the corner of a street. "Down there," he said, jerking his chin in the direction he meant. "It's the fourth house along. Be careful, and . . ." he paused, then added urgently, "If anyone asks you who told you how to get here, *don't* tell them."

"That would be hard," Iggy said. "Because you never told me your name."

The orange cat looked taken aback. "It's Tom," he said. "Or at least that's what the humans call me." He tapped the side of his nose. "No real name—can't have you blurting it out under torture, can we?" And it laughed as if this was some sort of hearty joke, jumped over the nearest hedge, and vanished, leaving Iggy staring after him in consternation.

The fourth house in the row had no shiny black car sitting outside. Instead there was a big yellow truck with a flashing orange light on top parked in the driveway, and some men in overalls were hoisting a rather scorched-looking vehicle onto the back of it. Iggy sat in the shrubbery and watched with interest. A thin woman in a smart pink dress was shouting at them, egged on by the thin girl he had last seen at Ben's house. She was carrying a thin and hairless cat.

It was Cynthia and the Sphynx.

Iggy shivered as the cat's sharp green eyes scanned the driveway, and he drew back deeper into the bushes.

Behind them appeared another girl. She was taller than Cynthia and had long fair hair caught back in a loose ponytail to show off a pair of very fancy feather earrings. He remembered her from the time when she had stuck her head up into the tree house. Then, she had been wearing a lot of sparkly purple paint on her eyelids; now it looked as if she'd been crying, for the black stuff she wore around her eyes was streaking down her cheeks.

For a moment, Ignatius Sorvo Coromandel's heart clenched.

"Ben wouldn't do such a terrible thing!" Ellie said, as if for the hundredth time. "He just wouldn't."

"If it wasn't him who burned Mum's Range Rover, why has he run away, then?" said Cynthia. "Answer me that."

"I don't know!" Ellie shouted. "I just don't know."

"Well, he'd better not come back," said the woman in the pink suit. "Or Aleister will beat him black and blue. As it is, your father will have to pay for the damage." Aunt Sybil eyed Ellie spitefully. "And on what he earns at that pathetic little local newspaper, it'll take him years. Years!" And she stamped off into the house.

Ellie sat down on the doorstep. "Has anyone told Dad that Ben's missing?" she asked her cousin.

"I doubt it," said Cynthia. "Who'd care?"

At this, the Sphynx stretched in her arms and gave

an evil grin, an expression that seemed much more emphatic without fur getting in the way.

"Nobody," it said quietly, as if to itself; but Ellie stared at it, and then at Cynthia, and when they both stared back enigmatically, she yelled, "I hate you and that rat of yours!" Then she ran down the garden path and out into the road.

Awful Cousin Cynthia and the Sphynx watched her go with identical little half smiles on their faces, then Cynthia turned away, went into the house, and slammed the door.

Iggy emerged from the shrubbery and ran out of the driveway. Ahead, far ahead, Ellie was walking at a determined pace in the direction of the town. "Oh, no," said Iggy. "I don't think I can go any farther on these feet." Even so, he gritted his teeth and ran after her. It took him some moments to catch up to her, though he was going at full speed. When he did, he was so out of breath he could hardly speak. "Ellie," he wheezed.

Ellie stopped. She looked around but, seeing no one there, started walking again, faster than ever.

"Ellie, wait," Iggy pleaded, limping after her.

This time she looked down. When she realized it

was a cat that had addressed her, she looked aghast. "I'm going mad," she said to no one in particular. "I'm as bad as Ben. Or Mum." She stuck her hands in her pockets and kept going.

At the bus stop, she sat on one of the little red plastic seats and stared down the road as if willing a bus to turn up.

Iggy made a last gargantuan effort and scrambled up onto the seat next to her. "Look," he said. "I wouldn't be doing this unless the situation was desperate, and it is."

Ellie's face went pale and panicked. Then she dug in her shoulder bag and took out a pair of earphones, which she stuck swiftly into her ears. A thin, tinny whine punctuated by a dull thudding beat filled the air between them.

Iggy butted her leg; she shoved him away. He dug his claws into her jeans and she got up and aimed a kick at him. From beneath the shelter of the seats he gazed imploringly at her, but she wouldn't look at him. Iggy nearly howled with frustration. "Ellie!" he cried. "Ellie Arnold!"

No reaction.

He took a deep breath and then, without even

realizing he was doing it, dug out of his memory a tiny nugget of information that Ben had given away to him in the tree house, before Ben had known what he was doing, or the power that it carried.

"Eleanor Katherine Arnold! Take those things out of your ears and listen to what I have to say!"

Chapter Eighteen

The Message

Three buses came and went as Ignatius Sorvo Coromandel told Eleanor Arnold his tale, and she did not notice any of them, just sat there on the bus seat with her hands pressed to her face and her dramatically black-lined eyes staring over the top at him.

"Poor Mum," she said.

A few seconds later she added, "Poor Ben."

Then she ripped off her earrings and stamped them

underfoot. Little bits of feather floated up into the air, were caught in the hot breeze from a car's exhaust, and danced across the road. Iggy watched them go, puzzled. "Those look like phoenix feathers. . . ."

"Those poor birds," Ellie said at last. "Brought all the way from their home in those horrid, airless boxes only to be killed and plucked. . . . I knew those feathers hadn't come from anything ordinary."

And she told Iggy about the jewelry and accessories that she and Cousin Cynthia had made secretly in Cynthia's den, stolen out of the boxes of unusually colored feathers and fur Uncle Aleister had traded in, which they had sold at school for extra pocket money.

"I didn't think about where they'd come from," she said, stricken. "I didn't really think at all. And you say that each creature my uncle and Mr. Dodds has brought out of Eidolon has made Mum sicker?"

Iggy nodded solemnly.

Ellie stuck out her hand. There was another bus coming along the road. "Get in my bag," she said, as it began to slow down. "Quickly."

Ignatius Sorvo Coromandel regarded her nervously and stayed where he was.

"Come on," she said, grabbing him by the nape of

his neck and stuffing him in alongside her makeup and her CD player. "We're going to the hospital."

Iggy stuck his head out of the top of Eleanor Arnold's bag and looked around. There were a lot of smells in this new place that he did not like at all: smells of illness and death and chemicals. The people they passed in the corridors were too preoccupied to notice a cat peering out of a shoulder bag. Some of them wore white coats or dresses and walked at a fast clip, or wheeled metal tables with sleeping people on top of them; others sat wearing ordinary clothes in lines of chairs and looked mainly worried or sad. The sharp scent of anxiety was everywhere.

At last they reached a room that contained nothing much more than beds. Some had curtains around them. Some had visitors sitting beside them. The one in the farthest corner by the window had a lot of equipment around it, including translucent bags dangling from silver poles with trailing tubes that led to a long shape covered by a yellow blanket. For a moment Iggy thought the bags were the same as the ones he had seen at the Pet Emporium, the sort Mr. Dodds parceled out goldfish in; but no matter how hard he squinted he could see no sign of fish in them at all.

A man sat by the side of the bed and the light from the window fell on his face, illuminating his haggard expression. Iggy ducked down and waited, not sure what to do next.

"Dad," said Ellie, and his head came up sharply.

"Ellie, love, what are you doing here?"

Ellie gave him a quick hug, then firmly drew the curtains around her mother's bed and sat down with her shoulder bag on her lap. Ignatius Sorvo Coromandel's ears popped over the top and the man smiled. He put his hand out to Iggy and let him sniff it. Then he stroked the little cat's head and the place under the chin that all cats like to have rubbed.

"I don't think you're supposed to bring pets in here," Mr. Arnold said softly, in case anyone was listening.

"I'm not a pet," Iggy said crossly, but all Mr. Arnold heard was "Meeeee-oww!"

"He's not a pet," Ellie said. "He's called the Wanderer."

At this, the shape on the bed stirred and murmured. Iggy stared. It was his first sight of the Queen of Eidolon, but he had to admit that she did not look much like a queen of anywhere at the moment. Her face was pale and thin, so that her cheekbones showed like knifeblades beneath lackluster skin. Her hair appeared lank and dull beneath the harsh hospital lighting and her eyelids were papery and bruised-looking.

"Dad," Ellie said, gripping his hand. "I know what's wrong with Mum—"

Mr. Arnold's eyebrows shot upward. He put a finger up to his mouth. "Shh. Don't wake her."

But Mrs. Arnold opened her green, green eyes and looked right up, transfixing him. "Hush, Clive," she whispered. "I'm awake." She pushed herself up a little in the bed. "Hello, Ellie, my brave girl." Then her gaze fell upon the little cat. "Hello," she said softly. "And who are you?"

"I am Ignatius Sorvo Coromandel, son of Polo Horatio Coromandel, and my mother is Finna Sorvo Farwalker," Iggy said, then added quickly, "Your Highness." He bowed his head.

Queen Isadora smiled weakly. "I knew your mother. I fear there must indeed be a tale to tell if . . . you are here." Each word was an effort.

Mr. Arnold stared and stared, unable to believe his

eyes, or ears. Was his wife really talking to a cat, and listening to its mews as if they meant something?

Suddenly Mrs. Arnold grimaced. "It's Ben, isn't it? He's in danger. I felt it, in . . . my sleep." She caught Ellie's arm, and there was sudden strength in her grip. "Tell us. Tell us everything you know."

So Ellie began to tell what she knew: about two worlds—one that was full of magic, and the grayer place they sat in now; about Mr. Dodds's Pet Emporium; about the true nature of Awful Uncle Aleister's import business and how he made money from selling the creatures of the Shadow World to the greedy and the immoral; how the balance of all things was being destroyed; and why Mrs. Arnold—known in Eidolon as Queen Isadora—was getting sick as her subjects failed and died in this world.

Mr. Arnold looked concerned throughout much of this explanation, then he looked appalled. When Ellie finished, he said sadly, "Why didn't you tell me, Izzy? I would have understood. At least, I would have tried to." He paused. "I worried that something like this might happen, that you'd suffer from leaving your home to live with me. But I thought you'd be sad, rather than ill. When you first got sick, I thought at first it must be flu or something, but then it got worse and worse, and I knew it wasn't . . ." He faltered, rubbed his forehead. "It's all my fault! If I hadn't stolen you away from your old life, none of this would have happened."

Tears shone in his wife's eyes, but she didn't seem to have the strength left to say anything.

Ignatius Sorvo Coromandel licked Ellie's hand. "Tell him that if he had not met your mother, then neither you nor Ben nor Alice would have come into the world; and that without you nothing can be put right. Sometimes things have to come to the brink of disaster before people realize how important they are."

And so Eleanor Arnold relayed these words to her father, and then told him the plan that Ben and Iggy had formed to begin to reverse the downward spiral of lost magic and lost lives.

"Yes," said Mrs. Arnold. "Yes . . ."

And then she sank back into the pillows with a sigh and fell once more into a deep sleep, which seemed less troubled than it had before.

Chapter Nineteen

The Prophecy

Ben leaned his elbows on the sill of the narrow window and stared out into the unfamiliar world beyond the tower room. It was all he had to look at, and all could do to take his mind off the rumbling of his stomach. He had been stuck in the Rose Room for a whole day now and hadn't had a thing to eat.

What he wouldn't give, he thought, for a dinner of Aunt Sybil's kidneys and cabbage!

But even as he thought about it, he knew he'd actually much rather have a hamburger, or some roast pork, or fish and chips, or even (and this was an indicator of just how hungry he was) a salad. . . . He tried to stop thinking about food at all, but visions of ice cream and chocolate cake and apples and casseroles and scrambled eggs on toast and Christmas pudding and Cornish pasties and all the delicious things his mother had used to make for them before she was ill danced through his imagination until his mouth was watering uncontrollably.

"Pull yourself together, Ben Arnold!" he told himself sternly. "You'll be drooling next."

"You already are."

The voice was tiny, at the limits of his hearing. He wiped his mouth instinctively and turned around just in time to see something scuttle across the room and disappear under the bed. Iggy must have missed a cockroach. He hoped that was the case. Then he hoped that he would never be so starving that he'd actually think about wanting to eat it. It was bad enough that he was hearing voices in his head.

His right ear itched, so he did what his father always told him not to, and stuck a finger in to relieve the irritation. When he took it out again, the voice said, "Such a rude boy." The sound trailed away to nothing; but when Ben put his finger in his other ear, leaving the right one clear, he heard another voice.

"Obviously thinks himself far too grand to speak to the likes of us."

This time it came from the far corner of the room, among the draped cobwebs hanging from the ceiling. Ben stared. He closed one eye, then the other.

"Stop winking at me. It's not polite!"

With his left eye he could see nothing beyond the soft gray shrouds; but with his right eye . . .

It was the biggest spider he had ever seen. And it was talking to him. Ben had never been much of a fan of spiders in the past; particularly the terrible tarantula that Awful Cousin Cynthia had owned, the one that had thrown itself beneath the wheels of Uncle Aleister's Jaguar. He wondered if it was poisonous. It seemed a good idea to be polite.

"Er, good evening," he said nervously. "My name is Ben. Ben Arnold."

"I know that. Do you think I'm a complete ignoramus? You should never judge others by your own standards."

Ben opened his mouth to defend himself, but the spider carried right on.

"What a to-do. No one's disturbed me for years and now in the space of just a few hours I've had boys and cats and goblins and giant Malaccan cockroaches and wood-sprites in my chamber. Not to mention *him*. . . ."

"Him?"

"The dog-man."

"Don't you mean the Dodman?"

The spider fixed him with several of its peculiar eyes in a way that made Ben feel thoroughly disapproved of. "I mean what I say, young man," it said primly. "You should learn to respect your elders. Especially those that have been extinct in your world for millennia!"

Ben stared at it. Extinct? For millennia? Did that mean it was dead—a ghost-spider? It didn't *look* dead: On the contrary, it looked alarmingly alive, and as if it might drop on his head at any moment and suck out his brain.

"Some of us call him the Dodman."

This came from somewhere on the floor. Ben felt as if he were being subjected to a very feeble stereo system.

The cockroach came out from under the bed and stood on the stone floor with a nervous sort of posture that suggested it might at any moment bolt back beneath it again. Ben supposed it was keeping an eye—or several eyes—out for Ignatius Sorvo Coromandel.

"Oh, what do you know?" said the spider in an impatient manner.

"I knew his mother," the cockroach replied, "and his grandmother knew my mother—"

"All right, all right," the spider said crossly.

"Excuse me," said Ben. "Must you talk over me as if I wasn't here?"

"Hark to the boy! Anyone would think he was a prince, the way he goes on," the cockroach mocked, waving its antennae about in what might have been a show of humor.

This made the spider laugh, a high, scritchy sound like the squeak of a finger on a wet windowpane.

"Apparenly I *am* a prince," Ben said gloomily. He had never felt less like one.

"Well, of course you are. You look just like your mother when she was young," said the spider. "Except that you're a boy."

"Same hair," said the cockroach.

"Same nose," agreed the spider.

"Same eyes—well, eye—"

"Please stop!" Ben cried. This was all too strange. He went and sat down on the edge of the bed, taking care not to crush the cockroach on his way. Odd to think it was supposed to have been his dinner. He thought suddenly that if people could hear their dinner talking to them in the Other World, there would probably be a lot more vegetarians around.

"Oh, dear," said the spider. "I think we've upset him. No need for that, young man. Chin up, as you people say. We spiders don't tend to use that expression. No chins, you see. . . . So someone has told you about the prophecy, have they?"

Ben gazed curiously up into the webs and noticed how intricately they had been constructed. It must have taken a lot of very precise work. All to trap a few flies. He looked at the spider consideringly. You would have to be careful around a creature like that.

"There was a dryad," he said at last. "In the forest. She called me 'one of the children of the prophecy.' But I still don't really understand what she meant by it."

Now the spider stepped onto the outside of her web and with an elegant move began to rappel down a length of her own silk till she came to the floor. Once there, she detached herself from the thread and raced across the floor, her eight legs a blur of motion. At the cupboard she stopped, edged inside the open door, and disappeared. She was gone for so long that Ben thought what he'd said had offended her; but at last she emerged, dragging something with her.

If Ben had been expecting treasure, he was disappointed to see just a grubby bit of cloth.

"Oh, the sampler. I'd forgotten the sampler," the cockroach said. "Show the boy, then; show the boy."

"Don't hurry me! This thing's heavy, you know." The spider lugged at the piece of material, moving it another fraction of an inch.

"Let me," said Ben. He took it out of the spider's many feet and smoothed it out on his knee. Once it must have been pretty, he thought—though he could not say he was much of a judge of embroidery—and it must have taken an awfully long time to stitch. When he looked at it with his left eye, it appeared to be merely a bit of grubby white cloth, about the size of a hand-kerchief, into which someone had sewn swirling patterns in different colored wools. But when he looked at it with his right eye, he realized that what he had at first thought to be patterns were in fact letters flowing into and around one another in an ornate script. He turned the material upside down and stared as the words came into focus:

> *Two worlds come together*
> *Two hearts beat as one*
> *When times are at their darkest*
> *Then shall true strength be shown*
> *One plus one is two*
> *And those two shall make three*
> *Three children from two worlds*
> *Will keep Eidolon free*

"What is it?" Ben said into the empty air.

But his heart was thudding, and he knew the answer before the spider said, "That's the prophecy, boy. You are one of the three. Your mother embroidered that when she was hardly older than you. But little did she know it was her own children of whom the prophecy spoke."

"But what part in all this can Alice play?" Ben wondered. It was hard to imagine how Alice could do anything helpful at all.

"Your little sister, is she?" the spider asked.

Ben nodded. "She's only a baby," he explained. "Ellie's my older sister."

The spider and cockroach exchanged significant glances. "What color eyes does the baby Alice have?" the cockroach asked innocently.

Ben had to think about this. Alice slept so much it was hard to think of her with her eyes open. He concentrated.

"Green, I think," he said at last.

"And your sister Ellie?"

That was easy. Ben saw her face coming through the floor of the tree house, covered in shimmery goo and spiky mascara. "Sort of hazely-brown."

"That explains everything," said the cockroach.

Ben frowned. "Not to me, it doesn't."

"Tut!" exclaimed the extinct spider. "Surely everyone knows that elves have green eyes."

"Oh." Suddenly it all made a weird sort of sense: It was his green eye through which he could see Eidolon properly. And he could imagine his mother as a girl, her bright-green eyes fixed upon her sewing, her face a study in concentration. She would be biting her lip just as his mother did when she was absorbed by something complicated. When he lifted the sampler to his nose, he was assailed by the scent of old roses. He closed his eyes and wished with all his heart that he was back at home and that nothing bad was happening, in any world.

And that was when the room flooded with a warm and rosy light.

"Oh, not again," said the spider in an aggrieved tone.

The cockroach ran for cover.

"Hello, Twig," Ben said.

"Got Iggy over lake," the wood-sprite told him excitedly. "Now back for you!"

Ben didn't much like the sound of that. "Um," he started. Unlike Ellie, who got on the bathroom scales several times a day and could tell you to the nearest gram what she weighed, Ben had no idea how heavy he was. What he did know, though, was that he weighed a very great deal more than a cat, even one as greedy as Ignatius Sorvo Coromandel. "I'm not sure you can carry me. . . ."

"Not carry," Twig said impatiently, in a tone that implied that Ben was the stupidest boy in two worlds. "Jump; swim!" And he indicated the window.

"You must be joking!"

"Joking?"

Ben did not think he was up to the task of explaining the concept of jokes to a wood-sprite from another world, so instead he just said, "There's no way I'm doing that!"

"It's the only way out," Twig declared stubbornly.

"I can't swim," Ben said, and then because that wasn't entirely true, added, "or rather, I can't swim a whole lake."

"Someone to help."

Ben gave Twig a disbelieving glance, then crossed to the window.

Down below—a very long way below—the lake lay gleaming and black, like a pool of oil. Ben shivered. Who knew what sort of horrors lay beneath that surface? Probably something like the Loch Ness Monster, or Jaws, or a giant sea serpent, or some other scary prehistoric creature. He shook his head and turned back to the room.

"I don't mean to sound ungrateful or anything, but no."

"Promised Iggy to get you home." The wood-sprite sounded as if it were on the edge of tears (if wood-sprites cried, that is). "Found help. It took a long time, very hard, and now you won't go."

"Ben . . ."

The word seemed to come from a long way off. It broke in the air like a wave breaking on a beach, a lilting trickle of sound.

Ben's breath caught in his throat. He whirled around and leaned out of the window as far as he dared. There was someone—or something—down there in the lake. Moonlight played on its pale head, on the ripples that spread out from its movements. Ben squinted. It looked like a seal. . . .

Or a selkie . . .

A trill of laughter floated up to him, followed by a waving flipper.

"Found her!" cried Twig in triumph. "Thought of plan: Bring friends!"

It was She Who Swims the Silver Path of the Moon.

"Oh, Silver—I never thought I'd see you again!"

"Do you remember how you caught me when I jumped from the great tree, Ben?" she called up.

"Yes . . ." He wasn't sure he liked the direction this was taking.

"I trusted you and you saved me. Well, now you

must trust me. If you jump, I will save you and carry you to the shore."

Now was not the time, Ben thought, to remember that it had been a stroke of luck that had really saved Silver, a branch that had caught her clothing and slowed her fall. Between the castle window and the lake there was nothing to break *his* fall. Nothing at all.

Twig flew up behind Ben, so that all the stonework was edged with his warm light. Ben had read a lot of stories in which the hero stepped through a magic portal: This was exactly what the window looked like now. But he was already in another world, and stepping out was a very scary thought indeed.

"Jump, Ben," the wood-sprite whispered.

"Think of your mother!" called the cockroach.

"Think of Eidolon!" cried the spider.

With his blood beating in his ears, Ben climbed on to the windowsill. Tall and narrow, it fit him like a picture frame. He looked down once more, saw how the selkie beckoned, and closed his eyes. Then, like a sleepwalker in a nightmare, he stepped into the void.

Chapter Twenty

Friends

The air rushed past Ben. His hair stood on end.

Just as he was thinking that falling was quite a pleasant experience, he crashed feet-first into the lake and the water swallowed him like the monster he had expected to find there. Down he went, heavy as a stone. There was no stopping him. The water, freezing and squeezing, got up his nose; he could not help but open his mouth to cry out, and then the water rushed in there, too.

I'm going to drown, Ben thought in panic. *I'm going to drown and my family won't know.*

Then suddenly something stopped his downward progress, something sleek and slippery and strong, and all at once he was borne up and sped along through the water's resistance, until at last his head broke the surface of the lake and there was air to breathe.

He coughed and spluttered. Then he opened his eyes and there was Silver's face, right by his own, and his arms were around her neck. Her big dark eyes blinked at him, and when she smiled her whiskers wriggled. Then she said, "Hold tight!" and they were off again, but this time it was more like flying than swimming. All he had to do was to hold on and the selkie did the rest, splashing with her powerful flippers.

The far side of the lake came closer and closer, and Ben was about to laugh in triumph, when a terrible baying split the night. He turned in dread, just in time to see the Gabriel Hounds come flying down over the battlements toward them.

"Oh, no . . ."

The selkie turned too. He saw her eyes widen,

then she struck out for the shore with even greater determination.

But Ben was unable to tear his eyes away from the spectral hounds, or from the dog-headed man in the chariot they drew. The Dodman's mouth was open in a shout of fury and exhortation as he drove the sky-yelpers onward; moonlight gleamed on his long teeth.

"Hurry, Silver, hurry!" he cried.

But a single selkie was no match for the speed of the Gabriel Hounds. Down they swooped, baying for blood; and Ben remembered that they had not been fed. He laid himself flat against Silver's back.

"Hold your breath, Ben!" Silver cried, and when he did, she dived.

Down they went into the cold blackness, but this time Ben dared to risk a look. With his left eye, all was dark and forbidding; but when he opened his right eye the scene nearly made him shout aloud in wonder. They were swimming through what appeared to be the ruins of an ancient city, for all around them loomed broken towers and abandoned houses like ghosts, lost gardens where fish darted between the skeletons of drowned trees. It made him think of the fish tanks at the Pet Emporium, with their pondweed and ruined plastic arches; but what he had seen there in poor facsimile was now displayed in the awesome grandeur of the original. For a moment he almost forgot to be afraid.

Above, the rainbow colors of the spectral hounds shot through the surface of the lake. Ben's lungs were bursting. He hoped the selkie would remember she had a human boy on her back, and not some weird sort of fish-beast that didn't mind breathing water. He dug his knees in to remind her of his existence, and up she went, flicking sinuously through the waves, a creature at home in her own element.

Up into the air they came, a little way ahead of the Gabriel Hounds. Ben turned back and found they were almost at the shore. What would Silver do then? He remembered the slow transition she had made from seal to girl, how she had had difficulty walking on her flippers. He could not let the dogs catch the selkie—they would rip her to shreds. . . .

"Silver!" he cried. "I can swim from here. Really I can. Save yourself, dive deep and get away."

But the selkie said nothing. Instead she veered so suddenly sideways that Ben was almost flung from her back. He had a fleeting vision of the leading pair of hounds just a few feet away, then a disorienting view of woodland. He thought he saw something pale move between the trees, but the glimpse was too quick to be sure.

Then Silver the seal barked into the night; and it was met by howls, not from above and behind them where the Gabriel Hounds were snapping at their heels, but from the shore. When Ben looked again he saw four great silver wolves emerging from the wood, and behind them two other, taller figures.

"I must leave you here, Benjamin Arnold!" cried the selkie. "I wish I could come with you, but I cannot. Good-bye, Ben, I will see you again!"

And she rolled sleekly so that Ben found himself fully immersed in the water once more. He flapped his arms. He kicked with his feet. He stuck his head out of the water and splashed and splashed. He tried to remember what his swimming teacher had told him when he kept sinking to the bottom; but somehow swimming at the local leisure center, with its dreamy blue water and neatly designated lanes, did not seem to be very useful preparation for trying to save yourself from a pack of rabid ghost-dogs and their mad master. Even so, he did his best, and a second later one foot struck the lake bed and he knew he was nearly there.

At the same moment, something caught at his fleece top, dragging him backward. He felt hot breath on the back of his neck.

"Do not kill the princeling!" commanded the Dodman. "I need him alive."

And that was when the four giant wolves Ben had glimpsed on the lake's shore hurled themselves into the water. Suddenly he was in the middle of a battle. Snarling muzzles, yellowed canine teeth, rancid breath, and furious growling surrounded him. The Gabriel Hounds roared and snapped. The wolves howled and bit. Ben was sure he was about to be mauled, but moments later there was a whine of pain and the grip on his jacket was released. At once Ben kicked free and, scrambling forward, found that he could stand. A moment later he was running through the shallows, and then he was on dry land.

When he caught his breath, he turned to see that the Gabriel Hounds were drawing back in fear from their adversaries, even though the Dodman stood and screamed at them from the chariot. The wolves stood resolute and unyielding, water sparkling in their shaggy fur. They looked magnificent, not at all like the straggly specimens Ben had seen in captivity at the local zoo.

"Come with us, Ben!" A deep voice thrummed through Ben's rib cage.

It was the Horned Man he had seen on his long and miserable journey to the castle. He stood just beyond the line of trees, his great antlered head limned in moonlight. At his side stood another creature straight out of the books of mythology that Ben loved so much. The top half of this figure was that of a young man, with a proud, fine-boned face and piercing eyes. Black hair fell to his shoulders and sturdy brown chest; but from the waist down he had the body of a powerful horse.

"Oh," Ben breathed in awe. "A centaur!"

"He is Darius," the Horned Man said, "one of the Horse People."

The centaur came forward. He bowed his head to Ben, then knelt on the grass. "It would be an honor to bear the son of Queen Isadora to safety," he said.

Ben did not know quite how to respond to this, but he made a fist of one hand and brought it to his chest, as he had seen a Roman soldier do in a film once, which felt right, somehow.

"Thank you, Darius," he said. "The honor is mine."

Gingerly, Ben climbed onto the centaur's back; and Darius rocked to his feet and turned to follow the Horned Man into the eaves of the wood.

In the space of just a couple of days, Ben thought suddenly, *I have flown on a dragon, swum with a selkie, and ridden a centaur.*

If it weren't all so dangerous and urgent, he would have been having the time of his life.

"Let us away before the Dodman can follow," said the Horned Man.

Ben chanced a last glance back over his shoulder, just in time to see the Gabriel Hounds breaking from their traces in a flurry before the four white wolves. Over went the chariot, and into the murky waters of the lake went the Dodman with a great cartwheel of arms and legs and a howl of rage.

Ben laughed in glee.

And then Darius kicked up his heels, and Ben couldn't do anything at all other than concentrate on how not to fall off.

Chapter Twenty-one

The Lord of the Wildwood

They emerged from the woodland onto the moors Ben had crossed as a captive just as the moon rose to its zenith. The centaur broke into a gallop, and the Horned Man ran along beside him, eating the ground away with huge, effortless strides. Their moonshadows stretched away from them, sharp and attenuated, companions to their flight.

Ben kept looking back over his shoulder.

"I am sure my wolves will hold the Dodman at bay," the Horned One said, and the moonlight glinted in his hazel-green eyes.

"Who *is* the Dodman?" Ben asked, his fists buried hard in the centaur's coarse mane.

"The Dodman, the dog-man, the Dead Man; there are many names for him," the antlered man replied. The leaves he wore rustled as he ran. Ben could not see how they were attached—whether they were some sort of clothing or an integral part of him. "But no one knows his true name, or his origin, which has proved to be unfortunate. For a time, that did not seem important—he was not always so powerful."

"Did he become powerful when my mother went away?" Ben asked in a small voice. He had a nasty feeling this was all his fault; his and Ellie's and Alice's.

The Horned Man nodded. "He hoped to wed her. He and Old Creepie had made some sort of cruel bargain. But fate tricked them, and Isadora escaped their clutches, though she did not know their evil plans. At the time we thought it a boon, but none could have foreseen the consequences."

Ben shivered. Then he wondered what would

have happened if his mother had married Mr. Dodds; would he have been born with a dog's head too? Perhaps he wouldn't have been born at all.

"Won't he punish you for this?"

The Horned Man laughed. "The Dodman does not rule the Wildwood, or ever shall. There are still places I can call my own."

"But if my mother is the Queen of Eidolon, is she not also Queen of the Wildwood?" Ben asked, confused.

"I have seen a thousand queens come and go in Eidolon," the Horned One answered without rancor or boast. "Your mother is Queen of Eidolon and she is also my Queen, and I owe her my love and my allegiance. For her part, she is happy to have a friend who maintains the guardianship of the wild places for her."

"Do you have a name?" Ben asked humbly. "I don't know what to call you, or how to thank you."

At this, the centaur gave a little buck of delight and turned his head to look at Ben. He winked. "The Dodman is not the only one with many names," he said. "You may call him the Horned One; Herne the Hunter; or Cernunnos, Lord of the Wildwood."

This was a bit overwhelming. Ben opted for the one that sounded most like a name. "Thank you for saving me, Cernunnos. But how did you know to come for me?"

The Lord of the Wildwood smiled. "One of the denizens of my forest sought me out. I think you know him: a wood-sprite called Twig. He said you saved him from the Dodman. I believe that one good turn deserves another."

Ben blushed with pleasure. It was something he had often heard his mother say.

Soon they were back in Darkmere Forest, and still there was no sign of pursuit.

They slowed to a walk, by reason of necessity as much as for a rest, for the trees here were dense and their roots treacherous to even the most nimble-footed.

The Horned Man led them through a great thicket of ferns whose curling fronds were weighed down by some form of fungus. He shook his head. "My forest has become darker and wilder than it used to be," he said softly. He brushed his fingers against the mildewed trunk of a hawthorn and lifted his hand to his nose. "And something has sickened it."

"I think," Ben said hesitantly, "that might be because my mother is sick. In the Other World."

Darius turned, and his eyes were wide. "The Lady is not dead, then?"

Ben's fingers tightened in the centaur's mane. "She wasn't when I left. But she was very ill indeed." A terrible dread seized him. What if his mother had died while he had been here? "I must get back," he said hoarsely.

"We have bound ourselves to your return," Cernunnos said solemnly. "You are a child of the prophecy. Our future rests in your hands. Yours and your siblings."

It was hard to imagine Ellie, let alone Alice, contributing much to the saving of Eidolon, Ben thought; but the world had revealed itself as such a strange place in the past few weeks that now he believed anything was possible.

They moved in silence among the trees and Ben stared around, wondering which of them harbored the dryad who had tried so bravely to save him from the Dodman, for he would have liked to see her again before he left her world. But none of his surroundings looked familiar, and Cernunnos did not seem pre-disposed to make a detour from their route, ploughing resolutely on through the forest.

They were making their way through an area of the forest where the trees were more widely spaced when the Lord of the Wildwood looked up suddenly and frowned. "Stay here," he warned. "Stay still."

Running as fleetly as a deer, he made off between the trees, his eyes searching the canopy as if he were tracking something overhead.

Ben stared upward. In the night sky he glimpsed a moving shape, black against the moon. He waited, holding his breath, all sorts of terrifying scenarios riot-ing through his imagination.

The centaur pawed the ground impatiently. "It is only a short distance to the Old Stone," Darius said quietly. "Do not worry, Ben, we will get you there." He paused, then added, "Or we will die in the attempt."

A few moments later Cernunnos returned. "It was a fire-drake," he said, "quartering the ground in search of something. Dragons are an ancient and unpre-dictable breed—it is generally better to avoid them than risk their wrath."

Ben remembered Zark burning the tires off Aunt Sybil's Range Rover. "I rather like dragons," he said softly.

On the edge of the clearing where the Aldstane's wild road had coughed Ben out, the Horned Man stopped and sniffed the air. "I don't like this," he said. "There are goblins about. I can smell them."

"That'll be Bogie and Boggart," Ben said. "They're working for my uncle. Or Old Creepie, or whatever he's called here. I don't think they mean to be as horrid as he makes them. They were going with him to trap another dragon for a customer."

"Customer?" Cernunnos frowned.

"Someone who pays money for something you've got and they want," said Ben.

"Money?"

Ben stared at the Horned Man. "You don't have money in the Secret Country?" He dug in his pocket and brought out a few coins. "We give people these and they give us . . . things instead."

Darius gazed at the coins. "Can you eat them?" he asked dubiously.

"No," said Ben.

The Lord of the Wildwood picked one of them

out of Ben's palm and held it up. It was a fifty-pence piece, newly minted. "It is rather shiny," he said after a while. "I suppose magpies might like such things. Or you could let it catch the light in a stream bed." He thought for a moment. "Though pebbles have prettier colors. What do you do with them, then?"

"Not much, actually. You just collect them, and pass them on."

"And Old Creepie is stealing away our creatures in exchange for such items?"

Ben nodded.

The Lord of the Wildwood's face contorted. "Then this is madness indeed."

"We're trying to stop him, my sister and I," Ben said, hoping that Iggy had reached Ellie and persuaded her to do as he asked. "If we can stop him and Mr. Dodds stealing magic out of Eidolon, Mum might get stronger; and if she gets better, then Eidolon might get better too."

"Queen Isadora must return to her people," the Horned Man said sternly. "Or there will be no Eidolon hereafter."

That silenced Ben. He had not thought things through that far. All he'd ever imagined was his mother getting better, but what would they do—he and his father and his sisters—if she had to leave them forever?

As they approached the entrance to the wild road, he felt suddenly miserable. The Eidolon part of himself was curiously reluctant to leave, even though the magical world was blighted and perilous. He almost wished he did not have to go home and face the awful truth of it all. But he knew that he must.

He slid down from the centaur's back. Then, squaring his shoulders, he touched the great stone that was the counterpart to the stone in Aldstane Park and watched as his hand passed into another dimension.

Above their heads sounded a great flurry of wings.

"Run!" came a voice from above. "He is coming! Go through the wild road now!"

Instead of doing what he was told, Ben stared upward into the night sky.

"Zark!" he cried. "Is that you?"

But there came no response except for a streak of flame, which burst through the air above them. Its fiery light revealed the Dodman, in the restored chariot drawn not only by the Gabriel Hounds, but by the four silver wolves as well. The wolves looked bedraggled and cowed, broken in spirit. Their heads hung down and their tails curled between their legs. Somehow the Dodman had mastered them, brought them to heel, and made them part of his wild hunt.

Cernunnos and Darius exchanged stricken glances, and it was the expression on the face of the Lord of the Wildwood that really made Ben afraid. Matters had taken an unexpected and terrifying turn. If Mr. Dodds could bind the great silver wolves to him, he had greater powers than even the Horned Man had suspected.

"Go, Ben!" Cernunnos cried. "Go through the wild road. We will guard your back!"

But still Ben hesitated. "Please don't put yourselves at risk for me." He remembered the way Xarkanadûshak had been brought low; he could not bear that the same fate should overtake the Lord of the Wildwood and the proud centaur.

"If we do not stand against him now, all will fail," the Horned Man said grimly. "But the Dodman is not yet ready to stand against me, for all that he dares to traduce my wolves. There will be a reckoning, but now is not that time. He puts on a great show of strength, Ben, but he will not fight me. And whatever happens here is not for you to witness. Go back to your world and do what you can there." And he pushed Ben into the wild road with all his might.

Chapter Twenty-two

The Aldstane

Tumbling over and over in the strange environs of the way between worlds, Ben felt no relief; nothing but despair. He had left others to fight his battles in the Secret Country, as he had in the Other World, the one he called his home. He had a long way to go if he was to become a hero, if he was to play his part in fulfilling the prophecy to keep Eidolon free.

Then he started to fall, but before he could prepare

for a landing, he hit the ground with a thud that knocked the wind out of him. "Ow!"

He stood up gingerly, dusting off his hands and knees. One of his elbows had caught the Aldstane on the way through and it hurt enormously. Quite why anyone should call that bit the funny bone, he could not imagine. Then some inconsequential bit of his brain reminded him that the armbone was called a humerus. Humerus, humorous. It still wasn't funny.

And it wasn't the time to be thinking about word-play, for something was going on. Ben stared around. He closed his left eye, then opened it and closed his right: There was no doubt that he was back in his own world, for the view out of either eye was the same. He was in Aldstane Park.

He could hear shouting and the sound of people— or something—running. There was a lot of worrying rustling in the undergrowth. Ben wondered if he had stumbled into something worse than what he had left behind. The next thing he knew, half a dozen goblins burst out of the rhododendrons.

When they saw him, the leading pair drew back.

"It's the boy," said the one he knew as Bogie.

"He's escaped!" cried Boggart.

"The boy?"

"The elf-boy, the Queen's son."

Now the other four drew close together behind Boggart and Bogie.

"He doesn't *look* like an elf," said one.

"He's only a half elf."

"Can we eat the boy half?" asked another.

"Nah," said Bogie. "He'll magic you."

Ben was pretty sure he couldn't magic anyone, but he said, "I magicked the Dodman, and I will magic you out of existence if you come anywhere near me."

"He magicked the Dodman!"

The goblins grew hushed. Then they spoke together in grumbling tones that were too low for Ben to hear, and he realized that whatever special powers he might have had in Eidolon were certainly no longer with him now. Even so, if he showed the slightest sign of fear, they would probably tear him to pieces. He remembered Boggart pleading with Mr. Dodds for a bit of "lovely fresh boy" and promptly pushed it out of his mind before his knees started trembling.

Now one of the goblins stepped forward. "Let us go," it said. "If you let us go through the wild road back to our forest, we won't come back."

"And what about your work for the old man?"

Boggart showed his sharp little teeth and hissed. "We don't want to work for him anymore. Nasty dragon . . ."

Ben looked more closely and saw that the goblin was wounded. In the darkness it was hard to see, but the arm that he clutched to his chest looked burned and withered.

"That will teach you for stealing away the creatures of the Shadow World!" Ben said sternly.

"What does he mean by steal?" Bogie asked, but none of his companions seemed to know—they shrugged and made faces.

"Taking what isn't yours," Ben said, feeling as if they were making him sound like a rather pompous schoolteacher.

They all looked mystified. "But a dragon isn't anyone's," said Boggart; and Ben couldn't think of an answer to that.

"You give me your word that you won't ever again do what Old Creepie asks of you?"

"What word?"

"Oh, this is hopeless. What will you do if I let you go?"

Bogie looked at Boggart. "Eat toadstools?" he suggested.

"Jump in ponds; chase fishes?"

"Tease the minotaur," suggested another.

"No, no, not that—remember what happened last time."

Ben felt dizzy. "Oh, go on then," he said, stepping away from the stone. He wondered what they would find on the other side but decided they were not courageous enough to get involved in any fight.

They approached cautiously, keeping their sly little eyes on Ben all the way.

"Um," he said, as a thought struck him, "just where is Uncle Aleis—Old Creepie, anyway?"

Boggart gazed over Ben's shoulder, his eyes wide. "Behind you!" he said, and leaped into the wild road.

Ben whirled around, expecting to see the horrible crouched old man with the long nails and overgrown teeth; but instead there was Awful Uncle Aleister, in a smart suit and long gabardine overcoat. He looked disheveled, as if he had been in a fight. His tie was askew, his pinstriped shirt was torn, and his nose had bled down onto the collar. He stared at Ben with loathing.

"Get out of my way, you vile nuisance!"

"No," said Ben, trying to sound braver than he felt.

"In which case, I shall just have to take you back with me!" Uncle Aleister declared. "And you won't be escaping this time, I can tell you. This time the Dodman and I will sort you out once and for all!" He laughed. "Come to think of it, it's what we should have done in the first place—the fewer of Isadora's children there are around, the less likely it will be that that ridiculous prophecy can ever come true!" And he advanced upon Ben in a menacing way.

Ben dodged behind the Aldstane. "Don't you come anywhere near me!" he cried.

"Boggart! Bogie! Brimstone! Bosko! Beetle! Batface!"

But none of the goblins were answering Uncle Aleister's call.

Blue lights scythed the air, illuminating the bushes with an eerie pallor; and now Ben could hear sirens.

"It's the police!" he cried.

"I know it's the police, you idiot boy. Why do you think I'm trying to escape to the Shadow World? Now get out of my way!"

But Ben was yelling, "Over here! Over here!"

Awful Uncle Aleister launched himself at his nephew. "You stupid little troublemaker. I'm going to feed you to a Tyrannosaurus rex." He grabbed Ben by the shoulders and shoved him toward the wild road.

"You don't want to go in there," Ben said. "The Horned Man is waiting on the other side. His wolves are there too, and a centaur."

He didn't think it necessary to explain that the wolves were currently harnessed up to the Dodman's chariot.

Uncle Aleister looked fearful. Then he got Ben in a headlock and, fumbling in his pocket, brought out a sharp little knife and dug it into the side of Ben's neck. "One more word," he threatened, "and you'll be dog-meat."

Then he stuck his head into the wild road and listened.

When he emerged again, his head was that of Old Creepie once more, pallid and bald, his brows looming over gleaming, sunken eyes; his yellow teeth all snaggled and fanglike—which gave new meaning to "long in the tooth," Ben thought, watching the illusion gradually fade.

"It seems you have not yet learned to be a liar, Benjamin Arnold," Uncle Aleister said. "Too much of your precious mother's blood in you."

He wrestled Ben into the bushes, backing him up against a tree.

Ben watched as the blue lights got brighter. The sirens sounded very close now; the police must be driving through the park. Car doors banged, then Ben heard running feet come crashing through the undergrowth.

"Over here!" someone shouted. "He went this way!"

Torches flickered through the leaves.

Then a policeman stepped into the clearing beside the Aldstane. Ben wriggled, but his uncle held him tight, and eventually the officer went away. Ben felt the arm holding him relax slightly, so he wrenched his head free and bit the hand that held the knife so hard that Awful Uncle Aleister swore. The knife fell to the ground. Ben gathered a breath to shout for help, but Uncle Aleister clamped a hand tightly over his mouth and nose. Blood dripped onto Ben's face. He couldn't breathe.

Just as he thought he might pass out, his uncle

grunted as if in surprise. A tendril of ivy seemed to have wound itself around his hand and was pulling it away from Ben's face. A moment later Ben found he could breathe, and then that he could move. With a desperate lurch, he dragged himself from Awful Uncle Aleister's grasp. He turned to see if his uncle was coming back at him. He could hardly believe his eyes.

The tree they had been standing against had wrapped itself around Aleister's legs and arms, pinning him to its trunk. Ivy wreathed his head and torso and pinioned his hands to his sides. His awful uncle's eyes bulged with shock and outrage.

Above his head, a second head revealed itself. Ben gasped. It had fine features and delicately waving hair, all of the same color as the tree within whose skin she stood.

"It's you," he said, amazed.

"I failed you in Darkmere Forest, and I knew I must do something to make amends," said the dryad, holding Awful Uncle Aleister so tightly that he squirmed in terror. "If Eidolon is to be saved, then we must all do what we can."

"You came through the wild road, without even knowing what you would find on the other side?"

"I followed you. The Lord of the Wildwood saw me go. I think he was glad you would not be entirely on your own."

Ben was astonished by her courage.

"I will go back, as soon as this miscreant has been dealt with and I know you are safe. The trees here have a little of the Secret Country's magic to them—it must have leaked through the way-between-worlds. I'll be all right, for a time."

She squeezed Ben's uncle so tightly that the air came whooshing out of him and his face started to go purple.

Ben decided that Uncle Aleister deserved the treatment he was receiving, so instead of asking the tree nymph to stop, he grinned and said, "Thank you, Dryad. You are incredibly brave. My mother would be proud of you." Then he cupped his hands around his mouth and yelled, "Police! Over here, over here!"

Seconds later, two uniformed officers came running, handcuffs at the ready.

"Help me!" wheezed Uncle Aleister, now more terrified by the tree than by any other prospect. "Help me—this tree is trying to kill me!"

The policemen exchanged glances. Then the

sergeant swung his flashlight beam up into Uncle Aleister's face. "Nutter," he said to his colleague. "Complete nutter." He looked at Ben. "Are you all right, son? Has he harmed you?"

"Not exactly," said Ben, watching out of the corner of one eye as the dryad faded back into the tree, leaving the policemen to extricate Uncle Aleister from the ivy.

"Ben!"

Ben turned around.

"Dad!"

Mr. Arnold came running full tilt into the clearing. "Oh, Ben, you're safe!" He hugged his son as tightly as the dryad had done, until Ben was seriously worried his ribs might crack. "I'm okay, Dad," he croaked at last. "Honest I am."

The two of them watched as the policemen hauled Awful Uncle Aleister out into the open and put the handcuffs on him. He glared at Mr. Arnold over their shoulders as they read him his rights. "Dodds will come for you and your family, Clive," he promised. "And when he does, a little crack on the nose like the one you gave me won't stop him."

"Painful, is it?" Mr. Arnold inquired innocently,

taking in the blood and bruising with some satisfaction.

"I'll press charges against you," snarled Awful Uncle Aleister.

The sergeant regarded him with a raised eyebrow. "Really, sir? I don't recall seeing Mr. Arnold hit you. But we saw you run slap-bang into that tree, didn't we, Tom?"

The other policeman nodded vigorously. "Got to watch where you're going in the dark," he said.

"Thank you for your assistance, Mr. Arnold," the sergeant said. "I'm glad your lad is okay. Can we give you a lift home?"

Ben shook his head. He looked up at his father. "We can walk home, can't we, Dad? After all, we've got a lot to talk about."

Mr. Arnold smiled. "Yes, we have."

They walked to the edge of the rhododendrons and watched the policemen put Uncle Aleister into the back of one of the cars. Then the convoy of vehicles trailed slowly out of the park, their blue lights swirling in the lightening air.

"Walk home?" came a voice out of the darkness. "I don't think we can have *that*."

Ben and his father turned around slowly, in a kind of dread.

Mr. Arnold gasped.

Ben grinned until he thought his face would split.

Above them were two gloriously colored dragons, their wings outstretched as they circled in for a landing.

"Zark!" cried Ben.

"And this is my wife, Ishtar," said Zark.

Ishtar glided to a halt in front of them, her scales a fabulous tapestry of blues and golds and purples, where her husband's were the color of flame.

"Hello again, Ben," she said, and Ben suddenly realized that Ishtar must have been the dragon he had seen on the other side of the wild road, the one he had mistaken for Zark in the gloom and panic of those last moments in Eidolon.

"Hello," he breathed, awed by her presence. "What are you doing here?"

"We've been very busy," Zark said, puffing his chest out proudly so that steam jetted out of his nostrils, followed by a thin line of flame. "We've been flying around your world rescuing the folk the Dodman stole away from Eidolon. We've already returned half a dozen saber-toothed tigers, a baby mammoth, some satyrs, and a small stegosaurus. Then Old Creepie and his goblins got hold of our friend Zoroaster and took him through the wild road last night, so we came back to free him."

Ben repeated this for his father, and Mr. Arnold stared and stared. Then he said, "I think your friend may have already got away. Half of King Henry Close has gone up in flames and one of Aleister's neighbors babbled something about seeing a dragon come rampaging out of a truck that was parked outside. Of course, nobody believed him!" He grinned. "Well, now I have seen everything. What a wonderful story to tell your mother."

"How is she?" Ben asked anxiously.

His father frowned. "Not well." Then he smiled. "But she's very determined to come home. They said she can come out of the hospital in a day or two."

Ben breathed a sigh of relief. It was a start.

"Well, don't hang around," Zark said impatiently. He dipped a wing to Ben, who climbed carefully onto his back.

"Not too high," Ben warned.

Ishtar offered a wing to Mr. Arnold. "It would be an honor to bear the father of the Prince of Eidolon," she said.

"Eh?" said Ben's father. But, even though he could not understand the language of dragons, he climbed aboard.

"Hay is for horses!" Ben laughed; and the dragons sprang into the air and wheeled away over Aldstane Park into the first glimmering light of dawn.

Epilogue

Two days later Ben's mother, known in one world as Mrs. Arnold and in another as Queen Isadora, returned to her family home. In her arms she carried baby Alice, and she managed for the first time in months to walk from the car right up the garden path and into the house, under the WELCOME HOME banner that Ben and Ellie had strung over the front door that very morning.

Mr. Arnold closed the door behind her. "Well,

we're all together again at last." He beamed.

Mrs. Arnold turned her face up to him for a kiss. Her cheeks were pink, Ben noticed, and her green eyes sparkled.

"Thank you, darlings," she said. "Thank you for being so brave. I know what you have done for me and," she paused, "for Eidolon."

Mr. Arnold looked at his feet, then forced a smile. Then he helped his wife to the sofa and made her a cup of tea. "Get comfortable," he said. "I have something to show you." He brought out a copy of *The Bixbury Gazette* and smoothed it flat upon the coffee table. "There," he said proudly. "Right on the front page."

DANGEROUS ANIMAL TRADE
RING SMASHED

ran the headline, and underneath that,

Pet shop a front for the sale
of illegal animals
Mr. Dodds's Pet Emporium on Bixbury High Street
was yesterday the scene of a major investigation

after police were tipped off by our own reporter, Clive Arnold, to the presence of certain dangerous animals being held illegally in the pet shop's stockrooms and at various private locations around the town. Police would not make details of the precise nature of their findings public, but Chief Inspector David Ramsay is quoted as saying, "Trust me, these aren't the sort of animals we want to have roaming loose on the streets of Bixbury. The consequences could be nasty. Very nasty indeed."

The creatures—including several large predators, some aquatic mammals, and what may have been a giant alligator—were being held in squalid and unsanitary conditions. Many were starving and others were almost dead from their ordeals. All those that have been recovered have now been safely rehomed, said a police spokesman, and other constabularies around the country will be mobilized to round up any animals that were sold prior to the raid.

There is currently no sign of the pet shop owner, Mr. A. E. Dodds, but police are requesting that anyone with any information as to his whereabouts contact the Bixbury Police Incident Room immediately. The public are warned not to approach him directly, since he may be armed and is to be regarded as highly dangerous.

Meanwhile, his trading partner, Mr. Aleister Creepie, has been taken into custody and is currently helping police with their inquiries. He will be charged tomorrow under twelve counts of contravening the Dangerous Animals Act. His wife, Sybil (43), and daughter, Cynthia (14), were taken in for questioning, but were released after a night in the cells and a great deal of complaining.

The Pet Emporium will be closed indefinitely. Chief Inspector Ramsay adds, "The police and people of Bixbury owe Mr. Arnold a debt of gratitude for his investigation into this disgraceful trade. His persistence and courage have undoubtedly saved many lives."

"The editor wrote it himself," Mr. Arnold said, "he was so pleased with the scoop. And, Izzie, he's promoted me to deputy editor!"

"Well done, Clive!" She squeezed his hand. "You are my hero."

Ben and Ellie exchanged glances. Ellie rolled her eyes. "God," she said. "If they're going to be all gooey, I'm off to watch TV."

But the story was also on the evening news, along with several reports of sightings of strange animals around the country.

"We've still got a lot of rounding up to do," said Ben. He grinned at his sister. "That'll be fun."

"Well, I'm not starting yet," Ellie said. "I'm going upstairs to do my nails."

Ben followed her up. "I'm going to play with my cat," he said.

"He's not 'your' cat," Ellie retorted.

"Well, he's certainly not yours."

"Cats belong to no one," someone said, and around the corner of Ben's bedroom door came a small black and brown cat with shiny gold eyes. It was Ignatius Sorvo Coromandel. "Though they don't mind pretending they belong to you as long as you feed them," he added hopefully.

Ben and his sister laughed.

The next morning Ben drew back his bedroom curtains and gazed out into a world that seemed to offer more hope than it had a week before. Everywhere the colors seemed just that bit brighter and the birds sang just that bit louder.

Iggy uncurled himself from where he had been sleeping at the foot of Ben's bed and came to look out of the window beside him. There was a particularly noisy blackbird chirping away on the garden gate. Iggy fixed it with a gimlet eye.

"How dare you wake me up with your racket! I'll have you," he promised, growling at it through the glass.

"I doubt that," said Ben. He tapped on the window to scare it away, but all that happened was that the bird lifted a few inches off the gate, flapped its wings wildly and fell, scrabbling from the string by which it was tethered. Ben frowned. Why would someone tie a blackbird to their garden gate?

He threw a coat on over his pajamas and ran downstairs with Ignatius Sorvo Coromandel bounding along behind him.

"Now, you're not to eat it," Ben warned the little cat. "It wouldn't be fair."

"All's fair in love and war," said Iggy cheerfully.

But it wasn't a blackbird at all. It was a mynah bird. It looked at the boy with its beady black eyes; then it looked at the cat and squawked, opening its bright orange beak wide.

"The Dodman sends his regards," it declared in an odd, mechanical fashion as if it had been taught the words by rote. "Squarrrk!"

"What?" said Ben, horrified.

"He is coming for your mother. Squarrrk! He will take her and with her power he will destroy all the magic in the world. There is nothing you can do to stop him! He will come when you least expect it, and if you get in his way, he will kill you. Squarrk!"

It cocked its head at Ben, hopped from foot to foot.

"Get this bleeding string off me, won't you, mate?" it requested. "I've done me bit now, delivered me message." It gave Iggy a hard stare with one of its shiny, orange-rimmed eyes. "Don't let that feline get me, will you, mate? I don't like the way it's lookin' at me."

"The cat won't harm you," Ben said sternly. "Tell me who gave you this message and I'll untie you."

The bird considered him, head on one side. "Well, you looks honest," it said at last. "It was Mr. Dodds himself gave me the message, and if you know the Dodman, you know he means what he says."

Ben felt a horrible wave of weariness engulf him. "Iggy, run inside and make sure my mother is safe."

The cat was gone no more than a minute. "She's asleep," he reported with a wide yawn. "As anyone sensible should be at this early hour." He fixed the mynah bird with an amber eye and the bird hopped around uncomfortably.

"Come on, mate," the mynah bird begged Ben. "Get us undone. Be fair. Don't shoot the messenger, and all that."

"Will you carry a message from me to your master?" Ben asked.

The bird fixed him with one of its beady eyes. "If you untie me I will," it promised with tremendous insincerity.

"All right, then. Tell the Dodman . . . tell him that the Prince of Eidolon sends his regards, and a warning. Tell him to leave my mother alone . . . or, or else," he finished weakly. He could not think of anything to say. "Do you understand that?"

The bird made a considering sort of noise, then repeated the message back to him, word for word.

"All right," said Ben. He undid the knotted string with which Mr. Dodds had tied the bird to the gate, and it flapped awkwardly away into the morning sky.

"Or else?" Iggy repeated derisively. "What sort of threat is that?"

He watched the bird go with narrow eyes.

"I know," said Ben with a sigh. "I couldn't think of

anything to say. Perhaps it was lying all along. Perhaps it made the whole thing up."

But in his heart he knew it hadn't. A shadow had fallen across his world again, a shadow that he hoped had somehow gone away.

"Oh, Iggy, the Dodman's been here. He's been to our house. He knows where my mother is. He's threatened to come for her. He's going to have to be stopped once and for all." Ben sat down on the grass with his head in his hands and tried to think.

"Come on," Iggy said kindly after a while, butting his head against Ben's leg. "Let's go in."

Ben attempted a smile. "Breakfast," he said, trying to sound more cheerful than he felt. "I can't think about any of this on an empty stomach."

Iggy nodded. "Food is often the best place to start."

So together the boy and the cat let themselves quietly into the kitchen of Number 27 Underhill Road and made themselves the sort of breakfast that was fit for a prince of Eidolon and a great explorer known as the Wanderer.

As they ate, they shared a thought: What in either world they would do now?

THE SHADOW WORLD

Contents

Chapter One

An Unwelcome Visit

Ben Arnold sighed and sat back against the wall of the tree house, brushing a strand of straw-blond hair out of his eyes. The book he had been holding slipped to the floor, where peachy midmorning light sliding through gaps in the planks illuminated a picture of a huge dinosaur confronting a band of ancient hunters dressed in animal skins. The tyrannosaurus, its alarming mouth agape to reveal an array of massive, sharp teeth, looked down upon the tiny ant-men out of one vast, intelligent eye. It looked slightly puzzled, Ben thought, as if it were wondering why these strange little creatures were making such a noisy fuss. Or even why they were there at all—waving their pathetic-looking spears even though all the dinosaur was doing was meandering along trying to find a little breakfast— since, according to Mr. Malarkey at school, dinosaurs and human beings had never even walked the earth at the same time in history.

Then another thought struck Ben: What if the author of the book had known that all along? What if the story was not actually set in this world at all, but in another place entirely—a place where miracles and monsters, dinosaurs and dragons, goblins and ghouls, selkies and saber-toothed tigers, all coexisted? A place he had once visited.

He looked up. Above him spirals of dust motes filtered down from the roof of the tree house, turning gold as they passed through the rays of sun. Just like little streams of magic. It made him think of his mother; and that made him feel sad.

"Morning, Sonny Jim!"

The head of a small black-and-brown cat with

shiny amber eyes appeared suddenly through the opening to the tree house.

"The name's not Sonny Jim," said Ben. "It's Ben."

This exchange had become something of a running joke between the two of them. He grinned, despite his gloomy mood.

The little cat—known by many as the Wanderer, and by Ben as Ignatius Sorvo Coromandel, or Iggy for short—regarded him with his head cocked to one side. After a while he said, "She has to go back, you know."

"I know. It's just . . ." Ben scratched his head. "It's just—well, I'm scared for her."

"Of course you are. She's your mother. But she's also Queen Isadora of Eidolon. The Secret Country is where she belongs."

The Secret Country. The Shadow World. Eidolon. As Iggy had once described it to him, it was a place that no true human being had ever seen; a world that existed everywhere and nowhere; that lay between here and there; between yesterday, today, and tomorrow; between the light and the dark; tangled between the deepest roots of ancient trees, and yet also soaring among the stars.

That had been before he had seen for himself the

magic that was Eidolon, and discovered that he was a son of that mysterious place, as much as he was of the world he was in now. They called him a prince there, but he'd never been called *that* here. Lots of other names on the playground, but never "prince."

He moved to make room for Iggy to sit beside him, and the sunlight fell across his face and shone into his eyes—one of which was a sensible hazel-brown, the other a vivid and startling green.

"I know that, too," he told the cat. "And I knew she had to go back soon, before she got any sicker. I just wasn't expecting it to be today."

"She sent me to fetch you. I think she wants to talk to you."

For a moment Ben felt a tiny stab of envy that his mother was also able to converse with the little cat. He had thought this ability his own private gift; but it seemed that anyone touched by the Secret Country could communicate with its creatures. Then his expression brightened as another thought struck him. "Perhaps she wants to take me with her. To Eidolon."

Ignatius Sorvo Coromandel looked at him sardonically. "In your dreams."

• • •

"Darling, don't you think you should take a warm coat?"

Mrs. Arnold laughed. "Don't fuss, Clive." She pulled herself to her feet, steadying herself against the bedside chair, and gave her husband a big hug. "Eidolon will provide for me."

"Yes, you keep saying that," Mr. Arnold said, almost crossly, "but what does it mean, 'Eidolon will provide'?"

"Exactly what it says. My country and my folk will look after me, I know it."

"Well, I'm packing your winter coat, anyway." Mr. Arnold stepped around Ben and Iggy and went thumping down the stairs.

Mrs. Arnold sighed, for a moment looking tired and wan; then she saw her son standing in the doorway with the little cat sitting smartly at his feet. She smiled. "Thank you, Iggy."

Ben hung back uncertainly. "Can't I come with you?"

Mrs. Arnold took her son by the shoulders and looked at him steadily. Her eyes seemed greener today than they had for months, he thought; and her pale cheeks were washed with pink. She was excited about going back to the Secret Country, Ben realized suddenly: She actually *wanted* to leave them for her original home. A lump rose in his throat and he swallowed furiously, unable to say anything.

"Iggy will carry messages for us, won't you, dear?" She reached a hand down, and Ignatius Sorvo Coromandel bobbed up on his hind legs to rub his cheek against it, purring like a motor.

"It would be my honor," he growled in his strange gravelly tones, which sounded just like the voice of an American detective who lived on whisky and cigarettes.

"Besides," Mrs. Arnold added, "you've already been very brave, Ben, rescuing my folk and getting them back to Eidolon; but I don't want you taking any more risks."

The evil pet shop owner Mr. Dodds (who in the other world stood eight feet tall, had the head of a dog, and was known as the Dodman), in league with Mrs. Arnold's brother, Awful Uncle Aleister (known in the Shadow World as Old Creepie), had been stealing magical creatures out of Eidolon and selling them. Dragons, to be used as garden incinerators; mermaids and selkies, to adorn rich people's lakes; sprites, to be used as fancy lamps; saber-toothed tigers and dire-wolves, to be hunted for sport; unicorns and satyrs, pterodactyls and dinosaurs, to be enjoyed by private collectors. But away from their home in Eidolon the creatures had sickened and died. And each death reduced the sum of magic in the Shadow World and made Mrs. Arnold sicker and sicker.

And that was not the worst of it.

Uncle Aleister was in prison now, and the Dodman had fled: No one knew where he was. But he had left an unsettling message for them.

Tied to the gate with a knotted string had been a big black bird with orange eyes: a mynah bird that Ben had last seen in the pet shop. "You have not heard the last of the Dodman," it had declared. "He will come for the Queen. And when he does, nothing in the world will stop him; indeed, nothing in *either* world."

Ben had been so horrified by this threat that he had kept it to himself, and with each passing day it had become more difficult to speak about. But now his mother was about to walk right into the Dodman's hands. . . . He hung his head.

Seeing his downcast face, Mrs. Arnold felt her heart pierced. She caught him to her. "Look after your sister and your father for me, won't you, Ben?" she said with her nose buried in his hair.

He stepped back sharply. "You said *sister*, not *sisters*—does that mean you're taking Ellie with you, then?" he asked jealously.

Mrs. Arnold smiled sadly. "No, love," she said. "I'm taking Alice."

Ben looked at her in horror. It was bad enough when she had been going back on her own, but how would a tiny little baby survive the dangers of the Shadow World?

"You're *what*?" Mr. Arnold had appeared in the doorway with his wife's soft blue wool coat folded over his arm. "Did I hear you right? You're thinking of taking the baby with you?"

"I *am* taking Alice with me, yes, dear."

Mr. Arnold sat down suddenly on the bed as if his knees had given way. "I admit that I don't understand all of this," he said quietly and with considerable restraint, "but I really don't think that's a very good idea. How will you feed her? What will she do for diapers? Where will she sleep?"

Mrs. Arnold patted his arm. "Eidolon will provide," she said. "Alice belongs in Eidolon. She will be its next Queen."

"What?" Ben's older sister, Ellie, stood in the doorway with her hands on her hips. Her cheeks were flushed and the makeup was smudged around her eyes as if she had been crying.

"Oh, Ellie."

"Why's *she* going to be Queen? Why not me?"

"Now, now, Ellie," said Mr. Arnold, "that's not really the point—"

"I want to go to Eidolon. Ben's been!"

Mrs. Arnold put her arms around Ellie, and Ellie promptly burst into tears.

Ben looked at his father. They both rolled their eyes. Ellie could be a drama queen, but Queen of Eidolon? Ben thought not.

Iggy jumped up onto the bed. "Now, now, Eleanor," he growled. "Queen Isadora must go back to her country. It will not be forever, and when the balance between the worlds is restored, you can visit her there. But it would be too dangerous for you now, for you have less of its magic in you than do Ben or Baby Alice; and your father would not survive

341

there long at all, being a Dull and entirely human."

Mr. Arnold heard all of this merely as one long and rather raucous meow, but Ellie narrowed her eyes at her brother. "I want—," she began, pouting; but at that moment the doorbell rang.

Mr. and Mrs. Arnold exchanged worried glances, then Mr. Arnold crossed quickly to the bedroom window. Outside, parked askew, partly on the sidewalk and partly across the next door neighbor's driveway, blocking the gate, was a large black Range Rover with shiny new wheels and shiny new paintwork.

"Oh no," he breathed. "It's Sybil and the awful Cynthia."

Chapter Two

Awful Aunt Sybil and
Awful Cousin Cynthia

"Just thought we'd drop by for a cup of tea," Sybil announced, walking straight past Mr. Arnold and heading into the living room. There, she eyed the brimming suitcase on the floor with interest. "Going somewhere nice, are you?" she called back over her shoulder.

Aunt Sybil had always been extraordinarily nosy, but her daughter was far worse. Awful Cousin Cynthia pushed her way into the sitting room and shoved her big raffia handbag at her mother, who peered into it unsurely, then clutched it to her large chest and watched as her daughter threw herself down by the suitcase and started poking through its contents.

First of all, Cynthia pulled out a pair of supple leather walking boots and a thin green cloak. These she discarded boredly, strewing them onto the floor along with a pile of baby clothes, which she'd also excavated. Other uninteresting items followed. But a moment later she came upon a battered old book. Her hand hovered over its ancient leather cover, then she picked it up and flicked through it with a puzzled expression on her face. No words appeared to have been printed on its pages, yet Cynthia's eyes scanned the open spread as if she were reading. When Ben came into the room, she closed it hurriedly and threw it down on the heap of clothes.

"Hey!" said Ben. "You shouldn't be—"

His next words were snatched away by sheer astonishment, for at the bottom of the case something gleamed invitingly.

"Oh!" Awful Cousin Cynthia exclaimed. Dislodging a toothbrush, a bar of soap, a towel, and a bottle of Calpol in the process, she grabbed something out and examined it in delight.

It was a crown. Not a heavy gold crown, studded with big flashy jewels and lined with velvet and fur, like the ones Ben had been taken to see in the Tower of London; but a delicate, spiky cap all of silver and crystal and a strange polished stone gleaming in different shades of gold and green.

With a sudden flurry of speed no one had seen from the invalid in many months, Mrs. Arnold spun through the door to the living room, pushed past the rotund shape of Awful Aunt Sybil, and snatched the crown from Cynthia's hands before she could plonk it onto her head.

"I believe that's mine," she said firmly, extracting it from Awful Cousin Cynthia's talonlike grip and burying it swiftly back in the recesses of the suitcase before Aunt Sybil could see what it was—though she craned her neck so hard it looked as if it might snap.

"Not for long," Cynthia muttered, fixing Mrs. Arnold with her malicious little eyes. "Not for long."

Mrs. Arnold held Cynthia's gaze steadily. Then

she said something so softly that no one else in the room could quite catch it, and Cynthia looked away suddenly, her cheeks blazing. Mustering as much dignity as she could manage in a miniskirt and a pair of clumpy platform wedges, which did nothing for her scrawny white legs, she retrieved her horrible handbag and minced out into the hall.

"Don't bother about a cup of tea, Mum," she said to Aunt Sybil, "they'll only try to poison us."

"Oh," said Aunt Sybil, looking very flustered indeed, "but I wanted to . . . ah . . . ." She stopped, her chins wobbling. Then she caught Mr. Arnold's arm and leaned in close to him. Even Ben, standing several feet away, could smell the waft of her awful perfume. "Clive, ah . . . you see, with Aleister . . . um . . . away for a time . . ."

"Three years, I believe?"

"Ah, yes . . . well, um, well I . . . that is, we, Cynthia and myself are . . . well . . . I'm coming up a little short on the bills this month and well . . . I wondered . . ."

Mr. Arnold's smile came slowly, and then widened and widened till it almost spread from ear to ear. He had endured Aleister and Sybil's taunts about his low-paying job at the local newspaper and his family's humble lifestyle for a very long time; and it had been more than a touch satisfying to help put an end to the trade in Eidolon's exotic creatures, which had been the source of Aleister and Sybil's much-flaunted and ill-gotten wealth.

"Sybil, dear, I'd love to help . . ." He spread his hands helplessly. "Perhaps if you sold the Range Rover, got something a bit cheaper to run. It is an awful gas-guzzler, and well, you don't really need an off-roader around Bixbury . . ."

Aunt Sybil's chest swelled alarmingly.

Ben intervened. "I'm sorry," he said, catching his aunt by the elbow and steering her out into the hall, "but we're already running late. Perhaps some other time?"

If Aunt Sybil was surprised by this sudden authority from her usually tongue-tied nephew, she didn't say so. Indeed, although her mouth kept opening and closing like a goldfish's, she left the house without uttering another word. Ben watched her get into the Range Rover and slam the door—rather more loudly than was necessary merely to close it.

Outside on the gatepost, Ignatius Sorvo

Coromandel stood with his back arched and the fur of his tail sticking out like a toilet brush, staring into the vehicle with loathing. He let out the most terrifying hiss, then a string of swear words that made Ben gasp.

"Wow! I didn't know cats *knew* words like that!"

Iggy swiveled a fiery glance at his friend, then transferred his attention back to the car.

As the Range Rover pulled away, Ben spied a familiar face peering out of a raffia handbag propped against the rear window. The face was small, triangular, and hairless. Wrinkles of skin pooled around its nose and slanted yellow eyes as it hissed back at the Wanderer.

Ben shivered, despite the sun on his back. "Oh no," he muttered. "It's the Sphynx."

Mrs. Arnold sat slumped on the sofa, rubbing the tops of her arms. Goose bumps had popped up all along her pale skin. She was trembling. Mr. Arnold sat down beside her. "Are you sure you're feeling strong enough to . . . er, travel?" he asked carefully.

She nodded. "I must. The time has come." She gripped his hand. "I'm sorry, Clive. I should have told you everything right at the start. But you'd probably have thought I was mad."

Her husband smiled lopsidedly, as if it were an effort. "But you *are* mad, my darling. That's why I love you. I always knew you were different from all the other women I'd met. But at least now I know why."

"Keep an eye on Cynthia, won't you? And I don't want Ellie or Ben going round to King Henry Close."

"I don't think there's much danger of that," her husband said grimly.

"No way!" said Ben, coming in with a now normal-looking Iggy in his arms. "I'd rather go to the *dentist* than round to Cousin Cynthia's!"

That made Mrs. Arnold laugh. "It *is* about time you had another checkup."

"Oh, Mum . . ."

She smiled. "Maybe when I come back," she said softly. Which made him feel a little better about everything.

Chapter Three

Aldstane Park

The Arnolds' rusty old Morris crawled through the streets of Bixbury, carefully avoiding the roads around King Henry Close. Mr. Arnold drove; Mrs. Arnold sat beside him with her winter coat folded in her lap; while in the back, Ellie and Ben sat all squashed up beside Alice's car seat. Ignatius Sorvo Coromandel had stretched himself along the car's back shelf and was watching the baby with curious amber eyes.

"Alice," he rasped, "can you hear me?"

In response, the baby laughed and babbled and banged her toy—a soft pink piglet in a dress and ballet shoes—against the front of her seat. In the sunlight her eyes were greener than ever, Ben thought, as green as limes, or frogs, or that green goo in tubs that he and his friend Adam had mock-fights with.

"What did she say?" he asked the cat quietly.

"Well," said Iggy, considering, "I think it went sort of like this: *La, la, gaga caa* . . ."

"Oh," said Ben. He thought about this for a moment. "And what does that mean?"

"Search me," said Iggy.

"Stupid," said Ellie scornfully. "She's only a year old. Of course she can't speak yet." She gave the baby a sharp look. "Queen-in-waiting or not."

At the top of the road, Mr. Arnold pulled into the parking lot and they all got out. Ben helped his father wrestle the suitcase out of the trunk while Ellie and his mother released Baby Alice from the straps of her seat.

Alice waved her arms around in delight. "*Ca* . . . *ca* . . . *cat!*" she suddenly said, quite distinctly. And in case anyone was unsure of what she meant, she pointed straight at Iggy, who was stretching out his back legs against the sun-warmed pavement.

Iggy stopped his exercises and stared at her. "What did you say?"

Alice folded the pig-doll to her chest. "Cat," she replied, entirely matter-of-factly, and gazed back at him out of the depths of her wide green eyes. "Cat."

"Oh my," said Mr. Arnold. He rubbed his hand across his face, then looked at his wife. "Did she really say 'cat' or am I going mad?"

"She did," Isadora said fondly.

"It's a bit . . . well . . . precocious at one, isn't it?"

Ignatius Sorvo Coromandel.

Ben heard this as a sort of tickle at the back of his skull, as if a small spider had got in there and was running around. He looked sharply around, but no one else appeared to have heard it. He frowned.

"She's a very special little girl," said Isadora Arnold brightly. She looked down at the baby and smiled. "That was a very good first word, Alice. I'm sure by the time we come back you'll have lots of other good words to show off to your daddy."

Mr. Arnold looked unhappy. "None of them are likely to be 'Dad,' though, are they?"

• • •

Ben watched as Ignatius Sorvo Coromandel—the Wanderer—took on the task of expedition leader and began a weaving trail across the park. Mr. Arnold followed, supporting his wife—who was still not very strong—with an arm around her waist. Ellie carried Baby Alice, and Ben lagged at the back. Partly this was because he was lugging the suitcase, which was pretty heavy, and partly it was because cold dread seemed to dog his footsteps, almost pulling him backward.

Aldstane Park did not look much like a place that would inspire dread; indeed, it looked very different from the last time Ben had seen it. Then it had been pitch-dark, except for the swirling blue lights of the police cars come to arrest Uncle Aleister. But now it was swathed in sunshine and covered with people. There were families picnicking on the grass, men with their shirts off and girls with their skirts hitched up over their knees to make the most of the sun, couples entwined around each other on colorful blankets, people throwing Frisbees, dogs chasing balls, and children splashing in the boating lake—where once upon a time Ben had seen a girl turn into a seal.

It looks so safe, he thought, *and all the people look so happy. They certainly don't look as if they know there's a standing stone among the rhododendrons that is the doorway to another world. A world full of wonders and weirdness. A world full of dangers. . . .*

And he felt the shadow of the Secret Country fall across him, chill and dark. But when he looked up, it was only a cloud that had passed across the sun.

For a famous explorer Iggy often proved to be remarkably inefficient at finding his way, and now was no exception. First, he took them on a winding route between the bushes that brought them out by an ice-cream van and a queue of noisy children; next, he circled around on himself till they finished up exactly where they had come in.

"Oh dear," he said, looking as embarrassed as only a cat can look. "I could have sworn the Aldstane was around here somewhere." And he started to groom a paw furiously in order to divert their attention from his error.

Ben sighed. "Follow me."

With the suitcase bumping against his leg, he led his family back into the cool darkness between the rhododendrons.

And at last there it was: a great finger of rock partially hidden among a grove of hawthorns. Pitted with age and patched with lichen, it was sunk deep in the earth, deep in the leaf mold. You sensed that, like an iceberg, there was more of it below the ground than appeared above.

A weary smile touched Mrs. Arnold's face. "Ah," she breathed. "The waystone."

She turned to her husband. "Do you remember when you first came upon me, Clive?"

"How could I ever forget?" Even as he spoke, Clive Arnold could picture the scene in his head: a delicate pale-skinned girl dancing with her eyes closed and her silver-blond hair lit by shafts of sunlight in a clearing in this very park, fifteen summers before.

"This was the stone by which I entered your world," she said softly.

"Cool!" said Ben. He grinned, despite his anxieties. "It's where I went into the other world, and where Iggy came in too."

Mrs. Arnold reached a hand down and stroked the fur on top of Iggy's head. The cat, who up to this point had still been looking slightly miffed that Ben had been the one to find the Old Stone rather than him, purred.

"Look," said Ben, pointing.

Partly obscured by the growth of lichen, a pattern was visible on the surface of the rock. It consisted of a lot of straight lines and angles and was topped by an arrow, pointing down into the ground.

Mrs. Arnold ran her hands across the stone.

"E-I-D-O-L-O-N," she spelled out.

"Eye-do-lon," said Alice. She gurgled delightedly. "Eidolon."

Ellie almost dropped the baby in shock.

"Whoo!" said Ben. His little sister had never seemed odd to him before—well, no odder than any other baby—but now he felt the hairs rising on the back of his neck. "Whoo, that's weird!"

"Clever girl," whispered Mrs. Arnold. "Such a clever girl."

Mr. Arnold had gone white. "Izzy," he said at last, "don't go. You've been better these last couple of weeks. Perhaps you'll just keep getting better if you stay here—"

He would have said more, but at that moment there was a shimmer of rainbow light around the base of the Aldstane, and something emerged from the stone.

Chapter Four

The Centaur

The first thing any of them saw was a leg, but it was not the leg of anything human. Sleek and brown, it ended in a shining hoof. A second leg followed almost immediately.

"What the—?" started Mr. Arnold.

A body was now beginning to appear: the smooth brown chest of a man that melded seamlessly into the powerful torso of a horse. A moment later the entire figure stood before them.

"Darius!" cried Ben.

"It's a cent . . . a centimeter . . . a sentiment . . . a . . . er . . . centipede . . . ," Ellie stuttered.

"Actually, he's a centaur," Ben supplied scathingly. "His name's Darius and he's a Horse Lord."

Ellie stared, her eyes getting rounder and rounder. She loved ponies and had just started to find boys very interesting indeed, but this amazing apparition appeared to combine the best of both worlds. The top half of the centaur was that of a young man, with a proud, fine-boned face and piercing eyes. Black hair fell to his shoulders and his tanned, well-muscled chest, but from the waist down he had the body of a horse.

"Hello," she said, blushing even more.

Darius clenched a fist to his chest and gave her his fierce smile. "Good day," he said. "Princess."

Ellie giggled and looked sideways at her mother. Then she put a hand to her mouth and gazed up at the centaur through her bangs, in what she thought was her most alluring pose, but to her disappointment the Horse Lord was not looking at her anymore.

"My lady, forgive me, I did not see you there. . . ."

With fluid grace Darius dropped to his knees

before his Queen, his head bowed and his fists crossed, but Isadora Arnold took two steps forward and touched him on the shoulder.

"Please get up, Darius," she said softly. "I have been away from my country for too long to expect such an honor."

Mr. Arnold looked from the centaur to his wife in some kind of shock. He had always loved and been amazed by Isadora, but he had never before seen her so regal or imposing. Even Ben and Ellie exchanged glances. To them she was "Mum"—a bit daffy; always talking to inanimate objects, as well as to flies and dogs and caterpillars; a mother who looked after them and laughed with them and was more likely to get tired than to get angry. It was hard to think of her as a queen, especially of a magical realm.

Darius got to his feet and stood there uncertainly. Then he said, "Cernunnos sent me through the wild road to fetch you—"

"Cernunnos is the Lord of the Wildwood," Ben interrupted knowledgeably. "He's big and sort of greenish, and he wears leaves, and stag's horns."

"Leaves?" Ellie sounded scornful. "Who'd want to wear leaves?"

But already in her head she was fashioning herself a fetchingly skimpy outfit of autumn colors designed to show off her dark hair and hazel eyes to their best advantage, the sort of dress that would beguile a young Horse Lord.

"He sounds a bit, well—wild," Mr. Arnold said nervously to his wife. "I mean, stag's horns . . . !"

"Cernunnos is my loyal friend," Isadora Arnold replied gently. "He guards the deep forest and takes care of my people there. He will take care of me and Alice, too."

"But—but you can't live in a forest!" Mr. Arnold said in horror. "I mean, where will you sleep?"

"The moss beds of Darkmere are famed throughout Eidolon," his wife said teasingly. "You should try them sometime; but"—she saw him open his mouth to say something—"but not now, Clive, dear; the Shadow World is not a safe place for those without magic at the best of times—and now is *not* the best of times." And she passed Baby Alice into Darius's outstretched arms.

The centaur cradled the child, smiling as she reached up to wrap her fingers in his long black hair.

Alice looked out at the assembled group as if she

were already Queen and they were all her courtiers.

"Da . . . Da . . ."

Clive Arnold held his breath.

"Da . . . Da . . ."

"Go on, love, say 'Dad.' . . ."

"Dar . . . ius!" Alice declared triumphantly.

And everyone laughed. Apart from Mr. Arnold. First of all he looked crestfallen; then he fixed the Horse Lord with a stern glare. "Just how did this Cernunnos know my wife was coming here today?" he asked, suddenly suspicious.

The young centaur returned Mr. Arnold's gaze steadfastly. "The Lord of the Wildwood did not know exactly when our lady would return, only that it must be soon," said Darius. "Since she has been away, my people have waited for her to come back to us, and many have sickened and died, or been stolen away. Without our Queen, we are diminished. But when Ben came to us, we regained hope; and every day since he returned to your world I have kept vigil by the entrance to the wild road and waited and listened until I felt the signature of her magic drawing near. There will be great rejoicing in Eidolon that its Queen has returned. Now we have a chance to unite our folk against the Dodman and drive him from the Shadow World forever."

Mr. Arnold looked puzzled. "The Dodman?" He turned to his wife. "Who is this Dodman?"

Isadora Arnold looked discomfited. "Maybe it was not entirely wise to mention that particular problem at this moment," she said to the centaur, who put a hand to his mouth, too late to draw the words back.

"He's awful," Ben said. "Over here he was just Mr. Dodds who ran the Pet Emporium, but over there he's about eight feet tall and has a great big dog's head! And he has some rather nasty goblins as his helpers, and some savage hounds—"

"That's quite enough, Ben," his mother said firmly. She put her arms around him and whispered in his ear, "I know all about the Dodman, and his mynah bird, and the message it carried. That's why I must go back now and face him." She stepped away and regarded her son with her head to one side. Then she dropped him a slow, conspiratorial wink.

"I don't like the sound of any of this at all," Clive Arnold said. "If you're determined to go, I feel I must come with you."

"Oh, Clive, I know you would if I asked you. But who's going to look after Ben and Ellie if you come to the Shadow World with me?"

Mr. Arnold hesitated. "I suppose Sybil—"

"No way!" chorused Ben and Ellie in one horrified breath.

Their father looked at them unhappily. "No, I don't suppose that would work." His shoulders sagged in defeat. Then he turned to address the centaur. "You'd better look after my wife and daughter," he said fiercely.

Darius bowed his head. "I would give my life for them," he said simply.

Clive Arnold nodded brusquely and blinked his eyes very fast as if he had something painful in them.

Ellie gave her mother a short, fierce hug, and wouldn't look at her.

"Take care of your dad for me, won't you, darling?" Mrs. Arnold asked her; but Ellie didn't respond, just stood there looking at her shoes. They were big cork-soled sandals with bright flowery patterns all over them, but even so Ben couldn't imagine why she found them so fascinating.

Now Mrs. Arnold came to her husband. "It won't

be forever, Clive," she said softly, and kissed him quickly before he could say anything.

Ellie looked up and rolled her eyes. But when she caught the centaur watching her, she blushed so hard that even her ears went red.

"Come along, Ignatius," the Queen of Eidolon said. "Time to go."

"What?" Ben couldn't believe his ears. He looked at Iggy, his heart sinking fast. It was bad enough that his mother and little sister were going away, but the black-and-brown cat had become his best friend. "Are you going too?"

Iggy shifted uncomfortably. "Um," he said. "Well . . ."

"If he's going to carry messages for me, he needs to know where I am," Mrs. Arnold said gently. "Or he'll never find me."

That was all very well, Ben thought, but knowing the cat's hopeless sense of direction, how would he find his way back? He'd probably end up in Alaska or Antarctica or Outer Mongolia. But Ben didn't say anything. He couldn't: There was a huge lump in his throat.

He watched as his father helped his mother onto

the centaur's back, and once she was up there, his father held his hand against her cheek. Then Mr. Arnold took Alice from the Horse Lord and passed the baby up to her mother. Ben gave the suitcase to Darius, who stared at it uncertainly, then fitted a hand around its handle and hauled it up into his arms, cradling it as he had the baby.

Mr. Arnold tucked the blue woollen coat tenderly around his wife, and Alice waved her pig-doll at him.

"Da . . . ," she said. "Dad. Daddy."

Mr. Arnold gave her a wobbly smile.

Then Darius turned and plunged into the standing stone. First his head and forelegs vanished, followed by the suitcase, the Horse Lord's long neck, Mrs. Arnold with Alice held tightly in her arms, and finally the centaur's powerful hindquarters and long black tail.

Ignatius Sorvo Coromandel jumped into Ben's arms and butted his forehead against his friend's cheek. "See ya later, Sonny Jim!"

Amber eyes blazed into Ben's and then the little cat, too, was gone, into the Secret Country.

Ellie and Mr. Arnold stared at the Aldstane in disbelief. Ellie walked all around the stone, testing the ground with her clunky sandals. Suddenly she exclaimed, "Oh!"

Her foot was nowhere to be seen.

"Ellie . . . ," said her father warningly.

She pulled her foot back and it reappeared, detail by detail.

"Come along," Mr. Arnold said quietly. "Let's go home." He looked absolutely exhausted.

"I'll come in a minute. I need a few moments to myself," Ellie declared with the tragic demeanor of a Victorian heroine.

Ben and his father exchanged glances; then Mr. Arnold shrugged. When Ellie got in one of her moods there was little point in arguing with her. "We'll wait for you by the car, then," he suggested. "Don't be long."

They made their way out of the rhododendrons and into the brightness of the park, where the sudden ordinariness of their surroundings—the Labradors and lovers and children with ice-cream cones dripping down their tops—seemed even more surreal after all that had just taken place. Ben and Clive Arnold walked in silence for a while until Ben, sensing the waves of sorrow emanating from his father, could bear it no longer. "Do you remember the dragons, Dad?" he asked in an attempt to cheer him up.

Mr. Arnold smiled, for a moment looking almost happy. He stared up into the brilliant sky. "It's hard to believe I've been up there on the back of a dragon named Ishtar." He paused, thinking. "She was an ancient Babylonian goddess, you know."

"Wow," said Ben, awed. "I didn't think she looked *that* old."

His father grinned, despite himself. "Not the dragon, silly. The Ishtar in *our* world's mythology. They called her the Lady of Battles."

The Ishtar Ben knew was Zark's wife. Ben had rescued the dragon Zark from the clutches of Awful Uncle Aleister, who'd been planning to sell him for dog food, since Zark hadn't been a great success as a garden incinerator, which was what Uncle Aleister had sold him as. He had, however, been a terrific success as a Range Rover incinerator. Ben remembered with some delight how its paint had bubbled and its tires had melted down into horrid black goo. Thinking about the dragons made Ben's heart lift. There were wonders in the world after all—in both worlds. Then he thought, *Perhaps all the dragons will unite to help*

Mum win her kingdom back. He imagined flights of them, like Second World War fighter squadrons, storming through the skies of Eidolon. . . .

Spreading his arms like a Spitfire, he went zooming and zigzagging through the picnickers all the way back to the parking lot.

Sitting in the old Morris, Ben and his father waited for Ellie. And waited. And waited. They often had to wait for Ellie—for her to wash her hair or "do" her face, or change her clothes eight times even though they were only going to the supermarket—but she couldn't have any of those excuses now. At last Mr. Arnold sighed and looked at his watch. "I'd better go back and look for her."

"It's all right," said Ben. "I'll go." It made sense: He knew exactly where the stone was.

His father tousled his hair then sat back in the car seat glumly, while Ben belted away through the gates.

Ben scanned Aldstane Park, looking for his sister's bright pink T-shirt among the crowds. But Ellie wasn't by the ornamental fountain. She wasn't at the boating lake. She wasn't sitting on the grass, nor on any of the benches beside the path. She wasn't in the queue at the ice-cream van. She wasn't hiding in the shadows between the rhododendrons, and she wasn't at the Aldstane, either.

Ben's heart began to thump, though that might have been because he was out of breath from all the running.

"Ellie!" he shouted, when he got his wind back. "Ellie, where are you?"

But the only sound that returned to him was the faint echo of his voice.

And there, at the base of the stone, was a flowered sandal.

Suddenly Ben knew, with a painful thump of his heart, that Ellie had gone through the Aldstane into the wild road beyond. She was in the Shadow World.

Chapter Five

In the Court of the
Dog-Headed Man

The Dodman sat back in the carved wooden throne in the great hall of Dodman Castle and stretched out his long, long legs. He had renamed the castle the previous day from its boring original name of Corbenic Castle and was still very pleased with the new version. He wondered why he hadn't thought of it before. . . . Old Creepie would have moaned on about it, that was why; he liked to stand by tradition, and the castle had been called Corbenic Castle since anyone could remember. Aleister Creepie was the Queen's brother. The castle had been his home too, when the pair of them had grown up here. But now Aleister had a rather different residence: a prison cell in the Other World, for the next three years. But the Dodman was not entirely unhappy about this, even though Old Creepie had been his ally. The situation had its advantages. Another of the royal family of Eidolon was out of his way. Now he had only to get rid of the Queen and her annoying family, and the Secret Country and everything in it would be his.

Not that he would stop there. . . .

The Dodman looked around at his motley courtiers. Lolling on the benches over the remains of a vast feast sat a number of squabbling goblins, two terrifically ugly trolls, and a cross-eyed giantess arrayed in a bizarre costume of leather and spikes. A pair of what appeared to be chicken's feet protruded grotesquely from her gaping mouth. They were still kicking.

The Dodman looked at the huge bones left over

from this feast, which lay scattered as though in a desecrated graveyard all over the long table and the floor beneath, and he gave the courtiers all a disgusted look, which went unnoticed. He had plans for this place, for his kingdom. Bit by bit, he would drain the magic out of the Secret Country so that none could challenge his rule. He had made a good start on this plan, keeping as much magic for himself as he dared, draining it out of the small folk he captured, drinking it down. One day, he promised himself, this hall would be crowded with the great and the bad of Eidolon—gorgeous, glittering, and greedy for the power only he could give them. That day must surely come soon. "Peasants!" he snorted, looking around him again and shaking his head.

"*Squarrrk!*"

The mynah bird that had been sitting on the crest of the throne behind him lifted suddenly into the air. "Peasants!" it echoed, taking roost up in the rafters.

The Dodman kicked the goblin lying on the floor in front of him, snoring drunkenly among the dogs, and, when it didn't stir, he put his feet up on it—which was the only thing it was useful for.

The dogs were the Gabriel Hounds, his spectral

hunting pack. They were not well behaved. No one had ever been able to teach these ghost-dogs any manners, and the addition of the Horned One's wolves had not helped matters. Today was not any different. A furor started up between the hounds and the wolves, and his unfortunate footstool was peed on once and bitten twice during the fracas before he could pull them apart.

There was a cough from the back of the hall, and the Dodman looked up. A visitor had appeared, materializing as silently as a ghost in the great hall's doorway.

It was the Sphynx.

"So, what news? Was the Queen preparing for a journey?" The Dodman's eyes—as round and black and shiny as a pair of giant ball bearings—narrowed minutely. "To Eidolon?"

"Yesss, master. I saw the thingsss she packed with my own eyesss. She had the Book with her and—"

"The Book, you say?" The dog-headed man grinned fiercely. "The Book of Naming?"

"Yesss, lord. There was no mistaking it." The speaker's voice lowered. "And she isss bringing the Crown of Eidolon back with her!"

"That worthless trinket!" the Dodman growled

dismissively. "I need no crown to be King of the Shadow World!"

In fact, he wanted the crown very much, but he knew it wouldn't fit him, not with his gigantic dog's head.

"Of course not"—the visitor paused—"sssire."

The Dodman's dog-mouth widened into a sharp-toothed smile. "Yes," he said, "I like the sound of that. *Sire.*" He sprang to his feet and at once the hounds and wolves were everywhere, snapping and snarling and picking fights with each other.

The creature started and ran pell-mell between the dogs and under the throne, where it sat quivering, its long thin ratlike tail sticking out into the light. After a moment it seemed to realize this and turned around quickly, before anyone could bite its bottom. Its wedge-shaped pink face and slanting yellow eyes peered out at the dogs.

"Don't let them get me, ssssire," it begged piteously.

In response the Dodman reached down and swept the Sphynx up by the loose skin around its neck, allowing it to dangle precariously over the snapping jaws.

"Now, then, little spy," he said, tightening his grip so that the creature writhed, torn between fear of the hounds and terror of the Dodman. "Who is coming with her? Is it the odd-eyed Princeling? Or maybe your friend, the one with the skinny legs and bad hair?"

The spy drew its feet up convulsively as one of the Gabriel Hounds got a bit too close for comfort. "My fr-friend?" it gasped.

The dog-headed man gave the visitor his ghastly grin, the firelight gleaming on his fangs. "Your little friend Cynthia."

"Cynthia? N-no. She would never travel with Isssadora. She hates the Q-Queen."

"Are you sure?"

"Q-quite sure," the spy replied nervously. As it felt the Dodman's grip relax slightly, it twisted out of his grasp, turned in midair, dug all four paws into his arm, and, righting itself, fled up along his shoulder and leapt onto the top of the throne, where it sat, shivering and glaring out at the scene below with loathing in its eyes.

The Dodman rubbed his arm where the cat's sharp little claws had dug into him. "You had better be right about this," he told it. "You say the Queen is coming soon?"

From its new position of relative safety, the Sphynx smiled enigmatically. "Oh, yesss," it declared. "She hasss already set out. She may already be in Eidolon, for all I know."

And before the dog-headed man could recapture it and ask it more difficult questions, it gathered its haunches and sprang over the pack of hunting hounds and ran across the great hall and out the door.

The Dodman watched it go. He knew it would be back, for it craved the treats he gave it in return for the information it brought him—the gnomes' eyes and fairy wings, the phoenix livers and fillet of mermaid tail, all manner of delicious items it could come by nowhere else in either world.

"Grizelda!" he yelled, and the giantess lumbered to her gigantic feet. "Leash the hounds and bring them to me. We are going to capture ourselves a queen!"

Chapter Six

In the Shadow World

One minute Eleanor Arnold had been looking at the old standing stone in Aldstane Park, and the next, some mad impulse had overtaken her and she had stepped *into* it, and been swallowed up by it in a way she could not comprehend. Whirling around and around as if on some weird fairground ride, she had felt sick with dizziness and thought she might faint. Air had rushed past her, warm with the scents of an English park, then turning chill and finally freezing, until at last the wild road had ejected her with such force that she had tumbled head over heels before coming to an abrupt halt. Now she sat on the ground, rubbing her knees and shins and staring about her with absolutely no idea where in the world she was. Her skin prickled all over as if someone had sprinkled itching powder inside her clothes. She looked about, scratching absentmindedly. Then she sneezed—six times.

"Wow," she said. "I must be allergic to something."

At school everyone had at least one allergy that they boasted about, but Ellie had never really had a proper one before.

On the other side of the stone it had been a hot and cloudless summer day, but here—wherever "here" was—it was decidedly wintry. An icy wind blew through the trees, rattling the dying leaves and whistling through the branches. Frost etched the bare soil. The ground was as hard as iron.

Ellie jumped up and almost fell down. Something was wrong with her balance! In the fall through the wild road it seemed that one of her legs had unaccountably grown longer than the other. Or had one got shorter? She stared at her feet. One of her sandals was missing. That was annoying! They were new, and no one else had a pair like them. They were her favorites. She looked around in search of the missing shoe. But she couldn't see it anywhere. In fact, she couldn't see anything very well. It was as if the fall had done something funny to her eyesight, so that for the first time in her life she needed glasses. She rubbed her eyes and blinked and looked around again, but still the world was slightly blurry and out of focus.

Usually not one to admit to being in the wrong, Ellie now suddenly regretted her rash decision to step through the stone. But for once there was no one but herself to blame. Indeed, there seemed to be no one else around at all.

"Mum?" she called. Her voice sounded for a moment like the plaintive cry of a seagull, and then it was whisked away to nothing by the wind. She called again, louder this time. "Mum!" And then, more hesitantly: "Darius?"

But no one answered.

Ellie, who was wearing only a short-sleeved pink T-shirt and a pair of thin cotton jeans, began to rub her upper arms vigorously. Perhaps it would be a better idea to go back. But there was no sign of the Aldstane at all. Hot tears pricked at the back of Ellie's eyes but she blinked them away fiercely. It would not do for anyone in this strange place to find her crying. Besides, crying made her eyes go all red and puffy, and everyone knew that was not a good look, especially if you wanted to make a favorable impression on a handsome young centaur.

"Well," said Ellie aloud. She often spoke to herself, it was a trait she had inherited from her mother, who spoke to all sorts of things, including herself, all the time. "I'll start walking in one direction and see what I can see."

She looked around, finding that if she squinted, the world seemed to come into sharper focus. She was standing in a small clearing between trees, but no matter in which direction she turned, trees and more trees were all she could see. No houses, no streets, and worst of all, no shops.

"Hmmm," she said, feeling dismayed. Given a choice of preferred environments, she would select first of all clothes stores, then makeup counters, shoe shops, and Internet cafés. Gardens came pretty low down on her list of favorite places to be; forests lower still. "It would be quite easy to get lost here."

Then she remembered something Ben had told her about a story in one of his books of mythology. She couldn't quite recall the point of the story, only something about a handsome youth and a king's daughter and a kiss and a labyrinth. It was the kiss she remembered most clearly; the rest of the story was a bit of a haze, but she thought the king's daughter might have given the boy a ball of red twine so that he could mark his route through the maze and not get lost. If she were to do something similar, she could at least find her way back to where she was now. . . .

But Ellie didn't have a ball of red twine, or indeed anything that might substitute for it. In her little handbag all she had was some makeup, a mirror, a pen, some chewing gum, and her cell phone. This last she seized upon with sudden excitement. She turned the phone on, punched in a number, and waited. And waited. And waited.

After a long time the screen blinked. Then it offered a message:

No network coverage

Ellie glared at it. Obviously the signal was a bit weak here. She walked on a little way and held the phone up, but the left side of the screen indicated no change to the signal strength. Annoyed, she tapped out a swift text message and pressed send.

For a long time she peered at the tiny blue phone, which seemed to be working very hard. Then at last something flashed on the screen:

Message not sent
Try again later

Ellie said a word her father would have told her off for using and threw the phone back into her bag. Perhaps if she were to head for higher ground she'd be able to get a signal.

She squinted about her. Trees. Trees. Trees. Some covered in moss, others in ivy. The ground looked pretty flat, but if she walked far enough surely there would be a hill. She started out in one direction, hobbling on her one remaining sandal (to lose both would be really stupid), then turned back. She really ought to mark her way somehow. . . .

She looked around desperately. Ivy! She could lay

a trail of ivy that she could follow back here if the route she chose turned out to be a false start. She grabbed a handful of ivy on the nearest tree and started to pull it away from the trunk.

"Ow!"

Ellie jumped backward as if something had bitten her. She looked around, but there was no one in sight. Frowning, she approached the tree again and checked behind it. Not a soul. Eventually she shrugged, decided she'd been hearing things, and gave the ivy another tug.

"Ow! Stop yanking my hair, you little witch!"

As if out of nowhere, a face materialized in front of her. Ellie shrieked and fell over in shock. When she looked up again, a figure was leaning out of the tree. Ivy flowed over her shoulders just like hair, her skin was as smooth and sheeny brown as the casing of a conker, and she wore a dress of bark and moss. Her hands were balled into fists. Her eyes sparked green fire.

"Oh, you're not the little witch. You smelled a bit like her, though."

Ellie frowned. Clearly the thing, whatever it was, was quite mad.

"How dare you attack me for no reason!" the tree-creature went on. "There's been too much of that sort of thing, and worse. But there will be justice soon, now that the Queen has come back to us, just you wait and see." And she shook her finger at Ellie angrily.

"The Queen?" Ellie's heart leapt. "Have you seen her? Which way did she go?"

"Why would I tell you such a thing?"

"Because she's my mother!" Ellie picked herself up and rubbed all the manky old leaves and soil off her best jeans with some annoyance.

The creature watched her with narrow eyes. Then she stepped out of the oak and made a progress around Ellie, examining her from top to toe. "You don't look much like a princess. . . ."

Ellie tossed her long dark hair and was horrified to find a spider hanging off it. She brushed it away in disgust. "Who are you to say that?" she said crossly. "You're just some tree-thing, all covered in scabby old bark and ivy—"

"And your eyes are the wrong color to be the true child of Queen Isadora. Besides, I am not a 'tree-thing.' I am a nymph."

Ellie had no idea what a nymph was, and cared even less. "I can't help the color of my eyes!" she snapped back. "My dad's got brown eyes. But he comes from . . . Earth."

The tree-nymph burst out laughing. "Is he a worm, that he comes out of the earth?"

"How rude you are! First you call me a witch, and then you call my dad a worm."

"And you call yourself a daughter to our Queen!"

"I *am* her daughter—her eldest daughter. Then there's Ben—he's a boy—and Alice, who's just a baby—"

"Ben . . . and a baby . . . Ah, now you're beginning to make some sense." The nymph leaned forward and scrutinized Ellie closely. One of her twiglike hands reached out and caught the girl by the chin, turning her head this way and that. The tree-nymph's fingers were cool and smooth against Ellie's skin, and the searching eyes were the rich green of new leaves, but Ellie wrenched her head away, and sneezed and sneezed and sneezed.

"Bless you," said the nymph. "There *is* something about you . . . But how did you get separated from the Queen, if she really is your mother?"

"She came through the wild road with . . . Darius, the Horse Lord," Ellie said quickly, feeling a blush coming on. "I followed a little later."

"I know the Horse Lord, Darius. And I know of the boy, Ben. Maybe you are telling the truth after all," the tree-nymph said at last. "It has been hard to trust anyone in Eidolon for a long time." She paused, considering, then appeared to come to a decision. "The Queen passed through this way, heading east, toward the domain of the Horned Man, Cernunnos. If you follow the sun as it goes down, you cannot go far wrong."

Ellie looked up into the wintry sky. It was cold and white, and if there was any sun at all, it was hidden behind thick clouds. She shivered. "I can't see the sun," she said miserably. "Which way is east?"

But the tree-nymph was not listening to her. She was staring above Ellie's head and her eyes were wide with consternation. In the distance behind her Ellie could just hear a faint wailing sound, like the cries of many lost souls tossed about in the wind, and even though she did not know what it could be, it made the hairs rise on the back of her neck.

She turned to follow the tree-nymph's horrified

gaze, but all she could make out was a fast-moving blur.

"Run!" cried the nymph. "Run, run for your life!"

But Ellie was still squinting for a better view. The moving shape came on and on, until at last she could just about make it out. Up in the sky, silhouetted against the white clouds, there appeared to be a great chariot bearing a number of bizarre figures, including one that looked just like a gigantic dog in a suit. The chariot was drawn by a pack of creatures that seemed to flicker in and out of visibility.

"Wow," said Ellie, initially impressed. Then she remembered what Ignatius Sorvo Coromandel and Ben had told her about Mr. Dodds, who in this other world stood eight feet tall and bore the head of a great black dog. A cold feeling spread through the pit of her stomach. "Oh no . . ."

In panic, she whirled around to follow the nymph to whatever place of safety she might have found for herself—and discovered that the tree-nymph had vanished.

"Thanks a lot!" Ellie hissed into the empty air. She had never much liked trees, and now they were pretty close to the top of her hate list. Awful Cousin Cynthia was first, still; closely followed by Cynthia's awful mother, Aunt Sybil.

Ellie hobbled back the way she had come, her handbag thumping against her hip, but the design specs for her pink-and-silver-flowered wedge-heeled sandals hadn't made escaping from monsters in aerial chariots a top priority. Even when wearing both, she could only manage a fast mince. In one, it was hopeless. Within seconds Ellie was sprawled in a heap amidst the tree roots and leaf mold, howling in pain and rubbing a turned ankle. The remaining sandal lay, broken-strapped, a little distance away. The Dodman was pointing triumphantly down at her, and the Gabriel Hounds were circling in on a space in the forest canopy and preparing to make a landing. . . .

Chapter Seven

The Wildwood

Many leagues west of where Eleanor Katherine Arnold was nursing her sprained ankle, Mrs. Arnold—known in Eidolon, the world of her birth, as Queen Isadora—thought she detected the passage of something sinister overhead and stared up into the dense web of branches, her keen eyes searching for the source of this unnerving sensation.

"Don't look up," Darius urged her softly, his

neat hooves picking a silent way through the frozen leaves. "It's the Gabriel Hounds. Remember: If they feel your eyes upon them they will become aware of you and be drawn back this way. We are close to Cernunnos's domain now, only a few more minutes and you will be safe in the Wildwood."

Isadora shuddered, and not just from the freezing wind. In the Other World there was a phrase for feeling so suddenly uncomfortable and scared. There it was said to be like someone walking over your grave, but in Eidolon they said, "I can feel the breath of the Gabriel Hounds on my neck." Now that saying was far too close to the truth.

"Are they looking for us?" she breathed. She glanced down at Alice, but the baby was fast asleep, clutching the pig-ballerina like a last vestige of her old life.

Darius turned to look at her over his shoulder. "I fear so, my lady. Though how the Dodman could have known you'd entered the Shadow World, I do not know. I took secret paths to and from the waystone and only the tree folk noted our presence." He paused. "Things have come to a terrible pass indeed if any of them would betray us to the Dodman."

"I am sure my nymphs and dryads would never fail us so," Mrs. Arnold said softly. But she could not help but frown.

They moved in silence into the shadow of the deep forest. Here the air was warmer, and from beneath the eaves of the ancient trees many eyes watched their passage.

Then the whispers began:

"*Look, it's her. It is.*"

"*She doesn't look much like a queen.*"

"*Look again; see her eyes.*"

"*Ah, green, so green.*"

"*It is the Queen.*"

"*It is, it is. It's Isadora.*"

"*Isadora. She's come back to us.*"

"*Isadora.*"

"*Queen Isadora.*"

Gnomes and goblins, sprites and dryads—one by one they slipped out of their hiding places, where long habit and a sense of self-preservation had driven them during all these years, and gazed in awe upon the Queen of Eidolon as she returned to this sheltered corner of her realm from a world of which they had no knowledge. One by one they came out, and one by one Isadora acknowledged them with a glance. To other eyes they might have seemed strange or ugly creatures indeed. Some had the rough, brown, lumpy skin of toads; some had ears that grew pointed and fleshy out of their heads like great mushrooms. Some of the fairies were ancient and toothless, their wings lacking lustre; some had lost their wings altogether and bore only long skeletal fingers from which the gauzy film had been eaten away by age or disease. Still others were pale and attenuated, as if they had grown up out of the light; and a few were bright and shiny and looked brand-new. But to Isadora each of them was brave and beautiful.

They walked farther into the cool depths of the forest and it was now with a grain of fear in her heart that Mrs. Arnold noticed over and over how there was mildew on the leaves of the bushes they passed, poisonous fungi and strangling vines leeching the life out of the trees on which they grew. No birds sang. Even the famed mosses of Darkmere were no longer the brilliant emerald they once had been.

Fifteen years! She had been away for fifteen years, and the health of Eidolon was failing just as her own health had while she was away from it. All those creatures stolen and dead, all their magic lost. A world abandoned to wickedness and greed, to her silly, weak brother and the dog-headed man who had exploited his ambitions so ruthlessly. She hoped she could set things right again; to have left Eidolon for love now seemed a selfish choice. But if she had not met Clive, then Ellie; with her moods and teenage tantrums, Ben, with his silly jokes and his kind heart, and tiny Alice, whose personality was yet to be determined, would not exist in either world.

> *One plus one is two*
> *And those two shall make three*
> *Three children from two worlds*
> *Will keep Eidolon free*

She remembered embroidering these words on a small square of white linen when she was little more than a child herself. Then, it had seemed just a nonsense rhyme. Now she wondered whether there could indeed be such a thing as a prophecy. *Three children from two worlds.* Ben and Ellie had already had a part to play in beginning the rescue of Eidolon, and Alice would one day be Queen after her, so perhaps it was true after all.

She sighed, missing Ellie and Ben already.

At last the path carried them past a stream. On its pebbled shores lay the silvery bodies of fish. Iggy sniffed at them and recoiled in disgust.

Isadora frowned.

"My goodness," she said. "If a greedy cat won't eat a fish, there must be something badly wrong."

"Greedy? Me?" Iggy stared at her reproachfully.

Darius turned his head. "We do not know why they are dying," he said, "except that they are already rotten by the time they die and any who have been so hungry as to try to eat them have ailed. Cernunnos fears the waters have been poisoned; even Ia the undine, that tough old biddy, has been under the weather, and the naiads have no more energy than to lie around in the shallows. No longer do we hear their laughter in the Crystal Pools, and the songs of the mermaids are gone from the Dark Mere."

Mrs. Arnold firmed her jaw. "These things must be remedied. The Dodman shall steal and poison and terrorize my folk no more."

She looked fierce and determined, but tears glittered in her eyes. Darius looked away sharply. It was too much to see his Queen weep: It spoke of hope-lessness, of despair.

At that moment a cry ripped through the still air—a great hullabaloo of triumph and bloodlust.

Iggy's fur stood on end from his ears to the tip of his tail. He knew that awful sound too well. "The Wild Hunt . . ."

Darius wheeled about, shading his eyes. "They must have happened upon some poor wayfarer."

Mrs. Arnold's hand tightened in the centaur's mane. "We must go to their aid!"

Behind them the Wildwood seemed to sigh, and when they turned back, a great dark figure had appeared between the trees. The Queen stared grimly ahead, but when the figure moved out into the light, her features relaxed.

"Cernunnos!"

The stag-headed man halted before her and dropped swiftly to one knee, so that the great branches of his antlers obscured his face.

"My lady, my Queen."

Slipping from the centaur's back, Isadora took two steps toward him and touched his shoulder.

"Lord of the Wildwood, rise. In this forest realm

we are equals: I would not have you kneel to me."

Eyes the color of a moorland tarn, brown as peat, gold as honey, found hers and he rose solemnly. "You must stay here, my lady, with Darius. Here you are safe. Unlike the unfortunate quarry the Dodman and his hounds have run to ground. I will discover who the poor soul is and whether they can be rescued."

And with that he was away, his feet as fleet and silent as a deer's, slipping swiftly into the shadows until he disappeared from sight.

Darius watched the Horned Man go, an unhappy expression on his handsome face, and Isadora could tell that whatever duty he felt to her and Alice, he badly wanted to follow the Lord of the Wildwood. Instead, he put the suitcase down by the side of the stream and began to pace back and forth in an agitated manner, as if he could not bear to be still.

Mrs. Arnold watched him. Then she turned to the little cat, who was now sitting on the suitcase, his tail flicking up and down.

"Run after Cernunnos, Iggy," she said softly, "and bring us news as fast as you can. I am sure that something is terribly wrong. I feel it here." She touched a hand to her heart.

Iggy shivered. His last encounter with the Dodman and his hounds had not been a pleasant one. He had a sudden unbidden and entirely illogical thought: What if it was Ben who was in danger? Galvanized by this, he jumped down from the suitcase, took to his heels, and bolted into the undergrowth.

The Horned Man's track should have been easy to follow for a cat of Ignatius Sorvo Coromandel's parentage, for both his mother and father were famous explorers, and such aptitudes often run in families. His mother, Finna Sorvo Farwalker, had founded a colony in the New West and discovered the wild road into the Valley of the Kings, while his father had climbed Cloudbeard, the highest mountain in Eidolon. But somewhere along the line Iggy had failed to inherit their skills, and before long he was hopelessly lost in the middle of a vast thicket of brambles.

Never one to admit defeat, Iggy plowed on, but the thicket became denser and denser, and soon he was forced to crawl on his belly. Snagging fingers caught in his tail and coat as if dragging him back. Something sharp embedded itself in the side of his neck.

"Bother!"

There were now so many bits of bramble and thorn stuck in his fur that it would take an age to groom them all out. He felt like a pincushion. There is very little in the world a cat likes less than to be uncomfortable; except, perhaps, to be hungry. It took a few stern words to remind himself that there was someone else—possibly Ben—out there experiencing a good deal more discomfort than he was, and he steeled himself to carry on.

"I wouldn't go that way if I were you!"

Iggy looked up, then to his left and his right, until at last he found the speaker.

A little red-and-white striped snake with a frilled collar of skin was watching him from a safe distance, its forked tongue flicking in and out of its mouth.

Iggy did not like snakes. He did not like the way they slithered, nor the way they coiled themselves around your leg if you trod on them by mistake, nor the way they tasted when you bit them, not by mistake. Chicken, indeed! Everyone knew that only chicken tasted like chicken: Snakes tasted of snake.

Besides, a red-and-white striped snake, especially one with that ludicrous frill, was probably poisonous. Putting his head down, Iggy rummaged farther into the thicket.

"I said, I wouldn't go that way if I were you!" the snake repeated, this time with an edge of annoyance in its voice.

"Well, you're not me," Iggy muttered.

Luckily, snakes tend to have very poor hearing, and this one was no exception, for it said no more and, giving what might have been in a creature with shoulders a sort of shrug, wove its way between some roots and disappeared.

"Good riddance!" Iggy declared firmly.

He shoved aside a particularly fierce blackberry runner, dislodged a large thorn from his head, and pushed onward until eventually he thought he could see daylight ahead.

That's a relief, he thought. *I was beginning to think I was in trouble there.*

But just as he was congratulating himself on getting himself out of a sticky situation, a truly horrible smell permeated the thicket. A sort of rancid, rotten smell that got into your mouth and nose and coated your fur with something vile and greasy.

Head down, teeth gritted, eyes watering from the stench, Iggy crawled the last few feet through the brambles into the pale winter sunlight and sat there breathing as shallowly as he could manage. Then he looked around him.

All about lay bones. Piles of bones; heaps of bones. Bones scattered as if someone had been playing a game with them. Bones discarded as if after a jolly good gnawing. Fish bones, sparrow bones, sprite bones, and the bones of things that looked as if they might once have belonged to something rather bigger—rats, maybe; rabbits or (and now he gulped) cats . . .

The next thing he knew, a huge shadow had blocked out the weak light of the winter sun, the smell had enveloped him like a cloud, and he was swinging up into the air by the scruff of his neck.

"Got you!" declared a guttural voice.

Iggy twisted his head to look at his captor—and immediately wished that he hadn't.

Chapter Eight

Prisoner

By the time Ben got back to the parking lot, his father was looking very worried indeed, and when he saw that Ben was on his own, he went pale.

Ben had been vainly hoping that maybe, just maybe, he had missed his sister among the crowds and that he would somehow find her back by the car, even though he knew deep down that he would not. "She's gone," he reported quietly. "She's gone into the wild road. Into Eidolon. She left this behind." And he held up the flowered sandal.

Mr. Arnold stared at it. All the color went out of his face. Then he let his head drop against the steering wheel and banged it there repeatedly. "Stupid, stupid, stupid girl!"

When he sat up again, there was a red mark with a Morris symbol imprinted on his forehead.

He lurched out of the car. "Well, I suppose we'll just have to go in and bring her back again."

Ben looked dubious. "Mum said it would be bad for you. Eidolon, I mean." He watched his father's eyes narrow. "It's just that you . . . well—you don't have . . ." He ground to a halt, not sure how to say it without hurting his dad's feelings.

"I don't have what?"

"You don't have any magic in you," Ben finished in a small voice.

Mr. Arnold snorted. "There's no such thing as magic, son," he declared. "Only tricks."

This from a man who had flown on the back of a dragon.

Ben shook his head. "There's magic in Eidolon, and everything that belongs to Eidolon. I've got some in me, and so have Ellie and Alice, because of Mum—but you haven't. And that's why the creatures of the Secret Country get ill when they're here: There's no magic in this world. So I suppose that's what Mum means—it'll be like that for you there. If you go into a world that is full of magic, you'll get ill, just like they do when they come here."

Mr. Arnold thought about this for perhaps three seconds. Then he roared, "Nonsense!"

He stomped around to the back of the car, opened up the trunk, and pulled out an anorak, an umbrella, a pair of boots, a flashlight, and a small rucksack. He put on the anorak and the boots—despite the boiling heat—stuck the flashlight in the rucksack, and turned to Ben, flourishing the umbrella. "Right!" he said. "Ready for anything." He dug into the other pocket and pulled out a packet of aspirin. "You see—if I feel ill, I can take a couple of these. Bound to be fine!" He beamed at his son, and Ben had the sudden sinking feeling that his dad was actually looking forward to having a bit of an adventure.

Reluctantly, Ben followed in Mr. Arnold's long stride, almost having to run to keep up with him. Was it so surprising that Ellie wouldn't do as she was told, when their father didn't listen to anyone either?

On the edge of the rhododendrons, Mr. Arnold had to give up the lead to his son, and Ben wove through the hawthorns and hollies to where the Old Stone stood, ancient and brooding in its shady place. His father, refusing to be in awe of it, marched over to the stone and started prodding it all over as if looking for a hidden lever or door handle.

"Here," said Ben.

At the back of the Aldstane he pushed one foot gingerly into the secret highway and watched his father's face change as his shoe vanished from sight. For a moment Ben thought he might have changed his mind, but Mr. Arnold said firmly, "We'd better hold hands. I don't want to lose you, too."

Together they stepped into the wild road.

Ellie wasn't fond of dogs at the best of times, and now was definitely not the best of times. Once, when she had delivered papers for some extra pocket money (a job that had lasted exactly one day), she'd had a bit of a run-in with the yappy poodle at Number 4, which had sunk its nasty yellow teeth into her new fake-fur coat and hung on for dear life, growling and drooling, until its yappy owner had come out and proclaimed that poor little Maurice had obviously mistaken Ellie for a bear come to maraud Lower Bixbury, and was only doing his job as a guard dog. Ellie had marched back to the paper shop, quit on the spot, and never worn the coat again.

But the dogs that faced her now were certainly not poodles. Despite the fact that they were sort of transparent, they looked as if they could do a lot more damage than Maurice. Luckily, they appeared to be harnessed to the big chariot that had just landed, for although they stretched their ghostly necks out at her and snapped and snarled and foamed at the mouth, they didn't seem to be able to reach her. Ellie drew a big sigh of relief.

But from behind the ghost-dogs there came leaping over the side of the chariot a host of creatures with dark green leathery skin and pointed ears. Before she could get to her feet, the goblins were confronting her, chattering and grinning and showing off their horrid pointed teeth.

"She doesn't look much like a queen!" one cackled.

"Too fresh and tasty . . ."

"Like a little nymph . . ."

"Or a mermaidy . . ."

"Without a tail . . ."

They looked down.

"No tail," they agreed.

One of them came forward and poked at Ellie's bare arm with a sharp black fingernail. "Mmmm," it declared. "Nice soft skin."

For a second all Ellie could think was: *Well, at least the papaya and parsnip body lotion works.* Then: "Whew!" She wrinkled her nose and drew back against the tree, so disgusted that she almost forgot to feel afraid. "You stink!" Then she started sneezing and couldn't stop.

The leading goblin cocked its head at her and grinned. It sniffed its armpit, gave a considering nod, and then offered this noisome part of its anatomy to its nearest companion for inspection.

The second goblin inhaled deeply and nodded. "Terrible," it agreed. "Really terrible."

Soon they were all smelling one another and giggling appreciatively.

"Vile!"

"Horrid!"

"Like rotten eggs!"

"No, like dead rats!"

"Bat poo!"

"Trolls' feet!"

"Dinosaur farts!"

"Minotaur wee!"

They looked at one another. "Nah," said the leading goblin, looking wistful, "not as good as that."

"I wish."

"He's the king of bad smells."

While the goblins debated this fascinating point, Ellie tried to get up. The ground was cold against her bare feet, but the offending sandal lay several yards away. As she put her weight on one foot, a searing pain shot up through the ankle she had twisted.

"Not so fast, my dear."

Suddenly a great black shadow blocked out the light and there was a heavy weight on her shoulder, pressing her back down onto the freezing ground. Ellie looked up, and wished she hadn't.

The figure that loomed over her stood over eight feet tall, and wore a sharply cut black suit topped by the long-snouted head of a jackal.

"You'll have a lot more to worry about than bad

411

smells where you're going!" the Dodman growled menacingly.

"Yes!" giggled one of the goblins. "We're going to mash you up with rats and lizards and worms and dead fairies, and put you in a pie!"

"You can't put me in a pie!" she cried in sudden outrage. "I'm a princess!"

Now all the goblins started to wheeze with laughter.

"A princess pie!"

"Yum!"

"With spider sauce!"

"BE QUIET!" the Dodman roared. He glared around at the pack of them. "Or I'll rip you apart and feed your giblets to the dogs."

That shut them up.

He leaned in to take a closer look at Ellie. Rage flickered in his shiny black pupils like inward fires, and Ellie closed her eyes in terror as his hot breath beat against her face, certain he was going to bite her head clean off. Then she sneezed, right in his face.

The dog-headed man recoiled in disgust, wiping his muzzle. "Princess, eh?" he growled.

Ellie cursed herself silently for her stupidity. Then,

gathering all the courage she could muster, she opened her eyes and looked him squarely in the face. "That's just something my friends call me," she said. "It doesn't really mean anything." Using the tree for support, she pushed herself to her feet and looked at her watch so that she didn't have to look at the dog-headed man anymore. Curiously, the readout said "4:25:03," which was the time when she had entered the way-stone in Aldstane Park. It felt much later than that here, for the sky was darkening; yet the seconds were no longer ticking by, as if time itself were frozen, or no longer relevant in this other world. Not wanting to think about the implications of this, Ellie added brightly, "Goodness, is that the time? I must go, or Mum and Dad will be worried."

The Dodman grabbed her wrist. His cold, sharp dog-nails dug into her skin. She shuddered.

"We don't have watches in Eidolon," he said, and his black eyes scanned her face avidly. "So where have you come from, I wonder, and how have you got here?"

Ellie felt her legs tremble. She remembered what the goblin had said about her not looking like the Queen. They must have come here looking for her mother. Tears began to well up inside her. She decided to let them fall. Crying often got her what she wanted, and what she wanted now was to escape from this horrible world.

"I . . . oh," she sobbed. "I got lost in Bixbury Park while . . . hiding from my friends and . . . sort of fell against this big . . . stone . . . and then next thing I knew"—she turned bleary eyes up to the dog-headed man—"I was here in this awful place. Oh . . . I'm lost—can you help me get home?"

For a moment it looked as if the Dodman's heart—if he had one—might be softened by her distress, for he hesitated as if considering her request. Then something stirred in the branches above her head and a familiar voice hissed, "Oh, I don't think that would be advisable at all, ssssire. The young lady you hold prisoner is indeed the Princesssss Eleanor."

Everyone looked up.

Ellie squinted hard. There was a small pale shape up in the tree, the shape of a pinkish creature with big pointed ears.

It was Cynthia's cat.

Chapter Nine

A Fish Out of Water

"Oh no!"

Ben stared helplessly up into the dark Eidolon sky, in time to see the spectral glow of the Dodman's carriage, drawn by the ghost-dogs, speed past overhead like a nightmare version of Santa Claus's sleigh and reindeer.

"What?" said Mr. Arnold, rubbing his eyes. He stared upward shortsightedly, rubbed his eyes again. "What is it?"

"It was the Dodman," said Ben grimly, staring after the disappearing apparition. "And the Wild Hunt. They must be out looking for Mum." He paused. *Or Ellie*, he thought.

"Ellie!" Mr. Arnold bellowed so loudly that Ben almost jumped out of his skin. "Eleanor! Where are you? Get back here at once!"

"Ssssh!" Ben looked around apprehensively. He grabbed his father's arm. "Someone might hear."

Tutting, Mr. Arnold clicked the flashlight on and shone it around the clearing. The light bounced from tree to tree, illuminating a strand of ivy here, a fallen log there, a patch of gnarled bark, the twiggy fingers of a leafless alder, a tangle of bramble runners.

"Darn thing!" Mr. Arnold declared. "Batteries must be as dead as dodos." He shook the flashlight violently, and its golden beam shot erratically around the clearing and up into the branches of a huge old oak, alarming whatever small resident was hiding there. Something long, thin, and pale scurried out of sight.

"But it's working fine," Ben said, mystified. He took the flashlight from his father's hand, swung the beam from one side of the clearing to the other, and gazed around. The trees stood out starkly against the empty night air, sharply delineated by the harsh yellow light. "See?" he said, holding the light steady so that it lit a circle of dying ferns.

"I can't see a thing," Mr. Arnold said crossly, taking back the flashlight.

Ben stood in its beam. "Can you see me?" he asked.

The light played across his features, illuminating his one green eye and one brown eye, the pupils gone to pinpricks in the glare.

Mr. Arnold frowned. "Not very well," he admitted. Suddenly he looked anxious. He rubbed his eyes again, held his hand up in front of his face. "It's very strange," he said softly, "but I don't seem to be able to see anything much here."

"Ah," said Ben. He closed the eye he thought of as his Eidolon eye, and at once the world became a bit blurry and distorted. Then he closed his Earth eye and looked around with his Eidolon eye wide open. Everything leapt into sharp focus.

He had forgotten about that.

"It's the Secret Country," he said. "It's different from home. You shouldn't be here, Dad, you're not adapted for it."

Mr. Arnold braced his shoulders. "Nonsense," he said. "It's just very dark and the flashlight isn't working properly. You lead on, son. I'll be fine."

Ben sighed. If he were to admit it to himself, he didn't have a clue where to begin looking for Ellie. He had hoped she would be on the other side of the waystone, lost and a bit anxious, ready to return home after making a silly mistake, but his sister could be remarkably pigheaded when she chose to be. He picked a careful path among the trees with his father's hand on his shoulder, and walked for several minutes amusing himself with the image of Eleanor's skinny body topped by a pig's head. A definite improvement, he decided at first. Plus, she'd have rather less use for her massive collection of makeup; although as soon as he thought this, the original image was replaced by an even more nightmarish one—of Ellie's new pig's face adorned with false eyelashes, shimmering green eyeshadow, and a lipsticked snout. *Gross!*

He was so carried away by these horrific details that he forgot to look where he was going—and the next thing he knew he had stumbled over something on the ground and his father had cannoned into him, knocking him flat. The flashlight shot out of his hand and rolled away.

"Ouch!" said Ben. Something hard was digging awkwardly into his kidneys. He sat up and extricated the object.

It was the other one of Ellie's ridiculous shoes, and the ankle strap was broken right through. Ben felt his heart beat faster. There was no way his sister would be parted from both of her beloved sandals unless it was in very exceptional circumstances. They were her favorites, though Ben thought they were horrible, with their chunky soles and lurid, swirling flowers. And they made her walk like a clumsy camel.

Retrieving the flashlight, he swung its beam around the area. The ground was rather churned up, as if by many feet, and farther back, where there was a space between the trees, two deep ruts had parted the frozen ground among the dead leaves, ruts that could have been made by huge wheels. *Like the wheels on a chariot,* Ben thought desperately, remembering the ghost-dogs' carriage. . . .

"Dad," he started, but when he turned back it was to find his father sitting on the ground, clutching his head and groaning.

"It's nothing," he said when Ben came over to him. "Just a bit of a headache. I'll be fine in a minute, once I've taken some tablets." He dug into his pocket and brought out the packet of aspirin he had brought from the car.

"Dad," Ben began again. "I think Ellie's been captured."

But Mr. Arnold did not seem to be paying attention. He was trying to dry-swallow one of the pills, but without any water to wash it down with, it stuck obstinately to his tongue, making him cough and retch.

"Dad—"

"Yes, yes," Mr. Arnold said impatiently, in between coughs. "I really must get rid of this headache. It seems to be getting worse all the time." He pushed himself to his feet and stood there, swaying unsteadily. "Goodness, I do feel rather odd." Abruptly, he sat down again.

Ben grabbed his father's arm and tried to haul him upright. "Listen to me," he said loudly, "I think the Dodman has got Ellie. We have to find her."

Mr. Arnold turned a wan face up to Ben. "I don't think I'm going to be much use to anyone unless I can get these pills down," he said after a while. "Do you think you could find a stream or something and get me a drink of water?"

Ben closed his eyes. It was all too much: His father was ill, his mother and baby sister and his friend Iggy had gone with the Horse Lord to who knew where, and his elder sister appeared to have been taken by the Dodman, and here he was in the dark, in another country. Suddenly, the Shadow World felt like the alien, wild, and terrifying place he had always known it to be in his heart of hearts.

It would have been easy to give up then, to admit defeat and slump down on the ground to await whatever fate might bring them. The human boy in Ben considered this option for perhaps three seconds, before the Prince of Eidolon took over.

"Dad, you have to get up and walk, whether you think you can or not," he said with sudden force. "These woods may once have been Mum's domain, but she's been away for a long time and all sorts of dangers lurk here now. We can't just sit here and wait for them to find us, and someone has to save Ellie. If you're not well enough to help me do that, I'll get you to the waystone and you can go back through the wild road into Aldstane Park."

It was probably the longest speech Ben had ever made to his father—worse even than explaining why he'd been given detention for misbehaving in class with some paper pellets and an elastic band that had made a brilliant catapult but had unfortunately over-shot his target—a horrible boy called Ian, whom he had once caught tying a firework to a cat's tail—and hit Mr. Mapp, the geography teacher, instead.

For a moment Mr. Arnold forgot how ill he was feeling, so overcome with surprise was he at the vehemence of his usually mild-mannered and slightly shy son. His mouth dropped open, but no words came out. Then, slowly and painfully, he shambled to his feet. "It was my choice to come," he muttered obstinately, "and I'll have to make the best of it. Besides"—he grinned weakly—"can't let the rest of my family have all the adventures while I sit at home, can I?"

Ben led his father through the trees until at last they came upon a lake. Ben sniffed at the water cau-tiously. "Only a sip," he warned, though it smelled okay.

Mr. Arnold took his headache tablets. As the two of them sat on the bank waiting for the pills to take effect, an almost-full moon slid out from behind her mantle of cloud and laid a silvery sheen across the water, illuminating the spiky reeds and the fronds of a willow that dipped its icy fingers into the lake. It was a tranquil place and Ben's heart started to beat at its normal speed, until something—a bat, or a very large moth—flittered overhead. For a moment he thought it might be the wood-sprite Twig. But even with his Eidolon eye he couldn't make out what it was before it disappeared into the trees.

"It seems beautiful here," said Mr. Arnold after a moment. His breath emerged in a great cloud of vapor. Then that vanished too.

"It is." Ben shivered. He wished he'd brought some gloves. He stuck his hands into his pockets and found there, among a number of assorted items, some toffees. He offered his father one and together they sucked the sticky paper off and sat there chewing silently.

"If you think this is beautiful, you should have seen it fifteen years ago."

The voice, which sounded rather as if the speaker were talking and gargling at the same time, seemed to be coming out of the deepest part of the lake. Ben stared. There was a splash, as if something had just submerged, then bubbles rose to the surface, limned in moonlight. These were soon followed by what appeared to be a head. Alarmed, Ben shone the flashlight at it. It must surely have been a very big fish indeed to have such a loud voice and to produce such large air bubbles.

From the middle of the black water, hands waved weakly in the sudden flood of illumination. "*Aiee!* Stop, please . . . The light, make that terrible light go away!"

Taken aback, Ben shut off the flashlight.

Once more in darkness, the figure regained some of its composure and stopped flapping its hands around. All Ben could see was what seemed to be a perfectly normal, human-looking head with a lot of white hair that floated limply on the surface of the lake.

"Who are you?" he asked.

The figure swam closer. "The question is, who are *you* to have the power to wield a sunbeam in the dark of night?"

Ben laughed. "It's not a sunbeam," he said. "It's a flashlight. It runs on batteries, and when I click this switch it comes on. Look . . ." He turned the flashlight on briefly and the circle of yellow light offered him the vision of a very old woman staring back at him in terror. Her eyes were droopy and red-rimmed and sore-looking, and her skin was crusted with scales.

"*Aieee!* Don't look at me!" She covered her face with her hands.

Ben turned the light off.

"What sort of fish is it?" his father asked, peering myopically into the darkness. "It's making a very strange noise."

"It's not a fish, Dad," Ben said. He shrugged. "I don't really know what it is."

"Fish? *Fish!*" The voice rose to a shriek. "Visitors to the Dark Mere never used to be so rude!"

"I'm sorry," Ben said. "My father cannot under-stand the folk of Eidolon: He is not of the Shadow World. My name is Ben. My mother—" He stopped himself in case he said too much, then added care-fully, "My mother comes from here, though."

"Ben, did you know you were talking to yourself? One of your mother's habits," Mr. Arnold said wist-fully. "They do say it's the first sign of madness."

425

"Sorry, Dad. You just can't hear what this . . . er . . . person is saying." He was about to say more when the creature in the water spoke again.

"Shine the sunbeam on your face so that I can see you," the old woman said.

Ben did as he was requested.

There came a sharp intake of breath from the creature in the water. "Ah, so you must be the Odd-Eyed Boy, the one they've been talking about, the one who escaped from the Dodman by diving off the battlements of Corbenic Castle. The one who swam the lake ahead of the Gabriel Hounds and summoned the Lord of the Wildwood to his aid. The one who flew on a dragon he'd saved from certain death, put paid to some of those no-good goblins, and imprisoned that miserable turncoat Old Creepie!"

Ben grinned. "Well, it wasn't quite like that; I had rather a lot of help—," he started.

"No need for modesty, young man. Or should I call you 'Your Highness'?"

"Oh no," Ben said quickly. "I'd much rather you didn't. But what can I call you?"

The crone slipped back into the water, made a

graceful turn, and with a splash, something silver gleamed in the moonlight. It was a tail: a great big fish's tail complete with interlocking scales and a huge curving fork at the end of it, just like the ones you see in storybooks.

"A mermaid," he breathed.

The old woman cackled, and Ben saw how there were gaps and stumps between her sharp, in-curved teeth. "Well, I was a maid once, but that was rather a long time ago now. My name is Melusine, but you can call me Mellie—they all do. Beautiful, I was then. Long golden hair and pearly skin, eyes that could drown a man. I could sing, too. Oh, how I could sing! Many's the unwitting goblin I've lured into my clutches with a song. . . ." She cleared her throat and began to croak:

> *"Come see, come see my loveliness*
> *Come swim, come swim with me*
> *I'll wrap you in a golden tress*
> *And take you home with me*
> *Through the lilies we'll dive down*
> *Down to where the fishies play*
> *And there in my fair arms you'll drown*
> *And nevermore see the light of day . . ."*

Ben gulped. It seemed highly unlikely that anyone would fall for that sort of trick, even if Melusine *had* been a great deal prettier than she was now and didn't sound like a rusty old gate hinge.

At this point Mr. Arnold interrupted. "Son," he said, and there was a distinct note of concern in his voice. "Did that fish just sing?"

"Er, yes, Dad. But it's not a fish. She's a mermaid called Melusine—Mellie for short."

His father gave him a weary look. "A talking mermaid? In a lake in another world?" He rubbed a hand across his face. "Well, anything's possible, I suppose."

"It is here," Ben agreed.

"Tasty little beasts some of them were." The old mermaid was still reminiscing wistfully. "Nowadays"—she gave a disgusted snort—"it's more like chewing old turnips. We've all got older and grimmer since your mother went away. It used to be that nothing aged here. It was charmed, they said, a world living under its own spell."

"Um, my mother's back now," Ben said. "She came back today."

"Oh, I know about that. There was quite a commotion."

"Commotion?"

"All the comings and goings among the woodland folk. Lots of scurrying and preening going on. Me, I'm too old and ugly for all of that sort of nonsense now. I don't like people looking at me anymore."

"You're not *that* ugly, Mellie," Ben lied chivalrously.

Melusine chuckled. "Nice of you to try to make me feel better, and just what I'd expect from a Prince of the blood. Always were a charming lot, your family." She paused. "Apart from Old Creepie, of course."

"I . . . ah . . . saw the Dodman and the Wild Hunt flying overhead earlier. Do you think they were looking for my mother?"

The crone cocked her head to one side. "I know the noise those hellhounds make when they're on someone's trail," she said after a pause. "They certainly caught something, but the Queen's safe in the Wildwood, and the Princess, too."

"Ellie?"

"Ellie?" Melusine echoed.

"Eleanor," Ben amended. "My older sister. She's . . . ah . . . a bit taller than me, and quite thin, and she was wearing—"

The mermaid shook her head. "No, no, it was a baby with the Queen; but there was another girl, almost full-grown, who was getting chased by the Wild Hunt, or so I heard from the oak-nymph."

Ben's heart sank. "He's got her, then," he breathed. "My other sister, Eleanor. The Dodman has got her and taken her to the castle."

"What's all this about a castle and Ellie?" Mr. Arnold seemed suddenly galvanized. "And the Dodman—is he the one with the dog's head and all the goblins? That doesn't sound good. . . ."

"It's not," said Ben.

With dread he remembered the deep, wide, chilly lake from which the forbidding castle walls rose like great cliffs, and the courtyard scattered with bones. It was miles away, through forest and over heath and plain. He had no idea in which direction it lay, nor how they could possibly cross the lake or get in to save his sister.

Melusine clucked her tongue. "There's been a lot of talk about goings-on at Corbenic. Fortifications, dungeons, strange monsters massing in the grounds, and the lake. He's gathering himself quite an army, the Dodman. And he's sucking the life out of Eidolon too.

Now he wants to extend his vile rule across all of the Secret Country, that's what I've heard." She paused. "So do you think that he has the Princess Eleanor?"

Ben nodded grimly.

"Then that is terrible news indeed."

Chapter Ten

In the Dungeons

"Can't have you leaping out of the window and taking a swim like your annoying little brother, can we?" the Dodman said, leering at Ellie. "So we're taking no chances this time. It's the dungeons for you, my sweet Princess of Eidolon."

"Sweet. *Squarrrk!*" echoed the mynah bird on his shoulder.

The Dodman cocked his dog-head to one side and

regarded Ellie out of the depths of one of those disconcerting black eyes. The flickering green flames of the wall candles leapt and danced, throwing bizarre shadows over everything. Green was not a color, Ellie decided, that brought out the best in anyone.

"A pity you do not resemble your mother more closely, for she was quite the beauty." He stared past her at the stone wall as if he could see the image of the young Isadora imprinted there. "She was extraordinary, you know, fifteen years ago. Her hair was as golden as a dragon's hoard; her skin was as pale and soft as a mermaid's belly; her eyes—"

Behind his back one of the goblins stifled a giggle.

The Dodman whipped around and fixed the offender with a gimlet stare, as if he might fillet him then and there, and serve his spleen up for supper.

"And her eyes were as green as a goblin's heart," he finished sharply.

"That's not a very nice thing to say about my mother!"

The Dodman's gaze swiveled back to Ellie, knife-like. "How old are you, *Princess*?"

"Fourteen."

The dog-headed man clenched his jaw. "If Isadora

hadn't conceived you, she'd have come back to me. She would have loved me, you know, if she'd allowed herself to follow the true inclination of her heart. She was always intrigued by me—if a little afraid. When she fled to the Other World it was only because she wanted me to pursue her. And pursue her I did—but I was late, too late. To think of that perfect beauty, stolen by a common human . . ."

"My dad's not common!"

The Dodman sneered. "A creature without magic? A denizen of the Other World? Each and every one as common as muck! Millions of them, all lumbering around without a clue as to the nature of the worlds, of their origins, of their pathetic purpose in life—and before you ask, that purpose is to bow down and acknowledge me as their true monarch; to crawl on their bellies and avert their eyes from me; to offer heartfelt prayers for my well-being, and that of my bride and our line of sons—"

"Your bride?"

"Bride, *squarrrrk!*"

Ellie felt her skin go cold and goose-bumpy all over. Her stomach turned over as if she might be sick at any moment. She felt dizzy.

The dog-headed man barked a sharp laugh. "Don't flatter yourself, my dear. You're much too young and scrawny for my taste, and, sadly, half-breed brunettes do nothing for me at all."

Ellie glared at him furiously. "I am NOT scrawny! I'm a perfectly normal size ten. Not that I'd marry you anyway, Dogbreath, not if you were the last . . . the last . . . creature in either world!"

The Dodman's eyes glinted in the gloom of the corridor. Then he licked his long black lips with a long black tongue. "So rude, and so ungrateful. You should think yourself lucky we came upon you in the Wildwood and brought you here to offer you the hospitality of our home, rather than leaving you there for the trolls and the saber-toothed tigers to find. They'd not have been so tender with your pampered skin. See, we have prepared the finest accommodation for you. . . ."

And he unlocked and pushed open a thick, iron-bound door.

It looked as dark as death inside, and it smelled awful. Ellie hated the dark. Though she didn't like to admit it, she was afraid of it, of the things that might spring out at her. At home she kept a little night-light burning by the side of her bed. But it didn't look as if the cell had any light in it at all. All she could make out was a semicircle of light on the ground in front of the door that showed bare stonework, its only carpet a layer of dust, dust that had been disturbed by the passage of many feet. Not all of them human, by the look of some of the prints . . .

"Make yourself at home, girlie," the Dodman growled. "Because it's going to *be* your home for a long, long time." He paused. "Unless your dear mother does the sensible thing."

"What do you mean?"

The dog-headed man's long-lipped smile widened until she could see every one of his gleaming ivory teeth.

"Grizelda?"

His voice resounded from the massive stonework like the voice of a dozen Dodmen, and somewhere in the gloom at the far end of the long corridor something stirred. It came closer.

For several seconds Ellie held her breath; then, when the creature stepped into the flickering light of the wall sconces, she exhaled in a great, shocked *whoosh*. Before her, limned by the weird green light of the candles, stood the ugliest thing she had ever seen in her life. She—or at least Ellie thought it was a she, for a massive bosom appeared to be trapped behind a tattered array of leather and spikes on the creature's torso—towered above even the Dodman, and her shoulders brushed the walls of the passageway on either side. Her hair, which appeared to be bright orange even in this odd candlelight, had been twisted into a hundred lumpy dreadlocks, wrapped around with bones and feathers and teeth. Her nose was more like a snout than anything. Her cheeks were like slabs of old mutton, and her smile was like a disaster in a graveyard. But despite the unfortunate features that fate had dealt the giantess, she did appear to have some vanity left in her, for her massive lips were smeared with bright red lipstick, some of which also coated her uneven tombstone teeth.

Ellie regarded this vision as steadily as she could, although maintaining eye contact was a bit difficult when the beast's eyes looked in two different directions at once. Then she said, forcing a friendly grin, "You know, that shade of lipstick really doesn't do anything for you at all." She dug into her handbag and from its depths retrieved an elegant silver tube.

This she pulled apart and twisted until the cosmetic within revealed itself as a rather smart shade of chestnut brown. "Here," she said, holding it out to the giantess, "try this color instead. I think you'll find— Oh!"

The giantess poised the lipstick tube at her mouth for a second, then the entire thing disappeared into her maw of a mouth. She chewed vigorously, the metal cylinder grating horribly against her teeth, then gave Ellie a ghastly grin.

"Tasty."

The giantess grabbed Ellie's handbag from her, dug around in it, and pulled out the mobile phone.

"No!" Ellie wailed, but it was already too late, for the hapless phone had also disappeared down the monster's throat.

Grizelda chewed the metal, plastic, and circuitry with the most blissful expression on her face.

"Yum!" she declared. She wiped the back of a huge hand across her mouth, then burped loudly. What Ellie had thought was red lipstick smeared itself grotesquely across her chin and some of it dripped onto her tunic, making a dark, shiny mark.

The Dodman rolled his eyes. "Honestly," he said.

"She'll eat anything. Give me the fairy, Grizelda."

The giantess looked puzzled; or at least her expression changed to one in which her lower jaw dropped open. Something was stuck between two of her bottom teeth. It looked suspiciously like a wing, gauzy and transparent. With a swift hand the Dodman caught hold of the trapped item, flipped it out from the giantess's mouth, and held it up. There was still a leg attached, tiny and delicate, shod with a long, spiky slipper of iridescent blue. Drops of red liquid oozed from it.

So the stuff all over the monster's mouth hadn't been lipstick at all, then. . . . Ellie shuddered. How *horrible*; how cruel.

"Oh, for badness' sake! When I tell you to bring me things, I mean *alive*, not chewed into pieces." The Dodman turned to the goblins and held out a huge key. "Boggart? Bogie?"

"Yes, lord?" two of the goblins chorused. They gazed with adoration at the key.

"Go and fetch me another fairy from the storeroom. A nice big strong one. Quickly, and you shall be rewarded!"

Bogie snatched the key from their master. Boggart

tried to snatch it from him. Fighting as to who got to wield the wondrous object that gave access to the most special place in the whole castle, the goblins turned and sped up the passageway, pushing and tripping over each other all the way.

The Dodman watched them go with narrow eyes. "Clowns," he complained bitterly. "Things will be different soon enough. When I have a better class of minion to choose from . . ." His gaze transferred itself to Ellie. "Well, my dear, in you go."

He gave her a hard shove and Ellie stumbled into the dungeon. Inside, she blinked and squinted, unable to adjust to the lack of light. Behind her, the dog-headed man clicked his fingers.

"I hope you still have the sprite, Grizelda."

The giantess mumbled something, discarded Ellie's now rather mangled handbag, then poked her huge fingers into a pouch at her side. She extracted something from it that emerged with a strange, scratchy squeal of protest. An odd pinkish light oozed past her fingers.

"Don't squeeze it so hard!" The Dodman prized the glowing thing from the giantess's huge mitt and held it up. Ellie stared at it. It was a large insecty-thing, with the iridescent wings of a gigantic dragonfly and a tiny humanlike face. Light pulsed out of it with every breath, light as red as blood. As if it could not bear to look at the awful thing that held it, it kept its eyes tightly shut.

"Twig?" Ellie gasped. Ben had told her all about his adventures in this peculiar world, about the friends who had helped him escape.

The sprite opened its eyes. They were big and dark and prismatic, many-faceted, like a ripe blackberry. It blinked at her and said something in its weird voice, something that sounded like "acorn."

"Acorn?" Ellie echoed.

The sprite nodded. "Not Twig," it wheezed, and the red light flickered. "His cousin, Acorn. They caught me in a net. In the Wildwood. Hurt me."

The Dodman shook it viciously. "I'll hurt you more if you don't stop your whining. Keep that light coming!"

He shone the sprite over Ellie's shoulder, and illumination immediately flooded across the cell room.

Ellie gasped. "There's no way I'm staying in here! It's . . ." Words failed her.

The cell was small, windowless, and filthy. An inch

or more of dust had settled on every surface like the matted gray fur of the world's grubbiest cat—on the narrow bed, which appeared to be no more than a stone shelf set into the wall; on the uneven flagstones of the floor; on a rickety table and chair; on an old tin bucket in the far corner.

Ellie's eyes fixed upon this last detail with dread and loathing. "What's that?"

The Dodman's smile widened. "That, my dear," he announced with some satisfaction, "is your en suite bathroom. Nothing but the best for the Princess of Eidolon."

"For the Princess, *squarrrrk!*" The mynah bird bobbed its head and fixed her with a shiny eye.

Ellie blinked back tears of rage. "One day my mother will punish you for this," she declared fiercely.

"She may try," the dog-headed man conceded, "but by then she will be powerless against me. I shall take her magic from her, bit by bit, when she gives herself up to me."

"And why ever should she do that? She will never give herself up to you."

The Dodman laughed. "Oh, I do not expect her to come willingly. I expect her to come for love."

Ellie frowned. That sounded like a contradiction if ever there was one. "Love? You must be mad. She will never love you."

"Me? Ah, no, my dear. I harbor no such delusions since she fled into the arms of your father. But she loves you. . . ."

The silence that settled over the scene at these words was broken seconds later by the sound of running footsteps. The goblins had returned.

"*I* caught it—let *me* give it him!"

"Nah, get off, I want the reward!"

There was a brief skirmish during which it sounded as if a lot of kicking and biting was going on; then something broke free of the goblins and came zigzagging crazily through the air of the corridor and came to rest on Ellie's shoulder. It was larger than the sprite and looked more like a tiny human being, apart from its long thin fingers and spiky toes, all of which were gripping her T-shirt as if its life depended on it.

"How sweet!" the Dodman sneered. "A Wildwood fairy come to pay its respects to the daughter of the Queen."

The goblins came charging up to him.

"I found it!" cried Boggart.

"So what?" shrieked Bogie, shoving him sideways. "I brought it. I want my reward!"

"You want a reward, do you, Bogie?"

The smaller of the two goblins nodded vigorously, and the sprite's red glow gleamed in Bogie's greedy eyes as he gazed adoringly up at his master.

"Give me the key." One of the goblins relinquished it to the Dodman reluctantly. "I think you *both* deserve a reward," their master went on smoothly.

Boggart and Bogie exchanged a surprised glance, and grinned from ear to ear, which was a long way.

As fast as a striking snake, the Dodman's free hand shot out and smacked both creatures soundly around their ugly heads.

"There's your reward! That's what you deserve for your clumsiness! What's the point of capturing a fairy for me if you squabble over it and let it go? Dolts! Dullards! Dunces!"

He lashed out at them with his boot and they backed away, quivering. They knew what the dog-headed one could be like in one of his tempers. Poor old Batface had copped for it last week and he hadn't walked the same since.

"Take this, and hold it steady," he told Grizelda, handing her the sprite.

"Then can I eat it?"

"No!" Ellie cried in horror. "No, you can't!"

The Dodman regarded her curiously. Then he gave her a lopsided smile. "Sweet . . . Well, maybe we won't let her eat it yet, if you behave, eh?"

He caught hold of her hair, wrapping a long hank of it around his fist, and pulled her head toward him. Ellie squirmed. "Ow!"

Something glinted silver in the darkness; then suddenly there was a knife blade before her face.

Ellie felt her knees go weak.

"No, please . . ."

She closed her eyes. There was a shearing sound, and abruptly her head was free of his grasp. Her eyes came open, to find the Dodman standing there before her with a knife in one hand and something dark and floppy in the other. Unconsciously, her hand went to her head.

"You cut my hair!"

"Be thankful it is only your hair, for the moment." He stowed the knife away and caught up the fairy, detaching its tiny hands roughly from the fabric of

Ellie's top. "Listen to me," he told it savagely. "You will go back to your Wildwood and you will find Queen Isadora and show her this." He wound the strand of hair around and around its slender body, making sure it did not interfere with the creature's wings. "Tell her that I hold her daughter Eleanor hostage and that if she does not give herself up to me by full moon, the next gift I will send her will be a rather more painfully acquired part of her pretty Ellie, followed by another and another and another." His grip tightened on the fairy until it cried out. "Have you got that?"

The Wildwood fairy stared at the dog-headed man with its great violet eyes. "This is a cruel thing you do, Dodman," it said, and its voice was surprisingly low for such a small creature. It turned its head to regard Ellie. "Forgive me, Princess. If I do not carry the message he will only find another to take my place. . . ."

"She mustn't come!" Ellie cried. "Tell her—"

One of the Dodman's hard elbows caught her in the ribs, sending her spinning backward into the cell. She fell back against the hard bed, gasping for breath.

"Enough!"

The cell door banged shut, consigning Ellie to

447

total darkness. The sound of muffled complaint came from outside, then the door cracked open and something small and pink and glowing came arcing through the black space. Then the door banged shut again.

Chapter Eleven

Trapped by a Troll

Iggy found himself staring up into quite the ugliest face he had ever seen in any of his nine lives. Under a shock of purple hair, it seemed to consist mainly of a mouth— a very large mouth containing a lot of long, sharp yellow teeth that stuck out at all sorts of angles—a hooked nose like the beak of some predatory bird, and a pair of bright, beady close-set eyes that were regarding him with an expression he recognized all too well.

Unadulterated greed.

449

"Help!"

What he had hoped would come out as a yowl that might be heard for miles emerged as a pathetic squeak, since his captor was holding him so tightly around the middle with its hard, horny claws that Iggy could hardly draw breath.

The monster's mouth opened wider, emitting a terrible stench.

"Yum. Cat," it said. "Haven't eaten cat for ages. What a treat."

It brought a squirming Iggy closer.

"Don't eat me," Iggy pleaded. "I'd taste awful."

"Awful?" The monster's huge brow drew itself into a puzzled frown.

"Like . . ." Iggy searched for a comparison that might delay the inevitable. "Like . . . old boots. I'm very scrawny, you see. There's not much meat on me at all. I'm all fur and bones. . . ." Even getting this out was an effort. He hung there, panting and hoping.

"Old boots . . . Hmmm . . ." There was a pause as his captor thought about this. Then its eyes gleamed. "I ate a pair of old boots once. Hundred-league boots. They belonged to a cat, as I recall. He was still in them at the time. Didn't taste that bad. A bit chewy. And the laces got caught between my teeth." It paused. "The whiskers did too."

Iggy stared at it aghast. "You ate Puss-in-Boots?"

A horrible noise reverberated through the air, as if someone had just switched on a giant engine. Iggy gulped. Then he realized the monster was laughing.

"Silly cat. That was just a story!"

A long gray tongue came out of the huge mouth, like a serpent emerging from a cave. Iggy watched in horrified fascination as it traveled across the horrible teeth and lips, leaving a slick of silvery slobber behind. He could imagine that tongue savoring him. It made him shudder.

"*And* . . . I'm—er, poisonous!"

"Poisonous? Whoever heard of a poisonous cat?"

"I'd give you a terrible bellyache if you ate me. You'd be sick for weeks."

"Sick? I'm never sick. My mother always said I had a very robust constitution."

It was hard to imagine that such a beast could ever have had a mother.

"How . . . how is your mother?" Iggy asked in a desperate attempt to engage the thing in polite conversation.

"I ate her, too."

"Oh."

The vast rumble of the monster's laugh thrummed through Iggy's bones.

"You really think I ate my mother?"

"Yes . . . er, no." Iggy felt like an idiot. This was hopeless. He braced himself. "Look, if you're going to eat me, just get on and do it. All I'm saying is that you'll regret it."

"Oh, I don't think so. Trolls aren't noted for their sense of regret."

Iggy thought hard.

"Don't you live under bridges and eat goats? You know, like in *The Three Billy Goats Gruff*?"

"Such a ridiculous story. You think I would let a nice juicy goat go safely on its way just because it said there was a bigger, tastier one coming along in a minute? You'd have to be pretty stupid to fall for that sort of trick." It squinted suspiciously at Iggy. "Do you think I'm stupid?"

"Of course not . . ."

"Of course not. Nah, I ate all three of them." And the troll licked its lips as if reminiscing.

"There's a lot more meat on a goat than on a cat,"

Iggy reminded it again. "And my fur would get stuck in your throat."

"Oh, I'd skin you first," the troll said cheerfully. "I'm not a complete heathen, you know. I never bother with skinning rabbits, since even the biggest ones aren't much more than a morsel—but a cat's a different matter. Bit special. Once in a blue moon sort of thing. In fact, I think I've got some rather good cat recipes somewhere. There's Moggy Meringue, though I'm out of dinosaur eggs at the moment. And Kitty Casserole . . . no, too many vegetables in that one. Vegetables—can't bear the things. Mother always said they were good for me, but I reason that being good's not really appropriate for a troll. Epitome of 'bad,' don't you think? So eating things that are good for you might take the edge off being bad, and I can't really afford that, you know. But there was one special recipe that didn't involve any veg, as I recall. One of the witches on the Blasted Heath gave it to me, and they certainly never ate anything so boring as a vegetable. Now, what was it again?" It rolled its eyes, consulting its capacious memory. "Ah, yes: eye of newt and toe of frog, tongue of dog and wool of bat, goes very nicely with a cat."

Iggy regarded him dubiously. "I don't think it would, you know."

"Well, trial and error is what good cuisine is all about," the troll declared cavalierly. "I shall have a cast about in my larder and see what I can find to stuff you with—make a bit of a feast of it. Might even invite Grizelda over for dinner." It thought about this for a moment. "On second thought, perhaps not. She doesn't really appreciate gourmet food, and you are quite small. I'm not sure there would be enough to go around. A couple of legs apiece. Tail for one and head for the other . . ."

Iggy felt faint.

The troll's grip on him tightened.

"Hmmm . . . Decisions to make. Let's put you away somewhere safe while I decide how I'm going to cook you, shall we?"

And he lumbered across the open ground to the entrance to a cave. Inside, there were a lot of big clay pots with lids on. With his free hand the troll lifted one lid and peered inside. "Fairies," he said thoughtfully. "Fairy mash, maybe, with a garnish of triffid and giant hogweed . . ." He replaced the lid with a clang and lifted the next one. "Ah, selkie flippers. A bit fishy with cat, I think . . ."

The next pot was empty.

"In you go, what did you say your name was?"

"I didn't."

"Be like that, then. I always like to know the names of those I eat. Names are special. They have power. Mother said it was what made me big and strong. I dare say you'll tell me before too long."

And he dropped Iggy into the pot. The lid shut out the light.

Chapter Twelve

A Deception

Cernunnos returned as the sun came up over the Wildwood, tinting every leaf and branch with an ominous wash of pale red light.

Darius looked up from his vigil beside the sleeping woman and her child. He knew at once that something was terribly wrong. The Lord of the Wildwood's face was grim.

The Horned Man put a finger to his lips and drew

the centaur aside. "Come with me," he said softly.

"But who will watch over Queen Isadora and the Princess Alice?"

Cernunnos lifted his eyes to the dawn sky. Above them two dark shapes circled silently, wings outstretched, like a pair of buzzards quartering their territory.

"Dragons? Can we trust them? Their kind have not always proved loyal."

"Xarkanadûshak and his lady will keep watch: They owe a debt to the boy, Ben, and his family."

In the shadow of a huge oak, its bark gouged and twisted by the centuries, the Lord of the Wildwood showed the centaur what he held cradled. It was a fairy, and it lay in the crook of Cernunnos's arm in a daze, its eyes tight shut and its mouth down-turned in misery. Something dark and sleek had been wrapped around its narrow torso.

Darius stared at it, uncomprehending.

"It is as I feared," Cernunnos said in a low voice. "The Dodman has taken a hostage, and not just any hostage, but the daughter of the Queen herself."

"Her daughter?" For a moment the Horse Lord's face clouded with bewilderment; then his eyes grew round. As if unable to help himself, he reached a hand toward the fairy, touched lightly the silken stuff around its body. "Eleanor? They have taken the Princess Eleanor? And this . . ."

"Is her hair, yes. Sent to us by the Dodman as a token of her capture. He will send worse next time. He said he would send her back piece by piece. . . ."

"Next time?" Darius echoed.

"If Isadora does not give herself up to him, by full moon."

"But she cannot, she has only just returned to us. And full moon is only two days away. . . ." But even as Darius said this, the image of a pretty dark-haired girl blushing at the Aldstane on the other side of the wild road floated before his eyes and his heart clenched inside him.

"Isadora cannot give herself up, no. We cannot allow her to become the Dodman's possession, and so she must not know of this."

The centaur regarded the Lord of the Wildwood in horror. "But we cannot keep such a secret from our Queen, it would not be right."

"There are greater rights in the world, Darius. The girl is a small price to pay for the future safety of all

Eidolon." Cernunnos bent so that his antlered head cast a long shadow across the forest floor, and with his free hand he scooped up a handful of fallen oak leaves, brown as nuts and crisp with frost. These he held out toward Darius, then let them filter through his fingers back to the soft ground. "All things have their allotted span in the world. They live, they die, and they give themselves back to the cycle of Eidolon, so that others may live." Between their feet, insects and worms moved where the leaves had been disturbed. A pair of eyes shone watchfully from the depths of a hole revealed in the roots of the old tree.

Darius swallowed his protest, though his brow was wrinkled by the turmoil of his thoughts.

As he struggled for words, the fairy stirred. It pushed itself upright and blinked.

"Can you get this stuff off me?" it pleaded, plucking at the hair.

Darius exchanged a glance with the Lord of the Wildwood, who nodded. Then he stepped forward and with careful fingers unwound the hank of Ellie's hair from the creature. The hair tingled against his palm like a live thing. He felt tears prick his eyes.

"What will he do to her?"

Cernunnos firmed his jaw. "Nothing, if we get to her first."

The Horse Lord's chin came up with a start. "You mean, we might rescue her?" he asked with sudden hope.

"That, or aid her on her way to silence."

"You cannot mean—"

"Hush. I pray that it will not come to that. But let us speak no more of this now. There are many ears in the forest and not all of them are loyal to our cause."

"But what about the messenger?" Darius regarded the fairy with concern.

"There is no need to talk about me as if I am deaf, or stupid, or absent," the creature said crossly. "I did not ask to be captured by the Dodman; and I certainly did not ask to have to carry such a horrid message, nor have that hair tied around me. It was pretty hard to fly with all that stuff on, I can tell you."

Cernunnos looked down at the fairy. "You did well, Nettle Blueflower," he said gently. "And now you must recuperate. I will send you with Beechnut and Quickthorn to the southern edge of the wood. Make sure you stay there until you are well."

"But I'm already feeling better," the fairy called

Nettle Blueflower protested. "I'm sure I'll be fine after a short nap."

"Even so," the Lord of the Wildwood reiterated, "it is my wish that you should travel south." And he summoned the two escorts, passed Nettle into their care, and he and the centaur watched as the trio flew slowly away, Beechnut and Quickthorn supporting the messenger carefully between them.

"I cannot risk him talking," Cernunnos explained softly. "If this news leaks out too early, it could be disastrous."

Darius transferred his intent gaze to the stag-headed man. "And they are truly taking him south? He will come to no harm?"

The Lord of the Wildwood regarded him curiously, and a shadow passed before his peat brown eyes. "Do you really believe I would bring deliberate harm to one of my subjects?" he asked.

Darius looked at the ground, feeling ashamed for questioning the Lord of the Wildwood. But there was still the matter of the Princess Eleanor, and he made a solemn promise to himself that he would do whatever was in his power to save her.

• • •

"My lady, I trust you are well rested?"

As the shadow of the Horned Man fell across her, Isadora opened her eyes. In the rosy light of dawn they shone the startling green of the buds on a spring larch. A night in the Secret Country had rejuvenated her.

She sat up and looked around. Baby Alice lay cradled in the nest of moss and clothes where she had laid her in the night, sleeping peacefully, forehead to forehead with her piglet-doll.

Isadora smiled. "I am well, Lord Cernunnos." Then she frowned, remembering. "Did you manage to save the poor soul whom the Wild Hunt were pursuing?"

"Alas no, my lady. The Gabriel Hounds were well away before we could reach them." It was an evasion, though not precisely a lie.

Isadora looked pained. She got to her feet, brushing leaf mold and dust from her skirts. "I cannot bear that such acts are carried out in my realm without opposition. We must do something to rescue the unfortunate captive. Tell me, Lord Cernunnos, how many of my folk have taken the Dodman's side against us?"

The Lord of the Wildwood shook his head. "It is

not just that he has gathered a horde of creatures to him, my lady, but that many have come to be born into Eidolon with no knowledge of anything but the ways of terror. Our greater task will be to persuade them that there is still hope in the world, that the future can be better for us all if they resist him and come over to us. But . . ." He hesitated.

"Go on."

"We are weak, my Queen. Magic has been leached out of Eidolon systematically by the Dodman's actions. He has stolen our folk out of this world and allowed them to fail and die in the Other World. And he has killed many and broken the spirits of more. Greed and laziness have claimed many souls. As we grow weaker, so he grows stronger, or so it seems; and the sum total of magic has dwindled. There will be less power for you to draw on now, and fewer to call to your banner, too."

"What are you saying, Cernunnos? That I have been away too long and that it is now too late to save my people?"

"No, my Queen. Never that. But we are not ready yet to take him on in open war."

"So we must allow whichever poor creature was

taken by his hounds to languish and die without our aid?"

"I fear we are not yet ready to storm Corbenic Castle."

Isadora's gentle face became grim. "Then we must find another way."

Darius stepped forward. "I pledge myself to the task of rescuing the captive, my Queen. I shall not rest until she is rescued."

"She?" The Queen's gaze became sharp as glass. "So you know who the captive is, then?"

The centaur shuffled his hooves under her scrutiny and the disapproving glare of Cernunnos. But just as she was about to question him further, there was a great deal of splashing and shouting from behind them, and Baby Alice awoke with a start and began to howl. Isadora scooped her up and walked back toward the stream to see what all the fuss was about.

A group of woodland folk had emerged from their dens and secret places and were braving the daylight to line the banks where the waters cascaded down into a sunlit plunge-pool. In the middle of this, looking rather wet and flustered, floated her husband, in a soaking anorak, with an umbrella held aloft—though if it had been meant to keep the worst of the waterfall off him, it hadn't worked. Two nymphs caught hold of the anorak and started to tow him to the shore, where they hauled him up unceremoniously and left him there like a beached seal.

"Clive!"

Mr. Arnold blinked and stared up at where his wife stood with Baby Alice cradled in her arms, shaking her head in disbelief, her hair made luminous by the sun. All he could make out was her silhouette, but it was a shape he recognized, in this world or any other.

"Isadora, my darling . . ."

Behind him, in the shallows, Ben watched this exchange with rising dread. In a moment he would have to tell his mother what had happened to her accident-prone family since they had last been together. It was bad enough that his father was here, and ill; but he knew the world would change shape as soon as he told her about Ellie. He turned to the old mermaid.

"Thank you, Melusine," he said. He paused as a thought suddenly struck him. "You don't know my friend Silver, do you?"

The mermaid considered this. "Silver . . . Silver . . ."

She shook her head and water droplets sprayed all around and fell like rain. "No, I don't think I recall that name."

"She's a selkie," Ben added.

"Oh, selkies," Melusine said dismissively. "Unreliable folk, selkies. They're only part-timers. Haven't got the same commitment or the stamina of us true mermaids. Really, if you're going to be something in life you should be that one thing and stick to it, I say, rather than chopping and changing all the time."

"Maybe you knew her father—He Who Hangs Around on the Great South Rock to Attract Females?"

For a moment a huge grin lit the old mermaid's face. "Now *him* I remember! Skerry, we called him. When he transformed, he was a real beauty: tallest man I ever saw, with a mop of wild blond hair and eyes the color of a summer sky. And he had a daughter, you say?"

Ben nodded, trying to remember Silver's true name. Then it came to him like a flash of light in the head, and he could see her in his mind's eye in her girl form, with her skin as pale as moonlight and her long hair clinging to her shoulders, and he smiled. "She Who

Swims the Silver Path of the Moon," he said happily.

The mermaid regarded him curiously. "I don't know her, my dear, but you obviously do, because you're blushing like a wood-sprite!" She cackled. "Well, if she takes after her father, she'll be a pretty thing for sure, so no wonder you're smitten."

Smitten? Ben blushed even harder. Ridiculous. He didn't even like girls. *But,* said a little voice at the back of his head, unhelpfully, *she isn't a girl, at least not half the time.*

"Ben?"

His mother's eyebrows shot up in surprise. Then she waved to him from the far side of the pool.

"I have to go," he said to the old mermaid. "Perhaps I'll see you again."

The crone laughed. "Not if I see you first, laddie," she said. "You're lucky I didn't sing you down to my lair this time." And she winked at him and dived out of sight, leaving Ben feeling rather bemused and even more anxious than he had felt before. Was everything in the Secret Country so scary? He waded out of the water toward his mother; but before he could reach her, a shadow fell across him.

He looked up. It was the Horned Man.

Cernunnos offered him a hand up out of the stream, and he grasped it. It felt hard and dry and warm, smooth as polished wood. The fingers tightened minutely. "Ben," the stag-headed man started quietly, pulling the boy onto dry land, "you will say nothing about Eleanor to your mother." His grip tightened.

Ben stared at him. "I won't?"

"You will not. She must not know, not yet. It is too dangerous."

"But Dad knows."

"Your father is sleeping."

The Horned Man pointed to where Mr. Arnold lay cocooned in the pile of blankets and clothes recently vacated by Baby Alice. His eyes were closed and he looked as if he were dreaming, for a huge smile was on his face.

"He will not wake up again until I allow it," Cernunnos said. "It is for his own good as much as for any other reason: He should not be here, as you should know." He fixed Ben with a stern gaze.

"I couldn't stop him," Ben said defensively. "I mean, I tried to, but he is my dad . . ."

"You must rescue your sister Eleanor from the

clutches of the Dodman," Cernunnos told him. "And you must tell no one. Darius will go with you."

"But . . . I can't lie to Mum. She always knows."

The centaur appeared at Cernunnos's shoulder.

"Then we must go now," Darius said simply, and reaching down, he caught hold of Ben and swung him up onto his back. Before Ben could utter a word of protest they were galloping away through the trees.

Mrs. Arnold watched them go with a puzzled expression on her face. Then she strode up to Cernunnos, looking very determined. "Where is Darius going with my son?"

Cernunnos turned to her. "I gather the Wanderer came after me and did not return," he said smoothly.

"I sent him, yes." Isadora frowned. "He really should have been back by now."

"I am sure they will find him and bring him back shortly. But in the meantime, I must ask you: Did you bring the Book of Naming with you?"

She nodded. "Of course."

"Excellent!" The Lord of the Wildwood's eyes gleamed. "Then we have him! We can Name our army at our will. The dinosaurs and dragons will have him out of Corbenic in no time. We shall drag him in chains across Eidolon, make an example of him before all the doubters. We shall extinguish the lives of those who have taken his side. We can show no mercy, or they will think us weak—"

"Cernunnos, stop." The Queen's face was pale, but her eyes were aflame with green fire. "We shall do no such thing. There has been too much coercion and violence in this world since I have been away, and I cannot condone more wickedness!"

"Wickedness?" Shadows passed across the stag-headed man's face like storm clouds. "Wickedness?" His voice began to boom so that his antlers rattled and shook. "The wickedness in your kingdom comes from the Dodman. He has been stealing your folk, selling them, killing them, torturing them, taking their magic from them. We need to Name our allies and make a stand."

"I will not compel anyone to our cause."

Cernunnos stared at her in disbelief. "But you have the Book of Naming," he pointed out slowly, as if to someone rather stupid. "You can summon them and then use your magic to compel them to your will. It's what the Dodman has been doing with the magic he's managed to extract from your hapless subjects!"

"The Book is an ancient volume that records and honors the true names of our folk," Isadora said gently. "It is not a tool for war and I will not use it as such. I will not misuse the magic of Eidolon as my enemy has done: it would make me as bad as he, and then to whom would the good folk of Eidolon look for guidance? No, we must persuade them to join our cause freely. It will require their courage and a difficult choice that they must make for themselves. I have been away too long to expect to command their loyalty."

"Persuade? That will take time—too much time!"

"Then we had better make a start," the Queen said softly, laying a gentling hand on his arm. "I will call them by their true names, but I will not compel them, do you understand me?"

The Lord of the Wildwood held her gaze for several long, defiant moments. Then he sighed. "You are our Queen, despite all the years that you have been away."

Together they crossed the sward to the suitcase and Isadora brought out the battered old leather-bound volume and opened it up. Where in the Other World its pages had seemed to a casual glance empty and unmarked, here they swirled into colorful life, offering a glorious confusion of pictures and script. Here, there was listed the true name of every one of Eidolon's creatures. The names came mysteriously into existence as soon as each new life came into the world; and faded just as mysteriously when a life was snuffed out. There were a lot of blank spaces among the pages now, far more than there should have been from natural causes.

Isadora had begun to turn the pages back, past "Dragons and Dinosaurs" toward "Sprites, Sylphs, and Small People," when the heading "Humans, Witches, Trolls, and Elvenfolk" stopped her in her tracks. There, in splendid living color, were tiny portraits of herself, her wicked brother, Awful Cousin Cynthia, and Ellie, Ben, and Alice.

The Lord of the Wildwood peered over the Queen's shoulder. He scanned the book curiously. Then his features sharpened. "I wonder . . . ," he said.

He took the Book from her and riffled through the leaves. Then he frowned and started his search again.

"That's strange . . ."

"What are you looking for?"

Cernunnos flicked another page open. "He must be here somewhere," he muttered.

The Queen smiled tiredly. "Did you really think I hadn't thought of that?" she said. "Searching for the Dodman's true name was the first thing I did. He's not in there."

"But that's impossible."

"Apparently not."

"But all the creatures of Eidolon are in the Book."

"Apart from him. Odd, isn't it? It's puzzled me for a long time."

The Lord of the Wildwood sighed. "It seems there are no easy solutions to our dilemma. We'd better make a start with our summons of the small creatures, then. Their movements will be less evident for the Dodman's spies to detect, and we can better shelter them here until we are ready to move against him."

Chapter Thirteen

Spies

"And you say the Dodman has captured the Princess Eleanor?"

"Yesss, mistressss. He holds her in the dungeonsss at the cassstle."

"Excellent! I shall be Queen soon enough at this rate. The Dodman will kill Ellie, and Isadora will die in the war that must soon come, and then I shall claim the throne."

The creature who in the Other World was known to Ben and Ellie as Awful Cousin Cynthia cackled gleefully and, making a fist, thrust one clawed hand into the air in a gesture of triumph.

"And what about Ben and the Baby Alisssse?"

"Ah, Ben. I have plans for Ben," Cynthia declared cheerfully. "And even a scrawny creature like you could probably deal with a baby."

The Sphynx had no hackles, for it had no fur, but the little ridges of loose skin around its neck flexed in irritation at this remark. If it had had whiskers, they would have bristled.

"Besides," Cynthia went on breezily, "no one would accept a baby as a queen; I've read my history books. They'd appoint a regent, or a regentess— someone to take care of the land while the little beast grew up. If it ever did." She held a hand out in front of her and admired it, though it was hard to see what there was to admire, for it was covered in scales and ended in long, horny claws the color of a fresh bruise.

In fact, it would have been hard for Ben and Ellie to recognize their cousin, for a strange and terrible transformation had taken place as soon as she'd crossed between worlds. Here, she was hunchbacked and spiky-nosed—as spiteful-looking on the outside as they knew her to be on the inside. Only her shock of orange hair remained the same; that, and her pale green gooseberry eyes, mean elbows, and her delight in tormenting things smaller and more vulnerable than herself. At the moment she was sitting on a log, holding a small greenish gray fairy, which was mewing as pathetically as a newborn kitten. The Sphynx regarded the fairy with interest. It hoped that when Cynthia had finished with the fairy, it might make a tasty snack. It watched curiously as Cynthia did something that was followed by a soft ripping sound. The fairy screamed. Cynthia examined the tiny, transparent wings thoughtfully, holding them up to the weak wintry sun.

"Hmmm," she said. "These would make great earrings."

She cast the damaged fairy down roughly, where it fell among a knot of three or four others in a similar condition. They made a space for it, and one of the larger ones put its arms around it to offer whatever comfort can be offered to a creature that can no longer do the thing it was born to do: fly joyously through the Wildwood like the very embodiment of magic.

The Sphynx stalked over to the group and assessed them with its angled amber eyes. It did not think it could eat them all at once, but it probably wouldn't have to seek food for another two days.

Cynthia grabbed its ratlike tail. "Go and get me some more," she demanded. "No, wait. I'm bored with fairies. What about a baby dragon? The hide would make a fabulous handbag!"

The Sphynx gave her a flat stare. Taking its time, it stretched out its front legs, then its back legs, then arched its back into a tight parabola. "I think not, mistressss. Even the babies are dangerousss; and their parentssss are edgy already. They know the Queen isss here, and they await developmentsssss, very alert, very watchful. What about a nice sprite, or a pretty little sylph?"

Cynthia clapped her hands together. "A wood-sylph! A wood-sylph! Yes, yes, yes! I can pull its hair out and braid it into golden chains."

Muttering darkly to itself, the Sphynx cast a last lingering, mournful look at the discarded fairies and stalked off into the undergrowth. Sylphs came in all sorts of sizes and could be tricky to catch. Also, the bigger ones tended to keep the little ones hidden away. But it knew where it could find some, left defenseless by the depredations of another of Eidolon's monsters. *Oh yesss*, it knew.

"It isss not right, it isss not fair, that she should treat me so. I who am the descendant of kingsss," the Sphynx growled to itself as it trod the fallen leaves of the Wildwood. It gnashed its sharp little teeth in frustration. "But I will have my due one day, when she isss Queen. Then I shall have my pick of all the lovely fairiesss, and the little mermaids, and the sprites, too. I shall have a troop of banshees to scare them out of the trees and into my clawsss! I shall eat only the tastiest pieces, and throw the rest away for the goblinsss to squabble over."

It could imagine this fine future now, without much effort. There would be a bed of red velvet close—but not too close—to the fire in the great hall, and the Gabriel Hounds would be kept chained safely out of the way in the courtyard. Unless it could persuade Cynthia to have them put to death . . .

But just how might one kill the ghost-dogs? If they were ghosts, then by definition they were already dead, and it is hard to kill something that is already dead.

And then there was the Dodman, too.

Maybe she will kill him, too, it thought, suddenly hopeful.

It paused in midstep.

"Yesss, once she hasss claimed the throne, she will not need him anymore."

Its eyes closed in pleasure. It was still purring to itself at this delightful thought when something grabbed it hard by the scruff of the neck, quite without warning, and swung it up into the air.

"And who is this miscreant?"

Darius turned to dangle the kicking captive in front of Ben's nose.

Ben stared at it. "That's the Sphynx," he said. "I doubt it's up to any good."

The hairless beast turned its cold yellow gaze upon him. "Good is for losersss," it hissed, twisting suddenly in the centaur's grip.

But Darius was too quick and too ready for it. "Oh, no you don't, little spy," he told it, clutching its scrawny body even more fiercely. "I've heard too many tales of the poor creatures you've caught and killed in our Wildwood."

Ben regarded the Sphynx with loathing. "What shall we do with it?"

"Turn it over to Cernunnos," the centaur said grimly.

At this, the spy cringed. Its mouth trembled. "Don't do that," it wheedled. "He'll crush me between his hard hands like an egg. He's cruel, the Horned One: cruel and pitiless."

"The Lord of the Wildwood is ever fair," Darius returned. "But I grant he will not look kindly on one who has pitilessly hurt and betrayed his folk."

"I was made to do it!" the Sphynx cried. "There is never any peace from either of them and their endless demands—"

It stopped in a rush, its eyes darting here and there in panic, realizing it had said more than it should.

"Them? Who do you mean by 'them'?" Darius cried.

"Well, Awful Cousin Cynthia, for one," Ben said. "It's her cat, after all. As for the other, well, I bet it's spying for the Dodman, too. I'd bet it knows plenty about what goes on at the castle."

He slipped from the centaur's broad back and came around to give the hairless cat a hard stare.

"What about my sister Ellie?" he asked furiously. "Have you seen her?"

"Oh, yessss. I've seen her."

"Where is she? Do you know where the Dodman has taken her?"

But the Sphynx's gaze became unreadable, flat-lidded. "I know many thingsss," it said cryptically. It paused, then winked unpleasantly. "I know, for example, what has become of your friend, the Wanderer. . . ."

"Iggy?" Ben was horrified. "What do you mean, 'what has become' of him?"

"Make the horse-boy let me go," the Sphynx teased, "and I'll tell you what I know."

But Darius shook the captive hard. "Tell us what you know now or I will break your scrawny neck myself!"

Ben turned anguished eyes upon the centaur. "Has something happened to Iggy?" There had been no sign of his friend in the woodland clearing where the mermaid had taken them down the stream and the waterfall to find his mother, but he hadn't thought anything of it at the time.

Darius looked uncomfortable. "Your mother sent him off after Cernunnos to find out who it was the Wild Hunt were pursuing. He never returned."

Ben felt as if his heart might stop. This news was even harder to bear than that of his sister's capture, for the Dodman would surely never kill Ellie, whereas anything might have happened to the little black-and-brown cat who, despite all his apparent toughness and absurd gravelly voice, really was quite hopeless when left to his own devices.

"Is he hurt?" he asked the Sphynx desperately.

The Sphynx gave him an evil grin. "Oh, he's probably more than hurt by now."

And that, no matter how much Darius threatened the hairless cat, or how much Ben cajoled it, was all the Sphynx would say.

Ben walked off to one side to think. He sat down. He closed his eyes. But nothing came to him. It was as if someone had spring-cleaned his brain and left it all shiny and tidy inside, but completely useless.

"Oh, Iggy," he whispered to himself. "What if I never see you again, my friend? Oh, Ignatius—" He clapped his hands over his mouth and leapt up. "Hold your hands tight over the Sphynx's ears!" he told the centaur urgently. "Make sure it can't hear anything."

Looking puzzled, Darius did as he was asked.

Ben took a deep breath, then called into the chilly air:

"Ignatius Sorvo Coromandel—if you can hear me, come to me now!"

It was Iggy's true name, and as such gave Ben the power to summon him three times, wherever he might be in this world or the next.

The shout echoed off the wintry trees and evaporated into the cold afternoon sky just like the vapor of Ben's breath. The centaur raised his head as if listening. They waited. And waited.

After a little while Darius shifted his grip on the Sphynx, which twitched its ears and stared at each of them suspiciously.

But nothing happened. Nothing at all.

Ignatius Sorvo Coromandel!

It came as if from a great distance—a thought more than a sound; like something in a dream; or an irritation at the back of the skull, like an itch he could not scratch.

Iggy had experienced this sensation before. Then, he had been chilling out on the shores of the Western Sea, watching the sun go down with a very pretty six-toed Jamaican Cat it had taken him three days' solid work to get close to; and he had not been at all pleased to hear the summons, which had dragged him halfway across Eidolon, through countless wild roads, a number of very scratchy bushes, across a wide moat (and everyone knew how much cats hated even a drop of water, let alone a whole lake of the stuff), past the snapping jaws of the Gabriel Hounds, and right into the clutches of the Dodman. And if that had not been bad enough, worse humiliation had followed.

Being flown through the air in a frilly bonnet drawn by a dozen struggling wood-sprites—all complaining about just how much some animals must eat in order to get to be so terribly heavy—had not been his finest hour. It made him blush (underneath his fur) even to think of it.

But right now, trapped in a clay pot in the larder of a very large, very ugly, and very hungry troll, he had never been so happy to hear a summons in his life. The problem was, he couldn't seem to do anything about it. The lid was heavy and firmly attached, and no amount of rolling around or kicking out would get the jar to topple over. He knew: He'd been trying for hours.

But it gave him new hope that someone, some-where in one of the worlds, cared enough about him to call him by his true name. He thought it was Ben, though the voice was muffled and distant. But then the significance of this struck him, and he thought, *If Ben is calling me, he must be in trouble!*

This gave him the energy to kick harder again at the inside of the pot, but still it did not budge an inch.

Iggy sat back down, panting with the effort. He could not help himself, and he could not help his friend. He was truly a sorry excuse for a cat. He sat, head down, contemplating his feet in the darkness, and listened to the sound of his heartbeat echoing off the heavy clay walls of his prison, imagining the sort of dishes a troll might make out of him—like Cat-in-the-Hole or Moggy Meatballs or Kitten Nuggets, or even simply Fillet of Feline and Frog Fries—until a thought penetrated the thick clouds of self-pity swirling around his brain.

"Idiot!" he proclaimed himself. "Iggy, you're an idiot!"

He wasn't the first to have made this observation, not by a long shot. There had been his father—Polo Horatio Coromandel—on several occasions, and his tutor Henry "the Navigator" Longshanks, who'd tried to teach him the finer points of stargazing (in which he had failed miserably); and countless others before and since. He'd begun to think they'd been right all along, but perhaps now was the time to prove them wrong.

He took a deep, deep breath, closed his eyes, and yowled as hard as he could: "*BENJAMIN CHRISTOPHER ARNOLD!*"

Chapter Fourteen

The Troll

Ben was so surprised he almost fell over.

"Did you hear that?" he asked the centaur.

Darius frowned. "Hear what?"

But Ben was already running, as if dragged by an invisible rope.

"Hey!" the Horse Lord shouted. "Wait for me!" And he gathered up his heels and galloped after the fast-disappearing boy, with the Sphynx yowling loudly in his fist.

Ben had not known he could run so fast. In fact, he wasn't entirely sure this sort of running had much to do with him at all. If he'd been able to run like this in the Other World, he'd have been a bit of a sports star at school, which he most definitely was not. But despite the exhilaration of being able to move so fast, it was a bit difficult keeping your eyes open for obstacles. Tree roots kept trying to trip him up, and rabbit holes—or holes where something rather larger than rabbits (he didn't like to imagine what) lived—kept trying to swallow his feet. After a few minutes of the relentless concentration it was taking to stay upright and without a broken neck, he was both breathless and exhausted. He had a stitch in one side under his ribs and his muscles were complaining at being used for exercise they weren't accustomed to. He wanted to stop—or at least slow down—but something wouldn't let him. It was not just the insistent voice reverberating around his head, calling his name over and over again, like a distant echo of the summons—but a physical sensation too, as if someone else entirely now had charge of his body.

And now ahead of him there loomed a considerable obstacle: a dense expanse of bramble and thorn. But even though he could see it coming at him, he didn't seem to be able to avoid it or even slow down.

"Darius!" he cried. "Help!"

He couldn't even turn his head, let alone diverge from his course. The thicket loomed up at him, spiky and destructive, without showing any sign of a gap or pathway into which he could dive. Some of the thorns were an inch long or more, some were covered with snagged swatches of wool or fur, and he could have sworn some were stained an ominous red. He closed his eyes, even though the thin film of his lids felt like scant protection, and waited for the impact.

The next thing he knew, there was a drumming of hooves behind him, a shout of warning, and then a strong arm encircled his waist and whisked him off his feet, and Ben found himself sitting astride the centaur's broad back once more. He breathed a huge sigh of relief.

"Thanks!"

"Here," said the Horse Lord, veering to a halt alongside the thicket. He thrust the Sphynx at Ben. "Take this creature and hold it tight. Keep one hand firm on the scruff of its neck and it should stop struggling so much. It's a cat thing: a reflex from the days when they were kittens and their mother picked them up like that."

It was hard to believe the Sphynx had ever been a

kitten, Ben thought. It looked as if it had come into the world as ugly as Yoda and as evil as it was now. He held it hard under one arm, with his fist clutched in the loose skin of its neck, and although it gave him a gaze that was full of hatred, it didn't seem to be able to bite him or do anything worse.

"Now, why on Eidolon did you take off like that?"

"Iggy called me. It's some sort of magical summons. It's still pulling at me now." Even so, he dug his free hand into Darius's mane in case he was suddenly dragged off.

The centaur nodded knowingly. "Ah," he said. "That explains that, then." He paused. "You told him your true name?"

Ben nodded.

"That was unwise. You should never give out your true name except to those you would trust with your life."

"I do trust Iggy with my life!" Ben returned hotly.

"Even so," the centaur said, "it is dangerous to give another such power over you: Imagine what the Dodman would do with such knowledge."

Ben shivered. "I'm *never* giving *him* my true name," he said.

"He will know it sssoon, anyway," the Sphynx hissed. "And then you will be at his mercy." It laughed—a high, thin sound more like the cry of a creature in pain than an expression of mirth. "Not that he has any!"

"What do you mean?"

But the hairless cat merely blinked enigmatically.

Ben gave it a hard stare, then transferred his gaze to the Horse Lord. "Darius, we must rescue Iggy."

"What about your sister? That was the task Cernunnos charged us with, not haring around trying to find your scatterbrained friend."

"I know," Ben said through gritted teeth. "But I won't be able to do anything until I've fulfilled the summons. As soon as I'm on the ground again, I'll be racing off into that thicket. It's hard enough staying on your back as it is: It's like getting pulled by a huge magnet."

"Magnet?" The centaur furrowed his brow.

"Don't you know about magnetic forces?" Ben asked, amazed.

Darius shook his head.

"Well . . ." Ben scoured his memory for what they had been taught at school about the scientific principle of attraction and repulsion, but all he could remember with any real clarity was how he and Adam had dropped their magnets into a big barrel of iron filings so that they came out like giant furry caterpillars. "Well, never mind about that," he said quickly. "Apart from anything else, Iggy is my friend and I won't rest until I've found him. Then we can go and help Ellie."

The centaur sighed. The will of these humans from the Other World was strong. But perhaps it was just such strength and loyalty that was required to combat the forces that stood against Eidolon. "All right, then, but if your friend is somewhere beyond this thicket then we have a bit of a problem."

"What sort of problem?"

Darius sighed again. "You'll see soon enough."

And he did. The centaur took a roundabout route that skirted the thicket between the slender trunks of a birch wood, then tracked in among a series of outcrops that ended in a cliff in which a large cave stood like a great black mouth. Bones were scattered all around the entrance to the cave—bones and feathers and bits of fur.

Aghast, Ben scanned the area for the unwanted sight of any chunks of black-and-brown fur, but there was none to be seen. There was, however, an awful smell and a cloud of vapor, amidst which a large dark shape could be discerned, bending over a steaming pot.

Darius came to a silent halt. Ben opened his mouth to say something, then suddenly found himself pulled from the centaur's back by an unseen force, and his feet took him straight toward the misty shape.

"Ben, no!"

Ben heard the whispered warning, but there was nothing he could do about it. Within seconds he had entered the foul-smelling cloud of steam. The Sphynx wriggled desperately beneath his arm, but he held on to it.

"Adder's fork and blind-worm's sting," a loud voice boomed out, and a huge shadowy figure threw something into a huge cauldron, which made it bubble and froth in a most disturbing way. The figure prodded them down with a long ladle, then squinted at the list in its hand. "What's this? Lizard's leg and howlet's wing. Howlet? Those witches have the most atrocious handwriting. Must mean owlet, baby owl. I'm sure I've got one somewhere. . . ."

It bustled off toward the cave.

Ben watched the thing move away, with the hair on the back of his neck standing on end. Whatever was it? It was huge! But he couldn't even turn around to look at it, for no matter what he wanted to do, his eyes were drawn to the cauldron. He stared at it in horror. Surely Iggy couldn't be in there? But the compulsion was drawing him toward the bubbling pot. With his heart in his mouth, he approached it. But the summons carried him past the cauldron to an area where a pile of utensils and jars had been piled in a higgledy-piggledy fashion. He found himself reaching out to a particularly large jar. . . .

"Hello, what have we here? A visitor? And a complete oddity at that. Can't say I've ever seen anything like you before. Though, come to think of it, you do have a look of Grizelda to you. She's much prettier than you are, though. . . ."

The thing stepped into his field of vision.

Ben stared at it openmouthed. He had never seen anything like it. For a start, it had noxious green skin, a ridiculous quiff of purple hair, and it was even taller than the Dodman.

"Don't worry, laddie. I haven't turned cannibal." It paused, then leered at him. "Yet."

"Cannibal? But I'm not . . ." He faltered, not knowing what it was.

"A troll?" The thing roared with laughter. "Well, we may not look much alike, laddie, but believe me, we're kissing cousins."

Ben screwed his face up in disgust. He didn't much like kissing anyone, and he certainly didn't fancy kissing a troll. Still, it was a relief that it wasn't going to eat him. He watched in trepidation as it reached over and dropped whatever it had in its hand into the bubble and froth of the giant pot.

"Scale of dragon, tooth of wolf. Yes, yes, that's excellent. Now, then, where's the main ingredient?"

The troll turned and lifted the lid off the big jar and withdrew something small and dark and kicking.

"Ben! Help me!"

Ben's mouth fell open in shock. Then: "Iggy!" he gasped.

"Oh, goodie," said the troll, "you know its name. That'll put a bit of power in the casserole." He bent and picked up a big, sharp knife. "Now, then, you hold it down and I'll skin it. Can't abide the fur, though it's a mucky task having to get it off."

"No!" cried Ben. "No, you can't. He's my friend."

"Friend?" The troll wrinkled its big knobbly brow. "What's that, then, a 'friend'?"

Ben had to think about that one. At last he said, "Someone you spend time with, and laugh and have fun with."

Still the troll looked puzzled.

"Someone you care about, and who cares about you?"

"Nope, no one I can think of," it said. It thought for a moment. Did Grizelda count? It shook its head rather sadly. Not really.

"Someone you'd count on to help you if you were in a spot of trouble—"

"Like now?" Iggy rasped. He eyed the knife in the troll's hand nervously. "*Now* would be a very good time."

From under Ben's arm there came a wheezing sound, like a squeezed bagpipe. "Hee hee hee."

A sudden thought struck Ben. He wasn't sure it was very ethical, but friendship was friendship. . . . "Tell you what," he said to the troll, "I'll do you a swap. I'll trade you this cat here for that rather furry one." He dangled the Sphynx in front of the monster.

The Sphynx wriggled and spat and tried to rake

Ben with its claws, but he held on tight.

Meanwhile, the troll peered at it dubiously. "Are you sure that's a cat?" it asked. "It looks more like a rat to me—a big rat, but a rat all the same."

"Oh yes," said Ben triumphantly. "It's a hairless cat. You won't even need to skin it: It's a ready-meal!"

The troll stuck the skinning knife back into the wood block and held out its hand to Ben. Ben stared at the hand cautiously. It was massive and hairy and green and scaly, and the nails were all black and broken. He wondered what you might catch from a troll. . . .

"Well, come on, then," the troll said impatiently. "Shake on the bargain. Don't they teach you any manners where you come from?"

Tentatively, Ben extended his free hand and watched as it was engulfed by the troll's massive mitt. The troll shook his hand so hard that Ben's feet came off the ground and he nearly fell over. The next thing he knew, the Sphynx was in the troll's grasp and every single one of Iggy's claws was digging into the skin of Ben's chest and arm. Then the little black-and-brown cat burrowed his head under Ben's armpit and trembled all over.

"It's all right, Iggy," Ben reassured him over and over, and at last Iggy withdrew his head and stared up at him with huge amber eyes. Then he braced himself.

"Thank you, Ben," he growled. "Of course I had my own plan of escape. But"—he gazed at the struggling Sphynx as the troll poised it over the bubbling pot—"I like yours a lot better! That was a clever move!"

Ben blushed, partly with happiness, and partly with embarrassment—it hadn't really been a plan, as such. Besides, he couldn't help but feel bad for the Sphynx. Although it was such a horrid little sneaking beast, it was still a living creature and did not deserve to die in a troll's vile stew.

But even as he walked back toward the watching centaur, a shriek split the air.

"*Cynthia Lucrezia Creepie!*"

In the direst of straits, the Sphynx had summoned its mistress.

Darius hauled Ben onto his back. "I do not think we want to stay around here to find out what happens next, do you?" he asked, indicating a small dark shape in the sky above them. Something up there was circling, and beginning to dive. Before either Ben or Iggy could answer, Darius broke into a swift canter that took them on a zigzag path between the slender silver birches away from the troll's den.

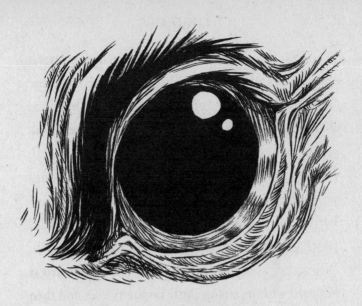

Chapter Fifteen

Ellie

In the confines of the stinking, windowless cell it was impossible to tell whether it was day or night. Ellie sat on the hard bed with her hands clasped together so tightly her knuckles hurt. She was shaking all over, for fear of the dark shadows and what might be hiding in them. If she moved, they would know she was there. So she sat still as a stone, trying not to cry: It wouldn't do to give Old Dogbreath that satisfaction.

Acorn the sprite clung to the edge of the bucket that the Dodman had so sarcastically referred to as her "en suite bathroom." For a time his pale red light had illuminated details she really didn't want to think about, let alone see. He hadn't been very talkative. In fact, after the Dodman had thrown him into the dungeon after her, he'd barely said a word, as if he blamed her for his woeful fate. The only thing he had said, which had not been exactly cheering, was, "Deep cells. Where they keep the dangerous ones." It had looked at her hard with its strange little raspberry eyes and then asked, "Are you dangerous?" And when Ellie had shaken her head and said no, not really, the sprite had nodded solemnly, then taken up its current stance, well out of reach, as if it did not really believe her.

After a while the sprite's light began to fade, plunging them into total darkness.

"Oh!" cried Ellie. "Oh, don't go out!"

"Not going anywhere," came back the tiny, scratchy voice. "Imprisoned here. Just like you." It paused. "*Because* of you," it added rather belligerently.

"No, I mean, put the light back on!"

Nothing happened.

Ellie was horrified. "Now!"

There was no change, except for a quiet rustling in the darkness, as if the sprite had folded its arms in annoyance.

Ellie stamped her feet. "Acorn, as Princess of Eidolon, I command you to turn your light back on right now!"

If anything, the cell got darker.

Ellie sat there, furious, for some minutes, waiting—but there was no change in the unrelieved blackness.

"Please," Ellie wheedled at last. She wasn't normally polite when she wanted something, but it didn't seem as if the sprite would react well to her usual tactic of throwing a tantrum. And she really, really didn't like the dark. "Oh, *please*, Acorn, just a little light."

Seconds later a faint greenish light pulsed out of the sprite, casting long, thin shadows across the floor.

"Thank you," Ellie said stiffly.

"Your family are trouble," Acorn said after a time. "Your mother abandoned us. Your brother got captured and had to be rescued. Now you, too."

Ellie frowned. "But Ben did save your cousin Twig."

"Only after your uncle stole him from Eidolon."

That was entirely true, but even so. "You can't hold

that against me!" she cried. "Ben and I call him Awful Uncle Aleister. We hate him, and what he did was terrible! Dad told the police and they arrested him, and now he's in prison!"

Acorn's eyes whirled and glowed as if he were digesting this indecipherable information. Then he said, "Your cousin, the witch, Cynthia: Her cat killed my brother."

Ellie had never heard Cynthia called a witch before, but now that she thought about it, her cousin *was* rather witchy, with her spiky nose and her carrot hair and her mean green eyes. She felt ashamed of the time she had spent with her, making jewelry out of the strange bits of fur and skin and feathers Cynthia had told her were "offcuts" from her father's import business, and then selling them at school. Because now she understood exactly where those "offcuts" had come from.

"I'm sorry about your brother," she said. "That's dreadful. Cynthia's cat is an absolute monster."

"Is evil spy," Acorn agreed. "Sneak around for the Dodman, watching, always watching. No one is safe when the Sphynx is around. If it doesn't eat you, it hides and listens and carries tales to its master. Dodman learns who is causing trouble, who is still

504

loyal to the Queen. And then the goblins come with their nets and sticks, beat and kill. Nasty creatures, have no loyalty to anything but their stomachs."

Ellie was shocked. When she'd thought about her mother being the Queen of a magical other world, this kind of brutality and terror had never crossed her mind at all.

"We must get out of here! I can't have Mum giving herself up to the Dodman to save me; she's got to stop all this!"

"What can she do?" the sprite said gloomily. "She away too long. No one believes in her anymore."

"She will take Eidolon back from the Dodman!" Ellie said furiously. "She *will* banish him to the Other World so that he's no more than pathetic Mr. Dodds, failed pet shop owner!"

Acorn's thin, wheezy laugh was not one of delight, but of disbelief. "Everyone is afraid of the Dodman and his monsters. They have lost hope for future. Cannot believe Queen will ever save them."

"But they *must* believe, or it will never stop. It'll just get worse and worse and the Dodman will be able to do anything he wants!"

"He already does."

"Well, I'm not going to let him. We're going to escape from here, you and I. Old Dogbreath isn't going to use *me* as a hostage!" And with that, Ellie marched over to the bucket and grabbed Acorn up. At once his green light turned a wild pink that flared out across the cell.

"Put me down!"

But Ellie was having none of it. Using the sprite as a torch, she examined every inch of the prison's walls, every chink between the massive stones, every bit of loose mortar, every crack and cranny and crevice. She was just working her way around to the last corner of the cell, when the sprite coughed and recoiled.

"*Woo!* What a stink!"

And just as he said this, Ellie smelled it too. It was hot and musky and very, very strong. She wrinkled her nose, and sneezed and sneezed and sneezed. The smell seemed to be coming from a narrow gap between the stonework at the top of the wall. Standing on the bed, Ellie peered into the crack, holding Acorn out in front of her to illuminate her search, her heart beating wildly. She had *known* there was something hiding in the dark: She could sense it lurking, breathing, waiting. . . .

At first she could see nothing; then something on the other side of the crack gleamed. She squinted, but her sight was poor at the best of times in Eidolon. She moved closer so that her nose was almost in the hole. The pink light from the wood-sprite flooded the dark space. And then the thing that was gleaming *blinked*.

It was a very large, very dark eye.

Ellie shrieked.

On the other side of the wall there came the sound of a profound sigh. Then she heard, "What did I do? All I did was blink. I didn't roar, I didn't paw the ground, I didn't chase. I just blinked. Just a little twitch of the eye and already she's screaming. Women: I'll never understand them."

Whatever it was, it sounded pretty miserable. Curiosity overcoming fear, Ellie applied her eye and the sprite to the hole again. "Hello," she said bravely, for there was a thick wall between her and the speaker. "Who are you?"

In the darkness beyond there was a heavy silence, as if the occupant of the next cell were thinking very hard indeed. Then a deep voice rumbled out. "Well, I could tell you I was a handsome hero, locked away by the Dodman and left to rot, but what would be the point in lying? You're in there and I'm in here and even if you want to run away from me you can't." It took a deep breath. "I'm the Minotaur," it admitted.

Ellie frowned. The name rang a distant bell in her head but she couldn't quite remember why. Something about an evil king who sent girls and boys into a labyrinth that they couldn't find their way out of, and something awful that lived at the heart of the maze. . . . What sort of awful thing was it, though? What had made it so terrible? She gave up.

"Oh," she said. "Well, hello, Minotaur. My name's Ellie, and my mother's the Queen of Eidolon."

"You're a *princess*?" The Minotaur sounded disbelieving. "Well, if you say so. I am, myself, a prince, of sorts, if not of such elevated status as yourself. Princess of Eidolon, indeed." It snorted.

It was a huge snort, the sort of snort a bull might make. A really big bull.

Acorn shielded her from the worst of the blast, which was just as well. "*Eeeeewwww!* Get it off me, get it off!"

Ellie stared at the wood-sprite in disgust. It had already been pretty ugly to start with, unless you had a thing for twiggy creatures with raspberry eyes. But

508

now it was covered from its head to its long, thin toes with thick green snot.

"Ugh!"

Ellie dropped the sprite without another second's thought, and wiped her hands instinctively down her jeans. Acorn gave her a furious look, then picked himself stickily up off the floor, walked disjointedly over to the bucket, scrambled up it, and nose-dived into the stagnant water inside to take a long and noisy bath.

"Sorry," said the voice on the other side of the wall. "I must be allergic to something."

Ellie made a face. Pathetic. *However*, she thought to herself, *whatever a Minotaur is, if it's in these cells, it must be the Dodman's enemy, and so by definition it must be my friend. However scary, or snotty, it may be.* She braced herself.

"So, why are you in here?" she asked boldly.

"The Dodman tried to make me work for him. But I bow to no man, and especially not to one with the head of a mangy hound." He paused. "Besides, he does not know my true name, and so cannot compel me. He captured me when I was being rather less vigilant than I should have been and tried to persuade me to his cause. He used the dogs on me after I killed a dozen of his goblins. Ghost-dogs are frustratingly hard to harm. He will go after the dinosaurs next. They may be more cooperative, being considerably more stupid than I."

"What did he want you to do?"

"Why, to fight for him, to destroy the creatures who would take the Queen's side."

"Are you very big and scary, then?" Ellie asked with a gulp.

"You could say that. Many are scared of me." There was a pause. "Though, really, there's little need. The stories about me are much worse than the truth."

"Stories?" Now she was interested. "What sort of stories?"

"If you haven't heard them, why should I tell you?"

There came a cackle from her own cell. "Are you all so ignorant in the Other World?"

Ellie whirled around. All of the sprite's sharp little teeth were showing in a not-very-friendly grin. He was laughing at her. She gave him a hard stare. "Why on earth should I know what it is?"

"Here, he is very famous," Acorn said. "A legend in his own lifetime."

Despite herself, Ellie was impressed. "Famous for what?"

"Eating folk." The sprite's little eyes were bright with malice. "Especially youngsters."

Ellie felt a chill run down her spine. "Do you?" she asked the chink between the stones, trying to keep the shake out of her voice.

"I'm not particularly proud of the fact," the creature in the other cell replied quietly. "And I wouldn't say I liked it much. Really I prefer a good patch of grass. Or some hay. Daisies, too. And meadowbells."

Ellie didn't know what meadowbells were, but—daisies? She frowned. "What are you, a cow or something?" Though she couldn't quite imagine a cow eating anyone.

"*Hmmph!*" The Minotaur snorted in affront and the sound thrummed through Ellie's bones. "A cow indeed!" He paused. "What is a cow, anyway?"

"Even babies in our world know what cows are," Ellie said contemptuously. "They're big four-legged animals that stand around in fields, and chew grass and make milk and stuff."

The Minotaur was none the wiser, so he said nothing. Curious now, Ellie looked through the crack

511

again, but this time all she could see was the merest slick of light from the shiny surface of a huge eyeball.

"I only have two legs," he said after a while. "You, on the other hand, from what I can see, don't look much like a princess of Eidolon. Apart from anything else, your eyes aren't green."

"I can't help that!" Ellie said crossly. "I'm the oldest of the three of us. Ben's got one green eye and one brown, but Baby Alice has the same green eyes as Mum."

On the other side of the wall there was a pause. Then the Minotaur said, "Three of you. That's interesting. And, may I ask, were you born in Eidolon?"

"Of course not! I was born in Bixbury General Hospital."

"I have not heard of this place."

"Bixbury, in Oxfordshire, England."

A puzzled silence.

Ellie rolled her eyes. "The United Kingdom, Europe. Planet Earth."

"The Other World?"

Ellie thought about this. "I suppose so," she said dubiously.

From the other cell there came a great sigh. "Three

children from two worlds! Perhaps you are the children of the prophecy."

"I don't know about any prophecy," said Ellie.

"It's known only to the older ones of Eidolon, and no one has ever really given it much credence. Really, it's more of a nonsense poem, a nursery rhyme told to babes in arms."

"Well, what is it, then?" Ellie asked impatiently. "I think if I'm in it I have a right to know."

The Minotaur took a deep breath, and said:

> *"One plus one is two*
> *And those two shall make three*
> *Three children from two worlds*
> *Will keep Eidolon free—"*

On the other side of the wall, Ellie made a face. "It's a bit vague, isn't it? It could mean anything."

"If you hadn't interrupted me, I'd have told you the rest of it."

"Oh. Well, I hope it's better than what you've already told me."

"Do you know something?" the Minotaur said. "You're really very annoying. I'm beginning to wish I hadn't given up eating people after all. In fact, I might just take it up again. Once I'm out of here."

Ellie bit her lip. "Sorry. Do tell me the rest."

"The last of it goes:

> *Three children from two worlds*
> *Three to save the day*
> *One with beauty's spell to tame*
> *One bravely to bring flame*
> *And one with the power to name.*"

Now Ellie's eyebrows shot up. "'Beauty's spell to tame.' I rather like the sound of that," she said softly.

"I don't think you'll be saving anyone," came the sprite's scratchy voice. "Stuck in here." It paused. "Anyway, you're not very beautiful."

"What would an ugly little thing like you know about beauty?" Ellie said sharply. "I read all the best magazines, you know. *Clobber* and *Warpaint* and *Hi!* There's not a beauty tip in the world I don't know. How to spend three hours achieving the 'Natural Look.' How to make your skin go orange without any smudges. How to stuff chicken fillets in your bra for a better cleavage—"

The sprite looked at her even more dubiously. "Chicken fillets?"

Ellie waved her hands at it. "Oh, I can't be bothered to try to explain to such an . . . ignoramus!" She thought for a moment; then her eyes gleamed. "But I have a plan. And you, Acorn, are going to be the one who carries it out!"

Chapter Sixteen

The Book of Naming

"Speckle Graywing! Lily Spearwater! Gossamer Moonhorse!"

The Queen's voice rose high as a songbird's, and Baby Alice clapped her hands in glee. "Gossma!" she declared happily. "Gossma, Gossma Moohoss!"

Moments later three streaks of light burst out of the pale clouds above, circled once, twice, then plummeted toward the clearing like falling stars, resolving at last into three exhausted and not-very-happy-looking fairies.

"Why have you summoned us?" asked Speckle Graywing, his curls of blond hair in disarray, his pale cloak tattered as if from a sudden flight through brambles, or a flight from the clutches of some taloned predator. He gazed around in amazement at the crowd already assembled there—the sylphs and the nymphs, the dryads and the gnomes, the sprites and elves, the centaurs and cats. They were thronged around every tree, seated upon each fallen log and hummock of turf; while mermaids and selkies jostled for space in the confined waters of the woodland stream.

"Yes, who do you think you are to drag us away without warning or request?" This came from the second of the fairies, tall and thin, her bony features set in a feral snarl.

"Oh, do stop moaning, Gossamer," said the third fairy. "See, it is Cernunnos himself who has called us."

"You need to clean out your ears, Lily. You must have got bees' nests in them!" Speckle declared furiously. "It was a woman's voice I heard."

"Bees don't make nests, stupid—," Lily Spearwater started.

The Lord of the Wildwood set down the Book of Naming he had been holding out for Isadora, put his hands on his hips, and yelled, "Be quiet, all three of you, and do obeisance to your Queen!"

"Queen? We have no Queen!" cried Speckle.

"Not since the last one deserted us," sneered Gossamer.

"Oh!" cried Lily Spearwater as her violet gaze settled at last on the small blond woman sitting on the log in the midst of the gathering, with a green-eyed baby in her lap. "Oh my! Oh my goodness, it is . . . it is Isadora of Corbenic, though"—her voice dropped to a whisper and she spoke behind her hand—"she looks so old and tired. . . ."

"There is no Corbenic anymore," Speckle said dismissively. "It's Dodman Castle now, and I can't see that changing anytime soon."

Isadora firmed her jaw. "It shall change," she said, and her voice rang out across the clearing. "It must. I will not see my country ruined by the Dodman and his ilk. But if it is to change, I will need your help—your help and the help of all the good folk of Eidolon."

Speckle folded his arms. "Why should we help you? You did not stay here to help us."

"Show some respect for your Queen!" the Lord of the Wildwood roared, advancing upon the belligerent fairy, who soared quickly out of his way and took roost upon the branch of a willow that wept over the water's edge.

"Cernunnos," Isadora said quietly, "what Speckle Graywing says is quite fair, and he has the right to an explanation, as do all my subjects who have answered my call." She looked up into the willow, where the two other fairies had joined Speckle. Then she looked around the clearing and raised her voice so that all might hear her words. "When I left Eidolon, I did not know that my absence would result in this cruelty and wickedness. I did not know that my folk would suffer as they have. I did not know that the Dodman would grow so powerful by diminishing the magic in my world." She hung her head. "I really did not know very much at all. I am sorry for my ignorance and I know how all of you have suffered. All I can say in my defense is that I left Eidolon for love, which is the best reason in any world."

At this, Baby Alice gurgled and cooed. "Mama, Daddy!" she said. "Ben, Ellie, Alice!" Alice's eyes now blazed an unearthly green. "The three!" she declared. "Save Eidolon."

Cernunnos's face went slack with astonishment, but after a few moments he recovered himself and said into the awed silence: "It may have seemed to many of us that Isadora left our world for so long that the magic of the Secret Country and its folk were left dangling over an abyss by the thinnest of threads, but while she was lost to us she brought three children into the Other World."

There was a murmur at this, then one of the dryads leaned out of her tree and asked, "*The* three? Do you mean the children of the prophecy?"

The murmurs grew in volume now as the older ones who were gathered there explained the meaning of this to those who had no idea what was being talked about, until Cernunnos waved his arms and called for quiet.

"It may be that they are indeed the children of the prophecy, the three who will weave the magic back into Eidolon and drive the Dodman and his kind back into the shadows whence they came. The three who will be our salvation." He dropped his eyes to Alice. "Of course," he added, "it may also be that it will take some time to win back our world from the clutches of those who are trying to destroy it, for as you can see,

Alice is very young indeed: too young yet to play any active part in the resistance against the Dodman."

At this, Baby Alice turned her luminous gaze upon the Horned Man. "Queen," she said, quite distinctly. "Me. Queen Alice." She reached out her chubby little hands and waved them in a wide, inclusive gesture that took in all the gathered souls. "Mine," she said.

Cernunnos laughed, rather nervously. "Well, Alice," he said, "we shall see about that in due course, I am sure."

"Now, now, dear," Mrs. Arnold said softly to her daughter, "let's not run before we can walk, hey?"

"Hay is for horses," said a white cat, one of a group of nine who were sitting by her feet.

The Queen laughed and reached down to her and stroked her head, and the white cat leaned her cheek into Isadora's palm. "Indeed it is, Jacaranda; and for hippogriffs and Minotaurs too, in a well-ordered world; and I hope Eidolon will be well ordered again soon, with your aid and the aid of all those gathered here."

"You will need more than a foolish old prophecy and a handful of fairies and tree-spirits and lesser beasts if you're to take on the Dodman and the monsters who will come to his call!" cried Speckle Graywing.

"Who are you calling a lesser beast, young man?" Jacaranda bristled fiercely, showing her hackles.

"Well, I can't quite see you taking on a Tyrannosaurus rex or a dragon, can you?" Speckle sneered. "One would rip your pretty white coat into shreds and the other would roast your skinny carcass and gobble you whole!"

"That's unkind," the Queen said sharply. "And I think you are doing Jacaranda a disservice. It is not always might that prevails in battle, but wit and courage, which the cats of Eidolon have in plenty."

"Even so," said Speckle, "you will need the greater beasts to join your cause if you are to challenge the Dodman, and I do not see even a single dragon here."

"Very true," said one of the female centaurs, pawing the ground with a neat hoof. "But that is because the Queen has not yet summoned them."

One of the gnomes shouted, "And then there's the trolls and the ogres, too!"

His companion elbowed him in the ribs. She looked exactly like him—leathery skin, long white hair, twinkly blue eyes, and hooked nose—except that she had no beard. "Do pipe down, Grot!" She stepped out of the ring of gnomes and addressed the Queen boldly. "It's good to see the bravery and loyalty of the woodland folk," she said, acknowledging the crowd with a wave of her gnarled hand, "but I agree that we will not stand long against the Dodman without allies from farther afield. We may not want the help of such as the trolls and ogres, for they were ever undependable and dark of heart, but I do not think we will fare well without at least the support of the fire-drakes."

Cernunnos stepped before the Queen and bowed his head. "Perhaps now is the time to summon the chieftains of the dragon clans," he said, "if we are to strengthen the will of your people."

"Perhaps," sighed Isadora.

"Though it must be said," the Lord of the Wildwood added quietly, "that dragons are volatile and arrogant beasts and can be very difficult to handle, let alone control in a limited space. Are you sure you will not change your mind and compel them as you summon them?"

The Queen looked around the clearing at the small creatures gathered there, her green eyes full of anxiety. Then she shook her head.

"No," she said. "Their choice must be a free one."

She sat Baby Alice on the ground at her feet, picked up the Book of Naming and turned its pages to the one that bore the legend "Dragons and Dinosaurs."

Chapter Seventeen

Terror

A great silver moon rose over the battlements of Dodman Castle, casting long thin shadows across the stonework like fingers of darkness. A tall figure stood silhouetted against the pale disc upon those battlements. It flung its head back and an unearthly howl ripped through the falling night; and all who heard it felt a sudden chill shiver through their bones.

As if awoken by the cry, a flock of bats came tumbling out of the crannies in the castle's wall and fled out across the lake in a clatter of wings. Somewhere in the woods beyond the lake's shore an owl hooted and was answered by the call of something Ben could not identify but that made his skin creep and crawl as if a parade of ants had got under his clothes and were marching up and down his arms and legs.

"I must have miscalculated. We are too late!" Darius cried, gazing up at the castle in horror.

"What do you mean, 'too late'?" said Ben.

"We need to save her before the moon is full."

Ben frowned. "Why? I mean, I know we need to rescue Ellie as fast as possible, but why by full moon?"

The centaur said nothing. He lifted his head and gazed up into the sky. A moment later a veiling cloud slipped softly sideways, and as it did so Darius gasped. "Thank the heavens, it is not quite full, but it will surely be so before too long. We do not have much time."

Iggy burrowed his head under Ben's arm. "I hate this place," he growled fervently. "Please don't make me swim that lake again."

This all came out as something of a mumble, but Ben hugged him anyway. "We have to find Ellie," he reminded the little cat.

"If he lays a claw upon her"—Darius turned his

head to look at the boy on his back—"I swear I will break every bone in his loathsome body. I will stamp him underhoof. I will trample him till there is nothing left of him but bloody rags."

Ben had never heard the centaur so fierce. Darius's eyes flared briefly silver in the moonlight and all at once he looked nothing at all like the friendly companion with whom Ben had shared so much of his time in Eidolon, but more like a savage creature from another world.

"I didn't know you liked her so much," Ben said. "You've only just met her."

His hands, knotted in the coarse black mane, felt the sudden heat rising from the centaur's neck, and he realized with a start that Darius was blushing.

"But she is the Princess," the centaur started. "She is a Princess of Eidolon, daughter to Queen Isadora. I am pledged to her cause and I cannot fail her. I must not!" He paused. "But she is also very beautiful."

Ben laughed. "Gosh," he said, "you must have terrible eyesight!"

From under his arm there came a great purr of delight. "Who'd have thought it?" rasped Iggy in his best gravelly tones. "A centaur falling in love with a human girl?"

"I am not 'in love,'" Darius said stiffly. "And anyway, she is not a mere human. Be careful what you say, cat, or you will be swimming the lake sooner than you think." He let that thought hang in the darkening air, then added, "Besides, we cannot allow the Queen to give herself up to the Dodman."

"What?"

Darius groaned. "I am an idiot. Cernunnos would have my hide for such indiscretion."

"Darius, I don't know what you're talking about. What do you mean about Mum giving herself up to the Dodman?"

Iggy squirmed free of Ben's embrace and ran up the centaur's neck. There, he dug his claws in and growled, "Is the Queen in danger as well? You'd better tell us, now!"

Darius winced. Then he sighed and hung his head. "You have a right to know. A fairy—Nettle Blueflower—carried a message from the Dodman to the Lord of the Wildwood. He said that unless the Queen submitted herself to him before the moon was full, he would harm Eleanor. He said he would send her back piece by piece. . . ."

Ben felt those last words echoing around in his skull.

Piece by piece. He imagined what the Dodman meant by that, and felt abruptly sick. It was horrible. He knew that his mother would never allow such a thing to happen. He swallowed as another thought occurred to him. "But we could never trust the Dodman to let Ellie go, even if Mum did go to him!" he cried.

"I know." Darius nodded. "And that is why Cernunnos thought it best she did not know what was in the message."

"Then she doesn't even know that the Dodman holds Ellie prisoner?"

Darius shook his head.

"Dad will tell her!" Ben said fiercely.

"Your father is asleep. He will not wake up until he leaves the Lord of the Wildwood's realm."

Ben stared at him. He understood why the Lord of the Wildwood had done what he had done, but even so it seemed to him wrong in a way he could not fully explain. He felt tears prick his eyes.

"So it's down to us to save Ellie, then," he said grimly.

"Take heart, Ben," rasped Iggy. "We will save your sister." He paused. "Though I do wish it didn't mean having to swim the horrid lake again."

• • •

The Dodman stared out over the moonlit lake. "Where is she?" he hissed, scanning the dark shore on the other side. He whistled and clicked his fingers and a great bird cast itself gracefully from the top of the tallest of the castle's towers, wheeled lazily downward around the spire, and came to rest on the crenellations a little distance away, where it folded its leathery wings and regarded its master with its head to one side. Moonlight played off one beady eye and down the length of its long, long bill.

"Boggart, a snack!" the Dodman demanded, and one of the goblins detached itself from the group lurking in the shadows and stepped forward, patting its pockets thoughtfully.

After a moment it pulled out a sack, and from that drew a small, striped catlike creature, which hissed and growled and showed its saber teeth.

The Dodman shook his head irritably. "We are not here for sport, Boggart! Let the beast go and give Terror something more suitable."

Looking puzzled, Boggart dropped the saber-toothed tiger cub on the ground and everyone backed away at speed. It ran around in furious little circles before eventually fastening its jaws in one of Grizelda's ankles and giving her a very nasty nip. Apparently not liking how the giantess tasted, it recoiled, spitting. Then it fled through the tower's door and down the stone steps. A few moments later there was a dreadful hubbub in the courtyard below followed by the yelp of a ghost-dog in pain.

The Dodman rolled his great black eyes. Then he cuffed Boggart soundly around the head. "A perfectly ordinary vampire chicken was all that was needed, idiot!" He turned on his heel. "Bogie!"

A second goblin came forward eagerly, flourishing a small feathered creature with wicked red eyes and a pair of sharp teeth protruding from the corners of its beak. The Dodman took it from Bogie's claws and tossed it to the thing on the battlement, which snatched it out of the air and swallowed it down in a single great gulp. You could track the course of the snack by the bulge that traveled, fighting all the way, down that long, leathery throat into the monster's gullet.

"You will overfly the forest," the Dodman instructed it, once it had wiped its beak once or twice against its featherless hide, "and look for the Queen.

See if you can mark her progress toward the castle. Then return here to me and tell me what you have seen. Go now."

"Yes, master!" the creature croaked, and gathering its haunches, it leapt off into the night.

The Dodman watched it go with some satisfaction.

"Well, let us hope that Isadora is doing the right thing," he declared. "Or it may have to be that a little part of her precious daughter will be leaving here soon without the rest."

The goblins all sniggered delightedly at that and started taking bets on which bit of Ellie their master might send with his message.

"Surely a heron should not be flying around in the dead of night?" growled Iggy.

Ben shut his left eye and stared upward with his Eidolon eye. He gasped, blinked; stared again. He remembered the pictures in the book he had been reading before he left the Other World. "That's not a heron!" he cried. "It's a pterodactyl!"

Darius shaded his eyes and watched the dark shape planing through the night sky. "Ah," he said softly.

"Yes, that is Terror. One of the Dodman's favorite spies. An ancient creature, cruel and wicked. We had better withdraw beneath the shelter of the trees till it is gone."

So saying, he backed quickly away into the eaves of the forest. From the safety of the darkness there they watched the prehistoric bird glide above them, the moonlight silvering its wide wings and glinting eyes, and Ben felt a shiver run down his spine.

A few moments later it flew directly overhead, and Ben held his breath, sensing its cold gaze on the back of his neck. But without hesitation it carried on in the direction from which they had traveled that day, toward the Wildwood. Through the canopy of branches Ben glimpsed it looking this way and that as it progressed, sometimes circling as if something had caught its attention.

"Cernunnos has his own lookouts posted through-out the Wildwood," Darius said quietly, as if reading Ben's thoughts. "The owls and wood-sprites will alert him to Terror's presence. Do not worry: He will keep your family out of sight. There is nothing more useful that we can do than continue with our task."

And so they emerged onto the dewy grass leading

down to the shore of the wide lake once again, and there Ben dismounted and set the little cat down on the pebbles at his feet, where Iggy at once set to dealing with his ruffled fur. Which was infinitely preferable to thinking about what might have to happen next.

Chapter Eighteen

The Dragons

"Sheherazade! Masaranshak!"

It was many long years since Isadora had had any dealings with the fire-drakes of her world, and then she had been little more than a child, and they had been figures out of legend, rarely glimpsed in her corner of Eidolon—at least around the tamer environs surrounding Corbenic Castle. Dragons were beasts about whom the great stories were woven; stories about treasure and treachery, about battles and broken vows, heroes and burning halls, fire and fear. She had never seen dragons any closer than the pair she had witnessed from her bedroom window, chasing each other, skimming their wing tips across the surface of the lake in the summer of the year in which she turned seventeen. For twenty minutes she had watched them in their mating game, and had thought them magnificent, noble creatures; a wondrous sight with the sun burnishing their colored scales and gilding the wisps of smoke that escaped their wide nostrils as they dived and soared. It was hard to equate such grace with the tales of murderous mayhem her old nurse had cheerfully regaled her with late at night, tales designed to chasten a child who would not go to sleep when told to. Even then, the stories had made the young Isadora's eyes sparkle with excitement and had filled her dreams with glorious images and the thrill of flight.

She shivered as, with all those present, she surveyed the night sky in anticipation mixed with dread.

Two dark shapes fled across the face of the moon, and still she held her breath. They circled lazily, then stooped like a pair of falcons diving upon prey. Air displaced from the great beats of their wings stirred the foliage around them like a wind; and then the first dragons she had ever summoned descended into the clearing.

Queen Isadora held her breath.

In a burst of jeweled color, the dragons landed.

"Who is it who has the temerity to summon us?" roared the first, and a thin sheet of fire accompanied his words, lighting up the dark air.

Isadora's eyes flashed. Above her head the dried winter leaves of an oak smoked and crisped. Two leaves burst into flame and spiraled down from the tree like falling fireflies. She stepped forward. "I have done so," she said bravely, gazing at this ferocious apparition. "I am Isadora, Queen of Eidolon, and I have called you here to ask you for your help."

The second dragon came up beside her mate and cocked her head to one side, regarding the Queen, unblinking. A long, thin black pupil split the gold of the iris, like a cat's eye in sunlight. At last she said, "Help? What 'help' is it that you need that you must summon dragons?"

"The Dodman threatens the very existence of Eidolon. He seeks to destroy its magic, and he is gathering his forces in order to do so. We must defeat him and drive him from our world. But we cannot do it alone, we cannot defeat him without the fire-drakes."

"Why should we care about the idiot dreams of the Dodman? He is but a puny little wingless man with the head of a jackal: He poses no threat to us."

"He is cunning and cruel, and his ambitions know no bounds. He has been destroying the small creatures, one by one. He has taken them from our world, and with each one that fails, magic is lost. Without magic, no dragons will fly in the skies of Eidolon."

The larger of the two dragons, his scales a brilliant emerald green, raised his head. Two wisps of smoke ghosted from his nostrils. "The Dodman is no threat to us," he declared haughtily. "We are too mighty for him. Or for you. Come, Sheherazade, let us leave these fools to their games."

The female dragon, Sheherazade, said, "I have heard some of this talk before, but it seemed like nonsense then, as it does now. And I do not take kindly to being called across half of Eidolon to answer the summons of some elf-woman who is no queen of mine, nor, for her long absence, of any others in this world."

Isadora went pale. Cernunnos put a hand on her arm. "Steady, my lady . . . ," he started, but two spots of hectic color had appeared in the Queen's cheeks.

"We are all of Eidolon," she said softly, but there was an edge to her voice. "And we all share responsibility for our world. I have been away, but now I am back, and I am Queen, and I swear I will stop the Dodman, whatever it may take."

Masaranshak coiled and uncoiled his long, scaly tail like an irritated cat making up its mind whether to bite someone. "Well, you must do so without our aid," he said. "Your quarrel is not ours. The Roix Clan have had no trouble from the one you call the Dodman, and we have better things to do than interfere in the petty squabbles of the unwinged."

"Halt!"

The voice came from above them, and everyone looked up. A great dark shape was looming closer, the moonlight shining off its scales, which gleamed in wonderful shades of crimson and gold.

"Do not challenge me, Xarkanadûshak!" Masaranshak bellowed, and a long spiny ridge running the length of his long neck rose just like the hackles of an angry dog.

Zark stared at the clan chief and his purple eyes whirled and whirled. "I am not here to challenge you,

Maz," he said grimly, "but to warn you. The Dodman
has his spy out, the vile pterodactyl, Terror. He is
searching for the Queen. If he takes her, his power will
be immeasurable. Ishtar is keeping him away for now,
but others will come. The Queen needs our help.
Would you be so cowardly as to deny her?"

The spines jutted dangerously, and little sparks of
fire shot out of Masaranshak's nostrils. "Just who are
you calling a coward, Zark?"

"Yes," hissed Sheherazade, "you can hardly speak
of cowardice, you who were too weak to stop the dog-
headed one from taking you captive! You bring shame
upon our whole race."

"Now, now, Sherry," Maz began, and his spines
lowered a few degrees. "Zark did go back into the
Other World to rescue the others who were taken—"

"Weaklings, all, to allow the Dodman to trap them
so! They do not deserve the name of fire-drake; they
are no better than worms!"

From the skies above the Wildwood there came a
harsh shriek. Then the darkness was split apart by a
sheet of flame.

Zark's head shot up anxiously, but in the aftermath
of the fire-blast there was nothing to be seen, and a

cloud had drifted across the moon. He dragged his eyes away from where his wife and the pterodactyl did battle above them.

"In ancient days we were one clan," he reminded Masaranshak. "Shall we not be so again, to the glory of our kind, united in the name of Eidolon?"

Sheherazade ruffled her wings impatiently. "No, we shall not. The Roix Clan have fought hard these long years for their territory and their rights, and we shall not be parting with either easily—especially to dragons of lesser heritage and abilities. Come, Maz," she declared imperiously. "I'm not staying here to listen to wheedlers and whiners."

And with that she bunched her mighty haunches and leapt skyward, to be followed a moment later by her mate.

Isadora watched them go in dismay. Cernunnos put a hand on her shoulder.

"They are but two among a dozen dragon clan chiefs," Zark said gently. "Not all may be as arrogant as these." He turned away so that none might see the doubt in his eyes. "At least, I hope not," he whispered into the dark air.

Chapter Nineteen

Old Friends

On the shores of the lake that stretched to the jagged outlines of the Dodman's stronghold, Queen Isadora's son had his own summons to make.

"She Who Swims the Silver Path of the Moon!"

Ben tried to call as quietly as he could, for fear that the Gabriel Hounds might hear him and give them away by baying their heads off. Then he thought: *Actually, if they do bay their heads off, that will be a jolly good thing!* He imagined them all running blindly around, bumping into one another and treading on one another's snapping jaws, yelping when they got bitten by the fallen heads. He was so taken up by this gruesome image that he didn't even notice when a pale shape broke the waters of the lake, followed by another, and another.

"Ben!"

It was barely more than a whisper, but it made Ben's heart skip a beat.

In the moonlight it looked for a moment as if the sleek head of a seal had emerged from the waters of the lake; then, as the magical air of Eidolon touched it, the long, full muzzle contracted and gave way to something much more human in appearance. Where moments before there had been great, sprouting whiskers there was smooth, white skin; where there had been huge black, glistening eyes, now there were eyes of a pale and gentle gray; and where there had been a mottled sheen, there was a flow of pale hair that cascaded from the top of the speaker's head to pool upon the surface of the water.

"Silver!"

And there she was: Silver the selkie, the girl who

was truly neither girl nor seal, but a tantalizing combination of both.

Ben could not help but grin from ear to ear. Despite the desperate situation they faced, he felt unaccountably happy, as if his heart had somehow grown too big for his ribs.

"Oh, Silver, you came!"

"How could I not? You summoned me. But, Ben, it is so good to see you." Her gaze rested on him gravely, then her wide grin matched his own and suddenly she was laughing, and it was like the sound of a mountain stream trickling down rocks. With a powerful flick of her body, she propelled herself up onto the shore, where the moonlight blurred the way the flippers changed to limbs and the sheen of wet skin gave way to the soft folds of a thin white dress.

A moment later she had hugged him so hard that he could hardly breathe. Even though she was now much more girl than seal, he could still feel the cold of her body seeping into him as if from the ocean depths. When she kissed him on the cheek, he could have sworn he felt the ghost of her whiskers against his chin.

At last she broke away from him and surveyed the other two members of Ben's expedition.

She nodded first to the centaur, then to Iggy. "Hello, Master Wanderer," she said, and the little black-and-brown cat yowled delightedly.

Behind Silver two figures were making their way into the shallows. The first was Melusine.

"Mellie!" Ben cried delightedly, and was about to step forward until he remembered the mermaid's last words to him, about taking him down to her lair, to eat him. "How . . . er . . . nice to see you again," he finished lamely, keeping well out of range.

Beyond Mellie, the third figure was imposing: at first glance as big as an elephant seal, or a walrus. But when Ben turned his Eidolon eye upon it, he could see that the top half, at least, was man: a great, tall, bare-chested man with a wild mop of curly blond hair and eyes that, even by moonlight, were the color of a summer sky. And those eyes were assessing him very carefully, as if weighing him up and taking stock of what he saw.

"Hello, Ben Arnold," he said. "My name is He Who Hangs Around on the Great South Rock to Attract Females—but you can call me sir."

Ben stared at him, not sure what to say to this.

The selkie burst into a great gust of laughter,

which sounded like the crash of surf against a reef. "Call me Skerry," he said at last. "I am Silver's father."

Ben smiled uncertainly. "It's nice to meet you, Mr. Skerry, sir." Remembering his manners, he started to extend an arm to shake hands with the selkie; then he saw the moonlight glinting off Mellie's sharp teeth close by—too close—thought better of it, and nodded respectfully instead.

"So, Benjamin," Skerry continued, "why have you brought us here? We were diving in the Western Sea, chasing some Greater Striped Catfish in and out of the rocks, and we'd only eaten one or two. So it's really not very convenient!" He inserted a finger into his mouth and drew out a shining white fish bone, which he threw over his shoulder.

Iggy shuddered. "My poor cousins," he said, then winked at Ben.

"Oh, Dad," Silver said crossly, "stop giving my friend a hard time. You know perfectly well it was me who asked you to come along. And I'm quite sure that if Ben's used a summons it must be for a very good reason. Although," she added, turning her candid gray gaze on Ben, a tinge of pink blooming in her cheeks, "it's always nice to see him."

"It *is* for a good reason," Ben insisted, feeling his own blush rising. "It's because the Dodman has got my sister Ellie."

"Oh!" Silver's hand rose to her mouth. "Oh, Ben, that's terrible."

"It gets worse," Iggy growled. "Unless we can rescue her by full moon, the Dodman is going to hurt her. He's using her as a hostage to make the Queen give herself up to him."

"Mellie told us that Queen Isadora had come home," Silver said softly. "But we already knew, for the air felt clearer, the winter sun is warmer, the water smoother, and the catfish seemed livelier than they used to be—"

"Very good sport," her father interjected. He regarded Ben, his blue gaze as keen as a hawk's. "And he's holding the Princess in the castle?"

"We believe so," Darius said.

"So you need us to carry you across the lake," Skerry said matter-of-factly.

Ben nodded. "Yes. I'm sorry to take you away from chasing the catfish."

Skerry placed a huge hand on his shoulder. "Do not apologize, young man. The catfish will wait until we've rescued your sister. Sometimes, though not often"—and one of his great blue eyes closed in a slow wink—"there are things that are more important than simple pleasure." He paused. "Do you know where they will have taken her?"

Ben shook his head. "I doubt it will be where they kept me," he said, "since I managed to get out."

"He will be taking no chances," Darius agreed. "There are dungeons, prison cells . . ."

Ben shuddered.

Skerry considered this. "I imagine those would be down in the foundations of the castle," he mused.

At this, Melusine snorted. "That is indeed a long way down, my dear boy!"

Skerry regarded her warily. "What do you mean?"

"There have been many fortresses where Corbenic now stands; fortresses lost to war and fire and flood, each built on the ruins of the last. I remember the old ways. In my youth—which was a very long time ago—the sealmen and I used to play nip-chase here."

She sighed as if remembering happier days.

"Nip-chase?" Ben asked curiously.

The old mermaid bared her long, sharp teeth at him. "If you caught one, you nipped him," she cackled.

"Just a little nip, no more than a caress . . ."

Ben had sometimes played kiss-chase on the school playground, which mainly consisted of him running away from the older girls as fast as his legs could carry him, for they seemed to like him a lot more than he liked them. That had been bad enough, but at least it had been on dry ground and no one had been trying to bite him!

"I don't know why, but those selkies used to try to get away from me any way they could," she sighed. "In and out of those ancient ruins we swam, and they would dash up into the tunnels and grow their legs back just to escape me."

Ben could quite understand why. If he'd been some poor selkie being chased by Mellie in her ravenous youth, he'd have been getting out of the water as fast as he could too.

"And might those tunnels lead up to the current castle's dungeons?" the centaur asked.

Melusine shrugged. "I don't know, but they must come out somewhere."

"Then lead on, my beauty!" Skerry declared with his most flattering smile. "The moon's not getting any thinner!"

"But, Dad—," Silver started, and her face was suddenly grave. "What about . . ." And she leaned in close to her father and whispered something to him.

Skerry grinned. "Nautilus? Where would the Dodman get a nautilus from? They've been extinct even in the Southern Ocean for centuries."

"Well, it's what I heard," Silver said crossly, folding her arms. "You never take anything I say seriously. And sometimes the mermen are right, you know."

Ben couldn't help but grin. Now the selkie sounded just like his sister. "Wow," he said. "I'd love to see a nautilus!" He could imagine one now, just like in the adventure stories he loved so much—a giant squid with its tentacles wrapped around some hapless ship, dragging it down to the ocean bed to devour everyone aboard. Hmmm, perhaps he didn't want to see one close up after all.

He almost jumped a mile when something grabbed him; but it wasn't a giant squid, it was Skerry's massive arm. A moment later he had been deposited on the big selkie's wide back and they were off into the lake, following the flick of the mermaid's tail. Ben turned just in time to see Silver catch a firm hold of Iggy, and Darius wading into the water behind the pair of them, and then Ben found he had to hold on tight, since He Who Hangs Around on the Great South Rock to Attract Females had transformed rather rapidly from man to seal, and had become as slippery as a fish.

The last time Ben had crossed the lake, it had been with the Gabriel Hounds snapping at his heels—and worse. He remembered how they had gained on him and Silver, how he had thought all was lost, and the way his heart had risen at the sight of the Horned Man and the centaur on the shore, flanked by a pack of white wolves. And then he remembered how the wolves had leapt into the water to do battle with the hounds, but how the Dodman had somehow managed to harness the wolves so that their tails quivered between their legs, and how from then on they did his bidding.

He shivered, expecting at any moment to hear the baying of the hounds, but their passage across the still waters of the lake was apparently going unnoticed. He was just about to relax and enjoy the strange sensation of traveling at speed on the back of the great selkie when a shriek split the air behind them, and when he turned to look back, he saw how a line of flame lit up the sky above the Wildwood.

Immediately, Skerry cried, "Hold on, Ben!" and dived.

Ben just had time to take a deep breath and think, *Oh, no,* because he did not much like getting his head underwater and had almost drowned in the local swimming pool when learning lifesaving (which was pretty ironic), when the lake closed over him and he was engulfed in a world of murk and shadow.

He had closed his eyes instinctively as soon as Skerry had dived, but now he opened his Eidolon eye cautiously and looked around. The selkie was barreling through the water like a torpedo, twisting and turning through tall weeds and columns of stone; but Ben felt curiously safe down here, for Skerry was clearly in his element, and the pressure of the water seemed to hold him in place on the selkie's back. He almost forgot to hold his breath when they passed beneath a great decorated archway and into what seemed to be an elaborate courtyard, long abandoned and drowned by the subsequent invasion of the lake. Statues lay toppled here and there among the weeds and rubble. He could make out the broken image of a man with a pair of dragon's wings on his back, and the slim figure of a woman in a long dress standing on a plinth. As they passed this statue, Ben stared and stared, for the face was just like his mother's. He opened his mouth in shock; and the water rushed in.

Chapter Twenty

Beneath the Castle

"Look at the state of you!"

The Dodman took in the tattered appearance of his spy with curiosity. The pterodactyl had flapped uncoordinatedly back to the castle and had barely managed to clear the battlements. He was clearly on his last wings. Or wing, for one was folded uselessly beneath him and was burned to an almost unrecognizable mess of charred bone and skin. The whole of one side of his leathery body was blackened, and he smelled even more appalling than usual. The dog-headed man wrinkled his muzzle in distaste.

"What happened to you? Did you fall in some troll's cookfire?"

Terror regarded the Dodman with an unblinking, expressionless eye, which gave the impression that had he been uninjured he might have skewered the dog-headed man with his murderous beak.

"*Cark!*" he cried. "Dragons. Over Wildwood. Four of them."

He neglected to explain that he had received his wounds from a single dragon, and a female one at that.

The Dodman frowned. "And the Queen?"

"No sign," squawked the pterodactyl. "But many creatures in Wildwood. Gathering."

"What is she playing at?" the Dodman growled. "Her daughter is in my dungeons under threat of death and she is throwing a party!"

Terror made a strangled noise, which might have been an expression of disgust, a laugh, or some other less obvious emotion. Then his legs gave way beneath him and he collapsed onto the stone floor, his breathing shallow and ragged.

The goblins, who until now had been keeping their distance, watched with interest. To them, the smell of barbecued pterodactyl wing was one of the most delicious things they could imagine in their wildest dreams (and goblins' dreams are wilder than most). Beetle stared at the felled creature with beady eyes; Batface was drooling openly. But it fell to Boggart, always the boldest of them, to put the question that each of them itched to ask: "Master, when he's dead can we eat him?"

The Dodman's face was like thunder as he considered how lightly the Queen was taking his threat. Time to send another, more graphic message. He turned sharply on his heel.

"Why wait till he's dead?" he said dismissively. What good was he with a broken wing? There were plenty more pterodactyls in the Shadow World to be captured and tamed and compelled to his will.

"And how is my little Princess?" the Dodman called through the cell door.

Inside, Ellie stiffened. She looked at the sprite. "Ready?" she whispered.

Acorn blinked his raspberry red eyes at her and gave a short nod.

"Actually," she called, "I feel dreadful!"

And as she said this, she realized abruptly that it was true. Her head felt as if someone had locked it in a vise and was tightening it, twist by twist. She swallowed. What if she was really ill? What if she died in here, in this horrid cell, in the dark, and no one knew? It was an awful thought.

There was a pause on the other side of the door. Then she heard the clanking sound and the grate of iron on iron as the key was inserted in the lock. Acorn launched himself from the edge of the bucket and hovered in the dark. Not even the faintest glow of pink emerged from him now and Ellie felt a sudden surge of admiration for the way he suppressed his fear.

As the Dodman opened the door and stared in, Ellie cried out, "Oh, my head!" and was promptly sick on the floor.

The Dodman stared at her with an expression of faint disgust.

"Your dear mother has not yet responded to our demands," he told Ellie smoothly, watching her wipe her mouth on the sleeve of her T-shirt. His great black lips curved back in a wide grin that showed off his array of ivory dog's teeth. "And the deadline is running out. The moon is almost full, but it seems that simple love for her daughter is not sufficient to bring her to me. I shall have to send her a more tangible message!"

Ellie was not quite sure what he meant by this, and at the moment she didn't entirely care.

"I really don't feel well," she croaked. "If I die, you won't be able to use me as a hostage."

The Dodman laughed callously. "She won't know that, though, will she? A dead girl's ear looks much the same as a live girl's ear, when it has been cut off."

Ellie's hands instinctively clamped themselves over her ears, and so she did not hear Bogie whoop triumphantly at winning the bet he had taken with Brimstone and Bosko—which meant that he would get their share of Moloccan cockroaches tonight at dinner.

Ellie stared at Acorn. "Go on!" she whispered. "Go now! Quickly!"

The sprite stared at her with its complex ruby eyes, and for a long moment of doubt she thought he would stay and watch the sport. But as the goblins advanced, giggling, into the cell, his wings flexed and he launched himself from the lip of the bucket, over their heads and out into the corridor, unseen by the motley collection of creatures gathered there, all of whom were peering into the darkness of the cell with undisguised anticipation. . . .

Acorn sped down the corridor, beating his wings with all the power that fear could lend him. He kept high up in the shadows beyond the lit sconces on the walls, in case any more goblins came wandering past. He hated goblins. He hated the Dodman, as he hated all the vile creatures in this castle. He was not an old wood-sprite, Acorn, and he had not known hatred for long in his life; but his faith in the world had been shaken by recent events and now it was hard to like or trust anyone. Which was why, now that he was free, he fully intended to stay free; to escape the castle as fast as he possibly could, return to the little copse where he had been captured, gather those friends and family he could find there, and persuade them to fly with him far away from this terrible place, away from the influence of the dog-headed one and away from the Queen and her followers. He did not want to be caught up in the war that threatened, for he had already seen too much horror and had no wish to see more. So the little Princess would have to fare as best she could without him. He had carefully made Ellie no promise that he could be kept to, and once she was dead, no one would know he had not done the thing she had asked of him.

Apart from the Minotaur.

He shook his head as he flew, as if to dispel that nagging thought. The Minotaur was never leaving the dungeons alive. And neither would he, if he did not find a way out soon.

He turned a corner, which offered the prospect of stairs up, stairs down, and a long line of locked doors. A pair of goblins lounged on the stairs that led upward, engrossed in a game that consisted of throwing a pair of bones up into the air and making bets on how they landed. It looked like the dullest game in the world; he could not imagine it would hold their interest very long. And so instead of flying past them, he took the passageway that led downward into darkness.

"Ben. Ben! Wake up!"

Something wet and warm dripped onto his cheek. Was it raining? But rain wasn't usually warm. And surely it didn't rain underwater, which was the last place he could remember being. Then something rough rasped his skin. He opened his eyes, not knowing what to expect.

Two faces loomed over him. Two pairs of eyes peered at him intently—one pair of black pupils ringed with amber, the others huge and gray. Then the amber eyes came closer, and something wet and soft and smelling of water and fish pushed against his forehead. It made a vast rumbling sound, like the engine of a truck.

A moment later another splash of warm liquid hit him squarely on the nose.

He pushed himself up awkwardly onto his elbows, blinking, and water ran out of his nose and mouth and hair.

"*Ugh!*"

"Oh, Ben, I thought you were dead!" Even with tears swimming in her eyes, Silver was grinning wildly.

"Yeah, you looked like a goner!" Iggy shook himself vigorously, sending a shower of lake water over everyone in his proximity. "Food for the fishes! Or"— and here he dropped his voice to a melodramatic whisper—"for the old mermaidy." He cocked his head sideways.

Ben stared past Iggy's shoulder to where Melusine lay in a pool, watching him avidly. Beside her, Skerry was helping Darius up out of the water, hauling him by the arms. The centaur's hooves slipped and slithered on the weed-covered ruins, then he was up and out of the water, his long black hair plastered to his shoulders.

Ben looked around. They were in a sort of cave, except that it was no natural construction, being full of masonry and stonework and columns in all different styles. It was quite dark, apart from an array of tiny bright gold lights dotted around the "cave" walls. Ben frowned. They looked like Christmas lights, the sort that people hung outside their houses to cheer up the neighborhood in the depths of winter. But surely they didn't have Christmas in Eidolon?

He was about to get up and investigate when one of the lights detached itself and flew at him. He put his hands up in front of his face instinctively to ward it off, but it didn't hit him. Instead, when he peered around his fingers, he found himself looking at a tiny creature with a glowing head.

"Wow," he said, impressed. How amazing to be able to light up your entire head. Imagine if people could do that: The Other World would be a much more cheerful place. "Hello."

But the tiny thing zigzagged away at speed to rejoin its fellows.

"Fire-fairies," Iggy explained matter-of-factly, licking the fur dry between his spread toes. "A bit like fireflies in your world. Very shy." He paused. "Tasty, though, if you can catch 'em." He looked at Ben enigmatically, his eyes as round as an owl's.

Ben stared back at him, horrified.

"Only joking," Iggy rasped. "Nearly had ya there."

Tunnels led away out of the back of the cave area—narrow and steeply stepped, leading away into pitch-darkness.

"Which one should we take?" Skerry asked.

A small voice in Ben's head went *Eeny meeny miny mo* and came up with the right-hand tunnel, but it was from the passage on the left-hand side that an ear-splitting shriek emerged.

High-pitched and full of pain, it echoed down the steep steps and out into the cavern where they stood. The fire-fairies shattered away from the walls as if an electric current had passed through them, and shot crazily about the chamber so that when Ben blinked, neon afterimages of their light trails showed on the inside of his eyelids.

"Oh my," breathed Silver. "What was that?"

Ben shook his head fearfully. "I don't know." He didn't think it sounded like Ellie; but he could not really ever remember his sister shrieking in such a fashion, even when she had been dressmaking for her dolls and had managed to stab her hand with some scissors. Even so, the hairs stood up on the back of his neck.

"Come on, Iggy," he said. "Cats see best in the dark. You'd better lead the way."

Iggy looked at him doubtfully, stuck his head into the tunnel, and promptly sneezed. "Must I?"

"For Ellie," Ben reminded him. "And Eidolon."

It is hard to see a cat's expression at the best of times, let alone in the dark of a cave, but Ben thought his friend looked both scared and resigned to the fact that he had to be their guide. In any case, Iggy squared his shoulders and stepped into the tunnel.

The air in the tunnel was chill and dank, pressing against skin and fur like fog. It smelled old and disused, as if nothing had breathed it in a hundred years. And it was very, very dark.

With a gulp, Ben took a step upward, his hands spread out on either side of him. The walls felt wet and slippery, as if they were alive and giving off a cold sweat in a similar state of fear to his own.

Up he went, feeling his way. Behind him was Silver; then Darius, his hooves clattering on the stone; and finally Skerry. They reached the top of one flight and then the steps bent around a corner so that the little illumination given off by the fire-fairies was lost to them and they proceeded in total darkness.

Until a series of strange pink shadows suddenly danced on the walls ahead of them, and then something small and glowing shot over their heads and carried on rapidly down the stairs.

Ben stared after it. "What was that?"

"I'll go and look," Skerry's voice boomed back.

There came the sound of his feet pounding down the stairs . . . then nothing.

"Let's keep going," said Ben. "He'll catch us up in a minute."

At the top of the stairs they emerged into a corridor that stretched to the left and right of them. Closed doors lined both sides. Faint light showed at the far right-hand end.

"That way," declared Ben grimly. "Run on ahead, Iggy, and see what you can see."

The cat squinted at him. "I can tell you're royalty," he said with a sniff. "Giving orders an' all." But he did as he had been asked, all the same.

He came back a moment later, looking nervous. "Goblins," he reported. "Guards, I suppose, though they don't look very professional about it."

Darius looked down at his hooves. "Even so, I don't think there's much chance of me creeping past them," he said dubiously.

Ben frowned. He hadn't thought about that. He was about to open his mouth to say as much when Skerry reappeared behind the centaur, clutching something triumphantly, something that lit the tunnel with an eerie glow. "My practice at catching flying fish came in handy." Skerry grinned, brandishing his prize.

Ben felt himself grinning foolishly.

"Twig?" he asked, hardly daring to believe his eyes.

"He says his name is Acorn," Skerry replied. "But he won't say anything else."

Indeed, the wood-sprite did not look at all happy with the situation, as Ben could tell from the red light exuding between the fingers of Skerry's huge fist, and from the way its face was screwed up, and its arms were tightly folded.

"Hello, Acorn," he said. "Do you know a sprite called Twig?"

"My cousin," Acorn replied shortly.

Ben nodded. "Then you might have heard about me," he continued. "I found Twig in the Other World and helped him to get back here. My name is Ben, and I promise we're not going to hurt you."

Acorn's beady eyes fixed upon him. "Another one," he said. "I might have known."

"Another one?"

"Your family bring trouble, every one of you."

Ben scrutinized the wood-sprite coolly, trying not to get cross. "Just how many of my family do you know?" he asked.

"Just the one, personally," Acorn said. "Eleanor, I think she said. Though now you have introduced yourself to me, I suppose I can claim two." He stared at Ben defiantly, then added, "All I want is to get out of here—which is just what I'd have done if the huge fishy lummox who's currently squeezing the life out of me hadn't caught me while I was trying to escape. It's not a lot to ask, really, is it, given all the trouble your family have brought our way?"

He closed his eyes as if pained. It seemed his plan of leaving this place quickly and quietly was bound to failure.

"Where is she?" Ben asked grimly.

The wood-sprite sighed and hung his head. At last he whispered, "You're too late, you know."

Ben remembered the terrible cry they had heard and his heart skipped a beat, then thundered against his ribs. "Too late?" he echoed.

At that moment a ferocious racket sounded above them, a snarling, yapping, howling, barking, roaring racket.

"The Gabriel Hounds," Silver said, her voice low with dread. "The Dodman's sending out the Gabriel Hounds."

Chapter Twenty-one

The Message

"Balthazar Mazurk!"

It was the Lord of the Wildwood who made the summons this time. The Queen sat on the fallen log, feeding her daughter. Behind her, Clive Arnold groaned in his enchanted sleep, one hand clenching and unclenching as if he fought an assailant in his dreams. She had thought that coming home to Eidolon would restore her health and her magic as well as her spirits, but nothing seemed to be going according to plan. Isadora felt helpless, as if the Dodman had somehow managed to leach out of her whatever little power she had left. One dragon they had called had simply circled endlessly overhead, as if trying to withstand the summons with all its might, had briefly touched down, then flown away again—and she had not had the will to call it back. Another had landed, stared at her without saying a word, then attacked Xarkanadûshak, before retreating with a bitten wing.

And where were Ben and Darius? she wondered, for the hundredth time. Surely Ignatius could not have been so very hard to find? Perhaps the Wanderer had lived up to his name. Or more likely Ben had got carried away with exploring the Secret Country. Although Darius should know better. The annoyance she had been feeling had now turned to an anxiety nagging at the corners of her mind.

She was brought back to herself by the beat of wings overhead. A glorious flash of turquoise shimmered through the trees and the dragon Cernunnos had called slid in to land as silently as a ghost. It stood there gazing around at the gathered crowd, taking in the unexpected company with an air of contempt. Its cat-eyed gaze came to rest for a moment on the stag-headed man, then it transferred its attention to the quiet figure seated on the log.

It curled its lip.

"All this fuss," it hissed, "over such a feeble thing."

The crest on its long neck rose in a line of frilled spikes and fanned back and forth: a magnificent array of jeweled lights.

Cernunnos looked alarmed. "A feeble thing? To what do you refer?"

The dragon snorted. Then it reached out a foreleg and uncurled a single long claw, which it pointed unerringly at Isadora Arnold. "Why, that feeble creature there! Such a hubbub everywhere about the returned Queen. I only came out of curiosity to have a look at it. Had I wished to ignore your summons, I would have done so. No one commands the Great Mazurk!"

"You know very well that is not true," Cernunnos countered. "No one can resist the calling of their true name." He flourished the Book of Naming, and the dragon's eyes glittered at the sight of it.

"Well, if you're going to compel me, get on with it," Balthazar Mazurk said proudly. "But I can tell you, as soon as the compulsion wears off, you're toast."

Behind the dragon, one of the fairies sniggered and whispered something to its neighbor. Without even bothering to look, the turquoise dragon twisted his head sharply and blew a stream of flame over its shoulder. Both fairies were instantly incinerated where they stood. The fern beneath which they had been sheltering remained completely untouched.

Wails of horror and distress rippled around the Wildwood clearing. Isadora shot to her feet. "No!" she cried.

The dragon gave her a dismissive glance then stared defiantly at Cernunnos, as if waiting for a reprisal and the chance to show all those present exactly what he was capable of if provoked.

"That was uncalled for," the Horned Man said, his face a mask of fury.

"That," said Balthazar Mazurk with satisfaction, "is how we dragons deal with insolence. Take care you do not call down my fire on yourself."

"Bad dragon." Alice regarded the great turquoise creature solemnly. Then she wagged a finger at it, just like a grown-up. "Bad!"

"Ssh, ssh," her mother chided quickly, shielding

her from the dragon's gimlet gaze with a protective arm, in case it decided to turn Alice into barbecued baby.

Xarkanadûshak stepped in front of his Queen and Alice. "We need your help, Balthazar, in bringing the Eastern Clans to our side against the Dodman."

"Why should we help you? We have problems of our own without getting involved in yours. The dinosaurs east of the Fire Mountains have united under a new leader and are trying to drive our clans out of our hereditary lands. The silly squabbles of the unwinged are of no concern while we have such matters to deal with. Unless"—and now his eyes glittered thoughtfully—"you do something for us first."

"What do you wish of us?" Isadora asked.

"Use your Book to find the true name of the dinosaur's chief. Then we can summon him to a place of our choosing. And kill him." Balthazar looked mightily pleased with himself for thinking of this brilliant plan. "When we have done that, we will come and lend you our aid."

The Queen looked shocked. "I don't think—," she started.

But Cernunnos was already leafing through the

Book of Naming. "Ah, dinosaurs," he muttered, finding the heading he was searching for. "Now, what type of beast is this new leader?"

"A tyrannosaur," Balthazar said eagerly. "A rex. Tall fellow, walks upright, big teeth, mean little eyes—"

"Cernunnos!" the Queen burst out. She plonked Alice down on the ground and stepped forward. "Stop at once. I command you!"

The stag-headed man stared at her in surprise. "But we need the support of the dragons."

"We cannot make such a bargain. It would not be right. To do such a treacherous thing would make us no better than those we seek to defeat. Now give me the Book." And she laid hands firmly on the great leather volume.

The Lord of the Wildwood stared down at her, his face darkening, and he did not let go. For a moment it looked as if he would wrestle the Book of Naming from her grasp.

Balthazar Mazurk watched this interchange with narrowed eyes. His tail flicked up and down with annoyance. "Tell me the name," he wheedled. "It's just a name. . . ."

At that moment Ishtar appeared overhead, her

scales gleaming in the moonlight. "The Gabriel Hounds!" she warned as she swooped toward them. "They are coming this way!" With a graceful sweep of her long wings she skimmed the treetops and soared up into the black sky again.

Balthazar Mazurk unfurled his wings. "It is already too crowded here for my liking," he said. "And I have no wish to make the acquaintance of the Wild Hunt, or whoever drives them. Farewell." He paused. "Or not, as the case may be."

Into the dark air he leapt and with two beats of his powerful wings he was away, just as the eerie howls of the hounds came cutting through the night.

As the Lord of the Wildwood stared up into the sky with apprehension, Isadora took the heavy great Book of Naming from his hands, laid it down beside her sleeping husband, arranged some moss over it, and spoke two queer words. At once, man, book, and moss blurred to a soft green mound, which would deceive the casual eye for a while, at least.

"Do you want me and Ishtar to see them off?" growled Zark, puffing out his chest.

Isadora picked up Baby Alice and smiled. "You are very brave; but, no, let us see why they come."

"You should hide yourself, my lady," Cernunnos said, taking her by the arm. "We cannot afford to lose you."

"I shall not run away," the Queen said proudly. "This is my home and I shall not hide in it. What sort of example would that be to my subjects? We must all face the thing we are afraid of or there is no hope of salvation."

But even as she said this, she felt her heart beating like a trapped bird and realized she was terrified of seeing the Dodman again. A shiver of loathing ran through her marrow, but she straightened her spine and turned her face to the sky.

The Lord of the Wildwood ran a hand across his antlers as if testing his weapons before a fight. Then he sighed. "Very well," he said.

He made a gesture, and at once centaurs and dryads came out of the dark eaves of the Wildwood where they had been standing, ready to form a protective circle around their Queen. Fairies hovered in the trees, and the other small creatures scattered for cover—but Jacaranda and the cats gathered at Isadora's feet.

Cernunnos regarded them with some amusement.

"The Gabriel Hounds are coming," he reminded them. "You cats had better make yourselves scarce."

Jacaranda licked one of her paws nonchalantly and rubbed it upon her cheek. "Oh, I think not," she said, standing her ground. "They are only ghost-dogs. We are too quick and clever for ordinary dogs—so what harm can their shades do us?"

Zark took several deep breaths, then turned away and surreptitiously blew upon a small pile of dry leaves, which ignited in a most satisfactory manner. While no one was watching, he stamped the flames out before they could catch hold. Then he fanned his wings and waited. If the Wild Hunt and their passengers gave the Queen any trouble, they would have a real fire-breathing dragon to contend with!

Above them the spectral hounds wheeled and dived, trailing a great chariot behind them. For a few seconds they disappeared amidst the forest canopy, and yelps and crashes could be heard as they descended; then a ghostly light penetrated the darkness, sending silvery fingers probing between the trees, and at last the Gabriel Hounds came into view: a pack of ghost-dogs, frost white with fiery eyes, ghost-slobber dripping from their jaws. The quiet of the Wildwood was shattered by their horrid howls. In the carriage they drew came a motley collection of creatures, but to Isadora's relief there was no dog-headed man among them.

Instead, a huge, ungainly creature clambered out of the carriage, flanked by a pair of goblins.

"Hello!" The giantess grinned around at the gathering good-naturedly, displaying her gruesome teeth. "What a turnout. You've done us proud. I wuzzn't expecting a party!"

"State your business," Cernunnos said sternly.

The giantess looked disappointed that matters should immediately get so formal. She'd been enjoying her new responsibility as an emissary; no one had ever asked her to do anything like this before.

"We brung a gift," she said. "From the Dodman." She rummaged in her sack, discarding a handful of feathers, a claw covered in fluff, a scrap of fabric, a small skull with some fur still stuck on it, and finally came out with something small and rumpled and brightly colored.

"And." Bogie nudged her with a spiky elbow.

"And?" Grizelda frowned.

"The *message*," he reminded her.

"Oh, the message." Grizelda looked unhappy. She screwed her face up with the effort of memory. "What message?" she asked after a long pause.

"Oh, for badness' sake!" exclaimed a voice that sounded unpleasantly like that of the Dodman.

Everyone in the clearing stopped what they were doing and looked around nervously, as if expecting the dog-headed man to materialize from out of nowhere.

"*Squarrrk!*"

A bright orange beak poked up out of the giantess's sack, followed by a black head with a pair of beady eyes. The mynah bird clawed its way out of the bag, jumped up onto Grizelda's shoulder, and stropped its beak briskly—once, twice, three times—on her leather jerkin. Then it fixed the Queen with its bright stare and said, sounding uncannily like its master, "Your daughter Eleanor is most disappointed that you care so little for her that you have taken no 'eed of our last message. *Squarrrk!*"

Isadora frowned. Cernunnos glared at the bird as if the very power of his gaze could render it silent; but the mynah carried on cheerfully. "You must come with us now if your daughter is to be saved. Ellie says"—and here it jumped up onto the giantess's head and hopped from one foot to the other—'Oh, Mum, Mum, 'elp me!'" This it delivered in a horrible falsetto that sounded only a little like Ellie; but the earsplitting shriek that it emitted after this plea made Mrs. Arnold's hands fly up to her face in distress.

Grizelda and the bird regarded the Queen hopefully; then the mynah's attention was distracted by something interesting in the giantess's tangled mat of hair. Fixing one bright black eye on its prey, it pinpointed it, then stabbed down sharply with its beak. Grizelda yelped and shook her head, but the mynah bird wasn't going to be dislodged. Digging its claws in, it squinted down the length of its orange bill at the wormlike thing it had caught, flipped it carefully sideways, and swallowed it with a single large gulp.

The giantess swatted at the mynah with a huge hand, and after a brief scuffle, the bird lifted off, then took roost on her shoulder.

"So you see," Grizelda said, remembering at last something of what she had been told to say. "You must come with us, or Eleanor will die. You for her. That's the deal. And to show that he means business, the Dodman sends you this gift."

And she handed the item to the Queen.

Mrs. Arnold reached out her hands to take the "gift" as if in a dream, but the Lord of the Wildwood snatched it away.

"Give me that!" Turning away from Isadora Arnold, he unwrapped it quickly and recoiled in disgust. "What is this abomination?"

"Let me see!" The Queen's face was as white as a cloud, but her eyes were dark with anger.

"You don't want to see it," Cernunnos began—but Mrs. Arnold had swiped it with quick fingers.

"What on Eidolon is it?" she breathed.

"An ear, I believe," the Horned Man said, gazing at the wizened, blackened, bloodstained thing in her hands.

Isadora's mouth twisted sharply as she examined the horrid object. "An ear it may be, but an ear from no human, and it is certainly not Ellie's ear–quite aside from the fact that it's dark green, it's not even pierced, and I can't remember the last time Eleanor left the house without wearing earrings. That is certainly not my daughter's ear. But for some reason it is wrapped in Ellie's scarf, the scarf I bought her for her birthday last year. And just how did the Dodman lay his paws on *that*? I don't understand. I left Ellie behind in the Other World. Has the Dodman traveled there and stolen her in this short time?"

Cernunnos could not meet her eye.

"Does he hold my daughter captive?" she demanded of him grimly. "Does he?"

The Lord of the Wildwood nodded unhappily.

"And you knew this?"

He opened his mouth to say something, thought better of it, and nodded again.

"You knew this and said nothing to me? Of my own daughter?" Two bright spots of pink had appeared on her pale cheeks. She looked absolutely furious. "How could you keep such a thing from me, Cernunnos? How dare you?" And she drew herself up before him, transforming suddenly from devastated mother to regal queen.

The Lord of the Wildwood grimaced. "How could I tell you? He wants you. It is the only reason he has taken your daughter, and if you give yourself up to him for her sake, then we are all lost. Tell me, what choice did I have? I would not willingly have lied to you."

Isadora gave him a hard look, then she transferred

her gaze to the giantess. "What is your name?"

Grizelda looked taken aback. "Um, er . . ." She scratched her head. "Ah . . ."

Bogie pinched her arm with his sharp little claws. "It's Grizelda, you dolt!"

The giantess nodded happily. "Grizelda," she repeated.

The Queen looked impatient. "Does the Dodman truly have my daughter, Grizelda?"

The giantess nodded vigorously.

"And she is still alive?"

"Um . . ."

"She is; yes, she is," said the other goblin, hiding behind Grizelda's vast leg.

"And whose ear is this?" Isadora demanded.

The goblin sniggered. "That's Bosko's, that is," he said. "Poor old Bosko. Now he's only got one."

The Queen shook her head sadly. Such cruelty, even to a goblin . . . "And if I come with you, he will let her go? Unharmed?"

"*Squarrrk!* If we bring you to the castle, Eleanor will be released. *Squarrk.* On this you have the Dodman's word. *Squarrrk!*"

"My lady, you cannot take the Dodman's word on

this matter: He has no honor!" Cernunnos cried. "If you go to him, what is to stop him from keeping you *both* captive?"

Isadora bowed her head, deep in thought. After a long pause she said, "We must make the exchange. My life for my daughter's."

A great sigh of distress swept around the clearing.

"My lady, you cannot!" The Lord of the Wildwood looked distraught.

"I must. And you, Cernunnos, must release Clive from his sleep and give Alice into his care. I had thought she would be safe here, but I see now that Eidolon is in a far more dangerous state than I had realized. I could not live with myself if anything were to happen to them."

"By all means send the man and the child back to the Other World," Cernunnos said quietly. "But if you are determined upon this course of action, then at least allow me and some others to accompany you, to ensure the exchange is made with honor and to bring the Princess Eleanor to safety."

Isadora gave him a wan smile. "Thank you, my friend."

Then she raised her face to the sky.

"Ishtar!" she called.

Zark's wife suddenly planed above them like a great, exotic gull, wide wings outspread. Gracefully she swept down into the clearing and landed neatly beside her mate. The two dragons butted their heads together affectionately.

"I have a favor to ask you," the Queen said. "Can you carry my husband and Alice safely home to the Other World?"

"Of course."

Her mate looked dubious. "But—"

"No buts, Zark," Isadora said briskly. "It's the only way. I'd like to see it done now, so that my mind can be at rest."

The Horned Man and the dragon exchanged a doleful glance, then Cernunnos bent and briefly touched Clive Arnold's forehead, muttering something under his breath.

Isadora's husband frowned in his sleep, grunted, and shrugged the Lord of the Wildwood's hand away. Turning on his side, he settled himself comfortably once more, and for a moment it looked as if he would never awaken again. Then his eyelids flickered and he groaned.

At once, Isadora was at his side. "Clive, Clive, wake up!" she whispered urgently.

At last he focused on her. A huge smile spread itself across his face. "Darling—"

"You must get up now and take Alice home with you," she said softly.

He frowned. "Yes, of course. And you're coming home too?"

She smiled sadly. "Yes," she said. "I shall be going home too."

"Excellent!" He sat up and reached for his anorak, but before he had time to put it on or say anything else his wife had passed Alice to him.

"Ishtar and Jacaranda are going to accompany you."

Alice clapped her hands. "Izzie!" she declared. "Ishtar!"

"Goodness," said her father. "That's a very fine word for a little girl." And he looked fondly at his youngest daughter.

"Da!" she said. "Daddy!" And grabbed his nose.

"Ow!"

Mrs. Arnold fixed her daughter with a firm, maternal gaze. "Now, Alice," she said. "Just you behave—for me, and for Eidolon."

"Eidolon," Alice echoed, and beamed.

With his free hand Mr. Arnold levered himself to his feet, and made his way over to the dragon, who was waiting with one shoulder dipped so that he could get on. His wife watched as he clambered awkwardly onto Ishtar with Baby Alice in his arms, and Jacaranda took up position at the base of the dragon's neck.

Alice never took her big green eyes off her mother. She waved her hands. "Don't go," she said suddenly. "Not to the Dodman."

Mr. Arnold became very still. He looked at Alice; then he looked at his wife. "What does she mean?" he exclaimed. "Isadora—"

"Go!" the Queen implored Ishtar. "Go, now!"

Whatever else Mr. Arnold had to say was whisked away by the sound of the dragon's wings as she lifted into the air.

The Queen of Eidolon watched them until they were no more than a tiny speck in the night sky. She blinked rapidly, then ran the back of her hand across her eyes.

"Now, then, Grizelda," she said briskly. "You must return to your master and tell him that we will make the exchange: my life for my daughter's. At dawn I will be upon the lake shore that lies to the south of Corbenic Castle, and there I will await him. He must bring Eleanor there at first light, unharmed, and I will then give myself into his care at the same moment as he hands Ellie into the Lord of the Wildwood's care. This is the bargain I will make. Is that clear?"

The giantess gazed at her, almost cross-eyed with concentration. "Dawn. Bring Eleanor, unharmed."

"South shore. *Squarrrk!*" The mynah bird bobbed and whistled.

The goblin named Bogie caught the giantess's sleeve and tugged hard at it with his spiky little claws. "No! We have to take her back with us. That's what Old Dog-Head said: 'Bring me the Queen, or I will eat your livers.' That's what he said!"

Grizelda looked puzzled. "He can eat my liver. I don't much like it, personally. Nice bit of stegosaur-steak-and-kidney pie, now that's a different matter, but liver—yuck!"

Bogie rolled his eyes. "Nah, stupid. He meant *our* livers." And he poked his finger into her capacious abdomen. "That liver. He'll hoick it out and fry it up!"

The other goblin shuddered. "He won't even stop to cook it," it said, grimacing.

Now the giantess began to look concerned. "*My* liver?" she echoed. "He's going to eat *my* liver?" She shook her head, laughed, gave Brimstone a massive wink. "You're having me on." And she gave him a good-natured punch on the arm that sent him flying in among the hounds, who all ran around and around one another, yapping and snarling. It looked as if a full-scale fight might break out at any moment.

Queen Isadora watched these antics in consternation. Could she entrust such a delicate bargain to such idiots? she wondered. That Ellie should be in the hands of creatures like these—who might do her harm without even understanding what they did—made her shudder. Then she reminded herself that all of them were her subjects. Like it or not, they were all Eidolon's folk.

And so she raised her voice and cried, "Go, now! Take this message back to your master without delay!"

At the sound of her voice, the Gabriel Hounds fell abruptly silent and immediately stood in line, haunches quivering. The two goblins shot her a look of surprise and scrambled into the cart. The mynah bird took off from Grizelda's shoulder, squawking loudly, "Message to the master! South shore at dawn. Bring Eleanor unharmed. *Squarrrrk!*"

And at last the giantess turned around, got into the back of the chariot, and sat down with such a thump that the whole frame shuddered and threatened to break apart.

A moment later they were gone, up into the lightening air.

Cernunnos and the Queen, and every creature of the Wildwood, or those summoned from beyond it, watched as the Wild Hunt was swallowed by the darkness—and dread showed on every upturned face.

Chapter Twenty-two

Rescue

Without a thought for the goblin guards, Ben hurtled around the corner and out into the candlelit corridor, shouting at the top of his voice, "Ellie! Ellie, where are you?"

Silver and Iggy hesitated no more than a second, then ran out after him, with Darius clattering along behind them.

Skerry rolled his eyes. "So much for secrecy," he

said. He shook the little wood-sprite. "Where is she, then?" he asked it. "I know you know."

Acorn's mouth twisted. "I was supposed to fetch help; though this wasn't quite what I had in mind." He laughed bitterly. "If I tell you, will you help me get out of here?"

The big selkie regarded him with his lucent blue gaze until Acorn felt a hot wash of shame flush through him. "Follow me," he said, and flittered out into the corridor.

At first the goblins couldn't quite believe their eyes. Out of the shadows, where there really shouldn't have been anything at all except perhaps a few spiders and maybe a couple of fire-fairies, came a yelling elf-boy, a cat, and a girl with flying hair and silvery-gray eyes. Any one of these on their own might have provided welcome sport and a much-needed midnight snack, but all three at once was quite a different prospect.

For a moment they dithered, then a centaur came charging into view.

Grabbit and Gutty exchanged a look of round-eyed panic, then took to their heels, their game of knucklebones discarded in a flurry. "Help!" they cried. "Help! We're under attack!"

"Come back, you cowards!" Ben yelled after them. "Tell me where my sister is!"

But the goblins weren't stopping for anything.

"This way."

The voice—scratchy and light—came from above. Ben looked up to find Acorn hovering over him in a blur of wings.

"I know where she is." He paused, blinking. "Or was."

Up stairs, around corners, down drafty passageways, and along corridors down which he had only recently flown in fear for his life, Acorn led them with his heart in his mouth. What if the Dodman had killed the Princess? What if he was still there?

But when he reached his destination, the corridor was dark and empty, the only visible movement the guttering of the last candle flame jumping across the walls.

"Ellie! Ellie!" Ben shouted.

His cry fell into a profound silence; then: "Ben?"

The voice came from behind the third door. It quavered with disbelief. Then there was a scuffle of movement, and more loudly it called, "Ben, is that really you?"

"It is! It is!" Ben almost laughed with relief. But his euphoria was short-lived. Ellie might be alive, but she was behind a locked door. He pushed at the door, thumped it, kicked it; to no avail.

"Stand aside," Darius said. He waited until his friends were out of the way, then he reared up on his great haunches and brought his hooves crashing down on the door.

The timber shuddered and rattled, but the door wasn't budging an inch. Again and again he thrashed at it, but all he managed was to dent and splinter the surface and make a din. And when Skerry tried to shoulder the door in, all he got for his efforts was a big splinter in his arm.

"Now what?" Ben asked.

"We need the keys," Silver groaned, and the two of them looked at each other in despair.

On the other side of the door, Ellie began to cry.

"How very interessssting!"

"It is indeed."

Cynthia's voice was thoughtful as she observed

598

from her vantage point, in the dark branches of a great oak some distance south of the clearing, how the lumbering giantess and the two goblins climbed back into the chariot after delivering what appeared to be some sort of message. A moment later the Gabriel Hounds were howling again, their cries ululating through the Wildwood, echoing off the trees, filling the night with their din.

Then she watched as the Lord of the Wildwood wrapped a fur cloak about the Queen's shoulders and gathered the centaurs. She watched as Isadora mounted one of the horse-men, and Cernunnos led a solemn procession out of the Wildwood, accompanied overhead by a lone, forlorn-looking dragon.

Soon the first hint of dawn was beginning to strike through the darkness, the edge of the rising sun sending a deep red glow into the blackness of the sky as if a forest fire were raging in the distant hills.

"Red sssky in the morning, Dodman'sss warning!" hissed the Sphynx, as if reading her mind. Its breath misted briefly in the chilly air.

"I am very curious," Cynthia declared, "as to exactly what is happening here."

The Sphynx grinned, baring its long yellow teeth.

Sometimes, Cynthia thought, it looked more like a rat than a cat, with its naked coat and skinny tail. It was one of the things she liked most about it. That, and its ability to sneak around unseen.

"Go and have a look. See if you can find out what is going on," she told it. "You're such a clever little spy."

"Yesss," agreed the hairless cat. "I am."

It licked the last smell of the terrible troll off its skin and stretched out its back legs, then its front legs. Then it ran straight up the trunk of an oak, digging its long claws into the bark for purchase—and the oak twitched and muttered in the deep, secret voice of trees in all worlds when they are upset by something, until the cat ran out along a branch and leapt neatly onto the outstretched limb of a nearby ash. In this manner it soon vanished from its mistress's sight into the dark mass of the Wildwood.

Cynthia sat back among the ferns, thinking. The Queen had not been wearing the Crown of Eidolon when she went with the centaur and the Horned Man; nor had she been carrying a suitcase, nor the baby. Many possibilities flickered through her head as she waited for the Sphynx to return with whatever news it had been able to glean.

She did not have to wait for too long before the hairless cat was back, its amber eyes flashing maliciously in the weird light.

"A new day isss dawning for Eidolon," the Sphynx reported gleefully. "The Queen hasss gone to give herself up to the Dodman in exchange for young Ellie."

Cynthia's straggly orange eyebrows shot up into her straggly orange hair. She stroked her long, crooked nose with a long and crooked finger. "Well, well," she said. "That's very curious."

"And," the hairless spy added, its yellow grin as wide as a goblin's, "they have left something very interesssting behind."

And when he told her what it was, Cynthia's grin soon matched his own.

"Right, then," Darius said firmly, sounding a good deal more confident than he felt. "Skerry and I will go and find the keys."

"But," came Ellie's voice on the other side of the cell door, "the Dodman's got them. Oh, please help me. It's as black as the grave in here and I'm afraid of the dark." It was a big admission for Ellie. She started to sob again.

The big selkie rubbed his face. "I'm sorry. I only came along for the ride," he said slowly. "Confronting the Dodman wasn't what I had in mind."

Darius gave him a hard look. "Go, then," he said. "Take your daughter and go back to your safe waters. Though I warn you that unless we can rescue Eleanor and stop the Dodman's plan, they will not remain safe for very long."

Skerry nodded. "You're right, of course, I know. But I've never regarded myself as any kind of hero. I like a quiet life: ride the occasional good wave, eat a few fish, catch some rays—that sort of thing."

"Dad . . ." Silver stepped in front of him. Her face looked fierce and her eyes flashed in the gloom of the corridor as if lit with some inner light. "Ben saved my life when I was taken into the Other World. We owe him this. And if you won't go with Darius, then I will."

Her father looked abashed. He gazed at her out of the depths of his big blue eyes as if seeing her for the first time. At last he grinned. "Well, I really wouldn't be much of a father, let alone a hero, if I let you go instead of me." He gave her a hug, winked over her head at Ben. "Look after her, won't you?"

Ben nodded.

Skerry pushed Silver away, ruffled her hair, then turned to the centaur. "Lead on, Darius. Lead on."

The centaur paused. "Take heart, Eleanor," he said, bending to speak into the keyhole. "We'll get you out of here, I promise, by hoof or by tooth."

Ben could feel his sister's smile, even though they were separated by a thick wooden door and walls of sturdy stone; then the centaur and the selkie were gone into the shadows, the sound of the Horse Lord's hooves ringing on the stone.

Silver watched them go, looking even paler than usual. "What if they don't come back? What if they get captured—or worse? What will we do?"

Ben squeezed her hand. He was glad she was a girl at the moment, because squeezing her hand was the only comfort he could think of, and squeezing a flipper wouldn't have been quite the same.

Ignatius Sorvo Coromandel rubbed his cheek against her leg. "Don't take on," he rasped in his best tiger growl. "Nothing bad is going to happen while the Wanderer's here to take care of you."

Ben and Silver looked down at the really rather small cat and burst out laughing.

"It's all right for you," came Ellie's voice. "You

603

can laugh all you want. You're not stuck in some horrible dungeon with nothing but a smelly bucket for company."

That sobered them. "Sorry, Ellie," Ben said through the keyhole. "Are you okay?"

"No, I'm not. It's dark and I've got a headache and I've been sick."

"We heard an awful scream earlier," Ben went on. "I was worried it was you."

"I think the Dodman did something to one of his goblins." There was a shuffling noise on the other side of the door, then something gleamed through the keyhole. "Oh, I can see you!" Ellie exclaimed with sudden delight. "Who's that with you?"

"This is She Who Swims the Silver Path of the Moon," Ben said proudly. "But she prefers to be called Silver. She's a selkie."

"Hello," said Silver.

"Hello. You don't look much like a seal," Ellie said, thus surprising Ben by knowing anything about the subject at all. He had thought she only ever read magazines about how to attract boys by wearing glittery purple eyeshadow and dieting till you looked like a wizened old stick—which had always seemed a deeply unlikely way of getting anyone's attention, unless you wanted them to laugh at you. "Oh, hello, is that you, Acorn?"

The wood-sprite circled around Ben's head. "I brought them," he said. Which was neither entirely true nor yet entirely untrue.

"Thank you, Acorn. Thank you from the bottom of my heart."

If wood-sprites could blush, Acorn would have done so then. "It was nothing," he mumbled.

"It's terribly dark in here without you," Ellie said miserably. "It's easier to keep your spirits up if you've got a little light."

"What about the fire-fairies?" Ben said suddenly, remembering the tiny light-headed creatures in the caverns below. "Acorn, do you think you could persuade a couple of them to come up here and slip in through the keyhole to give Ellie some light?" He reckoned they were small enough, and since if they could get in they could get out again, it wasn't as if they'd be in too much danger.

"Maybe," said Acorn, though he didn't sound very keen on the idea.

"Please," said Ellie. She paused, then added in a

small voice, "Unless you could manage to squeeze back in here?"

Iggy laughed cruelly. "I don't think there'd be much left of him if we tried to cram him through that keyhole!"

That made Acorn's mind up for him. Away down the corridor he flitted, a zigzag of pale green light that disappeared as soon as he rounded the first corner.

"Do you think he'll come back?" said Silver.

Ben looked at her in surprise. "Of course he will." But it was true that the wood-sprite didn't seem as friendly as Twig. He watched Ignatius Sorvo Coromandel wander off to sniff at the door of the next cell.

"There's someone in here," Iggy said, recoiling suddenly with a sneeze. "And they reek!"

"I heard that," Ellie said. "Don't be so rude! That's my friend, the Minotaur."

As if in response to this introduction, there came a tremendous bellow from the adjoining cell.

"Oh!" Silver jumped behind Ben, trembling. "The Minotaur! Don't let him get me!"

Ben frowned. He'd read a story about a Minotaur, a Greek myth about a hero called

Theseus, who had sailed to Crete with a group of young people who were to be that year's sacrifice to the beast; and somehow—the details of the story were a bit hazy—he had survived the ordeal, killed the Minotaur, and found his way back out of the maze in which it was kept. Oh, and won the heart of the king's daughter, though that wasn't the bit that interested Ben very much. Killing the monster had been the fun bit of the story, scary and exciting. However, he didn't feel much like taking on a real-life Minotaur. He was glad it was securely imprisoned, even if Ellie said it was her friend.

"Don't worry, Silver, he can't get you; and I won't let him."

Silver beamed up at him. "You are my hero, Ben."

Ben blushed to the roots of his hair. He was saved from further embarrassment by the sound of footsteps coming down the stairs. He looked at the selkie in panic. "We must hide!"

But there wasn't anywhere to hide. They couldn't run back the way they had come without being seen as they passed the stairs, and the corridor on which Ellie's cell was located came to a dead end beyond them.

"Stay here, Silver. I'll go and see who it is. If I shout, run as fast as you can back the way we came, and I'll hold them up so you can get away," Ben whispered, trying to sound braver than he felt.

He and Iggy ran along the corridor to the junction with the stairs. There they stopped. The footsteps were coming closer. More than one set. Ben counted. Three sets, at least, striking against stone, the echoes making it sound like even more. He felt his heart clench. He and Iggy exchanged worried glances, then Ben stuck his head around the corner and stared upward. At first he could see nothing, then . . .

"Skerry!"

The relief was so great that his knees went all wobbly.

Behind the selkie came Darius. As soon as Ben saw his face he knew something was badly wrong. "What? What is it?"

"The doors up above are locked. We couldn't get through."

"So you haven't got the keys, then?" said Ben in a quiet voice.

Skerry fixed his great blue eyes on him. "I'm sorry, Ben. We've done all we could, and now there's no more to be done. I'll take Silver now and we'll away. I'm sorry about your sister."

"Darius?"

But the Horse Lord just shook his head slowly. He looked utterly dejected. "When they built this place, they built it well," he said. "The doors are locked and bound with iron. If I could take the walls down stone by stone to save your sister, I would, Ben, believe me. Short of swimming around to the front of the castle and declaring war on the Dodman, I don't know what we can do."

No one said anything to this. No one had any ideas. Ben felt as if the inside of his head had been scoured out and left as empty and echoing as an old kettle. He looked from the unhappy faces of the centaur and the selkies away into the shadows of the corridor.

There, at the far end, something lit the gloom. Ben stared and stared. Then he fixed his Eidolon eye upon the distant glow. It was Acorn and a great swarm of fire-fairies, coming closer by the second.

Well, he thought, *at least Ellie will have some light to comfort her.* It wasn't much consolation, but it was something.

"Thank you, Acorn," he said as they approached. "Thank you, fire-fairies."

The fire-fairies jigged about his head, making mad zigzags of bright light in front of his eyes, buzzing like little bees full of joyous energy, and suddenly Ben couldn't help but smile, despite the dire situation they were all in.

"Follow me," he said, and they all streamed along behind him like a golden cloak.

When they reached Ellie's cell, the fire-fairies first flew in a stream of gold around Iggy, then around Silver, and then they danced up and down the door, then round and round, in what seemed a very disorganized sort of manner. But none of them went through the keyhole. They flew above it and below it, to the left and the right of it, but not one of them went in. Ben couldn't really blame them for not wanting to enter one of the Dodman's dungeons; even so, it was very frustrating to watch them having fun in their carefree, thoughtless way.

"What are they doing?" Silver asked Acorn, but the wood-sprite shook its head.

"They are as much of a mystery to me as they are to you," he said in his scratchy little voice.

"Well, you must have said something to them to make them come."

Acorn looked uncomfortable. "I only got as far as explaining that the Princess of Eidolon was trapped up here. Then they were flying so fast I could hardly keep up with them."

A great hum filled the air, as if all the fire-fairies had started to sing a single note at once; then there was a sudden blast of light accompanied by a strong smell of burning, and something went clattering onto the stonework in a great cloud of dust.

Silver sneezed hard, and Ben's eyes watered from all the dust and light. He blinked and blinked; then he stared.

Where the great iron lock had been, there was now a burnt and ragged hole in the cell's door; and through it he could see Ellie clearly, with a dozen or more fire-fairies zooming around her, weaving patterns of light in the shadows about her head—a pattern that looked remarkably like a crown. . . .

He burst out laughing, for now the door was swinging open and there were fire-fairies everywhere, making the cell as bright as day.

"Oh, Ellie!" he cried, and then he was hugging his

sister and she was hugging him—which was pretty strange, because generally they didn't even *like* each other most of the time.

Darius and Skerry gazed at the burnt-out lock, then at Ellie embracing her brother, and finally at what now appeared to be a dual crown of fire-fairies, which hovered over them.

"Well, I never . . ." The centaur shook his head so that his glossy black mane of hair tossed from side to side. "I thought I knew everything there was to know about the creatures of this world, but somehow they are always surprising me."

Skerry's huge laugh boomed out. "Task accomplished, then, and by the smallest of Eidolon's folk. So much for our brains and brawn, my friend!"

Darius smiled. His gaze met Ellie's, and at once she blushed and started fiddling with her hair. "I must look awful . . . ," she started.

Ben rolled his eyes. "Come on, then," he said impatiently, catching his sister by the arm. "Let's get out of here."

Ellie pulled herself free. "Not without the Minotaur."

Darius stared at her. "*Here?* The Minotaur is here?"

"If he is, he's best left here," Skerry said, frowning. "He's got a lot to answer for."

"He's been very nice to me," Ellie said.

"No doubt biding his time," said the selkie darkly.

Darius looked anxious. "He is very dangerous, and very powerful. If we get him out, how can we be sure he won't hurt anyone?"

"Simple," said Ellie briskly. "I'll make him promise."

Ben made a face. "Listen to Princess Ellie."

For once his sister did not rise to the bait, but walked straight past him to the door of the next cell. "Minotaur?"

A heavy sigh issued from behind the door. "You're free, then? Good for you. Maybe we'll meet again. Or maybe we won't. It's been nice knowing you"—it paused—"Princess of Eidolon."

Ellie loved the sound of that.

"If we help you to escape your cell, will you promise not to hurt anyone?"

"Anyone?"

"Well, any of my friends." She cast Ben a superior look that said, *So you'd better behave from now on. . . .*

There was a brief silence while the Minotaur

digested this. Then it said quietly, "If you can get me out of here, I will do anything in the world for you."

Ellie clapped her hands in delight. Then she turned to Darius. "You see?"

"If you believe that, you'll believe anything," Acorn said darkly.

Skerry walked over and caught Silver by the hand. "If that thing runs amok, there's nothing I'll be able to do to stop it, and I won't risk my daughter's life needlessly."

"No! I won't leave Ben!" Silver pulled away, but the big selkie was adamant.

"Ben may be your friend, but I am your father." He turned to Darius. "We will wait for you in the waters of the caves below. And if you do not come, well"—he shrugged—"at least as seals we can save ourselves."

The little selkie's huge eyes started to brim with tears.

"You'd better go, Silver," Ben said rather miserably. He hung his head, wondering if this was the last time he would ever see her.

As if she shared his thought, she broke suddenly from her father's grasp, ran to Ben's side, and kissed him quickly on the cheek. Then she turned and ran with Skerry down the corridor and disappeared into the shadows.

"Well, well," said Ellie. "Ben's got a girlfriend!"

Ben put his hand up to his cheek. It felt hot and red where Silver had kissed him. "I have not!" he denied furiously. But he could feel a smile bubbling up inside him.

"Come now," said the centaur. "No time for bickering. We must away as fast as possible, with the Minotaur or without him. What's it to be?" He turned to Ben.

"Let him out," said Ben as bravely as he could manage, though he was a bit worried, and not just by the beast's smell. "Nothing should be kept down here, in the dark and the damp. Acorn, can you ask the fire-fairies?"

But before he could even finish the sentence, the fire-fairies had flown to the door of the next cell and were already working their strange magic.

As the burnt-out lock fell away and the door swung open, Ignatius Sorvo Coromandel gazed into the cell and his eyes went huge and round. Then he fled down the corridor and leapt into Ben's arms.

Ben didn't even have time to chide him for his

cowardice before a huge figure ducked through the door, to emerge in a swirl of smoke and dust and fire-fairies; and then he couldn't even speak if he'd wanted to. A vast, rumbling bellow roiled out across the dungeons and echoed off the walls, and the sound thrummed in the bones of Ben's chest and up through the soles of his feet.

Golden light from the fairies and the dancing candles illuminated a creature as tall as the Dodman, walking on two legs like any man. But when he examined it with his Eidolon eye, Ben found that its head was the head of the biggest bull in any world, topped by a pair of monstrous black horns.

What Ben wanted to do when he saw this apparition was to run away, to pound along the corridor and down all those flights of stairs up which they had climbed, down into the caves and into the pool where Melusine and Skerry and Silver waited; and then swim the lake without anyone else's help at all until he was as far away from the Minotaur as he could possibly get. What he actually did, though, was to stand rooted to the spot, barely breathing, with his arms clutched tightly around the little cat and his eyes as big as dinner plates.

"Wow . . . !"

Even Darius gulped, and his voice sounded a bit shaky when he said, "Welcome back to the world, Minotaur. May I remind you that you are now in the service of the Queen of Eidolon."

The Minotaur slowly swung his huge head to survey the centaur with eyes of flame. "I am in the service of the Princess Eleanor," he rumbled, "and no other."

At this, a dozen of the fire-fairies circled around him, tracing in the dark air a golden floating heart.

Which made Ellie's eyes shine, even though her knees were knocking.

Chapter Twenty-three

Red Dawn

When the Dodman saw that the chariot drawn by the Wild Hunt did not contain the woman he had sent his messengers to fetch, he flew into a rage. Goblins scattered into dark corners of the castle, vampire chickens fluttered up to the rafters in a storm of feathers, and the white wolves who had once answered only to the call of the Horned Man slunk into the shadows with their tails between their legs

619

and their ears laid flat to their skulls. Even the guard trolls on the gate stood stock-still and pretended they were lumps of stone, in the hope he would not take his fury out on them.

Bogie and Brimstone had been preparing for this fearful prospect ever since they had left the Wildwood without the Queen. They had even made the Wild Hunt fly round and round in circles so they could think of a way to avoid their master's wrath. In the end all they had been able to fix on was this: "Leg it!"

As soon as the Gabriel Hounds landed, the two goblins were out of the chariot and scampering across the courtyard as fast as their fat little legs could carry them, leaving Grizelda to face the Dodman. Even so, they managed to somehow get tangled up in each other and fall flat on their faces.

The Dodman was upon them in a flash, planting a foot squarely on each goblin's back as if he would crush them into the ground.

"Where is she?" he boomed, and they could hear the spittle flying from his mouth and sizzling onto the cobblestones.

Unfortunately, he was standing on them so heavily

that they could not get any words out, which just made him angrier.

"WHERE . . . IS . . . SHE?"

With each word he stamped down hard, and groans of air came out of the goblins in such a rude manner that Grizelda started to giggle. She was still stuffing her fingers into her mouth in order (unsuccessfully) to stifle her laughter when the Dodman abandoned the two squashed goblins—who lay there for a few moments, looking rather flattened, before levering themselves to their feet and making their escape—and launched himself at her. Three inches away, he drew himself up and looked her squarely in the eye—which, given the size of a giantess, is no mean feat, even if you are eight feet tall with the head of a dog.

"Where . . . is . . . the . . . Queen?" he enunciated with great care, remembering that he was addressing a creature with a very small brain, despite the size of the rest of her.

Grizelda gave him a gap-toothed, lopsided smile. "With the Horned Man," she said. "In the Wildwood."

The Dodman's breath hissed out in a dangerous fashion.

Even the Gabriel Hounds quieted, sensing the

storm about to explode. But before the Dodman could lose his temper entirely and tear everyone present limb from limb, the mynah bird burst out of the giantess's pack and circled overhead, squawking: "Bring the Princess Eleanor to the south shore at dawn. Unharmed! Unharmed!"

The Dodman regarded the creature with a look that suggested if he got hold of it at least one person would be eating mynah bird that day, and that person probably had a lot of very sharp dog's teeth.

"Go on," he told it. "Then what?"

"The Queen will give herself up to you. That is her bargain."

Everyone waited, not daring to breathe, as they awaited the dog-headed man's response.

At last a calculating look slicked the Dodman's eyes. "Excellent," he said, rubbing his hands together. "That will do very well."

His grin was as long and gleaming as any crocodile's. He crossed the courtyard to look through one of the narrow arrow-slits in the stone walls there. To the north of the castle all was quiet and dark; but to the east, the first glimmers of red light had begun to enrich the night sky; and when he reached the southern wall and peered into the murky distance, he thought he could make out a group of figures emerging from the tree line there.

At once, he was all spring and vigor. "Right then, Brimstone, Bogie, Bosko, Batface!" he cried briskly to the hiding goblins. "Down to the dungeons. Let us fetch the Princess Eleanor and make our trade!"

He chased the goblins out of the shadows and they fled before him, one of them sporting a ragged bandage around its head, the others averting their eyes and trying to keep out of range of their master's booted feet. His moods were changeable at the best of times, and who knew when he would feel like taking off someone else's ear?

As the Dodman danced lightly down the steep stone stairs to the dungeons with the keys rattling merrily at his side, he sang to himself:

> *"We're going to catch a queen, tra-la*
> *With eyes of emerald green, tra-la*
> *Going to lock her in the cells, tra-la*
> *Full of lovely Minotaur smells, tra-la*
> *Going to take away her crown, tra-la*
> *Bring the whole world crashing down*
> *Tra-la, tra-la, tra-la, la, la!"*

"Oh my, it's the Dodman!"

Ellie looked fearfully at her brother. Ben stared at the locked door above them. The Dodman had the keys. . . .

"Right, that's it," Acorn declared, flittering above their heads. "I'm off. I'm not staying around here to be caught by the Dodman again."

But no one seemed to be listening to him.

Darius glanced at the door, then at the Minotaur. If anything could hold them at bay, it would be this monster; though how the dog-headed man had ever managed to capture it in the first place, he couldn't imagine.

"We must do everything in our power to protect the Princess Eleanor and her brother," he said to the Minotaur, who nodded his bull-head in assent.

Then Darius turned to Ben. "Take your sister and Ignatius down to the caves and join the selkies," he said urgently. "Get them to take you across the lake as fast as they can. The Minotaur and I will follow when we are able."

"No!" Ben said fiercely. "We won't leave you to fight our battles."

The Minotaur swung his gaze in Ellie's direction.

624

"You should do as the man-horse says. We will deal with the Dog-Headed One and his minions." His eyes gleamed. Then he pawed the ground, just as a bull might, except that his feet were those of a very large man. "I have been looking forward to this moment. It has been a long time coming."

Ellie paled, but she didn't want to appear scared in front of the handsome centaur or her new friend. "We're staying," she said, though her voice wobbled a little.

Ignatius Sorvo Coromandel gave her a ferocious grin. "I've got a few scores of my own to settle with the Dodman. I've been polishing up my claws especially."

The sound of footsteps was coming closer on the other side of the door. Keys jangled. Everyone held their breath and stared at the huge ironbound door.

It was a huge affair made from ancient oak wood, its surface pitted with age and wear, its long hinges and ringed handle rusted but sturdy. Scorch marks and clefts marred the wood, as if the door had survived through centuries of violent events. Ben hoped it would stand for a few minutes more.

The Minotaur grabbed hold of the iron ring and

took a firm stance. Darius arched his strong neck so that the tendons stood out on it like cords. Ben clenched his fists and listened to the sound of his heart thudding against his ribs. Ellie bit her lip.

At the sound of the Dodman approaching with the Gabriel Hounds howling and yapping and snuffing hungrily behind him, Iggy's hackles rose into spikes all the way down his spine and his tail fluffed up alarmingly, like an animal all of its own. All this time he had been thinking, for all his bravado, that if it really did come down to teeth-and-claw fighting, he might just run away. Now he felt his fur puffing up all over, so that his shadow loomed large against the door, and he began to feel a bit brave after all. Fighting chemicals poured into him, swelling his muscles—and probably his head, too. The mighty Wanderer had returned.

The Minotaur swung his great head around to look at his new allies. His eyes gleamed red as flame; but perhaps it was just the reflection of the fire-fairies.

"Get ready, then," he said.

He did not say for what. He did not have to. The key turned in the door.

• • •

As the sun came up over the eastern hills behind Corbenic Castle, Queen Isadora of Eidolon stood on the lake shore with Cernunnos, Lord of the Wildwood, and a phalanx of centaurs. She scanned the castle avidly, one hand shielding her eyes from the gaudy light.

"Red sky in the morning, dryads' warning," Cernunnos intoned, but whether this meant it was a warning to dryads or from them, Isadora did not know. All she did know was that the castle looked ominous and bleak, silhouetted against that glowing red sky. And there was no sign of the Dodman or her daughter anywhere.

Xarkanadûshak planed overhead like a hawk. He sideslipped across the lake, risking a swift pass over the castle battlements, then returned and landed gracefully beside them, shaking his head.

"I can't see anyone," he reported. "But there's a lot of noise coming from inside the castle somewhere, and the Gabriel Hounds are barking like demons."

"Perhaps Ellie has escaped," Isadora breathed. She turned shining green eyes on the Lord of the Wildwood.

"There's no way out except across the lake," said

Cernunnos. "And I fear that if the Wild Hunt are pursuing your daughter in the confines of the castle walls, it could be a very grim end."

Isadora shuddered. She knew how hounds dealt with foxes when they caught them in the Other World, and it was a violent, bloody death. Tears threatened. She grasped Cernunnos by the arm. "We have to help her. I must go." She turned to the dragon. "Zark, you could carry me—"

"No!" Cernunnos took her by the shoulders, blocking her view of the castle. "If you go to him, he will have both of you, and where is the sense in that?"

There was nothing she could do. Being queen of this world seemed to confer on her no special powers. What was the use of being a queen if you could not even save your own daughter? She hung her head and waited.

The Lord of the Wildwood narrowed his eyes. Perhaps if the Princess Eleanor were to suffer a grim fate at the hands and teeth of the Dodman and his monsters it would be best for all: Isadora would remain with him in the safety of the Wildwood, a rallying point for the creatures of Eidolon—more of whom would surely flock to her side in sympathy at the loss of her daughter. He could not help the small smile that twitched his lips.

The key turned in the lock, and someone pushed hard on the door—but it did not open. From the other side came muffled swearing followed by a yelp as a goblin was bashed for handing up the wrong key. More rattling. Another key in the lock, and a quiver as the door was pushed hard. Still no luck. The Minotaur's arms bulged. He dropped the centaur a slow wink.

"The Dog-Headed One will have to try harder than that," he said softly. "On his own he is a feeble creature, for all his size. You should all remember that. It is only by terrorizing others into his service that he gains his power."

On the other side of the door, there was considerable puzzlement.

"There's an appalling stench coming from somewhere," the Dodman declared disgustedly, wrinkling his big black nose. "Is it you, Bosko? Have you been eating rat droppings again?"

Bosko denied this vehemently (though he had).

"I know what that smell is," said Grizelda. "I should do: I dragged that net for miles, me and the ogres Oddspot and Offside. Over hill and down dale. I'll never forget it."

"What?" The Dodman was sorting through the keys again, frowning at the first one—which he just knew was the right one, even though it didn't appear to work.

"It's the Minotaur," the giantess went on. "I'd know that smell anywhere. . . ."

The Dodman's head came up sharply. "The Minotaur? But he's imprisoned safe and sound next to the Princ—"

He bent suddenly, withdrew the latest ill-fitting key from the lock, and applied his eye to the enormous keyhole. The next moment, he leapt backward with a look of utmost fury on his face.

"He's got out!" He glared at the goblins, who quailed away as if the heat in his eyes alone might sear them to little piles of ash. "And so has the Princess. But I locked her cell, I know I did!" He peered through the keyhole again. "And that little brat of a brother is with her! How did THAT happen?"

His fearsome gaze raked them all. The Gabriel Hounds began to whimper and their tails drooped and quivered. One of the goblins wet himself.

"Well? WELL?" he bellowed.

"Dunno," Bosko muttered, feeling the furious gaze upon him.

"No idea."

"Search me."

"Magic?"

"MAGIC?" The Dodman's boot found the last speaker, connecting with its large rump with an audible *squelch*. "Don't use that word around me! Well, however this fiasco has occurred, we'll soon put it to rights. And then I shall have *two* little hostages to play with. That should make Isadora come squealing to me for mercy. Grizelda, open that door!"

The giantess looked dubious, but she did what she was told. Or tried. She battered at the door with her fists, wrenched at the iron ring, tried to shoulder it open. A tiny crack of fiery light appeared down the edge on her last, most violent attempt.

"Hah!" cried the Dodman. "Put your back into it, woman!"

Grizelda pulled a face. Then she turned around and slowly applied her capacious bottom to the door, pushing backward as hard as she could. It creaked and creaked, and the fiery line grew wider. This time a couple of the fire-fairies buzzed through it, zooming over the Dodman's head, away and up the stairs into the glowing dawn. A moment later Acorn levered himself through and followed them.

On the other side, Ellie shrieked. With a massive heave, the Minotaur slammed the door fully shut again with a clang.

Now the goblins, with the Wild Hunt snapping at their heels and other more vulnerable regions, joined the giantess in pushing the door open—and it gave by an inch, and then another inch.

With a roar the Minotaur shoved it closed; but as he did so the Dodman's words drifted with horrible clarity through the gap.

"This calls for a dragon. If brute force won't solve the problem, then fire must!"

"Oh, no," breathed Ben, as the door slammed shut again.

"A dragon . . . ," said Iggy. "Now *that* would be bad." Abruptly, his fur subsided and he looked no longer like the mighty Wanderer, but like the small, frightened cat that he was.

"Take the children," the Minotaur said sharply, addressing the centaur. "I will hold the door."

"But—"

"Do not argue with me, horse-man." The

Minotaur's eyes glinted dangerously. "You never know what I might do."

Darius conceded to himself that this was true. It was hard to trust a beast with such a bloodthirsty reputation. He turned to Ben and Ellie. "We should do as he says."

Ben felt his heart grow large and heavy in his chest at the thought of leaving the brave Minotaur. Ellie ran quickly forward and planted a kiss on the bull-headed man's ugly snout. "Thank you," she said. "I'll never forget you."

Then another onslaught came from the giantess and her helpers, and the Minotaur turned back to his task.

Chapter Twenty-four

Nemesis

Down the corridors they fled, in darkness save for the bobbing lights of the few fire-fairies that darted ahead of them. Down through twists and turns they ran, down passageways and stairs, and once down a dead end when Iggy thought he knew better than the fire-fairies which way to go. Darius's hooves thundered upon the stonework, echoing so much it sounded as if a whole herd of centaurs were careering through the castle; but despite all the noise, Ben could hear his blood pulsing in his ears and his heart thumping, and he could see from Ellie's paleness that she was just as scared as he. He wasn't looking forward to the prospect of crossing the lake again; but if it came to a choice between that and facing the Dodman and all his hordes . . .

Down the final set of steps they dashed, with Darius shouting for the selkies to get ready for a quick getaway. But when at last they reached the cavern, it was silent and empty.

Ben stared around. The selkies were nowhere to be seen. "Skerry?" he called, and listened as his voice bounced off the dripping walls. "Silver?"

But there was no reply.

Darius frowned. "This is most unlike Skerry," he said. "However much he is concerned for his daughter, I'm sure he would never willingly abandon us."

Ellie stamped over to the pool and stared in, her lower lip stuck out belligerently. "Charming," she said. "Going off and leaving us here to fend for ourselves." She turned to her little brother. "Well, summon them, then," she said impatiently. "Go on, stupid!"

Ben felt like retorting that it hadn't been *him* who had stumbled into the Secret Country and ended up locked in one of the Dodman's dungeons, but he bit it back and applied himself to remembering the selkie's true name.

"Er, He Who Hangs Around on the Great South Rock to Attract Females!" he called a little nervously, for he found Silver's father just a bit intimidating.

Nothing.

"She Who Follows the Silver Path of the Moon?"

They waited in silence. And waited. And waited, but even Silver did not answer his call. Now Ben was beginning to feel anxiety gnaw at him. Where could they be? And how would they get out of here without them? Something must have happened—something terrible. . . .

Ellie put her hands on her hips. "Some friends they are!" she huffed. "They've just swum off to save their skins. They're probably having a lovely time playing in the surf on some beach on the other side of the world by now!"

"There must be a good reason," Iggy said, rubbing his head on Ben's leg for comfort. "They wouldn't be able to resist a summons unless something had happened to them that prevented them from coming."

"And," said Ben, "if anything *has* happened to them, it'll be your fault—since everyone's here trying to save you, after you so stupidly got caught by the Dodman!"

Ellie had the grace to look chastened. "So what do we do? I can swim—quite well, in fact; but this top will get ruined . . ."

Ben regarded her scathingly. "We're a very long way underwater and I nearly drowned getting here."

Ellie laughed. "You always were rubbish at swimming—"

Darius waved his arms in the air. "Stop, stop! Arguing won't get us anywhere. I wonder . . ." He waded into the shallows and stared out into the darkness. Then he turned back, a determined expression on his handsome face. "Princess Eleanor," he said, "if you will do me the honor of climbing onto my back, I will do my best to swim with you across the lake, and then I will come back for Ben and Iggy." He regarded her expectantly.

But Ellie was staring at something behind him and paying no attention at all to what he was saying.

Something huge was rising out of the pool,

displacing water in great sheets as it rose. Its skin was mottled and shiny. It had a beak for a mouth and two vast black eyes, one on either side of what must have been its head—though it was hard to tell where its head ended and its body began. It waved some of its arms in the air. There were a lot of them, almost too many to count, and they were long and snaky and covered in suckers like horrid red mouths, and fronds that looked suspiciously like fingers. In three of these vile tentacles, it clutched something greedily. But it still had a lot of unoccupied arms, and these were writhing up through the shallows in a questing sort of way.

Ben stared at it in horror. This must be the monster Silver had been afraid of encountering as they crossed the lake. The nautilus. Just like the one in one of his favorite books, which crushed ships and carried them to the bottom of the ocean.

"Look out, Darius!" he cried, too late.

As the centaur turned to confront the nautilus, two huge tentacles whipped through the air toward him. Darius reared up and beat down at the monster with his hooves, but the tentacles evaded him, snaking around as fast as thought—until one gripped him by

639

the neck and the other by a foreleg. For a moment centaur and nautilus stayed poised in a desperate struggle; then the monster tightened its grip on Darius, and with immense and terrifying strength lifted him right out of the churning water and hurled him through the air. He struck the rocks at the back of the cavern with a resounding crash, and lay still.

Ellie screamed. Then she ran to the centaur and knelt at his side, tears streaming down her face. Tentatively, she placed her hands on Darius's powerful neck and started prodding around. How did you check a centaur's pulse? No one had ever taught her *that* in first aid class. After a moment she looked back to Ben.

"I think he's still alive, but it's hard to tell. . . ."

Her tears had made what was left of her mascara run in black streaks down her cheeks, but for once Ben didn't feel like teasing her about it.

He nodded grimly, then returned his revolted gaze to the nautilus's occupied arms. For the thing trapped in the tentacle nearest to him was the old mermaid, Melusine. Her eyes were closed, and her great silver tail hung limp and dull. It didn't look as if there were any life left in her at all. "Oh, Mellie," Ben whispered.

She'd been pretty scary herself in her time, but now she looked as helpless and unthreatening as a dead fish. He turned his eyes to the second of the nautilus's victims, and gasped. As the air of the cavern began to dry the monster's prey, it was turning from a seal into a man.

It was Skerry.

Ben felt his heart thud: for now he knew, with an awful sick feeling in the pit of his stomach, what it was that the nautilus must be clutching in its third occupied arm.

Sure enough, as the water evaporated on the third still figure, he watched in horror as sleek gray flesh turned to pale pink skin and folds of white fabric, and silver-gold hair flowed out across the suckered tentacle—and even though it confirmed his worst fears, he could not help the loud wail of dismay that escaped him.

"Oh, Silver!"

And at once fear and horror turned to sheer fury.

"Let them go!" he roared at the beast, but it merely sent two of its tentacles out toward him, and he had to jump backward out of its way. "As Prince of Eidolon, I command you! Nautilus, let them go!"

For a heartbeat it looked as if the monster might comply, for it hesitated and its waving arms became still. Then it opened its strange beak of a mouth and an earsplitting sound—half shriek, half moan—filled the cavern. And it began to squeeze the life out of its victims.

Silver's eyes shot open and she cried out in terror, a cry that ended in a wheeze as the nautilus crushed all the remaining air out of her lungs.

Ben flung himself into the water. He ran at the monster and fastened himself to the tentacle holding his friend, battering his fists against it with all his might. "Let her go!" he yelled. "LET HER GO!"

By way of response, the nautilus merely whipped another of its arms in his direction. Ben ducked, stepping smartly sideways. His feet went out from under him on the weed-covered steps. Down he went, fast as a sinking stone. Water rushed into his mouth and nose. He coughed and spluttered, and more went in. He tried to stand up, but a tentacle snaked around his ankles and pulled him deeper. Twisting and scraping, he kicked out, got free, shoved himself away, choking and half-blind. The nautilus's arms came after him. Water tumbled about him, solid and bullying, as much an enemy as the monster itself. Ben tumbled over and over, his lungs burning, hit first by a tentacle, then by another. It was like being trapped in a revolving door. He grabbed at something blindly . . . and it grabbed him back.

For a moment Ben thought that was the end of it for him; that he would die here, held prisoner by the nautilus under the water until he drowned and went limp and became food. But as he felt the fight go out of him and the turmoil in the water began to clear, he realized that the thing that had hold of him was not a tentacle after all, but a flipper: a huge flipper. A vast, whiskery, tusked face was close to his own, and he realized it was Skerry—not Skerry the man, but Skerry in his true selkie form: a vast elephant-seal of a beast with huge black liquid eyes and whiskers everywhere. His mouth moved; then his eyes closed once more.

Nemesis.

Ben heard the sound as an echo in the cave of his skull. It did not sound much like Skerry, but lighter and younger and rather more human. Something else followed, but before Ben could think about it, his feet found something solid under them and he kicked off it as hard as he could, just as he had been taught in swimming classes. Seconds later his head broke the surface of the pool. Air rushed into his poor deprived lungs. He swallowed it down, then opened his mouth, took a deep breath, and lost it in a *whoosh* as a tentacle wrapped itself around him and started squeezing hard.

Some of the water that Ben had swallowed now shot out of his mouth in a great spout, just like water coming out of the mouths of the stone lions in the fountains in Aldstane Park. He almost laughed; then something shot past his ear—something that hissed and spat and yowled horrifically.

Some other monster must have joined the fray, just when he thought it couldn't get any worse. He twisted feebly in the nautilus's grasp to see what on Eidolon it could be.

It was Ignatius Sorvo Coromandel.

The little cat had become a crazed mass of talons and teeth. His amber eyes blazed like fires. He had attached himself to the tentacle that held Ben, with every one of his sharp little claws firmly embedded in the creature's flesh, and was biting and growling and hissing all at the same time. The nautilus's grip on Ben diminished a fraction as it tried to shake the furry demon off it, but Iggy wasn't letting go.

"Give up!" he yowled indistinctly between bites. "Release my friend Ben or you will die, you great big fat overgrown octopus!"

Unsurprisingly, this seemed to have little effect.

Now another voice added to the hubbub. Someone was talking softly in a singsong sort of voice, and the nautilus stopped its squeezing and thrashing and stilled, as if to listen. Then it started to sway, as if it were dancing. It waved its tentacles around its head, brandishing its victims, and all the little fingers on its tentacles waved as well, as if in rhythm with an unheard song. For a moment Ben could see nothing but water as the tentacle that held him dipped down to the pool; then he was up in the air, looking down on his sister from a great height.

"You really are a huge and ugly great octopussy thing, aren't you?" Ellie crooned, the flattering smile she gave the nautilus entirely at odds with her words. "Really, quite the most hideous creature I've ever seen, and that's saying something, considering the state of Mrs. McIntosh's vile poodle, Maurice, at Number Four."

As if delighted by these insults, the nautilus swayed closer to the speaker and its hold on Ben slackened.

Ellie batted her eyelids at the beast.

"There, there, lovely monster, nice monster, good boy . . ."

Now it was above her, the fingers on its four free tentacles waving like the fronds of some gigantic sea anemone.

Ben braced himself, felt the nautilus's tentacle twitch as if in response to his tiny movement, then hurled himself free and fell feet-first onto the hard stone floor of the cavern. Miraculously, the monster made no attempt to pick him up again as he rolled and fetched up alongside his sister, panting just as loudly as Mrs. McIntosh's smelly dog.

Ignatius Sorvo Coromandel landed neatly next to him, his fur sticking out all over him like a punk cat all spiked with gel.

"Wow! How did you manage that?" Ben looked back at the nautilus, and saw how its horrid eyes had grown heavy-lidded with great crescents of yellowish horn. Ellie seemed to have entranced it. Perhaps it liked being insulted by girls in clown makeup.

Ellie raised her eyebrows. "Oh, it was just something the Minotaur told me," she said enigmatically. "Something from a prophecy. I thought I'd try it out, since nothing else seemed to be working. Now you owe me your life." And she gave Ben her nastiest elder-sister grin.

Ben frowned. He couldn't remember the prophecy saying anything about Ellie being able to tame monsters of the deep. She must be making it up, as usual. He gave her a hard stare, but she just returned it coolly.

"Poor Silver," she said. "I think he's squeezing her to death."

Ben spun around to face the nautilus. Indeed, his selkie friend hung as limp as Mellie in the tentacles; and even her huge father seemed to be barely breathing. Ben felt his heart stop, then thunder urgently against his ribs.

"Nemesis, Lord of the Deep, release your prey!"

Ben had no idea where these words had come from: They seemed to leap out of his mouth of their own accord.

The mighty creature became as still as stone. Then it dropped the mermaid and the two selkies with a great splash into the pool.

"Xarkanadûshak!"

On the lake shore the dragon's head came up sharply, like a dog hearing a whistle beyond the range of human ears. His wings began to unfurl.

"No!" he protested. "Oh, no!"

"Zark, what's the matter?" The Queen was gazing at him in alarm.

"I have been summoned!" Zark's purple eyes whirled in panic. His haunches bunched themselves for takeoff.

Queen Isadora placed a hand on his trembling shoulder, but it would take more than that light touch to keep him on the ground. "By Ben?" she cried in sudden fear, but a moment later the dragon was unable to help himself. He soared into the air, his snout pointed directly, unwillingly, toward the castle, as if someone had attached an invisible wire between him and the distant battlements.

"By my son?" she cried again in anguish.

"I am sorry, my lady!" he called back. "He calls me against my will. I . . ."

But whatever else he said tumbled away into the rush of air displaced by his great wings, and, moments later, it was with sinking hearts that Isadora and the Lord of the Wildwood saw their most loyal ally, under the spell of the Dodman's summons, setting down at their enemy's side.

Chapter Twenty-five

Escape

"She's dead."

Ellie pronounced this with horror, then burst into tears. She had never actually seen a dead person before, especially not one with a long silver fish tail.

"Poor Mellie." Ben knelt beside her and slowly closed the old mermaid's staring eyes. There would be no more nip-chase for Melusine; no more bad singing; no more dragging of unfortunate goblins into her deep lairs for supper.

Behind Ben, Skerry was coughing like an old man with a bad tobacco habit, and Silver was pounding him on the back with flippers that were slowly turning to hands. Water gushed out of his mouth with every hit.

"Honestly, Dad," she kept saying, "every selkie knows to keep its mouth shut underwater."

"I was . . . *cough* . . . *cough* . . . trying to warn Ben . . . *cough!*"

Silver rolled her eyes. "Underwater, honestly." She laughed, then clutched her ribs. "*Ow!*"

"Warn me of what?" Ben asked Skerry.

The big selkie looked surprised. "Well, the monster, of course."

"I thought you told me its name."

Now Skerry looked puzzled. "I don't know its name," he admitted. "I didn't even believe it existed, despite what Silver said."

Ben frowned. So where had the name come from, then? This was all very curious.

Silver turned to Ellie. "I hope you can swim better than your brother," she said, "because I'm not sure I'm going to be able to carry you all the way."

"A brick could swim better than Ben." Ellie grinned between sobs.

"Thanks," said Ben. "Thanks a lot."

"I will carry the Princess Eleanor."

The voice came from the back of the cavern. Ellie whirled around, to find the centaur hobbling to his feet, pale and a bit dazed, and with a rather nasty cut on the side of his head.

"Oh, Darius! Thank goodness you're alive!"

The centaur laughed, then winced. "Just about. Alive enough, anyway, to offer my services, my Princess."

Ellie beamed, and completely forgot to blush.

Zark reared away from the dog-headed man in loathing. Little wisps of smoke trickled from his nostrils. If the summoner were not protected by the magic of the summoning, he would have barbecued the Dodman on the spot.

"What do you want from me?" he demanded. "I'm telling you now I won't do anything to harm Eleanor: I'd die first. . . ."

The Dodman laughed unpleasantly. Then he reached inside his jacket, drew out a brace of struggling fairies, and bit their heads off. He closed his eyes, sucked hard on their severed necks, and savored

651

the taste of their magic. When he opened his eyes again they were bright red, as if lit by some inner fire. "You will do whatever I wish of you, dragon, and then you may die. Quite horribly, if I have my way. And of course I shall. I always do. But there's really no need to toast the little Princess. Yet. Come with me."

Compelled by the magic and sickened by the wanton destruction of the innocent creatures, Zark followed the Dodman down the stairs, his wings grazing painfully against the walls on either side. Whatever else it had been built for, the castle had not been designed to contain dragons with any degree of comfort. Hounds and goblins squealed and fled at the sight of him, shoving past, getting underfoot, scrambling over one another to get away. No one liked dragons much. They had heard too many tales of roastings, and Boggart had been nastily burned by this particular specimen once before. Besides, fire in such close quarters was a worrying prospect, even at the best of times, let alone with the lord of the castle in such a bad mood, and a Minotaur on the loose only a few steps away. . . .

"Burn that door down!" the Dodman boomed as they reached the bottom of the stairs.

Grizelda, who was still leaning her considerable

backside against said door, slowly began to look alarmed. "Hold on—!" she began, but Zark's chest was already swelling up with combustible gases.

The first mighty blast burnt most of the giantess's hair and eyebrows off, and left a smoldering hole in the oak door the size of a goblin's fist. An eye blinked—once, twice—on the other side of the hole, then vanished.

"Again!" cried the Dodman.

Zark opened his mouth a second time.

At this point Grizelda wailed and pushed past him, shedding bits of charred clothing as she lumbered up the stairs, her hobnailed boots ringing on the stonework like hammers on an anvil.

Now the center of the door succumbed to the blast, falling away into charcoal and ashes. The Minotaur and the Dodman regarded each other steadily through the smoke.

Then, with a huge bellow, the Minotaur charged at the remains of the door, wresting the blackened timbers from the frame, and hurling them at the Dodman and his cohorts. In the chaos that ensued, the Minotaur turned and disappeared into the warren of tunnels below.

• • •

"I will take Ben," Skerry said, "if you can manage the Wanderer?"

Silver nodded. "Just watch your claws, little cat, eh? I saw the damage you did to the nautilus!"

Iggy grinned proudly and polished his claws on his coat.

"What do we do about this thing, though?" said Ben, staring gloomily at the pool, then at the nautilus, which was still lurking with its strange black eyes just above the surface, watching him, unblinking, its arms all hanging limply underwater. It was very unnerving.

"It seems to be enspelled," Darius said. He looked at Ben with a new respect. "Did you Name it, by any chance?"

"Yes," said Ben hesitantly. "And then Ellie sort of sang to it." Recent events were all jumbled up in his mind. He wasn't sure about anything anymore.

"It seems to have decided to do your bidding," the centaur told him. "Which is probably just as well—"

At that moment an almighty hullabaloo broke out. Bellowing, snorting, wailing, howling, screeching, gnashing, yowling, shrieking, noises filled the air. Up there in the dungeons, the door that had separated the

Dodman and his creatures and their friend must have been opened.

Ellie looked distressed. "What about the Minotaur?" she had just started to say, when the bull-headed man came crashing down the stairs.

"The Dodman is coming, and he has a dragon!" he cried, charging across the cavern. He skidded to a halt at the edge of the pool, his fiery eyes bulging. "What on Eidolon is that?"

"There's no time to explain. We have to get out of here!" Darius said, as calmly as he could manage. "Can you swim?"

"With these horns? I'd sink like a stone."

Ben and Darius exchanged looks. Then they both looked at the nautilus.

"It's the only way," the centaur said.

"I don't know if it'll do what I ask it," Ben replied quietly.

"We don't have a choice."

"Go," the Minotaur said. "Don't worry about me. I just came to warn you and make sure you got away. I'll hold them off while you make your escape."

"No," said Ben. "We're not leaving you. Nemesis, Lord of the Deep, will you please carry my friend the

Minotaur across the lake to the safety of the Wildwood shore, and then go back to where you came from and do no harm to any of our friends?"

The Minotaur eyed the nautilus uncertainly. "Me, go with that thing? I'd rather take on the Dodman." But he didn't sound entirely sure of that either. And a second later, he didn't have the choice. The next thing he knew, two of the nautilus's vast tentacles were securely wrapped around his torso and he found himself suddenly clutched to the monster's glutinous body.

"Take a deep breath!" yelled Ben, and then the nautilus and its passenger were gone in a great vortex of churning water.

Ellie made a face. "I'm so glad I'm coming with you," she told the centaur, hugging his neck.

Scuffling footsteps sounded on the stairs leading down to the cavern, accompanied by yelpings and the chattering of angry goblins.

"Ben!"

The voice was familiar, even through the echoey corridors.

Ben frowned. "Zark!"

"Get away, Ben!"

And then there came the sound of a dragon in pain, and the howl of a maddened dog.

"No time to waste. Come on!" Darius plunged into the pool, Ellie holding on for dear life.

"See you on the shore," Silver said to Ben. "Just remember not to open your mouth underwater this time, okay?" And she winked at him, tucked Iggy securely under one arm, and dived smoothly into the pool.

Ben cast one despairing look over his shoulder as the corridor behind them lit up with the red of dragon fire, and then he just had time to remember to take a very deep breath as Skerry leapt in.

I hate this, Ben thought as the water closed over his head, forcing itself all over him like a great cold glove. He closed his eyes. Perhaps if he really concentrated this time he could hold his breath without passing out. He felt the body of the selkie under him transforming from human to seal, the friction of skin giving way to sleek slipperiness; and he gripped as hard as he could with his knees and arms.

Chapter Twenty-six

Pursuit

The Dodman aimed a booted foot at Zark's belly. "You stumbled on purpose, dragon! To hold us up and allow your little friends to get away!" Then he let fly.

Zark felt the kick break one of his ribs, but he wouldn't give the dog-headed man the satisfaction of seeing his pain. Instead, he drew back his long muzzle and growled, being careful to show all his curving ivory teeth. How he wished he could bite the Dodman in two. . . .

"Back!" The dog-headed man waved his arms furiously at the jumble of goblins and hounds that had tumbled down the steps once Zark had unblocked them. "Get back up to the courtyard! Boggart! Beetle! Get the chariot, and Grizelda, and some knives! Harness up the hounds and the wolves. We are not finished here yet. And you"—he bent his face close to Zark's whirling purple eyes—"you will come with me, *dragon*."

"What is that? Look, over there, breaking the surface of the lake . . ."

Something had emerged from the depths and was heading at speed in their direction. No, not some-*thing*, but a number of them. The gray waters rippled with activity as these shapes cleared the shadow cast by the castle's tall walls.

The Lord of the Wildwood shaded his eyes. "I cannot quite make it out. . . ."

Now everyone was staring out at the lake, their eyes squinting against the bright morning light. Two of the Wildwood fairies soared into the air to get a better look.

"I can see Darius!" one of them cried. "And he's got a girl with him!"

"It must be Ellie!" Isadora's hands flew to her face. Her green eyes shone wildly.

"And there are two selkies, too. One of them's got a boy with it; and the other's clutching something too, but I can't quite see what it is."

"A boy?" The Queen went even paler than she had been before. "Are you quite sure?"

"Yes, yes!" the fairies chorused.

Cernunnos stared out at the scene, his face darkening. Then he nodded grimly. "It's Ben," he said, and his antlers rattled as he spoke. "Though how he came to be here, Eidolon only knows."

Isadora stood on tiptoe, trying to see her children better. "Come along, my dears," she breathed, not sure whether to be relieved or terrified.

A moment later there came the unmistakable sound of the Wild Hunt belling and calling, and a spectral procession launched itself off the battlements: a dozen ghost-hounds, yipping and slavering, followed by six white wolves drawing a chariot full of goblins brandishing wicked-looking curved blades, and a huge, dark, ragged figure. Behind them, a dragon sailed into the morning air, described a graceful circle, and then plummeted down toward the disrupted surface of the water.

"Oh, Zark!" cried the Queen. "Oh no!"

On the dragon's back, gripping tight to its crest with its hands and to its wide-bellied body with its spiky knees, was a single tall figure, every line of its body and its sharp-nosed head taut with murderous intent. . . .

"Look out!"

Ellie ducked as Zark's outstretched claws whizzed past her, catching a strand of her hair and tearing it away.

"Ow!"

"Blasted dragon, you missed on purpose!" The Dodman struck out with his boot as the dragon banked, catching the centaur a glancing blow.

Darius, his face gray with exhaustion, rolled sideways, almost dumping Eleanor into the water.

The dragon wheeled overhead, its wings beating the air fiercely.

"Zark, Zark! What are you doing?" Ben shouted. "It's us. Why are you doing this?"

"He's been summoned. He's acting under an unbreakable compulsion," Skerry said. "He can't help it. As far as I can see, he's doing what he can to avoid hurting anyone, but the Dodman's not going to let him get away with that for long. And here comes the Wild Hunt! Take a deep breath, Ben, we're going under again!"

Ben just had time to see the leading Gabriel Hounds inches above him before the water closed over his head. This time he'd forgotten to fill his lungs, and moments later his lungs were bursting. He held his breath as long as he could, then dug his knees sharply into the selkie. Skerry bucked and twisted, then shot to the surface.

Ben had time to take a single deep breath before the Wild Hunt was upon them. A goblin slashed at him with its sharp little knife, and Ben had the wit to flatten himself against the selkie's slick skin, before grabbing Gutty by the wrist. With a sudden jerk, he'd pulled the goblin out of the chariot.

At once, three of its fellows had Gutty by the ankles, not really trying to save him, but more to claw their way closer to Ben. Whoever captured one of the Queen's children would get a big reward: Their master had promised them.

Skerry made a sharp turn so that Ben lost his hold

on the goblin, but Ben managed to grab the curved blade—and then they were underwater again and barreling along. When Ben opened his eyes, he could see Silver in front of them with Iggy plastered to her side like a wet rag. Iggy had his eyes screwed tightly shut. He obviously wasn't enjoying himself at all. Ben almost smiled; but a moment later he could see Darius, his legs kicking feebly, and the water churning around him.

This time when they surfaced, it was to a cacophony of noise: Ellie screaming, goblins chattering, wolves howling, and hounds barking like banshees. Two goblins had hold of Ellie and were slowly dragging her from the centaur's back, while Darius was reaching around in vain behind him trying to hold her on.

"Help me!" Ellie shrieked. "Ben, help me!"

One of the goblins twisted its claws in her hair and yanked her head back. "Did he say he wanted her alive?" it asked Bosko.

Bosko shrugged. "He's so furious he won't care!"

Batface leaned out of the chariot and swiped at her with his curved knife, but Ben launched himself off Skerry's back with the stolen blade in his hand, and the two weapons clashed with a screech that shivered through the air—and Batface overbalanced and fell into the lake. Ben fell with him. Down they went, tangled up in each other, with Batface trying all the time to bite and stab. Ben twisted in the goblin's grip and kicked away from it, and then he was free of it and swimming in dark water, a long way out of his depth.

It took a moment to realize this; and then he panicked. At the swimming pool he had mainly swum widths in the shallow end, since he was, as Ellie had said, about as talented at swimming as a brick. Once, he'd tried lengths, but as soon as he'd passed into the deep zone and knew he could no longer touch the bottom, he'd got nervous and all his muscles had gone leaden. Luckily, he'd been on the outside lane and could grab the bar; but there were no bars here with which to pull himself out. He felt his legs going heavy, and then he started to sink. He dropped the knife and kicked out wildly, but to no avail; then he was underwater and going down. . . .

"Ishtar!"

The Queen called three times; on the third call a tiny dark speck appeared in the sky overhead and grew larger and larger with every passing second.

"I have returned your mate and kit," the female dragon said, as she came in to land. "Just as you asked me to." She sounded very annoyed.

"I am sorry to summon you," Isadora said breathlessly, "but I need your help. The Dodman . . ." Helplessly, she indicated the battle taking place on the lake.

"That's Zark!" Ishtar gaped, craning her neck. Her eyes bulged in disbelief. "What's he thinking of, carrying the Dodman around like that?"

"The Dodman summoned him," Cernunnos said.

"And how did the Dog-Headed One know my husband's true name?" Izzy asked sharply.

No one answered her. Instead, the Queen started to clamber onto Ishtar's back.

"What do you think you are doing?" the Horned Man demanded, clutching at her arm.

"I have to do something," Isadora answered fiercely, unpicking his fingers. She managed to get a leg up onto the dragon's withers, and swung herself up to sit astride its neck. "Since no one else is doing anything. Ishtar, as one mother to another, I implore you: Help me save my children!"

The great blue-and-purple-and-gold dragon

craned her neck around at the Queen, then nodded her assent. She reared up, beat her long wings so hard that the Lord of the Wildwood had to stand aside, and took off.

Staying high above the lake, Ishtar planed like a gull on a current of warm air, and the Queen of Eidolon peered down anxiously. She could see Ellie astride the centaur, and a selkie with a small dark cat stuck to it; she could see the Gabriel Hounds and the white wolves that had once belonged to Cernunnos himself, drawing a chariot full of goblins and a very strange-looking figure in charred clothing with a soot-covered face and bald patches. But nowhere could she see Ben, or, for that matter, the Dodman.

"*Ishtarrr!*"

Ishtar sideslipped swiftly, and not a moment too soon. Zark barreled past, neck outstretched and wings stiff and uncoordinated as if he were willing his body not to obey the compulsion the Dodman had placed upon him. The dog-headed man, known in another world as Mr. Dodds, leered at the Queen over his shoulder.

"Ready to give yourself up to me, are you, my dear? You didn't need to arrange your own transport, you know."

Isadora gritted her teeth. "You're a monster!" she cried.

"Ah yes, they do say that." Now the Dodman had steered Zark into flying a course parallel to Ishtar's. "Personally, I think monsters have had a bad press, often from nuisances like your own very dear husband. Him, I will deal with next. Oh, and the baby, of course. Once I've cleared away your family in this world." And he gave her his shark's grin.

"Where's my son?"

"Oh, drowned by now, I'd say. We saw him go down some time ago. And sadly there was nothing we could do to help him. Now"—and here a growl slipped out—"are you going to come quietly, or am I going to have to kill the worm you fly upon and take you by force?"

"Never!" cried Isadora. "Down, Ishtar, down!"

Zark's mate folded her wings back like a stooping hawk and plummeted toward the lake.

Grizelda never saw what hit her. Ishtar's talons raked out left and right, and over went the chariot— goblins, giantess, and all—into the lake. The traces got all tangled up with the wolves, who then started taking out their frustrations on the hounds harnessed in front of them. Soon, the entire Wild Hunt was fighting with themselves.

Ishtar skimmed past at speed and was gone before a single creature could lay a tooth or claw upon her.

"There!" cried Isadora. "Over there!"

She indicated a struggling figure a little way ahead of them. It was the centaur, battling valiantly on through the water toward the shore, though the last of his strength was waning. On his back, weighing him down, was not only Isadora's daughter Eleanor, but also three of the Dodman's goblins, squabbling over her. Beside them, Silver and Iggy were trying to help; but flippers and a small cat's fury were no match for three determined goblins armed to the teeth and greedy for reward.

Cernunnos and his phalanx of centaurs were wading out into the lake, but they would never reach them in time.

Yawing sharply, Ishtar made a low pass across the surface of the lake and grabbed two of the goblins in her talons. They squawked in horror as she tossed them aside and went in for the third. The last goblin, a mangled bandage flapping around its head, wrapped its arms and legs around Ellie and refused to budge. It had already lost an ear because of this scrawny little human, and it didn't want to lose anything else to the Dodman's rage.

Ishtar roared, and grabbed both girl and goblin up in her claws.

With the goblin obscuring her vision, Ellie had no idea what was going on. One minute she had been fighting for her life, the next she was in the air in some monster's grasp. She screamed and screamed.

"It's all right, Ellie," her mother cried through the din. "We've got you now, you're safe."

But Isadora spoke too soon.

Xarkanadûshak hurtled into his wife, howling all the way, compelled by the Dodman's will. In a great flurry of limbs and wings, both dragons crashed into the surface of the lake.

Vast plumes of water erupted into the air, as if the entire lake were trying to empty itself upward and change places with the sky. Everyone stopped what they were doing, transfixed by the shocking noise of it all. The Lord of the Wildwood stared into the confusion, searching desperately. Then he urged his centaurs forward.

"Find the Queen!"

• • •

Not many folk from either world know much about dragons. Stories abound, mainly of violence and treachery, of greed and arrogance. They are known for their destruction: for the breathing of fire and the eating of sheep and maidens. Among dragonkind, however, there are other stories—tales of courage and selflessness, tales of heroism and sacrifice.

When the Dodman gave Xarkanadûshak the order to attack his wife, there was nothing Zark could do but obey. But he did so shrieking a warning as he came; and although the collision appeared terrible to the onlookers, Ishtar moved fast, and it was a glancing blow Zark struck his wife, which sent Izzy and the Queen spinning harmlessly out of his way. Zark, however, carried on. Headlong he dived into the lake, dizzyingly fast, before the Dodman could make him do anything else. Down and down he went, driven by a compulsion all his own.

It is worth it! he told himself fiercely, over and over. *If I can rid the world of the fiend on my back, my wife and kids will lead safer lives, and so will the rest of Eidolon. My life is a small price to pay. My life . . .*

He tried not to think about that bit. A second later

he felt the Dodman trying hard to take control again, digging his horrid dog-nails into the sensitive places between his scales, biting and kicking.

For Eidolon, Zark thought. *For Eidolon and my friends and loved ones.* And he shut his mind to the Dodman and watched the lake-bed come looming closer and closer.

He had often wondered how his death would come to him. When the dog-headed man had captured him and sold him to the woman in the Other World, he had thought it would be there, tied to a fence post by a piece of frayed string among dead leaves and piles of rubbish he didn't understand, feeling his magic and his life leaking out of him moment by moment into the bad air. No one would even have known—had Ben not saved him. Now it was his turn to repay that deed. No one made songs for dragons who died a quiet death tied to a fence post far from home; at least this way he would live on in heroic tales.

He folded his wings as tightly as a furled umbrella, closed his eyes, and waited for the inevitable impact.

It never came.

The next thing Zark knew, he was flying through the water at a speed he could never have dreamt possible, and something had him firmly by the midriff, something that squeezed him with monstrous strength. Beneath the grip, he could feel the Dodman squirming, furious but feeble against this overwhelming force, and Zark could not help but crane his neck in curiosity. He felt the water bashing at the back of his head in their headlong rush. But when he stared around, it was not into the dead black pupils of the dog-headed one that he found himself looking, but a pair of mismatched eyes, one a sensible hazel-brown, the other a vivid Eidolon green.

It was Ben, and he was gripped in the snakelike arms of the same monster that grasped Zark and the Dodman. He should have been terrified, but instead he was smiling as hard as he possibly could with his mouth held tightly shut to keep the lake out of it. Then he tapped the great mottled arm that held him three times and pointed upward, and suddenly there was a great *whoosh* as the monster—a vast nebulous shadow beneath them—gathered itself and drove them up toward the light with phenomenal power.

They burst into the bright air seconds later, held aloft by the tentacles so that water streamed from them in sparkling rainbows.

Ben coughed and coughed; then he laughed and laughed. "Thank you, Nemesis!" he said. "That was brilliant!" His eyes were shining as he turned to Zark. "He saved me, you know, even though he's really scary. I was drowning again, and he dropped the Minotaur in the shallows and came after me."

The dragon blinked. Nemesis? Drowning? Minotaur? It was all too much to take in.

"And then we saw you crash into Ishtar and Mum, and it looked really bad, so we came to see what we could do, but when we got there Mum and Izzie were fine and Mum had got hold of Ellie, and so we came after you, because it looked as if you were going too fast to stop and I was really worried you were going to hit the bottom!" Ben finished in a great rush.

Zark didn't know what to say. He looked at his friend, and then he looked away.

A shadow passed before Ben's mismatched eyes. "You were . . . ," he breathed. "You were going to . . ."

The dragon nodded. "I could not kill him directly; but I thought if I hit the lake-bed hard enough and rolled, I would die there and trap him beneath me. And in time, and with luck, he would drown, and the world would be rid of him."

Ben regarded him solemnly. "That was really brave, Zark. But I couldn't let you do it. What would Izzy do? What about your kits?"

The purple eyes whirled and whirled. "Someone has to stop him."

Benjamin Arnold firmed his jaw. "Yes," he said. "That's true. Someone has to stop him."

He tapped the giant squid on its tentacle again, and its fringe of fingers flexed and swayed in response.

"Nemesis, will you please take me and the dragon to the shore and release us there? But keep a tight hold of the dog-headed one known as the Dodman. Do you understand me?"

The nautilus quivered and a weird chirrup emerged from its beak of a mouth.

Ben looked at Zark. "I do hope that means yes."

Two strange and motley groups had gathered on the southern shore of Corbenic Lake. On one side, away from the forest, was a sodden giantess, a pile of wet goblins, and some very miserable-looking hounds. A black bird with a bright orange beak flapped around overhead, shrieking. Only the words "Dodman" and "cowards" and "guts for garters" could be made out at a distance.

On the other side were a herd of centaurs with their manes and tails dripping puddles onto the stones, and six white wolves who had broken free of their traces and were now licking the remains of the lake and the taint of the Dodman off their fur. There were two dragons, one of scarlet and gold, the other of purple and blue, preening like eagles caught in a rainstorm; and two selkies, one big and one small, transforming moment by moment into a man and a pretty fair-haired girl. There was a pale woman in a soaking dress with her arm around a shivering girl in a pink T-shirt. Both were being wrapped in a cloak of moss and leaves by a tall figure with the branching antlers of a stag. Next to them there was a boy with straw-blond hair and mismatched eyes, who was squeezing water out of his sweater and grinning from ear to ear. A small black and brown cat sat at his feet, rubbing its bedraggled head against his leg over and over and over. And at the back of the group, in the shadows cast by the forest eaves, a vast figure with a massive bull's head and a pair of menacing horns watched over the scene with eyes of fire, but with a remarkably benign expression for one who owned such a fearsome and blood-thirsty reputation.

A sudden scream of outrage made everyone stop whatever they were doing and crane their necks for a better view.

Out in the deepest part of the lake, with Corbenic Castle rising behind it like a great golden mountain, a giant squid was wrestling a tall dog-headed figure into submission. The Dodman—held high in the air by a vast tentacle—was struggling valiantly: sinking his claws and teeth into the huge, rubbery arm; biting at the suckers and fingery things; kicking and squirming and cursing between grunts and growls and howls. It had been a bitter discovery to the Dodman that Naming the squid had absolutely no effect: for the Lord of the Deep was still safely under the compulsion placed upon it by Ben Arnold, Prince of Eidolon. And so the dog-headed man was taking out his frustration on the nautilus itself, who barely felt a thing. In its turn, Nemesis turned one of its huge black eyes upon its captive and regarded it with whatever degree of humor a giant squid possesses. Then it began to squeeze the Dodman just a little harder, and a little harder—until the dog-headed man stopped trying to harm it and hung there, helpless and panting, planning terrible revenge on everyone and everything in sight.

Ben picked up the little cat and cradled it against his chest.

"I'll never eat fish fingers again," he vowed solemnly.

"Fish don't have fingers."

The voice was soft and trilling, like the breaking of waves on a sandy beach. He turned around to find Silver smiling at him, all girl now, her pale gold hair glowing in the sunlight.

"You do!" Ben said, grinning from ear to ear.

"I am *not* a fish."

"You are sometimes. Sort of."

"And you are a horrid boy."

Ignatius Sorvo Coromandel turned to regard the selkie with his sardonic amber eyes. "That's not what you said before," he reminded her wickedly. "When you thought he had drowned."

She Who Swims the Silver Path of the Moon looked away. "I don't know what you mean," she said, flustered.

Ben looked at her. Then he looked at Iggy. "What are you on about?"

"Silver knows."

By now Silver was blushing furiously. "Shut up," she said to the little cat.

"What'll you give me," Iggy wheedled, "not to tell him? Will you bring me goldfish and silverfish and copperfish?"

"Yes!" said the selkie desperately.

"And catfish and dogfish and rabbitfish?"

"Yes!"

"And some of those fat little crabs from the beaches off Doubting Sound?"

"Yes, yes!"

"Goodness me," growled Ignatius Sorvo Coromandel, dropping Ben a great big wink. "She really doesn't want you to know how much she cares." And then he had to scamper off as fast as his paws could carry him, because when selkies have feet instead of flippers, they can move as quickly as any cat.

Epilogue

In the throne room of Dodman Castle an angry figure paced up and down, muttering to itself and glaring at anyone or anything that got in its way. No one dared say a word. Especially the word "nautilus" . . .

Nemesis had held on to its prize for long after the compulsion of Ben's Naming had worn off. The goblins had watched from the shore with macabre fascination, wondering whether or not the giant squid would finally squeeze the dog-headed one to death, and squabbling over who would dare to swim the lake and retrieve the keys to the castle's extensive larders.

But eventually the nautilus had grown bored, or decided it had something better to do, and after setting the Dodman down on the rocks below the castle (none too gently), it had dived down into the deepest part of the lake. No one had seen tooth nor tentacle of it since.

It was with considerable circumspection that the Sphynx entered the throne room, knowing all too well the Dodman's likely state of mind. He had lost his hostage (and a rather dangerous Minotaur in the adjacent cell), and he had almost had the Queen in his grasp, before losing her, too. But worst of all, he had lost his dignity. There were a lot of creatures spreading the tale across Eidolon of how a boy— believed to be the son of the long-lost Queen of Eidolon—had thwarted the mighty Dodman; of how the dog-headed one had hung, powerless, pathetic, and dripping, in the grip of a giant squid commanded by the young Prince.

None of this would have improved the Dodman's already bad temper.

The spy skirted the groups of sullen goblins (since

the lost battle, they had been on reduced rations as a punishment for their failure), avoided the tethered Gabriel Hounds—who watched him pass with hungry eyes and frothing jaws—and came to a halt at a safe distance from the pacing figure.

"Ahem," it said, and got ready to run beneath the throne in case one of those nailed boots that scraped and squeaked on the stones suddenly came its way.

The Dodman turned slowly.

His eyes—usually so fierce and shiny black—were dull and rimmed with red. It looked as if he had not slept in a week (which, in fact, he had not). He barely glanced at the hairless cat and continued his distracted pacing.

"What do you want with me, little sneak? Have you come to tell me how they snigger behind my back? How they flock to Isadora's cause now that they fear me no longer? How the Queen prides herself on my defeat?"

"Of coursssse not, master—"

"Because it is not a defeat. NOT, do you hear me? It is a . . . a . . . temporary setback, that is all."

"Yesssss, master. I came with newsssss that may brighten your day."

The Dodman stopped in midstride, turned, and regarded the Sphynx with renewed interest.

"It will take a great deal to brighten the gloom that has settled over me, little spy."

"If you would accompany me to the battlementssss, ssssire . . ."

Now the Dodman's eyes narrowed with suspicion. He surveyed the throne room to see if there was anything going on—but the goblins were as cowed and craven-looking as usual, and the giantess was snoring in a heap by the fire, on top of several squashed hounds. Was there a plot afoot, a plot to maybe tip him over the castle walls into the waters of the deep lake below? He shuddered. Ideas like this had been plaguing him by day and night; and being worse by night, he had ceased sleeping for fear that someone, somewhere, was hatching something to cause his downfall, now that they were less afraid of him than they had been.

"Why to the battlements, spy?"

"You will see, sssire. Sssomeone has a gift for you."

A gift.

As he followed the Sphynx up the winding stairs to the top of the castle, the Dodman ran through all the possibilities in his head. None of them seemed either likely or welcome; and when he reached the battlements, his spirits were not raised by the sight of a dark speck circling high up in the clear blue sky above him.

The weather in Eidolon had improved of late. Ever since the Queen had returned—more so since she had secured her daughter and retired to the safety of the Wildwood to fortify the resistance against him. It was yet another thorn in his side. Wicked deeds required foul weather—thunder and lightning, sweeping storms, driving rain—to quell the hopes of the small folk and make them seek the shelter he and only he could provide within these walls.

He squinted against the bright sunlight, shaded his eyes with a dark dog-nailed hand, and watched as the speck got larger and larger.

It was a thin, spiky figure with bright orange hair, all knees and elbows as it fought to control a classic willow-wood broomstick in the stiff updraft above the castle. A large parcel was balanced precariously in its lap.

"Ah," he said at last. "I see it is the little witch. Bad day, Cynthia." He inclined his great dog's head.

"Bad day, Dodman." And Awful Cousin Cynthia,

known by her true name in the Shadow World as Cynthia Lucrezia Creepie, gave the dog-headed man her most awful grin. Despite the existence in the Other World of plenty of good dentists and effective whitening toothpastes, it was a truly ghastly grin, full of slimy green-and-black teeth and too much gum. "I have something for you." She paused. "Though if I give it to you, you will have to promise me something in return."

The Dodman looked thoughtful. "Tell me first what the Queen and her vile brood are up to."

Cynthia looked annoyed. She ran an impatient hand through her carroty hair. "Ben and Ellie have gone back to the Other World to rejoin their father and the horrid baby. And to go back to school. Ha! Such a waste of time. And the Wanderer has gone with them." She laughed. "A useless bodyguard he'll be! Even my Sphynx could beat him."

The Sphynx looked uncomfortable at this idea. Among cats, tales circulated that Iggy had fought valiantly at Ben Arnold's side, taking on a huge tentacled monster single-pawedly, and later killing several goblins. However, since there had been no other cats present to witness these heroic events, he suspected these stories had probably originated with the Wanderer himself. . . .

"And the Queen?"

Cynthia shrugged. "With the Lord of the Wildwood, gathering her forces. There's word that she will try to persuade the dragons to her cause, but they are refusing their support so far."

The Dodman looked hangdog. "Dragons," he groaned. Even the walls of Corbenic Castle would not withstand the onslaught of dragons. "If she Names them, I am lost."

Cynthia's horrid grin widened. "Perhaps not. She refuses to compel them; and now she cannot!"

"Cannot?"

Cynthia unwrapped the parcel in her lap and held it up to his view, just out of reach.

The Dodman's eyes grew round with wonder. "The Book! The Book of Naming! Give it to me!" He fairly danced on the spot. "Oh, with the Book of Naming I can bring the dragons to my cause—even better, I can Name the dinosaurs! Imagine the Wildwood trampled to matchwood beneath the feet of a herd of brontosauruses! Imagine the centaurs devoured by Tyrannosaurus rexes! Imagine the Queen carried off by a pteranodon and brought to her wedding flanked by velociraptors!"

"Stop!" cried Cynthia. Beneath the Book, something else glittered. She fetched it out and set it on her head, where it rocked dangerously on her narrow skull. It was the Crown of Eidolon. "If you want the Book, you will have to make me a promise." She paused. "Actually, two promises."

"What?" He might have known there was a catch.

"First of all, you are to rescue my father from jail and return him safely to the Secret Country. And second, once we have dealt with Isadora and her brats, you shall bow to me as your rightful Queen!"

The Dodman regarded her askance. He'd been planning to spring Aleister from prison anyway, but it wouldn't do to look as if he were giving in to the little witch's demands too easily. "Well, now, that's a lot to ask." He stroked his hairy dog-chin thoughtfully. The second part of the bargain would be a lot more difficult to keep. . . .

"Promise me now, or lose the Book forever."

Cynthia hovered before him, and the sun glinted on the crown, almost blinding him with its brightness.

The Dodman crossed his fingers behind his back and gave her his finest smile. The sun of Eidolon gleamed on each and every one of his powerful dog-teeth.

"It is my pleasure, my dear, to make these promises to one as beautiful as you. Now, give me the Book and we can peruse it together in the comfort of my throne room."

Cousin Cynthia giggled and went all pink with delight.

It clashed horribly with her hair.

Dragon's Fire

Contents

Chapter One

Bad News

"No, no, Iggy, you're hopeless! How on Earth are we going to convince the neighbors you're just an ordinary cat if you can't even manage to chase a ball like a normal kitten?"

Ben shook his head at his cat in frustration. Some new people had recently moved in next door, and Iggy had complained that the woman kept giving him funny looks, as if she knew more than she was letting on, so Ben had been trying to teach him how to behave like a "normal" cat.

Now Iggy—known in another world as Ignatius Sorvo Coromandel, or the Wanderer—sat and watched as Ben got down on his hands and knees and tried unsuccessfully to fish the last ball of crumpled-up newspaper out from under the dresser where he'd just hit it. All this paper ball chasing was getting really, really annoying. He'd played along with Ben for a while, catching the ball, juggling it, running around, batting it from paw to paw like some clever furry soccer player; but now he was very, very bored. He'd managed to get rid of about a dozen of the irritating newspaper balls now—just out of Ben's reach beneath the carved Welsh dresser with all of Mrs. Arnold's best china on it—and Ben *still* hadn't worked out that he was doing it on purpose. Which was probably because Iggy had perfected the "oops-nearly-had-it-that-time, what-a-butterpaws-I-am!" technique of knocking each new ball just a bit too hard so that it shot across the floor and under the dresser.

Games. Humans seemed to love them. He couldn't imagine why. Safely unwatched, the little black-and-brown cat yawned grotesquely, then stuck his tongue out at the boy's back.

"I'm not an ordinary cat," he rasped, his voice all sandpaper and vinegar. "And I ain't no kitten."

Ben pushed himself back upright and stared at his friend crossly with his mismatched eyes, one a sensible hazel-brown, the other an odd and vivid green. "Well, *I* know that, and *you* know that, but you're supposed to be undercover! Cats with special wayfaring skills from the Secret Country are a bit hard to come by. You might find yourself getting caught and sold off . . . to some horrid pet shop or something."

Iggy sniffed. "That's not funny, Sonny Jim."

Ben had, in fact, rescued the little talking cat from Mr. Dodds's Pet Emporium, a strange shop full of peculiar and remarkable animals, many of whom had been smuggled in from the Secret Country of Eidolon, where all the magical and extinct creatures lived. But that had been before Ben had known anything about the Shadow World; or Mr. Dodds (who in the Secret Country walked eight feet tall and had the head of an enormous dog); or that his own mother was Queen of Eidolon, which made *him* a halfling prince—half of this world (since his dad was human) and half of the other: hence his different-colored eyes.

"Look, just one more try, eh?" said Ben, trying to sound reasonable. It was for Iggy's own good, after all.

"There's no more newspaper," Iggy growled. "You used it all up." He gave Ben a smug sort of look, though because of all his fur it was a little hard to judge his expression. Cats use their eyebrows a lot to express themselves, and they have the gift of being able to see exactly how another cat is using its eyebrows, but humans are a bit stupid like that and find it hard to tell just where a cat's eyebrows finish and the rest of its fur begins.

Ben laughed. "You don't get off that lightly; there's *always* more newspaper. It's under the sink." And off he went to the kitchen to fetch some.

Iggy watched the boy's retreating back furiously. Under the sink. He might have known. Everything that didn't have a proper place anywhere else in the house got kept under the sink. Sometimes he thought it was where *he* belonged. Iggy sighed and ambled over to gaze boredly out of the window.

Something moved, fast, a movement he caught just out of the corner of his eye. He blinked, then looked again, but all he could see was a falling leaf, a red and gold twist of fire, spiraling down out of the old oak tree to join a thousand other autumn leaves on the shaggy grass beneath it. Time was passing, in this world and the Shadow World. Who knew what might be happening in Eidolon now?

He stared at the tree, as if it might give up its secrets to him, but nothing else seemed to be stirring out there.

"Come on, Ig, pay attention!"

Ben held out another ball of newspaper and Iggy sighed. Turning his back on the window, Iggy tried to look alert and interested, but it was pretty hard. The ball went up into the air and he batted at it half-heartedly.

"Oh, Iggy, honestly!"

The thing had got itself caught up on the little cat's claws. Ignatius Sorvo Coromandel shook his paw in irritation, but all that happened was that the paper ball started to unravel itself. He stood on a corner and pulled at it with his teeth. Nothing happened. This was not very dignified, particularly for a cat of his prestigious heritage. His father had climbed the highest mountain in Eidolon, and his mother had been a great explorer, but here was their one and only son, the Wanderer, with a piece of dirty newspaper stuck on his paw. He growled at it, but that did not achieve anything at all. He gave it an extra-hard tug, and with a sudden roar, the paper ripped away from his grasp and lay there on the carpet, defeated at last.

"Grrr!" said Iggy, standing over it. "Grrrrr!!"

Ben shook his head. His friend had clearly gone quite mad. "Oh, Iggy, for goodness' sake, do stop it. It's only a bit of paper!"

But the little cat's muzzle was screwed up in an expression of sheer loathing. Ben sighed and bent to pick up the offending scrap.

"Oh no . . ."

There, square in the middle of the newspaper, on what had clearly been the front page of the *Greening & Bixbury Times*, was a grainy black-and-white photograph of someone horribly familiar. And under it ran the story:

Local Prison Breakout

"That's the beast who hit me over the head when I came through the wild road!" Iggy growled. "Grrrrrr!"

The wild roads run between our world and the Secret Country, and only a few folk know where their entrances can be found, or how to travel along them.

Ben had traveled the wild road into Eidolon through the great stone in Aldstane Park many times now, more or less safely.

"Yes, that's Awful Uncle Aleister," Ben concurred, studying the photo with a sinking heart.

"What does it say?" the little cat demanded in his gravelly voice. "He's still safely in prison, isn't he?" The fur had started to bristle on his neck.

Ben started to read:

Ardbar Prison was last night the scene of a dramatic jailbreak. Inmates report hearing a tremendous noise at around nine o'clock. "We thought it was a gas explosion at first," said Rodney Lightfoot (serving eleven years for cat burglary), "because the kitchens're in a right dodgy state here. Then someone said, 'It must be a bomb!' and then the power failed and all the lights went out. It was mayhem."

Prison Governor Collier takes up the story. "We implemented emergency measures and my officers immediately sealed the perimeter and encouraged the men to return to their rooms, where we locked them in for their own safety. However, when the backup generator kicked in and the floodlights came on, we found there was a huge hole in the east wing and that one of our inmates was missing."

Prison officer Mr. A. Tookey had come off duty earlier in the evening and headed as usual for the Red Lion public house. On returning to Ardbar to retrieve items he had left in the staff room there, he made a bizarre sighting: "There was smoke and dust everywhere, but out of the middle of it came a massive great ugly woman—at least I think it was a woman—I mean, some of the girls around here are pretty big, but even by local standards she was a real monster, about nine feet tall, with a load of orange and black hair and great big . . . er—"

"Grizelda!" exclaimed Iggy. "That's got to be a description of that awful ogress who hangs around with the Dodman!"

Ben nodded grimly. "It does sound rather like her." He read on:

"Anyway this, um, thing came out of there with a portly looking chap tucked under her arm. Then all the smoke and dust and stuff swirled out on the perimeter field, and I thought it was a helicopter or something.

Except it was really quiet, and those choppers generally make quite a racket. But when the smoke cleared, I got the shock of my life. It was a bl***y great monster with a pointy head and these huge, batlike wings, just like this picture of a dinosaur I used to have on my bedroom wall when I was a lad! And then the woman-thing sticks the chap on the dinosaur's back and off they all go, up into the sky."

There were no other witnesses to this strange account, and other regulars at the Red Lion report that the officer had "been really hammered" and was prone to exaggeration when "under the influence."

"Last year it was flying saucers," said barmaid Sally Ellery, rolling her eyes.

However, the *Times* can claim that our reporter spotted some enormous footprints in the grounds outside the walls of the east wing that did not resemble anything he had seen before. We called in dinosaur expert Professor Hugh Juggley Twitt to examine the evidence.

Professor Twitt was initially circumspect in his assessment. "They look rather similar to casts made of footprints found in the Midwest of America that may date back to the late Cretaceous period. But those prints belonged to a species of flying dinosaur called a pterosaur, which has been extinct on this planet for the best part of 150 million years. So, obviously, these can't belong to anything like that! It must be a hoax."

We pressed the professor for his opinion of what else might have made the marks, but he laughed nervously and said something about his reputation going up in smoke if we quoted him further, and left in a hurry, but not without taking several photographs of the footprints, "for future reference."

"Wow!" said Ben. "A dinosaur! Do you really think it is?"

"It's probably all a big mistake." Iggy wasn't going to linger on the subject. "What does the rest of it say?"

But there was no rest, for here the report was torn.

Ben glared at Iggy accusingly. "What have you done with it?"

Iggy glared back, then spread his empty paws at Ben. "I haven't got it! That's the whole of the bit you crumpled up to make a stupid ball for me to chase."

"Well, where can it be, then?"

The little cat shrugged. "I haven't eaten it, you know."

Ben stomped off crossly through the door into the kitchen and rooted around under the sink till he found the rest of the newspaper. He brought it back, and got down on his knees beside Iggy. Smoothing out the paper ball, he matched it up to the torn front page, and read on: "The missing prisoner is Mr. Aleister Creepie of King Henry Close, Bixbury, jailed earlier this year for selling dangerous animals. If you see him, please do not approach him but contact the police at Bixbury's incident room at once."

Ben and Iggy exchanged anguished glances.

"Oh, Iggy. It's true. Awful Uncle Aleister's escaped!"

Chapter Two

Bag-o'-Bones

At that moment the front door opened and Ben's father came striding in, followed by a thin, heavily perfumed woman with long red hair and a lot of teeth and a gangly youth wearing a pair of jeans so ridiculously loose that it looked as if they'd fly off him if he sneezed. Ben wondered if maybe the boy had got locked out of his house, trouserless, and had had to raid a fat neighbor's clothesline. Except that they *were* the neighbors.

Ben's family lived next door to them. Ben didn't like them much. There was nothing he could put his finger on, exactly, to explain why. They weren't as nice as old Mr. and Mrs. Thomas who used to live next door. Something about them just gave him the creeps. He turned around to gauge Iggy's reaction to the visitors, only to find that he had vanished. Or almost. The tip of his tail stuck out from under the sofa, the tuft of black fur a bit of a giveaway against the cream carpet.

"Ha!"

The scrawny youth, belying his lazy appearance, was on it in a flash, grabbing it with both hands. There was a terrible commotion, involving considerable hissing and spitting (most of it from Ignatius Sorvo Coromandel), then the cat flew out of the living room window, like a giant, furry bullet.

The red-haired woman started to sneeze and sneeze.

"Oh dear," she said at last, clutching Clive Arnold's arm. "I'm most terribly allergic to cats, and poor Robert is too."

"Poor Robert" did not seem to have suffered any particular ill effects following his set-to with the Wanderer, and it seemed rather perverse to chase cats if they made you ill, but Ben decided not to point this out. Besides which, how could anyone who claimed to be allergic to things wear so much horrible perfume?

Mr. Arnold patted her hand solicitously. "Don't you worry about that, Maggie. I'm sure Iggy will be perfectly happy to live outside."

Ben fixed his father with an appalled stare. "What do you mean?" he cried, all thought of Uncle Aleister suddenly flying from his head. "Iggy can't live in the garden, he lives here!"

"Now, now, Ben," his father chided. "We can't have Mrs. Bagshott sneezing her head off, can we? It's not very fair to her if she's going to be coming in all the time to look after us."

A fleeting image of Mrs. Bagshott's head flying through the air and out of the same window through which Iggy had exited like a great big firework distracted Ben for a moment; then he said stiffly, and probably rather rudely, "We don't need looking after. That's what Mum does."

For a moment Mr. Arnold looked a little dazed, as if he had somehow forgotten the very existence of Isadora Arnold.

Mrs. Bagshott smiled at Ben. It was not a very nice

smile: There were altogether too many teeth involved in it. "While your poor mother is away, Ben dear. Just to give your father a hand with the cooking and cleaning and all."

"Ellie can help with that," Ben said crossly, and rather chauvinistically, though he didn't really mean it. Ellie's idea of cooking was scraping burned chicken nuggets off baking trays she'd forgotten in the oven, and her room was such a mess, it really should have been the subject of one of those television programs where fierce women came around wearing aprons and rubber gloves and threw all of your most prized possessions away. "And anyway, Mum'll be home soon."

Mrs. Bagshott leaned toward him, so close that he could see what looked like pale blue veins under her gaunt skin and he could smell her breath, which was vile, and her perfume, which was enough to make you gag. "I wouldn't be too sure of that, young man," she said softly.

Somewhere upstairs, a baby started to cry.

At the sound, Mrs. Bagshott stiffened. Her pale eyes gleamed. Then she turned on her heel and kissed Mr. Arnold on the cheek.

"I'll be back soon," she promised, though to Ben it sounded more like a threat.

"Come along, Robert!" she called imperiously, and turned to leave, almost cannoning into Ben's older sister, Ellie, who had just come through the front door.

In what seemed like a rather bizarre dance routine, each of the two stepped first to one side of the narrow hall, then the other, trying to get out of each other's way and failing. Then Mrs. Bagshott took Ellie by the shoulders and pushed her out of her path before clacking away on her ridiculous heels.

"What was Bag-o'-Bones doing here?" Ellie demanded, dumping her schoolbag on the floor.

"Don't be so rude, Eleanor," Mr. Arnold said sharply. "Mrs. Bagshott is a very kind lady. She's offered to help around the house while Mum's . . . away."

"What have you told her?" Ben asked fiercely. "About Mum?"

Mr. Arnold looked vague. "Oh, nothing much. That she's traveling for a bit."

Ben and Ellie exchanged glances. "I hope that's all you told her," Ellie said grimly. "I don't trust her, and I don't like the way she keeps sniffing around. She's after something."

"Like a starving old dog," Ben added helpfully, warming to his sister.

Ellie snorted with laughter. "And her skinny son looks as if he could do with a bone or two to gnaw on!"

The usually mild mannered Mr. Arnold flushed a dangerous puce color. "Stop it! I won't have you speak about Maggie like that. She's . . . she's a lovely lady."

Lovely? Ben stared at Ellie, who rolled her eyes. "She's an ugly, smelly old bag," she said very quietly. "She reeks of disgusting perfume and I don't want her in the house when Mum's away."

There was a moment of terrible stillness, as if something massively heavy hung in the air between them all, ready to smash on the floor.

Clive Arnold's face contorted with anger. "You'll do as you're told when you're in my house, young lady. I'll have none of your princess antics here!"

At this, Ellie tossed her head. "I'll not stay where I'm not wanted," she announced. "I don't know what's come over you lately, Dad. If you change your mind and want to discuss matters civilly, I shall be in my room." And with that, she grabbed her schoolbag and flounced off upstairs.

Ben watched her go silently. It wasn't often that

he and Ellie agreed, but things had got a bit strange ever since the Bagshotts had moved in next door, replacing Henry and Maud Thomas, a nice elderly couple who wouldn't say boo to a goose (if there had been any geese wandering around Bixbury to say boo to). They had always been kind to Ben, even when he had burned their garden shed down and broken their garage window with his football (he never had been very talented at sports), and he rather missed them. No one seemed to know where the Thomases had gone, and their house had never had a FOR SALE sign outside, but then, quite suddenly, Bag-o'-Bones and Boneless Bob had appeared. It hadn't taken long for Mrs. Bagshott to appear at their front door with a bottle of wine ("I do so believe in the importance of being a *good* neighbor," she'd wheedled, batting her overly made-up eyelashes at Mr. Arnold), and after that she'd been around all the time. The evenings now rang regularly with the sound of her awful, cackling laughter.

There was a movement outside the living room window, and then a small, dark shape appeared on the sill. A bloom appeared on the glass as Iggy pressed his nose against it. He looked very cold.

"Dad," Ben started, "now that Mrs. Bagshott's gone, can Iggy come inside?"

"I think Maggie's got a very good point, Ben. Animals are dirty creatures and shouldn't be kept in the house. She keeps her house spotless."

"How do you know? Have you been in it?" This seemed to Ben almost as big a treachery as allowing the horrid woman into their own house.

Mr. Arnold shook his head. "Actually, no, er, not yet. But you can just tell." He blinked and ran a hand over his face. He was beginning to look more like himself, less red and strained. He stared around as if it was the first time he had been in his own front room. Then he said, "Why's Iggy out there on the windowsill looking half-frozen?"

Ben frowned. "You said he couldn't come in."

"Did I? I wonder why I said that?"

Ben decided to avoid mentioning Mrs. Bagshott. It seemed as if Dad had been having a bit of a problem with his memory ever since she had appeared. "Can I let him in, then?" he asked.

"Of course." Mr. Arnold looked confused, as if this was a most bizarre question to ask.

Ben moved toward the living room door. His foot

slipped on the piece of newspaper he had been reading to Iggy. He bent and picked it up. "Dad . . ."

"Yes, son?"

"Did you know about Uncle Aleister?"

"Uncle Aleister?" The confused look was back
again.

Ben flourished the newspaper article at him. "He's
escaped. From prison."

Mr. Arnold didn't say anything. He just took the
torn article from Ben's hands and studied it. "Ah," he
said at last. "Oh yes, I remember now."

"You knew?"

His father nodded minutely.

"And you didn't say anything? You didn't think to
warn Mum?"

Mr. Arnold set his jaw. A tendon began to twitch
in his neck. "Mag—er, Mrs. Bagshott said it would
only worry her."

Ben's skin crawled. What on Earth had his father
been discussing with Bag-o'-Bones? Another thought
occurred to him. "Dad, exactly when was it that Uncle
Aleister got out?"

Mr. Arnold tried to hide the newspaper from Ben,
but the date was clear on the masthead.

"That's over a week ago!" Ben's eyes grew round with alarm and outrage. "So an ogress blasts her way into the prison on some great big monster the Dodman's managed to get hold of to rescue Mum's horrible brother and you haven't warned her?"

His father looked flustered. Then he said, flatly and without any intonation at all, as if it was something that had been drummed into him by rote, "It wouldn't do her any good."

"She's got to know!" Ben shouted wildly.

Upstairs, Baby Alice began to wail even more loudly.

Mr. Arnold took his son firmly by the arm and shook him, quite hard. It didn't hurt, as such, but it was so unexpected that Ben cried out. His father had never in all his life laid a finger on him, even under great provocation (like when his dad had spent three months making a perfect scale model of a World War II Spitfire and had just finished painting it when Ben had helpfully put it on a radiator to dry, then forgotten about it, so that when he came back, it was a nasty, gooey heap, and the radiator was ruined).

"Now you've woken your sister! Shame on you. Maggie's quite right: You and Ellie are a pair of troublemakers and need to be taught some lessons! You shall go to your room and have no dinner, and I may think twice about letting you have any breakfast as well."

And with that, Mr. Arnold marched Ben up the stairs, never once easing his viselike grip on his arm, thrust him into his room, and turned the key in the lock outside.

Ben stared at the keyhole in disbelief. He didn't even know there was a key to his room. In fact, until just now he would have sworn there had been no lock. . . .

Something very odd was going on here. Something very odd indeed.

Chapter Three

An Escape

After a while something tapped the window, making Ben jump. But it was only Iggy, teetering uncomfortably on the narrow window ledge. How he'd managed to get up there, Ben couldn't quite imagine. The little black-and-brown cat meowed piteously and pawed at the glass. When Ben didn't move to open it quickly enough, Iggy ran a single wicked claw down the pane so it made a sound like a wailing banshee. Iggy watched Ben spring into action, and flung himself through the gap, spraying water everywhere.

"Ugh!" said Ben. "You're as bad as a dog. Perhaps old Maggotty Bagshott is right and it *would* be better if you lived outside."

Iggy fixed his erstwhile friend with a sardonic amber gaze and began to perform a complicated grooming process. His normally scruffy fur was looking even more unkempt than usual, sticking out in little spikes, as if he'd gone all retro-punk and applied a load of hair gel to it before coming in.

"You look horrible." Ben grinned.

"*You'd* look horrible if you'd been shut out in the rain," the little cat growled. He even sounded like a dog sometimes.

"Oh." Ben hadn't noticed it was raining. He stared at the window, where rivulets coursed steadily down the glass. The sun had gone down and it looked grim and wintry out there. In the Shadow World of Eidolon now it would be summer, and his mother would be in the dappled Wildwood, facing a terrible threat as the Dodman massed his terrifying army.

"Iggy, we must get a message to Mum."

Iggy looked at him askance. "You mean you want

me to go and find her?" He puffed out his chest proudly. "After all, I am the Wanderer. That's my job."

Ben snorted. "No, that's not what I meant. You're hopeless on your own: You'd get lost. No, we'll both have to go."

Nowhere in either world was safe anymore. There was war in Eidolon, and now even his own home was under threat. He could not explain to himself, let alone anyone else, exactly what sort of threat he thought that Mrs. Bagshott and her horrible son might pose, but his instincts told him something needed to be done, and that his mother was probably the only person who could do it. He watched a dribble of rain make its convoluted way down the dark pane to join the pool on the sill below, and the world inside his head felt as gloomy as the world outside.

Iggy followed his gaze. "But I've only just got dry." Cats hate to be wet.

"All right, then," said Ben. He pushed himself up off the bed, crossed the room, and dragged a raincoat out from his wardrobe. "I'll go on my own."

The little cat sighed. "Hadn't we better tell Eleanor?" he said, playing for time. Even five more minutes in the warm and the dry would help.

"I suppose so."

In the next-door room, music thumped softly. Ben made a face. His sister was playing a CD by a new band called the Secret Agents, and he didn't much like them. He tapped on the wall.

No response. He tapped harder. "Ellie!"

He heard the sound of footsteps, then the music went off. He tapped again. "Ellie, can you hear me?"

Nothing. Then a door opened and the corridor floor creaked. The doorknob to his room moved, but of course the door didn't open. The knob rattled harder.

"Ben? Why have you locked yourself in?"

Ben rolled his eyes. Honestly, girls could be so stupid sometimes. "I haven't locked myself in. It was Dad."

"Why?"

"I said we had to warn Mum about Uncle Aleister. . . ."

"What about him?"

"Old Creepie's escaped!"

"Escaped?"

"From prison. Over a week ago. It was in the paper."

"I didn't see anything in the newspaper about Awful Uncle A."

"I think Dad hid it. Under the sink."

There was a pause as Ellie took this in. Then she said, "Perhaps Bag-o'-Bones did it."

That wasn't a nice thought.

"Ellie, Iggy and I are going to Eidolon. To find Mum and tell her."

There was a moment's silence. Then Ellie said, "I want to come too."

"You can't. Who'll look after Baby Alice? You can't leave her to the mercy of old Maggotty."

"We'll take her with us."

Ben rubbed his face wearily. This was turning into an expedition, and he didn't want to be its leader. "She'll cry and alert Dad. And anyway, we can't take Alice into the middle of a war. We have to keep her safe, remember what Mum said? She's Eidolon's last hope."

An ancient prophecy in the Secret Country told of three children, and everyone seemed to think that he and Ellie and Alice were the ones it referred to.

> *Three children from two worlds*
> *Three to save the day*
> *One with beauty's spell to tame*
> *One bravely to bring flame*
> *And one with the power to name.*

Ellie had already decided that she was the one who held beauty's spell. Ben was not so sure, though Darius the Horse Lord and the Minotaur had seemed unusually impressed by her. He didn't even think his sister was particularly pretty, let alone beautiful. As to the other two talents the prophecy referred to, Baby Alice wasn't old enough even to hold a match properly, let alone "bring flame," and although she had uttered a few words, the last time had been several weeks ago, in Eidolon. Ever since returning to Bixbury without her mother, she had remained steadfastly silent, except to wail like any other baby from time to time. And Ben didn't have the faintest idea what he had to offer, especially since Mr. Jones, his history teacher at school, said he was so forgetful it was a miracle he could remember his own name.

"Anyway," he reminded Ellie through the keyhole, "you can't even see properly in Eidolon."

This was true. Ellie had brown eyes, like their father's, and for some reason they didn't work very well in the Shadow World. Ben had one hazel-brown eye and one that was bright green, like their mother's. He found that if he looked at things in the Secret Country with his hazel-colored eye they were a bit blurry but came into sharp relief if he looked at them with the green eye, or his Eidolon eye, as he liked to think of it. Both of Alice's eyes were a wild, other-worldly green; but who knew what a baby could see?

"I don't want to stay here on my own with old Maggotty Bagshott and Boneless Bob."

"Ellie, you need to be Mum's spy, her secret agent. How will we know what's going on at home if no one's here to witness it? Anyway, it's pouring with rain. Alice will get sick. And your makeup will be ruined."

There was a sniff from the other side of the door. "I suppose you're right," she said at last.

Ben breathed a huge sigh of relief. It was bad enough having to worry about Iggy getting lost or into trouble, let alone being responsible for his blind-as-a-bat sister and a baby. He bent down and applied his hazel-colored eye to the keyhole. On the other side, Ellie dabbed at her face with a tissue. "Anyway," Ben added with annoying reasonableness, "if you've got a cold here, you'd be horribly ill in the Secret Country."

"I haven't got a cold," Ellie mumbled indistinctly.

She moved out of sight, and seconds later he heard the door to her room close.

"You are an idiot," Iggy growled softly.

"I am?" Ben thought he'd handled it all rather well.

"She's not got a cold. She's crying. It's a bit much when even a cat from another world can tell the difference and her own brother can't."

He had a point. Rather than think about it anymore, Ben shrugged his way into his waterproof jacket. It was rather noisy, like putting on a bag of chips. He hoped his father wouldn't hear. Then he pushed open the bedroom window and got a faceful of rain. "Ugh."

"Why don't we wait for it to stop?" Iggy suggested hopefully.

It was tempting, but Ben shook his head. "Come on, Iggy, don't be a wimp." And with that, he flung one leg over the sill, then the other, and pulled himself onto the drainpipe.

He had forgotten about the drainpipe. Even on a dry day it could be slippery and awkward; in the rain it was positively treacherous. He missed his footing, grabbed desperately with both hands, and slid, at enormous and terrifying speed, down to the ground.

"Ow!"

Iggy, who appeared to have found his own way

down not involving drainpipes or falling, butted his head against Ben's knee. "Are you all right?"

Ben got gingerly to his feet. One of his ankles was stiff and throbbing, but it took his weight. He nodded bravely. "Let's go."

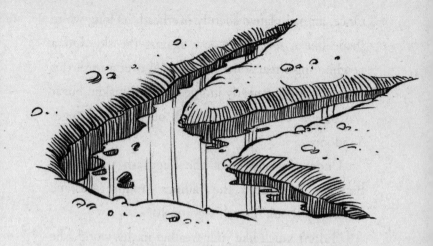

Chapter Four

The Aldstane

In the daylight, Bixbury was like any other small English town, bustling with traffic, with cars and motorcycles and buses carrying people to work, to school, or to the shops; but in the dark it was a very different sort of place, almost a secret country of its own. Shadows haunted the abandoned gardens, streetlights cast weird shapes onto the deserted roads, bushes rustled furtively, and rain pattered onto leaves.

Once, an owl planed silently overhead, its long white shape like a reverse shadow against the sky. On a neighboring street something tipped over a trash can with a crash. Ben nearly jumped out of his skin, but it was only a fox raiding the trash outside the Ganges Tandoori.

Under the shelter of the huge ash tree whose branches overspread the railings around Aldstane Park, Iggy shook himself vigorously.

"I don't much like your weather in this world," he said. "I'm not sure I shall come back when you return."

Ben swung himself up onto the most overhanging branch and looked down at the little dark figure on the pavement beneath him. "It must rain in Eidolon, too."

Iggy stopped his shaking and pondered. "It used to," he admitted. "Before the Queen left. Now all it does is thunder and throw down great hailstones in the winter. I can't remember the last time it rained in the Shadow World in the summer."

Isadora, Queen of Eidolon, had met Ben's father, Clive Arnold, on a visit to this world fifteen years ago. She had fallen in love, and abandoned her realm for him. She had stayed here long enough to have three children—and to become increasingly ill as the effects of a magicless world took their toll upon her. But the kingdom she had left behind had also suffered. In the time she had been away, others had turned her absence to their advantage: her brother, Aleister, for one; and his associate, the Dodman, who, owning no magic himself, wished to see all things of magic destroyed so that he could take Eidolon for himself. It was why Isadora had eventually returned, to try to put things right. It was why Ben and Iggy had to find her and tell her the odds had changed once more.

Ben's mood was somber as he tracked across the soaking grass of Aldstane Park with Iggy trooping bravely along at his heels, lifting his feet as high as he could to avoid getting too wet. Into the darkness of the rhododendron bushes they went, and the rain came down harder and harder, hammering against the great glossy leaves like a drum tattoo. The undergrowth got thicker and thicker, and the night darker still, until at last it seemed there was no moon and no starlight at all. Sighing, Ben dug into his pocket and pulled out his flashlight. The clearing in which the Aldstane was hidden was close now, he knew, but it was always hard to find, even on the brightest day.

He switched on the flashlight and swung it from side to side, but all he could see were wet bushes and brambles and fallen leaves. He turned around in a circle, then shrugged.

"I must have lost my bearings. What do you reckon, Iggy?"

But Ignatius Sorvo Coromandel had wrinkled his nose up and was looking agitated.

"Come on. You're the Wanderer. You're supposed to be able to navigate and find things." Though he knew that Iggy rarely lived up to his name. "Where's the Aldstane, Ig?"

But Iggy's tail was quivering and held low. He looked anxious.

"There's something wrong," he said quietly, and the growl seemed to have gone right out of him. "It smells wrong."

"What do you mean, 'wrong'?"

"I can smell Old Creepie. And something else . . ."

The hairs rose on the back of Ben's neck. He swung the flashlight wildly around, just in case Awful Uncle Aleister was lurking in the vegetation, though it seemed highly unlikely that anyone with any sense would be out in this weather.

"It's okay," Iggy said, regaining some of his bristle and bluster. "The scent's not recent."

"I bet he went back to Eidolon through the wild road here, through the Aldstane," Ben said, feeling a bit braver now. He stared around, following the flashlight beam until it came to rest on a hawthorn arch among the rhododendrons. "Through here!" he cried, recognizing where he was at last.

He could almost smell the leaf mold that surrounded the stone; he could imagine how its rough crystals would feel beneath his fingertips as he traced the ancient letters carved into its surface.

He ran forward, through the arch—being careful not to trip over the bramble runners that littered the ground—and suddenly came to such a violent halt that Iggy cannoned into the back of his legs and almost knocked him down. It was just as well he didn't, or Ben would have fallen headfirst into a great big hole.

They stood on the edge of the hole, uncomprehending. On the other side of it, the bushes had been flattened and trampled, the earth churned up by something vast and unforgiving.

But of the Aldstane there was no sign.

"Oh, Iggy. It's gone! The Aldstane, it's gone!" Ben's voice rose in despair.

"Yeah," the little black-and-brown cat drawled, "I think that's a fair assessment of the situation. Hole in the ground. No stone. Yep. It's gone. Gold star for observation."

Ben glared at him. "That's not very helpful."

He stomped over to where the bushes had been flattened and shone the flashlight around, examining the damage. The rhododendrons here had been ripped apart, gashed and crushed by something huge. Had the council driven a bulldozer into the park to remove the Aldstane for some strange reason of their own? He cast the flashlight beam around the churned-up earth and leaf mold, but instead of the trackmarks that might have been made by a bulldozer, he found . . . something else.

"Look at this!"

Iggy walked slowly around the ragged hole to where Ben stood. He stared at the footprint, wrinkled his nose, then started to groom vigorously. Ben watched him, bemused. Iggy inspected a front paw disconsolately. "Look at the mud on that," he muttered, wiggling his dirt-caked toes. "I'll never be clean again."

"Oh, Iggy, for heaven's sake! Is that all you can think about? My mum's facing a terrible war, our only way into Eidolon has disappeared, and all you do is worry about your fur being a bit grubby?"

"It's not just 'grubby,'" Iggy sniffed. "It's wrecked."

"I don't know how you can tell the difference. You're the color of mud at the best of times."

Iggy fixed him with a hard stare that reflected flat and hostile in the yellow beam of the flashlight. "I didn't sign up for any war." The fur was bristling all the way down his spine, Ben saw now. Iggy was scared. The instant of fury he had felt at the little cat's apparent indifference to the fate of the world vanished.

"Oh, Ig, I know. This is pretty big stuff."

"You ain't kidding," Iggy growled. "Have you ever seen one of those things? They're . . ." He stretched his paws wide, gave up. "They're vast."

"What things?"

Iggy snorted. "Dinosaurs." He stared down into the huge impression left in the churned-up ground. It had filled up with muddy water, but even so, it was unmistakable.

Ben shivered. "Dinosaurs?"

He gazed at the footprint. It was the biggest one he had ever seen.

"Dad took me to the Natural History Museum once," he said at last, remembering the giant skeleton that had taken up most of the main hall there.

"Believe me, you don't want to meet one of *these* on a dark night." Iggy stared around, as if half-expecting a dinosaur to come creeping silently out of the shadows.

"So you reckon it really *is* a dinosaur print, then?" Ben asked, squinting at it.

Iggy regarded him with his head on one side. "Well, let me think. Just a *little* bit big for a cat—and oh, look." He stretched out a paw gingerly and held it over the middle of the print, where it looked like a leaf floating on a pond. "Only three toes. I've got four, plus this dewclaw. . . . Dog? No, no nasty little dog claws. Just whopping great big ones. Bear? Jolly big one. Any escapes from the local zoo lately?" And before Ben could say anything, Iggy shook his head. "Nah, didn't think so. Which leaves us with . . . dinosaur."

Ben felt a certain strange excitement rising in him. Imagine, a dinosaur in Aldstane Park! Wait till he told Adam. Then he realized that he probably wouldn't be doing anything quite so ordinary as going to school and telling dinosaur stories to his best friend. Not for a while, at least.

He thought hard. Someone had removed the Aldstane. Deliberately. With a dinosaur. It must have been Awful Uncle Aleister. And he must have done it to stop anyone getting into the Secret Country. Or getting out. He shivered, thinking of his mother.

They *had* to find the Aldstane. Perhaps if they found it they could put it back. Without thinking this through, Ben strode off into the night, wielding the flashlight beam like a sword. Iggy watched for a split second, then bounded after him. He certainly didn't want to be left on his own there in the dark.

About thirty feet away they found the Aldstane, lying on its side, in the middle of a bramble thicket. The standing stone, which had once looked both majestic and eerie, with its time-pitted skin, its ancient carvings, and brooding presence, now looked defeated and sad. Muddy and manhandled, it lay face-down, so that its runes—which showed, if you looked very carefully, the letters EIDOLON and a smudged chalk arrow pointing down into the earth—were hidden. Now it looked like a discarded lump of old granite, a fallen war memorial, a tumbled giant. Ben felt a hard lump in his throat.

"So now what?" growled Iggy, breaking the mood. "I don't think we're going to be lifting *that*, do you?"

Ben shook his head miserably. Rain dripped off his hood, nose, and chin. "So, what do we do now? That's the only way into Eidolon. Well, the only one we know about, anyway."

Iggy was silent for a moment. Then he sighed. "Not quite the only one."

Chapter Five

Something Wicked

In another world an immense figure tapped his claws impatiently on the stone battlements of a tall castle, the sound echoing through the night. His long moon shadow jutted horribly across the cobbles and ended in a massive dog's head.

The figure turned to address his companion, whose shadow was smaller, slighter, and full of spiky angles.

"I have another task for you."

"I am not yours to command," the second figure said sharply. "Even though you managed, somehow, to summon me again."

She cocked her head and the moonlight fell across her face, which was long and thin and as white as bone. The witch, for this is what she was, studied the Dodman silently with her pale, cold eyes, until he felt sure she was trying to put some sort of spell on him. He stepped swiftly back into the shadows, as if by this simple action he could somehow dodge her sorcery.

Maggota Magnifica smiled, showing her teeth, which easily matched those of the dog-headed man for length and sharpness. Then she tossed her long red hair. "Don't you trust me, Rex?"

It was her special name for him and he hated it. She said it was the old name for a king, and that he should be flattered, but he could always detect an undercurrent of mockery in her voice when she used it. In the Other World there were pet dogs called Rex. He had heard their owners admonishing them outside the pet shop. "Now then, Rex, stop your barking. It's only a cat, and it's in a cage, so what good will barking do you?"

"Of course I trust you," he said insincerely.

"What information do you have for me from the Other World?"

"The man, Clive Arnold, is of no threat. There's not an iota of magic in him. The older girl is interesting, but her magic is weak. The boy has possibilities. . . . Yes, the boy has hidden depths, I think."

"And the baby?"

Maggota spoke quickly, too quickly. She waved a hand. "Of no consequence," she lied. "It's just a baby."

"I want all three of them, to make sure."

"All three? Isn't that just a tad greedy, my Rex?"

"All three!" he barked. "I don't want that infernal prophecy hanging over my head while I'm trying to take my kingdom."

She cast a sardonic eye at the dog-headed man. "Afraid of the prophecy, are you? Poor Rex. In that case, I'll do you a deal," she offered.

"Deal! I don't do 'deals'!"

"You will for me, or you will regret it. You shall have the boy and the older girl to do with what you will. But give me the baby."

He regarded her curiously. "What would you do with the little squalling thing?" Then he laughed. "Don't tell me you've become broody in your old age?"

"Old age!" The witch spat. "I'm in my prime!"

At this, the thing that till then the Dodman had thought to be a rather ugly scarf around the witch's neck raised its head and hissed at him, and he saw that it was in fact a particularly repulsive-looking snake, with an orange frilled crest and red and white bands around its body.

"Go back to sleep, Robert, my love." It regarded her with its beady eyes, flicked out its forked tongue, then tucked its head back in its coils. She smiled affectionately. "No, no, you are quite right: You are my baby. Do not fear being replaced. A witch is nothing without her familiar."

The Dodman watched this display with disgust. "Bring me all three children. I shall kill the boy and the girl. The baby you shall have, when the time is right."

Maggota's eyes flashed. "The time shall be my choice. Promise me truly or it shall be the worse for you! I shall bring the sorceresses out of the south and they will make your life a misery such as you could never imagine." The Dodman opened his mouth to speak, but she sent a little spiral of power through the dark air and he abruptly found he could not open his mouth at all.

In fact, he could not move. His jaws worked furiously as he tried to break the spell—to no avail.

She walked around him, shaking her head. "Rex, Rex, Rex. You forget your origins, but I do not. I know perfectly well why you summoned me to do your dirty work for you. You are a thing with no magic, and a thing with no magic cannot use a magic thing." She gave him her ghastly grin. "Isn't that right? Cynthia may have brought you the Book, but you cannot use it. And that is why you have not been able to summon the Arnold children. You are too stupid to hold the power you think you hold, Dog-Head. Now, remember your promise to me. And when you know in your black heart that you will hold to it, you will find the spell releases you." She leaned in toward him, so close that he could see the scraps of meat caught between her fangs, and kissed him on his shaggy brow. "And remember: I do this because it suits me, and because it amuses me. But if you try me too far, you will regret it deeply."

She clicked her fingers and sizzled away into the night air, leaving behind her a faint aroma of rotten flesh and perfume.

• • •

"Oh, for badness' sake, Father, don't be such a coward! They won't really hurt you—they're ghost-dogs!" shrieked Awful Cousin Cynthia. "Now, get me out of here!"

"Here" was a small and very sturdily constructed cage that sat at the foot of the Dodman's throne in the Great Hall of Corbenic Castle, which the dog-headed man had renamed Dodman Castle, in his own honor. Cynthia was crammed into the cage so tightly that her nose stuck out the front and her toes out the back. When the Dodman sat on his throne, he liked to put his feet up on her. Sometimes he rested the Book of Naming on top of the cage and put his feet up on that, too, just to add insult to injury, for Cynthia had brought him the Book in return for a promise: that she should have the kingdom once it was won. After all, she was of the royal blood, being Queen Isadora's niece. She hadn't reckoned, although of course she should have done, on the untrustworthy nature of the dog-headed man, who had no royal blood in him, indeed no magic at all, and not an iota of honor, either. He'd crossed his dog-claws behind his back even as he spoke the words of the promise. So even in Eidolon they counted for nothing at all.

And now she had lost her broomstick and her familiar, too. Without them she was powerless.

"My dear, I'm perfectly well acquainted with the Gabriel Hounds. I grew up with them, you know. Back, back, you monster!"

This last was addressed to a spectral-looking dog that had slunk up silently, its fangs bared in a ghastly grin. At the sound of the voice, the hound's grin widened. It paused, sniffed, then wrinkled its muzzle and started to growl. It remembered Aleister Creepie of old. Even as a boy he'd been cruel and spiteful: tying their tails together when they slept and sticking thorns in their noses. Ghost-dogs have long memories, especially for those who have harmed them; like most spirit-creatures they don't really have anything to do in the present other than nurse the grievances of the past, and where Old Creepie was concerned this hound had a list of grievances as long as its leg. . . .

"Hurry up! Quickly, he'll be back soon!"

"I'm trying, I'm trying, Cynthia dear. But it's an infernally tricky lock, and these nails aren't well adapted to the problem." In the Secret Country, Awful Uncle Aleister—who looked like the fat businessman he was in our world—turned into an ugly hunchbacked creature somewhere between a hobgoblin and a vampire. He had a big, fat, bald head and enormously long, but useless, fingernails. In Eidolon the outward appearance of folk tends to clearly give away their inner, true nature. Thus it was with Uncle Aleister, and also with the sorceress known as Maggota, who, in this world, appeared maggot-ridden, deathly, and grim as her name, while in the Other World—our world—she could appear (to Mr. Arnold, at least) to be a rather attractive redhead with an exotic taste in perfume and a sharp style of dress.

"Now, if we were in the Other World, I'd have you out of here in a trice, believe me!" said Old Creepie. But to be perfectly honest, he wasn't trying particularly hard to release his daughter, because he was more afraid of the dog-headed man than he was of the little witch.

"Just like you managed to get yourself out of Ardbar Prison?" Frustration made Cynthia sarcastic.

"Now, now . . . *Ow!*"

The ghost-dog had got hold of him by the seat of his trousers and given him a nasty nip in the process, which is generally known to be a very painful place to be bitten.

Old Creepie shot upright, clutching his bitten bottom, and aimed a kick at the ghost-hound. His foot went right through its ghostly outline, but it yelped and yelped, causing all the other hounds to join in the racket. They milled around, growling and barking and ready to fight anyone or anything that got in their way. Except for the creature that now strode into the hall. Even the sight of the Dodman's face was enough to make them slink away, tails quivering between their haunches, into the safe places out of the reach of his hobnailed boots.

It had taken the dog-headed man some time to capitulate to the sorceress's demands, and the battlements had been particularly—and possibly magically—cold, given that it was midsummer. When he had finally given in and been able to move, his limbs were almost frozen in place, and his nose was numb. None of this had put him in a pleasant frame of mind (if it could be said that he ever had such a thing). The Dodman had a great distrust of witches and their familiars. He did not understand their use of magic or their strange relationship, but he knew that one depended on the other. Which was why he had captured the creeping, slinking spy known as the Sphynx, who was young Cynthia's familiar, and separated it from its owner at the first available opportunity. Now it was in a safe place. A safer place even than its scrawny, wicked little mistress.

When the Dodman was in a foul mood (as he was now), it always cheered him up to see Cynthia Creepie reduced to the status of caged animal. He remembered how she had brought him the Book of Naming and expected him in return to be her subject when he made her Queen. As if such a spiteful, ugly little wretch could be a queen! Even though Isadora was his sworn enemy, he had to admit that she had presence and . . . well, nobility. Something about the way she carried herself, even under the duress of war or the burden of illness . . . the carriage of that beautiful head, that slender but resilient body, the flash of those magnificent green eyes. There had been a time when he had (fool that he was) believed that Isadora cared for him, that he was not just some dog-headed pet for her, nor (in her eyes) a buffoon. He had, in his delusion, even dreamed they would be wed. But then she had not only deserted him, but her entire kingdom, and all for the love of a common man, a pathetic being from the Other World.

He could never forgive her for such an insult. He would show her how wrong and stupid she had been in choosing such a worm over him—the fine, the relentless, the powerful, the merciless Dodman! He would grind her magic to dust. He would destroy her kingdom, its woods and lakes and rolling hills. He would drive its denizens into oblivion. He would stake out her children (ill-begotten, crossworld creatures that they were) on the hard ground before her pleading eyes. His wedding gift to her would be the destruction of her last connection with the Other World: She would witness her three children crushed beneath the vast feet of an army of dinosaurs. A bolt of ice shot through him then, an aftermath of the witch's spell. *All right, all right,* he corrected his imagination, *two of the children I shall stake out for the dinosaurs, and the witch shall have the other.*

And after that? His vision always failed him at this pleasurable point. But he knew he would think of something . . . suitable. And at that moment his eyes settled on the grotesque figure of Old Creepie.

"Ah, Aleister!"

Aleister Creepie darted away from the cage containing his daughter like a beetle disturbed when its stone has been lifted. In the brilliant black sun of the Dodman's gaze, he quailed. "I was just . . . er . . . checking that she was all right."

"Of course I'm not all right!" Cynthia's sharp little fists hammered the floor of the cage. Spittle flew from her mouth. "Let me OUT of here!"

"I see she can still caterwaul, so she must be as well as can be expected," the Dodman declared smoothly, regarding his captive with something bordering on affection. Really, he was quite getting used to her there, below his throne. She was almost a piece of the furniture now.

He strode to Old Creepie's side and put a long, dog-clawed arm around his hunched black shoulders.

"Aleister, my dear, bad friend. It's so good to see you back where you belong again."

"And not before time!" Aleister huffed. He couldn't help himself, however scared he was of his dog-headed associate. "I mean, dear boy, it was your fault I was in that place. You might have tried a little harder, a little sooner, to rescue me. You've no idea what it's like, in prison. It's . . . well, the food was quite revolting. And then—why—it's been over a week since Grizelda got me out, and not a word from you."

"Ah, yes, where is Grizelda? I have not seen her since I sent her for you."

Aleister looked abashed. "I . . . er . . ."

"What? Out with it!"

Old Creepie became flustered. He wrung his hands, but no words came out. "I . . . ah . . ."

"For badness' sake, Creepie, has the cat got your tongue?" The Dodman thrust his unpleasant muzzle at Aleister Creepie. "Because if you don't tell me at once, I can tell you the dog will have it!"

"You did tell me to cover my trail," Aleister started with a whine.

"What have you done? Where is Grizelda? Where is my dinosaur?"

"To make sure we weren't followed, I had them pull out the Aldstane."

"Good thinking." The Dodman was surprised at this level of foresight from Old Creepie. "Excellent. What did you do with it? Dragged it down after you? That must have made quite a crater when it came through the wild road. Hah! Probably flattened a few trees and some fairies in the process. I'd have liked to see that!"

"Ah, well . . ." Aleister was shifting awkwardly from

foot to foot now, as if he wanted to go to the toilet.

"Spit it out!"

"I . . . ah . . . left them to do that while I got into the wild road. You know, authorities probably hot on my trail and all that . . ."

"You left them?"

Aleister nodded.

"In the Other World?"

A dark patch appeared on Old Creepie's trousers. "Ah . . . yes."

"YOU LEFT MY DINOSAUR ON THE OTHER SIDE?" the Dodman roared.

Aleister Creepie covered his huge bald head with his hands. "And Grizelda, too. Don't hit me, don't hit me," he begged.

The Dodman stared at him contemptuously. "Well, that's just wonderful. I tell you to cover your tracks and you go and leave a thumping great dinosaur and an ogress behind in a world in which neither belong. Very nifty!" He struck his forehead. "With enough friends like you I could defeat myself in no time."

Old Creepie frowned, confused by this tortured logic. "I'm sorry," he wheedled at last. "I was trying to do the best thing." He brightened. "But at least the way between worlds is closed now. Isadora's right where you want her."

The Dodman shook his head piteously. "Really, Aleister, for someone with the royal blood of Eidolon running through his veins, you're remarkably ignorant about your own domain. There are a hundred wild roads—more. I dare say they'll find their own way back at last. There's no great hurry now. Your little daughter has been most helpful in supplying me with many more such beasts."

The Dodman bent down and waggled his fingers in front of his captive. Cynthia fixed him with her pale, gooseberry green eyes. If looks could kill, it really wouldn't have done the trick, though the Dodman might have suffered a small pain in his forehead. She was weak from fury, and lack of chocolate.

"Some father you are!" the little witch wailed. "How can you let him treat me like this? Get me out of here!"

Aleister Creepie coughed embarrassedly. "I must say, Dodman, old chap, it's really not necessary to put poor little Cynthia in a cage like this, you know. I'm sure she annoyed you in some way—badness knows she can be most annoying sometimes—"

"Thank you, Daddy!" Cynthia hissed furiously.

"But I'm sure she's sorry for whatever she said or did, now that she's had time for reflection. Won't you let her out, eh?"

"Oh, I don't think she's nearly sorry enough yet," the Dodman said softly. "Are you, my dear?"

Chapter Six

In the Wildwood

"Cernunnos!"

A young centaur came cantering through the close-packed birch trunks, twisting neatly this way and that to avoid their barred silvery trunks. Golden light filtering down through the delicate leaves dappled his long dark hair and brown shoulders.

At the sound of his name, Cernunnos, Lord of the Wildwood, raised his antlered head from the contemplation of an elegantly white-flowered plant growing tall in the shade.

"Darius, it's good to see you." He waited for the centaur to come to a halt beside him. "Look," he said, "wood asphodel. I haven't seen that bloom here for the best part of fifteen years."

Darius regarded the flower curiously. "Really?"

"It grows only where magic is strong and the air is pure. It is a plant peculiarly sensitive to magic."

"The Queen was here, yesterday. She came for a walk, and she seemed most distracted. I am sure it wasn't in flower then."

"How interesting." A complex expression crossed Cernunnos's face. "I wonder . . ." He looked deep in thought, his brows knitted together.

"My lord?" The centaur interrupted his reverie. "I came to find you because I am worried about her. She is exhausting herself, and I cannot stop her. We cannot let her harm herself."

"What is she doing?"

The centaur shook his head. "I am not sure, my lord. She is doing nothing . . . *physical*. She sits still, but the muscles in her face twitch as if she is under great stress. She will say nothing to me. Perhaps she will tell you."

They found Queen Isadora sitting on a fallen log in a sunny clearing. Her head was in her hands, but at the sound of their arrival she raised her face to them. She was paler than usual, and blue smudges pooled beneath her vivid green eyes.

Behind her, in the shadows, lurked something vast. If it had stood up, it would have been as tall as the Dodman, with the head of a bull. It sat quietly resting its forearms on its knees, but it looked as if it might spring into action at any moment, and that if it did, the action would be swift and violent.

Cernunnos nodded to the Minotaur (for that was what it was), then dropped to one knee beside the Queen and took her hands in his, where they vanished inside his huge, woody grasp. "My lady? You look tired. What have you been doing?"

Isadora smiled weakly. "Not enough. Never enough. But perhaps they are safe now."

Over her head, the Lord of the Wildwood and the centaur exchanged anxious glances.

"Who will be safe now, my lady?"

She smiled then, as if he had asked the most ridiculous question in the world. "Why, my children," she said softly. "Ellie and Ben and Alice."

"But the three are in the Other World," Darius reminded her gently. "They are safe there."

She gave a small, bitter laugh. "They should have been safe there, indeed, were it not for my own stupidity."

"What do you mean, my Queen?"

The face she turned to him was ravaged. "The Book," she whispered.

"The Book of Naming?"

She nodded. "It's lost." She had been putting off this evil moment for as long as she could; she could put it off no longer.

"Lost?" Cernunnos thundered. "What do you *mean* 'lost'?"

"I hid it before the battle. You will recall how we had already decided we would not use it to Name my creatures and compel them to join us."

The Lord of the Wildwood merely gave a curt nod to this, for he had agreed to no such thing. It had been the Queen's decree, and he still could not find it in him to agree with her decision.

"Well, I hid it away, and when we got back to the Wildwood after our small victory, all I could think of was Ben and Ellie, and making sure they got home safely to the Other World, so that I could concentrate on the hard decisions we must make in the war ahead of us." She hung her head. "I gave no thought to the Book for many days after that. There seemed so many other things to do—wounded creatures to attend to, reports to be had from our friends here and those who crossed the wild roads; and when at last I went to consult it, it was not where I had left it. Then I panicked, and thought I must have forgotten where I had put it, that I must have hidden it somewhere else. My memory is not all it was, I'm afraid. And so I searched, secretly, for I am ashamed to say I was almost more afraid of your reaction to the fact that I had lost the Book than I was for the consequences of losing it. And of course, I did not find it, though I looked everywhere."

She sighed deeply.

"So then I sent out the cats to search for it, and I am afraid that yesterday one of them—my faithful friend Jacaranda—came to me with news of its where-abouts."

The Lord of the Wildwood kept his voice low, but his eyes were stormy. "Tell me, my lady. What did the old white cat report?"

"Cynthia took it. Cynthia Creepie. When Jacaranda told me this, I must admit I felt a certain relief, for although my niece is not what I would call a pleasant child, I do not think she is yet completely wicked. I hoped I might go to her and persuade her to return it, whatever her reasons for stealing it. But I fear that what Jacaranda told me next destroyed even that small hope." She took a deep breath, then carried on swiftly, to get the awful thing said. "I'm afraid she has given it to the Dodman."

There was a shocked silence. Then Cernunnos threw back his head and gave a wild cry. It was a bizarre noise that rattled the very leaves on the branches overhead, and more of a deep-throated bellow than the high-pitched deer-shriek you might expect from a stag-headed man. The Minotaur leapt to his feet as if he thought the Lord of the Wildwood might do harm to the Queen. Isadora quailed away, her palms pressed against her mouth. The centaur put an arm out to steady her, but even his sun-warmed face was pale.

Then Isadora seemed to gather herself. She stood straighter. The worst was surely over now.

"What's done is done," she said at last. "What

remains to us is to decide what to do about it."

Cernunnos sat down heavily, as if his legs would not support him anymore. His great antlers lowered till they almost touched the ground. He did not speak, could not trust himself to say anything that was not angry and could not be forgiven.

The Minotaur watched him, his black eyes narrowed.

Eventually it was the centaur who said, "We must save our people. The Dodman will summon dragons and dinosaurs and all sorts of monsters to swell his vile army. We do not stand a chance. The small folk must find refuge; the rest of us must disperse far and wide. If we stay together in the Wildwood, all we will do is provide him with a fine target. He will use the dragons to torch every tree that stands, and the dinosaurs to crush and rend everything that moves. Nothing can survive dragon fire or the teeth and claws of the tyrannosaur."

At last Cernunnos raised his head. "Might you now tell me, madam, what it is that you have been doing? I know that some of your magic has returned. I saw the asphodels where you walked yesterday."

"I sent fading spells," the Queen said quietly.

A spark of hope dawned in his bleak gaze. He stood up. "Can you obliterate the entire Book?" he asked. "It were better it were destroyed than be in our enemy's hands."

She shook her head. "It has taken a full day and almost all the strength I have to fade a single page."

"And which page was that, my lady?"

She looked him straight in the eye, though his fierce, antlered head towered above her. "The page that lists the true names of my children."

His great, woody hands balled into fists, but she stood her ground. "That was a selfish act," Cernunnos said.

The Minotaur stepped swiftly between them. "It was the act of a mother," he said sharply. "How can you blame her for it?"

Isadora turned her limpid green gaze upon the bull-headed man. "It was the act of a mother *and* a Queen." She turned back to the Lord of the Wildwood. "Remember the prophecy," she reminded him. "It is the three who will save Eidolon. 'Three children from two worlds.' They are the future of our country, and so they must be saved."

Cernunnos snorted derisively. "The three! A silly,

half-blind girl, a young lad, and a tiny baby. Not one of them old enough or strong enough to bear arms. Not one of them possessed of true magic. What use are three halfling children to me? I need greater creatures than such at my command if we have any chance against the Dodman. A foolish rhyme is all that so-called prophecy ever was, and I will not place my faith in it, or in you, any longer."

Then he gave her the curtest of nods, turned on his hoof, and hurled himself off into the Wildwood.

The Queen stared at his retreating figure with dismay.

"Will he come back, do you think?" she asked. The way Cernunnos had spoken, as if he was in truth the ruler of Eidolon and not she, left her in little doubt of the answer.

Darius and the Minotaur looked at each other in shock. Then the centaur shook his head. "Cernunnos has been teetering on the brink of this decision for a long time, my Queen. He ruled the Wildwood during your absence. He finds it hard to share his power, and now he fears he has lost it all."

"And will you leave me too: you, Minotaur, and you, Darius?"

The Minotaur snorted. "Never!"

Darius bowed his head. "My Queen, no matter how bleak things may get, I shall not leave your side."

"Then that is something. We had better follow and give comfort to those who have stayed behind or are now lost in confusion. And when we have gathered those who remain faithful, we must leave the Wildwood. By dead of night, tonight."

Chapter Seven

The Minstrels

The rain was coming down hard now and Ben's raincoat was not living up to its name. He could feel a chill soaking into the shoulders of his sweater, cold water running down his back. They had been walking for what seemed like hours, at first through the suburban roads of Bixbury, where the streetlights gave the rain a watery, orange glow, so that it looked as if Gatorade was falling onto the wet cars and filling up the wide puddles. Then the streetlights became fewer and farther between, until at last they vanished altogether. Now there were no houses, no cars, and nothing but hedges and trees that loomed up like giants, and it was darker than anywhere Ben had ever been before. He was (though he would not admit it to anyone, and certainly not to Ignatius Sorvo Coromandel) just a little bit afraid.

"Where are we going, exactly, Iggy?" he said in as steady a fashion as he could manage, so as not to give the little cat the idea he might not entirely trust his wayfinding skills. Which, of course, he didn't. Iggy could get lost between the garden shed and the front gate. Ben was not at all confident that his friend had inherited any of his parents' expert explorer genes. Perhaps the Wanderer was really only an ironic sort of nickname for someone who got lost all the time.

The little cat didn't say anything, but he looked very purposeful, striding ahead of Ben with his tail in the air. He was as thin as a rat, his fur plastered to his skin, a state Ben knew he hated; but he didn't complain, which Ben thought was very stoic of him. He could feel runnels of rainwater trickling into the waistband of his jeans now, which was particularly horrible, and he definitely felt the urge to whine himself.

Going home was becoming a much more attractive prospect than walking around in the cold night rain, but he knew it wasn't really an option. He had to find Mum and tell her what he had found out—about Uncle Aleister, the dinosaur, and the Aldstane. And, a little voice in the back of his head added, about Mrs. Bagshott, too. The way she kept turning up. The fact that Dad seemed to like her visiting, that he talked to her about things he should not. The fact that he couldn't seem to see she was an ugly old hag. He hoped Ellie would be able to cope with her while he was gone.

If he ever got back to Eidolon again.

"Ig, where are we going?" he said again, a little louder and more firmly this time.

The little cat turned its reflective amber eyes upon him. "To the Minstrels," he said.

The Minstrels. A little shiver ran down Ben's spine, having nothing to do with the chilly rain. He had visited the Minstrels with his parents on his ninth birthday. Dad had driven into the countryside outside Bixbury in their old Morris Minor. Mum had packed a picnic. Ellie had been at Awful Cousin Cynthia's, playing at dressing up, since they were still best friends then, before Ellie had discovered where all the pretty feathers and bits of fur they used in their costumes came from (all the poor magical creatures Uncle Aleister had been shipping out of the Secret Country with the aid of the Dodman). And it was the year before Alice had been born, so it was just Ben and his parents and a wide summer sky at the start of the school holidays, and he had been very excited to have them all to himself, even though Mum hadn't been very well. She'd been complaining of headaches and not having any energy, and when it rained, her joints pained her. Dad told him she was "under the weather," which had confused Ben mightily, since wasn't everyone (who wasn't in a plane, or a spaceship, or a hot air balloon) under the weather? But he had only been young then, just turned nine. It seemed a lifetime ago: a time when he had thought that Mum's illness was just an ordinary sort of illness and that she would soon get well again; a time before he had discovered the existence of Eidolon; a time before he had got to know a talking cat, and a selkie called Silver; a time before he had seen real-life monsters, a war, or anyone die right in front of his eyes.

He hadn't really had any idea what the Minstrels were then. He'd thought vaguely when his parents suggested the outing that they might be going to a castle where people were all dressed up in medieval costumes playing instruments—because that's what minstrels were, wandering musicians out of history books—and he had been quite looking forward to seeing some for himself, especially if one of them had a sword and there might be a fight. So when they had parked alongside a country lane and climbed over a stile into a field where there was nothing but a few grim-looking gray stones in a circle, he had been rather disappointed.

They had had their picnic sitting in the middle of the stones, and his parents had given him his birthday presents there: a new cricket bat signed by some of the country's best players, and an anthology of poetry. He had hit some pebbles all around the field for a while with the bat, but he hadn't been very interested in the poetry book, even though it had a funny picture on the cover. And then his mother had walked around the circle, touching each stone she passed. "Come here," she had called to Ben, and he had left the grasshopper he had caught and run over to where she stood with her hands pressed up against the lichen-patched granite. "Touch this and tell me what you feel."

And he had put his hands where hers had been, and nearly been knocked off his feet by a sudden surge of electricity. Little hairs had stood on end all down his spine.

His mother had smiled and taken his hand away. Then she dropped him one of her long, slow winks. "That's what they call a piezoelectric shock," she said softly to him. "They say the crystals in the rock can conduct a current. But I know where that energy really comes from."

And for a few weeks after that she had seemed a lot more like herself: more radiant, more alive, and complaining less of aches and pains. But Ben had been scared by the stone he had touched. It had given him nightmares for months. The idea of coming back to that place in the dead of night was not a good one. Perhaps they should wait until it was light?

But just as he opened his mouth to suggest this to Iggy, the little cat became suddenly animated, shook himself vigorously, and vanished into the hedge to their left.

"Iggy?"

But he didn't reappear again, and there was nothing to do but follow. As he did so, the rain stopped quite abruptly and the moon slid out from her cover of cloud and shone a path across the road for him. And all at once, there was the field, and there was the stile, silvery gray in the moonlight, just waiting for him to climb over it. So he did.

There in front of him was an ancient circle: nine standing stones, none as large as the Aldstane, but in a perfect ring, as if frozen in the middle of a dance. Perhaps, he thought, they *had* been minstrels playing a jig, and someone had cast a spell on them, turning them to granite. Perhaps they were in there still, trapped and aware, but unable to do anything about their predicament.

In the middle of the stone circle stood Ignatius Sorvo Coromandel, and now he did not look like the rain-soaked, ratlike creature who had run along the road ahead of Ben. Now he looked tall and proud, and his tail was a flag. His ears were pricked and his eyes were as large and round as saucers in the moonlight. He looked the very icon of a cat, proud and solitary.

When Ben got within earshot, Iggy said triumphantly, "You see? I did it! I found them!" And he rubbed his head excitedly against Ben's leg. His purr rumbled in the night. "I could feel the stones," he said in awe. "They *called* to me."

Ben had no idea what that meant, but he stroked Iggy's wet little head anyway. "Well done, Ig. You really are the Wanderer. You managed to navigate your way here without a single visible star in the sky."

Iggy puffed out his chest. "Ain't I the cat's whiskers?" He chuckled. And then, finding this excruciatingly funny, he took to his feet and hurled himself around and around the stones, a little furry ball of energy.

Ben got dizzy just watching him. Suddenly he said, "You're running widdershins. Shouldn't you be running around the circle in the other direction? Clockwise, I mean."

Iggy came to an abrupt halt and stared at him, whiskers bristling. "What?"

Ben felt uncomfortable. He wasn't quite sure why he'd said that. The word "widdershins" had just come into his head. "It's something to do with bad luck, and witches," he said rather lamely.

"We don't have clocks in Eidolon," Iggy replied,

giving Ben a look. Then he backed away from the stones as if they might bite him.

"So now what do we do?" Ben asked, to break the awkward silence.

The little cat shrugged. "I don't know. One of them must lead into Eidolon. But which one?"

"We could try them one at a time," Ben suggested, and took a step forward.

"No!" Iggy's claws dug sharply into his leg.

"Ow!"

"Remember what I told you about the wild roads," the little cat said severely. "They run between the two worlds, this world and Eidolon, and some are new and some are as old as time itself. Some will take you to the Secret Country and set you down in a pleasant woodland glade. But nowadays some will drop you into a bottomless ocean or the depths of a volcano; and some will whirl you into Eidolon's history, centuries past. It depends how frequently they've been used, and by whom. Cats used to keep them all open and safe; but there are not as many of us in the Shadow World as there once were."

Ben's heart sank. "Then how are we going to get into Eidolon?"

Iggy looked away. "I don't know."

"But I thought you knew! You brought us here, after all!"

"I know only that there is supposed to be a wild road among the Minstrels by which the Secret Country can be gained. But I don't know which of the nine is the right one. I was hoping, maybe . . ." He paused.

"Maybe what?"

"Maybe you'd know."

Ben laughed bitterly. "Not much chance of that!"

"But you're her son, a Prince of Eidolon. Whereas I am only the Wanderer. That must mean something."

So far in his adventures between two worlds, Ben thought, that fact hadn't seemed to make much difference. "Couldn't you, you know, sniff out the right one? Cats have a good sense of smell, or so I'm told."

"What did you *think* I was doing when I ran around the circle? One thing I can tell you, though. There's a familiar smell here. Someone I know has visited the stones, and recently. I just can't quite put my paw on who it is."

Ben frowned. "Not Uncle Aleister? Perhaps he

came back to Eidolon from here once he'd pulled up the Aldstane."

Iggy paced over to the stones and walked about a bit, inhaling deeply. "No," he said at last, "though there is a faint whiff of something I can't quite identify. But the most recent smell is female. No doubt about it."

"Grizelda?"

Iggy snorted. "You think I don't know the smell of an ogre when I find one? Most insulting. I can see you have no faith in my professional abilities at all."

"Sorry, Ig. I didn't mean it like that."

Silence fell, and clouds drifted across the moon. Ben stared gloomily at the stones. They were all different shapes and sizes. None of them looked like the Aldstane, though that might not be much of a clue.

In the distant woods an owl hooted, and then there came a tiny, high-pitched shriek. Iggy's ears pricked up, all his ancient cat hunting instincts alert. Someone had caught a small rodent. Ben, having (for the most part) human ears, did not hear the dying vole, but the sound of the owl dislodged something in his memory.

"'The Owl and the Pussycat'!" he yelled suddenly.

Ignatius Sorvo Coromandel stared at him. "I do hope that's not the beginning of a terrible joke," he said, whiskers bristling.

Ben laughed aloud and started to run across the field. "It's a poem!" he cried joyously, and now Iggy knew his friend must be going quite mad, because poetry had never been something in which Ben had ever shown the slightest interest.

Ben had come to a standstill in front of one of the larger stones and was gazing at it intently. Iggy slunk across through the wet grass.

"It's this one. I'm sure of it."

"Oh, just like that you think you can tell the difference?"

"Mum was touching this stone and she called to me, and when I touched it, it gave me such a shock that I dropped the book I was holding and it fell open on 'The Owl and the Pussycat.' Just there." Ben pointed to a patch of bare earth on the other side of the stone. "Funny what you remember."

"You didn't tell me you'd been here before," Iggy said in an accusatory tone. "You didn't really need me at all." And his tail drooped sadly.

"Oh, Ig, I always need you. I couldn't have found

it in the dark. And I wouldn't have wanted to come on my own." He picked up the little cat. "Shall we try it?"

The amber eyes regarded him steadily. "Are you absolutely sure?"

Ben reached a hand out toward the stone, not quite touching it. Slowly the hairs on the back of his neck started to rise, but he wasn't sure whether it was because he was afraid, or because it was the stone that had caused the reaction.

"Hold tight, Iggy," he said, and his voice was shaking. "Here we go."

Chapter Eight

A Wild Road

Cradling Iggy against his chest, Ben stepped *into* the stone and suddenly there was no night or moon or wet field, but a blur of shapes, a flicker of light and shade. He would never get used to the sensation of being caught up in the power of a wild road. It was sort of exhilarating, and sort of scary, like a fairground ride that might run out of control. The first time he had stepped into the Aldstane, he had not known what to expect, and it had all been over so quickly, he hadn't had much chance to think about it. After that, when he had entered the wild road, he had experienced a second of dread and then the step into the void, but at least he had known where he would end up. This time was different.

Colors rushed at him. Shades of gray—the night colors of Bixbury's countryside—gave way first to golds and reds, then an astonishing blast of blue, as if an ocean were flashing past, until at last the hues paled and ran together in an extraordinary whirl. The wind of the wild road whipped at his face as if it would rip his eyelids off. It battered him so hard that his raincoat flapped as loudly as a ship's sail in a storm. He tumbled over and over, his feet kicking out into space. What had happened to the little cat, he did not know: Ben's arms had been thrown wide by the power of the wind, ripping Iggy from his grasp. There was nothing Ben could do about it. He cried out, but the very sound was torn away from him, and he was suddenly very frightened indeed.

To fall through a wild road between worlds was scary enough even when you knew where you were likely to end up, and that a friend was with you. But to fall alone into the unknown was terrifying.

And then, with sudden brutal force, he hit something very solid and everything went quiet.

Ben lay there stunned for several moments, not sure whether or not he was alive or just dreaming that he was. He moved his limbs carefully, but nothing seemed to be broken. Then he sat up and looked to see where he'd landed.

It was like nowhere he had ever seen in his life. He was on a wide, white beach, in the middle of a circle just like the Minstrels in his own world. Except that this was not a stone circle but one made of wood: ancient, black, seeping wood, stark against the white sand. On one side of the circle lay an expanse of pale blue sea. When he turned around, all he could see was a vast stretch of sandy dunes sown with strange-looking plants and a grass that was so gray, it was almost as white as the sand. There was no strong color anywhere except for the wooden circle. It was eerie and serene, like finding yourself in a faded photograph.

Ben got to his feet and shaded his eyes, for the lightness of everything was blazing. He closed his right eye, and at once spotted something he had not seen the first time looking. A tiny, weatherbeaten

DRAGON'S FIRE

shack among the dunes, surrounded by a broken fence and rambling weeds. The upturned hull of a rowing boat lay in what had once been a garden. And on it sat a small dark figure.

It was Ignatius Sorvo Coromandel.

"Iggy!"

Ben had never been so glad to see his friend in all his life. He started running up the beach, his feet slipping and sliding in the shifting sand. He had no idea where in the two worlds he was; all he knew was that wherever he was would be a better place with a cat by his side.

"Ssh!" The little cat jumped down off the boat and ran to him, his paws barely making an indentation in the sand. "There's someone in there." He indicated the shack. "I saw a face at the window."

"Perhaps we should just leave," Ben suggested nervously.

"I thought," Iggy said, "that whoever it was looked more frightened of me than I was of it."

"I'm not surprised. It's a bit weird here."

"Stay here. I'll go and have another look." Iggy ran back, wriggled through the broken-down fence, jumped up onto the boat, and then onto the narrow windowsill. He pressed his nose against the glass, then emitted a wail and promptly fell off.

"What? What is it?"

Ben ran into the remains of the little garden. Vines, columbines, and some other plant with long, spidery runners had taken possession of it now and seemed to be slowly dragging everything in it down into the sand. Ben had the unpleasant thought that he might be next if he stayed there too long.

"Them. It's them," Iggy whispered, hiding behind Ben's legs. His ears were flat against his skull. "Two . . . people. Old people."

"Not monsters of any sort? They haven't got— well, wings or horns or . . . big teeth or anything?"

"They look just like people from your world. You know . . . ordinary."

Trying to appear braver than he felt, Ben walked up to the house, trying not to step on too many of the spidery plants. He looked in at the darkened window, his heart hammering.

A pair of watery gray eyes peered back at him. They blinked. Then another face appeared.

"Oh my!" Ben exclaimed.

Without another thought, he ran to the front

door. It opened with a creak, but easily. From the gloom inside, two elderly people gazed back at him, holding hands as if in fear for their lives.

"Mr. and Mrs. Thomas!"

"Maud, it's . . . I can hardly believe it . . . it's young Benjamin Arnold, from next door."

"Ben?" The voice was quavery. "That nice little boy? Who broke our garage window with his soccer ball?"

"Yes, dear. I'm sure he didn't mean to."

"I didn't—," Ben started.

"I saw you!"

"I mean, I didn't mean to."

"That's all in the past, dear. He helped us mend it. And brought you some flowers."

The old woman chuckled. "That he picked from our garden."

Ben felt himself redden. He hadn't realized she'd seen that. It had seemed like a nice idea at the time.

"What's he doing here?" Maud asked.

"I don't know. What are you doing here, Ben? And, um, this may sound like an odd sort of question, but, um, exactly where is 'here'?"

Ben didn't really know what to say. "I'm not sure,

Mr. Thomas. It's certainly not Bixbury." He gave a little laugh. "How did you get here?"

The old couple exchanged a glance. "It's a bit hard to explain," Henry Thomas started.

"Nonsense," said his wife. "It was that awful woman."

"Mrs. Bagshott?" Ben asked with a sudden flare of instinct.

Maud Thomas regarded him suspiciously. "You know her, then?"

"She's the one who bought your house, isn't she? She keeps coming round to see Dad."

"Bought our house! Hah! That's what she's been saying, is it? Despicable old witch."

Something fell like ice into the bottom of Ben's stomach. Bag-o'-Bones was a witch. A *real* witch. How could he have been so stupid? And he had left Ellie and Alice to her mercies.

"Now, now, dear, be reasonable," said Mr. Thomas. "You don't *know* she's a witch."

His wife turned a furious gaze upon him. "Of course she's a witch! Do you think anything less than magic would have got me out of that house?" Her face started to crumple. "I was born in that house. I've lived there all my life. And I want to go home." She began to sob.

Henry Thomas took her in his arms. "There, there, dear. Of course you shall go home." He looked at Ben despairingly. "Ben's here to take us home, aren't you, Ben?"

Ben hesitated. What could he say? If he started to explain the situation, it would take as long as getting them back through the wild road. And he could hardly leave them here. All he had to do was work out which of the nine stumps in the wooden henge on the beach was the one that led back to Bixbury. After that, they would have to fend for themselves, he reckoned, while he went in search of his mother. (Though what they were going to do about Bag-o'-Bones was another matter.)

"Yes, of course," he said, trying not to worry about it all at once. "Let's get out of here, first of all."

Just as he finished saying "all," the door slammed shut behind him. A freak gust of wind. Surely.

He caught hold of the doorknob and twisted it. Nothing. He pulled, but it was stuck tight. Alarmed now, Ben ran to the window. And rather wished he hadn't, for it was the stuff of nightmares.

The entire garden was writhing. All over it, the spidery plants were on the move, snaking across the ground, binding the door and window shut.

"Oh dear," said Mr. Thomas over his shoulder. "That's what happened to us, too."

"The plants must have retreated in order to let you in," said Mrs. Thomas.

"Great," said Ben, unable to stop himself. "You might have told me."

He looked desperately for the little cat, who had been right behind him.

"Iggy!"

There was no sign of him, and no one responded to his cry. Ben stared and stared through a window crowded with jostling vines. For one long, horrible moment, Ben thought he detected a scrap of black-and-brown fur moving beneath a mound of twisting runners in the middle of the garden, but it turned out to be only a dead leaf. And then the vines had covered the glass, and he could see nothing at all, inside or out.

Behind him there was a click, then a bloom of light.

"Henry's always going on at me to give it up," said Maud Thomas, holding up a cigarette lighter, "but there are times I'm jolly glad I didn't. Being trapped here is bad enough, but being here in the dark . . ." She shuddered. Bustling about the tiny room, she managed to find a candle in an ornate golden holder. It seemed an incongruously pretty thing to be lying around in such a hovel, but Ben took it from her gratefully. He walked around the shack, peering at the walls in the vain hope of finding a way out.

Mr. Thomas laughed bitterly. "No chance of that, I fear," he said. "We've been here, well, I don't know how long . . ."

"Ages," said Mrs. Thomas. "Weeks, perhaps."

Ben looked aghast. "Weeks?" he echoed. "But how have you survived? I mean, there's nothing here, nothing to eat, no water. Nothing."

"It's very odd," said Mr. Thomas, "but you know, we just haven't been hungry at all."

"At first I thought it was just because we were too frightened to want to do anything as ordinary as eat, but it's more than that," said his wife. "Magic, Henry. It must be. I know you say you don't believe in it, but what other explanation can there be?"

"I've been giving it a great deal of thought," Mr. Thomas said in a tone that was meant to sound sci-

entific and rational. "And I've come to the conclusion we're in a place out of time. A sort of limbo.
Suspended animation."

"You're in Eidolon," said Ben. "It's the world that
was created when the big comet struck the Earth and
split it in half. This is the half that contains all the
magic and the dinosaurs and stuff. It's the Shadow
World. My mum's the Queen here, but she's at war,
and I need to find her."

Mr. Thomas gave his wife a knowing look. Then
he tapped the side of his forehead. "Poor lad."

"Did you bump your head, dear?" Mrs. Thomas
asked solicitously.

Ben cursed himself. It did all sound a bit mad
when you said it like that. But really, not that much
madder than saying Mrs. Bagshott was a witch. It was
all part and parcel of the same thing. But he really
didn't feel like explaining it anymore.

"Perhaps we could burn the door down," he said
instead, looking at Mrs. Thomas's cigarette lighter.

She put it hastily into her handbag and snapped
the clasp shut. "Ooh, I don't think that's a good idea,
dear. You'll remember what happened the year your
barbecue got out of hand."

Ben did. He and his friend Adam had decided to build a barbecue at the bottom of the garden and cook some sausages on it. Unfortunately, they hadn't taken into account the direction of the wind or the nearness of the fence, or the fact that Mr. Thomas's prized garden shed was on the other side of it. There had been a fire engine and lots of embarrassment.

"Well, we have to do something. I'm not just going to sit around here for weeks waiting for old Bag-o'-Bones to turn up!"

"Who?" Mr. Thomas frowned.

Mrs. Thomas gave a wheeze of laughter. "Oh, very good. Yes, she is a bony old crone, isn't she?"

Which surprised Ben a little. "Yes," he said. "I thought it was only me who saw her like that. Dad seems to think she's rather attractive."

"So did I," Mr. Thomas said quietly. "She seemed a lovely lady when she came calling that day. I invited her in for a cup of tea. How I wish I hadn't."

His wife grimaced. "You always were susceptible to a pretty face. But really, Henry, she must have put a spell on you, because she's a frightful-looking creature: all teeth and claws and rats'-nest hair."

Caught in the impossible position of having either

to admit to finding teeth and claws and rats'-nest hair attractive, or accepting the possibility that the woman really was a witch, Mr. Thomas had the grace to look shamefaced.

Ben, meanwhile, got down on his hands and knees and started prodding the floor. He got under the rickety old table in the middle of the room and felt around. There was an old carpet, rotted away to hardly anything, and a few unidentifiable objects that he really didn't want to examine too closely (they felt like bones beneath his fingers). He crawled farther and came up against a wall, turned, and bumped into Mr. Thomas's legs. "Sorry!"

The old couple watched him, bemused.

"What are you doing, Ben?" Mr. Thomas asked at last.

"Looking for a trapdoor," Ben said matter-of-factly. "I bet an old shack like this will have a smugglers' tunnel, down to the sea." Then he remembered that he was in Eidolon, and they probably didn't have smugglers here. But it was something to do, so he kept on looking.

And then, suddenly, as if the house was obliging him, he found the hidden door. Grabbing the candle, he showed the old couple excitedly. "Look!"

There was a rusty iron ring in the floor. Sand had gathered around the great square flagstone into which it was set.

Mr. Thomas looked at his wife. "I'm sure that wasn't there before," he said uncertainly.

"Well, it's clearly here now," she retorted briskly, and got down on her knees to help Ben clear the sand away.

Together, they pulled at the ring. Stone grated upon stone, and then it came free and they found themselves looking down into a deep, dark hole. Chill air drifted up out of it, bearing a scent of salt, seaweed, and dead things. The candle guttered, and went out.

Chapter Nine

Stealing Alice

The rain was lashing against the window so hard that Ellie barely heard the doorbell. Who could it be, so late? Perhaps Ben had changed his mind and been unable to climb back in. She pressed her nose to the glass to peer out, but the roof of the porch obscured her view. All she could see was a long black coat flapping in the wind, and then someone—Dad—had opened the door and the figure was inside the house.

She crept to the door of her room and opened it as silently as she could, only to hear a familiar voice in the hall below.

"Poor Clive, you look exhausted. And no wonder, when you've been managing so well, all on your own. You poor soul . . ."

"Yes, well, it's not always easy . . ."

The voices began to move away into the living room. Ellie strained her ears to catch: ". . . so difficult, yes, I know how it is . . . single-parent family . . . such difficult children . . ."

Difficult children! I'll give her "difficult," Ellie thought fiercely, balling her fists. She changed from her pajamas back into her jeans and sweatshirt, thrust her feet angrily into a pair of tennis shoes, and ran down the stairs as quietly as she could. On the threshold of the living room, she paused to listen.

"You put your feet up there, Clive dear," Mrs. Bagshott said soothingly, "and I'll make you a good stiff drink. That'll relax you nicely."

Ellie poked her head around the door, just in time to see Bag-o'-Bones heading into the kitchen with a bottle in her hand. It didn't look much like any of the bottles they had in the drinks cupboard (all of which

Ellie had secretly sampled one night when left to babysit, and had made herself thoroughly sick in the process). She stepped into the room. Her father was reclined on the sofa with his feet up on a brightly colored leather ottoman. In the other corner of the room, Boneless Bob sat coiled up on the floor in front of the television, flicking listlessly from channel to channel. Seeing Ellie, he ran a hand through his crest of red hair and flicked his tongue at her in a peculiarly repulsive way. Ugh! Ellie glared at him. Did he really think she would fancy a creep like him? Not in a million years. Not when there were handsome young Horse Lords in another world, or anything even remotely warm-blooded in this one. She tossed her head, dismissing him.

"Dad," she started, "if you're tired, why don't you go to bed? I'm sure Mrs. Bagshott would understand."

Mr. Arnold turned his head slowly, as if surfacing from a dream. He looked at his daughter and a puzzled expression crossed his face, as if he didn't recognize her and had no idea what she could be doing there.

But before Mr. Arnold could form a word, Mrs. Bagshott was back with a glass of foaming green stuff that looked, Ellie thought, rather revoltingly like a glassful of Fairy Liquid. This she handed to Mr. Arnold. "Drink that, Clive dear," she cooed. "It'll really take you out of yourself."

Clive Arnold took the glass wordlessly and tipped it toward his lips.

"No!"

For no reason that Ellie could put a name to, she knew it was imperative that her father not drink whatever it was that Mrs. Bagshott had prepared for him. She shot across the room, hand out to snatch the glass. But Boneless Bob was quicker. In a blur of motion, he had slithered out from his corner by the television, and before she knew it, Ellie was sprawling headlong over his out-flung leg and crashing headfirst into the sofa. Mr. Arnold spilled some of the green stuff down his shirt, but an awful lot of it had gone down his throat. He coughed and spluttered, and the glass flew out of his hand. It landed on the Chinese rug, the one with the border of pretty flowers that Ellie's mother particularly loved because, she said, it reminded her of the spring meadows of her home. Nobody at the time had realized she meant the meadows of Eidolon, for although they didn't really know much about their mother's past, the idea that she might be referring to an entirely other world would never have crossed their minds.

As it touched the silk of the rug, the liquid sizzled. Ellie stared at it in horrified fascination. Then it burned right through the fabric, and down into the floorboards. Within seconds, it had made a number of tiny holes right down into the cellar. Which was sort of interesting, because until that moment Ellie had never before realized the house *had* a cellar. She turned back to see what terrible effect the stuff had had on her father, but he had his eyes closed and was snoring loudly.

"Badness me," said Bag-o'-Bones with a malicious gleam in her eye. "I would never have imagined that Isadora would spawn such a clumsy daughter."

"I am not clumsy!" Ellie cried, leaping to her feet. "It was your horrible son. He tripped me up on purpose!"

"Robert would never do such a thing, would you, dear?"

But Boneless Bob just sniggered and flicked the remote at the TV. The channels jumped and came to rest on a station showing a film in which a hideous black dinosaur with a hooded figure on its back was flapping its way across a mournful-looking landscape in which three small figures cowered out of sight behind a bush.

"How curious," said Mrs. Bagshott, squinting at the television as if she wasn't used to focusing on such a strange object. "Isn't that Corinthius flying across the Great Mere? Though I don't recognize the rider. How did they ever get cameras into Eidolon?"

"Nah," said her son. "Nothing like it. Your eyes don't work too well over here, Ma. That's not a pterosaur, that's from *The Lord of the Rings*, that is."

Ellie stared at them. "Eidolon?"

Mrs. Bagshott's hand flew to her mouth in a show of shock. "Badness me, how indiscreet I can be. Did I say Eidolon?" She smiled, and as she did so the spell she had been using to beguile Clive Arnold wore right away, and Ellie saw her as she really was: Maggota, Witch of the First Order. Her face was a crescent moon of bone: a great hooked nose and curved chin, a Halloween pumpkin grin. Maggots writhed in her hair; rotten meat hung in scraps between her fangs. Ellie screamed.

Bag-o'-Bones snapped her fingers and her original guise resumed itself. The full spell worked only on those without a touch of the Secret Country, so Ellie could still sense the real horror behind the mask, but at least now she could breathe when she looked at the woman, even though her knees were still shaking.

"I wouldn't want you to die of fear, dearie," Mrs. Bagshott said. "At least, not just yet. Where's your brother?"

"He's . . . out," Ellie said, as resolutely as she could manage.

"Out? How very . . . unlikely, on a night like this. And his mangy cat, too, I suppose?"

Ellie nodded.

"No matter. You're either lying, in which case I shall find out soon enough; or you're not, and I shall find *them* soon enough. Now, go and get your little sister and we'll be off; there's a good girl."

"My s-sister?" Ellie stammered.

"The bay-bee," Bag-o'-Bones spelled out, thrusting her face at the girl.

"Alisssss," hissed Boneless Bob, and just for a moment Ellie thought she glimpsed a forked tongue flickering out of his mouth.

That did it. Ellie hated snakes, and she hated Robert Bagshott, and no one was taking Baby Alice anywhere. She drew herself up to her full height (five foot two) and took a deep breath.

"Get out of this house! Get out and never set foot in it again!"

Bag-o'-Bones laughed. "What a brave little creature it is. And how very stupid. We were invited in, dearie, and once you've invited a witch over your threshold, you're in her power and there's really nothing you can do about it. Tut, tut." And she tapped Ellie on the shoulder with a long, scarlet-painted nail, which looked, if you stared at it hard enough (and Ellie did), like a bony talon dipped in blood. "Didn't your dear mother teach you anything about magic?" She shook her head sadly. "She never *was* the most attentive student when it came to spellcraft, our Isadora."

"You know my mother?" Ellie regarded Bag-o'-Bones with loathing, although she was surprised to find that the revelation that the wretched woman was a witch was really no surprise to her at all.

"My dear, I was Isadora's magic tutor. For years and years and years. Until we had—how shall I put it?—a little falling-out." She gave Ellie her ghastly grin, revealing gums filled with flies' eggs and centipedes. "She had no sense of the practicalities of life. No realpolitik at all."

Ellie frowned.

"Oh dear, is that a word they haven't taught you at school yet? Such ignorance, such naïveté. Education standards really are quite woeful in this world. It won't be long before we witches can fly back in and reclaim what is rightfully ours. Practical politics, child. But she wouldn't play the game, wouldn't give and take. She could have had a legion of witches at her command with a little forethought, a little . . . compromise. Instead of giving my proposal the sensible consideration it deserved, she stamped her pretty little foot and got all hoity-toity with me. Had me thrown out on my ear. Me, Maggota Magnifica, oldest witch of the First Order! Listened to her brother, she did, little fool. Everyone knew he was in league with the Dog-Headed One, even then. Everyone but her. It's really no wonder Isadora's lost her realm!"

"Lost?" Ellie cried.

"As good as. That silly dog-headed creature's strutting about like a wolf around a sheepfold. He's got trolls and ogres, ghouls and goblins at his command.

Soon he'll have the dinosaurs and dragons, too. And what's she got? A Wildwood stag, who has long puffed himself up with his own ancient grandeur and wants Eidolon all for himself, a few measly fairies, and a rogue dragon or two."

"And the centaurs," Ellie added in a low voice.

"Neither horse nor man: a hybrid confusion and no use to anyone."

"And a minotaur."

Maggota exchanged a glance with Boneless Bob, who shrugged. "I thought he was held fast in the castle dungeons?"

Ellie raised an eyebrow. "I see you don't know everything," she said triumphantly.

"Be that as it may, your mother's reign will soon be over and mine shall begin!"

"Yours?"

"They are all so blind." Maggota smiled blithely. "They do not see what's truly precious or what's truly possible. It's a shame I am as old as I am now. Older than the hills, than the seas, than the mountains. How I would have loved to be Queen of Eidolon in my prime. Queen Magnifica. Even the name is perfect— such an improvement on Queen Isadora. I was such a beauty then. Or rather, I was maintaining the illusion of beauty just beautifully."

She stretched out a bony hand and regarded it solemnly. It flickered and for a moment Ellie saw it as it really was: a collection of dry bones and sinews stitched with ribbons of ancient skin. Then Mrs. Bagshott's hand was back in sight, complete with its long, red nails.

"It's all your wretched mother's fault!" she spat suddenly at Ellie. "If she hadn't upped and left the Shadow World for that . . . that useless worm over there"—she pointed at the snoring form of Clive Arnold—"I wouldn't have lost the power to hold it all together. Such a drain on our resources, stupid Isadora. She never understood her place in the scheme of things, the well of magic that springs from her. She is the source." She paused, cast a glance toward the ceiling. "For now. But I shall have my revenge. Now: Are you going to fetch your sister, or am I going to do it?"

And she treated Ellie to her best, unmasked smile.

Maggots spilled from between her teeth and fell squirming onto the carpet. Ellie imagined the maggots falling from the witch's mouth onto her baby sister's face.

"I'll get her," she said.

She went slowly up the stairs, trying desperately to think what on Earth she might do. Her father was clearly going to be of no help. He was comatose on the sofa, drugged by the horrid green drink. How could she save herself and Alice? Could she crawl onto the roof with the baby in her arms? Could she slide down the drainpipe like Ben had? Could she summon help? She did not know the Minotaur's real name, so that was no good. The Nemesis would be useless out of water. She knew the dragon Xarkanadûshak only as Zark, and try as she might to rack her brains, she could not remember the true name of his wife, either. How she wished now she'd paid more attention. She thought of the handsome Horse Lord, Darius. How she would love to see him now, have him carry her and Alice on his glossy brown back off into the night. But Darius was too short a name to be his true name, and he had given it too easily. Tears pricked Ellie's eyes. Princess of Eidolon, indeed! What was the use of being a princess if you were powerless and alone?

By the time she entered the baby's room, tears were streaming down her face. In the cot, Alice stirred and waved her fists. Ellie leaned in over the bars and touched her cheek. "I'm sorry, Alice, I just don't know what to do."

Alice regarded her older sister steadily with her wild green eyes.

"Ellie cry," she said. "Don't cry, Ellie."

Ellie blinked and tried to smile. Most of the time Alice was a very unremarkable baby, but sometimes she could surprise you.

"Come on. We'd better go with her before she puts a spell on us, and I'll try to think of something on the way."

Alice gurgled something unintelligible and Ellie picked her up, wrapped a warm blanket around her, and turned to leave.

A dark figure filled the doorway.

For a wild moment Ellie thought that help had somehow, miraculously come. But it was Bag-o'-Bones.

"You seemed to be taking a rather long time, dearie," she said. "I thought I'd come and . . . help."

She leaned in over the baby, but instead of cowering away and wailing her head off like any normal child at such a horrible sight, Alice laughed. "Witch!" she said delightedly. "Witch!"

Maggota's eyebrows flew skyward. "Great pits of

lizards!" she exclaimed, taking a swift step backward. "What a discerning child. Remarkable . . . quite remarkable." The witch rubbed her bony hands together, but despite her words she looked rather discomfited. "Come along then, let's be away."

"Away where?"

"Infinity Beach, dearie. For the time being. I have a little place there where I like to keep my precious things. I think you'll like it."

Chapter Ten

The Centaurs

The Minotaur shaded his eyes. "There is a disturbance on the hill."

Isadora followed his gaze, but all she could see was that some of the trees were moving more than the light summer breeze allowed for. "What do you see?" she asked after a while.

"I think . . ." He paused. He was not sure what he had seen, or whether he believed his eyes at all. For a moment it had appeared that a flock of birds had circled the woods there, then sailed across the sun. A flock of huge, ugly birds, like the biggest herons in any world. He shook his head. Ridiculous.

Darius scanned the area. "I can see nothing out of the ordinary," he admitted at last.

Isadora sighed. "Where will Cernunnos go first, do you think?"

The centaur turned his sharp brown eyes upon her. "I fear, my lady, he will go to my people. He will try to persuade them to his side."

The Queen looked shocked. "But the centaurs are my most important allies. Without their support I am lost. But you, you are their lord . . ." She left the rest unspoken.

"He knows that. He will try to turn them against me, against you. He will promise them swift, decisive action against the Dodman. He will call them to war."

Isadora looked dismayed. "He cannot do that! A few brave centaurs against the army the Dodman is gathering? They will be massacred."

"They are impatient, my lady. They want to do something, anything."

"But we must go there! We must stop them!"

The tendons stood out in the young Horse Lord's neck. He knelt suddenly at the Queen's feet.

Isadora regarded him with consternation. "Really, Darius, there is no need for that. You have proved your loyalty time and again."

Despite his concerns, the centaur smiled. "I just thought, my lady, that we would be likely to go faster if you were to get on my back."

Isadora colored. "Forgive me, Darius, I am still a little distracted. You are right, of course." And she gathered her skirt and climbed on.

They plunged through the sun-dappled woods, the small folk watching them curiously as they went. They had already seen the stag-headed man pass this way, at equal speed, and his face had been terrible to look upon, twisted into a furious contortion.

"What is happening?" one young female gnome asked timorously, watching them go. "I have never seen the Lord of the Wildwood in such a hurry, and then the Queen gallops by on a centaur, followed by a hulking great minotaur! Something is going on!"

"Nothing good, Toadflax," declared her neighbor, shaking his head. "Nothing good ever comes of such rushing about."

"Are they leaving us?" Toadflax asked, her eyes large with fear. She looked to where her children were playing, riding a pair of black-spotted frogs around a sunlit pool. "I cannot bear to live under such a cloud of fear. My poor babies have known little else all their lives, and just as it seemed a little of our long lost magic might be coming back too." And she called her children to her side. Remarkably, despite their fine game with the frogs, they came running at once, for gnome offspring are somewhat more obedient than human children. She sighed. "Maybe it would be better for all of us if Cernunnos and his precious Queen did up and go away and leave us all in peace!"

"Toadflax! Stop your mouth: You don't know what you are saying!"

One of the fairies who had been sitting in the tree overhanging the pool now flew down from his perch, his wings twitching angrily. "If they leave us, they leave us to the mercy of the Dodman, and he is a monster. He won't rest until he's rooted out every bit of magic in Eidolon and trampled it to bits. And that means you and me and every creature in this Wildwood."

Toadflax glared at him. "That's what *you* say. I'm

exhausted by it all. All I want is for all the unpleasant-ness to end so that we can live in peace."

"That won't happen until the Dodman has been well and truly defeated and the Queen takes back her throne," the fairy declared flatly. "Believe me. I've lost two brothers, an aunt, and three cousins to the Dog-Headed One. Do you know what he did to them?"

The gnome-woman shook her head unsurely. "No . . ." Another of the fairies intervened. "For goodness' sake, Catchfoot, don't frighten the children with your horrid tales!"

Catchfoot pushed him away. "People need to know," he declared furiously. "The goblins caught them and took them to the Dodman. And what did he do? Why, he bit their heads off. That's what he did!"

There were gasps of horror. The children immediately began to cry.

"Yes!" Catchfoot went on, making his point triumphantly. "He bit their heads off and drank their blood. Drained their magic. They say it makes him stronger. And you"—he turned to Toadflax, who had gone an odd shade of green, much paler than her usual color—"want to give up Eidolon to him! Well, I won't stay here and listen to such cowardly, treasonous talk. I'm going to follow Cernunnos and see what he's up to and what we can do to help bring down the Dodman!"

And with that, he soared off into the blue, followed by several of the other fairies, all muttering about the distressing lack of backbone owned by so many of the Queen's Wildwood subjects.

Toadflax stared around, but no one would meet her eye. "Well, what can I do?" she complained. "I'm just a poor gnome trying to raise my children on my own. It's not easy trying to stretch an acorn stew to last three days, and no one to bring me worms or anything good to eke it out."

But one of the other gnomes tutted angrily. "That's all very well, but you have to ask yourself what happened to your husband, Toadflax. What happened to old Crowfeather, eh?"

Toadflax squared her shoulders. "I don't want to talk about that in front of the children. As far as they're concerned, he's traveling."

One of the other gnomes guffawed. "That's a long road," he said sardonically. "One he's *never* coming back from."

Toadflax's lips set themselves in a hard, straight

line. "I'll thank you to keep your remarks to yourself, Oakum," she said, marching her children past him.

Oakum and the other gnomes watched them go. "What *did* happen to Crowfeather?" one of them asked curiously.

"He got trod on," Oakum replied unceremoniously. "By something very, very big. Something that had no business being in these parts at all."

"A dragon?"

Oakum rolled his eyes. "No, not a dragon."

"A troll?"

"Well, I believe a troll was involved, but we're used to them around here, great lumbering brutes. No, it was a blinking great dinosaur," Oakum said, lowering his voice. "A vast monster of a thing. What chance did he stand against that? What chance do any of us stand when they come crashing through the Wildwood?"

On and on they galloped, the centaur with the Queen on his back, her hands knotted in his mane. The Minotaur thundered behind them, his hooves pounding into the forest floor. They passed through stands of oak, ash, elm, and hartsfoot, through bramble and bracken and furze, past thorny brakes and tumbling streams where the ground grew steeper and boulder strewn. Stones skittered away beneath Darius's feet; Isadora ducked to avoid the branches of the gnarled and spiky trees that clung to the sides of precipitous ravines. The Minotaur simply blundered through them. And still there was no sign of Cernunnos, the Horned Man.

"Are you sure he has gone to the centaurs?" the Queen cried, exhausted and a little frightened by the speed of their pursuit. It seemed impossible that anyone could have run faster than Darius, even the Lord of the Wildwood himself. He had, however, been in a fury.

"Quite sure, my lady. His track is clear."

The Minotaur lagged behind them now. He was too big a creature to keep up with the fleet centaur, but they could hear his rough progress behind them. They plunged into a rocky dell, and at last even the centaur had to slow to pick his path more carefully without throwing off his precious cargo. Then the ground rose again and they reached the cover of the towering sapin trees that ringed the centaurs' domain. And at last there he was, Cernunnos, his antlered head bright against the dark foliage, his arms thrown wide

as he made some dramatic point. All around him centaurs had gathered—bay and black, gray and white,
dappled and painted, every hue of coat you could find
on a horse in our world, and a few (lilac, red, and
striped as vividly as any zebra) that you would not.
His voice rang off the trunks of the trees, rebounded
from the boulders, and echoed from the cliff walls.
His audience listened raptly to his every word. No one
even noticed the arrival of the two newcomers as the
Lord of the Wildwood roared, "And so we must wait
no longer in the shadows, cowering like mice as the
hawk circles above us, ready to stoop to the kill. We
must take the war to the Dodman. Aye, and we must
do it now!"

Cheers split the air. Some centaurs waved their
fists, others their shortbows.

Darius turned to the Queen. "We have come too
late," he said despairingly, "though I went as fast as I
could."

"None could have been fleeter," Isadora assured
him. "But perhaps they will listen to me."

She slipped from the young Horse Lord's back and
walked quickly into the circle of centaurs, her head
held high, her heart hammering.

"Centaurs!" she cried, and every eye turned toward her.

Some fell to their knees and bowed their heads. Others shouted, "War! For the Queen. We ride!"

"No!" She spread her hands. "Now is *not* the time to face the Dodman and his hordes. You are too few, though full of courage. He has arrayed an army of monsters, and he will have more—"

"Exactly!" Cernunnos stormed. "We must strike him now. Before he can summon more to his side. Before he can further use the Book." He gave Queen Isadora a hard and significant look, and she knew from that look with a sinking heart that he had told them of her folly.

She rallied herself quickly. "I say no. There has already been too much blood shed in this conflict, and I will not have my centaurs cut down in my name for the sake of needless action, needless glory. I have brought your own Lord Darius with me. Hear what he has to say."

Darius stepped to her side. He surveyed his centaurs, and saw from the set of their faces that they would be hard to sway. "Now is not the time," he said simply. "Our forces are few and feeble in the face of the Dodman's might. Besides," and he cast a cool look upon Cernunnos, "what would you do, swim the moat to the castle and batter uselessly upon its gate for him to let you in? Or stand forlorn on the lakeshore and tempt him out to slaughter you where you stand fetlock-deep in its waves? Then will the waters of Corbenic run red with your blood, all spilled in vain. I say we bide our time and seek a strategic advantage. I have spoken. I hope you have heard me."

A stillness fell over the circle as if the centaurs were deep in thought, which they were.

When they made no immediate answer, the Lord of the Wildwood tossed his antlers impatiently. "The Dodman has gathered his forces in the eaves of the forest on the far side of Corbenic. That is where we will take them, by night and by stealth. We can damage his army cruelly in this manner, for we know the secret ways through the forest and they do not. They will not expect an attack now. Let us take our advantage while we have it. I do not want to spend more of my days hiding in a hole, afraid to venture out, while he summons ever more terrible allies to his side. I say we strike, and strike now!"

Hooves began to stamp the ground; tails flicked the air.

Darius held up his hand. "Wait!" he cried. "We centaurs are few and growing fewer by the season. How many foals were born to us this spring?"

There was some muttering in the herd. Then someone called out, "Twenty-three."

"Twenty-three youngsters this year. Twenty-eight the season before. I remember when there were seventy foals in a season—one hundred, more. Shall we reduce our stock still further, and for no good reason?" Darius looked steadfastly around the gathering, but several of his centaurs would not meet his eye.

"Shall you dwindle fearfully into the darkness?" Cernunnos asked contemptuously. "Or will you set an example for your youngsters and go out and fight while you have a chance?"

"Against the wishes of your Queen," Darius reminded them sternly.

One of the older centaurs, his mane streaked with gray, his beard falling white upon his deep brown chest, stepped forward. He dipped his head respectfully to Isadora. "My lady. We are your subjects, this is true, and our blood is your blood to spill as you command. If you say we are not to fight, then I for one will stand by your word."

The Lord of the Wildwood glared furiously at the speaker. "You are old, Mentius," he said dismissively. "You are wise to know your limitations. Those with more vigorous blood in their veins will join with me to win back the Lady's realm for her, whether she wishes it or not." And he strode out of the circle without looking back to see if they followed him, almost colliding with the vast, dark shape of the Minotaur as he did so. The two great figures regarded each other wordlessly, then the stag-headed man pushed the Minotaur out of his way and stormed past him.

The herd of centaurs milled uncertainly. Then with a cry a dozen or more of the younger stallions galloped after Cernunnos. They were followed by others, and more again. At last only a handful were left, and some of those gazed waveringly after their departed friends.

"What has happened here?" cried the Minotaur.

"Ah," sighed the Queen. "They are going to fight the Dodman, though I begged that they did not go."

"Do not despair, my lady." The Minotaur's monstrous face was thoughtful. "Maybe the time is right and he will succeed. Maybe there *is* an advantage to be seized."

The Queen nodded. "I cannot believe it, but perhaps that is because I feel so weak in myself." She sighed. "If he fails, the Dodman's army will come after us, knowing we are vulnerable. We must gather those folk who will follow us, Darius, and find a place of greater safety."

The Minotaur gazed after the retreating centaurs, his eyes wistful. He had been imprisoned by the Dodman for a long time, cooped up in a tiny cell. He had scores to settle and a lot of unused energy to expend.

"I am going with them!" he announced a moment later.

Isadora stared at him in dismay. "But . . . I do not want you to." In the short time she had known the bull-headed man she had come to be fond of him, despite his grim and bloodthirsty reputation.

He bobbed his horned head impatiently. "I know, I know. But they will need all the help they can get. And what better to fight a monster than with another monster?" His huge black eyes gleamed with anticipation. His massive hoofed feet pawed the ground.

Tears welled in the Queen's eyes. "But, we need you . . ."

"To help round up the little folk?" The Minotaur snorted. "Do you think they will willingly come to me?" He laughed as her face fell. "You know the truth of it, my lady." He took her fingers in his, and they vanished inside those huge brown hands. "We shall bring you a great victory!" He turned to the Horse Lord. "I know I will leave her safe with you, Lord Darius."

The centaur regarded him angrily. "Go, then. Go and die with the rest of them."

"Ha! You wish you could come with us rather than nursemaiding the little folk!" the Minotaur cried, stung by his comrade's remark. Then he turned and galloped after the centaurs.

Isadora and Darius watched him go, and now the centaur looked more sad than angry.

"There was nothing I could do to stop him," Isadora said quietly. "He has his own strong will. It does not answer to mine."

The Horse Lord nodded. He touched her on the shoulder, then swiftly went among the remaining centaurs, dividing them into two groups. The first would lead the young centaurs and their mothers to the labyrinth of caves above the forest, where they might watch and wait. The rest he collected about him. "Tonight we will carry the small folk of the Wildwood, the old and the injured," he told them. "The Queen has two dragons at her command. They will spy out our way and guard our backs. The rest must follow on foot as best they can. None can remain safely in the Wildwood."

The centaurs bore this news with grim expressions, and went about their business swiftly and matter-of-factly, making their farewells, gathering small necessities, strapping on bows and swords and panniers of food.

Darius watched them, and though he appeared impassive, inwardly he was grieving. He had been raised in the Wildwood. He had never left its safety for more than a day; and neither had most of the creatures in this domain. "Where will *we* go, my lady?" he asked after a while.

The Queen looked at him long and steadily. Then she spread her hands.

"I do not know."

• • •

The Dodman balanced the Book of Naming carefully on the ground, just out of Cynthia's reach. She was a spiteful little thing. Unpredictable, too. He didn't want to risk her destroying such a precious item. He patted her cage absentmindedly, then sat down on it, facing the Book.

Its thick vellum pages stirred in the breeze, showing him an illustration of a troll here, a nymph there, then a whole array of other creatures. The images flickered unhelpfully and he glared at the ridiculous jumble of letters that accompanied them. He blamed his inability to use the Book on his lack of magic, but beyond that, he had never learned to read. It had never seemed a very useful skill, even if anyone had shown enough interest in his future to teach him.

They were on the shore of the great lake opposite Dodman Castle. He needed a bit of space for this. The last time he'd tried it, several goblins had got badly squashed and ended up having to be eaten for supper. The taste had been revolting. Filthy little beasts never washed.

"Call the next one!" he commanded Cynthia.

She cast a furious gaze up at him. "You promise you'll let me out when we've done this?"

"Of course."

"Show me your hands and say it again."

The Dodman gave her his best dog-smile, which was very, very wide and shiny. Then he stretched his paws out in front of him. "I promise," he said, without, this time, crossing his fingers.

"And you'll give me my Sphynx back?"

"Of course, my dear."

"All right, then," Cynthia said, watching him with narrowed eyes. She did not trust him (and quite rightly), but what choice did she have? "Turn over three pages from there. That's the tyrannosaur, Tyrant Megathighs III. That one there."

The Dodman gazed at the picture of the most fearsome dinosaur in Eidolon. Despite its ridiculous name, it really was the most satisfactory monster!

As Cynthia read the page carefully, the dog-headed man's smile turned inward and private. Crossed fingers! What a silly superstition. As if not being able to cross his fingers made the slightest difference. Foolish girl.

"Are you quite sure you want that one? He's very dangerous," she said at last.

"Oh yes." He nodded quickly. "Bring him to me. He's just what I need."

Chapter Eleven

Infinity Beach

Ellie was just a little disappointed that Mrs. Bagshott ushered them into a quite normal-looking car rather than onto a broomstick, though she drove it without touching the steering wheel once, instead staring very hard at the road ahead and muttering instructions at bends and junctions so that the car would lurch suddenly sideways, throwing everyone this way and that. But Baby Alice did not once cry; she just watched everything the witch did with fascination. Clive Arnold snored in the backseat with Boneless Bob. It wouldn't do, Maggota had declared, for him to raise a hue and cry when he woke up and found his family missing.

They went straight across the traffic circle on the outskirts of Bixbury, churning up the winter marigolds the council gardeners had so carefully planted the week before, and Alice laughed and clapped her hands.

Even in the dark, in the rain, with no headlights, Ellie knew this wasn't the way to Aldstane Park. "Where are we going?" she demanded again.

But Bag-o'-Bones had her attention fixed on the road ahead, and it was Boneless Bob who said with a horrible, hissing giggle, "You'll see soon enough!"

Ten minutes later they pulled over on a deserted country lane.

"Out you get!" cried Maggota.

Ellie stepped gingerly out of the car, trying to avoid the huge, muddy puddles that were everywhere, in the hope of keeping her pink tennis shoes clean. It was a vain hope. Within seconds the shoes were soaked through. She had no idea where

Maggota was taking them, and when they climbed the stile and jumped down into the soggy field on the other side, she was still none the wiser. All she could see through the dark and driving rain was a circle of stones which looked very ancient and broken-down and forbidding.

"But this isn't the Aldstane!" she cried.

"How remarkably observant the child is. Not the Aldstane, no. Not one ancient stone, but nine—a place of much greater power. My chosen road, of course. It keeps the riff-raff out. Not a place for the uninitiated, or the unconscious." And she cast a look back at where her son (who was evidently a lot stronger than his weedy frame suggested) was dragging Clive Arnold unceremoniously through the mud and wet grass.

Ellie shivered. Her first and only trip into Eidolon had been quite scary enough. She glanced down at the baby, but Alice's wide green eyes were fixed on the stones. She gurgled. She smiled. And then she pointed at one of them.

Moments later the witch walked up to the very same stone. How strange, Ellie thought. How did she know? Baby Alice could really take you by surprise on occasion. She wasn't like a baby at all sometimes. In fact, Ellie reflected, there were times when she looked positively ancient.

As if she knew Ellie's thoughts, Alice transferred her gaze from the stone to her elder sister. "Don't worry, Ellie," she said, and pulled her hair.

"Ow!"

"Get your carcass over here," the witch snarled. "And pay attention: Once you're in the grip of the wild road, keep your eyes fixed on a single point or you'll get dizzy. And hold the baby tight. Now, in you go!" And she shoved Ellie into the stone.

"Hold on, Alice," Ellie started to say, but the wild road had her and suddenly she was tumbling over and over and over. Colors rushed at her till she felt sick. She couldn't find a single point to focus on; instead her head whirled around and around till her neck was sore and her skull felt as if it might burst. The wind was so strong that it closed her nostrils tight against her face and stuffed itself into her mouth. She couldn't breathe. . . .

She came to lying facedown in sand, with cold water lapping about her feet, soaking through her tennis shoes and jeans. She had no idea where she was—

who she was, even. She lay there, stunned, trying to think. She recalled at last the witch, the stones, falling through the wild road. Then she remembered Alice. For a moment the awful thought that she might have crushed the baby beneath her in the fall occurred to her. She staggered upright, but there was no sign of her sister. No sign at all.

Ellie turned around and around. Her eyes weren't working very well, and that detail alone convinced her that she had landed in the Secret Country. She squinted, and after a while could make out a circle of what appeared to be stumps of wood sticking out of the sea, a long white beach, a wide gray ocean, and an expanse of sand dunes. A chilly wind had followed her out of the wild road. But, it dawned upon her horribly, Alice had not.

She cried her sister's name, but her wail of distress slipped forlornly away into the empty air, and there came no response. All she could hear was sea and wind.

Then Ellie heard a splash, and there within the circle of wood was her father, sitting upright with the water around his waist, still fast asleep. He had a long red and white scarf wrapped tightly around him.

The scarf stirred. It raised its head and flicked its tongue at her. The expression in its eyes reminded her of something. Someone.

It was Boneless Bob!

Ellie shrieked.

Before she had time to consider this bizarre transformation, there was a whirl of color and the witch appeared, perfectly composed, apart from the fact that her maggoty hair was standing on end, hovering just above the surface of the waves.

"Badness me!" Maggota declared. "It's high water. I really must remember to consult my tide tables next time." She glided to dry land and scanned her surroundings. Her eyes came to rest on a small wooden cabin among the dunes. Weeds had pushed their way through the sand and swarmed over its old fence, covering its garden and the shack itself. She frowned.

Ellie couldn't quite make out what the witch was looking at, but she had the distinct and eerie feeling that there was someone over there, looking at her.

"Alice?" she cried again.

Maggota's head swiveled, like an owl's, without her body moving an inch. "What?" She stared at Ellie's empty arms. "Where's the baby?"

A tearful lump got stuck in Ellie's throat. "I . . . I don't know," she stammered at last.

The witch's eyes flashed dangerously. "Don't know? What do you mean, you don't know?"

"I've . . . lost her."

"Lost her? Preposterous! I saw you both go in together, and there's only one place she can be. Here. That's where the road leads. Here. Infinity Beach." She stamped across to where Ellie stood, her eyes switching back and forth as if to catch Ellie in some deception. As if she might have her baby sister cunningly hidden about her person.

Then she turned suddenly and stared at the sea.

"Oh no!" Ellie wailed. She dashed into the water and fell to her knees in the circle of stumps without a thought, for once, of ruining her favorite jeans, her tennis shoes, or her makeup. She felt around wildly beneath the surface of the incoming tide, and when that yielded no result, took a deep breath and stuck her head under the water. Nothing. Nothing but her father's legs, his trousers flapping gently with the movement of the sea, and Boneless Bob's bobbing tail. Gasping, she emerged. Seawater ran down her face, mixing with her tears. And her mascara.

The witch flew above her, shading her eyes. "Bob!" she cried.

"Yes, Mother?"

"Search for the baby."

The snake regarded her. Then it looked at the ocean. Its bright orange crest rose and fell. It didn't look happy. "It'ss sso big—"

He had no chance to say anything else, for Maggota had him by the throat. (Snakes do have throats, though they're hard to distinguish from the rest of their thin, slippery bodies.) "My darling boy, you're so lazy," she said, staring him in the eye. "Now stop complaining and do what Mother says."

Boneless Bob flicked his tongue once, in what was either assent or insult, and slithered into the water.

"If she's in there, he'll find her," she declared, satisfied. "He's quite a marvel, my boy."

Ellie stared miserably at the encroaching sea. What if Alice drowned and it was all her fault? What would Mum say? She felt like the worst daughter in the world.

"Stop feeling sorry for yourself!" Maggota snapped. "Feel sorry for *me*! Now my plans are awry and it's all your fault. You people are such a nuisance."

She glared at Ellie, then at her unconscious father, and sighed. "Such a waste of my magic." She muttered something and Clive Arnold came dripping out of the sea. He rose into the air till he was over the witch's head.

Then he dripped on that, too.

"Ugh!" she cried, and sent him roaring up the beach toward the ramshackle cabin.

"Come along," she said to Ellie. "We have a little visit to pay."

Chapter Twelve

Third-Time Unlucky

With a final look back at Mr. and Mrs. Thomas, Ben lowered himself through the trapdoor and landed with a thump. It was farther down than he'd expected.

Mrs. Thomas peered down at him. She had relit the candle. "Here," she said, handing it down to him (it was quite a stretch for both of them), "if you're going to look for a way out, you might need this."

Ben took it gratefully. It *was* awfully dark. He

looked around. The tunnel he was in was long and narrow. Just at the edge of the candle's light it looked as if it went around a corner. The walls were hard and sandy. There was an old wooden box pushed against one side. He went to investigate it.

FINE OLD BERMUDA RUM, it read. It was empty.

Bermuda? Wasn't that in his world? Ben's geography was a bit hazy, he had to admit, but he could have sworn that was the case.

Just beyond the box was a door. Ben examined it. It seemed to be made of metal, and when he pushed it, it didn't budge, though he could find no handle or lock on it anywhere. High up there was a small peephole covered by a brass lid. Ben put the candle down and fetched the crate to stand on. Then he opened the peephole and peered in. It was very dark inside the room behind the door, but if he held the candle steady, he could see—treasure!

It was piled high from floor to ceiling. He could make out the glint of gold coins and vessels and bars in higgledy-piggledy piles, statues, boxes of jewels and precious stones, paintings, including a rather ugly one of a man holding his head and screaming, and something vast made out of loads of bright snakeskin.

"Wow!" breathed Ben.

He was beginning to enjoy himself now: He felt like an explorer finding a pharaoh's tomb.

The candle's flame shuddered suddenly. Ben's heart thumped. Just for a moment he thought he had seen something in the storeroom move. . . .

He jumped down off the crate, but luckily, the candle didn't go out. He listened. Was something breathing in there, or was it just the distant sound of the sea he could hear?

With a flourish of her hand and some words Ellie couldn't quite make out, Maggota banished the weeds that had swarmed up all over the shack, barring the door, which now swung open. Inside, Ellie could see something moving, but it was too large to be Alice.

Then someone appeared at the door.

Ellie cried out in surprise. It was Mrs. Thomas, their neighbor. The old woman's eyes went round at the sight of Mr. Arnold, who had, she was sure, been floating in the air a moment before, and was now propped upright against the cabin, for all the world as if he'd sat down to take in the view, except that his eyes were firmly closed. Puzzled, she glanced at Ellie, who was soaking wet, her hair hanging in rats' tails over her shoulders. Then her gaze settled upon the witch. "Oh, no you don't," she said, barring the door with her arms spread wide. "We made that mistake once before, welcoming you across our threshold. Well, you're not coming in this time."

Mr. Thomas appeared behind her. He stared in horror at the apparition at the door. "Is that what she looked like last time?" he whispered to his wife.

"To me, dear, yes."

Mr. Thomas shook his head sadly. "I really must get my glasses changed."

Maggota laughed. "Do you really think you can keep me out?" She pressed one bony finger against Mrs. Thomas's capacious chest.

Maud Thomas stood her ground. "Henry," she said. "There's something you need to do."

"What's that, dear?"

"Remember the garage window."

Mr. Thomas frowned. "The one that was broken by—"

Mrs. Thomas shot him a furious look over her shoulder. "Yes, dear. You remember how difficult it was to *shut* it."

Comprehension dawned slowly on Henry Thomas's face. He faded out of sight into the darkness of the interior. Moments later there came a muffled thud.

"Let me in," said the witch, pressing harder. "Or you will regret it."

At last Maud Thomas stood aside.

The tunnel had got very narrow beyond the door. It had curved around a corner and sloped down and down, and Ben now found himself having to shuffle along in a crouch. The sand underfoot was compacted as hard as concrete. There was a line of what looked like limpet shells clinging to the walls at about knee height. The tunnel took another turn and suddenly Ben could see light.

He grinned and started to run toward it (though running was rather hard when almost doubled over). After a moment he realized his feet were getting wet, and as he ran, water was beginning to splash up his legs. In fact, the closer he got to the source of the light, the more water there seemed to be.

A moment later he was wading, and it was becoming quite hard to move forward. He realized the sea was pouring into the tunnel.

Never mind, Ben thought, *at least I'll be out of here soon.*

By the time he reached the end of the tunnel, the water was up to his waist, and rising all the time. The light from the outside world was so brilliant that Ben couldn't see a thing. He dropped the candleholder and it vanished at once in a tumble of water. Rather than stop to find it, he reached out blindly with both hands and moved forward.

And ran smack into something immovable. It was a huge iron grille.

Behind him, in the distance, there came an indistinct thud.

Gosh, thought Ben, shaking the grille as hard as he could. *Wouldn't it be awful if the trapdoor closed and no one could get it open again?*

Inside the shack, Ellie stared around. "You haven't seen a baby anywhere, have you?" she asked the Thomases. "My little sister, Alice?"

They exchanged a curious look. "No . . . ," Mrs. Thomas said slowly. "Not a baby."

They didn't seem anywhere near as surprised to see her as she was to see them, Ellie thought.

The witch dragged the snoring body of Clive Arnold into the shack and closed the door behind her. She sniffed the air. "The baby's not here," she told Ellie sharply. She sniffed again. "But someone else is."

Mr. Thomas sat down hard on the floor and stared at her defiantly.

"Someone else? There's no one here but me and Maud, and now you and—" He gestured at Ellie. He had never known her name; but then, she'd never broken one of his windows.

"Ellie," Ellie said.

The witch waved her hands impatiently. "Enough of all this nonsense! You—up!" And she levitated Henry Thomas and left him hanging in the air. Then she flicked back the carpet. "Someone's been here and moved the stone."

She snapped her fingers and the huge slab hovered above the hole. She sniffed again. "Boy!" she declared triumphantly. "The perfectly lovely scent of boy!" And she grinned from ear to ear: an unnerving sight. "How very, very convenient."

Ellie looked fearfully at Mrs. Thomas. "Ben?" she mouthed silently.

Mrs. Thomas gave a single, tiny nod.

"Ah," Maggota sighed, without turning. "Ben. Yes, Benjamin Arnold. Excellent. Just where I want him. Well, he can await my pleasure down there in the dark, while I decide which one of you to kill first."

"*Kill?*" Ellie shrieked.

The witch regarded her askance. "Well, my dear, you're not much use to me. No magic to speak of and you even managed to lose the baby in a wild road. Extraordinarily incompetent. And as for these two useless creatures"—she indicated the Thomases—"if they'd had the sense to behave themselves, I might have let them live. But I happen to have a couple of potions that are an eye or two short, so they'll come in very handy for the store cupboard." She turned to regard Mr. Arnold. "I have other plans for your father." She lifted his chin with one spiky fingernail, but Clive Arnold, having no conception of the danger he was in, just kept snoring and snoring.

Ben ran back up the tunnel, but it wasn't long before he realized that the trapdoor—his only means of escape—really was closed. He was about to call out for the Thomases to open it, but above him he heard the unmistakable tones of Bag-o'-Bones, and then someone shrieked. For a moment he thought it was Ellie, but that was ridiculous. Even so, he dragged the crate over and stood on it, but he could only graze the stone above with the very tips of his fingers. He stood there, feeling useless, trying to think what to do.

Then someone called his name.

It floated through the close tunnel air like the answer to a wish. It was a light, musical voice with just a touch of the sea about it. It came from the end of the tunnel. Ben knew that voice. It made him shiver, not with fear, but with delight. Despite his fear of water (he was a useless swimmer), he jumped off the crate and started to wade toward it. He passed the strong-room door, and as he did so, there was an enormous thump and the door bulged. Ben started. If there was something in there, it was trying to get out; and if it could make a metal door bulge like that, it was something very big indeed.

"Ben!"

The voice came again, closer now. He kicked out and started to swim. Or rather, he started to push himself along with one hand against each wall. The current was strong against him as the tide rushed in to fill the tunnel. There came a particularly strong surge and Ben lost his grip on the walls and was tumbled over and over until he had no idea which way was up or down, nor which way back or forward.

Oh no, he thought, sinking fast. *Third-time unlucky.* (For he had nearly drowned in Eidolon twice already.) Then he banged up against something hard. He reached out and grabbed at it and found that it was the iron grille. The water roared and pushed at him, smacking his face into the grating.

"Ow!" he cried, forgetting that it is not a good idea to open your mouth underwater.

The sea rushed in, choking him. After that, it was all a bit of a blur. He opened his eyes and thought he saw a seal looking back at him. And then something caught him round the waist and hauled with terrific force, and the grating disappeared, and suddenly he was in the air and coughing up water.

Someone was laughing: a tinkling sound like a stream running over pebbles, and he stared and there was Silver; or rather, there was Silver's head, drying in the air, her pale hair merging with her mottled seal-skin where her body was still immersed. Then who had hold of him? He turned around and found himself face to face with a giant squid. It was the nautilus

Nemesis, and in one of his other tentacles he held the broken grille.

Ben grinned and grinned. He could not help it, no matter how awful things were. Seeing Silver always made him happy.

"Silver! Nem—" He managed to stop himself saying the nautilus's true name just in time. "Nice to see you," he finished lamely.

The selkie swam over and climbed onto the nautilus as if they were the best of friends (which perhaps they were now) and hugged Ben with flippers that gradually became arms as they dried in the chilly sea air.

"Thank you. Thank you so much!" Ben cried, hugging her back.

"Well, don't bother thanking *me*," growled an irritated voice from higher up. "After all, it was only me who had the wit to summon them."

Perched on top of the nautilus's head was a small black-and-brown cat.

"Oh, Iggy! You're so clever!"

Ignatius Sorvo Coromandel gleamed with appreciation. "Job well done," he congratulated himself.

Ben remembered the voices in the shack. "Well,

not quite—" he started, but Silver held a hand to his mouth.

"Stop, Ben," she said. "There's something else. It's . . . it's . . ." And she burst into tears.

Ben stared at her in dismay. Then he stared at Iggy, who pretended to wash his face. "What is it? Tell me!"

"Your sssissster."

Ben stared around. In another of the giant squid's free tentacles something red and white writhed. It was a snake, quite a big snake, with an ugly orange crest, which it now waved at Ben.

So it *had* been Ellie he had heard scream.

"Tell me what's happened to Ellie," he demanded, glaring at the horrid snake, which oddly reminded him of someone.

The snake's tongue flickered slyly. "Well, that I don't know. She's with my mother, who is, I am sssure, taking great care of her."

"Your mother?"

"Ah, yesss," said the snake. "I forget. You haven't had the honor to encounter Mother and me in our Eidolon forms." And it grinned at Ben in such a way that he was suddenly struck by its likeness to his horrible new neighbor, Bob. "Mrs. Bagssshot, otherwise known as Maggota, Witch of the First Order."

"Oh no," Ben groaned. "You mean Bag-o'-Bones has got Ellie?"

"Show ressspect!" the snake hissed. "Or she will make you."

"It's Alice," Silver sobbed, unable to bear the suspense any longer. "She's lost. In the sea. We think she's—" She couldn't say the word.

"Drowned for sure," said Boneless Bob cheerfully. "The baby. Your other sister—the one who thinks she's too cool to give me the time of day—dropped her in the ocean as she came out of the wild road. That's what I reckon."

"Drowned? Alice?" Ben stared at the snake aghast.

"We looked for her," Iggy said softly. "Silver and the nautilus looked in the sea, and I sniffed all around before the tide came rushing in. There's no sign of her at all. I'm so sorry, Ben." And he climbed down from his perch, negotiating Nemesis's strange face (carefully avoiding that cruel beak of a mouth, which might bite you in two by mistake, or on purpose), and nestled against his friend.

Ben closed his eyes. He thought about Alice and

her ways of surprising you with odd words. How she pinched your nose if you got too close and then laughed and laughed and laughed. How she seemed to see things no one else could see. How at home she had seemed in the Secret Country.

It was all too much. He had come here to find his mother and tell her that her evil brother had escaped from prison, and on a dinosaur, too; and now he would have to take her the worst news of all. He was too stricken even to cry.

Chapter Thirteen

The Darkest Hour

All the rest of that day, Isadora and the Horse Lord Darius and his centaurs gathered about them the denizens of the Wildwood. There was a lot of weeping and wailing from the female gnomes at the thought of leaving their safe forest nooks, which had lately been spruced up with hope and optimism, with the return of the Queen and her magic to their realm. There was confusion among the flying creatures, for could they not conceal themselves better than the rest and ride out whatever storm should come their way? But worst, there was despair from the dryads, who had never before in their long, long lives been forced to abandon their trees. Some opted to stay behind and take their chances, but most had already borne too much in the war against the Dodman to want to risk direct attack. Sprites and fairies, nymphs and satyrs, all had lost friends and relatives in the dog-headed man's quest to eradicate magic from Eidolon. They had heard terrible tales of what he had already done, or had seen such horrors for themselves. All had heard of the army he was gathering, of the monsters he daily summoned to swell the ranks. Things had been bad enough when their opponents had consisted of just a few bad trolls, the spectral hounds, Old Creepie, and a band of wicked goblins. But now it was rumored that dinosaurs and dragons were coming to his side; and surely even their returned Queen and their beloved Wildwood could not protect them from such foes.

It was a sorrowful procession that wound its way along the well-trodden woodland paths that night. Even the moon hid her face, leaving them in the pitch-dark. Her withdrawal left the pair of dragons who flew as sentries through the night sky above as invisible as bats in a cave. It was the wood-sprites who led the way through the forest, their pale green light making everything eerie. Branches became witches' fingers; roosting birds, demons crouched ready to spring; woodland pools, sucking mires that might swallow them all before dawn.

The Queen walked slowly at the head of the refugees, with Darius at her side. A small host of gnome-children had tangled themselves in his mane and were trying to sleep. Their parents sat solemn and silent among their hastily gathered bundles, attempting to accustom themselves to the odd sway of his movement and trying not to think about everything and everyone they had left behind. Above them, fairies wove and dived, flitting bright shapes in the dark canopy, while the dryads drifted alongside, heads down, weeping silently. No one spoke. Someone had tried to start a rousing chorus of "Woodland Creatures Free" some while back, but had at once been shushed into silence by half a hundred others. Even the sound of a twig breaking underfoot set everyone on edge, gazing fearfully into the shadows in case it had betrayed their presence to the enemy.

So when the silence was broken by the sudden crash of something large breaking through the undergrowth and the sound of stertorous breathing behind them in the night, panic reigned.

The fairies and sprites vanished into the night; dryads found the arms of a welcoming tree and slipped inside; gnome-children wailed in distress. Grim-faced, the centaurs drew their bows and short-swords and formed a protective barrier around the Queen.

Everyone waited in the thick darkness, not knowing what to expect. Then a huge figure burst through the trees. It was the Minotaur. One of his great bull horns had been cloven in two; blood washed his face. One arm hung useless at his side. He was weaponless. When he saw the guard with their swords drawn, his eyes rolled up white and he bellowed.

Centaurs and small folk cried out in fear. He was a terrifying sight—a monster looking for more blood to spill.

Darius let fall his sword and came forward, hands spread to pacify. "Minotaur, calm yourself. It is I, Darius. No harm will come to you here. Fear not."

The bull-headed man staggered and fell sideways, exhausted. Isadora broke through the rank of guards and knelt beside him. She brushed the bloodied forelock out of eyes that stared wildly and did not focus.

"Hush, now, hush," she said over and over. "You are among friends now."

Gradually, feeling the Queen's gentle hands upon him, the Minotaur began to calm.

"Tell us what has happened," Darius said softly.

The bull-headed man gazed up at him with haunted eyes. "Dead," he said in a voice that was barely above a whisper. "All dead."

"All?" the Queen echoed in horror.

The gnomes whom Darius carried in his mane and on his back began to wail.

"The centaurs?" Darius asked, dreading the answer.

"Every one . . ." The Minotaur coughed, and blood spattered onto the ground. "We did not stand a chance . . . they tore us to pieces . . . We were too few . . ."

At close quarters now it was plain to see where something with terrible claws had raked his side.

"He . . . the Dodman has . . . many monsters . . ."

"Dinosaurs?" the Queen asked in fear, but he did

not answer her, only groaned and groaned, both from physical pain and the horror of his memories.

"And Cernunnos? Where is the Lord of the Wildwood?" Darius prompted gently.

The Minotaur closed his eyes in pain. "Lost. I saw him fall."

The Horse Lord and his Queen stared at each other in shock. Around them, the Wildwood folk close enough to hear the terrible news began to weep. Word spread as fast as a forest fire. The fairies and wood-sprites hovered over the heads of the gathered crowd, many of the sprites showing the pale red glow that was their telltale sign of fear.

"We are all that are left," one of the old centaurs said to a companion. They stared at each other, thinking of all those who had left to fight—sons and nephews, daughters and cousins.

The Minotaur turned his ravaged head. "There was nothing I could do," he started, as if accused. "I—"

Isadora stroked his cheek. "Hush, now," she said. "Do not distress yourself further."

"They were all dead . . . and there were so many . . . I fled . . . I should have died with them. . . ."

And with a look of terrible anguish on his face, the Minotaur gazed at her. "Tell the Princess . . . Eleanor . . . I fought bravely." Then the great black eyes lost their focus, and he exhaled his last breath.

The Queen bowed her head and wept. The Horse Lord gently closed the staring eyes. "Poor fellow," he said softly. "He has seen such horrors." He picked up a handful of leaves from the ground and scattered them upon the Minotaur's chest. "He that has come of Eidolon returns now to Eidolon." It was what you said when someone died, but no one really knew where the bull-headed man had come from. He had come to them as a mystery, and died a mystery.

"We should bury him," Isadora said, gazing miserably at the noble creature.

"There is no time—"

And even as Darius said this, there was a flash of fire in the night sky, and when they stared upward, they saw for the briefest moment a dragon beset by flying creatures. Then another dragon came roaring through the trees.

It was Xarkanadûshak, the dragon Ben had saved in the Other World. He hovered above them, beating his wings furiously. Blood poured from a dozen small wounds. Smoke trailed from his nostrils. His snout was charred and soot had gathered between the scales on his face. He looked exhausted.

"Run!" Zark cried. "Run for your lives! We will hold them as long as we can!"

And he gave a huge flap of his long, leathery wings and soared up through the canopy into the night sky, screaming defiance at the creatures attacking the second dragon. With a mighty effort he hurled himself among them, slashing with his claws and shooting fire from his roaring mouth. The moon drifted out from her cover of clouds and at last they could see that the flying creatures were a flight of pterodactyls, with wickedly long, sharp beaks and terrible claws. Even though they were much smaller than the dragons they attacked, there were very many of them. One took the full brunt of Zark's fury and came plummeting down, trailing smoke and flames. They saw it crash into the trees away to the south, and then watched in despair as the trees there caught fire and burned like torches into the night sky, illuminating the horrors above.

"We must away!" Darius cried.

"But I know these dragons well," Isadora replied, staring up at the aerial battle taking place above them.

"It is Zark and Ishtar, his wife, and they have done me fine service. I cannot just desert them as they fight for their lives."

"There is nothing you can do," the Horse Lord replied, and indeed it seemed what he said was true.

Ishtar was tiring visibly, and seemed to have run out of fire. She turned and tried to fly away from her attackers, but they were too fast. Evading Xarkanadûshak with terrifyingly swift aerobatics, the pterodactyls sped after their wounded opponent, stabbing at her and swiping her with their claws like malicious crows mobbing a hawk. Three of them landed on her back and began to hammer at her head and neck with their vile beaks.

Zark threw off the pterodactyls who beset him and rocketed in to rescue his mate, but it was too late. Her wings drooped suddenly and she began to spin, slowly, very slowly, like an autumn leaf spiraling down from a tree. One by one the dinosaur birds peeled away to watch her fall. Zark stooped like a kestrel, his wings tucked close to his body, his neck stretched out in a hard, sharp line of desperation. But all his efforts were in vain. Ishtar crashed into the trees at appalling speed. Even at a distance, they could hear the way great branches were ripped apart by the impact of something huge and inert carrying everything in its path down to the hard, hard ground. Xarkanadûshak followed, howling his despair, his wings and feet pummeling the air in an attempt to break his own plunging fall. They saw the way he yawed sharply left, then right, to avoid the hazards of his path. Then he dived through the trees, disappearing into the darkness of the canopy close to the place where his mate had fallen.

Seconds later there came a terrible keening cry, and then there was a silence which was more terrible still.

Isadora's eyes welled with tears. "Oh no," she mouthed. "I must go to them." And she began to gather her skirts to run.

Darius caught her by the arm and pulled her back. "You must save yourself, my lady. Your duty is with these folk, who will not leave without you."

Overhead, the pterodactyls wheeled and shrieked their triumph as if to illustrate his words. Mutely, Isadora stared back into the dark where the dragons had fallen, disbelief and misery etched on her face. When she turned back to the Horse Lord, her eyes seemed like black, glittering holes in the whiteness of her face. She looked as if she had aged a hundred years in as many seconds.

"Such sacrifice shall not be in vain," she declared bitterly. "The Dodman must be made to pay for the blood he has spilled this day."

"He shall," Darius averred grimly. "Oh, he shall." And he retrieved his sword and ran a thumb down the sharp blade as if applying it to the Dog-Headed One's throat. He sheathed it angrily, then dipped a shoulder to his Queen. "Get on, my lady. We must make speed."

The gnomes who rode upon Darius rearranged themselves and their belongings swiftly to make space for her. When the Queen was safely on his back, Darius gave a signal and his centaurs kicked up their heels and followed him, their riders holding tightly to mane and tail and one another so as not to fall off. The fairies and wood-sprites flew above them, keeping noticeably closer now, not daring to fly high among the trees with such frightening predators aloft.

Along the ancient forest pathways they ran, dodging between the trunks of spruce and sapin, larch and oak, and beside them the dryads ran like shadows of the trees themselves, fleet and silent.

Gradually, they began to hear the unmistakable sounds of pursuit. At first it was the baying of the Gabriel Hounds that carried most clearly through the night air; then came a thundering that boomed and thrummed, making the ground tremble and shudder. Trees cried out and came crashing down, as if blundered into by something huge.

"Hold tight!" cried Darius, and broke into a gallop.

The Queen knotted her hands in his thick black mane and held on grimly, and the gnomes and gnome-children clung on to her. Between the uprights of trunks they ran, between thickets and over rocks and hummocks; and wherever they passed, new creatures joined their flight in panic, knowing nothing but that something terrible was about to happen, and was coming their way. Overhead, the ghost-dogs howled and streamed, and the flock of ancient birds glided, their black eyes glinting, their gaze malevolently trained on the ground below, their wicked beaks (bloodied now) eager for new prey.

They sped along, joltingly fast, led by the fiery red trails of the terrified wood-sprites who shot through the darkness like fireworks. Isadora gradually became aware that the spaces between trees were becoming wider, that the forest was beginning to thin out. Soon she could even glimpse through the gaps a wide and featureless terrain beyond—a great open tract of moorland.

"Darius!" she cried above the pounding of his hooves. "We have almost reached the Black Heath!"

The Horse Lord had bent all his concentration on the ground immediately before his feet, rather than gaze around and break their necks in a stumble. This was unwelcome news. With a lurch he pulled up, signaling for the rest of his centaurs to do likewise. "If we ride out onto the heath, in full sight of the enemy, we are lost."

"We must disperse," Isadora said bravely. "They cannot chase us all at once, and I fear it is me they most want to capture, or . . . ," she swallowed, "to kill."

There was a brief silence. Then one of the older centaurs concurred with a toss of his head. His flanks were heaving. Salty foam speckled his dark hide. "There are caves in the hills to the north of here. I know them well, for I was raised in this region. I can lead some of our folk in that direction. No . . . nothing very . . . big can enter there."

He avoided saying the word.

"Good." Darius nodded. "Take as many with you as you can."

"Go with them," the Queen told her nymphs and dryads. "There is no cover for you out there." And she gestured out to the heath.

Swiftly, the gnomes on Darius's back were transferred to another. A gnome-child dropped its doll of twigs and howled mightily, but there was no time to retrieve it, and their parting took place under the pall of this small but painful loss.

"You fairies and sprites," Isadora called, "can you fly a trail to the south and distract their attention as best you can? You will find a wide marshland there with a great river running through it. They cannot cross the river, for it is too swift, and the marshland is treacherous. Stay in the air, but beware those flying monsters."

"We are quicker than they," a fairy cried contemptuously. "If we cannot outfly them, we deserve to fail!"

"If we can, we shall lead them *into* the mere," another declared boldly.

"And watch them perish!" a wood-sprite finished, its red light washed through with pale green as a small measure of its courage returned.

"Then go!" cried the Queen, "with my love. Do what you can, but save yourselves."

And with that, the larger part of their gathering split away into two, the centaurs taking to their heels and heading north, the flying creatures to the south. The Queen and her Horse Lord and a small brigade of centaur-guards headed straight on to the farthest extent of the Wildwood—farther than any of them (save Isadora) had ever traveled before—and then out into the scrubland, where forest gave way to scattered trees and then petered out altogether into a welter of thorn and bramble, then gorse, then nothing at all but bleak, bleak moor.

"Once we are in the open, I will give them clear sight of us," Darius proposed breathlessly, "and when they give chase, we will cut back and bury ourselves once more among the trees. Once we have split their forces and sown confusion, we too should make for the caves."

"I trust your good judgment, Darius," the Queen replied, though the idea of fleeing out onto the empty moor filled her with dread.

Through the ferns and bracken they plowed like ships breasting a rough sea, then out onto the moonlit moors. For creatures born of the Wildwood, this was a grim and eerie place, with not a tree in sight, just tumbles of rock and bare earth, as if the world here had had its skin stripped back.

Above, the pterodactyls screamed in excitement. Two of them peeled away from the rest and headed back over the woods, no doubt to carry word of their sighting, and soon the crashing noises of pursuit came closer and closer. For a little while the sound was muffled by the forest; then the roaring and howling became suddenly sharp and imminent, and when Isadora turned at the sudden change in note, she saw the enemy clearly defined by the silver light of the moon.

The sight was so terrible that she could not suppress her cry of horror.

The Horse Lord wheeled around. "By all that is sacred!" he gasped, and the other centaurs stopped in their flight and stared where he stared.

On the edge of the moor, towering above the thorn and scrub, the Dodman sat upon his mount. He balanced high on its shoulders, held in place by a contraption of straps and harnesses, and in his dog-hands he carried a long, many-tailed whip weighted with spikes, with which he beat the creature that carried him mercilessly.

Twenty feet and more in height was this monster. It stood, slightly hunched, its huge legs bent as if ready to leap, its smaller arms caught up to its chest, claws curled. Its vast head swung slowly left then right, and even at a distance they could see how the moonlight rendered its massive reptilian eyes a flat and deadly silver. Then it opened its mouth and roared, showing teeth as long as swords and twice as sharp.

"He has a tyrannosaur," Darius breathed in dismay. "He has used the Book."

Now other figures emerged from the Wildwood, dinosaurs both large and small. Some were similar to the tyrannosaur, but smaller and with long, wicked faces, crouched as if waiting for a starting pistol to fire, when they would hurl themselves across that empty space like the wind. Others were huge, lumbering beasts that trod bushes and thorn trees underfoot as if they were grass. Hordes of goblins clung to their backs, chattering and waving their swords. A triceratops bellowed, its great rhinoceros-horns savaging the air.

"Oh, my heaven," cried the Queen. "It was

already too late for Cernunnos and the brave centaurs. The Dodman had summoned these monsters."

"It may be too late for us, too," the Horse Lord said flatly. "A tyrannosaur can run almost as fast as a centaur, and over a short distance the velociraptors can outrun us easily." He turned to his comrades. "Scatter!" he commanded them. "Fan out and double back when they have committed themselves to the chase. If you evade them, make for the caves and we will find you there."

"Go with blessing, my brave centaurs!" cried Isadora, and they bowed and ran.

"Now, my lady, if you have any magic left to you, I hope you will use it in our cause," said Darius, gritting his teeth. "For there is only so much that a strong heart and four legs can achieve against such odds."

Then he kicked up his heels and carried her on a breakneck path between heath and scrub, across streams and through mire and bog. Isadora focused hard. It had been a very long time since she had studied spellcraft under the tuition of Maggota Magnifica of the First Order of Witches, and since then the world had lost a lot of its magic. For a while she managed to maintain a weak invisibility spell, but it was hard to hold on to a galloping centaur and keep all her mind on it, so every few seconds it would disperse and they would reveal their position again. The Gabriel Hounds came flying out between the feet of the dinosaurs, their noses full of scent. No spell of invisibility was going to fox them. Next she attempted sowing spells of confusion in her wake, sending some of the pursuers in one direction and some in another, but still the Dodman, fixed in his purpose, drove his terrible mount onward.

Darius cut this way and that, but he could not shake his pursuers. There was no chance to double back toward the forest, and so on he went, and on.

At last, his breath laboring and his flanks salt-streaked and heaving, Darius climbed a steep and rocky hill, topped by a rock in the shape of a raptor's head. "If you have the power to summon a dragon, my Queen, now is the time to do it. Here at Eagle Tor is where we must make our stand, for I can run no more."

In a fluster, Isadora could barely remember the name of a single one. She bent her mind upon the dragons she had called to her, dragons who had arrogantly shown her their backs, or cruel words, before flying away again, refusing their aid. Would such a creature be compelled by a summoning? She did not think so. At last, and reluctantly, she cried:

"Xarkanadûshak!"

They waited, their heartbeats fast and loud in their ears, watching the dark sky. But all they saw was the pterodactyls gathering above, eyes glinting in anticipation. No dragon came.

It was not long before the tor was ringed around with dinosaurs, with spectral hounds and goblins and trolls—a dark tide surrounding their little island of rock. The Dodman rode toward them, stately on his giant tyrannosaur, his long, white dog-teeth flashing with triumph.

Darius drew his sword. "I am sorry, my lady, that it has come to this," he said. "It has been my honor to serve you." And he stepped in front of her to meet the monstrous army ascending the tor toward them.

Chapter Fourteen

Mummu-Tiamat

"Stay back out of sight," Ben warned Silver. He squeezed her hand, then let it go, feeling awkward. "I want to make sure you're safe. You never know what a witch might be capable of."

The selkie shivered.

"What about me?" growled Ignatius Sorvo Coromandel. "Don't you want me to be kept safe?"

Ben thought about this. "Well, you can stay with Nemesis too, if you like."

Iggy curled his lip. "I don't fancy my chances if he decides to go for a swim."

"Well, I can't carry you *and* the snake," Ben said crossly.

"What do you want with that horrible thing?"

"You'll see."

In the end Iggy balanced himself awkwardly on Ben's shoulder. "There," he purred into Ben's left ear. "Isn't that better?"

It wasn't, but Ben nodded. Then he gathered all his courage, turned to face the shack, and shouted, "Mrs. Bagshott! Come out of there and let my sister and my friends go free!"

A face appeared at the window of the shack, looking deeply surprised. There was a flurry of movement, then the door opened, and there stood Mrs. Bagshott in all her Eidolon glory: bones, maggots, and all. Ben couldn't help but stare.

"Robert!" she cried, then uttered something Ben could not make out that made the red and white serpent coil itself desperately around Ben's wrist.

"Ugh!" said Ben, who wasn't very keen on any sort of snake, let alone one that in the Other World was his horrible neighbor's horrible son. He held

Boneless Bob at arm's length, and shouted again. "Let them all go or the snake gets it!"

The sea was beginning to lap at the broken old fence surrounding the shack now. The strangling vines in what had once been its garden floated on the surface of the water like seaweed.

"Put Robert down or I shall pull out your sister's teeth, one by one!"

"If you harm one hair on Ellie's head, I shall kill your familiar." Ben was in no mood to trifle. "I hold you responsible for what has happened to my baby sister." And he gave the bit of Boneless Bob directly below his orange frill a hard squeeze.

Bob made a horrible squawking sound.

Maggota's hands flew in the air, weaving some sort of spell. Whatever it was came flying at Ben, but before it could reach him, something dark and swift leapt through the air in front of him, caught it, and came to rest on the fence post. It was Ignatius Sorvo Coromandel, and in his mouth he held an ugly bat-like thing, which flapped and flapped as Iggy's teeth closed on its wings. It had mad red eyes and leathery feathers, and when it opened its mouth to protest, it showed two nasty-looking fangs. Iggy bit down sharply and the thing went limp. Disgusted, he threw it into the water, where it floated like a black plastic bag.

"Yuk! Vampire chicken," he declared, spitting feathers after it.

Ben grinned at his friend, balancing neatly on the fence. "Thanks, Ig." He waved Boneless Bob in the air. "You'll have to do better than that."

The witch disappeared inside. When she returned a moment later, it was with Ellie in her bony clutches. "Perhaps I'll start on her eyes." She cackled. "Since they don't work very well here anyway."

"Ben!" Ellie shrieked. "Don't let her hurt me!" Her mascara had run so much that she looked like an anorexic panda.

Ben firmed his jaw. He held the dangling snake out and gave it a hard shake.

"What do I care about a ridiculous snake?" Maggota cried. "It means nothing to me. Go ahead, do your worst!"

"Don't take any notice of her," Iggy said softly. "It's her familiar; she can't do without it."

It was a terrible risk, but the loss of Alice had made him reckless. "Last chance!" Ben cried, squeezing till

Boneless Bob's long forked tongue shot out and waved around as if it were an entirely separate snake of its own.

Maggota's eyes bored into him. He could feel the intensity of her gaze like maggots crawling on his face. Something moved on his nose. Ugh! Maggots *were* crawling on his face! He very nearly dropped Boneless Bob then, but instead his start of horror made his fist close even tighter and Bob lolled suddenly limp.

Abruptly, the maggots vanished. So did the vampire chicken.

Ben stared at Iggy.

"Is he dead?" Iggy enquired curiously.

Ben examined the snake. It was a bit hard to tell. "Not sure," he whispered.

"Never mind," Iggy said cheerfully. "Everyone knows that witches are nothing without their familiars. It's where they store their magic. If a familiar dies or falls unconscious, they can't do much at all."

And indeed, when Ben looked back at the shack again, Mrs. Bagshott was holding on to the doorframe with one hand and Ellie with the other, but now it seemed as if she was holding on to them for support. She looked suddenly old, not just ordinary old, like Mr. and Mrs. Thomas, but OLD—like a withered tree, or like the fallen Aldstane.

He was about to press home his advantage and demand the release of her captives when suddenly the ground in front of the shack started to shake. Iggy took one look at it, then leapt from the fence post back onto Ben's shoulder and teetered there with his claws digging through Ben's so-called raincoat (which was now wet through). Ben didn't even think to complain: He was rooted to the spot. Earth and sea began to push upward, like a slow eruption; then there was a mighty roar and a head emerged from the ground.

It was huge and golden and covered in scales.

It was a dragon.

Ben gasped.

The dragon rammed upward and freed its shoulders, and stones and water began to tumble down into the hole it created for its huge body with every writhing effort it made to break free. It shook its head, and chunks of sand and rock splashed down into the incoming tide. Its eyes, as big as trash can lids and an unearthly shade of green, blinked rapidly, as if it was not used to daylight. It turned its head and looked at Ben. Then it opened its vast mouth and treated him to an array of teeth. A rumble filled the air. Ben felt it first in his breastbone, then it traveled all the way down till he felt his knees go to jelly. Was he about to be roasted? Or just have his head bitten off? He remembered his first encounter with Xarkanadûshak and how he'd been a bit worried even then about being barbecued, but this dragon was at least three times the size of Zark and looked a lot more annoyed. If this thing decided to roast him, it wouldn't just be a barbecue: It'd be Armageddon!

The shock of seeing it meant that it took him several moments to realize it was speaking. To him.

"Thank you," it said. "I take it it's you who broke her spell." It glanced at the limp snake Ben held in his fist. "Since you appear to have killed her traitor worm."

"Well, actually," said Ben, "I'm not sure it's—"

The dragon didn't let him finish. It leaned in closer to get a better look at him, and its eyes whirled like pinwheels. Ben felt his head going all loose and dreamy. He almost dropped Boneless Bob.

"Well, well," the dragon said at last. "A prince of Eidolon. That's an unusual thing to find."

Ben stood there stunned, not knowing what to say. At last he stuttered, "D-did she summon you here? The witch, I mean."

The dragon snorted. It puffed out its chest. "No one can summon *me*. *I* was here before the world began."

Ben couldn't make much sense of that. "Then how did you get trapped down there?"

"Greed," the dragon replied simply. It opened its mouth wider, showing all its teeth. Apparently, it was amused. "Always the curse of our kind. We do so love pretty things." It swept a wing in an expansive gesture. "Infinity Beach. Most beautiful place in Eidolon, and the most remote. I made it mine. I chased the dinosaurs out of it and made it my home. Mine, all mine. This beach, those dunes, everything, apart from that ugly little house the witch made to hide her comings and goings."

"And the Minstrels?" Ben asked.

The dragon wrinkled its brow. "The Minstrels?"

"I mean, the wooden circle . . ." Ben pointed to the almost-submerged stumps.

"Ah, those. No, the fairy folk put those there. They used to dance around them and leave me little offerings. To persuade me not to steal their children, I suppose. Though what would I want with a fairy child? Too small even for a tidbit; one bite and they're gone. No, it was the gold they brought me I treasured:

gold and jewels, precious stones . . ." Its whirling eyes went misty. "Gems and rare objects, golden fleeces, magic swords, antique statues, pharaohs' death masks—ah, they traveled far and wide to keep me in a good temper." It sighed, remembering. "Good times then, better times than these. Proper respect shown. I could breathe fire back then, fire that could singe the hair off a ghost-hound at a hundred paces. Mmmm, roast dog . . . that was a treat."

"Can't you now?" Ben asked, feeling faintly relieved.

"The witch took my fire. While I was sleeping." The dragon turned one of its remarkable eyes upon Maggota, who quailed.

"How did she do that?"

"You are too full of questions, Prince of Eidolon." The dragon shifted its vast bulk, sending ripples across the sea in all directions. There was the sound of earth moving and stones falling, and then its tail came free, sending the walls of the flimsy shack tumbling around the ears of those inside it. Someone shrieked.

Alerted by the familiar sound of fear, the dragon whipped around. First it eyed the Thomases, then seemed to dismiss them; *then* it focused on Clive Arnold, who had just sat up, yawning and rubbing his eyes.

"Goodness me," he said, "I must have fallen asleep on the sofa." He squinted around. "What's happened to the house?" he asked in confusion. "And what's that horrible-looking thing?"

The "horrible-looking thing" shook its golden head furiously and peeled its lips away from its teeth as if in preparation to eat him head first in a single swallow.

Ellie planted herself firmly in front of her father. "You leave my dad alone," she told the dragon fiercely.

"*Dad?*" Ben goggled. Was his father here too?

The dragon stared and stared at Ellie. Its eyes flared with interest. It regarded her first with one side of its head, then the other. "Another of the royal blood. How curious. What's your name, young beauty?"

Ellie smiled tremulously. She had been quite afraid of the monster till that moment, despite her bravado. Now it seemed rather charming.

"I'm Eleanor Arnold," she said, "Princess of Eidolon. Who are you?"

Maggota chuckled. "Bless the child. How are the mighty fallen! She doesn't know who you are, O Great One. Times really have changed in the Shadow World."

The dragon shifted its weight again so that its

huge golden head overhung the witch. Its shadow fell across her. "Yes, you managed to keep me imprisoned for a long time, didn't you, old woman? Did you think I would wither in this treasure tomb?"

"It was your own fault, foolish worm." Maggota grimaced. "Had you forgotten how stupid it is to invite a witch over your threshold?"

"I was blinded by the gifts you brought me," the dragon growled. "Gold was always something that tricked my wits. I have learned a hard lesson in my long confinement. But you, what have you learned, crone? The treasure you have stashed away for your glorious future is floating away on the tide"—and indeed, dozens of lighter items, like paintings and robes, were bobbing up and down in the water—"or sucked down into the earth, where such lifeless things belong. What good will your hoard do you now, old woman, with your familiar dead and your magic gone and a hungry dragon ready to bite off your head?"

At this, the serpent in Ben's hands gave a sudden convulsion. Boneless Bob was not dead after all.

"Ma!" he squawked, and even as he spoke, the witch seemed to grow in strength and stature.

Maggota shot a spiteful look at the dragon. "Not finished yet, Mummu-Tiamat. There—that's a surprise for you, isn't it? I spent a long time searching for your name."

Mummu-Tiamat shook out her wings. "You may well know my name, crone. Such things do not concern the Old Ones. In the ancient times everyone knew the name of the Mother of Dragons. Do not think it gives you any power over me. It was only a trick that caught me unawares. But now I shall exact my revenge." It turned to Ben.

"Tell me, Prince of Eidolon, shall I eat the worm first, or its mother?"

Ben was a bit taken aback by the question. He wasn't sure he wanted to see anyone eaten. "Um . . ."

Mummu-Tiamat laughed, and all around the sea stirred with her amusement. "If you're going to survive very long in the Shadow World, young man, you're going to have to be ready to make many more difficult decisions than that."

Ben held out the snake. "Here," he said. "Take it. I don't want it."

"No!" the witch shrieked. Something bright and spinning zigzagged through the air like a ball of lightning. The dragon swatted it boredly away. It fell into the water by Ben's feet with a monstrous sizzle. A huge cloud of vapor mushroomed into the air.

"No!" Maggota cried again, and this time her tone was plaintive rather than challenging. "Don't kill my son. He's all I've got."

"Ah," murmured Mummu-Tiamat, "how touching. You're trying to appeal to my maternal senses, witch, but it won't do you any good. Don't you know that half the time we dragons eat our young?" And the dragon gave her a ghastly grin. "Anyway, I've changed my mind. I'm going to eat you both!"

The Mother of Dragons reared up and grabbed Maggota, one of her great, clawed hands encircling the bony witch's waist.

"Wait!" shrieked the witch. "Don't eat me. What good am I to you dead?"

"What good are you to me alive?"

"I could give you back Infinity Beach."

"Pah! You have made it loathsome to me. I never want to see it again."

"I could restore your fire."

The dragon's eyes gleamed. She looked thoughtful. "Ah. Now that *would* be good. For me. But to extract a favor just for myself seems a little, how shall I put this? Selfish."

The witch looked crafty. "I know something the Boy wants to know."

Ben stared at her. "You know where Alice is?"

Maggota stared back. "Maybe." Though she didn't.

"Don't kill her," Ben implored Mummu-Tiamat.

"Don't listen to the dragon!" Ellie shouted. "The witch knows nothing!"

Maggota shot Ellie a look of pure venom. "Oh, don't I? I happen to know the Dodman's true na—"

"His true name?" Ben interrupted. He stared at the witch, then at the dragon, hope dawning in his eyes. "That could save the world!"

Maggota laughed, though it pained her to do so, so tightly clutched was she. "How naive the Boy is! How foolish!"

Mummu-Tiamat squeezed her till she choked. "You will be respectful to the Prince of Eidolon, crone. He saved me and I owe him a gift for that. So you are going to tell me what he wishes to know, and that will be my gift to him."

"Ow!" Maggota squawked. "Prince or no prince, he should know it's most rude to interrupt his elders.

What I was going to say is that I know something about the Dodman that would be very useful to him."

"And what would that be?" The dragon's eyes whirled.

"You must think I am stupid, to give away all my secrets so easily."

Mummu-Tiamat growled. "Give me back my fire, or I shall know you to be a lying and powerless creature."

"All right, all right." The witch said something strange, which sounded like *takat l'hisht*, and Boneless Bob twisted suddenly in Ben's hand. His eyes bulged till it looked as if they would pop out of his head. Then a little wisp of smoke emerged from the serpent's mouth, followed by the tiniest red flame, and smoke and flame fled across the space between snake and dragon and disappeared inside Mummu-Tiamat's open mouth. For a moment the extraordinary green eyes whirled faster than ever, then a golden light appeared in them. At last the dragon turned a beatific smile upon the company. She took a deep breath and directed a huge sheet of fire at the incoming sea.

There was a whooshing sound.

Then Ben yelped. "Ow! The water's boiling!" He bolted toward the remains of the shack and the safety of dry land.

But he found when he got there that no one was looking at him. They were all staring at the sea. Or rather, where the sea had been. There was now nothing but scorched sand all the way back to the wooden circle, inside which a very cross-looking giant squid and a rapidly drying selkie had been left beached.

But of Alice there was no sign at all.

Maggota regarded the dragon steadily. "I have given you your fire back, isn't that enough for now?"

The dragon rumbled. It shook its golden head. "I still owe the Prince of Eidolon a gift."

"Please," said Ben. "I don't mean to interrupt, but can I say something?"

The dragon and witch looked at him.

"Mummu-Tiamat, if you would be so good, I'd like you to carry me across Eidolon to find my mother."

"And that is to be my gift to you?"

"Well . . ." Ben hesitated, torn between the absolute truth and the need for a very small lie. He blushed. He was hopeless at lying. "I was going to ask you for something else, when we get there."

The dragon's eyes flared and for an awful moment Ben thought she was going to get angry and let loose her new fire. She gave him her cat-smile. "Ask me the thing you wish when we arrive, and I will consider it. But I promise nothing."

"Okay," said Ben in a small voice. Then he braced himself. "Now for you, Mrs. Bagshott." Ben gave a meaningful glance at the red and white snake in his hand. "Ellie and I will keep Bob safe, if you will, please, search for my sister Alice. Wherever she may be. And when you find her . . . her . . ." He couldn't finish the sentence.

Maggota fixed him with her gimlet eyes. "Her body, do you mean, Boy?"

Ben nodded miserably. "Bring her back to me," he finished almost in a whisper.

Mr. Arnold sat up straighter and squinted into the light. "Eh, what? Ben, is that you? And what do you mean by 'finding Alice's body'?"

Ellie began to cry. "We've lost Alice," she sobbed.

"Lost?"

But Ellie could say no more.

The witch watched all this with some satisfaction.

Then she said to Ben, "Boy, tell the dragon to put me down and I will do what you say. I, too, have an interest in your sister Alice. But if you harm my son, I shall know it at once and I shall find you, wherever you are, in the twinkling of an eye. I am not so stupid as to store all my magic in one familiar, whatever you may think."

Ben thought about this. Then he said, "Mummu-Tiamat, would you please release your captive?"

"Is that the boon you wish me to grant you, Prince Ben?"

Ben blushed. "Er, no, actually. It's just a request."

The dragon's eyes went round and round as if she was carefully considering whether she might still manage to eat the witch, and thus put an end to her troublemaking for all time, or whether she should honor the young prince and let Maggota go. In the end she uncurled her claws one by one by one and set the crone down on the scorched sand. Then she bent her huge head very close to the witch's ear. "But if I ever see you again," she hissed, still keeping her final claw firmly in place, "Maggota Medusa Magnifica, you are toast." Her long lips curled into a catlike smile. "You see," she whispered, "I know your true name too."

The witch looked shaken by this, but she bowed her head, and turned to leave.

"And, er, Mrs. Bagshott?"

Maggota turned back.

"Do you think you could take my dad and Mr. and Mrs. Thomas back to Bixbury?"

Maggota regarded Ben askance. "You'd trust me with that task?" Her eyes narrowed. "You are so very like Isadora. You believe there is good in everyone. I'm not sure that's wise in my case, but"—before he could interrupt her again—"but I will do this thing, and then I will look for Alice."

"And you will bring her to me?"

"Dead or alive."

Ben swallowed. "I am going to my mother."

The witch cackled. "I hope not, Boy. I have a fairly good idea of where she will be. But I will find you. And my son." And she gave him a horrible wink.

Ellie came to Ben's side. "Wherever you're going, I'm going with you," she said staunchly. "Only, don't make me fly on that thing."

Ben gave her a wobbly grin. He knew his sister was terrified of heights. "You can go with Silver and the nautilus."

Ellie regarded the giant squid dubiously, remembering the battle on the lake. "I'll probably get seasick," she said. Then she wiped her eyes fiercely with the back of her hand, smearing what little was left of her mascara over her face. "But I'm sure Silver will look after me."

"Mummu-Tiamat and I will be flying overhead," Ben promised.

"And what about me?" Iggy jumped down off the burned fence and stepped gingerly across the hot sand. He rubbed his head against Ben's legs. A purr like a rusty old machine starting up filled the air. "I can navigate for you."

Mummu-Tiamat snorted, and a little puff of smoke rose from one of her nostrils.

Iggy glared at the dragon. "I hope that was a hiccup and not a snigger," he growled, puffing himself up to his full (not very large) size. "I'm known as the Wanderer, you know."

Chapter Fifteen

The Dark Mere

The first time Ben had flown on a dragon's back had been when he was helping Xarkanadûshak to escape back to the Secret Country. He remembered how terrified he had been as they skimmed over the rooftops of Bixbury. It had been weird to see such familiar landmarks as his school and the football fields, the church and the supermarket car park from such a vantage point, let alone while he was trying to hang on to Zark's neck and not plummet to his death.

But flying on the back of Mummu-Tiamat was quite a different affair. It was a bit like suddenly finding yourself sitting in a comfortable open-topped limousine after bumping precariously along on a scooter. The Mother of Dragons was massively wide, and she flew with such smooth and powerful grace, her neck stretched out like a swan's in flight, that he soon found there was no need to be afraid of falling off. He had made a rudimentary bag out of his raincoat and stuffed Boneless Bob into it. The snake had immediately dived down a sleeve and had not re-emerged. Ben had tied the strings that fastened the hood around one of Mummu-Tiamat's scales for good measure. He had made a promise to the witch to keep her horrid familiar safe, and he intended to keep his word.

He turned around to see how Ignatius Sorvo Coromandel was faring, and found that the little black-and-brown cat was curled up in the wide space between the dragon's great shoulder blades, fast asleep. In fact, if you listened very hard, you could just make out his snores between wingbeats. Ben grinned. He was glad someone was untroubled enough to sleep.

For himself, he did not think he would ever sleep soundly again. Leaving his father had been difficult. Worse, now he had time to think about it.

Mr. Arnold, free at last of the witch's sleeping potion and the strange glamour she had cast over him, had not been in the best of tempers. And that had been before he realized that Alice was missing.

"I blame you for this!" he berated Ellie first of all, but then she had burst into tears again, and when Ben had bravely suggested that maybe if he had taken Ellie and Alice with him to Eidolon, then they would both have been all right, Mr. Arnold had exploded.

"It's this place that's the problem! None of this would have happened if you'd stayed in Bixbury, and now you're all coming home with me!"

"I have to find Mum," Ben said stolidly.

His father went red in the face. "Your mother's a grown woman; she can take care of herself. But Alice is just a baby. Whatever were you thinking of?"

Ben wanted to point out that in fact if it hadn't been for his father meeting his mother and keeping her away from her realm, things wouldn't have got out of hand in Eidolon and none of this would have happened. But then he realized that if that had been the case, then he, Ellie, and Alice would never have been born, and again, none of this would have happened. Which was very confusing. So in the end he stared at his feet and said nothing at all, and thought instead about his mother being "a grown woman." Did that mean she'd sprouted up out of the ground, like a plant? He was a bit hazy on the details of human reproduction (since on the day it was taught at school he and Adam had been sitting at the back of biology class, secretly letting the frogs out of their tank before they were dissected, and he hadn't been paying attention). Anyway, his mother wasn't technically human, if she came from another world, was she? And since he was half Eidolonish (if there was such a word), then perhaps *he* wasn't fully human either. Cheered, slightly, by this thought, he managed a weak smile.

"I'm sure Alice will turn up, Dad," he said. Curiously, when he said this, he suddenly felt it to be true, though he couldn't explain it to himself, or anyone else.

And it was at this point that Clive Arnold's fury revealed itself to be not true anger but terrible anxiety, for his face crumpled.

Maud Thomas put an arm around him. "Now,

now, Clive," she soothed. "Tears won't bring her back. Let's go home and wait for her, and let Ben and Ellie do what they have to do here." She turned to the witch. "Come along, Mrs. Maggot, or whatever you're called, and take us back to Bixbury. What we need's a nice, strong cup of tea."

Maggota gave Mrs. Thomas her most untrustworthy smile. "Oh, I could rustle one of those up for you in a jiffy."

Mr. Arnold had braced his shoulders and given her a hard stare. "I shan't be drinking anything *you* offer me in a long time," he said.

And then he had hugged both Ben and Ellie so hard, Ben thought his ribs would break.

Already, all this seemed like days ago, rather than a couple of hours. Being on a dragon's back changed your perspective on things. Ben had seen that Infinity Beach didn't really live up to its name, for eventually the vast stretch of white sand and dunes became a long spit of land sticking out into the sea, then an archipelago of islands, and then, finally, vanished altogether into wide blue ocean. Below them, at first a little way behind, Nemesis had plowed through the waves with Ellie sitting on top of his head and Silver, sleek in her seal form, swimming beside them. But as the dragon's powerful flight lengthened the distance between them, the nautilus had dived so that it could propel itself beneath the surface in its usual fashion. All except for the one long tentacle that it used to hold Ellie up out of the water, where she hung, as if by magic, above the tops of the waves, shrieking with a mixture of terror and excitement.

The longer they flew, the farther behind lagged the nautilus, the selkie, and his sister. Soon he couldn't see them at all. Iggy was fast asleep, the Mother of Dragons had her mind concentrated on flying—for the first time in who knew how many years?—and Ben felt suddenly as if he were all alone. Clouds scudded past him through the blue, blue sky; below lay the blue, blue sea; and the sun winking off Mummu-Tiamat's golden scales offered the only other speck of color he could see. All he could hear were the rhythmic beat of the dragon's wings and the little cat's snores, when the wind of their passage did not blow them away.

Everything seemed so serene. It was as if time itself had stopped and they moved through a space between worlds, a space in which there was no Dodman, no lost realm of magic, no war. In a way, Ben had never felt so calm. It was as if all worries, all fears, all problems had been suspended. It was impossible to believe, seeing all this comforting, quiet blue around him, that Alice could be lost. Even so, somewhere in the back of his mind the burden of the knowledge that he would have to tell his mother about her loss weighed as heavy as lead, immense and terrible and too much for him to bear. He had no idea what he would say to her. So he tried not to think about it at all.

For a little while, he slept. And as he slept, he dreamed. He dreamed he was in another world where the colors were different from this one, where the cold air tumbled around him in turbulent blasts, bringing all sorts of different smells with it. He was flying—not as he flew in the dreams he sometimes had at home, like Batman or Superman, or like James Bond with a jet pack—but on the back of some great creature that was not a dragon. How he knew this, he did not know, but the knowledge was deep inside him and he felt both powerful and proud, and not like his usual self at all. When he woke up, he was smiling.

"I don't know what you've got to be so pleased

about," said Ignatius Sorvo Coromandel. "It's freezing up here."

And indeed the little cat did look half-frozen in the moonlight, with the night wind whipping the fur back from his face and flattening his ears and whiskers. Ben found himself shivering, just from looking at Iggy. The next minute, Iggy was shivering too.

"Where are we?"

Iggy shrugged. "How should I know?"

"So much for being the Wanderer."

"It's dark."

"There are stars."

And there were. They shone brightly all around, and Ben seemed to be a lot closer to them than he had ever been before. He stared at them, but couldn't quite make sense of what he was seeing. He was used to finding Orion's bright belt of three stars and working out the constellations from the position of that. But try as he might, he couldn't see Orion at all. At last, by twisting right around on the dragon's back, he located three stars in a line, but they were pointing in the wrong direction. He stared. He frowned.

"Hang on," he said. "Why's Orion back to front?"

"Orion?"

Ben pointed out the belt of stars to Iggy. "In my world they slant the other way, and you see that bright one there? That's Betelgeuse. And that other one's Bellatrix. Except they're in the wrong place."

Iggy snorted. "How can they be in the wrong place? They're in the sky, aren't they?"

"No, no, I mean they're inside out, or something . . ."

Iggy rolled his eyes. "Are you sure you're properly awake? Anyway, that's not whatever you called it. It's the Minotaur. The three stars in a line are his sword."

None of this made any sense to Ben. He got as far as wondering whether Eidolon lay on the reverse side of the universe, and that idea hurt his head so much, he decided not to try to puzzle it out. Instead he said, "Why are we up so high?"

The little cat gave his raspy laugh. "Oh, you'd rather we plowed into Cloudbeard, would you?"

And when Ben looked down, there indeed was a range of snowcapped mountains right beneath them and the moonlight was frosting the snow with its glittering silver light. "Wow," said Ben, impressed. "Wasn't that the mountain your dad climbed?"

Iggy nodded proudly. "And now I'm flying over it.

Which means," he said, puffing out his chest, "that no cat has ever been as high up in Eidolon as me!"

It was getting hard to breathe, each breath feeling like cold needles in the chest. Ben's nose hair froze, which made Iggy laugh; then his whiskers froze, which served him right. At last the dragon began to descend into the warmer air on the other side of the mountains, and the rim of the sun showed in a thin gold-red band in the distance.

"But what about Nemesis?" Ben said suddenly. "I mean, he can hardly swim over the mountains, can he? What will they do?"

Mummu-Tiamat turned her golden head. "The sea will take them farther south of here. We will meet at the edge of the Dark Mere."

It was the first thing she had said since they left Infinity Beach, but she didn't seem inclined to speak further. Her eyes gleamed and whirled at the pleasure of finding the air beneath her wings, then she stretched out her neck and sideslipped swiftly, her scales like a coat of fire in the dawn light.

The Dark Mere was just as grim a place as Ben had expected it to be. Even in the light of a new day, its deep waters seemed as black as ink. Beyond it and a stretch of marshy mud lands lay the sea. Mummu-Tiamat landed on a rise of higher land overlooking the coast and immediately settled down to sleep, without a word to her two passengers. No birds sang, and nothing stirred, except the wind in the reeds.

Ignatius Sorvo Coromandel wrapped his tail around himself and hunched down next to Ben.

"Don't you want to get off and stretch your legs?" Ben asked. It was the sort of thing his father tended to say after a long car journey.

Iggy gave him a pitying look. "Here? You must be joking. There's quicksand and bogs, and if those don't get you, there are some pretty nasty things in the water. You've got frogs and leeches in your world; here we've got frog-leeches—they'll jump the height of a goblin and fasten on you and suck your blood till they pop."

Ben grimaced. Perhaps he'd wait till they were somewhere safer before he went to the loo.

So they waited as Mummu-Tiamat snored and Iggy rolled over on his back to let the sun warm his belly-fur; and Ben thought about the Secret Country, about its strangeness and its perils, about its beauty and its amazing (and sometimes horrid) creatures. He thought about wood-sprites and fairies, vampire chickens and frog-leeches, goblins and gnomes, nymphs and dryads, about Darius the Horse Lord and Cernunnos with his stag's head. He thought about the Minotaur and the nautilus, and about flying—on Zark, and then on the Mother of Dragons. He thought about magic, too, and the evidence for it he had seen. He tried to imagine what would happen if the Dodman used the dinosaurs to destroy the forces that stood against him and what Eidolon would be like without any magic left in it. No dragons would fly or breathe fire; no fairies or sprites would survive; the trees would wither without the care of their nymphs; the wild roads would fail. He would be stuck here forever. And so would Ellie. He had never felt bad in the Secret Country, but it made Ellie ill. He remembered how ill his mother had been at home, in a magicless world. It was clear that without magic she could not survive.

A dread like a cold hand wrapped itself around him, and he knew then that he would do anything he could to save her. But what could he do? He was just a boy, and she needed an army.

He hunched his knees up to his chest and stared out to sea. *Come on*, he willed silently. *Hurry up,*

Nemesis. But he didn't voice his thoughts, in case he summoned the squid and ended up drowning Ellie by mistake.

The sun rose ever higher in the sky. Some birds flew above them, and then veered sharply away when they saw the dragon. Ben watched them disappear with a vague disappointment. It would have been nice to see another living thing up close.

"Sprites," said Iggy, his eyes narrowed as he focused on the vanishing specks. Ben hadn't even known he was awake. "They're being remarkably antisocial."

Ben shaded his eyes. "And what are those, over there?"

Iggy turned to look at where his friend was pointing. Three small figures were silhouetted against the pale sky. "Fairies," he said at last. "They're a long way from home." He sat up, his brow furrowed, his whiskers drawn down. "I wonder what's up."

"Probably deserted. Cowards, the lot of them. No backbone. Or rather, such small crunchy little backbones. Sssssss."

Boneless Bob had poked his head out of the waterproof bag and was grinning widely. "She has no chance, you know, your mother," he said, regarding Ben with his chilly eyes. "I've seen what she's up against, the monsters the Dodman's gathering."

Ben stared at the red and white snake with intense dislike. "I know he has a dinosaur," he said at last, hoping this would shut Boneless Bob up.

"Sssssss!" the serpent hissed, and by the way it convulsed, Ben realized it was laughing. At him. "A dinosaur. Sssss! The boy knows nothing. He has *many* dinosaurs, the Dog-Headed One, large and small, those that run on the ground, and those that fly in the air. And what does Isadora have? Fairies and man-horses!"

Now it fairly whipped from side to side in mirth. Ben felt like throttling the horrid thing there and then, but he had made a promise. Iggy had not. With a single vicious pounce he had pinned the snake to the dragon's back. With infinite care he took its head between his jaws.

"You see," he said indistinctly around Boneless Bob's skull, "I'm just a cat. I haven't been going around making bargains with witches about keeping you safe, and my friend here can't be held to account for my actions. Quite fancy a chunk of snake for my lunch. I hear it tastes a lot like chicken."

The snake stopped wriggling abruptly. It tried to say something.

"Let him up," Ben said wearily. "He's vile and wicked, but you mustn't eat him. Yet."

Reluctantly, Iggy released the familiar.

"I was only passing on information," Boneless Bob whined.

"I'd rather you didn't say anything else," Ben declared grimly, and stuffed the serpent roughly back into the makeshift sack.

No one said anything more, for at that moment the dragon stirred and shook her wings. "Stop playing games on my back!" she admonished them. "The squid has arrived."

Mummu-Tiamat's eyes were better than Ben's. He squinted hard into the light, but for a long time all he could see was sea. At last he made out a wash of white water, and then a shape, and suddenly there was the nautilus, waving all his tentacles, with Ellie and Silver sitting on his head. As Ben watched, the selkie took Ellie by the hand and they jumped together into the sea.

Ben was impressed by the selkie's persuasive powers: It took a lot for Ellie to agree to get her hair or makeup wet. Let alone her precious clothes.

"We're coming with you," Silver declared before Ben could say anything. The long walk up from the sea had changed her completely into her human form, but Ben could see how down on the mudflats the trail of her flippers gave way to footprints. "Nemesis is tired, but if you need him, he will find a way to come to you."

"Does he speak?" Ben was curious.

Silver shook her head. "I just knew what he meant." She turned to the Mother of Dragons. "Mummu-Tiamat, Great One," she said, bowing reverently, "would you be so good as to carry me and the Princess Eleanor as well to the Wildwood?"

The Mother of Dragons showed her long row of teeth. "It is good to see that proper respect has not completely deserted this world in my absence." And she dipped a wing to enable Ellie and Silver to climb onto her back.

Ellie kept her eyes shut the whole way.

As the group approached the Wildwood, the dragon's wingbeats slowed. Mummu-Tiamat took a sharp intake of breath, then slewed sideways.

"What, what is it?" Ben cried, staring back at the

dark canopy she had just flown away from.

"Are you sure your mother is in the Wildwood, Prince of Eidolon?"

"Yes. She was with Cernunnos and Darius, the Horse Lord."

The dragon said nothing. She swung her head to regard him. "I hope for your sake she was not there recently."

"What have you seen, Mummu-Tiamat? Tell me! Show me!"

Something in the tone of Ben's voice seemed to arrest the dragon. "Are you sure you wish to know?"

Ben felt hollow with anxiety. "Yes. I must."

Slowly the dragon yawed around and glided back toward the forest. What Ben saw there made him gape in dismay. All around, trees had been burned and smashed. Charred trunks and blackened foliage lay scattered as if something vast and deliberately destructive had laid waste to the Wildwood. Smoke still rose from a dozen small fires. The smell was acrid and unpleasant.

Ellie opened her eyes. She squinted at the wreckage below. "Oh no." She reached for her brother's hand, squeezed it. "Oh, Ben, it's awful."

"What happened here?" Silver cried.

Mummu-Tiamat made no reply, but the eye that Ben could see as she made her spiraling descent had darkened ominously.

The devastation became clearer the closer they got. Some trees had been uprooted, others torn apart, their exposed flesh in shocking contrast to their burned bark. The ground was churned up. Here and there, dead things lay unburied and uncared for—families of gnomes overcome by smoke and fumes, wood-sprites limp on the branches where they had expired, a dryad who had stayed with her tree and burned inside it. Ellie's hands flew to her mouth. Ben's eyes felt raw, and not just from the smoke.

The Mother of Dragons drew in her wings and glided to a halt in a clearing where fallen trees lay scattered in all directions. The undergrowth here had been burned to the ground. Saplings lay black and flattened as if by vast feet.

Mummu-Tiamat looked around. "The burning was caused by dragon's fire," she said, her nostrils flaring.

"But why would any dragon do this?" Ben was horrified.

"I do not know. I do not think we should stay here. Let me take you away from here."

Ben shook his head. "No. I must find my mother."

Iggy jumped down from the dragon's back. "I will go and see what I can see," he told them. He picked his way gingerly among the debris, sniffing here and there. Then he scrambled up over a fallen log and disappeared into the forest beyond. They all anxiously watched him go. Silver started to shiver. Ben put an arm around her, and they all sat silently waiting for the little cat's return.

They did not have long to wait. Ignatius Sorvo Coromandel came running back into the clearing some minutes later as if he was being chased by demons.

"Something terrible has happened here," he gasped. "A battle . . . a massacre. There are dead centaurs and . . ." He could not finish.

"And what?" Ben's face was ashen, his green eye stark with dread.

"And the body of a dragon."

Chapter Sixteen

Xarkanadûshak

The Mother of Dragons gently lifted the burned corpse out from the litter of charred wood and detritus that covered it and laid it on open ground. It was a smallish dragon, maybe a third of Mummu-Tiamat's size. Great gouges rent its flanks, and one of its wings lay at an impossible angle. Its eyes were closed. Carrion birds had not been able to penetrate the scaled lids, though it looked as if something had tried to.

Ben fell to his knees beside it. "Oh, Zark. Oh no . . ."

His hand was shaking as he reached out to touch the body. He remembered how he had found the little dragon dying of neglect and lack of magic in the garden of a stately home in the Other World. He remembered how sad the dragon had been, and how hungry. How it had resigned itself to dying alone and far from home, far from its wife and kits. He stroked the blackened hide, and his hand came away covered in soot. Where he had touched them, the scales showed a dull bluish purple, the color of a bruise. Ben frowned. He rubbed away more of the char and again, the hues revealed were indigo and a dull gray-gold. It could not be Xarkanadûshak, for his scales were the color of flame. For a moment Ben felt an absurd, happy wash of relief. Then Mummu-Tiamat blew upon the poor dead face, and soot drifted up into the Wildwood air.

Ben's heart jumped and thudded. He knew this dragon. But it was the Mother of Dragons who named her. "Ah, my lady Ishtar," she breathed. "A terrible end for one so lovely."

It was Xarkanadûshak's wife. And now Ben felt terrible guilt for his moment of relief.

Ellie remembered how Ishtar had swooped down out of the sky over the lake to save her from the clutches of the Dodman's evil goblins. Queen Isadora had sat astride her: Together they had made an impressively regal sight as they screamed through the air. Ellie might be dead if not for Ishtar's courage, and what reward had the beautiful dragon received for her bravery and skill? Here she was, destroyed by Eidolon's horrid war, as dead as a spent coal. Ellie bent her head and her tears dripped with a little patter, like rain, onto the charred earth.

Ben remembered his father getting onto Ishtar's back, and how he had climbed onto Zark—how they had flown home together, side by side. It had been the first time his father had experienced for himself the magic of the Secret Country. He could not quite believe such a powerful, noble creature could have been reduced to this grim pile of smoldering scales.

"Good-bye, Lady of Battles," Ben whispered.

Mummu-Tiamat touched his shoulder with her claw. "Come away," she said. "I must consign her to our ancestors."

From a safe distance Ben and Ellie and Silver and Iggy watched silently as the Mother of Dragons gathered her wind. Even Boneless Bob seemed struck dumb by the enormity of the occasion. Then Mummu-Tiamat gave forth a great blast of dragon-fire so bright, they had to shield their eyes. When they looked back again, the fire had engulfed Ishtar's body and the flames were roaring away in brilliant shades of blue and gold and purple, as if the very essence of the fallen dragon, her magic and her grace, was burning before their eyes. Then, as swiftly as it had burned, the fire died away, leaving behind just a small pile of ash to be dispersed by the breeze.

The afterimage of the fire burned on Ben's retinas in bright zigzags of light. So when something came charging and roaring through the forest toward them, he could not for some time make out what it was. All he knew was that Silver and Ellie fled screaming, and Iggy jumped up onto his shoulder, trembling. The Mother of Dragons reared up on her hind legs and flapped her wings in warning at the intruder, but even this awesome display did not deter him.

"Where is she?" a voice bellowed. It was a voice Ben knew, though it was distorted by rage and grief. "Where is my wife? What have you done with her?"

It was Xarkanadûshak. He stood on the edge of the clearing with his flanks heaving and his eyes glowing and whirling. His mouth was charred and he was missing scales all over his body. One of his forelegs hung useless in front of him. In the claws of the other he held a straggle of withered flowers. Even the sight of Mummu-Tiamat towering above them all seemed to have no effect on his fury; all his attention was focused on the clutter of branches and burned wood where Ishtar's body had lain.

He rushed at the woodpile, casting aside the battered asphodels and lilies he carried, and dug through the debris with his one good arm. Then he turned and faced the silent watchers.

"Where is she?" he roared again.

"She is fire upon the wind, magic upon the air, spirit in the clouds," Mummu-Tiamat said softly.

Zark looked bewildered, as if the words had no meaning for him. Ben stepped forward. "Zark, it's me—"

He said no more, for the little dragon broke suddenly into a charge, his neck stretched out, his cheeks bulging as he gathered his wind.

"Get down!" cried the Mother of Dragons, and pushed Ben aside.

But the fire Zark released against her was a ragged,

pathetic thing—a lick of flame that might roast a fly, but nothing bigger. It caught Mummu-Tiamat on the chest and fizzled out in a second. Zark had used everything he had trying to light Ishtar's funeral pyre, and now he fell to the ground, hollowed out and breathing heavily.

"Oh, Zark!" Ellie was at his side now. She stroked his cheek and her tears fell upon him, leaving streaks in the soot and blood that covered his hide.

Iggy leapt down from Ben's shoulder and butted his head against the little dragon's rough scales. Ben followed behind, not sure what to do or say.

"I'm so sorry, Zark. About Ishtar. We all are," he managed at last.

Xarkanadûshak raised his head. He looked Ben in the eye. "She died for your mother. But it was for nothing. Now I will die too." And he hunched down as if waiting for death to take him.

"But what about your kits?" Ellie said softly. "If you die, what will they do without you?"

Zark just closed his eyes. "Go away."

"We won't leave you," Ben said firmly. "Not like this."

A growl built in Zark's throat. He swung his head

at Ben. "I wish you'd let me die in the Other World, Prince of Eidolon," he rasped. "Go away! If you hadn't saved me, I would never have owed you anything. Ishtar would be alive. I wish you and your family dead. As dead as she is."

Ben was shocked. He looked from Zark's mad, swirling eye to the calm face of the Mother of Dragons.

She pushed him aside with a wing. "Leave him. It is not Xarkanadûshak who speaks but his sorrow. There is little respite from that for him, for his world is a different place without Ishtar in it, and dragons have long memories." Then she leaned over Zark and breathed upon him. This time it was not fire that issued from her great mouth but a pale golden vapor that wrapped itself around him like a veil. The great swirling eyes lost their focus and slowly closed. His shuddering body gradually relaxed and finally his head fell sideways and hit the ground with a thump.

Ben stared in horror. "You've killed him!"

"Isn't death what he wished for?" the Mother of Dragons asked gently.

"Yes, but . . . he didn't mean it."

"Are you so sure?"

Ben didn't know the answer to that. He felt miserable to the core. "I hate this . . . ," he said at last. "This war. All this death. It isn't . . . it isn't right." He couldn't find the words to say exactly what he meant. The remains of the centaurs had horrified him: their brave bodies struck down and trampled underfoot by the Dodman's monstrous army, their gleaming hides muddy and crushed, their limbs contorted, their swords broken or stolen as booty. But at least he hadn't known any of them personally. To see Ishtar dead, and now Zark . . . Tears gathered and he gulped them back.

Mummu-Tiamat tossed her head. "There have always been wars. There will always be wars, in your world as in ours. When reason fails, violence triumphs, and there is no reason here. For myself, I do not like to see my dragons caught up in such pointless conflicts. We are so much longer-lived than others. The death of a dragon reverberates down the ages."

Ben stared at her, feeling bleaker than ever. He had, of course, been going to ask for her aid in bringing the dragons to fight for his mother against the Dodman, and that was to have been her gift to him for freeing her from the witch's cave. But now that he had seen one noble dragon brought to a futile death and another driven mad with despair, he knew he could never ask for such a sacrifice to be made. He hung his head. And that was when he saw Xarkanadûshak move. Just a little twitch of the ear, as if he were trying to dislodge a fly that had landed on him; but it was enough.

"He's not dead!" Ben cried joyously.

"Of course not. Did you really think after all I have said that I would take his life?" Mummu-Tiamat asked curiously. "He will sleep, for a long time, and that will ease his pain a little. I cannot afford to lose my dragons so easily, young man. Each of them is precious to me, for each of them is my child."

"Goodness," said Ellie, flustered by this extraordinary announcement. "How many children have you had? You've kept your figure very well, I must say."

Everyone burst out laughing. Ellie went red. It was the sort of thing people said in the Other World. Then she sneezed and sneezed and sneezed.

"I think she's a bit allergic to Eidolon," Ben confided to Mummu-Tiamat.

"Allergic?" The dragon regarded him quizzically.

"It makes her ill."

"Ah. Perhaps she should not be here, then."

Which was a perfectly logical thing to say. Ben sighed. "There's a prophecy, you see. And it's about us—me and Ellie and my little sister, Alice, who's missing." And he told the Mother of Dragons the prophecy:

> *"Two worlds come together*
> *Two hearts beat as one*
> *When times are at their darkest*
> *Then shall true strength be shown*
> *One plus one is two*
> *And those two shall make three*
> *Three children from two worlds*
> *Will keep Eidolon free.*
> *Three children from two worlds*
> *Three to save the day*
> *One with beauty's spell to tame*
> *One bravely to bring flame*
> *And one with the power to name."*

"I see," said Mummu-Tiamat slowly. Her eyes whirled with color. "Well, I hate to say it, but people are always making up songs and verses in Eidolon when they don't have enough to keep them occupied. Even dragons do it from time to time. There are some fine dragon lays I could recite to you, but they would take several days. There are prophecies by the cartload in this world, Prince of Eidolon, but none of them mean anything."

She tried to say it kindly, but Ben's face fell. The Mother of Dragons saw that he had been putting his fragile hopes in the childish verse, and that now those hopes were dashed. She put a wing around his shoulder.

"Never mind the foolish prophecy for now," she said to Ben. "Let us see if we can find your mother. You two"—this to Silver and Ellie—"stay here where I can find you. We'll be back shortly."

Ben and Iggy climbed quietly onto the big dragon's back and found themselves a vantage point at her right shoulder where they could watch the Wildwood pass by below. Mummu-Tiamat took off with a great beating of wings and soared into the still and silent air.

It was still and silent, they soon discovered, because nothing was alive in the Wildwood at all; or if it were, it was hiding. They passed over scene after scene of devastation, until Ben's eyes had grown round and hot with misery. Iggy turned his face away and buried his head in Ben's armpit. Down below were dead centaurs, dead fairies, dead gnomes, dead sprites, dead dryads, dead goblins, dead nymphs, dead trees, and once, even, a huge dead troll pinned beneath a burned and fallen tree.

But of Queen Isadora there was no sign.

"What do you think happened here?" Ellie asked. She peered around a burned tree trunk at the devastation.

Silver shook her head. "Don't ask me," she said. "I'm only a selkie. I don't understand any of it. All I understand is blue seas and sunny reefs and where to find the best rabbitfish. All this"—she gestured around, shivering—"all this destruction is beyond me."

Ellie (who rarely did what she was told) had wandered farther into the forest, squinting hard. Curiosity was one of her vices (along with vanity and picking on her little brother) and she didn't take well to being told what to do by a dragon who clearly thought more of Ben than her. But even a short way beyond the glade, she found herself rather wishing she had stayed put. Something in the trees above rustled, and Ellie's heart beat wildly.

"Was that you, Silver?" she asked, though she knew it was not. The sound of her own voice was not as comforting as she had hoped it would be.

"I'm right behind you," the selkie said. "I didn't hear any—Oh! What's that? Over there . . ."

"Where?" Ellie spun around and almost cannoned into her. "What have you seen?"

But Silver couldn't speak. She was gazing down at something lying on the ground and her face was twisted into an unrecognizable expression.

Ellie made her way to the selkie's side and stared at the huge, dark shape on the forest floor. Her eyes wouldn't focus properly: She couldn't make out what it was. She was just about to ask Silver and reveal just how hopeless her eyesight really was in Eidolon when she managed to make out a horn, and then a muzzle. "Oh . . ." She bent down, squinting hard, then recoiled, both hands flying to her mouth. "Oh no!"

Suddenly tears flooded her eyes. Surely nothing could kill something so big and fierce . . . surely he was only asleep. But she knew at once that he wasn't.

She remembered fire-fairies flying in a glowing golden heart around his head. "I am in the service of the Princess Eleanor," he had said. "And no other." And now here he was: the Minotaur, stone dead, stretched out on the hard, cold ground, where he could do service to no one other than the ants and the beetles. Tears came with a vengeance. "He was m-my friend!" she wept. "And I n-never g-got to know him properly. It's such a w-waste!"

Silver put an arm around her. "Come away," she said quietly. "This is all too horrible. Let's go back and wait by Zark."

And they stumbled back through the broken vegetation to the clearing where the Mother of Dragons had left them.

The selkie slumped down beside the hulk of the sleeping Xarkanadûshak and rested her chin on her knees. "This is like one of those nightmares in which I'm swimming through horrible black suck-weed that is trying to pull me down to the seabed and eat me," she said after a long silence that had been broken only by Ellie's sobbing. "And at any moment I'll break free of it and swim up into sunlight. But this isn't a nightmare, is it? It's real. It's war."

Ellie nodded and gulped. She wiped her eyes with the bottom of her sweatshirt. Without any makeup left on it, her face looked pale and vulnerable. "I've only ever come across wars in history books, and the teachers made it all so boring, so none of it seemed real. But people die, really die . . . And for what?" She'd never thought about war before in any serious way. It was a hard and horrible lesson to be learning firsthand.

"My grandfather told tales of a great war in Eidolon," said the selkie after a moment. "An uprising against the Queen of the time by a goblin chief who decided it was time there was a King. I never really paid much attention to the tales, either. It all seemed violent and ridiculous to me. I mean, what's the point of killing anyone just to be King? You're still you, and nothing has changed except that you've done horrible things and made the world a worse place just to live in a castle and have people afraid of you."

Ellie nodded slowly. "But this is different, isn't it? The Dodman doesn't just want to be King, he wants to destroy all the magic, too."

"And then what will be left?" said Silver angrily. "He doesn't even know what magic is. I believe every creature in Eidolon has some magic. It's why we don't do well in your world. So if he destroys too much of the magic, he'll make Eidolon like your world."

"Thank you," sniffed Ellie. "It's not that bad." She gave a huge sneeze. "And at least it doesn't make me ill."

"It makes *me* ill," said the selkie. "When your

uncle and the Dodman captured me and brought me through the wild road, I thought I was going to die."

"But it didn't seem to make him ill," mused Ellie, rubbing her eyes. "He and Awful Uncle Aleister were coming back and forth all the time."

"I don't know what he is," Silver said darkly. "Perhaps he's not from Eidolon at all."

"Well, he's not from *my* world! We don't have giant monsters with ugly great dogs' heads walking around as if they own the place."

The selkie shrugged. "He has to be stopped. But I don't know how. All this death and destruction, it can't be the way. That's *his* way."

They sat in silence for a time, pondering this, and thinking about Zark and Ishtar and the poor, dead Minotaur. Nothing stirred in the Wildwood. No birds sang. No sprites flitted through the canopy above them. It was as if every creature who had ever lived here had either fled or been slaughtered.

"If only we knew what the Dodman was or where he had come from," Ellie said at last. "That might give us some clue as to how to stop him."

"No one knows," the selkie replied gloomily. "I heard he just sort of appeared. At the castle."

The waterproof bag twitched. Then Boneless Bob's forked tongue flicked suddenly through the narrow opening where Ellie had knotted the sleeves to keep him in.

"I think he's trying to say something," Silver said. She reached out and loosened the knot a little, just enough for the familiar to poke his head out.

"My mother knows," he hissed.

"Your mother knows what?"

"She knows the Dog-Headed One's true nature."

"Whatever *that* means," Ellie snorted, regarding Bob with loathing. "What *does* it mean?"

The orange crest flicked and furled as if the snake was tucking its secrets away. "You'll have to ask her that," he said complacently.

Ellie and Silver exchanged glances. "I don't want to ask that old bag anything," Ellie said viciously. And she stuffed the snake back down into the sack and tied the sleeves tighter.

"I hope they won't be too long," Silver said, glancing around. "I never really liked the Wildwood. It always seemed so dark and dreary and closed in, even at the best of times. But now . . ." She shuddered. "It feels, well, haunted."

"I keep thinking I can hear something," Ellie confided. "But I think it's only Zark breathing, or the trees moving."

Silver listened intently, her pale hair tucked behind the pink shells of her ears. "No," she whispered after a moment, "I can hear something too."

They listened together. At first it really did sound like distant branches moving against one another, but it seemed to be coming closer. Twigs cracked as if someone was treading on them.

Ellie clutched the selkie's hand. "Whatever shall we do?"

Silver jutted her chin at the sleeping dragon. "Hide behind him."

They crept to the other side of Xarkanadûshak and peered anxiously over the great scaly hump of his back. At first they could see nothing at all, nothing but broken trees and smashed undergrowth. Then a bush on the edge of the clearing moved.

Ellie stifled a cry. "What if it's the Dodman?" she whispered. She certainly didn't want to find herself back in those dungeons. This time he might make good his threat to cut off her ear, or worse.

"It can't be the Dodman. Why would he be creeping around here all alone? He's got a great big army and a load of monsters at his command. Besides, he's a coward. He wouldn't be taking any risks."

It could be one of those other monsters, Ellie wanted to say, but she didn't dare open her mouth because she could feel another sneeze building up. It started as a tickle at the back of her nose, as if a bee was tiptoeing around in there; then it swelled up as if the bee had become the size of a small kitten. She pinched her nostrils shut. It was coming, it was coming . . .

"Achooooo!"

The noise rang across the clearing, bouncing off the tree trunks like a ricocheting bullet. Whatever it was that had been approaching stopped dead. A heavy silence fell. Silver rolled her eyes.

Then, very slowly, a figure emerged into the glade.

Ellie's eyes widened. "Oh!" she cried, and her cheeks went very red.

Silver watched in amazement as her friend got to her feet, threw her arms around the figure, and hugged it tight.

When Ellie stepped back again, a bit embarrassed by her own forwardness, her sweater was stained red. She stared at it as if she couldn't imagine how she'd got blood on it, then she stared at the newcomer. "Oh, Darius, you're hurt!"

This was something of an understatement. The centaur was covered in wounds. His handsome face bore a great slash, as if from a blade, or a claw, and the blood from it had dried like a mask. His body was covered in cuts and his fingers were red to the knuckle, the nails broken and bleeding, as if he had lost every weapon but fought on with his bare hands.

"Princess Eleanor . . ." He could not meet her eyes.

"What happened? Where's my mother?"

His reply was barely a whisper. His throat was raw from screaming at the enemy. "He has taken her."

"What?" Ellie was sure she had misheard.

The centaur swallowed the great lump that had risen in his throat. "The Dodman has her," he said more distinctly.

Ellie stared at him in disbelief. "No! Neither you nor Cernunnos would allow such a thing to happen, you'd die first—"

"The Lord of the Wildwood is dead, as is the Minotaur and most of my centaurs," Darius said flatly. "I took the Queen and the other Wildwood folk to find a place of greater safety, but . . ." He swallowed again, remembering, and closed his eyes. "What could we do against dinosaurs? He has so many of them, all different kinds, on the air, on the ground. They even killed Ishtar. . . .

"We split our forces, such as they were. The Queen and I fled out across the heath. We had planned to draw them out then double back and evade them, but they were too fast." He bowed his head. "We took a stand on Eagle Tor and there Isadora called for Zark to take us off, but he didn't answer her call. Perhaps he is dead too."

"He's not dead. He's over there." Ellie gestured behind her.

Darius frowned. "Well, he resisted her summons. Maybe he was unconscious."

"Or out of his mind. He was very upset about Ishtar." She caught his hand. "But, oh, Darius, tell me what happened to Mum. Is she okay? Is she still alive?" Her breath caught in her throat.

The Horse Lord swallowed. "I . . . I don't know. They surrounded us. I did all I could, except die. I should have died. Believe me, Princess Eleanor, I wished to. To have let him take the Queen without giving up my soul is the greatest shame to me. I killed I don't know how many . . . goblins mainly, two velociraptors. I wounded another, bigger dinosaur, but then he sent in a triceratops and my sword broke against its monstrous horns. I fought on without my blade, but they were savage. The great beast that the Dodman rode simply plucked us up. They took Isadora away from me and cast me away, like rubbish. . . ." His voice broke and he wiped a hand fiercely across his damaged face. "'Go back and tell them that I have their Queen,' the Dog-Headed One sneered. 'Tell them how mighty I have become, and that there is nothing left to them now but despair.' He left me alive to carry that message to the surviving folk of the Wildwood. But until I found you, I had yet to see another living soul."

Ellie went pale. "Oh, Mum . . . ," she started, and could say no more. She closed her eyes, swaying. Little black stars danced on the inside of her eyelids. *Don't be stupid,* she told herself sternly. *It's only silly women in old novels who faint at bad news. Pull yourself together.*

She blinked and tried to focus on Darius as if he might make the feelings of despair and dizziness evaporate; but although she could only see him through a blur, she could tell that he was watching her intently with tears in his dark brown eyes, and that just made her feel worse.

"Oh," she groaned at last, and sat down heavily.

"Now look what you've done," said Silver severely to the centaur. "Couldn't you have broken the news more gently?" She ran to Ellie's side and grabbed the girl's hand as if she would comfort her. Then she pinched the web of skin between Ellie's thumb and forefinger hard.

"Ow!" Ellie cried, leaping to her feet in outrage. "What did you do that for?"

Silver grinned. "Old selkie trick," she said. "If you want to stop yourself transforming back to being a seal for a minute or two. Hurts, doesn't it?"

"Yes," said Ellie crossly, pulling back her hand. "Anyway, I'm not a selkie."

Silver shrugged. "But it worked, though." She gazed up into the darkening sky. "Look, I don't want to be here when night falls. We'd better call Ben and Mummu-Tiamat, let them know there's no point searching the Wildwood for your mother."

Ellie scowled. There were times when she found Silver very annoying indeed, and she was just about to say so when the selkie hollowed her hands around her mouth and let forth an earsplitting cry.

It was the sort of cry selkies use to let others of their kind know that they have sighted prey—a fine swarm of rabbitfish, maybe, or a shoal of sea-toads—and it was designed to travel clearly across acres of rolling ocean. In the quiet of the late afternoon forest it was as sharp as a knife in the back.

Darius stared at Silver in disbelief.

"Good grief," said Ellie. "They'll think we're under attack."

"Did you have a better way of contacting them?" Silver glared at Ellie with her hands on her hips.

"Well, no . . ."

"Well, then. Mummu-Tiamat will know what it was, and she'll turn around and come back. Just you wait and see."

"I'm not sure it was wise to draw such attention to ourselves," Darius said quietly.

Silver held his gaze, and eventually it was the centaur who looked away. He shook his head wearily, then crossed the clearing to where Xarkanadûshak lay, unmoving. There, he went down on one knee beside the dragon and laid a hand gently upon his back.

"What happened to him?" he asked, looking back toward Ellie and Silver. "When last I saw him . . ." He bowed his head, remembering. When he had last seen Zark, it had been as the little dragon dived in desperation through the battle-ravaged canopy in pursuit of his stricken mate. It seemed an age ago, though it was only yesterday.

It was the sense of something in the air above that made Darius look up; then a shadow fell over him.

Silver and Ellie stared skyward expectantly. But it was not the Mother of Dragons who had cast the shadow.

Silver screamed.

It seemed to come out of nowhere, it was so fast and so silent. All Ellie could remember was the sight of herself reflected in one of its shining black eyes, and a long, bony beak, and wings that beat the air so hard that her hair stood on end in the backwash, as if she had been standing beneath the rotor-circle of a helicopter.

She saw, as if in slow motion, Darius charging across the turbulent space between them; but there was nothing he could do. The creature reached out with its wicked claws, dragged Silver off the ground with a determined lurch, and soared skyward again before anyone could stop it. All they could do was watch its spiky black silhouette flapping leisurely away beyond the trees.

Then it was gone.

Chapter Seventeen

Capture

"Put it on!"

"I will not!"

Isadora cast the froth of white muslin and lace in the Dodman's face. It hung on his muzzle for a few moments, looking distinctly strange, then tumbled in a heap to the floor. They both gazed at it, with very different emotions.

The dog-headed man was fast losing any patience

he had with Eidolon's Queen. He had thought to woo her, at first, and had been as gentle as he knew how: sending to the room in which he had confined her little treats—a necklace of mermaid scales and phoenix feathers, huge bunches of deadly nightshade, and finally, a pie made of wood-sprite hearts.

Isadora had torn the necklace apart with an exclamation of anger and had left the poisonous flowers lying where he had left them till they were wilted and withered. Hunger had driven her to cut into the pie. But when she saw what it contained, the blood drained from her face. That she should have come to this: The Queen of Eidolon, held captive by a monster in the very castle where she had run and played as a child, was now being fed the tiny hearts of her precious subjects. She sat down on the floor with her head in her hands and wept.

When the Dodman returned, sure to find he had won favor, he found her like this, and when he questioned why, she railed at him in fury, and he did not know what to do or say.

Eventually he picked up the dress from the floor and shook it out. A myriad of moths flew up from the folds of fabric. In the light, their wings sparkled and shone.

"Put it on," he said again, and now his voice was grim with intent. If she would not bow to gentle persuasion, he would bend her to his will.

Isadora shook her head. "I will not. It was my mother's and her mother's before her."

"I know. The Queens of Eidolon always wear this dress to be married in."

"I didn't."

The Dodman snapped his claws. "That? That was not a marriage. It was an abomination, a miscegenation. Different species cannot marry."

"Clive and I are not of 'different species.'"

"Clive! A worm. A mere human."

"He is not a worm," Isadora said firmly. "He is a fine man, the father of my children, and he is my husband whom I love dearly."

"You cannot love such a creature," he said dismissively.

"But I do."

"You have made a foolish error. You went away from here in confusion with your head all in a spin. He took advantage of you on the Other Side, and you forgot who you were and where you were from. But now you are back and you can make amends." He smiled indulgently, giving her the full benefit of his fine array of dog-teeth. "Soon the children will be no more and that will erase your error—"

"My children?" Isadora went white. "What have you done with my children?"

"Nothing. Yet."

She scanned his dog-face anxiously, but the flat black eyes gave away no clue. "Where are they?"

That was a good question. Maggota was taking her time. He avoided answering her directly. "Safe. Quite safe. For now. Wed me and you have the chance to put right all that you have done wrong. Put on the dress and we shall go down together, hand in hand, to be married."

"Married?" Isadora laughed. "By some troll or ogre?"

"Aleister will marry us," he returned smoothly. "He has the right, as the head of your family."

"Aleister?" she scoffed. "He will not do it. He knows I am already married."

"Oh, I think he will. Now, PUT ON THE DRESS!"

"My brother has no spine, that I know. But I cannot believe that he is evil through and through."

She took the dress from his claws. It seemed she

had little choice but to play his game. At least she would be out of this room, which she had loved so much as a girl, and which now offered only bitter memories. She remembered the last time she had been here, playing out a scene in which the same characters were in similar roles. It was fifteen years ago when the dog-headed man had fallen to his knees before her and pledged his heart, and she had laughed him out of the room. He was just a servant, a witch's drudge. She could not believe his arrogance. After that, she had felt his eyes on her wherever she went: cold eyes, calculating his next move. Then, one by one, everyone she cared about had mysteriously vanished, leaving only her brother Aleister, who was clearly in thrall to the Dodman. One day she heard them plotting to take her throne by marrying her against her will to the dog-headed beast. The next day she had taken a wild road into the Other World and met Clive Arnold. She had not returned until now.

In her absence, enraged by her escape, the Dodman had set about destroying all the magic in her kingdom. By the time she knew the truth of this, she had been rendered so weak and ill by his depredations, and by the difficulty of childbirth—first

Ellie, then Ben—that she had felt like lying down and dying, of shame as much as grief. But then along had come Alice, and although that had been the hardest birth of all, it was the one that had filled her with the most hope. One glance at those bright green Eidolon eyes, and she knew that the old prophecy she had once embroidered on a simple cotton sampler held the key to a new future, a future in which Eidolon should be saved.

My children, she thought now. *I pray that you are safe.*

"If you do not put on the dress, I shall be forced to do something very nasty indeed to little Cynthia."

The Dodman's cruel words cut into her thoughts. Such a threat surely meant that he did not have Ben or Ellie or Alice. This realization gave her courage.

"If I put it on, you must promise me you will let her out of that horrid cage."

"Certainly, my love, for she shall be your bridesmaid!"

"Bridesmaid!"

"She won't be happy, of course," he went on, shaking his head sadly. "She was intent on being Queen herself."

Isadora's eyebrows shot up. "Oh, she was, was she? And was that why she brought you the Book?" She laughed. "Poor, silly girl. She trusted you. I dare say you promised her all manner of things."

She saw the sly grin he tried to conceal, even as she shrugged into the dress.

"Ah, but you lied to her and crossed your fingers even as you promised," she said, pulling the white muslin down around her. As she did so, her Other World clothes began to disappear. It fitted her perfectly. It was bound to: There was magic woven through every stitch.

The Dodman gave a little growl. He did not like to be found out so easily.

"So why did you not kill her, as you have killed so many others, once you had the Book in your hands?" Isadora mused, and before he could reply, she had her answer. "Because you cannot read it. There is no magic in you." She watched his expression darken and knew she was right. "Such a shame for you that Aleister never persevered with his lessons. How cozy you would have been then, you and the boy you bullied all his life, summoning all the monsters of the world to do away with the rest of us. Do we really threaten you so fearfully, we of the magic?" And she reached out a hand as if to touch him.

The Dodman flinched away from her. Who knew what magic still resided in this Queen, no matter how weak she had become? He found he could not look her in the face, for the sight of her in the dress made him feeble in the legs. Strange sensations danced in his stomach. He braced himself and looked carefully to one side of her.

"You think you are so clever, you and all you magicked ones, because you are of the old stock, the ones who were here first. Well, I must tell you that your time has been and gone. Control is passing out of your hands. My Eidolon will be a different sort of world, a fairer world, in which magic does not confer power over others."

Isadora snorted her disdain. "A world in which power is taken by bullying and murder, a world in which power is horribly abused. You just want to destroy magic because you have none, and what you do not have or understand, you hate and fear."

The Dodman waved his fingers at her as if shooing away a fly. "What do I care for your moralizing, madam? You are my captive, and when we are married,

I shall be King and your body and realm will be mine. And yes, I hate all things of magic, but not just because I have none myself. I hate them because they are unnatural, vile, and sneaking. The world will be a better place without them, and you will be better too. Without the magic in you, you will love me, I know it."

Isadora shuddered. "You disgust me, and you always will, magic or no magic."

He grabbed her by the shoulder then and his cruel dog-claws dug sharply into her flesh.

"I want you to see something before we go down to be wed," he told her, dragging her out into the corridor. "And when you have seen it, then you will know you and your kind are defeated, and you will be able to better accept the inevitable changes that are coming upon Eidolon."

An unearthly shriek split the darkening air.

"What was that?" Ben stared wildly around, almost losing his grip on the dragon's scales in his startlement. Iggy slipped and scrabbled. "Hey!" he cried. "Watch out, Sonny Jim!"

The noise seemed to have come from where they

had left Ellie and Silver and the sleeping dragon.

The Mother of Dragons made a lazy circle and cast an eye back at the Wildwood. "A selkie hunting cry," she said, sounding puzzled. "How curious."

Ben realized she had never really seen Silver in her selkie form, but only as a girl. "That'll be Silver, then," he said. "I wonder why she's calling us." Something inside him felt tight and cold. "Can we go back, Mummu-Tiamat? I think something may be wrong."

The Mother of Dragons gave a great flap of her wings and headed back to the clearing. As they neared the site, Ben could just make out a familiar figure—half-man, half-horse—a centaur. Was it Darius? From high above it was hard to tell. The figure didn't stand like Darius, straight and tall. It looked smaller and less proud. Ben frowned. But the centaurs were their allies, so there could be no danger here, and whoever it was, perhaps he would have news of where his mother might be.

As Mummu-Tiamat came in to land, Ben jumped down, hitting the ground running, just like he had seen commandos do in war films. Unfortunately, he hadn't bargained on the fact that he was still moving and the ground was standing still. He hit hard, tripped over his own feet, and fell flat on his face. He got up slowly, waiting for Ellie to pour scorn on him in her usual fashion. But his ignominious arrival was met by an ominous silence.

He looked up to find the centaur looking down at him.

"Oh, Darius! What happened to you?"

The Horse Lord's handsome face was haggard. "I . . . ah . . . it's hard to know where to begin."

"The beginning's always good," Iggy suggested helpfully.

"The boy's mother!" a voice boomed. "Tell us what you know of the boy's mother."

Darius gazed at the giant dragon with dull eyes. She was the most magnificent creature he had ever seen, a legend made flesh. The very sight of her should have lifted his heart, but it was just too heavy. "The Dodman has her captive."

Ben felt the world collapsing around him. He grabbed hold of the centaur's arm. "What? No! It can't be—neither you nor Cernunnos would allow such a thing."

"The Lord of the Wildwood is dead," Darius intoned flatly. He had no wish to discuss the details again, even for Ben's sake, for nothing could change the facts. "So is the Minotaur, and most of my centaurs. We are defeated. And now there is other evil news—"

Ben felt dizzy. "A-Alice?" he stuttered.

The Horse Lord frowned. "No, not Alice. Silver."

"Silver . . . ?" Ben spun in a circle. Over by the bulk of Xarkanadûshak's sleeping form he could see his sister in a heap, her hair covering her face. But the selkie was nowhere to be seen.

He turned back to the centaur, hardly daring to ask his question.

"A quetzalcoatlus," Darius said baldly. "A flying dinosaur. It swooped down and took her. It came out of nowhere. There was nothing we could do."

"When?" The Mother of Dragons was at once practical. "How long ago was this? We heard a selkie cry out."

"That was before she was taken. She was calling for you."

"Foolish child! It must have heard her and gone to investigate." Mummu-Tiamat shook her head. "A shame. She was a pretty girl. Come, Ellie, Ben: We shall resume the search for your mother."

Ben was aghast at her hard-heartedness. "But we can't just let the dinosaurs take Silver. We must find her. We must save her!"

"She's gone, Prince of Eidolon. The quetzalcoatlus is probably eating her even as we speak."

Ben stared at the Mother of Dragons. "Mummu-Tiamat, I now ask you the favor you owe me for your life. Pursue the dinosaur and help me save my friend."

The dragon regarded him with one of her heavy-lidded eyes. "If that is what you wish, Prince of Eidolon. I would have thought you would be more concerned about the fate of your mother."

Ben felt a sudden pang of guilt. Did he care more about Silver than his mother? It was an impossible question to ponder. "I am . . . but, well, we can't just give Silver up without a fight."

Mummu-Tiamat sighed. "As you will. I fear it is a wild lizard chase and already too late."

Ben started to climb back onto the dragon, only to feel something pulling him back. He looked around. It was his sister and her eyes were flashing.

"Ben, the Mother of Dragons is right. We should be trying to save Mum. I'm sorry about Silver, really I am, but surely our mother's more important than a selkie?"

Ben took a deep breath. He loved his mother deeply, but he couldn't explain what he felt for the selkie. What he did know was that he couldn't just stand by and let her be eaten without at least trying to rescue her. He would never be able to live with the thought that he might have saved her.

"Look," he said, shaking Ellie's hand off, "it won't take long. They can't be that far ahead, and Mummu-Tiamat's faster than any old dinosaur. We'll overtake them, we'll rescue her, and we'll be back before you know it. And then we can make a plan for saving Mum from the Dodman." He couldn't even think about that at the moment: It was too big and too complicated to contemplate, especially with this new emergency on hand. He boosted himself up onto the dragon's back and found the Wanderer already there, waiting for him.

"Well, come on, then!" said Iggy impatiently. "We're wasting valuable time."

Ellie didn't know what to do. Part of her couldn't bear the idea of staying behind, in case another monster appeared; part of her needed to do something, anything. And beneath these warring sensations, another part of her yearned for none of this to be happening. She hesitated for just a moment, glancing at the Horse Lord. But Darius said nothing, just stared at the ground as if he wished it would swallow him up. "I'm coming with you," she declared fiercely. "She's my friend as well."

She handed up the sack containing Boneless Bob to her brother, then grabbed a scale with both hands and climbed aboard.

"Princess Eleanor!"

Ellie turned.

The centaur gazed up at her uncertainly, then turned away.

"What? What were you going to say?"

He turned back. "Don't go," he said in a low voice.

Ellie blushed. "Come with us. He can, can't he, Mother of Dragons?"

"We haven't time for this," Mummu-Tiamat said firmly. She fixed Darius with a glowing eye. "Stay here and look after my dragon, Lord Centaur. He will wake soon, and he will be grief-stricken and miserable. Take him with you to the rest of the Wildwood folk. They will take care of him. Do this for me. You have failed twice. If you fail a third time, you will have me to answer to."

Darius hung his head.

Despite his shock, Ben felt his heart go out to the centaur. He had taken many wounds. He looked ready to drop. As Mummu-Tiamat gathered her haunches to leap into the air, Ben called out, "It's not your fault, Darius! We'll get Silver back safely, and Mum, too. Just you wait and see."

He only wished he could believe his own words.

Chapter Eighteen

To the Rescue

The Dodman dragged Isadora to the top of the battlements and pushed her hard against the jagged crenellations.

"There!" he exclaimed, throwing an arm wide. "Now do you see? Those who were with me at Eagle Tor were mere skirmishers, no more than a small advance guard. These are the ones who will change the world with me. The ones who will rout all the magic out of Eidolon. Look on my army and despair."

The Queen stared out into the gathering gloom. On the northern shores of the lake surrounding the castle were gathered thousands of monsters. Isadora had good eyes: green eyes, Eidolon eyes. She could see goblins and hobgoblins, demons and saber-toothed tigers; trolls and ogres trussed up in armor. There were allosaurs and triceratops, velociraptors and megaraptors, tyrannosaurs and brontosaurs and stegosaurs. In the air above what had once been forest, banshees howled and trailed their tattered shrouds. Pterosaurs and pterodactyls wheeled like giant bats. Some that flew there *were* giant bats. Vampire bats.

The Wildwood had once extended almost to the shore. But now the trees were stripped bare, the plants beneath them flattened to hard earth. Other trees had been ripped out by their roots. A huge, ramshackle bridge now spanned the lake between the shore and the castle. Campfires burned, sending trails of acrid smoke and the smell of charred meat up into the darkening air. Isadora shuddered. Goodness only knew what those monsters were eating.

Even as she thought this, a great bird flapped

slowly overhead. In its claws something struggled.

"Help me!"

The voice was tiny, but it was familiar. Isadora strained her eyes. It was Ben's little selkie friend, Silver, in her girl form.

"No!"

The Queen turned to her captor. "Help me save her!" she commanded, and her eyes burned bright green.

The Dodman felt his legs tremble. He turned away, fixing his gaze on the prehistoric monster, but his eyes were not as good as Isadora's. All he saw was a small creature struggling helplessly. "Ah, my fine dinosaur, I see you have found some supper for your friends!" he called to the monstrous beast. "Feed well, my friend!"

Isadora cried out, "You cannot be so cruel!" But she knew he could. She dragged her hands free of him, hammered blows down upon his torso. "I will never marry a monster like you. Never! Save that poor child or I shall not go down with you."

The dog-headed man shrugged, but he kept his head averted. He had the measure of her magic now. It would not save her, or others. "My army must be kept fed and happy. And as for you, madam, know that you have no choice in the matter. I shall wed you and become King whether you will or not, and if you must be unconscious for the ceremony, I am sure that can be arranged."

The Queen started to cry. Not for herself, but for the poor selkie-girl, for her helpless subjects, her helpless world.

The Dodman risked a glance at his sobbing bride. Her eyes were downturned, but even so, the rising moon made her white form glow ethereally. He could almost see the elf-blood moving in her veins. He looked away quickly.

"I see that at last you understand the despair of the truly defeated," he said soothingly. "I will not ask you to dry your eyes and be glad for our nuptials, for the happy are strong, and that would never do."

Then he caught her fiercely by the wrist and dragged her behind him down the steeply winding stairs, down and down and down to the throne room below.

"Hold tight!"

The Mother of Dragons stretched out her long neck and her great long tail so that she formed a line as straight as an arrow in flight. The wind whistled past Ben's ears. When he looked down, it was to see Iggy's fur plastered so hard against his face that he looked more like a rat than a cat.

Ellie's eyes were squinched hard shut. She was beginning to wish she'd stayed on the ground with the handsome centaur.

Around them the air darkened and the moon came up. Try as he might, Ben could see nothing of the flying dinosaur who had stolen Silver. "Faster, Mummu-Tiamat!" he urged, without once thinking this might not be the most respectful way to address the Mother of Dragons.

Mummu-Tiamat made no response. She hurtled through the skies like a jet aircraft. At any moment Ben expected to hear a sonic boom as she broke the sound barrier, but all he could hear was the boom of his blood in his ears. He thought about summoning Silver: Would that save her? He imagined her flying through the sky to land beside him, breathless and grinning. But then he imagined her being whipped from the quetzalcoatlus's back and plummeting hundreds of feet to her death. He remembered how he had been summoned by Iggy when the troll was about to eat him, how he had been dragged through thorns and brambles and everything in the path between them, regardless of comfort or possibility. It was just too risky. So instead he shielded his eyes and stared out into the falling night and hoped and hoped.

The Mother of Dragons soared high over the Wildwood, so high that little clouds scudded past them. So high that it was hard to breathe. Ben had never been so high in his life as he had on the back of this magnificent dragon. He had never been in an airplane, for his mother had never been well enough to go abroad on holiday. And anyway, they had never had enough money.

Family life, in which illness and lack of money caused problems, seemed a lifetime, an eon, away. He wished with all his heart that he could return to that time of innocence, when it had all been someone else's responsibility, when the adults in his life had been there to take charge and make decisions. But he knew it was impossible. His mother was a prisoner of her deadliest enemy, and his father was able to do nothing in this magical world. Even his older sister was less effective here. Alice was missing, and now so was

Silver. It was too much for a boy of twelve to bear, prince or no prince.

He pushed his thoughts away; his despair, too.

"Can you see anything, Mummu-Tiamat?" he cried into the streaming wind.

"Over there," came back the dragon's voice. "Do you see the flickering lights?"

Down below and ahead of them, Ben could make out a great swath of darkness relieved only by a myriad of orange dots, like a swarm of fireflies against a black cloth. Beyond this was something wide and gleaming, then a darker lump with what appeared to be a fortress on it. It must be Corbenic Castle and the great lake that surrounded it! But what could the orange lights be? There was only Wildwood on the northern shore.

Mummu-Tiamat gave a titanic flap of her huge wings and dived toward the lake.

Ellie gave a muffled scream, and Iggy dug his claws into Ben's leg. "She's trying to kill us!" he meowed.

But Ben's attention had been caught by a figure moving away from the castle across the surface of the lake. From above it looked like a skinny crow carrying a twig for its nest, but within seconds he knew he was seeing the dinosaur that had snatched Silver.

"There she is!" he shrieked. "Go get her, Mummu-Tiamat!"

The dragon flicked her mighty tail and stooped like a hawk, and now Ben could say nothing at all. The skin of his face rippled and wobbled like a shaken jelly. Ben had once been on a fairground ride that had a similar effect and he hadn't enjoyed the sensation much. What he *had* enjoyed had been seeing his dad step down from the ride swaying and then tip over on top of some poor woman carrying two huge sticks of cotton candy for her children. It had taken ages to disentangle them. The children had thrown tantrums, and his dad's sweater had never been the same again.

Despite everything, Ben couldn't help grinning. They were gaining on the quetzalcoatlus with every beat of the great dragon's wings. They were going to catch it. They were going to save Silver!

The lake skimmed past below at impossible speed. Ben thought if they went any faster his ears would probably come off, a horrible but rather fascinating image. Knowing Eidolon, they'd probably take on a life of their own and go flapping away like butterflies.

Ben was just imagining this when Mummu-Tiamat pulled up so fast that Ellie howled and grabbed at him, and because he hadn't been paying proper attention, he lost his balance and slipped sideways. Suddenly he found himself hanging upside down, watching blurry shapes flee past him. Even as he was falling, he closed his ordinary eye and looked with his Eidolon eye, and suddenly the shapes resolved themselves into forest and campfires and huge creatures moving slowly around. Then there was a terrific pain in his leg and hands around his ankle, and between them Iggy and Ellie hauled him upright again.

"You idiot!" said Ellie.

Ben blinked and frowned, disoriented and confused. One minute they had been right behind the flying dinosaur, but now he couldn't see it anywhere. He twisted around and realized that the great dragon had wheeled about in a huge curve and that now they were heading in the opposite direction to which Silver was being taken.

"Mummu-Tiamat! Don't stop—we have to save her!"

The Mother of Dragons flapped her wings

implacably, and the distance between them and Silver extended itself with each beat.

"Mummu-Tiamat, go back!"

She made no immediate response. Then, "Did you see what was down there?" she said at last.

Ben thought about this. It had all been a bit of a blur. He closed his eyes, remembering. "Monsters," he said eventually. "Goblins and trolls and dinosaurs. Hundreds of them." He swallowed.

"Thousands," the Mother of Dragons corrected him grimly.

"I thought they were extinct."

"In your world. Not here. Here they thrive. They breed. Oh, how they breed!" Mummu-Tiamat spat. "A dragon pair may raise two kits in a hundred years, but those monsters . . . Clutches of eggs in the tens and twenties. Swarms of them, overrunning our ancient ancestral grounds, our sacred territory. They are a plague on the face of Eidolon, and every year there are more advancing: stupid, cunning, and greedy, and ready to pick a fight at the drop of a scale. No wonder he was able to persuade them to his side. I would hazard he didn't even have to summon half of them; give them the chance of fighting the dragons and they'd volunteer for the sheer pleasure of spilling our blood and taking more of our land."

Much of this long speech went over Ben's head, so all he really took from it was that dinosaurs and dragons didn't really like one another. It didn't seem anywhere near a good enough reason for turning tail and leaving his friend.

"I don't care about all that. All that matters is Silver. I won't leave her to be killed among monsters!" He felt his eyes fill with tears of frustration, and when the dragon said nothing, he screwed his fists up and hammered on her back. "Turn around, Mummu-Tiamat!" he cried.

The Mother of Dragons sighed. "I am carrying two children of the royal blood, to one of whom I owe my freedom. The cat and the snake mean little to me . . ."

"Oh, thanks," snarled Ignatius Sorvo Coromandel. "I'll remember that the next time you need rescuing from a witch."

The dragon ignored him. ". . . and there are plenty more selkies in the sea. But there is only one Prince and Princess of Eidolon . . ."

Actually, Ben corrected her silently, *there are two princesses. Or rather, there were . . .*

". . . and my duty is to keep you safe, to say nothing of myself—"

"You are a coward!" Ben was beside himself now; he hardly knew what he was saying.

"I am a realist," Mummu-Tiamat said tightly, keeping her temper with difficulty. "One dragon, two children, and a scruffy little cat are not going to go very far against a thousand hungry dinosaurs."

Ben took a deep breath. "The selkie is my friend. She means a lot to me, and she has saved my life not once, but twice."

"Twice?" The Mother of Dragons thought about this for several long, slow wingbeats. Then she began to turn. "A life-debt is a heavy thing, Prince of Eidolon. If you are set on sacrificing yourself for it, that is your choice. I will drop you on the edge of the forest."

Ben gulped. "Alone?"

The dragon flicked an eyelid at him. "It is your debt, not mine."

"But what am I supposed to do on my own against an army of dinosaurs?"

"You seem to be a resourceful boy, Prince of Eidolon. I'm sure you'll think of something." And she soared back toward the Wildwood, getting lower to the gloomy canopy with every flap of her great leathery wings.

Ben fell silent. He couldn't think of anything at all. It was as if his brain had slipped down into his stomach and he was now digesting it bit by bit. The inside of his skull where he believed his brain had once been now felt all shiny and empty and useless. He wasn't even sure he could speak.

There was a warm pressure on his arm. He looked down and found a small black-and-brown paw resting on it.

"I'll come with you," said Iggy.

"And I will too," said Ellie, taking everyone by surprise.

Mummu-Tiamat shook her head sadly. "If you are really determined to cast your lives away for no good reason, there's nothing I can do to stop you. I hope you rescue your friend. Perhaps we will meet again. In another lifetime."

She set the three of them down on the ground. They watched as she flapped slowly away.

The Law Book

Chapter Nineteen

The Law Book

All the usual suspects were gathered in the throne room of Dodman Castle. Eight spectral white dogs, known as the Gabriel Hounds, lay tangled up with one another in front of the fireplace, even though no one had been so organized as to light a fire in it for weeks and weeks. They were lazy creatures. Which was why a large band of goblins—including Batface and Bogie, Gutty and Grabbit, Beetle, Brimstone,

Barfer, and Blaggard—were congregated on the other side of the room. One of the ghost-dogs' favorite habits was biting goblins. Which they were very good at, despite having ghost-teeth.

The little witch, Cynthia Creepie, had managed to turn over in her wooden cage and now lay on her back, with her carroty hair poking through one end of the cage and her pointy feet out through the bars at the other end. Her father, Aleister, sat on the throne behind her. Absentmindedly, he had put his feet up on the cage (forgetting that it contained his daughter) and was coming to the conclusion that the Dodman had a point: having your legs stretched out really was quite comfy. His bald head (on which a delicate crown of silver and crystal was precariously balanced) nodded dreamily over the hands that lay folded in his lap. Really, the nails needed cleaning badly. Hygiene standards in Eidolon had fallen woefully low. Disgusted, he threw the hands across the room, where one of the Gabriel Hounds fell upon them in delight, then stood guarding them, fangs bared, in case any of its fellows fancied stealing such a tasty morsel. The rest of the wood-nymph they had belonged to, along with a dozen fairies, had been consumed last night by the

Dodman. He seemed to need more every day to keep his strength up.

"Aleister!"

Old Creepie shot upright in panic and the crown tipped dangerously low over one eye, making him appear both furtive and ridiculous.

The Dodman hauled Isadora the length of the chamber, glaring so furiously, it looked as if his eyes were on fire. "Take that off!"

Isadora regarded her brother curiously. "I wondered what had become of my crown." She glanced down at her sleeping niece. "She must have taken it when she stole the Book."

Aleister coughed. "Oh, I'm sure she . . . er . . . only borrowed it."

The Queen's eyes flashed. "Just as you are only 'borrowing' my throne, sweet brother?" She reached over and snatched the crown off his head. She turned the delicate web of silver and crystal over and over in her pale hands and then set it firmly on her own head. As she did so, she seemed to grow in stature and power. Old Creepie quailed away from her.

"I . . . er . . . just put it on for safety."

Isadora laughed. "Yes, well, you can see it wasn't fashioned for the head of any man, fat-headed or"—

she turned her fierce green gaze upon the Dodman—"dog-headed. The Crown of Eidolon passes from one Queen to the next. There has never been a King in Eidolon. And there never shall be!"

The Dodman growled suddenly. It was the sort of noise a mad dog makes before it bites. He loomed up over Isadora and raised his hand. Then he swiped the crown from her head and it went flying in a swirl of crystal, smashing into the wall on the other side of the room. After the terrible clatter, a heavy silence fell.

"That is a tradition I mean to break," he snarled. "When Aleister marries us, you may wear your little trinket, but I shall take your power and *I* shall be King. King Dodman the First. Yes." And he licked his long black dog-lips as if savoring his victory.

Isadora stared at him scornfully. "Never."

Aleister was frowning. "I hate to say anything, old chap, but . . ."

The Dodman rounded on him. "But *what*? Spit it out!"

"I can't officiate, old man. She's . . . er . . . already married. Technically, I mean. She already has a . . . er . . . husband. Don't think she can have another. . . ."

The Dodman waved a paw dismissively. "Counts for nothing. A Queen of Eidolon can't marry a worm of a human. Come on, Aleister, can't you see she's dressed for the occasion?"

"Hah!" cried Isadora. "This is a nonsense. You, sir, are a monster, and my brother is a fool. I am already wed, and nothing changes that." And she folded her arms and turned her back on the two of them.

Old Creepie gazed helplessly up at the Dodman, and what he saw in that monstrous face made him go pale, then bright red, which wasn't a pretty sight. "I . . . ah . . . Let me just . . . er . . . go and get the Law Book, old chap. Check the wording and such." And with this excuse, he slipped swiftly from the throne and sped across the hall remarkably smartly for one having such short, bowed legs.

The Dodman kicked the cage a ringing blow. Cynthia, rudely awakened, snorted and tried to sit up, which resulted in her banging her head hard against the bars. "Ow!"

"Don't you think you've tortured the poor child enough?" Isadora said over her shoulder. "Let her out of that cage!"

The Dodman favored the little witch with his

widest smile. "No, not at all. She shan't come out till our wedding. She's going to be your bridesmaid."

"Bridesmaid?" Cynthia screeched. "Whose bridesmaid?"

"Your aunt's, idiot, when she marries me."

"I've only got one aunt and she's already . . ." Cynthia's gooseberry green eyes almost popped out of her head. "You can't! You promised!"

"Oh, Cynthia." Isadora turned to regard the little witch pityingly. "Silly girl, for trusting such a monster."

"Silly you," Cynthia retorted. "For trusting me."

Isadora nodded. "Yes, I was foolish indeed. It is not a lesson I shall need to learn twice."

Her niece pursed her thin lips, wondering what that meant. She didn't get a chance to ask, for at that moment her father returned, bearing a large, grand-looking volume bound in thick red leather. He trotted to the Dodman's side and opened it at the page he'd marked. "See here," he said eagerly, turning it and thrusting it at the dog-headed man. "Here are all the rules concerning royal marriages in Eidolon." It had entirely slipped his mind that the Dodman could not read. His fingers traced the words. "The Queen has the right to take to husband whomsoever she chooses—be he elf or troll, giant, selkie, or any other creature of her choosing—"

"It doesn't say anything about human worms!" the Dodman sneered.

Aleister wetted his lips and read on: "Once the Queen has chosen her mate, he shall be her mate for life. Only Death shall part them."

The Dodman ripped the ancient tome from Old Creepie's hands. Then he flung it down upon the floor and jumped up and down on it. "That's what I think of your stupid old book and its stupid old laws!"

Aleister looked horrified. "But, old chap, it's the Law Book. It's sacred. It's what Eidolon was built on."

"Stuff and nonsense! Who cares about the past? It's the future that matters, and my future shall be glorious!"

There was a brief pause. Then Aleister suggested timidly, "Perhaps she could make you her chief counselor, old chap. There's a nice office you could use—"

The Dodman gripped him by the throat. "Perhaps Isadora could feed your liver to the hounds!" he roared.

The Gabriel Hounds raised their heads from what they'd been occupied with. Who wanted a pair of stringy old wood-nymph hands when there was an entire fat necromancer to be chewed upon?

Aleister looked as if he might faint. "I . . . er . . . don't think that would be a good idea. Look, old man, it's not my fault that you can't marry Isadora while her husband's still alive."

"Bravo, Aleister!" Isadora clapped slowly. "You tell him."

The Dodman's beady black eyes bored into him. Then he laughed. "What was it your precious book said again? About Death?"

Aleister retrieved the even more battered volume from the floor, found the page again after a lot of huffing and puffing, and read: "He shall be her mate for life, and only Death shall part them."

"Only Death shall part them! What a fine ring that has to it. Only Death shall part them." This he repeated over and over as he strode around in military style, his boots thumping the marble floor in rhythm to the words.

Aleister and Isadora exchanged a worried look. "You don't think . . . ," the Queen whispered, but the dog-headed man turned back sharply.

"You forget that dogs have extremely finely

attuned hearing," he said. "Think? Your brother rarely *thinks*, my dear."

"I do try—"

"Well, don't! I, however, have a brain that works remarkably well. And do you know the solution that this fine organ has offered me?"

They shook their heads.

"It's absurdly simple." And he clapped his hands as if to applaud his own brilliance. "I shall have your 'husband' brought here."

He paused to watch Isadora's face.

"And then I shall kill him, and you will know yourself a widow, so there will be no impediment to our marriage."

Isadora fainted clean away.

Chapter Twenty

Among the Dinosaurs

The eaves of the Wildwood were dark and eerie, and what little moonlight there was made Ignatius Sorvo Coromandel's eyes shine like headlamps. Ellie caught hold of Ben. "Just to make sure I don't trip over and make a noise," she assured him, but he could feel her heart hammering against his arm.

They walked as quietly as they could into the forest with the Wanderer leading the way. It was preternaturally quiet. No owls hooted, no sprites chattered, no insects chirred. Nothing stirred in the dark canopy of stark branches overhead: not a fairy, not a bird. Through the trees ahead of them they could see flickering orange light.

Ellie screwed up her eyes. "Is the Wildwood on fire over there?" she asked fearfully.

"Nah." Iggy's nose twitched. "Those are cooking fires. Things are being roasted on them."

Ben wondered what "things" those might be. Dread settled in the pit of his stomach, and then he started running, towing Ellie behind him, the makeshift sack containing Boneless Bob tucked firmly under his arm. Ignatius Sorvo Coromandel shook his head, then belted after them.

If they had been worried about alerting the Dodman's army to their presence, they needn't have been concerned. The camp was full of noisy hub-bub. There were monsters everywhere: a sea of brown and dark green, broken by the occasional glitter of lizard-scales or the magnificent striped coat of a saber-toothed tiger. Bands of goblins had lit cook-fires, several of which had got out of hand and set fire to trees in which pterodactyls were roosting for the night. There was a great deal of squabbling and squawking about this, and one group of pterodactyls had killed an unfortunate goblin in retaliation and were currently engaged in eating him piece by piece.

"Ugh!" exclaimed Ben. He looked away, distressed by the sight, even though the victim was a hateful goblin.

"What?" said Ellie.

"You don't want to know," her brother replied fervently.

"Can you see Silver?"

"I sincerely hope not." Ben searched the rabble in front of them, but there was no sign of her in this quarter of the enemy camp. Which was probably a good thing. Here, there were mainly goblins, a few smaller trolls snoozing in heaps, and some enormous, slow-moving creatures stripping the last remaining leaves from a large tree.

Ellie clutched Ben's arm. "What on Earth are those?"

"Don't worry about them: They won't eat you. The really big one there's a brontosaurus, and the one next to it, with the beak-thing, is an iguanodon. They're herbivores. They don't eat meat."

Ellie's eyebrows shot up. "Oh, you mean vegetarian. Like Melissa, in our class. Wow."

"They must have been driven to the edge of the camp because they've run out of stuff to eat," said Ben. He paused, staring at them. "The one we're looking for, the one that took Silver, must be closer to the center."

They skirted the edge of the camp, keeping downwind all the time. As Iggy pointed out, he didn't really want to be sniffed out by a horde of hungry goblins and eaten for dessert. An area of huge boulders, which must once have formed the walls of a long-dried-up river, provided them with cover as they made their way closer to the heart of the enemy army, and soon they were seeing all sorts of extraordinary creatures. Satyrs had mock-fights with one another, butting their heads together and locking their goats' horns, watched by a swarm of hungry-looking vampire bats. Beyond these loomed the allosaurs, as tall as the trees against which they lounged on their powerful haunches. One of them opened its mouth to laugh at something its comrade had said and moonlight glinted off its long, serrated teeth. There were armor-plated stegosaurs and triceratops, a sad-looking diplodocus nosing around in the vain hope of something to eat, and a horde of small raiders that Ben did not recognize but that looked rather like miniature tyrannosaurs darting between the feet of the others, stealing whatever food they could lay their little clawed hands on. Some of them wore scraps of fur and bone and hair around their necks.

"I like their necklaces," Ellie whispered, after one had passed close enough for her to peer at it. "I've seen things like that at Top Shop. Jungle Chic, they call it."

Iggy favored her with a hard stare. "That's not fashion," he said scathingly. "That's our friends."

Ben closed the eye he thought of as his Earth eye and focused with his Eidolon eye. He recoiled. The little raptors were sporting sprigs of centaur hair, wood-sprite husks, fairy bones, gnome ears. "They've taken trophies," he said, disgusted. "Bits and pieces of the woodland folk they've killed."

"Oh . . ." Ellie felt sick. It wasn't all that different from the jewelry she and Cynthia had made with the feathers and bits of fur Uncle Aleister had brought home for them. There were girls in her class still wearing their earrings made out of mermaid scales, their necklaces of unicorn horn. Except then she hadn't known that was what they were. And now that she did, she couldn't bring herself to tell them.

They edged closer. Close enough to hear a pair of allosaurs having an argument.

"I want to go home."

"Stop whining, Ancasta. We can't. We've been over this a thousand times."

"And you've never given me a good reason for us being here. I mean, look at the company we're keeping—stegosaurs and eoraptors—idiots and thieves. Very noble!" And she folded her arms and glared at her companion.

"We're here to support the clan-chief. As you know."

"Well, it's not *my* fault he got summoned, is it? It's not even our war!"

"Be quiet!" The larger of the two allosaurs looked over his shoulder. "You'll get us into trouble."

"You're such a wimp, Pertinax. Mother was right. I should never have mated with you."

"Wow," Ben whispered. "This is great. I can understand dinosaur."

Iggy rolled his eyes. "They're not speaking 'dinosaur,' Sonny Jim. They're speaking Eid, like everyone in Eidolon."

The two allosaurs had moved closer. "We could just . . . go," said the female, Ancasta.

Her mate stared at her. "And leave our comrades in the lurch?"

"They don't want to be here either. Maximus said so yesterday. No one knew it was going to be like this. They're ready to leave."

"The Dodman will reward us when he wins."

"Oh, yes? And how's he going to do that?"

Pertinax looked nonplussed. "Well, I'm not sure. But that's what they're all saying."

"That puny dog-headed creature's got nothing I want," Ancasta said sullenly.

"He could drive the dragons out of the Eastern Quarter. We could move back there, have some babies . . ."

The female tutted. "He's not going to bother doing that. What's in it for him? Anyway," she sniffed, "I'm not sure I *want* babies with you, not unless we can live somewhere really special. Kits need space and light, somewhere to run around in safety."

Her mate hung his head, looking dejected. Then, as if he had suddenly come up with a winning argument, he looked up, his eyes gleaming. "He could take back Infinity Beach for us."

"The stuff of fairy tales," Ancasta said scornfully. "It doesn't even exist. It's just some mythical paradise they wave in front of you to make you hate the dragons for stealing it away."

Ellie's fingers tightened on Ben's arm. "Infinity Beach. Isn't that—?"

Ben nodded. "Ssh—look, something's coming."

The allosaurs had stopped their bickering. Creatures everywhere were staring up into the dark sky.

"Is it Mummu-Tiamat? Has she come back?" Ellie asked hopefully, but whatever it was was much too small to be the Mother of Dragons. It circled over the army camp, then flapped toward them.

Iggy bristled as moonlight delineated the dark shape. "It's that horrid bird!" And he started to chatter furiously. "You should have let me eat it the first time!"

Ben reached out a hand and folded it over his friend's muzzle to keep him quiet. He could still feel the little jaws chattering involuntarily. Iggy was a cat and he hated birds—he couldn't help himself—and in this case, Ben couldn't blame him. It was the

Dodman's mynah bird. He remembered how it had turned up one day on their garden gate back home in Bixbury, bearing a nasty message from its master.

The bird hovered for a moment over the gathered troops as if searching for someone in particular, then came arrowing down.

"Come on!" said Ben. "It'll be carrying a message from the Dodman and we've got to know what it is."

They reached the very last boulder that would afford them cover, but it was too far away from where the mynah bird had come to rest for them to hear anything except the thud and shuffle of feet, the breathing of vast lungs, and the roar of other voices.

Ben tugged at his hair in frustration. "Stay here," he warned Ellie. "And you, Iggy, stay with her."

"But—"

"Please, Iggy. I'll be okay. Anyway, there's no point in all of us getting caught." And before anyone could stop him, he was gone.

He almost got trodden on by a diplodocus that wasn't looking where it was going; and luckily, because it wasn't, it didn't see him. He dodged sideways to avoid the swinging, spiked tail of a stegosaur and ran slap, bang into the backside of a triceratops. It turned around, very slowly, and surveyed him with its tiny black eyes. But although a triceratops has the most enormous skull, it has a very tiny brain, and so by the time it had got around to thinking, *I wonder what on Eidolon that was?* Ben was long gone, hiding behind the trunk of a burned-out tree. He looked up at it. Then he stuffed the waterproof bag down into his sweater and started climbing, slowly and quietly. It was like climbing the giant ash tree on the edge of Aldstane Park, the one like Yggdrasil out of the old Norse legends. The one Silver had had such trouble climbing because of her flippers. He remembered how she had jumped off the overhanging branch and how he had caught her, and the memory brought tears to his eyes. "You are my hero, Ben," she had told him. But the situation they had faced then had been nothing compared to this.

He tried not to think about what would happen to him if he was seen, and applied himself instead to searching for the selkie in a sea of monsters. He gazed and gazed till his Eidolon eye hurt, but if Silver was anywhere among them, she was well hidden.

Something vast loomed up in the thickest part of the throng, and the eoraptors and velociraptors, the stegosaurs and allosaurs, goblins and goat-men and saber-tooths all made way for it. Ben gasped. It was the scariest-looking dinosaur he could ever have imagined: a vast tyrannosaur, towering thirty feet high with a massive skull, bone-crushing jaws, and cunning eyes. The mynah bird had landed on one of its outstretched, clawed hands.

"Greetings, General. I bring word from the Dodman. *Squarrrk!*" it declared, and the army fell silent.

"Speak on, bird," the tyrannosaur rumbled. "Tell us what our master has to say."

"He says, *squarrrk*, that tomorrow at noon there will be a wedding feast at Dodman Castle and a coronation, for tomorrow he shall be crowned King of Eidolon. You and three of your chosen commanders are invited to attend."

There was a murmur at this news. Ben frowned. "But who would marry the Dodman?" he said to no one in particular.

"Sssssssss!" hissed Boneless Bob. "Sssstupid boy! How does the Dog-Headed One become King?"

"I don't know," said Ben.

"By wedding a Queen."

"But . . ." Ben's heart thumped. "What, you mean *Mum?*"

"Yesssssss."

"But he can't. She's already married."

"I'm sssure he won't let that sssstand in his way. Looks like you're about to get a ssssstepfather."

Things in Ben's world were getting worse and worse.

The tyrannosaur grinned widely, giving everyone an unwelcome view of its masses of sharp, sharklike teeth. "Excellent. I like a good feast!"

"But," the bird continued, "you must bring a gift: a tribute fit for a King."

"What sort of gift?"

"He said 'be imaginative.' *Squarrrk!*" The mynah bird unfurled its wings. "Tomorrow at noon. With your tribute. Don't be late!" And with that, it launched itself into the dark air and flapped away again.

"What shall we take him?" the tyrannosaur mused.

"Gold!" called one of the dragons.

"Jewels!" cried another.

The lizard-king rolled its eyes. "Pah! You dragons are so predictable. Can you think of nothing but treasure? He can't eat gold and jewels at a feast, can he?"

There was a brief silence, then a flurry of suggestions.

"Goblin pie!" yelled a troll.

"Fried troll's feet!" retorted a goblin.

"Roast brontosaurus with all the trimmings, garnished with dragons' eyes and stuffed with stegosaur steaks," an allosaur suggested wickedly.

The tyrannosaur laughed. "Have you ever tried brontosaurus? They taste like mud, my friend, roasted or raw. Awful. No, that would never find favor with such a sophisticated traveler as the Dodman. He's been around, the Dog-Headed One. He's eaten the best that Eidolon has to offer, and I even heard he's supped in the Other World—"

"How about vampire vindaloo?" growled a saber-toothed tiger. It had once got lost in the wild road system and found itself in the Other World, where it had sampled a few sheep on Bodmin Moor before nipping into a local town and falling into company with a pair of urban foxes who knew of all sorts of good things to eat.

"Sweet and sour satyr!" suggested its mate, warming to the theme.

"Mmmm, interesting." The tyrannosaur stroked

its chin thoughtfully, and the satyrs started backing away and making excuses about other places they needed to be.

A figure appeared suddenly on the lizard-king's shoulder. It was small and hairless with big, pink, triangular ears and eyes of a virulent yellow. It was wearing a harness of leather straps, which were fixed to the wide collar the tyrannosaur wore about its neck, as if the small creature were a pet, but also a prisoner.

"If it please you, ssssire, I have an excellent idea," it hissed into the tyrannosaur's ear.

Ben stared. He knew that creature. It was the Sphynx, the horrid, bald cat that belonged to Awful Cousin Cynthia and spied for the Dodman. The waterproof bag under his arm rustled, and Boneless Bob's head popped out.

"The Ssssphynx!"

Ben transferred his gaze to the witch's familiar. "You know him?"

"He's my brother," Bob said. If a serpent could show emotion, it seemed anxious. Its orange crest rose and fell uncertainly.

"There's not much of a family resemblance," Ben

said unbelievingly. "I mean, you're a snake and it's a . . . well, a cat, sort of."

Bob gave him a pitying look. "You don't understand much about this world, do you? Does Old Creepie resemble your mother? No, well, shush, I want to hear what he has to sssay."

The tyrannosaur reached up, grasped the hairless cat, and held it up before its face. "Out with it, then, spy!"

The power of the lizard-king's bad breath made the Sphynx's eyes cross. It struggled against the scaly grasp, then went limp. "I saw a quetzalcoatlus land a few moments ago," it gasped. "It was bearing a very tasty-looking prize."

The tyrannosaur's eyes gleamed. "What was it?"

"A sssselkie-girl. Her name is Ssssilver, and she is a friend of the Queen's ssson. I am sssure she would make good eating."

The lizard-king considered this for a moment. Then it rumbled its appreciation. Its voice boomed out across the camp. "Bring me the selkie. Now!"

There was a lot of flapping and squawking behind the tyrannosaur; then the crowd parted to reveal the most massive, hideous-looking bird. Forty feet long and a dozen high, it lumbered toward the lizard-king in a fashion that reminded Ben of the bell ringer in a production of *The Hunchback of Notre Dame* he had once seen; but it was much, much uglier than even Quasimodo. It had a long head with a bony crest, a horrible, long beak, and not a feather in sight. Its leathery wings were half-folded and it used its pinions to propel itself awkwardly across the ground. Ben soon saw why: In one of its great claws it held its prey.

Silver.

Dwarfed by the monstrous bird's mantled shoulders, she lay there in her girl form, her pale hair spilling down to the ground, too frightened even to cry out, her liquid eyes huge in her face.

The tyrannosaur strode forward. It bent its vast head to examine the object, poked her once in the stomach, and grinned from one scaly ear to the other. "Excellent!" it roared. "A bit small, but very succulent. Give her to me!"

But the quetzalcoatlus wasn't giving up its prize that easily. It glared up at the giant lizard with its small, bright eyes. "Mine," it stated, and its beak clacked sharply. Speech was difficult for the flying creature; it had a long way to go on the evolutionary ladder.

The tyrannosaur regarded it magnanimously. "Yes, it's yours. But if you give the selkie to me, Montezuma, you shall accompany me to the feast tomorrow night and take the credit for catching it. It will be a great honor for you."

The huge bird turned its head and looked suspiciously at the lizard-king, first with one beady black eye, then with the other. Then it shook its beak. "Me. Eat now." And it lifted back its bony head as if to deal the selkie a killing blow.

"No!" The shout had escaped Ben before he could prevent it. His hands flew to his mouth as if to stuff the word back in again, but he was too late.

Beneath the tree a satyr stared upward. Ben flattened himself against the trunk. The goat-man squinted. The cold, yellow, vertically-pupiled eyes scanned the branches. He looked straight at Ben for a heartbeat, then his gaze passed over what he had taken to be a burr in the wood, and he shrugged. "One of those wailing banshees," he announced to his friends, and they returned their attention to the quetzalcoatlus, relieved that someone else was going to be the victim.

"Last chance, Montezuma. Will you give me the selkie or must I take her from you?"

"Mine! Mine! Mine!" The creature stamped its clawed feet in fury.

The tyrannosaur moved with lightning speed, and suddenly the flying lizard had no head. There was a vile crunching sound and then Ben could see a huge lump moving down the monster's gullet. The rest of the quetzalcoatlus collapsed in a heap. Before the goblins could move in on her, the lizard-king scooped up the selkie and held her up for inspection.

For a horrible moment, Ben thought it was going to give in to temptation and bite her head off too, but the tyrannosaur merely weighed her and then pronounced, "She's not very big—a mere morsel for me. But she's big enough to feed the Dodman."

Ben's eyes filled with tears. "I have to save her!"

Something caught him by the sleeve. When he looked down, he found Boneless Bob's fangs clutching the fabric. He pried them off, wiping the snake-spittle away with the other sleeve in case it was poisonous.

"She's my friend. I have to do something."

"Let me go and I will save her for you."

Ben stared at it. "Why would you do that?"

"I have my reasonsssss."

"How can I trust you?"

"You can't."

"Then why would I let you go?"

"Look, I have an idea, okay?"

"But if I don't keep you safe, Maggota will harm my family."

The snake's crest flared up around its head like a huge orange collar. "If you want to ssssave your friend, you'll just have to take that rissssk."

Ben looked at the tyrannosaur, and the selkie in its awful grasp; then he looked at the horde of dinosaurs; then he looked back at the snake. He couldn't move very far among this army unhindered, but a slithering sneak like Boneless Bob could. They'd probably regard him as one of them. A monster. They were probably right.

"Okay, I agree," Ben sighed at last. "I must be mad." He shook the serpent out of the makeshift bag and watched as it coiled and uncoiled itself on the branch of the oak tree, flexing its sinuous spine this way and that.

"Thank you. I'll ssssay one thing before I go. Gordon Gargantua."

Ben frowned. "What does that mean?"

"You'll know when the time comes." And with that, it wound its way smoothly down the tree trunk and disappeared in a flicker of red and white and orange into the dark mass of monsters below.

Within moments it had fetched up at the feet of the tyrannosaurus.

"Greetings, General Tyrant Megathighs."

The general looked down. "Who are you?"

The Sphynx on his shoulder stared so hard, it looked as if its yellow eyes would fall out.

"Ask not who I am. Ask what I can do for you."

"And what can you do for me, worm?"

"It would be inadvisable to give the selkie to the Dodman while she's alive and kicking. She may look delicioussss raw, but selkie-meat is notoriously tough. If you boil her, she will become a sssseal, and where is the magic in that? And if you roast her, you will spoil her delicacy. It isss a conundrum. But I can help you ssssolve it."

"And how might you do that, worm?"

"I can bring you the best chef in Eidolon."

"A chef?"

"A troll, my lord."

The Sphynx's ears pricked up. It remembered the troll. Specifically, it remembered being traded by the nasty prince for the worthless Wanderer. It wasn't sure it ever wanted to see that troll again. The troll might decide that hairless cat made the best accompaniment to Seared Selkie.

"And where is this troll?" The tyrannosaur scanned the massed ranks of his army. He could see at least a dozen, right off. But they all looked far too stupid to be chefs.

"If you release the Sphynx, I will bring him to you."

The lizard-king's little eyes narrowed. "Why?"

"He issss my brother."

The tyrannosaur laughed. "As if that means anything. I ate *my* brother!" And it threw its head back and laughed. All around, the other dinosaurs bellowed their approval of this "joke." Then it reached up and broke the leather straps that attached the Sphynx to the vast collar around its neck.

Not quite believing its luck, the Sphynx sat there, blinking.

"Go wait for me in the oak tree behind those satyrsss, brother," Boneless Bob hissed. "I shall be back in three shakes of my tail." He wriggled at speed into the thickest part of the crowd and disappeared.

The Sphynx didn't need telling twice. It leapt down from the shoulder of General Tyrant Megathighs III and belted through the ranks like a skinned rabbit. Three seconds later it was sitting on the same branch as Ben, its sides heaving.

Ben regarded his new neighbor with distaste. "Just don't say anything," he warned. "We're in this together now."

The crowd parted to make way for a gigantic troll. It had noxious green skin, a shock of purple hair, and a lot of yellow teeth that stuck out at all sorts of angles. Ben recognized it immediately. It was hard to forget. He watched as the troll greeted the tyrannosaur and bent its hideous face over Silver.

". . . lots of choices," it was saying, and started counting them off on its warty fingers. "Selkie stew, selkie and goblin bake, selkie stuffed with liz—" It hesitated. "Ah, probably not a good idea in the circumstances. . . . Selkie, coriander, and prune tajine, selkie sticks and chips . . . ah, I have the very thing! Coronation selkie! Perfect! Just the thing: You sear the meat, then cook it very gently for a long time in a saffron-flavored sauce, add some sultanas and a few fairies' eyes for luck, and hey presto!"

"Now look here, whatever your name is . . ."

"Gordon," said the troll, and the hairs on the back of Ben's neck rose all of a sudden.

"Gordon. Just take her and do what you have to to make it a really special dish. Because otherwise my colleagues and I will be eating roast troll tonight, do you understand me?"

The troll nodded vigorously. It was a bit bemused as to how all this had happened. One moment he had been checking his store cupboard and listing the ingredients he needed to stock up on (cats' tails, minced mermaid, and green lentils); the next he had been running as fast as his huge feet could carry him at the behest of a small red and white snake. Still, it wasn't every day the troll got his hands on a fresh selkie. Pretty little thing too. He took her eagerly from the tyrannosaur's claws, then found himself sent by his summoner in quite a different direction from his cave and kitchen. It was a nuisance, but there didn't seem to be anything he could do about it.

Ben waited until the troll turned away and headed in his direction. As the troll came abreast of the satyrs Ben yelled, "Gordon Gargantua!" and the troll fetched up against the tree with a tremendous thud that shook Ben and the Sphynx right off their branch. The hairless cat did what cats do—twisted in midair and landed neatly on its feet—but Ben hit the ground so hard that all the air was knocked out of him.

"Pick me up," Ben wheezed, "and run!"

"What?" said the troll. "You'll have to speak up. I'm a bit deaf."

His fall had attracted the attention of a dozen sharp-sighted trolls, the satyrs, and an inquisitive velociraptor.

"I said, 'Pick me up and RUN!'" Ben yelled, using up every scrap of air in his lungs.

Chapter Twenty-one

The Getaway

"Run till I say stop!" Ben instructed the troll. It was the only order he could think of for the time being.

Gordon Gargantua was not built for running. It is not a sport at which trolls excel. They have stout bodies and legs like tree trunks, very good for long-distance walking or for stomping on creatures who have annoyed them, but not the best for evading a horde of fleet-footed dinosaurs and goblins. Ben, straddling the troll's thick, warty neck, drummed his feet against Gordon's shoulders. "Faster!"

The Sphynx, determined to make good its own getaway, had fastened itself to the seat of the troll's capacious trousers and was clinging on for dear life.

Silver, held tight in the crook of Gordon's arm, turned to look up at Ben. Her eyes shone. "Thank you, Ben! I don't know how you managed to save me, but thank you!"

"Don't thank me yet," he warned her. "We still have to escape."

Their hunting instincts triggered by the sight of something running, a pack of velociraptors and eoraptors had taken up the pursuit, followed by a dozen curious goblins. None of them were much interested in taking down and eating a troll, but it looked as if chasing it and frightening it to death might be good sport and a change from all the dull waiting around.

Gordon swatted away a small dinosaur that had got too close, and it went flying head over heels among its fellows, causing several of them to stumble and fall. This just served to make the rest of them more determined to harry the troll. They redoubled their efforts, making little clacking noises deep in their throats, which Ben took to be some sort of growl or threat.

"Through these boulders," Ben told the troll. "Follow the dried-up riverbed toward the trees there." That was where he had left Ellie and Iggy. He hoped fervently they had stayed where he had told them to. There would be no time to search for them, for he saw when he looked back over his shoulder that the chase had now been taken up by a pair of allosaurs, who were outstripping the smaller dinosaurs and the goblins and looked hungry enough to eat them all—troll, boy, selkie, and hairless cat—without a second thought.

The troll lumbered painfully through the boulders, driven by the force of Ben's compulsion, knocking his elbows and hips all the way in the narrower stretches. The clatter of his big, bare feet scattering rocks underfoot counterpointed with his grunts of pain and the soughing of the air in and out of his mouth. Gordon Gargantua was not in good shape. At one point he clutched his chest with his free hand, and Ben was afraid the running had given the troll a heart attack, if trolls had hearts, that was. But, "Stitch!" moaned Gordon, massaging his ribs. "Oh, let me stop!"

"We can't!" Ben yelled in his less-deaf ear. "Keep going!"

Other creatures had joined the pursuit now: a pair of saber-toothed tigers loped along, as curious as any cat as to what was going on, and a lot more goblins had joined the pack, including a particularly evil-looking one with only one ear.

This goblin peered hard at Ben, then announced, eyes wide with amazement, "I know that little beast. It's the Queen's son!"

This news traveled fast among the pursuers. Ben could hear snatches of their breathless conversations.

"Are you sure, Bosko?"

". . . Isadora's elf-boy . . ."

". . . halfling prince . . ."

". . . reward from the Dodman . . ."

"Oh no," Ben groaned. He thumped Gordon on the shoulder. "Can't you go any faster?"

Gordon turned a pair of bloodshot, watering eyes upon him. "If you wanted a faster getaway vehicle, you should have summoned a blinking dragon!" he wheezed. "It's not fair. I was just minding my own business . . . few household chores . . . sweep out the cave a bit . . . hadn't planned on running a blinking marathon . . ." Then he couldn't say any more because the ground rose suddenly and it was all he could do to keep moving at all.

Ben stared around at the rocks. He had been sure this was where he had left Ellie. It was so dark, he could hardly see a thing and the boulders all looked so similar. He risked a shout.

"Ellie! Iggy! Where *are* you?"

Nothing.

Typical. His sister never did what she was told.

Something caught his foot and yanked it so hard, he almost fell off the troll. He looked down and found one of the goblins climbing up the troll's back, flourishing a wicked little curved knife. He caught its arm and managed to wrench the knife out of its grasp, then kicked out frantically and dealt it a blow on the shoulder, but still it kept coming. With a yowl the Sphynx jumped on its head and raked at its face and the goblin fell off, howling.

The unpleasant yellow eyes gleamed in the moonlight. "You owe me one, Isadora's ssson," it hissed.

Ben nodded. "For now," he said.

An eoraptor attached itself to the troll's right leg. Silver grabbed a dead branch, snapped it off, and battered the thing till it fell away, chattering furiously.

"Ellie!" Ben yelled again, and this time he thought he heard a reply somewhere to their right. "That way!" he instructed the troll, and hauled on its hideous purple hair as if on a horse's bridle to make it change direction.

There was a shriek and a horrible snarling noise, and then the moon came out from behind a cloud, and there was Ellie backed up against a tree, surrounded by a band of velociraptors that were gazing at her rapturously, obviously looking forward to a tasty snack. Above her, Ignatius Sorvo Coromandel sat on a branch, his fur bushed out till he was twice his normal size, hissing and spitting and howling imprecations but being of very little practical use.

"Gordon Gargantua: Grab that girl and that cat and let's get out of here!"

The troll waded into the midst of the velociraptors and laid about them with Silver's stick till they turned tail and watched vengefully from a distance away, waiting for the rest of the pack to catch up. Gordon picked up Ellie, set her on his shoulder, and reached for Iggy.

The little black-and-brown cat retreated till he was

squashed up against the tree trunk. "Are you crazy?" he asked Ben. "You're sitting on the troll that tried to cook me, or didn't you realize? Do you want to be put in a pot and made into prince rissoles?"

"Haven't got time for this, Ig. Get down here."

Iggy shook his head. Then he stared past the troll and saw what was following it. About a hundred hungry-looking dinosaurs and goblins. "Oh." He closed his eyes and jumped onto Gordon's head, scrabbled desperately in the snakelike hair, then fled down his neck to Ben. The next thing he saw was the Sphynx. All his fur that hadn't been standing upright now rose as if electrified. "The world's gone mad. What's *he* doing here?"

The hairless cat snarled at him. "Jussst keep out of my way, Wanderer."

Ignatius Sorvo Coromandel gave the Sphynx a hard look, then turned his back on him. "Suits me."

Gordon Gargantua ran. He ran until his legs felt like lead, till he thought his heart would burst. It was all very well for the elf-boy to keep apologizing, but it didn't help that he kept drumming his feet and yelling, *Faster!* The troll was beginning to feel as if his body was no longer his own. Under normal circumstances there was no way he would entertain the idea of running twenty yards on his own, let alone the mile or more they had already covered with him carrying an elf-boy, a girl, a selkie, and two cats.

A few of their pursuers had got bored with the chase and fallen away, and some of the dinosaurs seemed to have used up their best turn of speed and were lagging, but the goblins just never seemed to tire.

At last they came into a clearing and Gordon simply fell down in a heap. Ben and Ellie and the cats went flying, but Silver found herself trapped underneath him.

"Get up!" Ben cried desperately. "Get up and run!" But all that happened was that the troll's legs waved pathetically in the air as if miming the motion of running.

"Can't," he groaned, and lay there, panting.

Ben scanned the midnight air for the Mother of Dragons, but all he could see was unrelieved blackness.

"Mummu-Tiamat!" he yelled. But there was no answer.

The goblins were closing in, and if they stayed here any longer, the dinosaurs would catch up too, and then they'd all be eaten alive. Had it really come to this? There was just one possibility, and he knew it was a slim one. There was nowhere large enough here for the Mother of Dragons to set down in, and getting to the edge of the Wildwood before the goblins overtook them would take a miracle. But it was the only chance they had.

"Iggy, climb the tallest tree you can find and try to signal to Mummu-Tiamat. We need her to pick us up. Say . . ." He paused, thinking. "Say 'The Prince of Eidolon requests a great favor from you, and he will be indebted to you forever if you grant it.' Or something like that. Be respectful. But make her come!"

Ignatius Sorvo Coromandel regarded him with glowing amber eyes. "I hate climbing trees."

"Ssssssss!" laughed the Sphynx. "And he calls himself the Wanderer!"

The little black-and-brown cat drew himself up to his full height (about twelve and a half inches) and growled. "We still have scores to settle, Baldy, and if you want to do it now, that's fine by me."

"Iggy! Stop it. There's no time for this now. Please, try to find Mummu-Tiamat. We're depending on you."

Put like that, what could Iggy say? His fur subsided. "Okay, okay, I'm going." And he took to his heels and fled into the depths of the Wildwood.

Ellie had managed to extricate the selkie from under the troll's groaning bulk.

"We'll fight them!" Silver said through gritted teeth. "They're not taking me again without a fight."

"Nor me," said Ellie fiercely, though she didn't feel very fierce.

They armed themselves with the biggest sticks they could find.

They did not have long to wait. Moments later the monsters appeared. At once, an eager pair of goblins broke ranks, dashing in and trying to snatch Ben, but Silver thrashed out with her stick and one of them fell away shrieking and clutching its head. Three velociraptors crept around behind the troll and tried to bite him, which galvanized Gordon to lumber to his feet. He grabbed two of the raiders and banged their heads together so hard that they couldn't walk straight when he threw them down again. The third retreated.

Now the saber-toothed tigers decided to try their luck. They slunk along on their bellies, haunches waggling as if ready to spring, but the Sphynx positioned itself in front of the others and hissed something at them in a language Ben couldn't understand. The tigers blinked their huge amber eyes, then sat down and started to groom, like a pair of domestic cats caught doing something they shouldn't.

But there was nothing the Sphynx could say that was going to put off Boggart and Bosko and the rest of the goblin troop. Ben saw them conferring; then a great roar of laughter went up and they started closing in.

Ben turned to scan the forest behind them. "Oh, Iggy, where are you? Where's Mummu-Tiamat?" But nothing stirred in the canopy, and with a sinking heart he turned back to face the pack of marauders.

Ignatius Sorvo Coromandel was not the best tree climber in either of the two worlds. He didn't mind the going up too much, but he didn't like teetering on the top of a tree, and he *definitely* didn't enjoy the coming down, which often entailed an awkward, falling run and a less-than-elegant jump. This was fine on a fifteen-foot cherry tree and not such a good idea on a hundred-foot Wildwood oak. That thought was always in the back of his mind as he made the ascent. It made him nervous and tense and his muscles moved jerkily, making the branches rustle and vibrate just when he didn't want them to. At one point he almost managed to shake himself off, then he got the wobble under control and continued upward, pulse racing. The other thought that fluttered around in his head was that he wouldn't be able to see the dragon, or if he *could* see her, that he wouldn't be able to make her come to him—after all, she'd said she didn't care about him or the snake, so why should she listen to him? And if she didn't come, he'd be stuck up a tree and his friends would be lost to the goblins and dinosaurs, and it would all be his fault.

The branches began to thin out, and he was just about to pounce out of the canopy into the clear air toward the top of the big oak when he saw something outlined against the moon. At first he thought it was an odd branch sticking upward instead of outward. Then it moved. It was tall and thin and strange-looking, and then it turned slightly so that the moonlight lined its features and he saw that it was a pterodactyl trying to tuck its head under its wing to roost for the night.

Ignatius Sorvo Coromandel cursed his luck. Of all the trees in the forest to have picked to climb. He froze against the trunk, wondering what to do. Should he make his way down again and try another tree, or wait and hope that the monster would fall asleep? Either would take more time than he had. It called for desperate measures. Positioning himself so that he was hidden by the last of the oak's leaves, Iggy dug all his claws deep into the trunk and began to shake it. At first the movement was barely noticeable, then the tree's top began to sway as if caught by the lightest of breezes. Iggy began to feel dizzy, but he pushed harder and harder. The pterodactyl stirred. It brought its great heronlike head out from under its wing and looked around with its tiny, beady eyes. Iggy hoped it was as unintelligent as it looked. If it figured out that none of the other trees was swaying, it would start looking for the cause. Which wasn't very far away and rather edible. He pushed this thought aside, closed his eyes, and shook the tree with all his might till he thought his backbone might snap with the strain of it. The topmost branch started whipping from side to side as if a brisk wind had started. Then momentum took over and the swaying increased. The pterodactyl squawked its displeasure. It spread its wide wings for balance and clacked its bony beak. Then it took off into the night, complaining as it went, to look for a more comfortable spot to get some rest.

Iggy climbed slowly to the crook of branches the pterodactyl had vacated. His head was spinning and his stomach felt as if it were at sea. He stared out into the night sky. Something was moving out there, something long and bulky—a huge object planing silently through the dark air.

It was now or never. He took the biggest breath his little lungs could manage. "Mummu-Tiamat! Mother of Dragons!"

The great shape seemed to pause in its flight, then it sideslipped and began to make its way toward him. Iggy's heart lifted. He might just turn out to be the hero in this drama after all.

"You may as well give up, elf-boy!" one of the goblins snarled.

"No point in you *all* getting badly hurt for no reason!" another shouted.

"Nah, give up peaceably. Shame to spoil good

meat!" suggested one of the allosaurs. And they all sniggered.

"It'll be you who gets badly hurt!" Ben yelled back hotly. "I can promise you that!"

The laughter became a little more nervous. Then Ben heard one of the goblins tell its neighbor, a sly-looking velociraptor, "That's the Prince of Eidolon, that is, Queen Isadora's son. We capture him, the Dodman will be well pleased."

"You'd better watch out," another said. "He's got magic, he has. The last time I saw him, he had a dragon with him. Poor old Boggart got burned all down his front."

"Least it wasn't his back. He's no coward, our Boggart."

"He's no beauty, either. Some say the burning was an improvement!"

The goblins were in high spirits at the thought of capturing a princeling. And they'd eat the selkie straight off. No point wasting a nice, fresh seal-girl on the Dodman, especially cooked in a nasty sauce. The girl—well, the girl was another matter.

"Poor old Bosko didn't do so well out of his encounter with Isadora's offspring, did you, Bosk?

Heard you wailed like a banshee when the Dodman took your ear."

A smaller, one-eared goblin hissed at this and tried to stab the speaker with its dagger. There was a brief and vicious fight, which Bosko won, against the odds. He leered in the direction of Ben, Ellie, and Silver.

"See this?" he called, indicating the ragged flap on his head. "I look like this because of you lot. Lucky little princess still has two nice, pink ears, thanks to me, though I reckon one of them would suit me very well. In fact, I quite fancy a matching pair—get rid of this old thing." He turned to the allosaur behind him. "What do you say, Pertinax, will you keep her ears for me when you chew up the rest of her, eh?"

The allosaur grinned horribly at Ellie, showing off its best assets: a lot of very white, very pointed teeth.

Ellie shuddered. "Nobody's having my ears!" she shrieked. "Or any other part of me. And if any of you vile creatures comes anywhere near me, I'll hit you so hard, you won't know what day it is!"

"Ooh, 'vile creatures,'" said a velociraptor to its neighbor, not taking its eyes off Ellie. "Is that what we are?"

Bosko turned to one of the other goblins, mock-puzzled. "What day is it, Bumface?" he asked theatrically.

Bumface shrugged. "No idea."

Bosko laughed. "So much for that, then, girlie. Now, let's be having yer ears!"

And they started to close in.

As the dark shape sailed closer to the tree, Iggy frowned. He was beginning to have second thoughts, though it was a bit late for that. He didn't remember the dragon having such a long tail. And its body was, well, fatter. He opened his eyes as wide as possible to get as much moonlight into them as possible (for this is how cats' eyes work, unlike humans, who tend to squint) and felt a shudder of dread run through him. There were two figures on the back of the Mother of Dragons, if that was who it was coming toward him, at speed now. But they had left her alone. Or rather, *she* had left *them* . . .

Perhaps, Iggy rationalized to himself, perhaps she had gone back for Zark and Darius. But he wasn't managing to convince himself. He got ready to bolt down the tree.

But then the shape glided into a ray of moonlight, and Iggy found he couldn't move his feet. He couldn't move a single muscle, not even his tail. He was transfixed.

"Hello, Iggy," said a voice he almost recognized.

Chapter Twenty-two

The Elf-Girl

Ben was beginning to panic, though he wouldn't admit it to himself, let alone anyone else. There were so many of them. If it had just been goblins, he'd have been less worried. Though goblins were vicious, they were also rather stupid, and could be easily frightened. But it didn't look as if anything would frighten the velociraptors or the allosaurs; and the great, armored triceratops that had just lumbered up to join them looked like a bulldozer. If it tried, Ben thought, it could crush all three of them, and Gordon Gargantua too, without even knowing it.

The troll had got to his feet. "Now what?" he asked Ben. His great, hairy mitts hung limply by his sides, and his face was hangdog. He was just awaiting instructions, Ben realized, still under the compulsion of his summoning, even though he was exhausted.

"Try looking really scary," Ben told him in a low voice. "Roar at them a bit, or something."

The troll frowned. Then he screwed his face up in an alarming fashion and emitted a huge belch. It smelled awful, but the goblins didn't seem much impressed.

"Is that the best you can do?" jeered one.

His neighbor let rip a monstrous burp, and they all laughed, and the next minute they were all burping and farting and roaring with amusement. The allosaur took a deep breath and it seemed as if all the air that had ever been in its stomach came flying out at once. The force of the blast actually knocked down several goblins.

The Sphynx bolted up a tree and sat there, shivering. It would wait this out and side with the victors. It was beginning to look pretty obvious who they would be.

Gordon Gargantua began to cry. Tears like giant raindrops ran down his face. "I don't want to die," he said. "There are so many more recipes in the world. So many more interesting things to eat."

Ben didn't know what to say. "Just . . . just sit over there," he told the troll as kindly as he could manage. He was clearly going to be of little further use to them.

Ben flourished his stick and the curved knife he had taken from the goblin who had climbed the troll's back. He glared at Bosko. "Your dinosaur friends look hungry!" he shouted. "But with my magic knife here I can cut you so you never stop bleeding, and how do you know they won't then all fall on you and attack you like sharks at the smell of so much blood? I've heard that's what carnivorous dinosaurs do."

The goblins had a brief discussion as to what "carnivorous" might mean, came to the conclusion that they had no idea, and that it was just a big word for showing off, and turned defiant faces to Ben. "Nah, that's Putrid's knife, that is," said one of them. "It ain't magic at all."

Without warning several of the goblins flew at

Ben, spitting and snarling and lashing out with whatever weapons they carried. Ben parried one dagger with his "magic" knife and watched with satisfaction as it skated up the blade of the dagger and caught the goblin a nasty blow on the forearm. The goblin fell away, howling that it was going to bleed to death, but another goblin took its place at once, and Ben found himself cutting and thrusting with both dagger and stick. Another goblin went flying as Silver gave it a tremendous blow.

"Iggy!" Ben yelled into the night. "Mummu-Tiamat!"

But if anyone replied, the response was lost in the ferocious howls and roars of their attackers. They had been driven back several paces now. Soon their backs would be up against the forest trees and they'd have nowhere else to go. Things were looking grim. A vague plan began to form itself in Ben's head. It was a truly desperate measure, one that should be taken only if all else was lost. It would be his one chance to save Ellie and Silver.

He fought on desperately, and hoped against hope that some miracle would happen.

• • •

Iggy stared and stared, unable to believe his eyes. Of the three figures in front of him, he recognized only one, and it wasn't the one who had greeted him. The one he *did* recognize was hard to mistake. She was vast and terrifically ugly, with wild orange and black dreadlocks, bald bits where her hair had been burned down like corn-stumps, and a face covered in warts and wens. As far as he could recall, her name was Grizelda. And the last time he had seen her, she had been driving a chariot drawn by the Gabriel Hounds through the air above the lake at Corbenic Castle, fighting against his friends, on the Dodman's side.

The second figure was a slight, pale elf-girl with brilliant, uptilted green eyes and hair so blond, it was almost white. This was the one who had called him by name, and he had no idea who she was.

The third creature was a monster of terrible proportions: a huge flying dinosaur with the flat, black eyes of a predator and a forty-foot wingspan.

It was most certainly *not* the Mother of Dragons.

They had beaten off dozens of the goblins, but it made no difference. Ben's arms felt as if they were on fire, the muscles hurt so much. He tried to take no notice, but the blows he was landing were less and less effective. Soon they would be overwhelmed, for the canny dinosaurs were waiting only for the stupid goblins to break down their defense. Then they would close in for the kill and Ben knew that there would be nothing he could do about it. He glanced around at Ellie and Silver and saw how exhausted they were. It was now or never.

He caught Gordon Gargantua's eye. "When I say the word," he hissed, "you run. You pick up Ellie and Silver and you run as far and as fast into the forest behind us as you can."

The troll looked forlorn. "I'll try."

"You'll do it," Ben said fiercely. "Because if you don't, I shall order you to pick a fight with that huge allosaur over there, and it will rip you limb from limb. Do you understand me?"

He whacked another goblin's dagger away, and the shock from the blow ran up his arm, making it so numb, he almost dropped the stick.

"Did you hear that, Ellie, Silver?"

They nodded mutely.

"You get as far into the Wildwood as you can. Dodge in and out of the trees and keep shouting for

Iggy and Mummu-Tiamat. They will rescue you, I know they will. You'll be okay."

"But what about you, Ben?" Silver cried, her eyes huge.

"Don't worry about me," Ben said grimly. "I've got a plan."

"I was looking for a very large dragon called Mummu-Tiamat," Iggy said nervously.

"And what would a cat be doing consorting with dragons?"

"Arranging a rescue mission," Iggy said, trying to sound official. "For my friends. They're surrounded by—" He was about to say "monsters" but realized just in time that she was actually sitting on one, and might not actually be on their side. "By enemies," he ended carefully.

"Enemies? Oh dear." The girl frowned. "What sort of enemies?"

"A lot of goblins, and satyrs and . . . er . . . dinosaurs." There was no avoiding it. "There's a whole army of them down there. The Dodman's army."

"I see," the elf-girl said. "Well, we can't have that." She put two fingers in her mouth and whistled loudly, and seconds later another large shape glided into sight.

This time it *was* the Mother of Dragons, and she had come to the elf-girl just like a well-trained dog coming to heel. Iggy felt even more nervous.

"Mummu-Tiamat," the girl said. "We are going to need reinforcements. I have something I need you to do for me." And she leaned forward and whispered something that Iggy couldn't quite catch, though he tried very hard.

At once the great golden dragon turned and flapped urgently away.

Iggy's eyes boggled. "You gave the Mother of Dragons an order and she didn't burn you to a crisp?"

The elf-girl regarded him with her extraordinary green eyes. "Of course not. How absurd. Now then, Ignatius Sorvo Coromandel, please get on my pterosaur and we can go and save Ben and Ellie and Silver."

Iggy's head was in a whirl, and not just because of the casual use of his true name to compel him to leap from the top of a hundred-foot tree into thin air. Luckily, he landed foursquare on the back of the pterosaur, in the space between the elf-girl and the giantess. He was about to ask a very important question when the air was stolen right out of his mouth by the sudden downdraft of the dinosaur's descent.

Ben could put off the evil moment no longer. "Goodbye, Ellie," he called. "Good luck." He risked a glance at the selkie. "See you again, Silver." He tried to smile, but his mouth wasn't working properly. It seemed to know better than the rest of him that it was unlikely he would ever see either of them again.

He took his welling emotions out on a goblin, giving it such a whack that his stick broke in two. So that was that. He took a deep breath.

"Run, Gordon Gargantua! Take Ellie and Silver and run!"

The troll lumbered to his feet in a disjointed, puppetlike sort of way, picked up its passengers, and pushed aside the goblins who got in his way. These went flying into the goblins attacking Ben and caused a very useful diversion. By the time they had extricated themselves, the troll had vanished into the dark forest and Ben was dashing full tilt in the opposite direction, yelling, "Come on, then, you slackers! Catch me if you can!"

He slammed into an unwary satyr and it fell over backward, hampering the allosaur who had had a clear run at Ben. The allosaur growled and promptly bit the satyr in half. Out of the corner of his eye, Ben glimpsed the cloven hooves vanishing into the monster's maw. His heart raced. He was going to die just like that. He could imagine the jaws closing on his midriff, their crushing force, the teeth penetrating his skin, the chill as it severed his top half from his bottom half . . .

It made him accelerate. His feet hammered the ground. He was running faster than he had ever run in his life. Which wasn't really surprising, given the circumstances. When he'd run the hundred meters at school and got beaten by most of his class, he hadn't had a pack of vicious monsters on his heels. If he had, he'd probably have broken the county record.

A velociraptor came at him and he ducked sideways and dodged around a rock; a goblin tried to jump on him, but he hurled himself out of its way. Something attached itself to his leg. Without a thought he kicked out and bashed it against a boulder and felt it fall away. A vampire bat tangled itself in his hair and he swatted at it in disgust.

Then something landed on him hard, pinning him to the ground.

"Gotcha!" snarled a voice.

As soon as the pterosaur landed, Iggy was eager to be off it, but he didn't seem to be able to move his feet.

The elf-girl turned around. "Off you go, then, Iggy. Go and find them. We'll be right here."

This seemed to break the compulsion. Iggy didn't need telling twice. He belted through the trees, yelling, "Ben! Ellie! Silver!"

At last someone called back to him. "Is that you, Iggy?" It was the selkie's voice. There was a lot of crashing through the undergrowth, and then suddenly there was the troll.

"Thank goodness," sighed Iggy. And he sat down and gave himself a quick impromptu grooming. It was good to look your best when taking the credit for saving the day.

But Gordon Gargantua ran right past him. The ground rumbled as he thundered along. Ellie called something as they overtook the little cat, but Iggy was in the middle of washing his ears at the time and didn't quite catch it.

"Eh? Hang on!" yowled Iggy. "I'm here! Come back!"

Indignant, he got to his paws and stalked after the troll, muttering as he went. At least they were safe; that was the main thing, and there didn't seem to be anyone in pursuit.

By the time he reached the edge of the forest where they had landed, the troll was doing his best to run right past the pterosaur, too. But the elf-maiden put up her hand. "Halt, Gordon Gargantua." And the troll came to such an abrupt standstill that Ellie and Silver were catapulted right off it.

Ellie sat up and brushed at the knees of her jeans. Then she looked around. When she saw the massive dinosaur with Grizelda on its back, she shrieked.

The elf-girl laughed.

"Oh, Ellie, don't be such a scaredy-cat."

Ellie narrowed her eyes at the elfin creature, but it was still hard to make her out in any detail. "Who on Earth are you?"

"Good question—well phrased. Who am I, on Earth and in Eidolon? Well, can't you guess?"

Ellie put her hands on her hips, cross now. "Look, we haven't got time for riddles right now. My brother is back there fighting off a horde of monsters single-handedly. Can you help us rescue him?"

"Ben isn't with you?" The elf-girl's face crumpled. "That spoils everything. I was looking forward to telling him about the wild roads." She turned to the selkie, who was looking very forlorn. "Hello, She Who Swims the Silver Path of the Sea. It's a pleasure to meet you at last. I've heard a lot about you. From Ben."

"Please," said Silver. "Please, whoever you are, help us. We must rescue him."

"Well, get on board, then, all of you. Gordon, come here and help them up."

The troll did as he was told.

"Gordon?"

He looked up. Then his face split in a huge grin. "Grizelda!"

"It is you!" The giantess grinned back, which was not a pretty sight.

The troll, however, seemed transfixed.

"Wait for me!"

Everyone turned hopefully, but it was not Ben who had shouted but a small, hairless cat.

The elf-girl regarded it solemnly. "Cousin Cynthia's

familiar," she said accurately. "How interesting. Have you decided to change your wicked ways?"

The Sphynx gazed at her, slack jawed. The skin at the back of its neck began to wrinkle. If it had had hair there, it would have stood on end. Its eyes went very wide. Then its haunches quivered low to the ground and it started to back away.

"Ah, Abu al Hôl, Father of Terror, which of your nine lives are you up to now? Can you afford to waste one?"

The Sphynx sat down. It looked terrified.

"Come up here," the elf-girl bade him. "I have uses for you, little spy."

Against its will the hairless cat found itself bounding up the pterosaur's haunch. It sat down beside its summoner and its skin rippled with fear.

Ellie and Silver exchanged glances. Whoever this tiny, fragile-looking creature was, she seemed very impressive.

"Corinthius, up and away!"

The winged dinosaur bunched its leg muscles and leapt into the air.

Chapter Twenty-three

A Tribute Pit for a King

The witch appeared in a whirl of teeth, hair, and rotting-meat perfume. In one bony claw she still clutched a half-drunk cup of tea.

"You took your time!" the Dodman roared. He stared around behind her. "Well, where are they, then?"

"They?" Maggota batted her hideous eyelids at him.

"Don't play the innocent with me. I sent you to fetch them. Where are they?"

The witch wagged a bone-white finger at him.

"Third and last time, Dog-Head. Be careful you don't annoy me too much and waste your last chance. The children—ah yes, the children. Shall we say I experienced a little local difficulty with the children. . . ."

"You've lost them!"

"Not . . . exactly."

The Dodman stamped his dog-feet in fury. "I am surrounded by idiots and incompetents!" He gritted his teeth. "I have one last task for you. It shouldn't be too difficult, even for you. Fetch me Clive Arnold."

The witch rolled her eyes. "Well, you might have said before and saved me the effort. I've only just taken him back to the Other World."

The Dodman frowned. "What do you mean?"

The witch waved her free hand. "It's far too complicated to go into now." In fact, it was plain embarrassing. To explain what had happened would be an admission that her powers were not what they were. And that would never do. When she got her hands on the baby, she would show them all!

"Clive Arnold. Nothing more?"

"Clive Arnold. Now."

The witch drained her tea, tossed the empty cup to the Dodman, and was gone before he'd even caught it. He turned it over in his hands, sniffed at the dregs suspiciously. Was it magic, or poison?

The pterosaur put down neatly in the clearing where they had fought the goblins and dinosaurs, its nose almost touching the trees on one side and its tail on the other. But other than a broken stick and a scrap of bloody fabric, they found no sign of Ben.

No one was left there except for a goblin sitting against a tree, moaning and nursing its broken leg.

The elf-girl slipped down from the flying dinosaur and approached the goblin. The rising sun outlined the elf-girl in golden light. The goblin shielded its cat-slit eyes, then hissed.

"Putrid Agaricus!"

The goblin paled at the use of its true name. Up till then it hadn't even known it had one.

"Tell me where the boy called Ben is."

It narrowed its eyes at her. "Why d'you want to know?"

"He's family."

The goblin hawked, spat, then bent its head to examine the result. "Blood may be thicker than water, but snot is thicker than blood," it said cryptically.

"Tell me!" the elf-girl shouted, and the goblin clutched its shattered leg.

"He ran. He bashed me, and he ran, that way"— he gestured toward the rocks—"and the others all chased him."

"And what lies that way?"

"Why, our army, of course. What planet have you been on?"

"Till most recently, Earth. Mainly."

The goblin frowned. "Earth?"

"The Other World, I believe you call it."

"You don't want to go there. I've heard it's full of all sorts of monsters."

The elf-girl laughed. "That's what they say about Eidolon."

She went back to the pterosaur and spoke to the Sphynx. "Abu al Hôl, I have a job for you—just the right task for a spy. Run into the enemy camp and find Ben. Tell him this from me. . . ." And she hollowed her hands around one of its big, triangular ears and whispered something. Its yellow eyes flared.

"Then come back here immediately. Do you understand me?"

The Sphynx nodded once, very fast. It couldn't

wait to be away from her disquieting presence.

"If you are not back here by the time the sun clears those trees, I will summon you. And you will be sorry." And she reached out to lift it down from Corinthius's back.

The hairless cat recoiled from her touch, then hurled itself to the ground and fled. They watched it go in silence. Then: "Who *are* you?" Ellie asked curiously. "I mean, you seem familiar in a weird sort of way, but also very strange." She squinted, trying unsuccessfully to focus on the elf-girl's face.

"Don't you recognize me?"

"I . . . er . . . I don't think we've met before."

The green-eyed girl laughed.

"Don't you know your own sister, Eleanor Katherine Arnold?"

Ellie frowned, wondering if she'd heard this right. Then she thought, *Perhaps Mum had a secret child in the Secret Country.*

"You don't seem very happy to see me again," the elf-girl pouted. "I suppose I have changed a bit. I was a lot smaller the last time you saw me, when Maggota Magnifica stole us away, and you dropped me in the wild road."

Ellie felt dizzy. "That's . . . that's . . . impossible. You can't be Alice. Alice is a baby."

The elf-girl clapped her hands. "A baby! I *was* a baby, that's true. Oh, but that was ages ago. I've been all over the place since then. The sights I've seen!" Her green eyes shone vividly in the dawn light. "I've been to the pyramids and Knossos; I've been to Tibet and New York and Marrakech; I've been to the bottom of the sea and the middle of the Rub al-Khali and to Samarkand and the top of Cloudbeard. It's been fascinating."

"But . . . it was only two days ago that we lost you." Ellie was bewildered. "How could you go to all those places in two days?"

"The wild roads, silly. They go everywhere. And they're full of magic."

"Oh, I see," said Ellie faintly, though she didn't.

"And now I'm stuffed with magic. Magic and experience. You have to grow to make room for it all," Alice said wisely, as if it were the most normal thing in the world. In two worlds.

Ellie just didn't know what to say. Or think. It was the selkie who said, all in a rush, before bursting into tears, "Well, I hope all that magic and experience is going to save Ben. Because he's the bravest person I know and he doesn't deserve to die among a pack of the Dodman's monsters."

"Nobody deserves that," Alice agreed solemnly, and green fire flashed in her eyes.

"What have you got there? Leave it alone!"

Reluctantly the velociraptors fell away. One of them wiped its mouth reflectively. Blood stained its sharp white teeth. The boy tasted good. It was a shame to give him up, even to the General.

"It's just a boy, Lord Tyrant. Nothing you'd be interested in."

"I'll be the judge of that. Let me see it."

The tyrannosaur dragged away those who were too slow to respond and tossed them aside. Ben lay crushed and bitten on the ground, barely breathing.

"It's just a scrap of a thing, General," the velociraptor wheedled. "Let us eat him."

"It's the . . . Queen's son!" puffed a goblin, dodging in between the tyrannosaur and the boy. "He's our prisoner. The Dodman will reward us for him."

Tyrant Megathighs III bent his fearsome head to regard the goblin eye to eye. "I think you'll find he's my prisoner now, goblin. Step away!"

Bosko glared back, greed making him brave. "The

Dodman is my master, not you. And I declare this boy as our tribute."

"Ah yes, the tribute. Where is my selkie?"

Bosko was at a loss. He looked to the other goblins for help. They looked away. "I . . . er . . . it wasn't my fault!"

"And the troll?"

The allosaur Pertinax shook its head. "It ran, my lord. It took the selkie and the girl, and ran into the Wildwood."

"How could you lose anything as big as a troll? Are you an army of dimwits? You shame me. You shame yourselves. You shame our leader."

And with that, he picked up Ben and stalked away, calling back over his shoulder, "Pertinax, Ancasta: You will come with me."

The allosaurs looked at each other. What did he want with them? They could not imagine it was anything good.

When the Sphynx returned, it was not alone. Draped around its neck and body like a weird, ragged scarf in lurid hues of red and white and orange was Boneless Bob.

Alice folded her arms. "There you are! I wondered where you'd got to. Well, where's my brother?"

"Is he alive?" cried Silver.

"The General has him prisoner."

"Who's the General?" asked Ellie.

"A huge tyrannosaurusss rex," hissed Boneless Bob.

The selkie moaned. She would not forget that monster in a hurry.

"They're taking him to Dodman Castle," added the Sphynx.

"He's going to be a wedding presssent!" said the serpent, its neck-frill flaring.

"A tribute for the King," the hairless cat corrected.

"Who's getting married?" Ellie asked curiously. She wasn't interested in the "King" bit, but she liked weddings, and had already planned out exactly what she was going to wear and who she was going to invite (and, more importantly, who she wasn't) to her own. She didn't have a boyfriend yet, and had in fact only ever kissed one boy properly, when tipsy on cider and black currant at Katie Manning's party; but that was a minor detail.

The snake hissed with laughter, then stopped

suddenly as Alice narrowed her eyes. "Queen Isssadora."

"Mum? But that's impossible. She's already married. To Dad."

"The Dodman doesn't care about that."

Ellie shrieked. "She can't marry the *Dodman*!"

Alice's pale pink mouth set in a hard straight line. "No, she certainly can't." She turned to the pterosaur. "Corinthius, we have a journey to make."

Chapter Twenty-four

Killing Time

Clive Arnold was asleep when the witch came for him. It was six thirty in the morning and he'd been tossing and turning for the two small hours he had slept, his head filled with fears for his family and with bad dreams.

In one dream he'd been walking alone in a wood on a bright, sunlit morning, and heard singing. The song had made his pulse race; he did not know why. He ventured farther into the wood, in pursuit of the singer, and then suddenly he glimpsed her, dancing barefoot, her eyes closed and her pale hair flying. Legs trembling, he had walked toward her, on tiptoe, trying to make no sound and hardly knowing why. Like this, he came at last into the little clearing where she danced, and just as he appeared, her eyes flew open. They were eyes of the most startling green, and at that moment he felt that all the breath had been sucked out of his body.

In the dream it was Isadora, and then it wasn't Isadora. She was a Queen, then a woman, a Queen, then a woman. She bloomed with health, then became frail and ill. It was as if someone was flicking a switch back and forth, showing one image, then another. He called her name, and she stared at him as if he were a monster, and when he called out to her, to reassure her, she screamed, and he took a step toward her and found himself falling, falling, falling . . .

. . . and then he wasn't falling anymore but flying, like a bird, with the wind pressing against the bare skin of his face and arms. For a moment or two it was exhilarating. He felt a tremendous sense of freedom, of possibility—that everything was going to be all right. Then he looked down. The ground beneath him was a *very* long way away. Somehow he could tell this, even though he couldn't really see very well. In his dream he shook his head, because his eyesight was perfectly good. He didn't even own a pair of glasses. A little voice in the back of his head reminded him that his eyes only worked in his world. And then he woke up.

He *was* flying. That much was clear. And not in any aircraft, either. He looked down: nothing but a blur of clouds and the misty green-brown of land a long way below. He tried to look up, but it was hard to move his head. Something was hauling at it. He wrenched his neck sideways and stared. And stared.

Maggota grinned back at him. She was very close, horribly close. So close, he could see her in all her full and gory detail.

"Welcome back to Eidolon, Clive dear," she purred, and some maggots fell out of her snakelike hair onto him.

Luckily, the wind blew them off his face before he had a chance to retch. Which was just as well, since if he had thrown up, it would have gone all over him and spoiled his clothes. Except that he wasn't wearing clothes, as such. He glanced down to find that he only had on his pajama bottoms. Perhaps he *was* still dreaming after all.

The witch's insistent tug on his hair (which was how she was pulling him along) dispelled this vain hope.

"I do hope you don't mind the lack of ceremony," she went on. "It's all been a bit of a rush."

"I don't understand," Mr. Arnold moaned. "You took me home. We even had a cup of tea, and then you . . . you disappeared. I thought you'd gone for good."

"For good?" Maggota laughed. "I never go for good. For bad, for kicks, or for laughs, but *never* for good. Good is for fools. You and your family seem very attached to the idea of good, which is why none of you are likely to survive in this world. Or the other. Really, you haven't got the sense you were born with. If, indeed, you were born with any." She clucked her tongue disapprovingly. "I mean, really, inviting me in for a cup of tea, after all you've learned about inviting a witch over your threshold!"

Clive Arnold closed his eyes. "It was just good manners," he said faintly.

Maggota laughed. "You see? There you go again: such reliance on the concept of good. Good and goodness: the weakest of the weak."

"You're wrong. It's the strongest force there is."

"Well, all it's going to do is get you killed."

"Killed?"

The witch gave him a ghastly grin. "It's really best not to ask."

They started to descend and the wind rushed past Clive Arnold's ears like a hurricane. He opened his eyes and saw a large building rushing toward him. Dark shapes moved around on top of it, but when he tried to focus on them, his head hurt and he had to close his eyes again. Which was probably a good thing, since the shapes were dinosaur guards—a troop of velociraptors and a squadron of pterodactyls, patrolling the battlements and keeping watch for any unwanted visitors.

The next thing he knew was hitting the ground with rather more force than seemed necessary, and being tugged down a flight of seemingly never-ending steps, up which roiled blast after blast of different smells. Some were delicious and made saliva gather in his mouth; others made him want to gag.

"Ah," said Maggota knowingly. "It seems we're just in time."

"In time for what?"

"The wedding feast."

Clive Arnold frowned. "What wedding feast?"

"No need for you to concern yourself with that," she said briskly. "Because, though it can't take place without you, you're not actually invited."

The kitchen staff at Dodman Castle had been up all night and were now at their wits' end. The Dodman did not keep a very orderly kitchen at the best of times, and he wasn't known for his management skills. Hence those who "ran" the kitchen tended to be the wilier goblins who knew that working there meant having access to the larder and avoiding getting trampled on by dinosaurs, and a couple of trolls who'd decided they'd rather cook than fight. Unfortunately, the goblins had had rather too much access to the larder and had been stuffing their faces on a regular basis, becoming decidedly tubby, and leaving very little in store. When the Dodman had come storming into the kitchen the night before to announce that there would be an enormous feast the next day, he'd found most of his staff snoozing off the remnants of the last roast ox, their guilt made all the more obvious by the pile of bones they'd fallen asleep on. It had not made him very happy. He had kicked awake the three worst offenders—the appropriately named Gutty, Grabbit, and Butterball—upended a tureen of cold gravy on the snoring trolls, and informed them all that unless they had a spread fit for a King arrayed in the throne room by noon the next day, he personally was going to see to it that his guests fed upon roasted troll stuffed with Gutty, Grabbit, and Butterball.

Muttering unhappily, Butterball had taken the keys and gone to inspect the larder. He had returned shortly afterward (wiping his mouth surreptitiously) and reported that it now contained only three dried fairies, a couple of boiled wood-sprites, some rotting apples, and a mermaid that was beginning to smell. (And if a goblin says something is beginning to smell, you had better believe it's more than half rotten.) None of which was going to make a feast.

They put their heads together. Gutty suggested running away. One of the trolls nodded; the other punched it on the arm. "He'll only summon us back. And then he'll be really, really angry. And you know what happens then."

They all fell silent. Till last week there had been seven of them working in the kitchens, but now there were five. The Dodman had fed the other two to the Gabriel Hounds after he'd caught them frying fairies.

It wasn't the cruelty that bothered him, it was the waste of their magic. He had decreed that all fairies, sprites, and other creatures of magic were to be killed by him personally before they were cooked. It was the only way he ate now—biting off their heads and draining their magic. The goblins had come to be grateful that they had no magic in them. It didn't seem to do you any good round here.

Then Grabbit had had a brilliant idea. They might not have anything useful in the larder, but the dungeons were stuffed full of captives taken in the war against the Queen's forces. . . .

Isadora woke before dawn, stirred by the aroma of something truly terrible. She tried to stretch, and found that she couldn't. The Dodman had left her bound by sturdy leather cords around her wrists, telling her that if she was so attached to her throne, then attached to it she should be. She looked at the complex knots and wondered whether she even had the strength to summon up the magic to unravel them, decided that she didn't, and fell back against the carved wood. Her nose wrinkled.

"What is that dreadful smell?" she whispered to herself.

"Roasting centaur," came an indistinct voice by her feet.

She looked down to find her niece, Cynthia, awake and staring at her upside down with eyes that reminded her uncomfortably of boiled gooseberries.

"I beg your pardon?"

"You should," Cynthia said rudely. "You *should* beg my pardon, leaving that Book lying around so temptingly, and the crown, too. How could I resist stealing them? It's all your fault. If it wasn't for you, I wouldn't be here in this horrid cage." And she started to cry.

Isadora forbore saying that it was Cynthia's greed, ambition, and naïveté that had got her into the cage, since pointing it out would only upset her more. And really, was it the child's fault if she had inherited these characteristics from her greedy, ambitious, and rather stupid parents? Aleister had never been the sharpest needle in the pack, while his wife, Sybil, had all the imagination and individuality of a traffic warden, which was exactly what she had been when Aleister had met and married her. Isadora sighed.

"Roasting centaur," Cynthia said again, more

clearly, "and the last of Cernunnos's wolves."

Isadora closed her eyes. "How . . . terrible."

"Oh, you'll be surprised at what you'll eat when you're really hungry. I went three days without a bite to begin with. But he just force-fed me. With juiced fairies," she added malevolently, as her aunt's eyes opened wide in horror. "Not that he cared whether I lived or died. Just to keep my magic up. So that I could read the Book of Naming for him."

"So it's you who summoned his monstrous army?"

Cynthia nodded. "Well, not all of them," she added modestly. "Some of them just joined up for the chance to kill dragons and for the promise of land."

"What land?"

"Oh, they want all the land east of the Fire Mountains, where they've been at war with the dragons for ages, but I don't think he ever promised them anything specific. They're not very bright, most of these dinosaurs."

"But I only ever had two dragons at my command. They killed Ishtar. I don't even know what happened to Zark, except that he didn't come when I called for him."

"Good!" declared Cynthia. "They'll be the ones that wrecked Mum's Range Rover. Serves them right."

It seemed the Queen was wrong. There was no good left in her niece at all.

"Does he really mean to kill Clive?" she asked.

Cynthia wriggled and turned over with difficulty. "He will stop at nothing to get what he wants."

"And what *does* he want?" It was a question put into thin air. She did not expect an answer.

"Everything. Your throne. Your realm." She paused. "You."

Isadora shuddered. She had never felt so powerless in her life. Not even when she had been so ill in the Other World and had been taken to the hospital. Even then there had remained a small well of strength at the core of her, the willpower to survive. For the sake of her family. And where were her family now? She had not the least idea. An enormous tear spilled down one cheek and rolled off her chin. It fell, like the patter of a raindrop, onto Cynthia's forehead. There was a moment of silence in which Isadora managed to stifle a sob, then the little witch said very softly, "If you got me out of here, I could help you."

"And how would you do that?"

"Let me out and I'll show you."

Isadora smiled. "You must think me very foolish."

Cynthia considered this. "Not really. Just too good for this world."

"There was a time when that would have been a compliment." The Queen closed her eyes, concentrating. She had no expectation of help from her niece, but she did not approve of keeping anyone or anything in a cage, no matter how annoying they were. At last she felt her magic return.

She freed her own knots first, then, panting, bent to examine the cage's lock. One of the Gabriel Hounds growled a warning, but she paid it no heed. The tumblers in the lock clicked over one another, realigned themselves, and abruptly the hasp sprang open.

Cynthia stared at it, unbelieving. Then she reached out of the cage, removed the lock, and wriggled free. She gazed at her aunt in surprise. "I didn't really think you'd help me. After all, I haven't . . . I haven't been . . . very nice to you."

Isadora smiled. "There's no point in adding to the distress in the world. Even the tiniest improvement is still an improvement. I'm not asking anything from you in return. Everyone should get a second chance. What you choose to do with your freedom is up to you. Everyone has a choice as to how they act in the world. In *either* world."

Cynthia regarded her aunt suspiciously, not at all sure what to make of either the sermon or her new-found freedom. In the end she bobbed her head awkwardly, then dashed for the door.

The hounds watched her go curiously, but a look from the Queen kept them silent.

She had not freed Cynthia a moment too soon. The door at the other end of the hall burst open and in strode the Dodman, with her brother Aleister clutching at his elbow. Behind them was a frightful apparition with wild red hair, a mouthful of fangs, and a clawed hand that was propelling along the fourth member of the group.

"Clive!"

Isadora fairly flew the length of the throne room. Goblins, hounds, and saber-toothed tigers scattered from her path. Evading the burning gaze of the dog-headed man, she ran to her husband and threw her arms around his neck.

"Oh, Clive, I'm so sorry!"

Clive Arnold blinked. He held his wife at arm's length, where he could see her better, and gave her the

bravest smile he could muster. Given the circumstances (being hauled from his bed in the witching
hour, hurtled through space into another world, and
presented to a monstrous figure that looked as if it had
a dog's head—a fact he attributed to his terrible eyesight in this place), it was a bit of a wobbly smile, but
it made Isadora's heart turn over.

"Don't be sorry," he said softly. "Whatever happens, I know it's not your fault."

"Oh, but it is. It's all my fault. If it wasn't for me,
you wouldn't be here. None of this would be happening."

"If it wasn't for you, none of my life would have
been worth living." And he touched her tear-stained
cheek with a gentle finger.

"The children?" Isadora whispered. "Are they . . . ?"

Clive Arnold braced himself. He had no idea
where in either world Ben or Ellie were, and no idea
how he was ever going to tell her about Alice. As it
happened, he didn't have the chance to say anything.

"Ah, how touching!" The Dodman's growl was bitter. "Make the most of your last few seconds together."
He turned to the boggle-eyed goblins. "Shall we give
him to the saber-tooths?" he asked with a cruel smile.

The goblins chuckled at this. It would probably be entertaining, but ever so messy. This thought gave them pause. Who would have to clear up the mess? They would. It wasn't even as if they'd get a chance of leftovers; the tigers never left anything worth having. Once they'd had their way with the human, there wouldn't be as much as a little finger left.

The Dodman strutted to the cage. "Now then, Cynthia, what are the names of these saber-tooths again?" He stopped in midstrut. He stared at the empty cage. Then he picked it up and shook it, as if his captive had somehow managed to shrink herself to almost nothing and hide in a corner of it. Then he stared around the throne room. The goblins wouldn't meet his eye. The hounds shuffled nervously. Only the tigers regarded him unblinking.

"Where's my little witch?" he roared. Then something else struck him. "And where's my Book?"

Maggota clapped her hands together in sudden delight. "You really, really shouldn't underestimate us witches, Rex, dear."

He glared at her. Then he transferred his gaze to Isadora. His teeth flashed dangerously. "This is *your* doing!" he accused.

She returned his look coolly. "I know nothing about the Book's current whereabouts," she replied truthfully.

"I don't believe you!" He stamped his feet. "Damn you! Nothing will stop me!" He caught hold of the nearest goblin, wrenched its nasty little curved knife away, and flourished it so that the blade glinted in the light. Then he ran at the little group, pushed Isadora roughly aside, and grabbed painful hold of her husband.

Clive Arnold had had enough of being towed around by the hair. It wasn't as if he had much of it left, and he was quite attached (literally) to what remained. He balled a fist and slammed it into what he hoped was the dog-headed creature's massive chin.

Unfortunately, because the Dodman was so much taller than he was, and because he couldn't really see what he was hitting, it was not much more than a glancing blow. It did, however, surprise the Dodman so much that he let go of the man, and bit his own tongue. So hard that it bled. Blood oozed out between his black dog-lips and dripped down onto Clive Arnold's head. Within moments he was the most ghastly sight.

Everyone held their breath. Then Isadora hurled herself between them, shrieking, "Don't kill him! I'll change the law. You can have the throne. You can have it all; just don't kill him!"

In response the Dodman merely snarled. "I *shall* have it all and I don't need your permission or your precious law to take it!"

Maggota pulled the Queen aside. "There really is no point in prolonging the agony, my dear. Accept your fate. Accept his fate"—she nodded her crescent moon of a chin at Clive Arnold—"and let it go. You should have understood you could never marry outside Eidolon and expect to keep any of it. Such a waste of your magic. Such a trial for the rest of us."

Isadora turned. "My marriage and my children have been no waste of my magic or my life," she said furiously. Then her eyes narrowed as she recognized her old teacher. "So it's true what they say, that Eidolon does hold a mirror up to the nature of its folk, Maggota of the First Order. Your inner wickedness has made itself very evident indeed over the years."

"Hoity-toity!" the witch clucked. "You won't be saying things like that when he's got you chained up in your chambers and I'm the only company you've got."

Isadora's eyes glittered. "As if I would ever again wish for your company!"

"Now, now, be polite, or extracting your magic from you may not be as painless as you'd prefer."

"Faithless old crone! How could you ever choose to take the side of such a creature as him? One set on rooting out and destroying all the magic in our world? He will destroy you, too, you fool!"

Maggota raised an eyebrow. "Be careful who you call a fool, Isadora, lest you be the thing you decry. You forget who you are talking to!"

"Enough of this!" the Dodman roared. And he fitted the claws of his huge left paw over the crown of Clive Arnold's head and pulled it back, exposing his pale and vulnerable throat. "Say good-bye to your first husband, Isadora. At least you won't be widowed long!" The blood sprayed from his mouth as he chuckled and raised the curved blade.

At that moment something whizzed through the air of the throne room. It seemed to have come from nowhere and it moved so fast, it was impossible for anyone without good Eidolon vision to be able to tell what it was. Certainly, Clive Arnold had no clue. All he knew was that at one moment the dog-headed monster had been hauling his head back so hard, he thought his neck might break, and the next he found himself staggering forward into his wife's arms, inexplicably free. There was a great deal of commotion, a lot of barking and snarling (and not all of it from the oddly pale dogs that seemed to litter the hall), and a shout of triumph.

"Cynthia!" cried Isadora, her amazement clear in her voice.

The little witch hovered well out of the long reach of the Dodman's grasping claws. She had gratefully retrieved the broomstick from where it had been thrown on the woodpile outside. In her lap she cradled a large leather-bound volume. This she was currently flicking through with some urgency, using the knife she had whipped from the Dodman's outstretched hand as a bookmark.

Dragons, Trolls, Goblins, Dinosaurs, Nymphs, Fairies, Sprites, Centaurs, Selkies, Merfolk, Banshees, Vampires, Elves . . .

"You're not in here!" Cynthia accused the dog-headed man furiously. "How can you not be in here?"

He'd never left the Book of Naming in her possession

long enough for her to discover this lack before. He'd always watched her too carefully for that, and she knew that while the words were no more than a meaningless jumble to him, he would certainly spot a picture of himself if she came to that page.

"Well, of course he's not, child!" Maggota chuckled. "He's not really *from* here."

At this, the Dodman spun around. Red lights lit his black eyes from within, like demon-fire. "What do you *mean*, I'm not really 'from here'?" he roared. "I've lived here all my life!"

The ancient witch looked crafty. She hadn't yet decided which side she was on, or how to use the knowledge she had tucked away up her sleeve (which was long and ratty and full of spiderwebs).

"Then how can I kill him if I can't Name him?" shrieked Cynthia, incensed.

"Now, now, Cynthia, dear," her father exhorted nervously. "Stop your little game now. Delightful prank, ha ha! But time to make your peace now, eh? Say you're sorry and give the Dodman his knife back, and let him get on with the business at hand."

"The business at hand? You mean killing Uncle

Clive? Or Stupid Uncle Clive, as you always used to call him?"

Old Creepie looked distinctly discomfited by this awkward revelation. "Sorry, old chap," he said to Clive Arnold, as if somehow calling him names was much more serious than suggesting he be murdered by a monster; but Mr. Arnold merely laughed.

"That's all right, 'old chap,'" he returned sarcastically. "We always called *you* Awful Uncle Aleister."

"And for good reason," Isadora said grimly. She pushed her husband firmly behind her. It wasn't his fault he couldn't function well in the Secret Country. If he lost his temper and struck out again, he was as likely to floor her as he was to hit the Dodman. "Give me the knife, Cynthia."

The little witch looked at her distrustfully for a moment, then zipped neatly down and dropped the blade into her aunt's hand. Isadora held it in front of her purposefully, though she wasn't quite sure what she was going to do with it. Then she summoned the best of her magic, cloaked her husband with as much invisibility as she could muster, and drew herself up in front of him, offering the Dodman the most regal image of herself that she could possibly project.

Chapter Twenty-five

A Meeting of Monsters

It was into this bizarre scenario that Tyrant Megathighs III suddenly appeared. A huge leg (as befitted his name) arrived first, followed by his massive head, crouched to fit through the main door to the hall (which, although designed to permit the entrance of ceremonial coaches and sedan chairs, had never been designed to allow a tyrannosaurus rex to pass with ease), and at last the rest of him followed after some clever contortions. He was accompanied by the allosaurs Pertinax and Ancasta, with their captive in tow behind them. The tyrannosaurus rex's massive bulk seemed to fill the hall. Its head grazed the ceiling. Cynthia retreated into the farthest corner, where her eyes gleamed out of the shadows like a particularly malevolent spider.

The Dodman turned at the intrusion, his expression forbidding. "Get out!" he yelled. "You're too early."

The tyrannosaur was taken aback. Had it not been expressly invited? And while the sun had not been directly over the castle, the smells of the feast being prepared were undeniable. The dog-headed man was often in a vile temper of late, but it knew how to win his favor.

"Sire," it growled, bowing deeply. "I have brought you the tribute you demanded." And it waved the allosaurs forward.

They had meant to garland their tribute in flowers since, as Ancasta pointed out, you should always wrap wedding gifts nicely, but most of the flowers in Eidolon had died the moment their Queen had been taken captive, and so they had resorted to what they could find on the outskirts of the Wildwood, among the trampled vegetation and the burned trees. Thus it was that Ben Arnold, Prince of Eidolon, stumbled into the throne room wound around with stinging nettles, ferns, and thistles, his arms and legs bound by chains of twisted ivy.

There was a thin cry, and the goblin knife Isadora had been holding clattered to the ground and skated away across the floor.

The Dodman's grim expression changed to one of beaming munificence. "Ah," he breathed. "Tyrant, you have outdone yourself!" He strode forward to inspect his gift.

Ben looked up at the dog-headed man defiantly and willed himself not to be frightened. Even though the Dodman loomed eight feet tall, and had the head of the ugliest dog imaginable, the first time Ben had encountered him he had been working behind the counter in a Bixbury pet shop and had looked like a rather ordinary sort of person (apart from his teeth). The last time he had seen the Dodman, in his current form, the nautilus had been waving him around in one of its tentacles. He might be a monster, but he was not *that* scary. His knees stopped knocking abruptly. He summoned his courage and took a deep breath.

"Don't you dare touch me!" he said furiously. "You've got no right to be here. This is my mother's castle, my mother's realm. You have brought war to a peaceful world, destroyed the magic that makes it special, killed hundreds of innocent folk, compelled others to do things you haven't got the guts to do yourself, and for what? To be King of a ruined, miserable place, surrounded by goblins and monsters who don't follow you because they like you or believe in what you stand for, but because they're scared of you or held by the magic of their true names."

At this, the two allosaurs exchanged a glance. With a self-righteous expression, one said quietly to the other, "I told you so."

"But what happens when the compulsion of their summoning wears off?" Ben continued bravely. "Who's going to stick around then? And where does that leave you? A King with no subjects. A King of a wasteland, of a kingdom that's blasted and wrecked. Is that what you want?"

For a moment it seemed that the Dodman dwindled. In a fairytale he would have been diminished by the power of the prince's fervor, revealed by these clear and ringing words as the mean and insubstantial villain that he was. Shame would have shrunk him to nothing. But this was no fairytale, and the Dodman had no shame. Instead of diminishing, he seemed to grow, his evil cast about him like a great cape of darkness. He drew back his black dog-lips to reveal an array of long, sharp, white dog's teeth. Then he threw back his head and howled, an eerie sound that echoed around the rafters and shivered the marrow of every creature in the hall.

"Yes!" he hissed. "Yes! That's exactly what I want. I hate all you little bright, shiny, happy, magic-filled creatures. I hate the world you've made. I want to see it in shreds, in ashes. No one cares about me, so I care for no one. Your mother ruined my life. Now I'm going to ruin everything and everyone she ever cared about."

A terrible, heavy silence fell. The sound of pages being frantically rifled in the air above their heads was suddenly very loud. Cynthia was searching, searching, searching. . . .

The Dodman fixed the little witch in his sights. Then he turned to the giant tyrannosaur. "Kill her!" he screamed, pointing up into the dark corner of the roof. "Kill her and bring me that Book!"

The tyrannosaur seemed to hesitate for a second, as if the compulsion that bound it was wearing thin. Everyone seemed frozen, holding their breath, waiting to see whether the dog-headed man still held his power. Then the monstrous dinosaur sprang into action, crossing the space between it and Cynthia in a single, terrifying leap and swiping her off her broomstick and into the air with a wicked, curled claw. Cynthia screamed. It was the last sound she made. Down into the monster's tooth-filled maw she went, head first, her shriek suddenly and horribly cut short by the crunch of its jaws. The broomstick clattered to the floor, followed a split second later by one of her shoes, which had flown off at the impact.

With the other clawed hand, Tyrant caught the falling Book as neatly as a conjuring trick and passed it to the dog-headed man.

Everyone stared in horror. They had all seen terrible sights in this war, but to see death come so close and so suddenly in such an enclosed space was shocking. Ben felt as if his ribs had been bound with iron, not ivy; his feet made of lead. He could not move, could not breathe.

Someone sobbed, a racking sound like the swinging

hinges of a rusty gate. It was Old Creepie, Cynthia's father. He sat on the floor as if his knees had given way (which they had), and his hunched back shook and shook. Pale-faced, Isadora laid a hand upon her brother's shoulder.

The Dodman regarded this familial act with scorn. His lip rippled and curled. Then he laughed. The horrible sound filled the empty space where Cynthia had been. "Right, then," he said. "Who's next?"

His gazed fixed upon Clive Arnold, no longer fully hidden by the shielding magic of his wife.

"Him!"

The tyrannosaur bent to inspect its prey, which was shimmering in and out of visibility in a most disconcerting way. It swiped a hand down just as the Queen leapt up and pushed her husband sideways. The tyrannosaur knocked them both flying. Clive Arnold landed a little distance away on his backside with a thud, and the spell shattered, leaving him in full view of the beast.

Tyrant grinned and lumbered forward.

"No!"

Without a moment's conscious thought for what he was going to do, Ben hurled himself onto the floor, executed the most perfect commando roll (this being the only way he could move fast at all, with ivy tied around him), grabbed the fallen goblin knife, and swung it in a single, shining arc up and then down.

Goblin knives are very sharp, and this one had been honed on a pair of stegosaurus spikes the previous day. The power of the blow delivered by Ben's desperate hand and the keenness of the blade had driven the knife right through the armored scales of the tyrannosaurus rex's leading foot and pinned it neatly (and very painfully) to the wooden floor.

Tyrant roared in agony. He beat the air with his scaly fists, but he could not move. At least not without ripping his foot in two.

The Dodman growled his frustration. "I am surrounded by incompetents!" He thrust the Book at Maggota. "Name them," he instructed her, pointing at the allosaurs. "They look as if they should be able to take off a head or two without much difficulty. Start with Clive Arnold, then take the boy."

Even Maggota seemed cowed by the demise of the little witch. Taking the Book of Naming from him, she bent her head over it and her bony fingers moved among its pages.

One of the allosaurs stepped forward. "There will be a lot of allosaurs in that volume, crone. It will take you longer to find our names than it will be to snap your head off, so do not think to try to compel us." It folded its arms, glaring.

The other allosaur winced. "Ancasta, do stop."

Ancasta turned to it. "Shut up, Pertinax. Shut up and think for just a moment. Did you hear what the Boy said?"

Pertinax nodded unwillingly.

"Do you want to raise your young in a wasteland? Well, do you?"

A tiny, joyful light lit the male allosaur's gaze. "No, dear."

"Well, then." Ancasta glowered down at the dog-headed man. "What you are doing is wrong, and I want no more part of it and neither does my mate. There's been enough pointless bloodshed. We're leaving."

And she turned to go.

"No!" roared the Dodman, quivering with fury. "Tyrant, drag that pathetic pin out of your foot and kill them. Kill them all!"

The tyrannosaur made a terrible, agonizing lurch.

Chapter Twenty-six

Alice

The gigantic tyrannosaur ripped its foot clear of the
dagger and hurled itself at the two allosaurs. There
was not a great deal of difference between their sizes.
Tyrant topped his erstwhile captains by maybe five
feet, but his jaws were massive, and he was both
enraged and compelled by his Naming. The hall thundered as they roared and stamped, moving around one
another, half-crouched, like professional wrestlers.

The goblins pressed themselves against the walls to avoid their lashing tails, a blow from which could club a dozen of them immediately unconscious. The saber-toothed tigers, deciding that discretion was the better part of valor, snaked furtively between the dinosaurs' feet and fled out into the courtyard. The Gabriel Hounds, meanwhile, clambered upon one another for a better view, baying for blood.

Into this chaos stepped a small, pale figure, weaving a path between the stamping feet and swinging tails, the claws and jaws and roars of the dueling dinosaurs.

In a high, clear voice she addressed the chief offender. "Tyrant Megathighs III, desist!"

The huge tyrannosaur hesitated, blinking.

The Dodman barked out a laugh. "Whoever you are, dwarf, you should know you cannot compel a creature that has already been Named. This dinosaur is under my control!"

If this were the case, Tyrant did not appear to realize it, for his little clawed arms had dropped to his sides and his eyes had swiveled, puzzled, to survey the tiny girl. She smiled at him. His jaws worked, as if they were munching something (perhaps the last strands of Cynthia), then he returned a toothy grin.

The Dodman was horrified. What was going on? "Get out!" he shrieked. "This is my throne room, *my* castle, *my* fight. You weren't invited!"

"Oh, I know," said the elf-girl sweetly. She turned her lambent green gaze upon the amazed spectators. "But I decided to drop in anyway."

Isadora's eyes—the same color as those of the elf-girl—went very round. How could this be? In any other world she would have thought her sight deceived, but this was Eidolon, and magic was suddenly running strongly in her veins. Besides, a mother always knows her child. "Alice," she breathed at last. "Alice!" And she ran across the throne room with her arms outstretched and swept the tiny blond creature into her embrace.

Ben stared and stared. *Alice?* But Alice was a baby, and lost, lost in the wild roads. He rubbed his eyes with his free hand and stared again. The green-eyed girl winked at him, just the sort of wink his mother used to give him, and something inside him (who knew what?) recognized his little sister. Though she was not so little anymore.

"Hello, Sonny Jim," growled a gravelly voice at his

feet. Ben looked down and found a small black-and-brown cat gnawing through the cords of ivy that bound him. "It *is* Alice, you know. Weird but true."

The Dodman turned his fiery gaze upon Maggota. "I've had quite enough of this," he snarled. "Name her and have her throw herself off the battlements."

The elf-girl extricated herself from her mother and her crystal laugh rang out. "Go on, then, Maggota Medusa Magnifica. Name me!" And she giggled and giggled as if this was all part of the best game in the world. In any world. Which, perhaps, it was.

Maggota Magnifica dropped the Book of Naming with a clatter. It landed on one of her long, bony feet, and must have hurt quite a lot, because it is a very big book, but she didn't wince or make a sound. Instead she just stared at the blond-haired child in awe, and not a little fear.

Alice shrugged. She waved a finger and the Book came flapping toward her like some great, ungainly bird. "I don't think we'll be needing you anymore," she told it sternly, tapping it once on the spine. The Book snapped shut and vanished in a cloud of dust.

The Dodman took one look at this small act of magic, turned, and ran. The door at the other end of the throne room heaved itself shut before he could slip through it. He spun around, arms splayed against the wood, chest heaving. His eyes bulged.

"Beetle, Brimstone, Batface, and Bogie, take her prisoner and bring her to me!"

The goblins sneaked a peek at the little elf-girl, then at the rage-filled face of their master. She didn't look as scary as the dog-headed man, and surely four of them could deal with her? They advanced cautiously, wary of magic tricks.

"No, you don't," Ancasta said sharply. She scooped up Bogie and Batface, one in each clawed hand, then gave her husband a meaningful stare.

Pertinax, who had never much liked goblins, and found working with them rather beneath his dignity, picked up Beetle and Brimstone and held them at arm's length, where they kicked feebly.

Alice clapped her hands. "Thank you, but there's no need to hurt them. There's been too much of that going on here." She turned back to the main door. There, peering in rather nervously, were a selkie, a rather short-sighted girl, a hairless cat, and a striped snake, as well as the saber-toothed tigers, for they suffered from the relentless curiosity of all their kind and could not bear not knowing what was going on.

"Come in, come in," Alice declared cheerfully. "Everyone's welcome!"

"No they are NOT!" roared the Dodman, for whom the situation had passed from the surreal to the plain embarrassing. Even if he managed to kill the little creature and its mother, there would be talk the length and breadth of Eidolon about this incident. How a little blond-haired child had appeared out of nowhere and marched right into his castle—his heavily guarded castle—and ordered his own particular bodyguard of monsters around, made fun of him, *ridiculed* him. He would be the butt of a thousand jokes; he would be a laughingstock. Enraged beyond measure by this idea, the Dodman hurled himself across the chamber at Isadora.

"Mum!" Ben warned, but she was enraptured by Alice. She turned too slowly and found herself suddenly in the Dodman's arms. No tender embrace this, but a hard forearm across her throat so that she could barely breathe, and one of her arms twisted painfully up her back, imprisoned there by a savage paw.

He snapped his claws at the ghost-dogs, and like dogs everywhere, they responded to the master they had always known and jostled around the Dodman and his prisoner, haunches quivering, tails held low. They didn't bark (for once) but maintained a puzzled, attentive silence. *What now?* they seemed to ask. *We will do whatever you ask of us, but we don't understand any of this at all.* Ghosts of any kind do not retain much of what little intelligence they had in life. All they keep is a remnant of what they were, a tiny essential flame. Ghost-dogs are simpler than most. They require only food and fighting and a master's orders in order to carry on their reduced existence.

"I am going out to my army now, and I am taking her with me," the Dodman announced. "You can keep this filthy castle. I never liked it anyway. But if you make one move, one little step toward me, or even waggle your little finger to make a spell, I will snap her neck like a stick." And he thrust his long jaw at Alice provocatively, as if daring her to laugh at him.

Alice wasn't laughing now. Her pale, glowing face had become grave. For a moment she looked as if she had never been a baby, had never even been human. Her eyes became the deep, marine green of a storm at sea, her features sharp and taut. The playful child was gone, replaced by an eldritch creature eons old.

Then, like waves erasing patterns on a beach, the ancient being was gone. She gestured to the door. "Go, then. Go and find your army. They are waiting for you."

"Alice, you can't—," Ben started, but she silenced him with a look.

With the Gabriel Hounds snapping and snarling around him, threatening to bite anyone who tried to harm their master, the Dodman made his way to the courtyard door, his captive held tight against him.

Ellie and Silver pressed themselves flat against the carved statues as he passed. Ellie gazed at her mother, tears running down her cheeks, but in response, Isadora turned her head a fraction, gave her the tiniest smile, and dropped a lazy eyelid, as if she didn't mind at all that she was going to die, now that her kingdom was passing into the keeping of her youngest, strangest child.

The saber-tooths growled at the ghost-dogs, but they did nothing to hamper their progress, and after the odd procession passed them by, they turned and followed them.

As if a spell had been broken, Ben took to his heels. He ran the length of the throne room, down the long, dark passageway beyond, and out into the court-yard. "Mum! Mum, no!" he cried. And then he stopped. When he had entered the castle just a little while ago (though it felt like an age ago) as the captive of the tyrannosaur, the courtyard had been full of the Dodman's minions. There had been goblins on guard with pikestaffs, dinosaurs plated with armor, ptero-dactyls patrolling the air, and a squadron of trolls manning the bridge across the lake. On the iron spikes above the main gate a row of heads had leered down into the courtyard, no doubt removed from prisoners taken in battle, all dark and rotting like overripe fruit.

Now it was like walking into a completely differ-ent world. The goblins were still there, but they were all sitting quietly cross-legged on one side of the courtyard, as if they were at a Sunday school outing, watched over by a group of centaurs. Their weapons lay stacked in a neat pile well out of reach. There wasn't a dinosaur in sight, except for Ancasta and Pertinax and the tyrannosaur, who had followed everyone out-side to see what was happening.

And when Ben looked up expecting to see the spiky outlines of prehistoric birds in the sky, he saw instead a dozen or more dragons quartering the air above the castle. Between them, sunlight sparked off the wings of a myriad of fairies and wood-sprites. A lot more of them appeared to have survived the Dodman's ravages than anyone could ever have hoped.

On the bridge that spanned the lake from castle to shore the guard trolls had either thrown down their spears or were leaning on them and chatting good-naturedly to Gordon Gargantua and Grizelda. A phalanx of dragons was marching across the bridge now, led by—

"Zark! Oh, Zark!" Ben felt his grin stretch right across his face.

The little dragon was thinner and his glowing red scales looked duller than they had been even when Ben had found him in the Other World, but his eyes were shining, and no longer crazed with grief. He held up a claw to salute Ben and puffed out a little smoke, just to show he still had it in him. Beside him, with one hand on Zark's shoulder, walked a centaur, his dark head thrown back, his carriage proud, a bow slung across his back and a short sword in his hand. It was Darius. Yet despite his warlike appearance, no blood stained the bright metal of his sword.

The Dodman looked wildly about him, trying to take all this in. His jaw dropped in shock. He came to an abrupt standstill as if he had been shot. Tremors ran through his muscles, as if even his body was rebelling against him. Taking advantage of the sudden laxness of his grip, Isadora elbowed him hard in his stomach, and when he grunted in pain, twisted out of his grasp and ran to Ben's side. He barely seemed to notice he had lost her. He turned around and around and saw grinning faces wherever he looked. He closed his eyes, squinching them tight shut, then opened them again, in case it had all been an illusion, or a nightmare. But the scene that met his bewildered gaze remained the same. He looked for an escape—saw none. Every exit was blocked by Wildwood creatures or dragons, and he could not swim. He threw back his head and howled like the dog he was.

Chapter Twenty-seven

Transformations

The dragons have come! This was the thought that played over and over in Ben's head. They had come from all over Eidolon, and no one had compelled them. Or rather . . . He shaded his eyes and gazed up into the blue air again, and there she was, a great, glorious, golden zeppelin of a dragon.

"Mummu-Tiamat!" he cried, but she had already dipped a wing and was spiraling down.

She landed in the courtyard, making it suddenly rather crowded. She lowered her head first to Queen Isadora, then to Ben. "I hereby repay my debt to you, Prince of Eidolon," she told him, rumbling a laugh. "It was your sister Alice's idea. But I knew what your heart's wish was, even though you never said it aloud. And having witnessed your bravery in going to save your friend, I could hardly refuse."

Ben was overcome. It was, indeed, exactly what he was going to ask as his boon: that she bring her dragons to fight for his mother in this war. Except that it had seemed too great a thing to ask when he saw Ishtar dead and Zark mad with sorrow. He didn't know what to say. It was more than he could ever have hoped or dreamed. He blushed. "Gosh, thank you," he said at last. And no one even seemed to have been hurt. "How . . . ?" he began.

It was as if she could read his mind. Perhaps she could, which was an uncomfortable thought. Her golden eyes whirled. "How did we make the Dodman's army capitulate without spilling an ocean of blood?"

"Well, yes."

"Perhaps you should ask your charming sister, since she had a hand in it." The Mother of Dragons nodded to his right, and he turned and found Ellie there beside them.

"Ellie?" How on Earth could useless Ellie have changed the minds of a thousand dinosaurs?

"I used the word 'charming' for a reason," added Mummu-Tiamat, reading his thoughts again.

"Alice came and rescued us on her pteranodon, Corinthius, which she said she found wandering in the wild roads," Ellie said. "With Grizelda, of all people. Apparently Uncle Aleister made them pull up the Aldstane and then they couldn't get back into Eidolon the usual way and they tried a different way and got lost, and that's when Alice found them, after I'd dropped her when we went through the Minstrels—"

"What?" cried Isadora. "I don't understand—"

Even Ben was frowning. He waved a hand. "Never mind about all that now, Mum. We'll explain later, but it'll take a while. Get to the dinosaur army bit, Ellie," he suggested.

Ellie grinned at them. For some reason she didn't seem to be sneezing or squinting anymore, Ben noticed. Something had changed in her. And was it his imagination, or were her eyes just a little greener?

"So when we found out they'd taken Ben captive and were bringing him here, Silver and I wanted to come to the castle immediately and rescue him, but Alice was very firm about it. She said we had to deal with the larger situation first, then get down to the details. She's quite scary, Alice."

Isadora laughed. "She is!"

"So we got Corinthius to land near the enemy army, and Alice took my hand and we stood side by side in front of them all, which was pretty terrifying, I can tell you," said Ellie, flicking back her hair proudly. "And then I greeted them and they all sort of stared at me, mesmerized—"

"How come that little trick didn't work when we were beating them off with sticks?" Ben asked crossly. He thought back. Odd, now that he came to think about it—the dinosaurs had left Ellie alone, concentrating their efforts on him and Silver. And he remembered how Nemesis had gazed at her; Mummu-Tiamat, too. But she never seemed to have the same effect on goblins.

Ellie shrugged. "I don't know. I don't understand any of it. Anyway, while they were all standing still looking at me, Alice sort of concentrated on them one by one, and then she Named all the clan-chiefs. I don't know how she knew their names, so don't ask me. And then Mummu-Tiamat arrived with Zark and all the dragons, and Darius brought the centaurs, just to make sure there wouldn't be any trouble."

"And as witnesses," the Mother of Dragons added loudly, "to the Dodman's demise."

The dog-headed man came slowly out of his trance. He turned his head to look at her. "So burn me," he said flatly. "Burn me and get it over with, you overstuffed lizard."

Mummu-Tiamat took a deep breath, filling her enormous lungs.

"No."

Alice stood there between them.

"No," she repeated. "It will not end like that. *That* is his way, not mine." She indicated the line of rotting heads. "If you must use up the dragon's fire you have just drawn, Mummu-Tiamat, use it for good," she suggested.

The Mother of Dragons let a single curl of smoke escape one nostril. "You *are* a strange one," she said, shaking her head. "I see a change is coming to the Secret Country."

"Yes," said Queen Isadora, taking Alice's hand. "It is."

So instead of burning the Dodman, Mummu-Tiamat incinerated the obscene heads. A swath of clean black ash drifted down, leaving the spikes on the main gate hot and gleaming.

The Dodman cringed. "Well, what are you going to do with me, then?" he demanded, his paws balled into fists.

Isadora and her youngest daughter exchanged a glance.

"Hmmm." Alice stroked her pointed little chin. "It is a bit of a puzzle, that." She turned back and called down the hallway, "Maggota Magnifica, I need your help!"

Seconds later the bony old witch appeared. Boneless Bob—her beloved son and familiar—was coiled once more around her neck. She regarded Alice and her mother suspiciously. "What do you want from me?"

"I believe you know the Dodman's true . . . nature," Alice said softly. "He appears to be the only being in this world I cannot Name, and I don't understand why."

At this, a gleam of hope lit the Dodman's flat black eyes.

"Well, now, child," said Maggota Magnifica, stretching out a vile, bony hand in front of her and examining it carefully. She flexed the cadaverous fingers with their bloodred nails. "What will you trade me for this most valuable piece of information?"

"Be careful, Alice," Isadora warned.

Alice smiled. "The thing you want most."

"Alice!" Her mother looked seriously worried now.

Maggota frowned. "The throne?"

"You don't really want that," Alice said, shaking her head.

Didn't she? The witch mulled this over. It was true. She didn't. She thought again. Then her eyes lit up. "Ah, yes. Complete sovereignty over witches of every order. That they bow down to me and hail me as First Witch."

Alice shook her head again. "No, I don't think so."

Maggota glared at her. "What do you *mean*, you 'don't think so'? Who are you to tell me my heart's deepest desire?"

Alice gestured with her hand and a tiny silver- and pearl-inlaid mirror bloomed in her palm. She held it up to the witch's ravaged face. Maggota cackled. "You think I'm going to give away my priceless knowledge for a paltry little mirror?"

"No," said Alice simply. "You're going to trade it with me for what you see reflected there."

Frowning, Maggota grasped the child's hand, brought the mirror up to her nose, and turned it this way and that, as if to discover her best possible angle. If anyone else had had Maggota Magnifica's hideous mug, thought Ben, and had examined it as minutely as the witch was doing now, they would probably have thrown up, then smashed the mirror into a million pieces, but the witch seemed absolutely enthralled by her own reflection.

She widened her eyes, brushed back her vermin-infested hair, and drew back her poisonous purple lips to reveal her meat-encrusted fangs.

"Exquisite," she breathed. "Perfection."

No one laughed, which was a miracle in itself.

She handed the mirror back to Alice. "It's a deal," she said, thrusting a bone white hand at her. Alice took it, without blinking, and shook it hard. Then she bent upon Maggota her lambent gaze and waited.

Everyone waited. The air felt heavy and still, as if no one was daring to breathe.

"You cannot Name the Dog-Headed One, because he is not a natural being."

Well, that was just stating the obvious, Ben thought contemptuously. Whatever it was that Alice had given the witch in return for such useless information, he hoped it hadn't been important.

But Maggota had not finished. "I made him, you see," she admitted.

"*Made* him?" whispered Isadora faintly.

"Made him," the witch repeated. "An experiment. Which got a bit out of hand." She shrugged. "I really didn't expect him to turn into such a monster. He was quite sweet, in the beginning."

"But . . . how?"

"Oh, I borrowed an orphan boy and a puppy from the Other World—"

"*Borrowed?*" cried Isadora, aghast.

"I was going to take them back," Maggota said defensively. "But the experiment was such a success and all the other witches made such a fuss of him, I thought, well, I thought I'd keep him."

Alice gazed at the Dodman, who looked as if he

might burst with all the different emotions running through him. "Did you know?"

He made no response, just trembled from head to toe.

"Did he?" she questioned the witch.

"Oh, no," she said breezily, waving a dismissive hand. "Of course not. How could he, once I'd switched the heads?"

Ben felt sick. Did that mean that somewhere there was a monstrous dog running around with a boy's head stuck on it?

"The other creature died," Maggota carried on, answering Ben's unspoken question, "so I couldn't really return either of them. But as the Dodman got bigger—older—he became very . . . difficult . . . headstrong." She laughed. "Headstrong, ha! And not very nice with the other . . . children."

"You can say that again."

They turned to find Old Creepie standing there, his eyes burning. "He was horrible to me. Kept biting me, making me do things for him. Bringing him fairies to torture, sometimes making me do it for him. All sorts of dreadful things."

"You could have refused," Isadora said gently.

Her brother turned woeful eyes upon her. "You have no idea," he said grimly. "No idea at all." He turned to the witch. "It *didn't* die, the other . . . thing. We just told you it did, and you were too busy with all your pupils to have time to see for yourself whether it was true."

Maggota looked appalled. "Where is it?"

"In the dungeons," the Dodman said suddenly. "We hid it there. It's not seen the light of day since."

Isadora sat down suddenly and put her head between her knees. "This is . . . terrible." After a while she looked up and fixed the witch with her flashing eyes. "Maggota, how could you misuse your magic so horribly? It is forbidden to make a living thing. Why, it was the first thing you taught me. . . ." She paused, thinking. "And that is why; because you had already made him and knew what you had done. Is it any wonder he hates all things of magic and has set out to destroy them?" She shook her head wonderingly. Then she turned her pitying gaze upon the dog-headed creature. "I can't imagine why, after all that he's done, but I feel very, very sorry for him."

The Dodman stared at her. Then he growled. A white froth appeared along the line of his long, black lips. "I don't want your pity!" he howled, and flecks of froth sprayed everywhere. "I just want you all dead. Every one of you." And he ran at the Queen as if he would bite her head off.

Alice held out a hand, and he stopped as if he had run into a wall.

"Go and fetch the poor beast you have kept in the dungeons," she told her uncle. "Do it now."

Aleister bobbed his head and scuttled away, taking four goblins with him.

No one said a word while he was gone. Isadora got to her feet and brushed at the wedding dress, now dirty and torn. She walked to her husband's side and laid her head upon his shoulder, and though he didn't have the least idea what was going on, Clive said nothing but encircled her with his arm and squeezed her tight, which was exactly the right thing to do.

Maggota stroked her familiar and stared at the ground, no doubt considering when she might ask for her reward. Boneless Bob's eyes slid back and forth shiftily.

Ellie hugged herself, since no one else was there to do it for her, and it seemed a bit much to cross the entire courtyard to ask the Horse Lord if he might. She blushed at the very thought.

The Dodman remained motionless, held by Alice's spell, though his black eyes flared with furious light as if his brain was in overdrive trying to make sense of all he had heard. Ben could not take his eyes off him, so fascinated and horrified was he by the witch's tale.

For her part, Alice stayed exactly where she was, thinking hard.

At last Old Creepie reappeared. He looked even creepier than usual, as if struggling under a great weight of guilt, and serve him right, thought Ben. Behind him shuffled the most miserable-looking thing he had ever seen.

It made its way on all fours, and its dog-legs were thin and bowed, shaking with the effort of moving. Its flanks were moth-eaten and ribby, its spine bowed, and its head . . .

Ben had to look away. He knew that if he looked even once into the poor, malformed thing's eyes, he would have nightmares for the rest of his life. So he looked down, and found Ignatius Sorvo Coromandel there, looking up at him. He bent and stroked Iggy's head, and Iggy bumped his forehead against Ben's leg, and thus they comforted each other.

Alice was made of sterner stuff. She crossed the courtyard and stood before the other poor monster Maggota had made. It looked up at her wonderingly, its red eyes blinking painfully in the bright sunlight.

"Come with me," she said gently, and laid a hand on its terrible head.

The dog-man followed her to where the Dodman stood frozen in time. Alice touched each of them in turn. She frowned, concentrating. Then her wide green eyes popped open.

"Alexander George McEwan. Napoleon Rex Barker. Be yourselves."

A vortex of air enveloped the three figures. Dust whipped around and around, masking whatever transformation was underway at the heart of this storm. There came a noise like a thunderclap, and then silence.

Alice stepped away, leaving behind two figures huddled together on the ground. One was a sandy-haired boy, with pale blue eyes and a dusting of freckles. In his arms a Doberman puppy writhed and yapped.

Four-year-old Alex McEwan stared around

uncomprehending. His blue eyes widened till it looked as if they might pop out of his head. Dragons, dinosaurs, horrible little dark green wizened creatures with sharp teeth, horses with men's torsos and heads, a nasty old woman with a hooked nose and a snake around her neck, ugly giants . . .

It was all too much. He started to wail in anguish.

The puppy, by contrast, seemed entirely unconcerned. Its long, pink tongue lolled out of its wide, black mouth in delight at all these exotic sights and smells. Its stubby little tail wagged and wagged.

"Right," said Alice, wiping her hands on her dress. "Aleister. I cannot bring Cynthia back for you, and I'm sorry about that. This is your chance to make up for what you have done. Corinthius will take you, and little Alex and his puppy, Rex, back to Bixbury, where you and Aunt Sybil will look after them."

"But . . . Sybil hates dogs, won't have them in the house—"

Alice put her hands on her hips. "Uncle Aleister. Do you want me to do some magic on you? Or on Aunt Sybil?"

"No, no," he said hastily. "Er, come with me, little boy, nice doggie . . ."

Alex McEwan stared at the bald, hunchbacked monster advancing upon him and wailed even louder.

"Oh, for goodness' sake," said Alice. She stalked over to the child and tapped it once on the forehead. It fell immediately into a deep and dreamless sleep. Then she turned to Old Creepie. "When he wakes up, he won't remember any of this. He won't remember anything at all. You are henceforth banished from the Secret Country. Your task now is to go back to the Other World and raise him as your own. Make his life as nice as possible."

"But . . . how will I make a living? We haven't got any money. . . ."

"Being happy is not about having money," Alice said sharply. "I think you will find that you will manage. And you will like yourself a great deal more if you can do this well. It's a better reward than you deserve."

"You could sell the Range Rover," Ben chipped in helpfully.

"Buy something cheaper," suggested Ellie.

"Maybe a bicycle?" Isadora said brightly. "They're much more environmentally friendly."

"A tandem." Clive Arnold grinned wickedly.

Ben imagined fat Sybil Creepie pedaling away on the back of a tandem and had to muffle a giggle.

Alice looked severely at each of her family members in turn. "You are not being very nice," she said crossly.

Epilogue

A few weeks later (though it felt like a lot more) Ellie and Ben were sitting in the tree house in their back garden at Gray Havens, 27 Underhill Road, Bixbury. A huge sheet of paper was spread out across the wooden floor. Ben had set himself the task of charting the Secret Country. He hadn't told anyone (he knew what they would say), but he meant to go back to Eidolon sometime soon to have an adventure of his own, one that didn't involve hostile monsters or getting lost. Iggy might well boast that he knew the place like the back of his paw, but Ben wasn't taking any chances. Ellie was helping because she liked drawing and her writing was neater than Ben's, and Ignatius Sorvo Coromandel was doing what he excelled at—making matters worse—by walking up and down the map, leaving not-very-helpful footprints all over the place.

"Oh, Iggy," Ben sighed. "You've knocked over Cloudbeard again."

"Cloudbeard" was a small cone of cardboard set near the middle of the sheet of paper, and it marked the highest point in the mountain range that Ben had drawn in between the Dark Mere and a wide expanse of ocean. Toward the top of the sheet (depending on which way you were looking at it) there was a long line of silvery white on which Ellie had written in her best handwriting "Infinity Beach." She had also drawn in a tiny hut, although strictly speaking it wasn't actually there anymore. For verisimilitude (and just for fun), Ben had added a number of his collection of plastic dinosaurs, which included a bright green triceratops, a stoplight-red tyrannosaurus rex, and some smaller, unidentifiable brown creatures that might (if you looked closely enough) turn out to be cows from his old farmyard set. They made it look more inhabited, which is what it was, now. Mummu-Tiamat had graciously waived her right to the enormous beach and the swath of dunes and backcountry beyond, ceding it instead, at Ben's suggestion, to the dinosaurs, with Pertinax and Ancasta to have first choice as to which bit of it they wanted to live in. He hoped they would be happy there and raise the babies they had mentioned.

"We're not all monsters, you know," Ancasta had said, rolling her eyes, when he had thanked her for her intervention in the throne room at the castle.

This left the Eastern Quarter free for the dragons to roam without having any more border wars, and everyone seemed more than happy, for now, with the arrangement.

As for the castle . . . Ellie had drawn in the island in the middle of the lake where Corbenic Castle used to stand, before it was renamed Dodman Castle, and became the center for all the cruelty emanating out across the Secret Country. Their mother and Alice had decided to dismantle the castle. "There is too much pain here," Alice had declared. "I don't want to live in a place where each stone has a memory of horror."

Isadora had agreed, even though it had been where she was raised. And since she would be leaving Alice to be the Queen of Eidolon, despite her apparently tender years, and would only be visiting the Secret Country from time to time, it was only right that Alice should decide exactly where and how she wanted to live.

Surprisingly, Alice had declared she didn't want a castle at all, but was going to spend part of her year in the Wildwood, living close to the folk who had survived the war against the Dodman, and part of the year traveling from one province of Eidolon to another, to ensure that all was well and that dangerous pressures were not building up between (say) the dragons and the dinosaurs, or the factions of witches down in the south.

Most surprisingly of all, she had reappointed Maggota Magnifica First Witch, and given her the beauty she had shown her in the little mirror. "Because," Alice had explained, "our appearances in Eidolon reflect our inner nature; so now that you are a lot nicer to look at, I hope you will be a lot nicer to be around, too."

Ellie approved of this, though she was a bit jealous, and had secretly asked Alice if she had a spell that could change the length and line of her nose, which she felt was rather too snub to be truly pretty. Unfortunately (or fortunately) for Ellie, a certain Horse Lord had been within hearing of this request, and had immediately stuck his head through the bush that had up till then been shielding him from view and asked Alice on no account to do any such thing, because he liked Princess Eleanor's nose just the way it was.

Which had just made Ellie blush a lot and grumble about people rudely eavesdropping, but secretly she had been very gratified by Darius's remark, and replayed it in her head every night before she fell asleep.

"What I don't understand," Iggy said, sitting down suddenly in the middle of the map and thus obliterating everything from Corbenic Lake to the sea, "is what Alice sees in that horrible Sphynx. I mean," and he licked the side of his paw and ran it rather vainly across his cheek, making the black fur there even more shiny, "he's extremely ugly *and* a villain to boot. His outside definitely mirrors his inside."

Ben was silent for a moment, remembering how

he had gone back into the throne room after all the drama and found the hairless cat sitting disconsolately beside the broken broomstick. It kept rubbing its little bald head against Cynthia's discarded shoe, and meowing pitifully.

"I think," he said carefully, "that Alice feels everyone should have a second chance. And anyway, she said that a spy always comes in handy, and it was rather a good spy."

"Hmph," said Iggy. "She could have picked me as her familiar."

He looked very put out about it.

Ben and Ellie exchanged glances. "Yes, but Iggy: If Alice had decided you were to be her familiar, you wouldn't have been able to visit Ben and me, or go where you want. In fact, you wouldn't be able to be the Wanderer at all," Ellie pointed out.

Iggy made a face. "I suppose not," he conceded, though his vanity was still hurt that the new Queen of Eidolon had picked a hairless cat over him. He puffed out his chest. "Anyway," he went on, "at least everyone knows now what nonsense that prophecy was."

"Oh yes?" said Ben politely. He had now heard this theory of Iggy's about a hundred times, but was determined not to spoil the little cat's justifiable pride in his act of courage.

"Well, maybe not entire nonsense," Iggy conceded, "but shall we say, not entirely accurate? Beauty's spell to tame—well that must be Ellie . . ." He always said this because it made her smile, and more likely to give him an extra sardine at teatime. "And one with the power to name is clearly Alice. Everyone is agreed on that." Everyone was. "But all that stuff about one bravely to bring flame—well, that was *me*, that was!"

"Tell me again how you did that, Iggy," Ben said gently, because he knew it made the little cat happier than anything else he could do for him, except, perhaps, rubbing his tummy after he had overeaten.

"Well, when you sent me to find Mummu-Tiamat and I climbed that tree—"

"And found Alice on Corinthius," Ellie prompted.

"And found Alice on Corinthius," Iggy went on. "It was me who told her about the army and your situation, and it was because of that that she sent Mummu-Tiamat off to fetch the dragons, which is what I take 'bringing flame' to mean. So really, it's me who should take the credit for that bit of the prophecy after all." And he smiled proudly and puffed up his chest.

"Yes, Iggy, you did a very brave thing, climbing that big tree and driving off that nasty pterodactyl and summoning Alice and the Mother of Dragons to save the day," said Ellie, grinning at her brother. "Poor old Ben, not a hero after all."

Ben grinned back. "That's okay," he said cheerfully. "I never really wanted to be a hero anyway."

Ignatius Sorvo Coromandel sniffed. "I should think not. You're not cut out for being a proper hero at all. Not like me. Goodness knows what would have become of you if I hadn't been there to save the day."

"Look out, Iggy!" Ben cried suddenly. "There's a dinosaur right behind you."

Iggy's coat stood on end, all the way from his tail to his nose. His ears went flat. He began to tremble all over. Then, with a yelp of terror, he dug his back feet into the map and launched himself for the door like a black-and-brown furry bullet, leaving two paw-size holes in the map they had so carefully made.

The little plastic tyrannosaur that had been menacing Iggy promptly fell into one of the holes. Ben looked at his sister. Ellie looked back. Then they burst out laughing.

"So much for heroes," said Ben, and went back to the map.

About the Author

Jane Johnson was born in Cornwall and has three degrees: in English Literature, Old Icelandic, and teaching. She has worked for many years in the book industry in the United Kingdom, first as a bookseller, but more recently as a publisher and a writer for children and for adults. At George Allen & Unwin Publishers she was the editor who looked after the works of J. R. R. Tolkien and was responsible for commissioning artists John Howe, Ted Nasmith, and Alan Lee to illustrate Tolkien's books. It was these commissions that won her an invitation to visit the production of Peter Jackson's movie trilogy of *The Lord of the Rings* in New Zealand, and she was so entranced by the experience that she returned many times to watch the filming and offer her expertise. Eventually, under the pen name of Jude Fisher, she wrote the worldwide bestselling Visual Companions that accompanied the three movies.

Under the names of Jude Fisher and Gabriel King she has written seven novels, including *The Wild Road*, *Sorcery Rising*, *Wild Magic*, and *The Rose of the World*. As Jane Johnson, she has written for both children and adults: In addition to the Eidolon Chronicles, she has a new children's book, *Maskmaker*, forthcoming in 2010.

In 2005, while researching a historical novel based on the experiences of a family member stolen by Barbary pirates from the Cornish coast in the seventeenth century and sold into the white slave trade in North Africa, she visited Morocco and there met and married her Berber husband. The novel she went to research, *The Tenth Gift*, has since been published in twenty-six countries across the world. *The Salt Road*, her epic novel set in the Sahara, will be published in 2010, and she is now at work on her third Moroccan novel. She and her husband, Abdellatif, and their Norwegian Forest Cat, Finn, now split their time between London, Cornwall, and the mountains of Morocco.

You can visit her websites to find out more and view her photos at janejohnson.eu and janejohnsonbooks.com.